D0340732

Betsy: Bride of the Vampire

Also by MaryJanice Davidson

BETSY THE VAMPIRE QUEEN (SFBC Exclusive Omnibus):
UNDEAD AND UNWED
UNDEAD AND UNEMPLOYED
UNDEAD AND UNAPPRECIATED
UNDEAD AND UNRETURNABLE

THE ROYAL TREATMENT
THE ROYAL PAIN
THE ROYAL MESS

DERIK'S BANE

HELLO GORGEOUS!
DROP DEAD, GORGEOUS!

SLEEPING WITH THE FISHES
SWIMMING WITHOUT A NET

With Anthony Alongi

JENNIFER SCALES AND THE ANCIENT FURNACE
JENNIFER SCALES AND THE MESSENGER OF LIGHT
THE SILVER MOON ELM: A JENNIFER SCALES NOVEL

Betsy: Bride of the Vampire

MaryJanice Davidson

FANTASY

This is a work of fiction. All of the characters, organizations and events portrayed in this novel are either products of the author's imagination or are used fictitiously and are not to be construed as real. Any resemblance to actual events, locales, organizations, or persons, living or dead, is entirely coincidental.

UNDEAD AND UNPOPULAR Copyright © 2006 by MaryJanice Alongi
  Publication History: Berkley Sensation hardcover, June 2006
                           Berkley Sensation mass market paperback, May 2007
UNDEAD AND UNEASY Copyright © 2007 by MaryJanice Alongi
  Publication History: Berkley Sensation hardcover, June 2007
                           Jove mass market paperback, April 2008
UNDEAD AND UNWORTHY Copyright © 2008 by MaryJanice Alongi
  Publication History: Berkley Sensation hardcover, July 2008
DEAD AND LOVING IT Copyright © 2008 by MaryJanice Alongi
  Publication History: Berkley Sensation trade paperback, April 2006

First SFBC Science Fiction Printing: November 2008

All rights reserved, including the right to reproduce this book, or portions thereof, in any form.

Published by arrangement with
Berkley Sensation
An Imprint of Penguin Group (USA) Inc.,
375 Hudson Street, New York, New York 10014, USA.

Visit The SFBC online at http://www.sfbc.com

ISBN 978-1-60751-248-6
Printed in the United States of America.

Contents

Undead and Unpopular

For Mr. Fogarty,
who got me my first rejection slip.

Acknowledgments

No one comes up with a book totally on their own—if that was the case, authors would get 100 percent of the royalties. Some of the people who helped themselves to my cut, or should otherwise start charging me for their services:

My editor, Cindy Hwang; the entire Berkley Sensation team; my agent, Ethan Ellenberg; Darla (from Team Laurell K. Hamilton); my PR guru, Jessica; my husband, Anthony; my sister Yvonne; and the rest of the good-looking bums who comprise my family.

Special thanks to my grandpa for inspiration. If he can escape from a nursing home, I can make my deadlines.

Author's Note

Betsy's thoughts about Antonia and Garrett's new relationship make reference to the novella "A Fiend in Need," an April 2006 anthology release from Berkley titled *Dead and Loving It*. This book takes place about two months after the events of that novella.

Also, zombies do not actually exist. Um, right? Please, God.

"And the Queene shall noe the dead, and keep the dead."
—THE BOOK OF THE DEAD

"Keep your friends close, but keep your enemies closer."
—SUN TZU,
The Art of War

"Victory is mine!"

—STEWIE GRIFFEN,
Family Guy

Chapter 1

There's a zombie in the attic," George the Fiend informed me over breakfast. His voice was a calm pond, and he wiped blond strands out of his face carefully as he peered at his knitting.

"Sure there is," I replied. My casual response was, I decided much later, a massive mistake. I mean, here was this guy (vampire) living in the house owned by my best friend with at least three other people (two more vampires and a surgical resident), telling me what the problem was (a zombie), in plenty of time to do something about it, and I totally blew him off. Were this a horror movie and I, Betsy Taylor, Queen of the Vampires, was on the screen pulling this crap, everybody in the audience would have thrown their popcorn and Sno-Caps at the screen.

But this wasn't a movie, so I screwed up in an honest sort of way.

Also, I was distracted, crow-like, by the big shiny thing on my finger: my engagement ring. Pretty silly for someone who was supposedly already married (to the prophesied Vampire King for the next thousand years) and officially engaged (to same, one Eric Sinclair) for several weeks. But, my God, getting Sinclair to cough up a proposal had been hard enough. I was still stunned he'd come up with a ring, too.

In fact, I was still tingling from our whole previous evening together, a wacky outing involving blood-drinking, sex, a stop by Caribou Coffee for hot chocolate, and The Ring: a delightfully shiny gold band strewn with diamonds and rubies.

I'd had to make a Herculean effort not to squeal when he slid it onto my finger (where it promptly slid off; I have freakishly small hands). Now here it was, a day later, and I couldn't stop staring at the thing.

Also, it wasn't really breakfast, since neither George nor I were eating and it was eleven o'clock at night. But we still called it breakfast, since that's when Marc (the surgical resident) would often get up and have a muffin before his overnight shift.

George—well, actually, we learned his name was Garrett shortly after he began speaking—went back to the lovely baby blue afghan he was knitting, which matched the fine sweater I wore that evening. I, in turn, went back to the guest list. Not for my wedding. For my surprise birthday party. Which wasn't a surprise at all, but I wasn't telling.

It was a short list. My mom; my dad; my (sigh) stepmother, Antonia; her BabyJon; my landlord, Jessica; my fiancé, Eric Sinclair; Marc; my sister, Laura; Garrett's mate, the other Antonia; our friendly neighborhood police officer Nick; Sinclair's friend Tina; former vampire hunter Jon; and of course Garrett. Almost all of these people I had met *after* I died.

Of course, half of these guests *were* dead people. Even Marc, who was alive, often put it, "Why not be dead? Most of my exboyfriends act like I am anyway."

Jessica and I kept trying to fix him up, but the few gay guys we knew were not Marc's type. Not that we had any idea what Marc's type was. On top of that, fixing people up is hard. Almost as hard as—well, trying not to drink blood.

I tapped my pencil on the pad, trying to come up with a plan to tell Eric before the wedding that I had decided to completely give up the blood-drinking thing. I figured being the vampire queen had a few advantages—as it was, every vampire I'd ever known had to drink every day, even Eric. But I could go up to a week without so much as a drop of O-neg, without any shakes or desperate pleas for stray rats. So in honor of my birthday, and of being in this shit queen job for a year, I figured I'd give it up completely. I would be in a blood-free zone!

But Eric would be tricky. Normally he ignored whatever I did, but during our intimate moments, someone always got bitten. Sometimes more than once. It squicked me out to try to explain it, but drinking during sex just made the whole thing better—

"Lame, Betsy," Jessica said, coming into the kitchen and glancing over my shoulder as she headed for the espresso maker. "I can't believe you're making a list of birthday presents. Miss Manners would be rolling in her grave."

"Miss Manners is still alive. Besides, it's not a list of presents. It's a list of people you're going to invite to my surprise party."

Jessica, a painfully skinny nag with gorgeous skin the color of Godiva milk chocolate, laughed at me. "Honey, it hurts me to say this. Like a sliver in the eyeball. But we're not. Planning. A party."

"Although," I added, "you don't have to try too hard to get the Ant there. I wouldn't mind if she missed it."

"Sugar." She gave up the espresso maker as too complicated— this was a nightly ritual—and fixed herself a glass of chocolate milk instead. "You made it perfectly clear two months ago: no party. And we believed you. So stop making guest lists and worrying about your stepmother showing up. It's not happening."

"Are we talking about the nonexistent surprise party?" Tina asked, startling me as her bare feet slid noiselessly across the spotless shamrock green kitchen tile.

"I'm putting bells around your pretty, petite ankles," I told her.

Jessica had nearly choked on her drink, Tina had so startled her. She took a breath and said, "She tells us our lives won't be worth living if we throw her a party, then she makes a guest list."

"Constancy, thy name is Queen Elizabeth," Tina murmured as she slid her tiny butt onto the breakfast nook bar stool next to George—dammit, I mean Garrett. She was dressed like the most tempting college student in creation, as usual—long blond curls, big pansy eyes, knee-length black skirt, white designer T-shirt, bare legs, black pumps. Most college students nowadays hadn't witnessed the Civil War, but undead bombshells like Tina just didn't let go of their perky tits.

"What do you want for your birthday, Majesty?" she was asking me as I stared jealously at those ageless melons. Her duties nowadays were the equivalent to serving as "best man" to Eric, whom she had turned into a vampire decades ago. Nowadays, instead of sucking his blood, she limited herself to smoothing out the morning edition of the *Wall Street Journal*, fixing his tea the way he liked it, and setting out gobs of paperwork for him to look through. "Some nice shoes, I suppose."

"You suppose wrong," I replied. "I want peace on earth, goodwill toward men."

"Do they have a store for that at the mall?" Jessica asked innocently. "Or maybe one of those sales carts in the walkways, right next to the portrait artist and the guy selling T-shirts with pithy sex jokes?" She was shamelessly stealing peeks at the memos Tina laid out neatly on the marble countertop.

"It'd be the only thing they don't have," I said. "Tina, Jessica, I know you. I know I told you not to throw a party, and that therefore you will throw one. But if you want to keep up the deceit—fine. No party. Instead, find a quiet moment to pray for the aforementioned world peace and global harmony, or failing that, snag me a fat gift card from Bloomingdale's."

"Or perhaps a pair of the new Prada loafers," Jessica added.

"No, I'm sick of loafers. Spring is here—I want some strappy sandals." Which was kind of silly—I couldn't wear them with socks, and these days my extremities were pretty icy. But still. I was sick of winter, and this was Minnesota—we had at least two more months of snow.

"Right," Jess said. "Because you don't have enough of *those*."

"Why don't you take one of my existing pairs and shove them up your cute black butt?" I suggested sweetly.

"Well, Ms. Taylor, why don't you take your delicate ivory nose and—"

Tina interrupted the argument du jour. "Majesty, are there any designer shoes you don't like?"

Garrett cleared his throat as he started a different stitch—knit, garter, crochet—it was all the same to me. "She doesn't care for Rickard Shah sandals. Especially the gold ones."

"This is true," I confirmed. "They're all like something out of the *Boogie Nights* prop drawer. I mean, what year is this? I'd pay two hundred bucks *not* to wear them."

"No need for that," Eric Sinclair said, ignoring my yelp and Jessica's flinch. He was worse than Tina. Where she slithered silently, he teleported like an alien. A tall, broad-shouldered, dark-haired, dark-eyed, yummilicious alien. "You have a thousand pairs of sandals."

"Do not. Leave me alone and read your papers."

"Guest list?" he asked, leaning over my shoulder and peering at my pad. "But you don't want a party."

"You're damned right I don't!" I slapped my notebook shut. In fact, I didn't. I was pretty sure. "How many times do I have to say it?"

Don't get me wrong: I can hear myself. And I'm very self-aware, regarding all my little tics and annoying quirks. Nothing triggers Maslowian self-actualization like getting body-slammed by a Pontiac Aztek.

But no matter how bad I sound to myself, I can't help it. My situation is impossible. You'd be amazed how often I'm ignored, even though I am the so-called Queen of Vampires. Repeating myself ad nauseum is one of the many ways I try to make myself heard. I am too new to the game to be quietly tough, like Sinclair. Not smart, like Tina. Not wealthy, like Jess. Not an all-seeing ghost, like Cathie. Not a clever doc, like Marc; or an indifferent psychic werewolf, like Antonia. You know what it's like to be called a queen and have the least to offer among all the people you know? It's a huge ego hit.

"We got it, Betsy," Jessica was saying. "No party. Fine."

"Fine."

"Why are you—" Sinclair caught Jessica's frantic arm waving. "Never mind. Are you ready for our guests?"

"Guests?" I tried not to freak out. They *were* throwing me a party! Bums! And throwing me off by having it two weeks before my actual birthday.

He sighed, which was about as close as he got to a blitzing tantrum. "Please don't say '*guests?*' like you don't remember the European delegation coming at midnight."

"And Sophie and Liam," Tina added, looking over her own memos.

"I know. I *know*." I did know. Sophie and Liam I didn't mind—Sophie was a charming vampire who lived in a tiny town up north with her very alive, thirtysomething boyfriend, Liam. They'd been a couple for a few months, and a while back they'd helped us catch a real creep, a vampire who got his rocks off dating college girls, charming them into deep love, then talking them into killing themselves.

Sophie, in fact, had kind of renewed my faith in vampiredom. It seemed to me that most of us were jerks, men and women who found sexual pleasure in felony assault. But Sophie was made of purer stuff—the evil that supposedly consumed the undead didn't seem to touch her.

So her coming tonight, along with the pleasant (if somewhat dry) Liam, was great by me.

But this European delegation was just what I didn't need: a bunch of ancient vampires with stuffy accents dropping in to irritate me two weeks before my birthday. As if turning thirty last year (and dying) hadn't been traumatic enough.

"I didn't forget," I said. Truth. I just had been trying hard to ignore it.

He smoothed his dark hair, which was already perfectly in place. Uh-oh. Something was up. "Um, Jessica, I wonder if you could excuse—"

"Don't even," she warned him. "You're not kicking me out of my own house to have a dead-only meeting. Marc depends on me to pass on full reports of the crazy shit you guys are up to."

Eric said something to Tina in a language I didn't know. Which meant, anything but English. She replied in the same gibberish, and they talked for a minute.

"They are totally debating whether to kick you out or not," I said to Jess.

"Duh."

"Let's speak our own language: we'll call it English, which really fucking rude vampires don't understand."

I glared at the two of them, but Tina and Eric kept babbling. I wasn't sure if they were ignoring me or honestly hadn't heard, so I took the mature route and just spoke louder.

"IT'S PROBABLY A SAFETY ISSUE. YOU KNOW WHAT ASSHATS THOSE OLD VAMPIRES CAN BE. THAT'S WHY THESE TWO GET OFF ON INVITING THEM OVER. ANYWAY, ONE OF THEM WILL PROBABLY TRY TO CHOMP YOU, AND WE'LL HAVE A BIG WICKED FIGHT, ALL OF WHICH WE CAN AVOID IF YOU JUST HANG IN THE BASEMENT WITH GARRETT."

"No, no, no. My house. No offense, Garrett."

Garrett shrugged in response. He hadn't offered much since his Shah sandal observation, and stuck to his knitting. He had been spending more time than usual in the kitchen: his girlfriend, a werewolf who never turned into a wolf, was in Massachusetts. Apparently her pack leader's wife had had another baby. She bitched, but she went. Garrett stayed, which was fine by me—it wasn't like we didn't have the room. Antonia could come back with half the pack and we'd have the room.

I had to admit, I had no idea what Antonia (the werewolf, not my stepmother) saw in him.

Side note: how weird was it that I knew two women named Antonia? Jessica claimed it all had Some Deeper Meaning, but I figured I was just lucky.

Back to my fretting about Garrett. Don't get me wrong. I mean, he was great-looking (it was the rare vampire who wasn't), but I had the impression he wasn't the sharpest knife in the drawer. Not to mention, a few weeks ago he'd been running around on all fours and drinking blood by the bucket. Antonia was smart and, even if she'd been a drooling idiot, she could see the future. Hello? *See the future.* She could have had anybody, I figured.

She would have disagreed. Violently. It was amazing to me that a great-looking brunette with the body of a swimsuit model who could *see the future* had rotten self-esteem, but there it was. And who was I to judge? Garrett and Antonia had a good thing.

"Very well," the questionable prize I was dating said at last, in English. "You may stay. But Jessica, please watch what you say and do. Don't look them in the eyes for long. Speak only when spoken to. Yes, sir; yes, ma'am."

"Sit up. Arf," I teased.

"What about her?" Jessica cried, pointing in my general direction. "She's more in need of an etiquette lesson than I am."

"Yeah," I said, "but I'm the Queen. With a capital fucking Q. Hey, you're looking me in the eyes for too long! Eric, make her stop!"

"Give me a damn break," she muttered, and went upstairs making gagging noises.

Chapter 2

The doorbell rang as I watched Jessica rant her way up the foyer stairs. She had seemed especially prickly in the past few weeks. Not that I wasn't used to her speaking her mind; she was my best and oldest friend—we'd shared lipstick in junior high. Which, given our skin hues, was a true testament to our friendship (and more importantly, our ability to find common accessories). But it seemed like everything I said and did was going beyond surface irritation, and digging deep inside her annoy-a-meter.

"It's Sophie and Liam," Tina informed us from the foyer.

"Oh, good," I said, following everybody (except Garrett, who was deep in mid-afghan) out of the kitchen. "The fun meeting first."

"Nonsense," Eric said. "All meetings are fun."

I snorted, but didn't say anything. Truth be told, I was too busy looking at his black-panted butt, which was very fine. He was wearing a dark suit as usual, a perfect complement to his dark hair and eyes. He was so broad through the shoulders I often wondered how he fit through doorways, and had long, strong legs. I pondered the fact that I'd resisted his evil charms for so long.

Although these days, it felt like he was resisting mine. He'd dodged every wedding meeting we'd had. At least we'd agreed on the date: July 31. Sometimes it seemed like forever, and sometimes it seemed like the date was rushing up on me. And I was virtually planning the entire thing by myself (well, with Jessica's occasional help). He had no opinion on flowers, food, drinks, tuxes, gowns, ceremony, or the wedding song. If I didn't know for sure he loved me, I'd think he didn't—

"Your Majesties," Sophie was saying, bowing to us both. Tina had opened our enormous cherry front doors, and there were Sophie (Dr. Trudeau—she was a vet) and Liam, uh, whatever his last name was.

Sophie was dressed in a sharp navy suit with a cute short skirt, matching turtleneck, black tights, and black (ugh!) running shoes. I know it's practical for career women, but sneakers with suits? Jesus couldn't possibly weep harder than I did. Like all vampires, Sophie was ridiculously beautiful, with black hair (done up in an unfashionable bun) and pale, velvety skin. Her dark eyes didn't miss a flea. Which, in her line of work, was probably really good.

Liam was in jeans, leather jacket, and beat-up loafers. Which reminded me again that I was ready for spring, and sandals. It was always startling to see his youngish face (Late thirties? With the farmer's tan, it was hard to tell.) juxtapositioned against his prematurely gray hair.

Tina led us all into a parlor (there were at least four; don't get me started) and the first thing Sophie did when we were all seated was hand me a copy of that day's *Star Tribune*. "Would you please sign your article?" she asked pleasantly in the charming French accent she had never lost, not even after all these years here in Minnesota.

Eric muttered something under his breath that, luckily for him, I didn't catch. I had a weekly "Dear Betsy" column for vampires. It was supposed to be published in an undead-only newsletter, but someone had leaked it to the *Trib*. The editor had thought it was hilarious and published it. Most people who read it thought it was a tongue-in-cheek thing. This was the only thing that spared me from Eric and Tina's wrath.

"I'd be glad to," I said. "Uh . . ." Tina handed me a pen. I never had a pen, a leash, or a stopwatch when I needed one. "Thanks." I scribbled my signature on the latest ("Dear Betsy, my friends keep insisting on having their book club meeting during daylight hours. Should I tell them what my problem is, or lie?") and handed it back.

"Heh," Liam said. "Bet the librarian didn't like that much."

He was talking about Marjorie, who ran the vampire library down in the warehouse district, and the column, which was in a paper anybody could read, anytime. And he was right. She had been furious. She was still trying to track down who'd given my columns to the *Trib* editor. I didn't think it was a deep dark plot or anything; accidents happened. I was alone in this theory. Which was why I kept writing the columns, no matter how irritated everyone got.

"Never mind," Tina said hastily. "How are you both?"

"We're real good," Liam replied in his flat Midwestern drawl. Looking at him, you'd never know he was rich. His dad had invented the first pocket calendars with three-hole punches, or some such thing. "Real good. And you're looking good. The same, in fact."

"Oh, well." I modestly patted my hair. There were a few advantages to being a vampire, and not looking my age was big number one. I'd never need highlights again. "What can I say? How're things up in Embarrass?" What a dorky name for a town.

"The same." Not real chatty, this guy.

"Majesties," Sophie offered. "We have a reason for stopping by, if you don't mind."

"And miss all the scintillating small talk?" Jessica muttered from the back of the room. She had used her brief time upstairs to freshen her jack-o'-lantern lipstick.

"Truth be told," Liam said, ignoring the snarky comment, "it's about me. And my age. Sophie's—well, you know—but I'm not exactly standing still. We were thinking about her turning me. We wanted to know, er, um, well, what you thought about that."

At first I had no idea what he was talking about. "Turning you into what? A Republican?"

"A vampire, dumb shit," Jessica said. I bit my tongue and let that one pass, but made a mental note to get her alone and find out just what had made the incredible upward journey deep into her large intestine.

My jaw went slack with horror as I turned back to the happy couple. "Why would you want to do *that*?"

They looked at each other, then at me. "Not everyone has the same view of the undead as you do, my queen," Sophie said. "And I have lost too many lovers to death."

"Oh," I said, because nobody else was saying anything. "Well, that's a shame. Uh. Liam? You, uh, think this is a good idea, do you? Because loving a vampire and being a vampire—those are two very different things. One can be very nice. The other can be pure hell." Eric moved perceptibly at this comment, but didn't say anything.

"I'm not real keen on giving up salmon hash and fried eggs," Liam replied. "But I'm less keen on giving up Sophie. The idea of eternal love—it's . . . well, it's—"

"He's dying," she explained.

"What?" Jessica and I squawked in unison.

"He's only got thirty, forty years left—assuming he doesn't get run over by a bus or hit by lightning." Or have a heart attack from all the fried eggs. For the first time, her smooth face was anxious. "I don't think we dare wait much longer."

Leave it to a vampire to think a healthy guy in his late thirties or early forties was on his deathbed. "Uh . . . Sophie . . ."

Eric spoke up for the first time. "Dr. Trudeau, you know the risks."

She nodded.

"Right," I said. "The risks. The many, many risks. Let us count the risks. Such as." I coughed, stalling for time. "Well, the risks are . . . very risky."

Jessica rolled her eyes, but Tina kindly jumped in. "Sophie, Liam, as Her Majesty is trying to explain, vampirism is a virus—and some people don't catch it. They just die. And young vampires are feral—they don't know themselves, or anyone. Only the thirst. The Queen here is the exception."

"Which is why she's the boss lady around here," Liam said. "But it's a risk I wanna take. I don't much care for the other choice."

"Dr. Trudeau, you may do as you wish," Eric said, not bothering to consult with me, as usual. "It's not for us to deny you a chance to be with your love."

"Good luck," Tina added.

"Whoa, whoa!" I cried. "That's it? We're not going to talk about it for, I dunno, more than *twenty seconds*? I mean, they did come to consult with *me,* didn't they?" Facing dubious looks from my friends, I turned desperately to the new arrivals. "Liam, come on! We're talking about your potential death by maiming, here! Sophie, think about it—how you'll feel if it doesn't work out."

"Of course, if Her Majesty orders us not to do it, we won't do it," Sophie said stiffly.

"I don't give out orders like that," I said, appalled. What was it about vampires, they couldn't take care of themselves anymore, make their own decisions? "I'm just saying, think it over. Liam doesn't look like he's going to keel over, you know, right this second. What's the rush?"

"I think Betsy's right," Jessica said. Everybody squinted at her, and she continued. "Sorry, I know this is vampire business, and I'm just a mangy human, but from my point of view, it seems like maybe you could think it over a little longer. You've only known each other a few months. Lots of people get married after that long, and then divorce. This seems like an even deeper commitment. What happens if the two of you outgrow each other?"

"No chance of that," Liam said.

"Sophie . . ." I trailed off. I tried to imagine how I'd feel if Eric was human, and I knew I'd outlive him. Possibly by centuries. Could I face him getting old and dying on me? If there was any way to prevent it—"Sophie, it's not for me to tell you yes or no."

"Of course it is," she said, surprised. "You're the queen."

"Right, right. And I really appreciate you coming here . . ." And dumping this ginormous problem in my lap. "But you guys are adults, it's your choice. If you want to go ahead and bite him, it's up to you. I'm just saying—" What *was* I saying? Think it over? Wait for Liam to get older? Who was I to tell them no? I was sort of shocked they'd stopped by to ask my permission about something that was so completely none of my business. "I don't know," I finished, giving up. "Do what you think is best. I'll back you up, whatever you decide. And I believe my fiancé has already agreed with my edict," I added with a sidelong glance at Eric, who held his tongue.

"Thank you, my queen. We will be going forward, I think, but your support means the world to us."

"Yup," Liam said.

"And—"

The sonorous, long door chime rang again.

"Excuse me, Dr. Trudeau." Eric turned to me. "Our other guests have arrived."

Great. More vampire fun and games. Tina got up. "I'll see them in, Your Majesty. Dr. Trudeau. Liam." She excused herself, leaving a nice awkward silence for the rest of us.

"So, uh, when are you going to do it?" I asked. I looked nervously at the plush carpeting, the ornate upholstery, the beautiful tapestries. What if they decided to do it *right here*, right now?

"Soon," Sophie replied.

"Do you want to, uh, stay here while Liam, uh, recovers?"

"Thank you, my queen, but I think we'll be best suited at our home."

"Okay. And you'll, uh, make sure he doesn't hurt anybody when he's, you know, nutty and out of his mind with blood lust?" For the next ten years?

Liam winced (well, he blinked), but Sophie soldiered on. "My queen, I have experience in these matters. Guarding young vampires—I—all will be as you wish."

Yeah, right. That'd be a fucking first.

"Guess we'd better hit the road, hon," Liam said, standing. Sophie stood. We all stood.

"Thank you for your time, Majesties, and your counsel."

"Are you heading straight back to Embarrass?"

"Tomorrow. Sophie don't like to leave the animals too long."

"Best of luck, Dr. Trudeau." Instead of bowing as he usually did, Eric held out his hand and, surprised, she shook it. "Please keep us posted."

"Thank you, Majesty. We will, Majesty."

"Liam." They shook. They were about the same size, though Liam was a lot narrower through the shoulders.

Liam smiled at us, and the corners of his eyes went all crinkly. I thought of him as a nutty thirsty ignorant young vampire and wanted to cry. But maybe it would work out. Maybe, ten or twenty or a hundred years from now, everything would be fine and they'd be happy together.

And maybe we'd be going north for a funeral in a few days.

"Well, uh, talk to you soon." Maybe. *And if you get out, I'll be staking you soon. But never mind.*

"Yup," he said, typically laid back. *Yup.* Like being chomped and turned was as routine as fixing the wood-chipper out by the cabin.

"Are you sure you don't need anything?" I asked.

"Nope."

Tina came in just in time to prevent my hysterical sobbing. Which was just as well; I had nothing else to contribute. She was trailed by half a dozen stately vampires. I knew from Tina's briefing—and by the way they held themselves now—that they were very old, very powerful dead guys (and two gals). The youngest was something like eighty-seven. Which was about as old as Eric.

It was hard to take them all in at once—I saw a bald guy with dark skin, a couple of brunettes, a redhead with freckles (an undead Howdy Doody!)—

"Majesties," Tina began, gesturing to the group that had filed into the room. "May I present our European brethren: Alonzo, Christophe Benoit, David Edourd, Carolina Alonzo—"

Tina did not get the chance to introduce the last two; upon Carolina's introduction, Sophie shot across the parlor and was upon Alonzo in a hot fury of teeth and claws.

Chapter 3

I barely had time to get a look at Alonzo—a blade-thin, fine-looking guy with skin the color of good espresso and yellowish eyes, before Sophie was doing her level best to claw his face off. Her speed was devastating. I think only Sinclair could have stopped her but he just watched. All he said was, "The French," with a shrug.

So, as usual, I was the one stuck with the moral high ground. "Stop, stop!" I shrieked. "Sophie, what are you doing? Get off him!"

Meanwhile, Sophie was going for his eyes and a stream of presumably impolite French was pouring from her spittle-ridden mouth. Alonzo did not appear immediately hurt, and appeared able to fend her off. However, she consumed enough of his attention that he did not say a word.

Liam took a step forward—to restrain the love of his life, or help her, no one knew—but Tina wisely knocked him back onto the couch. Jessica scanned the room for something to throw, or, perhaps more sensibly, hide behind. Eric watched, Tina alongside, and the other vampires observed the skirmish anxiously, chatting to themselves in various European languages. (I think they were European languages. Hell, it could have been Asian, or Antarctican. What am I, a linguist?)

Liam got up off the couch, looked at Sophie and said, "Hon, don't do that," and started forward again. I tried to grab one of them and got an elbow in the cheek for my pains, which would have given me a massive shiner in the old days, and that's when Eric finally said something.

"Enough."

In the movies, everybody would have stopped; Alonzo did, but Sophie was still shrieking and clawing at him, and I saw her tear a huge strip of skin off his shaved scalp.

Eric stepped forward, grabbed her by the right elbow, and tossed her away from Alonzo as easily as I'd have tossed a cardboard box. She caromed off the wall and looked ready to keep rumbling despite herself, but I gamely recovered and stood by Eric's side. I tucked my hands into my armpits so no one could see how they were shaking and piped up loyally, if shakily, "Sophie, he said enough. These are guests in my home."

"*Our* home," Jessica piped up, glaring at me and ignoring all of Eric's previous advice on the care and handling of ancient European vampires.

"Bastard!" Sophie was as wild-eyed as a rabid cat; I'd never even heard her raise her voice, never mind totally lose it like she'd done.

Alonzo calmly pulled the hanging flap of skin off his head (*blurrrggghhh!*) and said in a pleasant Spanish accent, "The pleasure is mine, señorita."

"You dare, you *dare* speak to me? You dare look at me, be in the same room with me, and not beg my forgiveness?"

"We have met?" I couldn't believe how mild-mannered this guy was. And his very voice suggested a man who could sing, dance, and swordfight all at once—yum. I mean, boo!

A sluggish trickle of blood inched toward his eyes, and one of the vampires behind him handed him a spotless white handkerchief. Of course, anybody else would be slipping on a gigantic puddle of their own blood (head wounds in particular looked so frightening), but not a vampire. And certainly not this vampire. He calmly blotted his head for a moment, watching Sophie with his cat eyes.

"You don't remember, swine, bastard, monster?"

He shrugged with suave innocence.

"August 1, 1892? You were visiting Paris. You went to a tavern. You—"

"Oh," he said carelessly. "The bar girl."

"Don't tell me," I said.

Sophie pointed a trembling finger at Alonzo. "He killed me. He *murdered* me."

"Oh, hell," Jessica said, which exactly echoed my sentiments.

Chapter 4

$\mathcal{E}$ric and Tina had steered the Europeans into another parlor; I'd grabbed Sophie and hustled her upstairs. Jessica had followed us. Our last view of Alonzo was an indifferent cock of an eyebrow as he watched her hiss at him on her way out of the room.

"Okay," I said when I finally had her settled in a spare bedroom, and then I realized I had no idea what else to say. "Okay, uh. Sophie. Okay. You okay?"

Sophie dropped to her knees, as startling a thing as had happened in the last twenty minutes, and it was already one for the diary. "Majesty," she said, her fingers digging into my thighs, actually ripping through my jeans, and she didn't notice. "I beg you to kill him—or let me kill him."

I grabbed her wrists and tried to pull her to her feet. Her wavy dark hair had come undone from the bun and was flying everywhere, pouring down her back like a black river. Her eyes stared wildly past my own, into some other space. "Sophie, come on. Please get up. Listen, I can't just—you know. He's—part of a delegation."

I couldn't believe it: I had turned into a politician.

"Oh yes, I see," she said bitterly, staring at the floor. "Diplomatic immunity and all."

"Look, we'll get to the bottom of this. I promise. We'll—"

"There is nothing to get to the bottom of." She climbed slowly to her feet. "He murdered me and you will either punish him or you won't."

"It's just that he's—they're—important. I can't just march down there and, you know, punch him in the brain. Sophie?"

Too late; I was talking to her back. Jessica gave me a wide-eyed look and followed.

We found the correct parlor in short order. Just about everyone was seated comfortably, except Liam. He was standing in a corner and looking at Alonzo with a look that bordered on predatory.

"We are going now," Sophie was saying. If Liam looked like a pissed-off panther, she was looking downright murderous.

"Adios," Alonzo said amiably. If he had had a drink in his hand, I am sure he would have raised it.

"Alonzo," Sinclair said, with a small note of reprimand.

"I will see *you*," Sophie promised, "again."

They left. I glared at Alonzo, who shrugged and smiled politely.

"Tina, perhaps you could get our guests something to drink," I practically snapped. Tina stared at me for a short moment, but then quickly nodded and left the room. Good—she understood I needed to assert authority here. Jessica remained comfortable on a velvet chaise longue, but that didn't bother me—I didn't need the Europeans to see me bossing around a "sheep."

I turned to Alonzo. "This is quite a spot you've put me in."

"Us," Sinclair said.

"Right. Did you do it?"

Alonzo shrugged again. His scalp had grown back. Pretty quick, for a vampire—to get that kind of healing, most of us had to feed first. "I'm sure she's right," he said. "I don't remember everyone I've—"

"Murdered?"

"—bitten, any more than a man of romance can remember all the women he has slept with. But I do not dispute her account."

"Then we have a serious problem. You may have wasted your time making this trip."

"With all respect, Your Majesty, killing people—making vampires—is what vampires *do*."

"*I'm* a vampire," I corrected him sharply, "and I haven't done anything of the kind."

"You are young," one of the women—Carolina, it was—spoke up.

"Don't patronize me, you arrogant Spanish bitch." Sinclair's fingers closed over my upper arm and squeezed; I yanked away. "You have already insulted one of my subj—one of my friends, and you've been here, what? Five minutes?"

"We can leave," another vampire said silkily.

"Great! Don't let the heavy cherry doors hit your bloodsucking asses on the way—"

"Perhaps we can reschedule," Sinclair interrupted. "Given recent events."

I glared at him. "Fuck rescheduling."

"Such American charm," Alonzo began, "but if I might correct Her Majesty on a point of etiquette—"

"Thanks, I'm sure I'd find it fascinating, not; and also, in case you missed the memo, I don't take etiquette tips from murderers."

The dark pools of his eyes narrowed. "I will only take so much insolence, even from a supposed queen."

I rolled up the sleeves of my special, Garrett-knitted, baby blue sweater. "Hey, you wanna go? Let's go. But you won't be picking on a kid waitress this time."

"If Your Majesties wish us to leave"—another vampire—Don? David?—"then of course we—"

"What a shame," Tina interrupted politely as she entered the room with a tray of teas and wines. It was as if she had heard the entire conversation—and of course, her ears were good enough that she probably had. She promptly set the tray down on the coffee table and rubbed her hands together. "It seems these drinks will go to waste. But not every diplomatic mission succeeds at first, am I right? This one may take a bit of extra time."

"If you have a spare decade." Jessica smirked from her chaise longue. I couldn't tell if she was happier to see these vampires leave, or to see me fail. Either way, the way she blatantly ignored Eric's advice annoyed me.

"Please come with me, ladies and gentlemen," Tina motioned out of the parlor. "You can get back to your hotel all right? Do you require transportation?"

"Possibly off the tip of my foot?" I asked, dodging as Sinclair reached for me again.

They all stood and bowed. I had never seen sarcastic bows before. Asshats. Then they trailed after Tina like the pack of dogs I was beginning to think they were.

"Not exactly the Yalta Conference of 1945," Sinclair spat. I couldn't decide if he was looking at me with deep sympathy, or fathomless disappointment.

Chapter 5

I popped a new piece of strawberry Bubblicious into my mouth and chewed frantically. Like constant tea-gulping and daily manicures, this was one of the many ways I tried to distract myself from the near-constant urge to drink blood.

Come to think of it, tea wasn't a bad idea right now. And Tina's tray was still there, so I got started.

"What are we going to do?" I cried, chomping and gulping and examining my nails. "We can't let him get away with it. Poor Sophie."

Sinclair was rubbing his temples the way he did when he felt a migraine coming on. No doubt, my actions were blameless in this case. "Elizabeth, where to begin. First, Alonzo is under your protection as much as Dr. Trudeau is. Second, he's a member of a very powerful faction—"

"Yeah, yeah, I know. We have to play nice."

"More than that," he said quietly. "We must determine if they are a threat to us. Rather, how large a threat."

"What?"

Sinclair was prowling around the (second) parlor like a leashed tiger. "As you probably do *not* recall—"

"Hey!"

"—they came by to pay their respects, but they took their time. You and I have been in power for a year."

I slumped lower on the couch. "Don't remind—wait. You think they should have stopped by sooner?"

"I know they should have. Taking this long is a borderline insult."

"They wanted to see if you guys could keep the top spot?" Jessica guessed, getting up from her chaise longue long enough to sample some of the wine Tina had brought in.

Sinclair and Tina nodded. Their nods were so hypnotic, I almost nodded myself.

"I believe I convinced them of my staying power when I visited them last summer," Sinclair was droning, "and certainly, I was able to avoid a coup at the time—"

"Thanks again," I said brightly.

"But now they're here. Ostensibly to pay their respects."

"But maybe to see if we've got what it takes," I said.

"Exactly."

"Well." I hated saying anything nice or close to nice about the Euro-asses, but still . . . "They're here now. Right?"

"They're probably still in town, somewhere," Tina muttered.

"And I don't know that *borderline* insult is the right phrase, Eric."

"One thing at a time. What are we going to do to Alonzo, on Sophie's behalf?" I asked.

"What do you propose we do to him?" Sinclair replied.

"Huh." That was a stumper. Execute him in cold blood? Spank him? Banish him? Lock him in a room with Sophie and let her finish what she tried to start? "Huh," I said again.

"Can you even *do* anything? I mean, all respect to Sophie, but Alonzo killed her . . . what? Over a hundred years ago? Way before you guys were on the scene. And like they said—it's what vampires do. Not you, Betsy. But you know." Jessica sounded as doubtful as I felt. "Can you punish him for hurting someone decades before you were born?"

"A thorny problem," Sinclair admitted. "I have to admit, one rarely faced. Often, a vampire sired by another either joins forces with that elder, or completely ignores the connection. Many, in fact, do not even remember their sire. Sophie does not fall into any of these three categories."

"Ya think?"

"Darling, no one can understand you with that wad in your mouth."

I had made the huge mistake of trying to blow a bubble, and now it felt like yards of gum were tangled around my teeth. I fingered the chunk at the back of my mouth, glared at Sinclair, and tried to look both authoritative and sympathetic, all at once. "We gotta talk to Sophie again," I mumbled. "And the Europeans, I guess. We can't just leave it like this."

"We will," Sinclair promised, but for once, he looked like he didn't have a clue what to do. As frightening as Sophie's breakdown had been, watching him now actually made me feel worse.

Chapter 6

So I'm meeting Dr. Sophie here to try and talk this whole thing out." I took a sip of my daiquiri. "What. A disaster."

It was the next evening; my sister Laura Goodman and I were having drinks at my nightclub, Scratch. It was finally running in the black, which had taken some doing, believe me. Vampire nightclubs were awful—blood-drinking, rapacious murder, disco. I had literally killed to get the clientele to behave.

At least I had a little money left at the end of each month now—I didn't need it, but every girl likes to have a little independent income of her own.

Laura nodded sympathetically. A real bear for sympathy, was Laura. She was a precious-looking lanky blonde with sky blue eyes and a flawless complexion. Long lashes shadowed her eyes and her pretty mouth was turned down in a frown as she considered my problem. She smelled, as she always did, like sugar cookies. She used vanilla extract as perfume. It was an idea I was toying with myself. Not vanilla, but something else out of the pantry. Lemon zest? Paprika?

Laura was my half sister by my father. Her other parent was the Devil. Yes, I do mean that literally. Long story. She was a sweet-looking cutie-pie with a lethal left hook and a murderous temper. The beast only showed about one time in a hundred; but when it did, enemies died.

"She's coming here tonight?"

"Yeah." I checked my watch. "Any minute. And what the hell am I going to say to her?"

As my eyes wandered around the bar, I noticed all of the vampires in here with us looked tense. Like I cared. I had bigger problems, and if vampires came to the Queen's club because they were too scared *not* to, it was a nice damn change.

Of course, they might be afraid of Laura—she'd killed a number of them a couple of months ago. In this very nightclub—why, right over there. She was quite good at it.

I guess that sounded cold, and I didn't mean to be. I tried to treat vampires like everybody else. I really did. They wouldn't let me. It was just—why did so many of them have to be such unrepentant murderous assholes?

Case in point: Alonzo. He didn't even *remember* killing Sophie at first. Bad enough to be murdered, but to have your killer be so thoughtless and casual about it?

"I'm sure you'll think of something," Laura said, which was nice, if totally unhelpful. "Do you want me to leave?"

"Well, it's just that this is, uh, Sophie's private business. I just wanted to explain why we couldn't hang together tonight, even though we made plans."

"That's all right," she said at once. "I'll go to the evening service instead."

I finished my drink. "Back at church again?" Thank goodness. Her attendance had been off since I first met her, and I was starting to think I was a really shitty influence. Although, as Jessica pointed out, Laura could have a lot worse habits than occasionally skipping the nine o'clock service. Freebasing cocaine was the example she'd used.

Laura looked hurt. "I only missed a few times."

"Right, right. Honey, I'm in no position to judge." I couldn't remember the last time I'd attended church services, although nothing about my vampire-ness prevented me from doing so now. Crosses, holy water, Christmas trees—none of that stuff could hurt me. "I was just. You know. Commenting."

"Well, I'd better go before your friend gets here." She rose, bent, kissed me carelessly on the cheek. "We'll reschedule, yes?"

"You bet. Say hi to your folks for me."

"I will. Say hi to my—to your folks, too."

Oh, sure. My stepmother, who'd given birth to Laura while possessed by the devil and then callously dumped her in a hospital waiting room, and my father, who had no clue Laura existed. I'd get right on that. Then I'd cure cancer and give all my shoes to charity.

I watched her go. I wasn't the only one. Clearing my throat

loudly enough to be heard, I glared at the guys scoping my sister's ass until they all went back to their drinks. Sure, the package was nice, but it was the inside that concerned me. Not only was Laura the Devil's daughter, she was prophesied to take over the world. Her way of rebelling against her mother was to be sweet, and *not* take over the world. Which was a good thing.

But we all wondered if—and when—she'd crack under the pressure.

As she marched out, Sophie marched in, ignoring the surly hostess and zooming in on my table like a Scud missile. She stood over me with her arms crossed and said, "Is he dead yet?"

"I forgot how you take your coffee," I replied, not terribly surprised. I mean, after last night, I'd had an idea how our little meeting would go. "Besides, you could probably use a drink."

She plunked down in the seat next to me. "I fed earlier," she said absently. "Liam insisted."

"I meant like a martini or something."

"In fact," she went on like I hadn't spoken, which was very unlike her—she was usually the soul of French courtesy, "I had to persuade him to let me come here alone. He may have followed me anyway. He—he is most cross. As am I."

"Honey, I was there. I *know* you're pissed. And I feel shitty about it. I really, really do. I'm open to options. What can we do?"

"Hand me his head."

"See, that's just not helpful. You've got to work *with* me, Sophie."

She didn't smile. "With all respect, Majesty, if you are unable—or unwilling—to assist me, then I see no point to this meeting."

"The point is, I'm upset that you're upset and I wanted to talk to you about it. Come on, we'll figure out a compromise."

"Majesty." She speared me with her gaze. "There can be no compromise."

I made listless water circles on the table with my glass. "That's the spirit."

"I am not . . . blind to your position. But you must understand mine. He foully murdered me and must not get away with it."

"Well if you, uh, think about it, if he hadn't killed you, you never would have come to America or met Liam or any of that stuff. Made a new life."

"I had to make a new life," she said as if speaking to a child—a mean, dumb child—"because *he stole* my old one."

"Yup, yup, I hear you."

"I understand your hands may be tied politically." She smiled thinly. "I am, after all, French."

I laughed.

"But understand me: if you cannot act, I will."

"See, uh." I picked up my empty glass, fiddled with it, put it down. "You, uh, can't do that. I mean, I forbid it. Now, I know it—" I was talking to air. She had gotten up and zoomed to the door so quickly I couldn't track. Vampires sometimes seemed all legs to me—it was like they could take one step and be across the room.

"Hey, you can't do that!" I yelled after her. "I've given you an order! I've decreed! You can't ignore a decree! You'll cause all kinds of trouble! Sophie! I know you can still—what are *you* looking at?"

The vampire at the next table, a skinny blond fellow with a mustache right out of the 1970s, was unabashedly staring. "I like your shoes," he practically stammered.

Mollified, I waved the approaching hostess away. Guy needed a shave, but he had taste. I was wearing my usual spring outfit of tan capris, a white silk T-shirt, and a wool blazer, but I was shod in truly spectacular tan suede Constança Basto slingbacks. Five hundred forty-nine dollars, retail. An early birthday gift from me to me. Sinclair, that sneak—it *had* to be him—kept tucking hundred-dollar bills into the toes of my pumps, and I had quite the Shoe Fund by now.

I crossed my legs and pointed my toe, an old trick that called attention to my (if I do say so myself—there were *some* advantages to being a six-foot-tall dork) good legs. "Thanks," I said.

"I have something for you," Nineteen Seventies said, reaching under the table, and coming back up with—ugh—a muzzled toy poodle. It was wriggling like a worm on a hot sidewalk and making little burbling noises around the muzzle.

"Get that away from me," I almost yelled. I wasn't a dog person. I especially wasn't a fan of dogs that only weighed as much as a well-fed lab rat.

Nineteen Seventies enfolded the curly, trembling creature into his bony arms. "I thought you liked dogs," he said, sounding wounded.

"They like me," I retorted. Another unholy power—dogs followed me everywhere, slobbering and yelping. Cats ignored me. (Cats ignore everybody, even the undead. There's something Egyptian in all of that.) "I *don't* like them. Will you put that thing back in your pocket?"

"Sorry. I thought—I mean, I came here with a boon because—"
"A boon? Like a present? I don't want any presents. Or boon. Consider me boonless. She Without Boon. And if I *did* want a boon—which I don't—I'd rather have some Jimmy Choos."

He nodded to someone else at the bar, a short brunette with disturbingly rosy cheeks, and she rose, came over, got Sir Yaps a Lot, and discreetly vanished into a back room somewhere.

"Jeepers," Nineteen Seventies said. "I guess I messed it up all the way around."

"Messed *what* up?"

"Well . . ." He stroked his mustache, a loathsome habit I had no intention of sticking around long enough to break him of. "Everybody says that if I'm in town, this is the place I have to come. And that it's best to, you know, spend a lot of money here and all that."

"Oh." Who was "everybody"? The all-vampire newsletter one of the local undead librarians put out? Street gossip? My mother? What? "Well . . ."

This was my chance to say, don't sweat it, my good man. I'm just an ordinary gal, not a dictator-for-life asshole like Nostro was. You don't have to do anything—just try to keep your nose clean. You certainly don't have to come to my bar. But thanks anyway.

"Drink up," is what I *did* say, and sure, I felt a little crummy about it, but hey, everybody's got to make a living.

Chapter 7

I groaned when I pulled into my driveway. It wasn't even nine o'clock and the whole evening was crumbling apart. I hated how things had gone with Sophie—and what was I going to do if she disobeyed me? "Disobeyed," ha! Even the word was silly. Everybody said I was the queen, but in my head, I was still Betsy Taylor, shoe fashionista and part-time temp worker. It had been almost a year since the Aztek had creamed me, but it still felt like about two days.

Meanwhile, there was a Ford Escort in my driveway, one that smelled like chocolate. Detective Nick Berry, Jessica's new boyfriend.

Marc's beat-up Stratus was parked next to it. Lucky Marc, he'd missed all the excitement the night before, but it looked like he was on days again for a while.

And a rental car—a Cadillac, no less. The Europeans were back.

It took a long moment for me to open the door of my car. I damn near put the engine in reverse and got the hell out of there.

In the end, I got out and trudged into the mansion. Where was I supposed to go, anyway? This was home.

I zeroed in on the conversation—the third parlor, the one that took up a good chunk of the first floor. I could hear Marc squawking like a surprised goose: "Whaaaaa?"

I hurried down the dimly lit hallway.

"You guys *saw* Dorothy Dandridge?" he was saying as I entered the parlor. He was delighted and surprised, jumping up on the couch cushions like Tom Cruise with a boner. "You saw her live, on stage?"

"Yes, on a visit to New York City." Alonzo was watching Marc like an amused cat. He was sleek and cool in a black suit, black shirt, black socks and shoes. I didn't know the brand—men's shoes all look the same to me. His were spotless and polished to a high gloss, the bows in the laces perfectly tied. "She was wonderful—a joy."

"It was the last time I saw you," Sinclair commented, "before last year." He was more casually dressed—an open-throated shirt, dark slacks. Shoeless and sockless. This was a message, I knew, one for Alonzo: *I'm not worried enough about you to dress up.*

"Correct, Majesty," Tina said courteously. "We left for the West Coast right after."

It occurred to me, not for the first time, that I had very little clue what Sinclair—my fiancé and current consort—had done in the decades before we'd met. One night I'd have to get his whole life story out of him. It wouldn't be easy. When there wasn't a crisis at hand, he was about as chatty as a brick.

"You *saw* her." Marc couldn't get over it. *Boing, boing* on the couch. "Live and everything. Did you get to meet her?"

"Did you bite her?" I asked. I had no idea who Dorothy Dandridge was.

"That's the tragedy of her," Jessica said. She was on the couch beside Marc, trying not to be pitched onto the floor with all his antics. As usual, her hair was up—skinned back so tightly her eyebrows arched—and her mouth was turned down. She was dressed in her usual "I'm not really a millionaire" style: blue jeans, Oxford shirt, bare feet. In the spring! It made me cold just to look at her and Sinclair. Tina, at least, had wool socks on. Marc hadn't even taken off his tennis shoes. "That you've never heard of her."

"I didn't *say* that," I said.

"Oh, please, it was all over your big blank face." Her broad smile was forced—it was clear the barb was genuine, and not at all a joke.

"What is *with* you these—" I began, forgetting all about Alonzo, Sophie, bare feet, only to be interrupted when Detective Nick came back into the room.

"Thanks," he said cheerfully. "I was in the stakeout van half the day—no time to take a—oh." He slowed down. "Hi, Betsy."

I stifled a groan. Nick was a whole new problem, his own subset, you could say. I'd known him before I died. I'd bitten him right after I'd died, and it had driven him nuts. Literally crazy. Sinclair had had to step in with a bit of vampire mojo to make him all right. The official line was: Nick never knew I died, didn't know we were all vampires.

But we all wondered if he was going along with the party line, or fooling us. Normally I'd think nobody could get past Tina's bullshit radar, but Nick was a cop. They paid him to lie. And Jessica had decided to *date* him. Because, you know, my life wasn't stressful enough.

He held out his hand, and I clamped on it and escorted him to the parlor door. "Great to see you again." I had no intention of introducing him to Alonzo, the Amazing Spanish Killer Vampire. "Guess you two want to get to your date, huh?"

"Actually . . ." Jessica began with a mischievous glint in her eyes.

"Well," Nick said as I hustled him out, "the show starts at ten, so we thought we'd stay and visit for a few . . ."

"Right, don't want to miss it, have some popcorn for me, bye!" I hollered as he practically went sprawling into the hallway. Jessica rolled her eyes at me and followed. "See you later!"

Much later.

"That was—" Tina said, stopped, and put a hand over her mouth so I wouldn't see she was fighting a grin.

"Efficient," Alonzo suggested.

"You hush. You're still on my list, chum."

"Oh, Majesty." He clasped his heart like a player in a bad opera. "I would gladly cross seven raging oceans to be on any list you might have."

"Are you trying to pick me up?" I asked irritably, "or overthrow me?"

"Can we not do both, darling Majesty?"

"Say that now," Marc said cheerfully. As usual, he was clueless—or didn't care. He just loved the whole vampire politics thing. It was a lot more interesting than his day job, saving lives.

"Don't you have some patients to intubate downtown?" I asked him pointedly. "Or some dates to fondle uptown?"

"If I did, do you think I'd be here?" Damn. So reasonable, and the truth besides. He looked at Eric and Alonzo again. "So tell me about the show. Where did you see Dorothy? Did she look fabulous? She did, didn't she?"

"I was there for other reasons," Sinclair said. "I must admit I paid little attention to the stage goings-on."

Marc groaned and covered his eyes. His hair was growing out—he'd been shaved bald when I first met him—and his scalp was almost entirely black now, with an interesting white streak above his left eyebrow. His green eyes were shaded with long black lashes—guys always got the good eyelashes—and he was dressed in the scrubs he'd worn to work. They made him look doctor-like and professional, which was good, because he was actually a few years younger than I was, and sometimes patients had a hard time taking him seriously.

They should see him now, bouncing on the couch and grilling an undead Spaniard about somebody named Dorothy.

"As I was saying, it was in New York City," Alonzo said, smiling as Marc sighed and squealed like a bobby-soxer. " 'La Vie en Rose.' Could it have been . . . 1950? Yes, I think so."

"Oh, man, this totally makes my night. It was a shit night to put it mildly. I'm on my third set of scrubs."

"Oh, a lot of patients?"

"Bus crash. A lot of DOTS. Just really a downer."

"DOTS?" Alonzo asked.

"Dead on the Spot," Sinclair and I answered in unison. Thanks to Marc, we were up on all the medical slang.

"That sucks," I continued. "Maybe you should skip work for a while, Marc."

He shrugged. "They're hauling in a shrink for us to talk to, you know, talk about how helpless and arbitrary the whole thing was." He seemed to make a determined effort to look cheerful. "Anyway, you were saying about Dorothy, Mr. Alonzo . . ."

"She was wonderful," the Spaniard said at once, and I almost liked him for his obvious attempts to cheer Marc up. "Illuminating, gorgeous. It was impossible to take your eyes off her. Unless you were the king," he added, with a nod in Sinclair's direction.

"Thanks for not killing her and dumping her in an alley somewhere," I observed sweetly.

"Her neck, her voice box, was a work of art," he said, having the colossal gall to sound wounded. "Risking damage to such delicate organs with my teeth, even for the sake of eternal life, would have been sacrilege."

"And ending Sophie's life was not?"

Marc shook his head sadly, unwilling to completely damn this magnificent Spaniard. "Sophie's a great chick, man. You shouldn't've killed her. A great chick."

"Who would, if my math is correct, be at least fifty years under her cold, stony grave by now had I not turned her. Assuming she died of natural causes."

"That wasn't for you to decide," I said sharply. "Vampires can drink without killing people. You didn't have to take it that far."

He spread his hands. "This argument is pointless. The girl is dead. She hates me for it. There is nothing I can do about this now."

Marc looked at me. "Good point." I could see he was half in love with Alonzo already.

"Go make yourself some Malt-O-Meal," I snapped. "This is vampire business."

"Hey, I know when I'm not wanted." He didn't move from the couch.

"You're not wanted," I said.

"Oh." He got up. "Well. It was nice to meet you. Maybe you can tell Betsy and Sophie you're sorry and, you know, hang out for a while."

"Perhaps." Alonzo held out a hand, and Marc shook it. "A pleasure, Dr. Spangler. I look forward to our next conversation."

Marc was staring raptly into Alonzo's golden-colored eyes. "Yeah, that'd be good. I'm off for the next two days, so maybe—"

"Maybe," I said, seizing him by the back of his scrubs, "you shouldn't break your dating drought with this guy."

"Hey, I deserve a social liiiife," he trailed off as I practically threw him into the hallway. It was my night for tossing men out of the room, it appeared.

I stuck a finger in Alonzo's bemused face. "Don't even think about it."

He licked his thick lips. Which probably sounded gross, but it wasn't—it actually called attention to his lush mouth. "I assure you, Majesty, I do not make a move toward that delicacy of a man without your express permission."

"Ha!"

"But it is the truth," he said, sounding vaguely hurt. "Why else am I here, if not to make amends for yesterday?"

"To figure out how to kill me, after a rotten evening?"

He smiled at me. It was a nice smile; lit up his whole face and made him look like a pleasant farmer from Valencia instead of a rotten undead fiend from hell. "Oh, Majesty. Forgive me if I patronize, but how young you are to me. There was nothing rotten in last evening. Just a simple misunderstanding. To kill you in response—forgive me, to try to kill you in response—would be an overreaction of the worst sort."

Tina and Sinclair looked at each other and I could sense their unspoken agreement: *it's a peace offering. Take it.* As usual, when I was the only one who felt a certain way, I got pissed.

"Look, we can't just paper over this, okay? You weren't here two minutes before you plopped a big steaming pile of shit into my lap. Last night was *bad,* get it?"

"Majesty, lopping off heads and cutting off penises and flaying strips of skin and drying them out like jerky, then making innocent children chew on them, *that* would be bad. Not being allowed to feed until you lose your mind, fighting over victims like dogs in a pen, that is bad. Do you understand this?"

"Alonzo." I ran my fingers through my hair and resisted the urge to kick the couch through the wall. "Okay, I understand. You are trying to put this in perspective. So try to see mine. You hurt my friend. You killed my friend."

"When you were not in power, when I did not know she would be your friend."

"Agreed. But dude: she is gunning for you."

"And you will allow that? Am I not your subject as much as she is?"

"Maybe a caged death match?" Marc hollered from the hallway.

Tina got up and firmly shut the door.

"Perhaps a formal apology?" Sinclair suggested.

"I would do that," Alonzo said at once. "It would be my honor to do that, to help Her Majesty and His Majesty find a way through this . . . difficult situation."

I sighed and looked at Tina and Sinclair. Of course they would want this to end here, with a hint of a chance at agreement, so we could move on with diplomatic relations.

I gave them both a look. Tina had turned Sinclair; they were best buddies. Of course he would think Sophie and Alonzo could Just Get Along.

"You didn't see her tonight. She is beyond pissed. And she's pissed at *me,* because I'm not helping her. Yet," I added, hoping to wipe the smile off his face. Unfortunately, since I wasn't cutting off his penis or making him eat his own skin, he was in a pretty good mood.

"Where's the rest of the Undead L'il Rascals?" I asked, because more surprises, I so did not need.

"We felt it was better for me to return alone to make amends, as I was the one to, ah, incur your wrath." He almost laughed when he said *wrath.*

"Alonzo, I am fond of Sophie as well," Sinclair commented.

Finally, the lurking smile was banished. Alonzo looked contrite. "I cannot undo the past, Majesties. If you will it, I shall seek out the lady and apologize. And make amends."

"Make amends how?"

"However you wish. My fate," he said simply, "is in your hands."

I glared. "Stop being nice about it."

"Of course, as you wish. I shall endeavor to stop the niceness of my apology immediately."

Before we could go any farther down this insane road, there was a long, sonorous *gong* from the foyer, and I nearly groaned. The front door. Terrific.

"You know what? I'll get it. You guys"—I motioned to Tina and Sinclair—"should Alonzo be strung up by his balls? Discuss."

"I would be against that particular course of action," I heard him say as I left the room.

My evil-o-meter must have been on the fritz, because I didn't realize it was my stepmother until I'd swung open the door (these old fashioned mansions didn't have any peepholes—something we probably should have rectified when we moved in).

She was holding my half brother, BabyJon, a chubby three-month-old infant who was squirming and wailing in her arms.

"You take him," she said by way of greeting. "He's just being impossible tonight, and if I don't get any sleep, I'll be awful tomorrow for the foundation meeting."

"It's not a good—" I began, then juggled the baby as she shoved him into my arms. "Antonia, seriously. This really isn't—"

She was backing down the front steps, wobbling on her high heels. If it hadn't stuck me with permanent baby duty, I would have wished her to fall down. "He'll need to eat in another hour," she said. "But it's not like it's really an imposition, right? You'll be up all night anyway." She'd navigated the steps in her tacky brown pumps, and now she was practically running to her car. "I'll pick him up tomorrow!" she yelled, and dove into her Lexus.

"It's not a good time!" I hollered into the spring night as gravel sputtered and tires squealed. BabyJon was chortling and cooing in my arms. And—was that?—yep. Shitting. He was shitting in my arms, too.

I trudged back to the parlor, laden with bags of baby crap and, of course, the baby.

Alonzo looked mildly surprised. "I thought I smelled an infant," he said, which was creepy in nine ways.

Tina looked away, nibbling her lower lips. Sinclair looked resigned.

"I'm, uh, going to be babysitting tonight. Starting right now. Which does not get you off the hook," I added. "But we'll have to finish this up later."

"You have a baby?" Alonzo asked, looking befuddled.

"It's not *my* baby. It's . . . ugh. You know what? Never mind. Our discussion is over. Go apologize to Sophie, if you think that'll make things right. Just . . . do it and mind your own business."

BabyJon, perhaps in agreement, barfed all over me.

Chapter 8

I had other plans for us tonight," Sinclair said, looking nudely aggrieved.

I had just plunked BabyJon into the port-a-crib in our room, none too happy about current events. I was trying not to drool at my fiancé, who was standing, hands on hips, beside our bed. His dark hair was mussed from where he'd pulled his undershirt over his head (vampires layered), which was the only indication that he was annoyed. With his broad shoulders, long muscled legs, and big, uh, nipples, he could have been a lumberjack slumming in the state capital. All he needed was the axe. And possibly the blue ox.

"This wasn't exactly how I pictured spending the evening, either."

"Must he sleep in here with us?" Sinclair continued.

"He's not exactly sleeping," I mumbled, as BabyJon cooed and chortled in the port-a-crib.

"Why not put him down in another room?"

"Why do that when I can put him down here?" I looked at the baby. "You're fat and you don't know how to use toilet paper."

"I am quite serious, Elizabeth. Put him down somewhere else."

"Eric! Be sensible. What if something happened to him? This is an eighty-room mansion. What if he chokes? I'd never forgive myself if I couldn't get to him in time because I couldn't remember what door I put him behind."

"You have super speed and super hearing." Eric sighed.

"It's just one night. We're supposed to be together for a thousand years, you can't ditch sex for one night?"

"It is the third night," he retorted, "this week. At this rate, in a thousand years we'll have missed sex one hundred fifty-six thousand—"

"Jeez, okay, I get your point, so what? I should put him on the doorstep from now on?"

"You could try telling your stepmother no."

"It all happened so fast," I said weakly. "And you want him to have to spend *more* time with his mother? Unfeeling bastard! Besides, the baby brings the family, uh, closer together."

"Which I would understand, if you had the slightest desire to be closer to Mrs. Taylor."

"It's one night," I said again. Okay, three—in addition to the surprise she'd dumped on me tonight, we'd actually planned for the baby to stay tomorrow night and Monday. I decided not to bring this up just now. "Come on, babe. He's the only little brother I've got. Maybe he's our heir!"

BabyJon farted.

"Our heir," Sinclair observed, "is a hairless, incontinent monkey. With frog legs."

"That's not true! He looks like a real baby now." About the incontinence, I couldn't argue. But BabyJon had plumped up beautifully, and wasn't so yellow and scrawny anymore. He had a mohawk of black hair and bright blue eyes. He didn't look like my dad or my stepmother. But who could tell with babies? They usually didn't look like anybody.

"You only like him because he prefers you to all others," Sinclair pointed out.

"Well, sure. Duh. Come on, it's a little flattering that I'm the only one he can stand. I mean, how often does a girl find someone like that?"

"*I* prefer you above all others."

I melted. *Goosh*, right into a little puddle on the carpet. At least, that's what it felt like. "Oh, Eric." I went to him and hugged him. He was stiff in my arms for a moment (not in a good way), then hugged me back.

"You have to admit," I said, nuzzling his chest with my nose, "it's brought us together."

"Us being you and Mrs. Taylor."

"Yeah. I mean, my whole life—since I was a kid—we've basically stayed out of each other's way, when we weren't torturing each other. Now we're almost . . ." I was stumped. "What's the word?"

"Civil."

"That's it."

He was stroking my back with his big hands and I leaned further into him. He dipped his head, kissed me, sucked my lip into his mouth, plunged his fingers into my hair, and I responded eagerly, hungrily, touching him wherever I could reach as we—

"Arrrrgggggh," BabyJon said, and an unmistakable, mood-killing odor filled the air.

Sinclair pulled away. "Perhaps he should see a doctor. Certainly there must be specialists for this sort of thing."

"Eric, you're just not used to babies. Stinking up the room is what babies do. And changing them," I said, stepping toward the diaper bag, "is what I do, apparently."

"I'm going to take a shower," he sighed, and trudged into the bathroom.

"Thanks for nothing," I told my brother, who stuck his tongue out.

Chapter 9

Aw," Laura the Devil's Daughter was saying, chucking BabyJon under the chin. "Ooo's a wittle ittle cutie-pie? Is it ooo? Is it?"

"Stop that," Sinclair ordered from his breakfast nook bar stool, "or I will kill you right now."

Laura ignored him. "It *is* ooo! So key-yute!" She shifted him to her left hip and looked at me. "I ran into Mrs. Taylor on the way in. She invited me to a fund-raiser she's chairing."

"She did?" She didn't invite *me*. Not that I would have gone. But still. She wasn't dumping BabyJon on Laura every two days, but who got the invite? Hmmm? That's right, the devil's daughter. "I don't know why she even bothered to stop by. I mean, she had him at her house for, what? Six hours?"

"And now," Tina said, "he's baaaaaack." She snickered at Sinclair, who ignored her.

"Laura, it is quite remarkable." It was the next evening, and he was paging through the *Wall Street Journal*. "You appear to have the capacity to melt the iciest, most unfeeling exteriors."

"You shouldn't be so hard on yourself," I teased.

"I was referring to Mrs. Taylor."

"Did you work things out with Sophie?" Laura hastily interjected. She slung BabyJon over a shoulder and patted him. The smell of burped-up baby formula mingled with the aroma of fresh-squeezed orange juice—Laura's favorite drink.

"Uh, no. No word from Sophie."

"I'm sure it's just a matter of time," she said unhelpfully.

"Right. Actually, it's super tricky because the guy she's so pissed at, he's a big European mucky-muck and super-charming, too. I mean, he's sorry. He says he'll apologize. What am I supposed to be, be all *off with his head*?"

"Technically, you're allowed," Tina pointed out.

"Well, the new boss is *not* the same as the old boss. Which is my whole new, you know. What's the word?"

"Platform," Sinclair said.

"Right. Sympathetic understanding, in. Beheadings, out."

"I'm glad it's your problem and not mine," my sister said cheerfully, because she'd taken Unhelpful Pills this week.

"Actually, Laura, I am glad you stopped by," Sinclair said, glancing at his watch. "We need to have an important, private meeting among the household. I was hoping you could take the infant for an hour or so."

"His name's BabyJon," I said, "not 'the infant.' And what are you talking about? What meeting?"

I heard a car door slam outside and, annoyingly, Tina and Sinclair looked completely unsurprised.

"Of course," Laura was saying. Anybody else so unceremoniously getting the boot would be a little offended, but you had to do a lot worse than that to Laura to irk her. "Glad to help out." She scooped up the diaper bag and left with BabyJon, just as Jessica walked into the kitchen, still in her coat and rubber boots.

"Good evening," Sinclair said.

"Hey," I said, as Jessica dropped her purse on the table and went immediately to the teakettle on the stove.

"Hey," she replied.

"Jessica, we're glad you're here." Tina glanced at me, then continued. "We've been wanting to talk to you. For some time."

We had? Right. We had. I'd been meaning to get her alone and ask why she'd been so bitchy lately. Looked like Tina and Sinclair had noticed, too.

"Super," she replied with a noticeable lack of enthusiasm.

"Dear, is there anything you want to tell us?" Sinclair asked, folding his paper and then folding his hands in front of him.

"Your rent's due?" she suggested, adding a hefty dollop of cream to her tea.

"The check is on your desk. Something else."

"What is this," she joked, "an intervention?"

I didn't know *what* it was. But I could see the white Walgreens prescription bag peeking out of her purse. All of a sudden, I didn't want to be in this meeting.

"In a manner of speaking," Sinclair replied, "yes."

"Jess, you've been a little, uh, touchy lately." I coughed. "Is anything up?"

"No."

"Perhaps," Sinclair said gently, "we can tell you."

She sat. Shrugged out of her coat. Looked at him. For the first time, I noticed the dark circles under her eyes. She hadn't been sleeping well.

What else hadn't I noticed?

"Why don't you?" she replied. "Tell me, I mean."

"As you wish. At first, the change in your scent appeared to be the product of stress. But after consulting with each other, Tina and I quickly recalled the last time we sensed this—condition—in a living human."

"You quickly recalled?" Jessica teased, except she didn't sound much like she was teasing. "Or did you slowly recall?"

He ignored her and continued. "It was shortly after we arrived upon the West Coast, and found temporary shelter in the basement of a nursing home. There was a woman there who suffered for a long time—"

"Can we get to the point?" I hissed, squashing the urge to pull all the hair out of my head. There was no way this story was going to end well.

Jessica shifted on her bar stool and looked at me. I could tell she really, really wanted to say it. But she couldn't.

Sinclair let his hand slide across the marble counter and rest on top of hers. "You have myeloma."

"What?" I said.

Jessica didn't take her eyes off me. "Blood cancer."

"*What?*" I screamed.

Chapter 10

"I knew you'd be like this," Jessica insisted.

"Oh my God. Oh my God!" I was lying on the cool kitchen tiles, a cold cloth on my forehead. "I can't believe this!"

"Darling," Sinclair said, kneeling beside me, "you are my soul and my life, but this is not even remotely about you."

"How can you *say* that?" I cried. "My best friend is *dying*—"

"I'm not dying," Jessica said sharply. Far above me, perched upon her bar stool, she looked more than ever like an impatient Egyptian goddess. "I knew it, I *knew* it. This is how you get. This is why I didn't say anything."

"How could you keep this from me?" I screeched upward. "I told *you* when *I* died."

"I'm not dying," she said again, louder. "I've been to seven different specialists and they're all pretty optimistic."

"Seven? Specialists?" I rolled back and forth on the tile and groaned. "They all knew before I did? I'm like, *eighth* on your to-know list?" Tenth, I realized, when you counted Eric and Tina. "This is horrible! What kind of friend can I be? I've been sitting around chatting with Spanish murderers and you've been hauling your buns to cancer doctors?"

"I wouldn't put it quite like that," she admitted.

"How long have you been sick?"

"I got the diagnosis a month ago." To Sinclair: "Here we go."

"A month ago? Month? As in four weeks, as in thirty days?"

"Thirty-one," Tina pointed out helpfully.

I ignored her. "You didn't think you could *mention* it? You had other things on your mind? Why the *hell* didn't you say anything?"

I felt faint, but I was already lying down. That was something. *"How could you do this to me?"*

"I'm sorry." Jessica sniffed. "I guess I was being selfish."

"You're goddamned fucking right you were!"

"Elizabeth."

I turned on them like a rabid hyena. "You guys *knew*? You *knew* and you didn't *say* anything?"

Jessica looked thoughtful. "You two haven't been spying on me or anything, have you?"

"No, of course not," Tina said. She was patting my hand, kneeling on my other side. Jessica slid off the stool and stood at my feet. Tina looked up at Jess and added, "We didn't need spies to figure this one out."

"Also," Jessica said, "that'd be a crummy thing to do to your friend."

"Yes, yes. As Eric suggested, your scent has been a little ane-mic lately. There are multiple reasons why this might be, but each reason has its own particular, well, sub-scent. When Eric and I put our heads together, we matched yours with the woman in that nursing home. She also suffered from myeloma. It's rare to be that close to someone who has had it for so long, but the sub-scent is distinctive."

"And Betsy's the Queen, and you vampires should always tell your Queen everything. So. One way to look at it is that *you* guys should have told me."

The corner of Jessica's mouth twisted in a wry smile. "That's right, they're the ones who screwed up, not me. It's all on them."

"Nice try," I yelled from the floor. "You are still in a shitload of trouble, birdbrain. I can't believe this is happening to me!"

"I know," she sighed. "What a terrible week you're having."

I glared up at her. "When I get off this floor I'm kicking the shit out of you. Then you'll *really* need a doctor."

She grinned down at me. "Happy birthday."

Chapter 11

The kitchen door swung open before Jessica, Eric, Tina, or I could say another word. "I'm home!" Antonia the werewolf called, Garrett right behind her.

"Not now, Toni."

"How many fucking times I have to tell you? An-TONE-ee-uh. Just because your lousy stepmother has the same name doesn't mean I have to change mine."

"Not *now.*"

"Oh." She looked down at me. Garrett did, too. "Jessica finally told you, huh?"

Eleventh!

"Duck and cover," Tina muttered, but I was in no condition to launch myself at our resident psychic werewolf.

"You saw it in a vision?" Jessica asked.

"Hell, no. You smell totally bland. What, you guys didn't know?" Toni was looking around at all of us. With her short, Aeon Flux–like dark hair and big brown eyes, she should have looked more innocent than she sounded. And I didn't know what was up with the old T-shirt and Daisy Duke shorts (and flip-flops! In April!) but right now, her grotesque fashion screwup was the least of my problem. "Huh. Guess I should have said something before I left."

"Think so?" I snarked from the floor. "As your punishment, you are now and forever known as Toni."

"The hell!"

"Jessica's sick," Garrett said helpfully. "Also, there's a zombie in the attic."

"Shut up. Help me up. Goddammit, I'm kicking some serious ass in a minute."

"I'm outta here," Toni said at once, turning to leave. "Just wanted you to know I'm back from the Cape."

"Well, *thanks for sharing*." God, she was the most fucking annoying person in the fucking history of fucking people! Ever! Though, to be fair, I may have been feeling overly sensitive at that moment.

"Come on up to the bedroom and welcome me back," Toni was saying to Garrett as they left the kitchen. *Ugh.* I prayed I wouldn't be able to hear them doing it.

"What are your immediate plans?" Sinclair asked Jessica as he grabbed my elbow and lifted me effortlessly to my feet. Apparently, I was done wallowing.

"Chemo, probably. We're still figuring out options."

"How sick are you?" I asked anxiously.

"Not sick at all, compared to how I'll feel when they shoot radiation into me," she said with glum humor. "I'm just tired a lot these days. I actually thought I might be . . . well . . ."

"Pregnant?" Tina suggested quietly.

Jessica nodded. "Yeah. I'd been tired, and I'd—well, there were other symptoms. And Nick and I—anyway. I was wrong. Definitely not pregnant."

"Does Nick know?"

She looked away. "Nobody knows except you guys."

"Oh." I knew Jess very well, better than anybody (I was pretty sure), and I knew why she hadn't said anything. I didn't like it, but I could figure it out.

"If you thought you were carrying his child, then perhaps you should tell him you're ill."

"I don't want to. I didn't want to tell you guys, remember?"

"Oh, I remember." I still had tile marks mashed into my butt, for God's sake.

"It's like—it's not real if nobody alive knows. Right?" She smiled crookedly, dark eyes filling with tears. "It's not happening to me if the only people who know are dead."

I felt like a total toad, watching her cry. "Come on, don't do that." I hugged her. Had she lost weight? Was she bonier than usual? I was embarrassed that I didn't know. And why hadn't *I* smelled anything different? Sure I was still rather new at this, but couldn't I learn stuff like that? Was I that damned selfish? So wrapped up in my own troubles that I didn't care when my best friend caught cancer?

And hey, *could* you catch cancer? I didn't know a thing about it. That would change as soon as I could get my ass to a computer. Or my hands on those seven fucking specialists.

"You're living with the king and queen of the vampires, a werewolf, an actor, *and* a doctor."

"And a Libra," Tina piped up, a rare joke.

"Right. We'll help you. We'll fix it."

"You're an idiot," Jessica sobbed in my arms.

"That's the spirit!"

"I'm sorry I didn't tell you," she finally offered. *Finally.* "It's just all this stuff with Sophie and Liam and Alonzo. And your birthday and your wedding. I didn't want to be the downer, you know?"

I knew. And that's when I got my idea. My really, ridiculously, atrociously bad idea.

Chapter 12

$\mathcal{S}$ inclair and I were walking up Hennepin Avenue. The cops had done a great job lately in cleaning up the neighborhood; but you could still find trouble if you knew where to look. Minneapolis wasn't Cannon Falls, after all. It was still an American city with a nightlife.

"I know what you're thinking," he said at last.

"Prob'ly," I said, staring at the surprisingly clean gutter. I was profoundly bummed out. Myeloma—technically cancer of the bone marrow, and the blood plasma cells there—was serious. My research had been a total downer.

It could infect everything, and it carried with it fun symptoms like fatigue, pain, dehydration, constipation, susceptibility to in-fection, and even—ding, ding, ding!—kidney damage.

The good news was, Jessica's cancer was slow, which gave her and her doctor—and me—time to figure out options.

But right now, I could only come up with one.

"You're thinking of turning her."

"I'm still getting over the shock of finding out she's sick. How come you didn't say anything?"

"It wasn't my secret to tell," he replied simply.

"I really hate you sometimes."

He didn't say anything.

"I just—I can't lose her. My best friend! I mean, I always knew, since I'm immortal and she's not, that it was a problem I'd have to face. But not *now*. She's only thirty, for God's sake!"

"Young," he agreed.

"I'm not ready to have this happen *now*. And I don't want her to be sick at all. Maybe—maybe I can fix it."

"And maybe you do your friend a disservice," he said quietly. "Maybe you should let her solve her own problems."

"Not knowing what to wear on a date is a *problem*, pal. This is a fucking *disaster*."

"This week has certainly had its twists and turns."

"Oh, boy, don't get me started." We walked along, headed toward burned-out streetlights. "How would I even do it?" I asked. "I've never made a vampire before. Hell, I'm trying to get off the whole blood-drinking thing entirely."

"Which is why we're walking down Hennepin at two A.M.," Sinclair pointed out. "As opposed to being home."

To get back at him for not giving me a heads-up about Jessica's *fucking fatal illness*, I'd told him about my zero blood diet. He'd taken it pretty well, but I knew why.

He didn't think I could do it.

He couldn't do it, which was why we were out prowling in the wee hours.

The scene when I'd told Sinclair about my new "no blood all the time" slim-down plan (does OB-negative running down my chin make me look fat?) had been, like all the dramatic scenes in my life, anticlimactic.

We'd been necking in the shower and he'd moved in for a bite and I'd avoided him so deftly I nearly went ass over teakettle. He'd had to grab me to keep me from plunging through the shower curtain like Janet Leigh.

"What in the world . . . ?"

"Don't do that."

"As you wish." He'd let go. Then grabbed me again when I slipped again.

"I think we'd better rinse off before I kill myself."

He was standing under the shower, blinking water out of his eyes and staring down at me. "What is the matter, Elizabeth?"

"Nothing. Nothing! Uh. Nothing."

He hummed and looked at the ceiling.

"We're going to be in the shower until I spill it, aren't you?"

"In a manner of speaking."

If I'd been alive, I would have taken a deep, steadying breath. Instead, I counted backward from five, but by the time I was down to two, I couldn't wait any longer. Besides, the water was going to

get cold any second. "I'm giving up blood drinking for my birthday."

"Giving up."

"Yeah."

"For your birthday."

"Yeah."

He rubbed his chin and I realized I had never seen Sinclair
shave. Did vampires grow beards? I hoped not. Blech.

"No more victimizing would-be rapists?" he finally said. I
could tell he was hoping that would be the end of it.

"No more at all. I mean, I'm the queen, right? There's perks,
right?"

"Perks."

"Don't say 'perks' like there's a roach crawling around on
your gums. Yeah, perks! And I figure, if I'm this all-powerful
kick-ass queen you and Tina keep babbling about—"

"I never babble."

"—I should be able to decide when and where I drink blood."

"True."

"Or *if* I drink blood."

"Ah." He peered at me closely, almost as if seeing me for the
first time. Except he looked at me like that at least twice a week. It
was nice, if odd. Nobody in the world looked at me like that. "Are
you the queen of the vampires if you don't drink blood?"

"If a tree falls in the forest and no one's around, does it squick
you out by sucking out a hiker's blood? Come on, it's not that big
a deal. Right? I mean, you know I'm nuts about you. It's not personal. In fact, it has nothing to do with you."

"Nothing to do with me," he parroted.

"Look, don't be like this, okay? I'm sorry, I shouldn't have
picked the next time you wanted a chomp to tell you the feed store
is closed, but there's been a ton of stuff going on." I reached out and
wiped soap off his shoulders. His broad, broad shoulers. *Stay fo-
cused, idiot.* "You know I love everything we do in bed. And out of
bed. And in the shower. And in the parlors. And—well, I adore
every second of it. But I really need to do this. I still don't feel like
drinking blood is part of who I am, so . . . so I'm not going to do it."

"You have shampoo on your ear," he informed me, and that
was the last he'd said on the subject.

Now here we were, stalking prey for him.

Personally, I'd rather be back in the shower.

"So what's it like? Making a vampire?"

"Anticlimactic."

"Mister? Could you give me a hand?"

"Here we go," I muttered. Well dressed as we were, we must have looked like pigeons ready to be plucked.

She was tall, with dyed black hair. Torn stockings. Thin as a two-by-four. No coat, the better to see your boobs with, my dear. Her arms looked like windshield wipers.

"Yes, miss? Do you require assistance?" Sinclair let her get close.

"No," she replied, and I heard the pop of the switchblade. "I need your wallet."

"There are shelters and counselors available to help you," he informed her.

Her pimp was already flanking us in order to take us by surprise (so he thought), and as he made his move I backhanded him without even looking. It was easy. He spun and crashed to the ground.

Meanwhile, Sinclair had relieved the "professional" of her knife, picked her up so her feet dangled above the cracked sidewalk, and sank his teeth into her throat. She squealed and kicked, but I knew from experience it was like trying to get free from a tree.

I felt my own fangs pop out and had to look away.

I could (maybe) give up blood; Sinclair could not. But taking blood was downright sexual for us, so we'd compromised: we'd go out together. One-night stands only for him.

Did I like it? I did not. I fucking hated it. I should be the one he was growling over, the one in his arms. By choice, I was not. But I felt like a pimp.

He pulled free and her head lolled against his shoulder. He looked at me with a vicious gleam in his eyes, blood staining his grin. "Like some? There's plenty."

Yes! Hand her over! No, hell with her, bite me now, and I'll bite you, and that's how it'll be for a thousand years . . .

"Let her go."

He dropped her. "As you wish." He bent, tucked a business card from the nearest shelter into her top, straightened. Licked his teeth. "Ummm. She needs more fatty acids in her diet. And less crack. Shall we go?"

I shivered. "Eric, I love you, but sometimes you give me *such* a case of the creeps."

He smiled at me. "Good."

Chapter 13

We took our bloodlust straight to the downtown Marriott, where Sinclair, the sneaky bastard, had booked a room. We'd barely made it through the door when we started tearing off our clothes, groping, kissing, sucking—everything but biting. And God, it was hard. It was like jerking off and not letting yourself come. Why, why, why was I doing this?

Because I would not be ruled by my fiendish bloodlust. I was the queen; it had to count for something. I was my own person, not a slave to my hungers.

I managed to keep those coherent thoughts until Sinclair tossed me on the bed, ripped through my skirt and panties, pushed my legs apart, and stuck his tongue inside me. I wrapped my legs around his neck and rode his mouth, both of us clawing through the bedspread. Then he was rearing over me, holding me apart with trembling fingers as he rammed into me with no finesse whatsoever. I didn't hold it against him.

O Elizabeth you queen you brat you darling

"Back atcha," I groaned while he pumped and worked between my legs, while I bit my own lip so I wouldn't bite him, wouldn't eat him like the wolf ate Red Riding Hood.

Another weird queen thing: I could read Eric's mind during sex. He couldn't read mine. Yeah, that had gone over well. I'd finally told him, at the worst possible time, but the good news was, he hadn't had the worst possible reaction. We'd patched things up, but it hadn't been easy.

I can't believe I'm going along with your stupid bid for independence I should have you over my knee this minute

"Later," I panted. "You can spank me later."

I will you brat you lovely you darling

I yelled at the ceiling as I came, yelled and clutched at him and tried to pull him farther into myself. He slid his hands beneath my ass and pinched me viciously as he shuddered into orgasm.

"Owwwww."

He rested his forehead on mine for a long moment.

"What was that for?" I bitched. To hell with afterglow.

"You deserve that and worse," he said, rolling off me. "Cutting me off from my favorite blood source. Why don't you take my testicles while you're at it?"

"Stop whining. If you really minded, there wouldn't be a thing *I* could do about it."

He smiled thinly, and contemplated the ruin of our clothes. "You really think so, don't you, darling?"

"What are you bitching about? You got fed, you got laid. No baby in sight. The whole night in front of us—alone."

The smile came again, a little more real this time. "Sometimes," he said, "you almost make sense."

"Yeah, well, sometimes I have panties on. What'd you do, eat them? There's scraps of clothing all over the place."

"I took the liberty of packing a bag."

"Well, thank goodness. You didn't, uh, *like* that whore, did you?"

He pulled me on top of him and suddenly I was looking into his black eyes, which, since I had just been looking around for my underpants, was startling. "You know my heart and my soul," he said quietly, tenderly. "You can read my mind, something no one else on the planet can do. There is. No. Comparison." He shook me a little at each word to make his point. "Though I must say I find your insecurity quite charming."

"Shut up. I'm sorry to make you drink from strange women—"

"*I* don't mind," he said silkily.

"—it's just something I have to do for myself, you know? Not drink, I mean. I know it seems dumb to you—what'd you call it? My stupid bid for independence? If I was you, I'd probably think it was dumb, too. But it just seems—this whole past year—like I've been on a ride I can't get off. This is something I can control. I'm sorry if it screws you over." To my surprise, I suddenly felt like crying.

He hugged me to him. "Darling, don't do that. I know what

it's like to be a slave to the thirst. I think what you do is wondrous. I'll support you as long as you—"

"Can hold out?"

"—decide to stay with this course of action," he corrected himself.

"Thanks. For a puke, you can be pretty nice sometimes."

"Crumbs from the lady's table," he said with grim good humor, and got up to find the overnight bag.

Later, we made love again, slowly and tenderly, sliding against each other and purring like the big predators we were. And for a whole night, I didn't think about BabyJon or Sophie or Alonzo, or even Jessica.

Chapter 14

There's a zombie in the attic," Cathie said, and I nearly yakked up my gum. She was a ghost—literally, the spirit of a dead person—and as she spoke she floated through the wall, into my bedroom. Cathie had been a tall woman, almost as tall as me, with honey-tinted hair pulled back in a perpetual ponytail, a green sweatshirt, and black stretch pants. Barefoot. For eternity! At least her feet were attractive. They were little and pretty, with unpolished but nicely shaped toenails.

"This is no time for your quirky sense of humor," I snapped as I lugged a pile of near-empty journals into my closet. It never failed—I'd buy a new journal, write like a madwoman for ten pages, then lose total interest in the process. Three months later, I'd start the whole process all over again. I think I just liked buying new notebooks.

"Well, well! You seem touchy! What's the matter, didn't get laid last night?"

It was scary how much she sounded like me sometimes. Maybe that's why she totally got on my nerves. "That's not the problem at all. I just hate it when you dart out of solid walls to tell me ridiculous stories."

"Well, it's not like I have a choice," she said crossly, floating through my bathroom door and then back out again. "After all, the shortest distance between two points is a straight line. You'd walk through walls, too, if you could. And it's not like I can ring a doorbell to get your attention. As for the zombie—is it my fault you're in denial about reanimated corpses?"

"*I'm* a reanimated corpse," I said glumly. "Let me deal with that. There's no such thing as zombies anyway."

Cathie stuck her head into the wall (probably just to creep me out, since she knew it drove me crazy), pulled it back out, and said, "Why do I bother?" and stuck it back in. "Where is everybody?"

"Sinclair isn't up yet, ditto Tina, Jessica's at an appointment, Marc's at work, Toni and Garrett haven't left her bedroom since she got back, and I *was* enjoying my privacy."

"Too bad. I'm bored, and you guys are exciting company."

She'd been killed by a serial killer a few months ago, and had come to me for help. Unlike other ghosts who came to me for help, once she got what she wanted, she stayed. I wasn't a vampire queen, I was a damn soul collector. Nobody left; they all just chained themselves to me like eternal chattel. But they were all too fucking sassy for the phenomenon to be flattering.

"I bring good news from the underworld," she was booming in a terrible Vincent Price imitation. "All's quiet on the Midwestern Front."

"Yeah?"

"Well, there have been ghosts, but I've been helping them."

"You've been helping ghosts who seek my favor, without even telling me? So you're like my—"

"You know those Hollywood assistants who handle all the producer's problems so she can concentrate on making movies? That's what I do now. I help the little people."

"You want to make movies?" She had lost me. And so soon in the conversation, too.

"No, dumb shit, I'm like the assistant who tends to the little people."

I felt my eyes bulge. "I don't think you should call them that."

"I'm doing you a favor, okay? Usually these ghosts just want someone to listen, maybe point them in the right direction. You've got higher priorities right now, I gather."

"Well, thanks." I must not have sounded convincing, because she glared at me. "No, really. Thanks. The last thing I need this week is another needy ghost dropping by for favors."

"You're welcome. It's actually kind of nice. They can see me and talk to me, just like you. I mean, look at my options! I have to talk to you, or I can talk to them."

"Well, you've made the right choice," I said with faux enthusiasm.

"Don't get too down. At least your hot, hunky boyfriend can see you and touch you. Your friends can see you and touch you. What have I got? A distracted vampire with a long to-do list ahead of me and my problems."

"Cathie, that's not true!" I couldn't believe I was getting a lecture from a woman in a green sweatshirt. "I solved your problem right away, didn't I? The bad guy's dead, if memory serves."

"Yeah," she said, cheering up. "Your sister cracked his head open like an egg."

"So what do you want from me now?"

"I dunno. But there's got to be more than *this*." She sulkily floated through the wall.

"Tell me about it!" I shouted after her.

Chapter 15

Because things weren't awful enough, an hour later Marjorie the scary librarian popped by and chimed the bell. I put my foot down: no. Just because people—

"Very old, very powerful vampires," Sinclair interrupted.

—stopped by without proper planning or scheduling—

"She says it's an emergency. You want her to plan her emergencies?"

—didn't mean I had to drop everything and rush to the parlor.

"No one was in the parlor," Marjorie announced, pushing open the swinging door into the kitchen, "so I let myself in."

Tina followed closely on the librarian's heels with a pained, helpless expression. I gave Sinclair a look.

"Ah," he began. "Marjorie. So good to see you again. But perhaps now—"

"Majesty," the elder vampire said, dipping her head. "Very rude to barge in, I know; but what I have is extremely important."

"Of course it is," I sighed. "A nice new crisis you're gonna drop in my lap."

"Are you suggesting, Majesty, that I should let all important matters run their course without your intervention?" She smiled a little and fiddled with her sweater cuffs.

No, just call first.

Marjorie looked around the kitchen approvingly. The big wooden table in the center had plenty of chairs for all of us. More than enough to hold Sinclair, Tina, Jessica, and me. Everybody else was—heck, I didn't know, what was I, the fucking family calendar?

Marjorie was a severe-looking woman of ordinary height, dark hair with gray wings at the temples, and sensible shoes. She ran the vampire library in the warehouse district—the biggest, I had been told, in the Midwest.

She tried to keep tabs on all vampires, recently turned or otherwise, kept their mortgages and bills paid up (in the case of new vampires, that was especially nice . . . if they ever came back to themselves they would find a home and their credit rate unaltered), kept nice neat computer files (or, in earlier ages, carefully maintained paper files) on everyone she could. How *did* she do that? No one knew.

Anyway, she had been around before Nostro's time (Nostro=deceased disgusting despot), and before Nostro's sire's time, too. She had little interest in explicit displays of power, which was probably good news for the rest of us. Just stayed in her library, organizing lives, collecting a different sort of power—one that wasn't so intrusive, but nevertheless caught our attention when gently applied.

Anyway, she had that look of relieved approval because she saw a traditional scene that must have warmed her heart: the king and queen, with lackey (Tina) in attendance, with presumed blood-sheep (Marc and Jessica) close at hand.

"Nice to see you again, Dr. Spangler," she said, since I wasn't reintroducing her to anybody.

"Hi, uh—sorry, I—"

"Marjorie."

"Right." He'd been heads together with Jessica until a few seconds ago, but now he was looking downright flustered. Marjorie had that effect on humans. She could snap her fingers and Marc or Jess would have obediently opened a vein. "Nice to see you again."

"Thank you."

A short silence followed while Marjorie waited for us to dismiss the peons.

"So," I said before Eric could speak, because he actually *would* have dismissed the peons, "what brings you to Summit Avenue?"

"This," she said, whipping out—a gun! A knife! A brick!

No, my nerves were just a little overwrought. It was—

Tina frowned, causing a neat wrinkle to form between her eyes. It made her look positively ancient—twenty-five instead of her usual eighteen. "That's a book catalog."

"Correct."

"Thank all that is holy and unholy," I proclaimed with even less patience than usual, "that you didn't waste a second getting this over here! Why, we've been combing this entire mansion, top to bottom, for a book catalog. Our need has never been more dire."

"Specifically," Marjorie said, slapping it down on the table, "it's the Berkley Fall catalog for this year."

Sinclair closed his eyes.

"Yes, well that is the Holy Grail of book catalogs," I said, still walking the line between playing along and suggesting to this woman that she leave before my head exploded.

Sinclair didn't say anything, but his grim look and slight shake of the head suggested he knew where this was going.

I didn't. Marjorie waited for me to catch on. I quietly trusted she had packed a lunch. Finally, she said, "Page forty-seven."

Nobody moved. Apparently she was talking to me. I picked up the slick catalog and thumbed to the appropriate page. And nearly dropped it like it had turned into a rattler. "Okay, I can see why you might think this is . . ."

"A catastrophe?" she said sharply.

". . . bad. A little bit bad."

Undead and Unwed by Anonymous was splashed across a two-page spread. *Hilarious new take on the vampire genre!* was printed across the bottom, along with other critical comments ("abrupt transitions make for a rollicking ride all the same" and "low on plot but high on fun!").

There was also a quick paragraph: "Playing along with the 'true autobiography' approach, the author poses the clever conceit of suggesting herself queen of the mythical undead. One of the fall's brightest!"

"Somebody wrote a book about you?" Jessica asked, staring at the catalog spread. "Wow!"

"Not wow. The opposite of wow." *What would that be,* I asked myself wildly. *It's not like you can just spell it backward and hope that works. Maybe invert it—owo? As in, "owo is me"?*

"Majesties. I don't question your judgment—"

"But you're going to."

Marjorie looked as anxious as I'd ever seen her. "How could you let this happen?"

"It was—" *A favor for a friend,* I started to say, but Sinclair stepped on that in a hurry.

"Can the book be pulled?"

"It's not *our* book," she pointed out, sounding pissed. "You may as well ask if the new Stephen King can be pulled—we had nothing to do with it."

"*Can* the new Stephen King be pulled?" Marc joked. He was an "old-school" King snob—nothing good since *Pet Sematary*, he once claimed. I kept buying them, though. Letting go of King was like letting go of your favorite greasy spoon hangout. You don't. They're still open, so you keep going, out of pure love and memory of the good old days.

I looked at the spread again. Dark blue cover, silver lettering. "The first true tale from the undead trenches." Sure.

I knew who had written it: Jon Delk, formerly of the vampire-hunting Blade Warriors, current hot author. Not that he knew it—thanks to a bit of quick memory wiping.

Of course, the source *behind* the author had been me.

A few months ago, Jon had come by to talk me out of marrying Sinclair. A college student by day and ferocious vampire hunter by night, he'd sworn off the stake a few months ago. Meeting me had made him see a whole new side to vampires, I gathered. These days he and the rest of his little Cub Scout den from hell asked questions first and staked later.

Grateful for Delk's change of heart, I'd told him my story, which he used for a college paper. Then the manuscript disappeared, and Sinclair made Jon forget he'd written it. Problem solved. Right?

A fresh new take on the vampire tale from someone who's actually been there, according to *Publishers Weekly*.

"Jon's gonna be pissed," I said, shaking my head.

"Only if we tell him."

"Of course we're gonna tell him! We can't not tell him. That would be—"

"The feelings of the infant who wrote this are the least of your problems," Marjorie pointed out sharply. "I can assure you, the vampire community will not be happy about this. We have spent a millennium in hiding; you've been in power for about a year, and now—"

"*Charming anti–Anne Rice tale from a vampire with real world problems!*" Marc read helpfully.

"We need to deal with this now," Sinclair said quickly. "If we cannot stop the book's publication—"

"What's the spin?" I asked.

"Do you even need any?" Jessica asked. She looked a little like a cornered mouse when we all stared at her, then spoke up again. "Nobody's going to think there are *really* vampires running around. I mean, look at this ad. If you were reading it, would your first thought be, *oh my gosh, this is real, cover the kids in garlic and sprinkle the doorstep with holy water?* No way. It's obvious that it's a fiction book pretending to be nonfiction."

"Except," Marc said, "it's nonfiction pretending to be fiction."

"Right, but what live human being—other than the very few of us who already know—will realize that? Of course, if you try to get the book pulled, that really *will* get people interested. Who's trying to stop this book? Why? Are they a satanic cult? Do they worship vampire mythology?" She paused for dramatic effect. "Then: why do they act like vampires? Do they really think they are? And wow, why don't any of them have suntans?"

Marjorie leaned forward and whispered in Sinclair's ear. He nodded.

"What? What was that? Don't keep secrets. Are you keeping secrets? Marjorie, don't you know the whole 'share it with the class' rule?" I said.

"I was only asking," she said, "if your friend knew she was ill, and I was speaking privately because it was off the topic, and I didn't wish you to think I wasn't paying attention."

"Thanks, but I did know," Jessica said. She even smiled. Marjorie didn't, and I realized Jessica had made a classic mistake where vampires were concerned. Marjorie may have sniffed out Jessica's cancer, but she didn't give a shit if this specific bloodsheep ever recovered. She was just curious about Eric's feeding habits.

"Getting back to business," Tina said. "I think Jessica makes an excellent point. Trying to restrain a book only increases its impact."

"Very well," Marjorie said. "I only wished to bring this to your attention. What you do with this information is entirely up to you."

"Somebody better bring it to *Jon's* attention," I muttered, closing the catalog and trying to hand it back.

She gave me a chilly smile. "No, thank you, Majesty. I have plenty of copies."

"Well, thanks for bringing that extra special bit of fun into our lives," I said back, with equal warmth. Which was to say, with no warmth.

"Any excuse to spend extra time with Your Majesty."

"I'll see you out," Tina said, rising and gesturing to the door.

"Thank you," Sinclair said politely, staring down at the catalog with a thin twist of his mouth, "for stopping by."

"Yeah, thanks loads."

"Majesties. Dr. Spangler. Miss." And off she went, ready to spread more joy to other vampire households.

Chapter 16

There is a book about you?" Alonzo asked, his dark Spanish eyes aglow.

More pop-ins! Oh, wait. It was possible Tina had mentioned the Europeans had scheduled another meeting. At least we were in one of the parlors this time, instead of being ambushed in the kitchen by bitchy librarians. In fact, this was my favorite parlor (who knew I'd ever live in a house where I'd have a favorite parlor?), with the cheerful candy-striped wallpaper and blond wood furniture. Big east-facing windows let in tons of natural light (I assumed), and the room was heated by a gorgeous, midnight blue ceramic stove in the corner.

I was beginning to feel like I was spending half my (new) life in parlors. Thank heavens we had four, or I would get bored with the wallpaper. Now the idea of opulent mansions suddenly made sense.

"Really and truly," I answered Alonzo. "Look: we only told you guys so you wouldn't freak out if you, you know, happened to be in Barnes and Noble looking for some light reading before you iced the girl at the coffee counter."

"I appreciate the genuine concern in your otherwise needlessly provocative statement," Alonzo said. He shot his cuffs and looked at his watch, a big chunky silver thing that looked like it weighed down his wrist. He did it so often I assumed it was some sort of tic.

"Provoke this," I retorted.

"The book is not quite out yet," Sinclair pointed out, clinging to hope like a balding man with a sparse comb-over.

"Yes, it's a bright new fall offering," I added. "Place your orders now. Beat the rush!"

"I'd like to beat *you*," Sinclair muttered, which I didn't think was very unifying of him. Then, louder, he added, "We are, as you say, keeping you in the loop."

In fact, there had been a wicked big argument about it. My initial take was, let them read about it on the *New York Times* bestseller list. Who cares about their feelings? I mean, Gawd. Look at the sitch. We've got bigger problems than a book about my alleged (what was the opposite of alleged?) life story. Like Jessica being *deathly friggin' ill*. Sophie needing revenge. The Europeans needing to kick me out and take over. Maybe on that last one; it was possible they only needed to clear customs on the way home. Anyway, a book nobody would think was true was the least of my problems.

Tina and Sinclair were adamantly opposed to my own superior point of view. Like parrots playing off each other, they kept telling me in grating and repetitive ways that it was better to tell these Europeans about the book before they found out themselves and used our silence. Use it how, they didn't elaborate.

Anyway, since my number one complaint about being dead was that nobody told me anything, I eventually agreed to let Alonzo and the others know. For once, *I'd* called the meeting (well, Tina had called for me). For once, *I* was expecting company. Yeah! How 'bout *that*?

"I confess," Alonzo was saying, "I have no idea what to say. This is an unusual problem." He gave me an admiring look.

"Listen, totally off the subject, can I ask you something?"

"Majesty, I am at your disposal."

Now was the perfect opportunity. Jessica was asleep—or, at least, in her room. Marc was working. It was just us dead people.

"What's it like, to make a vampire?"

"Oh, well." Alonzo looked uncharacteristically flustered, and ran a hand over his smooth head. "I never, ah, stayed to take care of one. That is to say—"

"You always chomped and moved on."

"Would you ask a lion to sit with the corpse of the gazelle, as the hyenas and vultures tore at the tendons?"

"People aren't gazelles," I pointed out, restraining my temper with some difficulty. *You brought it up, you brought it up.* "So there might be other vampires running around, ones you made?"

"It is likely," he said reluctantly. "In my youth. Now, of course, I have much more control over the thirst."

"See, I avoid that whole thing by not even drinking. You should try it!"

"This, what you say, 'avoid the whole thing.' This is physically impossible." Frustration, intrigue, admiration, and rage crossed his features all at once. It made his eyes go really squinty and he was rubbing his head so much I wondered if he was trying to start a fire up there.

"Feeding leads to killing. It happens time and time again, vampire after vampire. I can't even imagine," I said, speaking more to myself than anyone in the room. "Killing somebody. I mean—"

Okay, I had killed someone. Two someones. Wait, four, if you counted vampires. Hmmm, official Gray Area ahead. But they were all self-defense, right? And the vampires were already dead, right? Neither of which Alonzo could claim about Sophie.

"Walk with me?" the Spaniard asked, getting up smoothly from his spot on the love seat.

"Yeah," I said, standing up an instant later. "Sure. No problem."

Sinclair raised his eyebrows at me, but didn't say a word or make a move.

So we went.

We'd put our coats on; he had put back on the slightly muddy but still meticulously crafted black wingtips he had left in the hallway upon his entrance. For myself, I'd slipped into a somewhat fashionable pair of bright red rubber boots—it was wet out. Spring in Minnesota meant thaw, and thaw meant mud.

"At last," he teased when we had walked a block without saying anything to each other. "I have spirited you away from the king."

"Yeah. I don't even know why we're talking. I sort of thought when I first met you, that we'd end up at each other's throats. You know, after Sophie had her turn."

"Have you decided what to do with me?"

I nearly walked into a melting snowbank. "Seriously? You're asking me?"

"I am but a loyal subject. Your will is my will."

"I appreciate the thought." And, weirdly, I did. "Is it real? I mean, is it genuine? If I said, 'Okay, Alonzo, I'm going to cut off your head because you were a bad vampire a hundred years ago,' you'd just go along with it?"

"Well," he admitted, neatly avoiding a sample of thawing dog poo that had likely been there since January, "I wouldn't calmly kneel before you and wait for the sword to swing, but I respect the power of the monarchy."

"In other words, you don't think I'd be so cruel."

"No," he replied. "I don't think you would be so cruel. In fact, I am counting on it."

"You really don't think I'd do anything to you?"

His words came out with careful measure. "That would be an overstatement. I do not think you would kill me in cold blood."

Well, nuts.

"It would be easier," I said with a sigh, "if you and your friends were the bloodthirsty monsters I thought you were at first. Maybe the six of you could leave town in a trail of blood. Then killing would be easy."

"This should not concern the others," he said emphatically. "This is a matter between me and Dr. Trudeau. And your Majesty, of course."

"Is that why you came over tonight by yourself?"

"You only sent for me."

"You're the only one whose name I can remember," I admitted, and he laughed.

In the distance, I could hear barking and yowling and toenails clicking on sidewalk. I figured we had about two more minutes before all the neighborhood dogs descended. There was a reason I didn't like taking walks.

"Let's head back."

"We only just—"

"Dude, trust me. You do not want to be here five minutes from now. We can talk more in the garden behind the mansion. Behind the fence."

He obediently turned with me as I did a one-eighty and started heading back up the sidewalk to the house. He was right; it was a little silly. We were barely out of the shadow of the mansion. I had barely talked to him about anything. Wait—had it been my idea to go for a walk? I tried to remember. No. He'd asked me.

"I have another question for you, Majesty."

"Oh, great. My turn again. Except we're not playing a game."

"About that, *señorita*, you are wrong. But here is my question: are you going to turn your friend into a vampire? Or wait for her to die and bury her and mourn her?"

"How do you even *know* about that?"

"You mean, before you asked me what it was like to make a

vampire? I guessed. I know she is ill, and after seeing you and her in the same room, I could make some assumptions."

The mansion loomed larger before us, the dark and forlorn branches of surrounding trees still waiting for rebirth. The baying of dogs was coming closer.

He broke the silence again. "You do not seem the type of lady to give up her friends so very easily."

I chewed on that one for a moment. The thing about Alonzo was, even when he said something nice, it wasn't like he was sucking up. Maybe it was in the translation of his ideas from Spanish to English; but his well-crafted words betrayed a certain attention for my well-being. In fact, he made for a pleasant change from most vampires here in America, who either (a) ignored me or (b) tried to kill me.

"I only just found out my friend was sick," I said finally. "I don't know what I'm going to do, yet."

"I beg your pardon. But I believe you do."

We stopped together at the iron gate on the west side of the house. It led to the brown and lifeless gardens behind the house. But neither of us reached for the latch. Instead, we watched each other for several seconds. *Game indeed,* I thought.

"Well," I said finally, "you're assuming my friend will even go along with it."

"She has a choice?"

"If she didn't, she wouldn't really be my *friend,* would she?"

"Your uniqueness," he offered, "is both blessing and a curse. Blessing, in that you are different from others, which I always see as a positive. A curse, in that you generate problems of your own making—problems that vampires like me do not trouble with."

"For example?"

"I have never known a vampire to remain friends with a human—certainly not long enough to consider a careful plan to turn that friend."

"Never? And you've been around, what? A hundred years? Two hundred? And in that time, you've never made a friend and then wanted to keep them around?" My situation with Jessica couldn't have been that out there . . . and neither could Sophie and Liam's.

"Not a living human," he answered with arms stretched and palms up. "And when you generate two estimates of my age, you would do well to round to the higher one." One of the hands lifted higher than the other.

I laughed.

"There's us," he said, finally swinging open the gate and entering the garden, "and there are them. The two cannot mix. No good comes of this. Your situation—forgive my boldness, Your Majesty—I see your situation as the inevitable, and unfortunate, end result of your unreasonable attachment to your human friends. Someday, you will end up in the same place with your doctor friend. Each of these endings will devastate you, weaken you—and to no good purpose."

"I don't see it that way at all." I felt a little defensive, but also grateful to this vampire. Which was amazing in and of itself. But Alonzo was giving me the first chance I had really had to organize my thoughts. A rare and wonderful thing, in my case.

"How do you see it, my queen?"

My thoughts assembled rapidly as I said the words, and I felt more secure in my opinion with each new idea. "I gain strength from my friends, not weakness. My 'situation' with Jessica is not the 'end result' of anything. It's a step in our journey together. Maybe she dies, maybe she lives. But she is an essential part of me, either way. What am I without these friends?"

"Faster, stronger, generally superior," he suggested.

"Superior," I muttered. "I'm afraid I don't like that word very much. Especially when vampires use it."

"Oh dear." He gave a knowing smile as he walked beside me on the dead garden path. The baying of the dogs faltered in the distance. "No wonder you had a problem with the former regime."

Chapter 17

We slipped into the back entrance of the house and just sort of stood around for a moment in the mudroom. I wanted to go to the kitchen and hang out with Jessica for a while—give her a chance to maybe tell me how the doctor's appointments were going. How everything was going. The thing about Jess—you couldn't force information out of her. She'd tell you or she wouldn't. I planned to make the atmosphere as welcoming as I could.

Anyway, I was pretty much done with Alonzo. I'm sure he was done with me. And Sinclair wasn't the "hey, let's go play golf in the dark" kind of guy. In fact, I had never seen Sinclair with one man friend. In further fact, as far as I knew, Tina was his only friend.

Anyway, Sinclair was done with Alonzo. Tina probably wasn't even there—she was tracking Jon down for us.

So it was that part of the party where you want your friends to leave, and they want to leave, but it was too early to look at your watches.

"It's getting late," Alonzo said, stealing another glance at his big silver watch. *Thank God!* Normally that weird tic of his made me wonder if a bomb was set to go off somewhere. But this time I welcomed it. "And unlike some, I must feed before dawn. With your permission, Majesty . . . ?"

"Of course. Um, try not to kill your food." I tried to say it as a joke, but it probably sounded like an order. Enough—I was too emotionally exhausted to try to explain. Let him figure it out. "Thanks for coming over."

"The pleasure was mine." He smiled at me, showing me how

very pleased he was. "I was waiting and waiting for the phone to ring. And now, I will go back and wait some more."

"Hmmmph." I was 98 percent sure he was fucking with me, but he had enough slipperiness in his tone that just made it quicker to repeat, as I did, "Thanks for coming over."

He went. I listened for Sinclair but he didn't pop out from a hidden shadow the way he usually did. Nobody was pulling up in the drive. Tina was standing unobtrusively in the short hall to the kitchen, ready to spring forward with a cup of tea. Guess she'd quit looking for Jen for the night.

I slung my coat into the mudroom closet, kicked off my boots, and made for the kitchen.

Sinclair was there, sitting with Marc and Jessica and reading Sun Tzu's *The Art of War*. His sleeves were rolled up. His feet were bare. He looked as comfy as ever.

Not that I wanted him breathing down my neck, but . . .

"Shouldn't you be, uh, waiting breathlessly to hear about my walk with Alonzo? Did he swear allegiance? Did he bone me at the intersection of Dale Avenue?"

"Oh." He turned a page. "About the first, Alonzo is gradually falling under your spell."

"My spell?"

He looked at me innocently. "Why, dear, your natural charm. No doubt you had it before you were a vampire queen; but it's all the stronger now. No one of any intelligence can resist you for long."

See, there it was again, just like Alonzo—the 98 percent certainty that this guy was just fucking with me. I just waved a hand and let him continue.

"I only have to wait a few more days, and then he will be yours and, by association, ours. As for the latter, if you wanted to use your walk to, ah, show carnal interest, there is nothing I can do about it. And if you bit him, or allowed him to bite you—"

"Fat goddamned chance."

"Yes, well." He shrugged. "I was not especially worried."

"Okay, there's got to be something between total disinterest and hanging all over me. This"—I gestured—"isn't it. But anyway, even though you seem, uh, not too worried about it, I'll tell you how the walk went."

"The walk with the guy who's going to fall in love with you?" Marc asked.

"He's *not* going to fall in love with me. Besides, I think he's—

I mean, if he was going to fall in love with anybody—which he's
not—look, can we stay on track, please?"

Just then I saw Marc slip Jessica something small and white—
it looked like a business card—and whisper to her. I cut myself
off. "What was that? Are you telling secrets? What did you tell
her? *Share with the class!* Are you getting sicker? You're not getting sicker, are you?"

I couldn't smell *anything* different about her. Of course, I
didn't go out of my way to smell my girlfriends, so I didn't exactly have a baseline for comparison purposes. But still. You'd
think I could tell something.

"Take a pill," Marc said. "I'll give you one. I was giving her
the business card of a guy I want her to see. He's a really good
doc—my dad saw him."

And is still alive, right? I was embarrassed to ask. I knew
Marc's dad was sick, but surely I would have heard if he'd died.
Somebody would have told me, right? We share with the class!

"How's your dad?"

"He's really good." Weirdly, Marc said this in an almost glum
tone. "They got him in this new place, he likes it a lot. It's a real
house, not a hospital or anything. He's one of a couple guys who
lives there, and the nurse who owns the place keeps an eye on
them, you know, makes sure they get their meds and see their
docs, but she's not, you know, taking care of them in an obvious
way. If he wants to retreat to his own space and watch a baseball
game, he can. Or he can eat in the dining room if he wants company. It's a pretty good compromise."

"That's great." I said this with total sincerity. And it was, beyond obvious reasons: so, so great to hear good news for a change.
"You should bring him by to—"

"Meet all my cool new vampire friends?" Jessica smothered a
snicker as he continued. "Honey, he had a huge problem with my
lifestyle when I was just gay. Now I'm gay and living with vampires."

"Well, it's not like you're sleeping with any of us." I shrugged.

"Hmm." His eyes searched the hallway behind me. "So,
what's Alonzo's story? Did he go home? Is he sticking around? I
just thought—"

"Alonzo's not an option, Marc. Honestly."

"Yeah, well. You never know. You know how it is. You're new
in town, you don't know the good bars, you—"

"Go out and kill a waitress for the fun of it?"

"Still working through that?" Jessica asked.

"Well, no matter how we deal with it among vampires, I'm sure Marc can agree that murder is a really great reason not to date a guy, doy!"

"Oh, I dunno. That whole 'falling for the dark side' thing worked out kind of good for you," Marc said, his gaze sliding to Sinclair for a moment.

My mind went blank. A cliché I completely understood: I could feel my brain trying to make words and not coming up with a thing. Nothing. Empty. *Nada.* Finally I managed, "Do as I say, not as I do. And Eric's a good guy. When he kills in cold blood, he does it for a good reason. You know, like love in his heart."

"Ah, darling," Sinclair said, gaze on his book.

"And I know he's cute and all," Jessica said, "Alonzo, I mean, but I don't think he *dates.* You know, those types have minions and contemporaries, but I don't think there's much emotional attachment anywhere, with anyone."

"True," Sinclair said, still not looking up, "but do not discount Dr. Spangler's scruffy Gen-X charm."

"No, you don't," I said, ignoring how Marc suddenly looked pleased and puffed up a little. "I'm on to you, bud. You're not sneaking under Alonzo's radar by having one of us date him."

Shit, when Detective Nick asked Jessica out, Sinclair practically drove her to her date. He *loooved* the idea of a cop being on our little "go, vampires!" team.

"So he's headed back to the hotel?" Marc pressed.

"After a quick stop to commit felony assault," I said glumly.

"You two are getting so chummy," Jessica said, "I'm surprised he didn't ask you to go with him to rustle up some dinner."

"No thanks."

"You talked to Sophie's people lately?"

I slunk into one of the chairs. "What people? It's her, and it's Liam. And no. All's quiet from their end. They're waiting, I guess. For me. To do whatever."

Like Alonzo. Like all of us: stuck in the same web of waiting. If I could get my hands on the guy who made the web, I'd throttle him.

"So, what?" Jessica asked. "Did Alonzo try to jump your bones?"

"Or did a slobbering horde of golden retrievers descend on you before he could make his move?" Marc piped up.

"Shut up, shut up. He didn't make any moves. He didn't do

anything. He asked me some stuff and I asked him some stuff. And then we came back."

"What 'stuff'?" Jessica asked, suspicion making her tone heavy.

Oh, whether or not I was going to put the chomp on you, nothing to worry about. "Vampire stuff," I said, and wouldn't say more, no matter how much she bugged me. Which, by the way, was a considerable amount.

Chapter 18

It was the next night and we were back in the kitchen. Half the table (and it was a big table) was covered with liquor bottles and half-full drinking glasses. It looked like we were all going on a bender, but the truth was, Marc was trying to teach us how to make rainbows.

Jessica was having a bit of success; she'd get her rainbow halfway made and then the grenadine would sort of squiggle into the rest of it.

All my rainbows looked like mud. I was so fucking thirsty I didn't care; I drank the mistakes. The real tragedy was, I didn't feel anything close to drunk.

"Just—okay, watch me again. See? You slooooowly let it sort of dribble off the spoon. Otherwise it'll all moosh together."

"I can get the first layer," I said, watching Marc (who had put himself through med school tending bars) carefully build a rainbow-colored drink of grenadine, vodka, that blue stuff that looked like Windex, sweet and sour mix, and something else I didn't know the name of. I wouldn't have wanted to drink it (well, I was drinking it, but if I were still alive these concoctions would have had me on my ass) but once Marc made it, it sure looked pretty. "Then it all goes to hell."

"Free booze and a metaphor for life, too!" Jessica watched her rainbow come apart, rushed it to her lips, and then made a face and put the glass down. "Why are we all learning how to make a drink none of us like to, um, drink?"

"I saw one of the bartenders at Scratch make one and thought it looked cool. Once I was sure one of the layers wasn't blood—"

mmmm, blood, precious blood

"—I thought it'd be fun to try. And I wasn't going to ask that vampire how to do it. She's fairly surly as a bartender, and worse when she's hostess."

Where had *that* come from? Actually, I was starting to think about blood a lot more and more. You know those cartoons when the wolf looks at his friends and they turn into rib roasts and stuff before his eyes?

Jess and Marc were starting to look *reeeally* good.

"Maybe if you were a little friendlier to the Scratch vampires," B-positive—I mean, Marc, began, "they'd treat you—"

"Look, nobody's trying to kill me right now and that's just fine. If they don't *like* me, that's just how it goes. I got over needing people to *like* me in tenth grade, when I spied the captain of the cheerleading squad on her knees in front of the offensive line of the football team under the bleachers, one day after school. I figured that wasn't the life for me."

"Of course," Jessica observed as she experimented with different rainbow colors, "she somehow still pulled off Miss Congeniality two years later."

"What was your secret, Betsy?" Marc's eyes glittered with a fascination. "Did you do the defensive line instead? I hear that's where all the votes are."

"Honey, you tell me. You probably blew more guys in high school than I did."

He laughed. "Miss Congeniality! Seriously, that's great! Do you still have the crown and sash? I could get a date in no time if you'd lend me those props for five minutes."

I drank another failed rainbow and ignored an empty bottle of vodka as it tumbled to the floor and rolled under the table. "Forget about it."

"Yeah, but just think—"

"Marc, I said fucking forget it, okay? Do I have get out the hand puppets? Knock it off!"

"Jeez, Betsy, I was only kidding around."

I resisted the urge to throw my empty glass at him. I wasn't mad at him. I wasn't mad at anybody. I was just . . .

Just really thirsty.

"I'm sorry," I said, not meaning it, but that was what people said in such circumstances. "I'm a little on edge these days."

"Sure, no problem. I had half your problems, I'd stress out, too."

Well you don't so why don't you SHUT THE FUCK UP?

"Uh-huh," I said brightly. The smell of all the booze was making me a little light-headed. Not to mention the smell of B-positive's aftershave. I probably shouldn't have been drinking so much on an empty stomach. Not that I could get drunk. Well, maybe I could. Eventually.

"Yeah, uh, Betsy, we've been meaning to talk to you about this." This from myeloma. I was pretty sure I could smell it now.

"About what?"

"Your no blood-drinking thing."

"It's not a *thing*, it's a lifestyle. You know," I added brightly to Marc, "like yours. I'm *choosing* not to drink blood."

Marc almost dropped the grenadine. He turned to give me his full attention when Jessica jumped in with, "Nuh-uh! Picking a fight to get out of talking about this won't work."

"Right," Marc said, looking less convinced. "That won't work. Bitch."

Nuts. "Oh, come on, you guys!" I rested my forehead on the table. "I figured you'd be supportive."

"Supportive of you breaking Sinclair's heart and making yourself nuttier than you usually are? Honey, your temper these days is almost as bad as mine."

"Well, why don't you shut your fucking face, then?" I straightened up in a hurry as my vision cleared. "Sorry. That sort of slipped out."

"Great," Marc mumbled. "Vampire Tourette's syndrome."

"And Sinclair's heart isn't broken. And even if it was, it's none of your business."

"How's he supposed to feel when you tell him not only are you going on a hunger strike, he is, too, unless he cheats on you with other people?" Marc demanded.

"What part of 'none of your business' do you not get?"

"Ha!" Marc wiped off his lips and began refilling another glass with yet another perfect rainbow. "We have to live with you guys, you know."

"No," I said pointedly. "You don't."

"What's *that* supposed to mean?" Jessica asked.

I rubbed my eyebrows. "Nothing. It's not supposed to mean anything. Sinclair's heart isn't broken."

"He's been moping around this place like he heard yellow was the new black," she added.

"We worked that out. We have a plan for him getting his blood."
Marc snorted. "Yeah, I'm sure it's not awful."

I threw my hands in the air. "So, what? What are you telling me? Start drinking again? Hurt more people? Maybe kill someone by accident if I go too far?"

"What happened between Alonzo and Sophie won't necessarily happen to you."

"I *knooow*," I said. I was a little astonished. One thing had nothing to do with the other. I had started my hunger strike way before Sophie even got to town. Right?

"Moderation," Marc was babbling. "Everything in moderation. Besides, aren't you the only vampire who only has to drink once or twice a week? How are you going to kill somebody doing that?"

"I plan," I said grimly, "on being the only vampire who doesn't have to drink at all."

"Well, it's making you nuts," Jessica snapped, "at the worst possible time for me. And if I find one more piece of chewing gum on the banister, I'm evicting you. I figure you've gone through twenty packs in the last two weeks alone."

"You're counting my gum wads?" I felt my eyes narrow. I didn't make them do it; they sort of went all squinty on their own. "That doesn't strike you as, oh, I dunno, anal-retentive?"

"Doesn't your depositing them all over the house," she snapped back, annoyingly unafraid, "strike you as incredibly selfish and slovenly?"

"For the lasht time, thish ish none of your bithneth."

What the—? Horrified, I felt my mouth.

Marc was pointing at me, eyes big. "Your fangs are out! You got so pissed your fangs came out!"

"I thought they only came out when you smelled blood," Jessica said, still remarkably unmoved.

"They do," I replied, feeling. Cripes, it felt like I had a mouthful of needles. "But Sinclair can make his come out whenever he wanth. Maybe thith ith part of a new power."

"And maybe you're, I dunno, *losing it!*"

"Calm down. Thereth nothing to worry about."

"Nothing to worry about?" Marc was as hysterical as a woman who missed all the really good Thanksgiving sales. "You should see yourself!"

"Well, maybe I'll go take a walk." Oh, and run into that cute Mrs. Lentz in her bouncy, thin-strapped jogging bra while she walks her border collie. Normally I went for guys but her shoulders were so lovely and bare—

"You can't go out looking like *that*."

I was hurt. Well, pretending to be. "Are you thaying I thould be athamed? Thith is who I am now."

"Yes," Marc said, and Jessica swallowed her laugh. "You should be very, very ashamed. You should go to your room and hide your head until the shame passes. And until you don't look like you're trying out for the next *Dracula* remake."

A sly thought popped into my head, there and gone, one

Eric would understand, and so would Alonzo

too slippery to hold on to. Probably just as well. These days, none of my thoughts were nice ones.

"Doeth anybody have thum gum? I'm freth out."

"Sure," Jessica said brightly, as if a wonderful idea had just occurred to her, "and hey, maybe this time you can stick the wads in a garbage can, if you want to avoid eviction." She slid a brand-new pack of strawberry Bubblicious toward me.

"I'll second that motion," Marc mumbled. "Honestly, Betsy, do you know what they *put* in that stuff? The artificial gunk that slides down your throat, leaving the hard, gray crud behind?"

"Thut up," I told him, reaching for the pack. "Thith ithn't very conthructive."

"Yeah? Constructive is the last damned thing on my mind. This place drives me nuts sometimes: nutty vampires, a bitchy werewolf, a zombie, a grumpy billionaire, and a vampire on a hunger strike."

"You have to admit," Jessica said, starting to put away the liquor bottles, "there's never a dull moment. What's the polar opposite of a dull moment? 'Cuz that's what we got around here. All the time."

"I don't think you should call Garrett a zombie. He's a little slow, but—hey! Don't take the vodka."

"You can have it back," she said in her annoying Mommy voice, "when your fangs go away."

"I can have it back right *now*, honey."

Marc put his hands over his eyes. "Don't fight, you guys. No more. I'm sincere here."

She slapped my hand when I reached for it. "No! Bad vampire!"

I glared. "You know, most sensible people would be scared of me."

She laughed at me. "Most sensible people haven't seen you dancing the Pancake Dance in your granny underpants on New Year's Eve."

"Hey! Your fangs are gone." Marc digested what she'd just said. "Granny underpants? You?" Apparently me doing the Pancake Dance wasn't so hard to believe.

"It was just that one time," I grumbled, the last of my mad-on vanishing as quickly as it had come upon me. "All my thongs were in the wash." What had I even been so mad about, anyway? I couldn't remember. Jessica and Marc were the greatest. I was lucky to have friends like them. They were—

The kitchen door swung open, framing the former head of the Blood Warriors. "I don't understand," Jon Delk said. "You're saying I published a book?"

—sunk. We all were.

Chapter 19

Thanks for coming so quickly."

Delk hadn't taken off his coat, and had tracked mud all the way (groan) to the kitchen. His full name was Jonathon Michael Delk, but too many people in his life called him Jonny. So he was going all tough guy now and insisting on the moniker Delk. I couldn't blame him: I had a silly first name, too.

"She said you were in trouble," J—er, Delk was saying. "But it sounds like that was just another vampire trick to get me to—"

"I said the Queen needed you," Tina corrected him with more than a little sharpness. Tina didn't care for Delk, given his vampire-slaying past. No doubt the car ride up from the farm had been a carnival. Not least because she and Eric thought it was perfectly fine to leave Jon out of it. But I just couldn't do it. He had written the book. It was being published. How could I keep my mouth shut about it?

"Delk, sit down."

"What's going on?" He shook the catalog at me, dropped it on the table, and rubbed his hands together; they were red with cold. "One minute I'm home, the next I'm in the car with Tina—"

"Do you want something to warm up with?"

He gave me a look I supposed he thought was subtle. I was feeling sicker and sicker by the moment, and it wasn't all the failed rainbows. Delk had a bit of a crush on me, and if he had come charging up to the Cities because he thought I was in trouble—well, that was just too damned sweet.

In fact, he'd shown up here a few months ago when he heard about my impending unholy nuptials. The gist of our conversation:

DELK: You can't marry Eric Sinclair.
ME: Just watch.
DELK: He's a bad man.
ME: You don't know from bad.
DELK: You're making a mistake.
ME: Shut your head.

Not exactly Tristan and Isolde, but it passed the time around here.

Then, inexplicably (except I was pretty sure I knew why) he hung around the mansion. Started interviewing me for a class project. Eventually produced a book. But then Sinclair—

"Tina, would you leave us alone for a minute?"

"I'll go see if the king is available," she said, backing out of the kitchen, looking at Delk the way a cat looked at a really big rat. *I can take you. I might get hurt, but that's all right.*

We were alone. Except for Marc and Jessica, shamelessly eavesdropping outside the kitchen door. I couldn't do anything about that, so I addressed the problem at hand. "You wrote the book. It's coming out this fall as a paperback everyone thinks is funny fiction."

"You're saying someone used my name on their book?"

Oh, boy. He was standing there, so earnest and flushed and blond and *young*, I almost couldn't bear it. He was a nice kid. I liked him a lot. There never would have been anything between us, and not just because of Sinclair, but I still liked him and sure didn't want to upset him.

I could almost hear Sinclair in my head: *Then don't.*

Too bad.

"I'm saying you wrote this book, this *Undead and Unwed*. Someone—probably you—turned it in to a publisher, and now it's going to be on bookshelves this fall."

"But—I mean, I did a paper for class before holiday break—"

"You turned the paper into a book. You followed me around for days, transcribing my life story, putting your own spin on it. You had, like, three hundred pages."

He was blinking so fast, for a second I thought he had something in both eyes. "But I don't remember that! I'd remember if I wrote a book, right?"

"Yeah, normally. Except Sinclair made you forget you'd written it. And since you didn't remember writing it, you didn't think to warn us that you'd sent it in to get published."

"*Warn* you? I—" He walked dazedly back and forth by the table for a moment, not quite pacing. He looked like he didn't know what to do with his hands. "Sinclair made me forget?"

"Well." Tell the truth and shame my sister's mother, wasn't that how the saying went? Sure, we could be done now, but I didn't want any part of this conversation left undead. Whoops—Freudian slip. *Unsaid.* Another surprise down the road I didn't need. "Tina found the electronic version of your manuscript—she was looking for it, or something like it—and told Sinclair. He mojoed you into forgetting all about it, and then they deleted your work. They thought all of your work."

"Did you call me down here," he whispered, "because you just found out and you want my help to stop them?"

"Ah, no. See, after they did all that, they told me. This was around Christmas. And at first I told Sinclair to undo his undoing, if you get what I mean. But then I remembered."

"What?"

"I remembered I'm the queen and I'm responsible for all the vampires," I said simply. "So I let it all stand. It was shitty for you, but I thought if the book got out that would be shitty for all vampires."

He was clutching the back of one of the kitchen chairs and I saw all the knuckles had gone from pink to dead white. All the color had fallen out of his face, except for two patches of red way up on each cheek.

"Are you okay?" I asked, dumbest question of the year, no doubt. "Maybe you better sit down."

"You—you *let*—him—*do* that? To me?"

"Well, I didn't know about it until afterward," I began lamely, "but—"

He actually swayed a little while he hung on to the chair. I edged a little closer, figuring I could catch him if he fainted. He *looked* like he was going to faint. After he threw up. "You *let* him do that—let him into my fucking *mind*—and then you had the chance to *help* me and you took *their* side?"

"I—yeah. That's more or less it."

"You didn't help me—you let him—and you didn't—"

"Delk, I think you should sit down before you—"

"*Shut! Up!*" he screamed at me, the cords standing out on his neck. "You aren't *even* sorry! Because if you did it, if you fucked me over to help all of goddamn vampire-kind, you *can't* be sorry."

"I'm sorry you got stuck in the middle. I'm sorry there's a

book out there that you don't remember writing. A funny book the critics like," I added, trying to find a speckle of good in this whole awful nightmare. Oooh, and there was something else! "You kind of got the last laugh, because the book is coming out anyway, and the vampires who know about it are pretty annoyed, so—"

"So everything you let him *do* to me was for nothing."

"Okay, that's another way to look at it."

He wiped his nose with the back of the hand not holding the chair. "I can't believe this," he whispered.

"I'm really sor—"

"I can believe that bitch snuck around in my files, and I can believe that prick jumped into my mind, but you! You're supposed to be the good one! I-I thought you—you aren't supposed to be a bad guy! You're supposed to look out for me, *and* for vampires—they're all the same to you, right?"

I stammered, trying to say five things at once.

"Right?"

"Delk, I—"

He wheeled around and almost slipped in one of the little puddles he'd made.

"Please don't leave! Please, let's talk some more."

He barked an incredulous laugh, staggered for the door, and shoved against it, hard.

Unfortunately, it only moved about a foot before it thudded into something.

"Aagghh!" I heard Jessica say from the other side, then another thud as she fell down. I rushed over, held the door open, and saw her rolling back and forth on the floor, hands cupped around her nose. The blood, it was—it was *sheeting* down her throat and onto her shirt; the blouse was already wrecked.

Marc was crouched beside her, doing the doctor/mom chant: "No, I won't touch it, just let me look, no, I'm not going to touch, just get your hands down so I can see, let me see."

That was no ordinary nosebleed. It was just—it was everywhere. I whirled upon Delk. "She's sick! And you practically broke her nose—she didn't do *anything*. And she's *sick*, you asshole!"

Before I knew what was happening, I had seized him by the shirt and was holding him right up to my nose. "You thouhd have kept your handth to yourthelf."

"Betsy, don't! It was an accident, come on, it's—" Jessica choked a little from her spot on the floor and spat blood. "It's a swinging door, for heaven's sake. I'm surprised this doesn't happen every week. Come on, put him down."

I threw him away from me. He bounced off the wall (and I'd be lying if I didn't admit it felt good to watch him fly like a paper airplane, and where had all my sympathy for him gone?) and crumpled to the floor in a heap.

I knelt by my friends. "Jeth, are you all ri—"

"Look out!" she screamed, and I turned just in time to get shot.

I'll bet Marc is sorry he skipped work today, I thought, toppling into Jessica's bloody face and knocking her down again.

Chapter 20

I woke up just in time to hear Jon's bellow of pain and the instantaneous dull "snap" that came with it.

Get up

I tried to move.

Get up or they'll kill each other. Really kill each other.

My entire chest felt like it had been drenched in kerosene and then lit. And not in a good way, either. I tried to sit up.

"Better not," Marc said, and I realized he and Jessica were both kneeling over me. "I think your heart's busy growing back."

"Help me up," I groaned.

"Bad idea," he said, but he carefully pulled me to my feet. It seemed to take a long time.

"Jess, you okay?"

"I'm fine. Nothing's broken." She looked awful—blood all over her clothes, blood drying across her face—but at least it wasn't fresh blood. "I know this isn't the time or place, but that really squicks me out."

"What?"

"You're licking blood off the back of your hand," Marc murmured.

Yeesh! "Sorry." I made myself stop. Just as well; it hurt to move. Luckily I didn't need to breathe, because I bet that would have hurt like crazy, too. Now where was I? Something important. Like, life or death important. Oh, yeah . . . "Stop, you guys! Cut it out. Sinclair, let him go."

Not that I could see what was going on, but it wasn't hard to guess.

I limped toward the kitchen door (which had started all the trouble, come to think of it) and pushed it open. Sinclair was just leaning down to pick Jon up off the tiles, ignoring the loaded gun pointed at his nose.

"Ah, you're up and around," Sinclair said, looking over at me. "Splendid."

"Just . . . stop. Okay? Come on. I got shot, you broke Delk's arm, Jess got a nosebleed. We'll sprain Marc's ankle and make Tina have a haircut and then everybody's even, okay? Please don't," I pleaded, as Sinclair reached for his prey again. "It's so awful right now; please let's not make it worse. Besides, aren't you dying to rush over here and make sure for yourself that I'm all right?"

I could see him think about it. The gun might have been made of candy for all he noticed it, but I knew Jon's bullets were hollow points stuffed with holy water. One probably would have killed Sinclair. As usual (happy sigh), when I was concerned, he didn't give much of a shit about his personal safety.

And yup, he was actually wrestling with his lovely desire to check on me. And his strong male urge to pull Delk's head off his shoulders and use it as a soccer ball.

"Please," I said again, and abruptly Sinclair straightened up, leaving the other man flat on his back and waving his gun at nothing. He crossed the room and grabbed my hands, then held them out so he could stare at my chest. Marc had ripped my shirt open while I was out; luckily, it was a bra day. I looked down; no hole. Just a few trickles of dried blood.

"*Are* you all right?"

My Ipex bra would never be the same, but . . . "Sore as hell."

He shook his head. "You are miraculous. The bullet should have killed you. At the least, you should not be healing so quickly, especially as you haven't had any blood in—four days?"

I made a face. "Don't remind me."

He kissed me. "I am thankful for all your peculiarities." He said it with a fervor that made me smile, but a cold part of me wondered what Delk must think of all this cooing vampire affection. Not much, I imagined.

"I'll see the boy out," Tina offered. She'd come in, unnoticed as usual, and was standing by the back stairs. "The boy," heh. No more of "your friend" or "the young gentleman" or "Jon" or even "Mr. Delk." Nope, the gloves were off.

"No, you won't," I wheezed, because she looked positively

drooley at the thought of getting Jon alone for a moment. "I'll see him out." I was pretty sure I could make the walk from here to the front door without falling down.

Pretty sure.

"Well, *I'm* not going to," Jessica said. "Marc, you help her."

"I've got patients here."

At some point, Jon had climbed to his feet. The gun was still out, was swinging wildly as he tried to point at all of us at once. His other arm was bent at a nauseating angle; I wondered how he was able to get to his feet, never mind stand and keep the gun up. His face had gone the color of oatmeal. Sweat was standing out on his forehead in big drops. "Nobody sees me out! None of you *freaks* come near me. I'll see myself out."

"Well, all right, don't make a big thing of it," I said crossly. "You know, I *should* be yelling at you for shooting me, but I'm going to let the whole thing go. Now we're even for everything, right?"

"Fuck you," he replied, sounding cool and tough, and we all pretended not to see the tears rimming his lower lashes. "You're only alive because I—because I didn't want you dead just yet."

"Whatever sustains your fragile young male ego. But I think you'd be better off coming back here with an improved attitude."

"You'll see me again," he promised. "With attitude and more." Then he let the gun sort of drift to his side—it was probably way too painful to put it, one-handed, back into a shoulder holster—and simply walked away. On his way through the foyer, he steadied himself once on the banister—and drew his hand away in disgust, shaking stale gum off his fingers.

"And you wanted to evict me," I gently chided Jessica.

Delk stumbled up against the giant front doors, wrestled with the nineteenth-century knob, swore at the latch, got the door open, swore some more at us . . . and was gone.

"He's got a lot of personal growth ahead of him," I observed. My chest felt a lot better; had the bullet gone through me? It must have. I hoped so; I didn't want Marc or anyone else digging around in there to find it again.

"The infant is lucky he chose to leave."

"We did some pretty shitty things to the infant, in case you forgot. Or don't you care about that?"

Sinclair was eyeing the ruins of my ripped shirt, the blood-stains. "No," he said flatly. "I don't care about that."

Chapter 21

We can't let him live," Tina said.

"Sure we can."

"Majesty, be reasonable. I know you are—were—fond of the child, but he is a *dangerous* child."

"I still consider him a friend, okay? Friends have falling-outs. Or would that be fallings-out? Anyway, we don't always get along a hundred percent of the time. Look at me and Jessica!"

"Duh *not*," Little Miss Myeloma said, her voice muffled through the ice pak Marc had slapped over her face, "drag meh en-toh this."

We were in the (first) parlor. We'd picked it because there were two couches, and Jessica and I both needed one. Shit, I needed a hospital ward. But a couch that smelled like dust was the best I could do, right now.

"Surely after what happened today you do not still consider him an ally?"

"Eric, try to see his point of view! If someone's keeping score, we're ahead of him on points, okay? So, seriously: don't go after him, you guys. Don't order another vampire to do it, either. Jon's out of bounds as far as the vampires are concerned."

"Foolish sentimentality."

"Hey, I'm mad at him, too, okay? He shot me. In the chest. With holy water. But I'm not going to kill him."

Everybody looked at my chest.

"No, seriously. He didn't mean to do that. Or he meant to, but he knew it wouldn't kill me—he was scared, okay? Scared and humiliated, which is just the worst combo ever. At least the worst part's over."

"Worst part?" Jessica mumbled around her ice pack.

"I was really dreading telling him. I did *not* want to do that, boy oh boy. But at least it's out."

"What I'd like to know," Marc said from his chair by the fire, "is what he was doing here with a gun in the first place."

"Are you kidding? That kid's always got about nine guns and knives on him. Those farm boys are tough."

"Right," Marc allowed, "but a former Blood Warrior shows up, and you guys don't even frisk him? Make him walk through a metal detector? Something?"

"We knew he was carrying. Mostly because he's *always* carrying. But we never frisk anybody."

"What, that's a rule now?"

"Sure," I said, and Sinclair nodded, backing me up.

"Come on, guys! The Queen of England's a tough cookie, too; but she puts people through a metal detector and a security check before they can talk to her."

"If the throne is so easily taken from us," Sinclair explained, almost exactly the way he explained it to me, "we would be poor monarchs indeed."

"In other words, if someone gets the drop on you in your own house, too bad for Betsy and Sinclair, but they should have been able to take care of themselves?"

We looked at each other. "Basically," I answered, "yeah."

"Great," Marc muttered, and slumped lower in his chair. "Those of us caught in the crossfire appreciate the attention to detail."

"Although," I said, looking at Jessica's face—what I could see around the ice, "maybe we should change that rule."

"If we cannot protect our allies," Sinclair said, "the same rule applies."

"Tough luck, guys," I said in a fake-bright laugh, and they both laughed.

"Getting back to the issue of the child," Tina said, harshing our buzz as usual, "I really think you should reconsider. He—"

The phone rang. She picked it up, glanced at the caller ID.

"We're kind of busy," I said, a little sharply. The phone was a whole thing between Tina and me.

"But—"

"If it's important, they'll call back."

"But it's your mother."

I practically snarled. The phone, the fucking phone! People used it the way they used to use the cat-o'-nine-tails. You had to drop everything and answer the fucking thing. And God help you if you were home and, for whatever reason, didn't answer. "But I called!" Yeah, it was convenient for *you* so you called. But I'm in the shit because it wasn't convenient for *me* to drop everything and talk to *you*, on the spot, for whatever *you* needed to talk about.

Unfortunately, Tina was the type who lunged for it every time it so much as peeped. She couldn't stand the sound of a ringing phone. Always tracked me down: it's so-and-so. Well, I'm *recovering from a fatal chest wound, take a message.* But it's your mother! Yeah, well, she'll call back. But she's on the phone *now.*

I practically snatched it from her. "Hi, Mom, this really isn't a good t—"

"Your grandfather," Mom said in the doleful voice reserved for announcing funerals, "has escaped."

"Escaped what? Mom? He's got three kinds of cancer, he's eighty-nine, and he's hooked up to forty different machines. What are you talking about, escaped?"

"Someone's coming up the driveway," Tina said in a low voice.

"Well, go take care of it."

"And if they need to see you, Majesty?"

I cupped a hand over the mouthpiece. "Read my royal lips, Tina: *this is not a good time.*"

"What?" my mom said.

"I wasn't talking to you, Mom. See, the reason I sound all distracted right now is because *this is not a good time.*"

"Well, why did you answer the phone then?" my mom asked reasonably. "Just let it ring."

"*Gah!* Tell me about Grandpa, please."

"Well, you know he doesn't care for that nursing home."

"Right. So what else is new. The guy's got three kinds of cancer. And frankly, it probably isn't much fun for the nursing home to have him there."

"This is true," Mom replied promptly. She had, after all, been raised by the gentleman in question. "Anyway, he doesn't like it there. The animals are the least of it."

I had to laugh. The animals! Apparently all these studies had been done about how soothing and restful nursing home inmates—uh, residents—found live-in cats, dogs, and birds.

So my grandpa's nursing home adopted all these strays, and told incoming residents, *why, of course you can keep your angry, incontinent, biting dog Nibbles! No problemo! Bring all his brothers and sisters, too! Share them with the other residents!*

On paper, this is a swell idea. What the genius who did the study didn't take into account was: Grandpa Joe. Maybe he had only nice, soft-spoken old ladies and gentlemen in the study.

Grandpa had grown up on a farm, and had a very pragmatic view of animals: *if I can't eventually kill you and eat you, you are taking up valuable air and space.* My mom never had a pet—not so much as a goldfish in a bowl—the entire time she was growing up. Neither had I, until I'd moved out after college and picked up Giselle the cat from the pound.

The animals had pretty much taken over the nursing home. They had the run of the place, and took ruthless advantage of it. And they certainly made the staff feel better. *Ohhh, how cute, that cat is helping that man with all the terminal illnesses!*

So now, my grandfather, who should be enjoying his autumn years, has to boot a snoozing golden retriever out of his bed if he wants to snag a nap after lunch.

"Well, he just couldn't take it anymore," Mom was saying. "So he unhooked all the equipment he was on—"

"Um, hello, didn't any alarms go off in the nursing station?"

"Well, hon, you know how understaffed they are. And Grandpa lulled them into a false sense of security by pulling his leads out a bunch of other times."

"Like the boy who cried wolf," I suggested. The angry cancer-raddled animal-hater who cried wolf, repeatedly, to fool his captors. I mean the nurses. "Except a whole bunch of times."

"Right. So nobody thought much of it when the alarms went off—they figured Joe was up to his old tricks again. So he got into his chair—"

"He can transfer by himself now?" I knew all the lingo from a brief, but memorable, stint as a volunteer at that very home.

"Yes. So he got into his wheelchair and—you know. Escaped."

"Just wheeled himself out past the border guard, huh?"

"Exactly. You know—oh, look, that sweet old man is coming out to see the world."

"Morons," I decided.

"Yes, but they couldn't know. They aren't family. Anyway, out he goes—"

"Out*side*?"

"I know, I know."

"It's twenty fucking degrees outside!"

"Well, more like ten there." There being Brainerd, Minnesota. "But sadly, your grandfather did not foresee his old enemy, fatigue, when he made his daring dash for freedom."

"Where did he think he was going to go in a hospital johnny?" I wondered. Dumb question. For Grandpa, being half-naked was irrelevant. Being master of your own destiny was all! "How far did he get?"

"About three blocks outside the home and then fell asleep. A family on the way to visit a relative ratted him out."

"Vile informers!" I cried.

"So the nurses came to get him, and wheeled him back, and tucked him back into bed—he was so exhausted he didn't even wake up—and imagine how completely irritated he was when he woke up with a cat on his pillow!"

I shuddered, imagining Grandpa's wrath. As a member of The Greatest Generation, he wasn't adverse to blowing shit up to get his way.

"The important thing is, he's okay."

"Betsy, what am I going to do? He hates it there. I mean he *hates* it. How can I keep my own father in a place that he hates?"

"You could revel in the payback for a horrible childhood?" I guessed.

"Elizabeth." On this, as in very few other things, my mom had no sense of humor. I guess when you spent your childhood dodging fists and trying not to get kicked down stairs, it wasn't much fun to joke about it later. "You're not helping."

"Come on, Mom, it's a nursing home. He's lucky he's not in a hospital. Actually, he's lucky he's not dead."

"That's true," she said doubtfully.

"Although, if he's peppy enough to escape, he maybe could be moved some other place."

"Maybe. But where? Any place private is too expensive."

"Yeah." I looked over at Marc, who was tenderly touching Jessica's nose and murmuring to her. She in turn had just finished telling him a heartwarming Grandpa Joe story she had previously heard from me, probably the one involving grenades and the minister. "Listen, I've got an idea about that. My roommate, Marc, has a—"

"Oh, that clever doctor. Did I tell you I met the perfect man for

him? He's a grad student, getting his doctorate in Japanese literature—"

"Yeah, that sounds really fun and useful. Listen, his father has
this place—they must have some like it up where Joe is, but if not,
maybe we could move him down here . . ."

"What kind of place?"

I told her. And that was how I ended up with my Grandpa Joe
living four miles away from my vampire-infested house. Which
may or may not, now that I look back, have been a greater hazard
to my health than having my heart temporarily blown up by holy
water.

I never did find out who had popped in for a surprise visit.
Which was fine with me. More surprises, I so did not need.

Chapter 22

You realize of course that, once he gets transferred down here, you'll have to visit him. When he was a four-hour drive away, that was one thing, but now you could walk there in ten minutes."

"Shut up," I moaned, "shut up, shut *up*."

"I have to admit," Jessica went on cheerfully—why wouldn't she be cheerful, the swelling had gone down and *her* grandparents were dead. "I'm amazed he's still alive. Didn't they tell you *last* year that he had only months to live?"

"Three months," I remembered. "They gave him three months."

"Wow. And now here he's going to be living with Marc's father!"

"Yes, it's all a rich tapestry of horror and survival. Where's a perfectly made rainbow drink when you need one?"

"Marc's sleeping," she said, "and you can't blame him. Guy finally gets a day off, and spends it taking care of his roommates."

"Finally, having a doctor in the house pays off."

"I know I'm feeling better—how about you?"

"Fine." Which was true. When I'd risen that afternoon, it was like nothing happened. If not for the ruined T-shirt and sports bra in the garbage, I'd guess nothing had happened.

Sinclair had seen for himself, pulling off my bra the minute our bedroom door had closed, going over my chest and back inch by inch. Which had turned into him going over my crotch inch by inch. Repeat as needed. The evening had turned out so terrific, it made it almost—

No, I didn't mean that. It wasn't worth it no matter how much sex I'd had. I didn't mind getting shot nearly as much as I minded Jessica and Delk getting hurt.

And oh, boy, the look on Delk's face in the kitchen as everything dawned on him. That was one I'd take to my grave. Assuming I ever went there for any other reason than to visit the currently premature tombstone.

"Delk will be back," Jessica said, trying to cheer me up.

"Yeah, I know. That's what I'm worried about."

The phone rang, and I gave the wall extension an ugly look. It rang again. Jessica got up and said, "I know, you're not here. It might be about your grandpa's transfer . . . hello?"

I stirred my tea, and simmered next to it. Like Korben Dallas in *The Fifth Element*, I was sure all communications were ultimately bad news. Why hasten it by cutting out the middle man?

"Uh-huh," Jessica was saying. "I'm not sure that's—uh-huh . . . yeah . . . yeah, but—listen, I'm just not sure if—let me just ask her, okay? She's right—hello?"

Jessica hung up and looked at me.

"Hours later or a day late?"

"Your stepmother won't be able to get the baby for another couple of hours." Jessica looked at the clock on the wall. "It's still early. I guess she—uh—lost track of—look, this doesn't prove your stupid telephone theory, okay?"

I could hear BabyJon's fretful squealing getting closer and closer. Then the kitchen door opened and Sinclair poked his head in. "The baby wants you," he called, and the door swung shut. Then I saw the door open again as Sinclair held the port-a-crib in his arms. It was a little too wide, fully open and extended, to go through the door, so Sinclair squished it a little and it popped through.

I leaped to my feet as Jessica cracked up. "You carried the whole crib down here? Stop that, you're *folding* him up in it!"

"He has plenty of room on all sides," Sinclair said, louder, to be heard over BabyJon's escalating wails.

"Just pick him up! Or leave him there and come and get me, jeez." I picked him up and he quieted. "Don't blame you for that one, yes, Uncle Sinclair is a big poopie-head, isn't he?"

"I am not his uncle," he replied, making a beeline for the liquor cabinet, "and if I was, it would be Uncle Eric."

"It's Uncle Schmuck right now, bud! I can't believe you just dragged the whole thing down here, all unfolded and everything . . ."

"He seems fine," Sinclair said, dumping a shot of brandy into an empty teacup, which he then filled with hot water from the kettle.

"We're out of English Breakfast, so ha."

"I will struggle along." He gave the baby a look. "You are expecting your stepmother presently, yes?"

"She's running late."

"Hours late or a day late?"

How well they were coming to know the Ant! It was enough to make me want to cry. No, that was the smell BabyJon's diaper was giving off. "Hours," I said, nearly choking.

"I think that kid does have supernatural powers," Jessica observed as I gagged and looked around wildly for the diaper bag. "Powers in his pants."

"You guys. He's just a baby, doing what all babies do." I could hear the resonant chime of our front door bell. "Maybe that's the Ant!"

Sinclair called something out to me, but I didn't hear it. Okay, wasn't listening. Anyway, I practically galloped through the rooms and the halls that led to the front door. All would be forgiven if I could get out of changing this one sinister diaper.

I swung open the door.

"Majesty," the strange but familiar vampire said. She had a calm center that resembled Alonzo's. Had she been with the European delegation? Yes, I believed she had. Her small stature and close-cropped carroty red hair jogged my memory along. "I beg your indulgence in coming by without an appointment."

"Uh." I shifted BabyJon to my other arm. "That's okay. Uh—"

"Carolina."

"Right. Carolina. What's up."

"I was just—" She looked around on the front step.

"Oh! Sorry, come in."

"Thank you, Majesty." She followed me in and swung the big door shut. "I will not keep you long. I was only wondering if you had decided Alonzo's fate." She seemed perfectly calm, but she couldn't have been. Unless she saw me as no threat whatsoever, and decided to swing by the mansion on the way to Caribou Coffee.

"You were? Wondering, I mean?"

"Yes, ma'am. We all are. Alonzo most of all, of course, but he has surprisingly little to say about you, which is frustrating for the rest of us, as you can imagine." She gave me a small, hopeful smile as if to say, *Isn't all this just so silly?*

"Well, it's nice of you to check in."

She shrugged. "He is my cousin."

"Oh! I didn't know that."

She looked puzzled, and rubbed her nose for a moment. Then rubbed it again. Maybe she was trying to get rid of the freckles. "We were introduced."

"Right, right. Well, about that—I'm sorry you guys are sort of stuck there waiting—you don't have to—" I realized what I was saying and stopped. Of course, they had to. She in particular, if they were family. Family! Real honest to God family; here I'd thought I was the only vampire with blood relatives. And what were the others supposed to do while this little Sophie/Alonzo/Liam triangle was resolved? Blow town and leave their buddy to swing?

But they couldn't exactly go around doing their normal vampire things while this was hanging over their head. And they had to be wondering if they were all going to be painted with the same brush when, and if, Alonzo was punished. Trouble was . . . "I didn't mean to leave you guys all waiting."

"Majesty, it is too bold of me to come by and ask your intentions, but it would not be the first time my curiosity led me down a sorry path."

"Yeah, sorry about that."

"Do you smell something horrible?" she asked, looking at my brother.

"Yeah, well, he's had a lot of bottles today—"

"That is your *brother*?"

"Yeah. Look, that's a whole other—"

"I thought you only had a sister."

"Right, the devil's daughter, but—"

"But how interesting! You must tell me more."

BabyJon blatted and I felt his diaper get warmer. And heavier. *No! Hull integrity would not hold! She's losing it, Captain, she's losing it!*

"Carolina!"

She jumped, and I continued before she could react further. "Look, I'm sorry, but I just can't talk to you right now. Everything's just a mess: my best friend's horribly sick and my other friend's got a crush on Alonzo, I'm stuck babysitting hours past what I agreed to, this kid is shitting up every diaper he gets near, one of my subjects wants to turn her human boyfriend, my birthday's at the end of the week and I'm off blood, my grandpa's sick and he's moving in just down the street, I got shot in the chest with holy water by a young farm boy with a crush on me, and my life story is the promising new fall book. On top of that, I haven't done a fucking thing to prepare for my wedding in three months. It is—how do you say this in Europe?—just *not a fucking good time right now.*"

Carolina had backed up until her back was flat against the door. "So sorry to intrude," she said.

I took a step forward, fragile baby-and-poop bomb bouncing tenderly in my arms. My mouth was beginning to hurt. "Sometimes, I just feel like I'm going to break, you know what I mean? Can you imagine?"

"Yes, Majesty."

"Really, you can? Because I figure it's gotta be something pretty fucking spectacular when a Vampire Queen lights up. I mean, just goes off the deep end. Lets the blood boil and the teeth fly. Have you ever acthually theen that happen?"

"I cannot say that I have, Your Majesty."

My tongue played around the sharp edges of my teeth. Her scent was fascinating—she had turned when young, and even the passage of centuries of evil deeds could not cloud a certain divine innocence. "Would you like to? You and I can lock ourthelves in a thpare room, and I can focuth on your particular thituation and conthernth, and we can thee who leaves the room a few hourth later. Hmm?"

"I will go now. See? I am making no sudden moves." She slowly turned and reached for the doorknob. She was far more facile with the nineteenth-century technology than Delk had been; she was immediately back in the safety of open air. "Good . . . evening . . . Majesty . . ."

The door clicked closed.

"I think," Sinclair's smooth voice came from behind me, "you are finally getting the hang of this, my love."

As my fangs slowly receded, I didn't know whether to thank him or throw the baby-bomb at him.

Chapter 23

Laura, I'm so sorry to do this to you again."

"Betsy, it's fine. I'm delighted to help out." She nuzzled the baby. "And delighted ooo see ooo again! Is ooo my best wittle boy? Is ooo?"

"Really, really sorry. But I had plans for tonight and frankly, if I don't do this now, I'll never psych myself up to do it again."

She had all the baby crap, was hauling it (and BabyJon) easily into the front hall. "Betsy, will you stop? It's my pleasure to help out. You'll let his mom know?"

"Yeah, well, she's not gonna be happy when she finds out I shirked BabyJon on you. Just remind her not to shoot the messenger."

Laura laughed, shaking her blond hair away from her face. "Goodness! I'm sure she'll be fine. You know, Betsy, Mrs. Taylor isn't nearly as bad as you—"

Okay, if I had to get the "give your stepmother a chance" lecture from someone who hadn't grown up with her, I was going to pop a blood vessel. "Yeah, well, thanks, I owe you, bye!" I gave her a helpful shove.

I closed the big front door and leaned on it. Right. BabyJon given the bootie: check. Sinclair off with Tina somewhere: check. No pop-ins that I knew of: check. Marc at work: check. Toni and Garrett prowling around outside, him to eat and her for kicks: check (I made a mental note to make sure those two were only fucking with bad guys). Cathie-the-ghost nowhere in evidence: check.

Jessica knitting in her room: check.

She had a largish room on the second floor, the one with the blue and gold wallpaper and all the trim and old furniture in blond wood, as if the Scandinavian carpenters who built this mansion so long ago were thinking of their wives' hair when they designed and built it.

I rapped on the half-closed door and went in at her, "C'mon in."

Crocheting in bed was a new thing. Usually she brought her yarn bag into the kitchen with us, or went into the basement with Garrett, or took it to a craft class. But Marc had explained that she got tired earlier, and took longer to get going when she got up.

"Got a minute?" I asked.

"Uh-huh."

"I can't tell where the one on the bed is, and the one you're working on starts," I joked. It was true, though: she was lying on a navy crocheted coverlet, and crocheting another one, this one red.

"Yeah, well, you're an idiot." She grinned.

"Uh-huh." I barely heard the insult. I started to sit on the bed, then got up and sort of prowled around the foot of it for a moment. "Listen, Jess, I've been doing a lot of thinking lately. I mean, a *lot.*"

"Do you need some Advil?"

"This is serious!" I almost shouted at her. "Listen—I can't believe I'm even talking to you about this—"

"No," she said.

"What?"

"No. You can't bite me. You can't turn me into a vampire. I won't allow it."

My oft-rehearsed speech disappeared in a whirl of relief and indignation. "What? How did you know? Oh, those big-mouthed idiots!"

"Yes, that's how I'd describe Tina and Sinclair. Come on, Betsy. Nobody had to tell me. It was so obvious—not only are you having private conversations with experienced vampires, but frankly, every time you look at me it's like a dog looking at a raw steak."

"Huh."

"Yeah."

"Listen, I'm sorry about the looks, but I've done some research, and the risks—"

"Are a lot higher if you bite me, than if I treat my cancer."

I opened my mouth.

"Because pretty it up how you want, you're still killing me, right?"

I closed my mouth and she went on, in a nice but totally firm way. "Even if I come back after. And if I *do* come back after, there's no guarantee I'll be me, right? In fact, it sounds like for at least the first few years, I'll be a mindless blood-sucking automaton. No thank you."

"Anything sounds bad when you put 'mindless' and 'sucking' in front of it." I flopped down on the end of her bed. "Jeez, days I've been working up to this, grilling everybody, screwing up the courage to talk to you about it, and you're all, 'yeah, I knew what you were going to say, and by the way, no.'"

"It's not my fault it's pathetically easy to read your minuscule mind."

I gave her a look. "I guess this is the part where I'm all 'you *will* be mine, O yes' and you're all 'eeeek, unhand me, I'd rather die than join in your unholy crusade.'"

"No, that was last winter when you wanted me to go Christmas shopping in early October."

"Christmas shopping in October is just efficient."

"Trust you"—she sneered—"to get *grotesque* and *efficient* mixed up."

"Why do I want to save you and keep you around for eternity again?"

She shrugged. "Beats me."

I looked at the ceiling, because I didn't want to look at her. I didn't want to try to figure out if her color was off, if she'd lost weight. "Jessica, this thing might kill you."

"So your response is . . . to kill me?"

"It's a chance for some kind of life. A life where your best friend is the queen. That's got to be worth something."

She nudged my shoulder with a toe. "You're glossing over all the things that could go wrong."

"Well, so are you!"

"There's time. Time to fight this. I'm sorry—I can see it's been a little on the agonizing side for you. But typical Betsy—you assumed this was something *you* had to decide. It's my life, and my death, and I'm choosing to stand and fight." She smiled. "Besides, if you turn me into a vampire, I don't think we can hide that from Nick. And then he'll know for sure!"

"The least of my problems," I said glumly. Then I said, "You haven't told him yet?"

"I'm saving it," she said, suddenly glum, too, "for our two-month-aversary."

What a phenomenally bad idea. Also, none of my business. "If that's how you feel . . ."

"That's entirely, exactly how I feel. So no sneaking around and leaping out at me from the shadows to try and turn me, okay?" She picked up her afghan, and got back to work.

Good example for all of us.

"Okay," I said, getting up and walking toward the door, "but if you change your mind and decide you want to be foully murdered—"

"I'll run up to your room first thing," she promised.

Mollified, I left.

Chapter 24

I didn't get far.

"Hey," Cathie said, walking through the wall at the top of the stairs.

"Hey."

"I wasn't eavesdropping," she began defensively.

I groaned.

"Well, I wasn't. I was coming to get you."

"Why?"

She shrugged. "No ghosts around to talk to right now. Which leaves you. Hey, I'm not happy about it, either."

"So when you weren't eavesdropping, what didn't you overhear?"

"That you aren't going to turn Jessica in to a vampire. Good call, by the way. Which reminds me, are you ever going to do anything about the zombie in the attic?"

"Are you ever going to drop the joke? I mean, I know you guys all know I'm scared of zombies, but this is just—"

"Betsy, I'm serious. There's a zombie in the attic."

I swallowed my irritation. Cathie had had a hard life. Or death, rather. She was lonely. She was bitchy. I was the only person she could bug. Talk to, rather.

"It's not funny anymore," I said, as nicely as I could. "And it never really was. So can you please drop it now?"

"Come up to the attic and see."

Aha! The surprise party. It was on me at last, like a starving wolf in the moonlight. Fine, I'd play along.

"Okayyyyy, I'll just pop up into the attic to check on the zombie." I looked around. We were at the top of the stairs; there were closed doors on both sides of the hall. "Uh, where *is* the attic?"

"Come on." She floated off.

"Gee, I hope nobody jumps out at me or anything. Certainly not with the new Prada strappy sandals in ice blue . . ."

Cathie shook her head. "Oh, honey. If I wasn't so bored I'd never do this to you. But I am. And so I am."

She gestured to the door at the end of the south hall. I opened it and beheld a large, spiderwebby staircase. The stairs were painted white, and in serious need of a touch-up.

"Okayyyyy . . . I'm coming up the stairs . . . here I come . . . suspecting nothing . . ."

There were light switches at the top of the stairs, which was good, because even though I could see in the dark pretty well, the unrelieved gloom of the attic was a little unnerving. I couldn't even hear anybody breathing. Maybe they were all holding their breath. My live friends, that is.

Like any attic, it was filled with generations of accumulated crap. Dust covered everything: broken pictures, beat-up desks, sofas with the stuffing popping out of the cushions. It appeared to run the length of the house, which meant it was ginormous.

Out of force of habit, I put my hand up to my nose and mouth, then remembered I never sneezed—unless something threw holy water in my face, anyway.

I took a few steps forward and heard a scuttling from behind a scratched wardrobe missing a door. Ugh! Mice. Please not rats. Just little harmless field mice who had decided to stay in the mansion for the winter. I didn't mind mice at all, but rats . . .

And what was that other smell? A layer of rot above the dust. Had someone, ugh, left their lunch up here or something? Fine place for a turkey sandwich.

Cathie pointed. "He's right over there."

"Oh he is, eh?" What a crummy place for a birthday party. But I had to admit, I would never have snooped up here for presents. "Well, he'd better watch out, because here I come."

I marched a good fifteen feet and shoved the wardrobe— which was huge, much taller than I was—out of the way. "Surpri— what the . . . ?"

At first I was genuinely puzzled. It was like my brain couldn't process what it was seeing. I'd expected: banners, presents, a group of my friends and family huddled, ready to leap up and yell "Surprise."

What I got: a hunched figure, wearing rotted clothes—
everything was the color of mud. Slumped shoulders; hair the
same color as the clothes. And that *smell*. God, how could the others stand it? Surely even the live people could smell it.

The figure pivoted slowly to face me. My hand was back up,
but this time to prevent a gag instead of a sneeze.

I could see bone sticking out of the remnants of what might
have once been a white dress-shirt sleeve. Bone? That wasn't
bone. It was something else, something gray and weird. It was—

"Nice zombie costume," I managed. Complete with authentic
stink and rotted clothes and—this was a great touch—graveyard
dirt in the wig.

"Betsy, that's what I've been trying to tell you. It's not a costume. It's a real live zombie." Cathie was circling it admiringly.
"The things you see when you're dead! I thought it was a movie
thing."

"Nuhhhhhhhh," it said. It reached toward me. It had long fingernails, so long they started to curve under, like claws. There was
dirt under every one.

I backed up a step. It compensated by taking a step closer. I
couldn't bear to look in its face—and then I did. At first I thought
he—he was wearing the decayed remains of a suit—was smiling.
Then I realized one of his cheeks had rotted away and I could see
his teeth through his face.

I had thought I was frozen with fear. No, that was too simple a
word: terror. Absolute numbing terror. It was silly, but I had a lifelong terror of dead things. Especially zombies. The way they kept
coming toward you
(the way this one was coming toward me now)
and the way they reeked of the grave
(the way this one did)
and the way they moaned and reached for you and nothing
stopped them, no matter what you did, they came and came
(the way this one was coming)
and I thought I was frozen with fear, thought I could never
move, but somehow I was backing up. Internally, yeah, I was
frozen, I couldn't make myself speak, scream, figure out where
the door was, reason, think. But my legs were moving just fine.
And that was good. Because if that thing touched me, I would die.
Die for real. Die forever.

It
(he?)

reached still, and I was backed up against one of the dusty couches, and its hand brushed my shoulder, and then my internal freeze vanished like an ice cube on a July sidewalk and I let loose with the loudest scream I'd ever heard anybody scream. I sounded like a fire alarm.

I fell back over the couch and hit the floor, raising a cloud of dust. I was trying to back up and stand up at the same time while the zombie calmly walked around the side of the couch and kept coming. As a result, I was leaving a Betsy-wide track through the dust on the floor as I shoved myself along the floorboards.

I screamed again. This time words. But more fire alarm than words, because Cathie said, "What?"

I chewed on the phrase, actually coughed it out of my mouth: "Go get Eric!"

She rushed toward me—it seemed to take her forever to cross the fifteen feet or so between us. "Betsy, I can't!"

"Then get Tina! Get Marc! Get the Ant! I don't give a shit! *Help!*"

Suddenly, her hands shot through the zombie's chest. It kept coming.

"I can't! Nobody can see me but you! What do you want me to do?"

I'd shoved myself into the far wall and clawed my way to my feet. God, the stink! I could handle almost anything else except for the stink, the godawful, rotting, disgusting, fucking *stink*. "I don't know," I said, and never had I been so angry about being so dumb.

"Well, kill it! In the movies, the good guys shoot them in the head."

I didn't say anything, just knocked away its arm as it reached for me. Cathie finally remembered: "You don't have a gun. Okay, but you're not without skills. You're a vampire. Break his neck!"

But then I'd have to touch it. I couldn't bear to touch it. I'd go crazy if I had to touch it.

I grabbed its wrist and pushed. Hard. It went sprawling off into a broken coffee table, and smashed to the ground.

Okay, I'd touched it. And it hadn't been so bad. Okay, it had been crawly and awful—like touching a shirt full of squirming maggots—but there were worse things. Like—like—

I couldn't think of anything worse.

I looked at my hand and saw there was dirt and skin on the tips of my fingers. I started to cry and frantically wiped my hand on my jeans.

"Maybe it isn't trying to kill you," Cathie said helpfully from right beside me. "Maybe it's trying to communicate. You know, like I was. Maybe it came here because you're the Queen and you can help it. Please stop crying. Betsy, come on. It's not that bad. It's just a zombie. It can't even do anything to you."

Couldn't do anything? It was hurting me just by existing. It was—my hysterical brain groped for the word and caught it. It was an *abomination*. It was wrong for this thing to be anywhere, never mind my attic. It went against everything right and good and sane and normal.

It was getting up. It was coming toward me again. It was saying "Nuhhhhhhhhh" again. It was trying to touch me again. I cried harder. It seemed that crying like a B-movie heroine (the ones who always got saved at the last minute, but who was going to save me?) was going to be the way I dealt with this. Well, that was all right. Crying didn't hurt anybody. Crying never—

"Betsy, will you for Christ's sake do something!"

Here it came again. Here it reached again. Here it was touching me. Here it was showing me its teeth. Here it was pulling on me. Here it was making an odd noise—ah. It was trying to smack its lips, but they had rotted away. Smacking its lips the way a hungry fella smacked his lips as he contemplated Thanksgiving dinner. Or a big steak. Or—

Me.

Its hands were on my shoulders. The stench rose, almost a living thing. I raised my own hands. It pulled me close. I put my hands on either side of its head. It slobbered without saliva. I twisted. But of course it didn't die, of course it leaned in like a grotesque parody of a vampire and bit me, chewed on me, ate me while I screamed and screamed, while Cathie darted around helplessly and watched me get eaten, while—

—it fell down, its head twisted around so that, if it were alive, it would have been looking down on its own butt.

"Now that's what I'm talking about," Cathie said. "Whew! I thought you were really going to—Betsy?"

I had walked stiffly over to one of the couches. Sat down, almost impaling myself on a broken spring. Cried and cried and rubbed my hands on my jeans. They would never be clean. My fingers would always stink. They would always have dead meat and graveyard dirt on them. Always. Always.

Chapter 25

I sat on the couch and looked at the (dead) zombie. I never, ever wanted to get away from a place more than I wanted to get out of that attic, but I couldn't make myself get up and make the long walk to the door at the top of the stairs. The only thing I had the strength for was sitting on a filthy, broken couch that was so dusty I didn't know what color it was under all the dirt. That, and looking at the zombie I'd killed.

I suppose part of me was waiting for it to get up and come at me again. Like Jessica would get up and come at me if I'd gone through with it, if I'd ignored her wishes (as, truthfully, I'd been tempted to do) and made her a vampire. She wouldn't be Jessica anymore if I did that; she'd be a slobbering, crazy vampire. Fast forward ten years, by then maybe she'd have a little bit of control over the thirst. Then her new life would begin: being more careful about meals. Never aging, but getting old just the same. Pulling further and further away from the mortal Jessica, my friend, the older she got. Getting sly, like Eric and Alonzo.

Alonzo. He had made a vampire without a single thought to the consequences: for Sophie or for himself. He had killed her and gone on his way, and he had to pay. That was it, that was how it was: he fucked up, and he had to pay. What if it had been Jessica, dead in some alley in France how many years ago?

And how could I have gone to her room and asked her to let me do that? I deserved a zombie hiding in my attic. I deserved a hundred zombies.

"Why do you think it was here? How did it get in, and get all the way up here without anybody seeing?" Cathie was chattering nervously and looking at me the way you looked at a recent mental ward escapee. "What do you think it wanted?"

"I don't give a ripe shit," I said, and stood.

It took a long time to find the door.

Chapter 26

"Can I tag along?" Cathie asked, drifting beside me.

"I don't care."

"Well, I just thought I'd ask. Are you okay? You're done crying, right?"

"No promises." I could hear the phone ringing as I went downstairs. I'd heard Tina and Sinclair come back, which was too bad because it meant somewhere in this big house, Tina was sprinting to get the phone before it clicked over to the machine.

"I'm not here!" I yelled. Sinclair was standing at the foot of the stairs, looking up at me, still in his overcoat.

"It might be important," he teased, well aware of my antiphone leanings. Then he wrinkled his nose. "What is that smell?"

"It's a long damn story, and I'll tell you all about it on the way—"

"On the way where?"

"But will you just hug me right now?"

"Darling, are you all—" He almost staggered as I flung my arms around him. I tried to squash the traitorous thought

(why didn't you save me?)

and concentrate on the good things: Sinclair's arms around me, his good clean scent, the polar opposite of the zombie.

Cathie coughed. To be honest, I'd forgotten she was there. "I'll just, uh, catch up with you later." She vanished into the stairs.

Sinclair was rubbing my back. "What is it?"

"Alonzo has to be punished."

He pulled back and stared at me. "Does this have anything to do with Jessica turning you down?"

Now I was the one staring. "How did you know—okay, apparently I'm traveling through time about half as fast as the rest of you, but how did you know she'd say no?"

"Because," he replied, "she is a billionaire who works, even though she does not have to. I never imagined she would lie back and let you try to fix anything for her, much less something like this."

"Well, I don't want to do anything to her."

His perfect brow wrinkled. " 'Do' anything?"

"It's part of the long story. But if you were dying, wouldn't you—"

"She maintains she is not dying, only ill. Is it for us to argue?"

"No way. I just wish I'd figured that out a little earlier." I leaned my head against his neck. "I guess I thought maybe since she saw me get better so fast after Delk shot me—"

"*No one* should decide to be turned based on *your* experiences, my darling. You are unique."

"But maybe a vampire I turned would be like me!" God, what was I saying? Had I learned nothing from the Unpleasant Attic Incident?

No, I didn't want to turn Jessica. But I didn't want to watch her die, either. It was too awful, like having to choose your own manner of death: Ah, Miss Taylor, will you be choosing beheading or exsanguination today?

"No one is like you. You may check the Book of the Dead," he added, "if you require another source."

"Ugh, pass." The Book of the Dead was a tough read.

"So she did refuse you."

"Repeatedly." And a good thing, too.

He shrugged. "She has faith in modern medicine. It's not entirely misplaced."

"Yeah." I straightened his lapel, which was already perfectly straight, and felt his arm steal around my waist. I pushed him away, gently. "You need to get Tina. I've made a decision about Alonzo."

"I trust you will let me in on it?" he asked lightly, but he was giving me an odd look. "If it is not too much—"

He cut himself off. We both looked as Tina came hustling out of kitchen and almost ran through the hall, actually sliding to a stop in her stocking feet in front of the steps.

"Majesties!"

"Whoa, who died?" It was a joke, but then I remembered the

company I was in, the events of the past, uh, *year,* and my life. "Oh, God. Who *did* die?"

"No one. I heard you wanted me and came as fast as I could. And Alonzo called to say he would be here in an hour."

"Not soon enough," I replied. "Let's go."

"Wait, we're meeting him?"

"Yeah. Right now. Get your coats. Come on."

"What's happening?" Tina asked.

"I was not aware you were meeting with him today," said Sinclair.

Me neither. Well, if Alonzo was open to a meeting, that was fine with me. "Listen, he killed Sophie and there has to be a consequence. Not a Nostro consequence, but still. So, he has to pay. Literally pay. And I was thinking, he's probably built quite a little holding for himself over the years. Right?"

"Right," Tina replied, and Sinclair nodded.

"Okay. So: he gives all his property and money to Sophie. And has to start over."

Sinclair blinked.

"Oh, Majesty," Tina began dolefully. "That is—we're talking millions. Possibly billions. And he would have nothing?"

"He'd have more than Sophie did. A cousin, friends to help him. A way to get back on his feet. Or maybe he never will. That's not my problem. He has to pay for what he did. And that's how it is."

Sinclair was looking at me like he'd never seen me before. Tina's eyes were practically bulging in surprise.

"I will support you, Elizabeth, if you feel this strongly about it."

And Tina said, "Your will is our will, Majesty."

And that was that.

Chapter 27

We pulled up to the hotel, Sinclair (reluctantly) handed his Mer-
cedes keys to the valet, and walked into the hotel. It was one of
those hotels that look like a nice big brownstone on the outside, a
place where families lived. It cost, Tina had told me, twelve hundred dollars. A night. I assumed the beds were made of gold and
the staff tucked you in every night with hot cocoa and kisses.

"A zombie," Tina murmured. She looked like she was having
trouble processing everything that was happening at once. I hoped
she enjoyed being a member of the "I'm freaking out" club. "I had
no idea they even existed."

"We will take care of that—"

"Too late," I said.

"—after we take care of this. Perhaps I should tell him," Sinclair was saying as we trooped to the elevator. "Be the heavy, as it
were."

"I'm not afraid to tell Alonzo that we're punishing him," I retorted. Shit, after the Unfortunate Attic Incident, I wasn't afraid of
anything.

"Small bites, Majesty," Tina murmured.

The elevator came—ding! The doors slid open. Before I could
let Tina in on my new "not afraid of nothin'" mind-set, Sinclair
muttered the rare epithet.

Tina looked. I looked. We all looked. And after the night I'd
had, I really wasn't all that surprised.

"He's pretty dead," I observed.

Chapter 28

Alonzo was in two pieces in the elevator. There was also a bloodless hole in the middle of his forehead. Sadly, he wasn't the first dead vampire I'd seen. I was mostly numb—no idea how I felt about Alonzo being dead, how he got that way, or what to do next. Not even taking the elevator up to the fifteenth floor (*WITH THE DEAD VAMPIRE INSIDE*) moved me. Well, moved me much.

Did I feel bad about a killer getting killed?

"Thorough job," Tina said, squatting beside Alonzo's head.

"Yep," I confirmed. So the killer had shot him to, I dunno, distract him, and then cut off his head while Alonzo was still trying to grow back his brain. Obviously, someone had known what he (or she) was dealing with. There was very little blood, which I'd expect, but the other five European vampires were scared shitless, which I didn't expect.

At least it was very late—not much staff to deal with. And we'd jumped in the elevator and taken it up before anyone in the lobby had seen.

Carolina and the others were sort of milling about in the hallway, if shifting back and forth and occasionally murmuring to each other could be called milling. I guess that was milling. What was milling? They weren't back there polishing grain, after all. They sure were taking the news like cool customers.

Wrenching my brain back to current events, I forced myself to look at Alonzo's body. The elevator door had been propped open, so unfortunately it was easy to take in.

The body was dressed up, he had his shoes and socks on. His head was about two feet away. One eye was wide with surprise;

the other one was rolled up, looking at the ceiling. Well, he wasn't really looking at the ceiling. It just looked like he was looking at the ceiling. In fact, it looked like one big dead vampire in the elevator.

Alonzo had been killed in the private elevator, which was solely for the use of the guests on the suite floor. Tina had checked; the vampires were the only ones staying in the hotel suites.

Had they heard anything? If they had, they hadn't volunteered anything yet.

Anyway, the elevator had been brought back up to the fifteenth floor, where we all were, but there wasn't any police tape or anything because the vamps wanted to keep this one in-house. I had no idea how they could keep something like this from the cops (it wasn't a vampire hotel, after all) but I kept my mouth shut. Police involvement could only cause complications. Especially if Alonzo was correctly identified: hmm, a hundred-year-old dead guy who doesn't look a day over twenty-five! Now there's a stumper! Say, all you others, would you mind coming in for questioning? For about five-to-ten with time off for good behavior?

"What happened?" I asked.

There was a long silence while the Europeans looked at each other, and I was beginning to repeat my question, louder, when Carolina said, "Well, ah, Majesty, Alonzo called you and he left. And then he died."

So *that's* why they were so twitchy. Funny; I'd imagine ancient vampires didn't much care about imminent death, but I'd found the older they were, the more they thought they were entitled to live. It was amazing, when you sat down and thought about it.

"You guys, relax. I didn't do it. None of us did it." I looked at Sinclair and Tina, who I just remembered had mysteriously disappeared earlier tonight before Alonzo's death.

"None of us did it," Sinclair echoed. Right! Besides, he and Tina were always mysteriously disappearing. If Tina hadn't been gay, I would have had to keep a much closer eye on—

"The monarchy had nothing to do with this," Tina reiterated. I was glad she seemed to know all about it. "We assumed he had been killed in a dispute with one of you."

"Why would one of us kill Alonzo?" Carolina asked. "Why would I kill him?"

"To get in our good graces?" Sinclair suggested.

"Family doesn't always get along," Tina added.

"And for the same reasons humans kill," I said. "For money? To get property? For love? Hate? Jealousy? Revenge?"

Carolina was shaking her head; they were all shaking their heads. "No, no. Alonzo was—any differences we had were worked out decades ago. You were the only cause—that is to say, we had different opinions on what to do."

"Because of the situation with Dr. Trudeau," Sinclair said.

"That was her name? The brunette from your parlor?"

I looked away and counted to five before talking again. "What happened?" I asked, wondering if vampires had a CSI-type team they could send out for to, I dunno, vacuum for fingerprints or whatever.

"We had risen, of course, and were preparing to go out and get something to eat. David—" Carolina, the group's unofficial spokesvampire, nodded to a tall, quiet (but then, they were all quiet) gray-haired vampire who looked like a used car salesman in a good suit. "David was having someone come up; the rest of us were going out in a while. Alonzo was going to wait to dine, though, he wanted to leave right away. He was excited. He said you wanted him to come over. He—he was excited," she said again. "He was looking forward to seeing you again."

I turned to Tina. "For the record, not that I think you'd be so obvious and sloppy, but did you call Alonzo, pretending to be me, to lure him out away from his buddies, ambush him in the elevator on his way down, shoot him in the head, then cut his head off?"

"No, Majesty. I had to go to Best Buy and get a new DVD player for the game room."

"I can verify her story. I went with her." Sinclair sniffed down at Tina. "You are a gem in all things but one: you will insist on buying American."

"Can we focus, please? So after a while, Alonzo went skipping out the door, all happy to come to my house, and then a while later we came up with—blech—his headless body."

"Yes, there he was," used car salesman said. David! His name was David.

"And none of us did it," I clarified, "and none of you guys did it."

"If one of us had a grudge," Carolina pointed out, "we would hardly wait all this time, until we were here under your watchful eye, and kill him in a strange country in a strange hotel room. This draws your attention to us at a time when we have little interest in being noticed."

"Good point," I admitted. That "no attention" thing made sense, too. Getting noticed was a great way to get singled out and, well, just check the elevator for why it was bad to get noticed.

"We will take care of this," Sinclair told them. "We have a small team coming to tend the body. Do you wish to take him back to France?"

"Why?" Carolina asked. "He is dead. What difference does it make where his body is?"

Nice epigraph: *You're dead now, and who cares? Not even your cousin.*

"If you did not kill him," she continued, "then his properties are on the table, so to speak. Speaking for myself, I am most anxious to return and look into disbursement issues."

The three of us looked at each other. These guys didn't know that I had planned to give all Alonzo's stuff to Sophie. But now that he was dead, there was no reason to avenge the good doctor.

"You're not sad he's dead because you want his stuff?"

"His being dead solves a rather large problem for you, too, Majesty."

Larger than you think, honey. I pushed the thought of Sophie— an obvious suspect—aside for now. "Yeah, but—come on, the guy's dead. A friend of yours—family member—for decades? Perhaps a century? Don't you owe him something? Don't we all? I barely knew him and I sort of liked him, when I wasn't thinking about—" Shooting him, I'd started to say, but probably that wasn't the best way to go. "Look, there's got to be something. I mean, I'm glad you guys aren't in a killing psycho rage because of this, but the poor guy got iced in a hotel elevator, for God's sake."

"What is it you want us to do?" Carolina asked. Her expression made it clear she could not think of a single idea that appealed to her.

It took me a moment, but then I realized what this group needed. What Alonzo needed. What *I* needed. "Okay, let's—okay, everybody bow your heads. Bow your heads! Okay. Uh, dear God, please—"

"You're praying? We can't pray," David said.

"Not to mention, I don't think Alonzo is with . . . Him," Tina added.

"Shut up, you guys. I'm sure you won't burst into flames if I do all the talking. I see heads are up. They should be bowed. Bo-wwwww." All the heads dropped like they were on a string, except for one. Sinclair's. He was looking at me and struggling valiantly not to laugh. I glared at him, but he wouldn't bow his head. Typical. I'd let the Big Man handle him another day.

I bowed mine and looked at my clasped fingers. "Heavenly Father, you may have noticed our friend, Alonzo, has run into a spot of misfortune. We're not sure where he is, but regardless, please bless him and look after him, forever and ever, and please let him be happy where he is and not scared or lonely. And, um, thanks again for all the help you've been giving me on the whole fasting-for-my-birthday thing. Amen."

"Okay," Tina said. "Now that the . . . the royal prayer is out of the way, perhaps we can get back to the business at hand."

"Which is what? We talked to these guys, other guys are coming to take Alonzo's body—we're not cops, we're not forensic scientists, and we're not journalists. We're—"

A phone began to ring. I glared around at them. "You guys! Shut that off. Hotel room phone, cell phone, whatever it is, kill it, just don't get me started on phones. Will you—"

After a few seconds of looking around, everyone looked straight down. The phone continued to ring.

It was coming from Alonzo's body.

Chapter 29

The dead man's pants are ringing," Tina said, somewhat need-lessly.

"Maybe it's a sales call," I said. "They have the worst timing."

Sinclair stepped into the elevator, fished around blank-faced in Alonzo's pants for a minute, then pulled out a small ringing cell phone.

He flipped it open and said, "Dr. Trudeau?"

Ooooh, snap! Except—

He held it out. "It's for you."

"Did you tell her that now isn't a good time? I mean, just because the phone is ringing doesn't mean—"

"Elizabeth."

"Okay, but I'm just saying. I mean, obviously this is an impor-tant call, but in general, if it's *really* important, they'll call back." I took the cell phone from Sinclair, who looked like he'd be happy to make me eat it. "Hello?"

"Hello, gorgeous," Liam drawled. "You having fun in the ele-vator?"

"Uh, is this the part where you taunt me and leave me clues?"

"Not hardly. I did it. Sophie wanted to, so I'm afraid I had to send her on a bit of a wild-goose chase so I could take care of things for her—"

I looked around at the others. "When you use euphemisms like 'take care of it' and stuff, are we, I just wanted to make sure, are we talking about the same thing?"

"I cut the smug bastard's head off," Liam said. "After I stuck my .38 in his forehead and pulled the trigger."

"Oh. Well, it's good that you got that out of your system." I
didn't say his name out loud, though why I was trying to protect
the maniac was beyond me. "So, uh, what now?"

"Now nothing, blondie. I just wanted to call you and let you
know in case your barrel was swinging over to Sophie. Now listen
close, 'cause there might be a test later: I did it. Sophie had nothin'
to do with it. She didn't ask me to do it and she didn't know I was
gonna go out and take care of it tonight. I told her you called and
were looking for her—"

"That seems like a popular strategy today."

"—and she scooted right over to your place. Then I called
Alonzo—"

"How'd you get the number?"

"He *gave* it to Sophie. Called *her* cell—she's listed up in Embarrass, since she's gotta be accessible—and left her the number
in case she wanted to 'work things out.' Boy, if I didn't want to kill
him before, I sure woulda after that."

"I, uh, gave him your number. He was supposed to call her and
set up a meeting and apologize."

"Too late now," Liam said, totally unmoved.

I turned and walked a little ways away from the group. "Then
you came over here and did it?"

"Yep. Then I came back to our room, told Sophie, and we lit
on out of here. But I didn't want you guys wondering. It was me."

"Your friend must have flipped right out of her gourd," I said
in a low voice, but who was I kidding? They were vampires. They
could probably hear both ends of the conversation.

"Yep, she was pretty pissed at me. Still is. But we'll work it out."

"How does this affect your—your earlier plans?"

"Dunno." I could almost hear him shrug over the phone.
"Don't much care right now. She'll turn me when she gets around
to it. Right now, we gotta get in the wind."

"Maybe you don't have to—"

"You ever seen a vampire have a nightmare, Bets?" His voice
was lower, too, either because he didn't want Sophie to hear or in
response to mine. "It's awful. It's about the worst thing you ever
saw. You have nightmares, Bets?"

"No," I said truthfully. "I don't dream anymore. I didn't think
any vampires dreamed."

"Lucky," he said, and hung up.

I closed the phone and turned back to the group. "Okay! Where
were we? Right, we were leaving."

"Dr. Trudeau's lover." Carolina, looking very relieved, glanced around at the others. "Of course! We should have guessed much sooner."

"What, you're happy?"

"No, just . . . reassured. Vengeance for a loved one is—"

"An understandable motive," Tina interrupted. "Like being interested in taking over his properties."

"Right," Carolina said, completely missing the sarcasm.

"We're going," I said.

Chapter 30

"**W**ow!" Jessica said. "That is—wow! Liam! Sneaking over and icing the vampire—who'd have thought?" She answered her own question. "In retrospect, everyone. And it's *so* slick."

"Slick?"

"Well, Bets, what are you going to do?"

I opened my mouth, but Jessica rushed ahead. "Punish him? You can't do anything to him—he's human. If he was a vampire, you could do something, but he's not in your, what do you call it, jurisdiction. Turn him over to the cops? For what, killing a dead guy? Assuming you could find the body—which I bet, thanks to Sinclair's little gray men, I bet you can't—you sure don't want a forensic guy poking around in it."

"You're giving me a headache," I muttered.

"Sophie didn't do it, so you guys can't be pissed at her or punish her or anything. And someone *did* kill Alonzo, avenging Sophie. The Europeans won't expect you to do anything—they gave you a big hint when they were all uncaring about what to do with his body. In fact . . ." She shot Sinclair a sly look. "Am I right? Did you tell her?"

"I haven't had the chance, and besides, you're obviously dying to."

"I hate when you go all Sherlocky on me," I grumbled.

"They're gone! Aren't they gone?" she asked Sinclair. "I bet they beat feet out of here this very night."

"They are gone," Sinclair confirmed.

"What? Already? It's only—" I looked at my watch. It was

eight-thirty the next night. Once we'd left the hotel, the evening had been a bust. Sinclair made feeble mention of tracing Sophie's cell through Alonzo's cell, but I waved that away (could it even be done? I didn't know from cell phone technology). Let it go. They were long gone from here, anyway, and Liam probably wouldn't have been dumb enough to hang on to whatever phone he'd used to taunt me from Alonzo's pants. "How do you know?"

"I have been keeping an eye on them, of course," Sinclair replied, looking surprised at my abysmally stupid question. "They departed as soon as the sun set."

"They just took off? Without a word to anybody?"

"Of course." Sinclair was looking like the cat that had eaten fifty canaries.

"But it was such a big deal when they came. And now they're just—what? Sneaking out of town? Aren't they afraid that'll make us mad?"

"They know it won't."

"It won't?"

"Look at it from their point of view, Majesty," said Tina. "They are not remotely sure of your power base. They wait almost a year before coming to pay tribute. While they are here, you show evidence of fasting, prayer, powerful allies—vampire and human—live through an attack by a vampire killer—"

"Delk wasn't trying to kill me," I protested. "He was just having a really shitty day."

"—publish your life story, maintain a cop and a doctor as blood-sheep—"

"The hell!"

"—kill a zombie sent here for obviously sinister reasons—"

I'd told them about Zombiefest in the car on the way to Alonzo's hotel. They had both been flabbergasted. Both denied ever seeing a zombie in their long, long lives. "We don't know if it was sent, or just wandered in."

"And, when presented with a moral dilemma, you arranged for the death of a contemporary."

"But I didn't!"

"From their point of view," she reminded me.

"Well, how dumb are they?" I muttered.

"Frankly," Sinclair said, smiling, "I am surprised they did not skulk out of town quite a bit earlier."

"So—you're happy? You're happy that those guys think I'm a royal murdering jerk."

"You should be very happy they think that—if you can bear it, Miss Congeniality."

I stuck a finger in his face. "I told you about that privately. It's private. Private information! *Not* for sharing with the class!"

"You should never have told Jessica, then," Tina piped up, "because she told everyone that story."

"What?" Jessica cried when I looked at her. "You were in the Burnsville paper, for God's sake. It's not like it was a Pentagon secret."

I turned to Sinclair. "So do we ask Sophie and Liam to leave? Banish them?"

"They banished themselves," Sinclair said quietly. "They did not return to their home in Embarrass; no one has seen them in days. Too bad; I have questions."

"Questions like what?"

"Like how a farmer of modest means could have killed one of the oldest, most powerful vampires on the planet."

"A classic assassination," Tina pointed out. "He just walked up to him and—well. Alonzo was distracted, apparently. Perhaps Liam got close to him with a lie—I'll be your driver tonight, orders from the Queen, she's the one who had me call. Something. Anything."

"And he isn't a farmer," I said. "He lives in a small town, on a farm, but he doesn't work the land. He's retired from the Air Force, Sophie told me." I nearly groaned as I remembered *what* she had told me. "Where he used to teach small arms."

"Small arms?"

"Handguns," Tina clarified. "Hmm. In hindsight, someone should have been watching those two."

"I guess I thought Sophie would just wait around for—" *What? For me to make a move? For justice?* "Indefinitely," I finished. "I should have known none of this would sit well with Liam. And he wouldn't think killing Sophie's killer—I mean, I don't get the idea that it's going to be weighing heavy on his mind, you know?"

"Did killing Nostro weigh heavily on yours?" Sinclair asked.

I shook my head; if he was looking for answers, he had the wrong girl. "I'm so fucking thirsty right now," I admitted, "it's hard to get worked up about anything."

Jessica edged away.

"I don't think you have to worry," Tina teased. "You smell so bland and tasteless right now."

"Hey, that's right!" She brightened. "Vampire repellant."

"You've always been repellant," I told her gently.

"Oh, that reminds me. We're redoing the parlor—"

"The second one?"

"No, the first. All the foot traffic in there just reminds me how awful the wallpaper is. Anyway, once the walls were stripped the workmen found something really interesting."

"Interesting how? Interesting bad? Termites? What?"

"Come and see," she invited.

I followed her, groaning. What fresh hell was this? Couldn't I ever get a break? And why was Jess even bothering me with this stuff? She knew I was bored to death by anything having to do with the house; not to mention, if there was a real problem it would be her, not me, who would have to take care of it financially.

"Whaaat?" I whined, following her into the parlor.

"Surprise!" a dozen people yelled back. I stared; there was a big HAPPY BIRTHDAY swag on the far wall; the place was full of multicolored helium balloons, and people were throwing confetti at me. The walls, needless to say, were not stripped at all. Lying bitch.

"You'd think it would be harder to fool a vampire," my mother was saying, a colorful conical hat perched incongruously in her white hair. "But no."

"If the vampire is Betsy," Sinclair said, coming up and putting an arm around me, "it is not so difficult."

"Shut up. Jeez, you guys! I said, I said no parties." I was trying not to grin like a chimp. Aw! They'd gone to all this trouble. Balloons everywhere. Streamers. The aforementioned swag. A big table at the far end full of all kinds of pop and wine and even sandwiches. And a big cake at the end—double layer, chocolate frosting. If I knew Jessica's maniac attention to detail, the inside of the cake would be chocolate, the layers filled with chocolate buttercream. Hopefully someone had a blender nearby and could toss a piece in for me.

There was also a gallon of chocolate ice cream in a tub of ice. Now that I *could* have, once I mixed it with some milk and made it into a shake.

"Well, I can't stay," the Ant was saying, giving my mom a narrow-eyed look of (mature!) distaste. "I only came to drop the baby off." The baby had gotten hold of his birthday hat and was busily chewing on the end of it. I wondered how he'd like chocolate cake. How could I slip him some? It would blow all the circuits in his little head. And the kid would love it. Hee!

"I'll take him. Please, Mrs. Taylor? It's Betsy's special night."

"Oh, well, uh." The Ant looked flustered; BabyJon had only spent the night at home and, more and more frequently, my house. "Well, Laura, if you don't mind. He can be a handful."

"Oh, it's no trouble." She bent down and scooped him out of his car seat. "I'd love to have him overnight!" She took the hat away from him and he wailed. She whipped a bottle (where had she been keeping it? Her pocket?) into his mouth and the wail was shut off as he sucked energetically.

"Sorry I'm late," Detective Nick said, rushing into the room. I was amused to see him out of breath. "Did I miss the part where everyone yells surprise and she freaks out? I love that part."

Honey, you should have seen me last night.

"I ran from the car," he was saying apologetically to Jessica. "Sorry—got hung up at work."

"Hey, you're here. Have some cake." Jessica hugged him, and over her head Sinclair shot me a look. I knew what he was thinking: Nick hadn't been in the room when my mom had made her ill-conceived comment about vampires. So he missed it, so he was still fooled. Or he was still fooling us.

An issue for another time. The larger concern: the Ant wasn't leaving. She and Laura were burbling over BabyJon and the Ant actually took her coat off. Weird! Further proof that Laura's devilish charm worked on anybody, no matter how freakish or awful.

"Your father couldn't make it," my mom said through tight lips. "He's sorry." Wow, if I had a dollar for every time I'd heard that growing up—wait a minute. I think Sinclair *did.*

"It's fine." I meant it. It would be just too weird to have my dad there, too, along with—

Let's see, there was Nick. Jessica and Tina. Sinclair, Marc. The Ant, BabyJon. Cathie—yes, she had just floated in, and was waving to me across the room and talking to another ghost, a much older woman who kept pointing at me and gesturing urgently. No doubt a problem Cathie could handle herself, as she had suggested before.

Marjorie the librarian, scarfing up the free wine. Toni and Garrett. No Sophie and Liam, of course, but I actually looked around the room anyway. It made me sad; under "normal" circumstances, they could have—and would have—come. And obviously, no Delk.

I cheered up a little when I saw Carolina! Wait a minute,

wha—yep, there she was, standing awkwardly in front of a bowl of potato chips.

I gestured and she came over to me at once, looking almost relieved. Not one for parties, this one. Or nervous about *this* party. "What are you doing here? I heard you guys were all on a plane out of town."

"Oh, well." She shrugged and looked down. "The others were in rather a hurry to get back—the business, you know, and various personal issues. But I—I wanted to see you, when you weren't under so much stress."

"Well, I'm glad you came." She smiled uncertainly and I took her hand. "Really, Carolina. I'm glad you're here."

"Oh, well," she said again, and looked away with a slightly more real smile. "Really, I couldn't stay away. It's been—it's been many years since I was at a birthday party. And never a surprise one."

"Yes, lucky me." I gave Jessica and Sinclair a sideways look. "Well, this one wasn't supposed to be. I remember saying repeatedly—"

"Oh, knock it off, bitch, you know you love it." Jessica waved my objection away. "Tell me you didn't love it when you saw all the shit on the walls and all these people here for *your* birthday."

"Yeah, well, my birthday isn't until tomorrow."

"A masterful way to throw you off guard," Sinclair put in (not that anybody was talking to him). "Which succeeded brilliantly, I might add."

"This is good practice for our wedding rehearsal," I told him, which wiped the smirk off his face. The big day was three months away, and I doubted if he knew what time it was or where to show up.

"So, thirty-one," Marc said, coming up to our little group.

Carolina laughed out loud, earning mystified looks from my mother. I loved it—the one nice thing about ancient vampires is, they could make you feel young.

"Hey, I didn't not invite you over to my forbidden surprise party to have you insult me. God, look at all that pop. I could really use a big glass of Coke with a ton of ice."

"And I would get it for you," Sinclair said, "except that is not what you *really* want."

"Can you step out in the hall with me?" I asked seriously. "I wanted to ask you something about Liam."

"Oh." Sinclair looked surprised, then set down his wineglass, took my hand, inclined his head to the group, and said, "Excuse us."

He led me swiftly to the hall and asked, "What is it? Did he call again? Threaten you?"

"No, dumb ass. It was a ruse. A ploy, a subterfuge." I slung my arms around his neck and pulled him close. "It's my birthday and I wanted to get you alone."

"It is not technically . . . mmmm." He shut up (finally) and we kissed, made out, groped, and groaned in the hallway like a couple of teenagers sneaking out past curfew.

"Oh, Elizabeth, I do love you. I—ah!" He groaned as my teeth broke the skin on his neck, as I pulled the blood from him in a sweet winey flow, as I fell off the blood wagon with a big old crash. Sinclair was right beside me for the fall.

"I've been thinking," I murmured, licking his throat, his lower lip, the tip of his right fang. "This fast. It didn't prove anything. It didn't make me a better vampire." If anything, it made me a bitchier one. "It's not where and when you drink blood, it's—" I couldn't think of the rest of the platitude. How you drink it? Who you drink it from? If you have it in a fancy glass with a cocktail umbrella? Whatever. I was distracted. Possibly because he had bitten me, was sucking on my throat so hard he'd pulled me to my tiptoes. "Anyway," I managed, trying not to flail and gasp, "I'm going to drink again, but only from you. And you'll drink only from me. Right?"

"Mmmm," he said, his mouth busy on my throat.

"And we'll have a better life together than most, I bet."

He pulled back and looked at me. There was a spot of blood just below his lower lip in the shape of a comma. "No one, ever, could have a better life together. Not if they have you, Elizabeth."

"Well, then, aren't you the lucky fella." I laughed and kissed away the bloody comma. "Let's see if you say that three months from now."

"Er, three months?"

"Sinclair!"

"Right. Ah, the magic of three months from now. I await breathlessly."

"Very funny. We already don't breathe." I tried to wrestle out of his embrace, but he held fast. "Unf! Ergh! Sinclair: you *have* put this on your calendar, right?"

"Darling, it's been there for ages, I swear! Stop wriggling. Our magical, culturally meaningless evening looms before me like a sweet hippopotamus of joy."

I was soothed by his tone, then digested his words and redoubled my efforts to get away. "Dude! I wouldn't marry you if you begged for it."

He laughed and let me go. "But I would, you know." He looked at me with slightly narrowed eyes, that considering look I knew so well. "Beg for it."

I loved that look. I loved him. I started to step back into his embrace, but he seized me before I could, yanked me to him, and thrust his mouth into my neck with the speed of a striking snake. His teeth were so sharp I barely felt them penetrate. Well, I felt them penetrate, but not in my neck, if you know what I mean.

He had thrust his fingers into my hair and was holding me by the head, the other arm so tightly around my waist it was a good thing I didn't need to breathe. He drank from me like a man just out of the desert, squeezed me to him with desperate hunger, and I loved it, I would have let him hold me like that all day, take from me all night.

We were almost wrestling, moving in a tight little dance in the hallway, and I struggled free enough to bite him back, to feel his cool blood on my tongue like a rich dark wine, to feel it racing through my system, making me stronger, making me better, making me more.

Vampire.

"The party," I groaned.

"Fuck the party," he growled back.

"We can't stay out here making out."

"Exactly so. Let's go to bed."

I managed to wrench free—mostly because he let me—and stood back, wiped my mouth, and checked my shirt for blood stains. His tongue darted out and caught a rill of blood, and I fought the urge to leap back into his arms and bite it.

I remembered there were more than a dozen people less than ten feet away. Thank goodness for thick doors and walls! Yay, old houses! Like I said. "We'd better get back to the party."

"In a moment. I wanted to ask you. Will you tell me the entire story? The tale of you and the zombie?"

"Oh. I thought I—"

"You gave Tina and me the Cliff Notes version. And we both pretended not to notice that you nearly had a breakdown—and then there was Alonzo to deal with. But I want to hear everything."

"You'll laugh at me."

"Yes, of course."

I smiled; I couldn't help it. "Okay, but later. And with all the lights on. In our bed. And when I start to freak out all over again, tell me something that pisses me off."

"I will."

He picked up my hand—the one with my glorious engagement ring—and kissed it. "With me it's spiders."

"Really?"

He almost shuddered. Eric Sinclair, badass vampire king, afraid of Charlotte! "All those legs," he muttered.

I hugged him. "I won't tell a soul," I whispered. "But for crying out loud, we've got to get back to my party. It's the only thirty-first birthday I'm going to have, you know."

I stepped back to straighten my clothes, which didn't last long; he snatched me back into his arms so quickly I couldn't dodge, much less keep away. "Oh, the party. Never mind the party."

"Mind *me*, then," I said, and kissed him.

"I do mind you," he replied, and we got busy in the closet under the stairs, and it was only later that I thought about what he said and got pissed, but he just laughed at me.

Undead and Uneasy

Thanks to my long-suffering husband (fourteen years of marriage by the time you hold this book in your hand, poor bastard . . . my husband, not you), my supportive family, Jessica, and my readers . . . long may your credit cards reign.

Acknowledgments

This book was written alone, but several of the usual suspects helped, either by making suggestions or telling me to get my big butt back into the office chair. In no particular order, they are: Tony; Chris; Liam; Yvonne; Mom; and my Dad, the artist formerly known as King Al (see *The Royal Treatment*; *The Royal Surprise*).

But it's also dedicated to friends I've never met. All the members of my Yahoo group, for starters. This is the nicest group on the Internet, sharing pictures, stories, and, best of all, book recommendations. I also post new chapter excerpts and drop annoying hints about upcoming books and plot developments to the Yahoos. If you'd like to join, you can check it out at maryjanice-subscribe@yahoogroups.com. Special thanks to Terri, Mippy, and Jose, who always put a smile on my face.

Another ridiculously supportive group is the Laurell K. Hamilton forum (www.laurellkhamilton.org). I mean, these aren't even her books, this is *her* website to promote her work, and not only does she make room for a Web page of mine, but everyone there is super nice: they support me, buy my books, discuss same, meet me at book signings, and ask for autographs. Weird. But nice.

Frankly, the romance world is full of warm, supporting authors. Among the best of the best: Charlaine Harris, Susan Grant, P. C. Cast, Nora Roberts, Lori Foster, and Christine Feehan.

I write the books, but no book can get on the shelves, or stay on the shelves, without phenomenal PR representation. In this I am blessed with Julia Fleischaker of Berkley PR and Jessica

Growette of J.A.G. Promotions. Their job sucks, because they do the hard work and I get all the glory.

Speaking of sucky, horrible jobs with no glory (no, Mom, I'm not talking about you), there's my editor, Cindy Hwang, and my agent, Ethan Ellenberg. Both have had more than their fair share of migraines, thanks to yours truly.

But this book, and all the ones before it, would not have been possible without e-publishers and e-books. They took a chance on this writer when no one knew me, and I appreciate it.

This past summer I went on my first book tour, which was harrowing yet thrilling. And a lot of the things you're about to read in this book were directly inspired by questions and comments readers asked me at signings and readings. So thanks for caring enough to show up, for caring about characters enough to be concerned about them, and finally, thanks to David, who cornered me (in the very nicest way) at a book signing and begged me to get Marc Spangler hooked up. He was not alone in this request and I, the obedient author, obeyed.

Also, thanks to Martha Stewart, whose Wedding DVD was a great help in figuring out what Betsy's gown, cake, and bridesmaids' dresses would look like.

Thanks to Jamie Poole for thinking up The Betsy, a delightful cocktail that lubricated my creativity on more than one occasion. Take that however you like.

And finally, a tip of the hat to my readers, especially those of you who've been at this since the original *Undead and Unwed*. This is a book that goes where the first five really haven't. That's not to say we won't have fun along the way . . . Those of you who've been with me before know this universe is always a good time.

And the Queene shalt noe a living childe, and he shalt be hers by a living man. —THE BOOK OF THE DEAD

A cat's a better mother than you.
—MARGARET MITCHELL, *Gone With the Wind*

A gloomy guest fits not a wedding feast.
—FRIEDRICH VON SCHILLER

Lisa, vampires *are* make believe. Like elves, gremlins, and Eskimos. —THE SIMPSONS, "Treehouse of Horror IV"

With enough courage, you can do without a reputation.
—MARGARET MITCHELL, *Gone With the Wind*

To challenge the Queene, thou shalt desecrate the symbole.
—THE BOOK OF THE DEAD

Crying is all right in its own way while it lasts. But you have to stop sooner or later, and then you still have to decide what to do. —C. S. LEWIS, *The Silver Chair*

You are cordially invited to
the wedding of

Elizabeth Anne Taylor
and

Sinclair

607 Summit Avenue
Midnight
July 4, 2007

RSVP by June 25, and don't be one of those jerks
who doesn't RSVP and then shows up with
three people. Seriously.

Prologue

Once, there was a beautiful queen who was as terrible on the inside as she was glorious on the outside. She was vain, wicked, cold, and selfish. Her greatest pleasures were her coalfire earrings, terrible unwieldy things that swung past her shoulders. Each stone was as big around as the ball of the queen's thumb, and it was said more than a thousand men died mining the bloodred rocks.

So conceited was this queen, and so greatly did she love her coalfire earrings, that she threatened a curse upon any who might steal them from her. So naturally, her people waited until the queen died before taking them.

The four thieves (who in truth cannot be called grave robbers, because no one waited until the hated queen was buried) went to her unguarded body and helped themselves. The body was unguarded because the parties celebrating the new monarchs (the dead queen's cousin, a plain but generous woman; and her husband, a shy healer) were in full swing, and no one especially cared about guarding a dead jerk.

The first of the four dropped dead before he could mount his horse. The second of the four died after his tent mysteriously caught fire the next night. The third made it to the coast, sold the earrings for a splendid sum, and promptly dropped dead of a brainstorm, what today is known as an aneurysm. What happened to the fourth is not known.

The man who bought the earrings had them in his shop for three and a half days. He sold the earrings to a man of some wealth and standing, just before his shop was struck by hundreds of successive strokes of lightning, sparing his life but driving him out of business forever, and leaving him with a lifelong fear of flashing lights and loud noises.

The man of wealth and standing was the manservant of a European prince (history is vague on which one). He delivered the earrings to his master, and one hour later, the prince ingested a lethal amount of tainted meat, along with half of one of the earrings, which was later extracted during the autopsy.

The earrings eventually reached London, but not after causing a series of increasingly odd and gruesome disasters along the way, including but not limited to a pig plague, a tomato blight, a series of foals born with five legs, multiple drownings several miles away from any natural source of water, and a viciously quick mammal that no one ever saw clearly enough to describe well.

The day the jewelry went on display at the British Museum in their Return of Egyptian Antiquities Exhibit, the head of security suffered a fatal heart attack, the gift shop girl went blind, and three tour guides were stricken with crippling dysentery.

The earrings stayed in the museum for many years. Probably. The earrings, it seemed, disliked staying in one spot, and curators were known to snatch themselves bald looking for the jewels.

They turned up once in the Neanderthal exhibit, twice in the men's urinal on the second floor, six times in the gift shop (by now word of the "cursed" earrings had spread, and no museum employee, no matter how long her hours or how low her pay, dared touch them), and four times in the cafeteria (where an unwary museum guest nearly choked to death on one). They also went on an unscheduled, miniature tour around the world, disappearing and being found in no fewer than eight exhibits: Japan, Rome, Manila, Greece, the Americas, Britain, the Pacific, and the Near East. Each of the other museums, aware of the artifacts' history, returned the jewels to Britain quickly and without comment.

Eventually the British Museum came under new management (the last curator having taken forced early retirement for mysteriously losing his fingers and his sense of smell) who, in an attempt to score points with the House of Windsor, made a gift of the earrings to Diana, the Princess of Wales.

Some time later, they came into the possession of a very old, very curious vampire who had the idea of breaking the earrings into a series of smaller stones and shipping them in twenty-five different directions around the planet. You know, just to see what would happen.

One of the stones ended up in Minnesota, right about at the turn of the twenty-first century. Nobody knows the exact date, because those involved in the shipment arrangements simply cannot be found.

Chapter 1

There are three things wrong with that card," the king of the vampires told me. "One, my love for you is not anything like 'shimmering amber waves of summer wheat.' Two, my love for you has nothing to do with adorable, fluffy cartoon rabbits. Three . . ." And he sighed here. "Rabbits do not sparkle."

I looked at the shiny yellow card, aglitter with sparkling bunnies. It was the least objectionable of the pile of two dozen I had spread all over our bed. What could I say? He had a point. Three of them. "It's just an example—don't have a heart attack and friggin' die on me, all right?"

"I do not have," he muttered, "that kind of good fortune."

"I heard that. I'm just saying, there will be a lot of people at the wedding"—I ignored Sinclair's shudder—"but there will also be people who can't make it. You know, due to having other plans or being dead, or whatever. So what you do is, you send a wedding announcement to pull in all the people who couldn't come. That way people know we actually did the deed. It's polite." I racked my brain for the perfect way to describe it so my reluctant groom would clamber aboard. "It's, you know, civilized."

"It is a voracious grab for gifts from the crude and uncouth."

"That's true," I acknowledged after a minute, knowing well where I was in the Wars of the Couth. Come on, we all knew he was right. There was no point—*no* point—in all those birth and wedding and graduation announcements beyond, "Hey! Limber up the old checkbook; something new has happened in our family. Cash is also fine."

"But it's still nice. You didn't fuss nearly so much about the invitations."

"The invitations have a logical point."

"The invitations are weird. Just 'Sinclair,' like you don't have a middle or first name. Why wouldn't you put your full name on the thing?"

"Our community knows me as Sinclair."

"Our" my butt. He meant the vampire community. I couldn't resist one last dig. "I'm marrying Cher!"

"Don't tease."

I bit my tongue for what felt like the hundredth time that night . . . and it was barely 9:00 p.m. With the wedding only three weeks away, Sinclair, my blushing groom, was growing bitchier by the hour.

He had never liked the idea of a formal wedding with a minister and flower girls and a wedding cake frosted with colored Crisco. He said that because the Book of the Dead proclaimed him my consort, we were already married and would be for a thousand years. Period. End of discussion. Everything else? A waste of time. And money. Tough to tell the greater sin in his eyes.

After what seemed like a thousand years (but was only one and a half) I'd gotten Eric (yes, he had a first name) to profess his love, propose, give me a ring, and agree to a ceremony. But he never promised to take his dose without kicking, and he sure never promised to get married without a heavy dose of snark.

I had two choices. I could rise to his bitchy comments with a few of my own, and we could end up in a wicked big fight, again. Or, I could ignore his bitchy comments and go about my day, er, night, and after the wedding, Sinclair would be my sweet blushing boy-toy again.

Then there was the honeymoon to look forward to: two weeks in New York City, a place I'd never been! I'd heard NYC was a great place to visit, if you had money. Sinclair had gobs of money to his name. Ew, which reminded me.

"By the way, I'm not taking your name. It's nothing personal—"

"Not personal? It is my name."

"—it's just how I was raised."

"Your mother took your father's name and, even after he left her for the lethal flirtations of another woman, kept his name. Which is why, to this day, there are two Mrs. Taylors in town. So in fact, it is *not* how you were raised."

I glared. He glared back, except his was more like a sneer. Since Sinclair looked like he was sneering even when he was unconscious, it was tough to tell. All I knew was, we were headed for yet another argument and thank goodness we were doing it in our bedroom, where one of the house's many live-ins weren't likely to bother us. Or, even worse, rate us (Marc had given our last fight a 7.6—we started with an 8 based on volume alone, but he had taken four-tenths of a point off for lack of originality in name-calling).

We lived (and would presumably for the next thousand years—hope Jessica was paid up on her damage insurance) in a big old mansion on Summit Avenue in St. Paul. Me, Sinclair, my best friend Jessica, Marc, and a whole bunch of others I'm just too tired to list right now. I adored my friends, but sometimes I couldn't help wishing they'd all just disappear for the sake of some peace and quiet.

Retreating to the master suite, where we were currently arguing, was an acceptable substitute for actual solitude. I'd never seen a divine bathroom before, much less been in one, but after taking a bath in the eight-foot-long whirlpool tub, I'd come to believe God could act through bubbles.

The whole place was like a bed-and-breakfast—the fanciest, nicest one in the whole world, where the fridge was always full, the sheets were always fresh, and you never had to check out and go home. Even the closets were sublime, with more scrollwork than you could shake a stick at. Having come from a long line of tract housing families, I'd resisted the move here last year. But now I loved it. I still couldn't believe I actually lived in a *mansion* of all things. Some of the rooms were so big, I hardly noticed Sinclair.

Okay, that was a lie. Eric Sinclair filled every room he was in, even if he was just sitting in the corner reading a newspaper. Big— well over six feet—with the build of a farmer (which he had been) who kept in shape (which he did): wide, heavily muscled shoulders, long legs, narrow waist, flat stomach, big hands, big teeth, big dick. Alpha male all the way. And he was mine. Mine, I tell you!

Sinclair was seventy-something—I was vague on the details, and he rarely volunteered autobiographical info—but had died in his thirties, so his black hair was unmarked by gray; his broad, handsome face was without so much as a sun wrinkle. He had a grin that made Tom Cruise look like a snaggle-toothed octogenarian. He was dynamite in bed—ooh, boy, was he! He was rich (possibly richer than Jessica, who had arranged for the purchase of this mansion). He was strong—I'd seen him pull a man's arm off his body like you or I would pull a chicken wing apart. And I mentioned the vampire part, right? That he was the king of the vampires?

And I was the queen. *His* queen.

Never mind what the Book of the Dead said, never mind that he'd tricked me into the queen gig, never mind what other vampires said; shit, never mind what my *mom* said. I loved Eric (when he wasn't being a pud), and he loved me (I was almost positive); and in my book (which wasn't bound in human skin and written in blood, *thank you very much*) that meant we collared a justice of the peace and got him to say "Husband and Wife."

Two years ago, I would have said a minister. But if a man of God said a blessing over Eric Sinclair, sprinkled him with holy water, or handed him a collection plate, my darling groom would go up in flames, and it'd be really awkward.

Anyway, that was the way I wanted things. The way I needed them. And really, it seemed a small enough thing to ask. Especially when you look at all the shit *I* had put up with since rising from the dead. Frankly, if the king of the vampires didn't like it, he could take a flying fuck at a rolling garter belt.

"If you don't like it," I said, "you can take a flying fuck at a rolling garter belt."

"Is that another of your tribe's charming post-ceremony activities?"

"What is this 'my tribe' crapola?" I'd given up on the announcements and had started folding my T-shirts—the basket had been silently condemning me for almost a week. Jessica had hired plenty of servants, but we all insisted on doing our own laundry. Except Sinclair. I think Tina (his super-butler/major domo/assistant) did his. He could hold his damned breath waiting for *me* to step up.

I dropped the fresh, clean T-shirt so I could put my hands on my hips and *really* give him the glare. "Your dad was a Minnesota farmer. This I'm-an-aristocrat-and-you're-a-peasant schtick stinks like a rotten apple."

Sinclair, working at the desk in the corner (in a black suit, on a Tuesday night—it was the equivalent of a guy getting up on his day off and immediately putting on a Kenneth Cole before so much as eating a bowl of cornflakes), simply shrugged and did not look up. That was his way: to taunt, to make an irritating observation, and then refuse to engage. He swore it was proof of his love, that he'd have killed anyone else months ago.

"I am just so sick of you acting like this wedding thing is all me and has nothing to do with you."

He didn't look up, and he didn't put his pen down. "This wedding thing is all you and has nothing to do with me."

"I'll bet you haven't even worked on your vows yet."

"I certainly have."

"Fine, smart-ass. Let's hear them."

He laid his pen down, closed his eyes, licked his lips, and took a deep breath. "Alas, the penis is such a ridiculous petitioner. It is so unreliable, though everything depends on it—the world is balanced on it like a ball on a seal's nose. It is so easily teased, insulted, betrayed, abandoned; yet it must pretend to be invulnerable, a weapon which confers magical powers upon its possessor; consequently this muscle-less inchworm must try to swagger through temples and pull apart thighs like the hairiest Samson, the mightiest ram." Opening his eyes and taking in my horrified expression, he added, "William Gass, 'Metaphor and Measurement.' "

Then he picked up his pen and returned to his work.

With a shriek of rage, I yanked my engagement ring off my finger, yelped (it stuck to my second knuckle), and threw it at him, hard.

He snatched it out of the air without looking and tossed it back at me. I flailed at it, juggled it madly, then finally clenched it in my cold fist.

"Oh no you don't, love. You insisted on a gauche representation of my feelings and you *will* wear it. And if you throw it at me again," he continued absently, turning crumbling sheets of parchments, never looking up, "I will make you eat it."

"Eat *this*." I flipped him the bird. I could actually feel my blood pressure climbing. Not that I had blood pressure. But I knew what it felt like. And I knew I was acting like a brat. But what was the matter with him? Why was he being so cold, so distant, so—so Sinclair? We hadn't even made love since . . . I started counting on my fingers and gave up after I'd reached last Thursday. Instead we were sharing blood without sex—a first for us. It was like—like being used like a Kleenex and tossed accordingly.

What was wrong with him? What was wrong with me? I was getting everything I ever wanted. Since I woke up dead, right? *Right?*

I was so caught up in my mental bitching I hadn't noticed that Sinclair had advanced on me like a cat on a rat.

"Put your trinket on, darling, lest you lose it again."

I ignored the urge to pierce his left nostril with it. He was *soooo* lucky I liked rubies.

I managed (barely) to evade his kiss. "What? You think we're going to have sex now?"

"I had hopes," he admitted, dodging a fist.

"Don't we have to make up before the makeup sex?"

"I don't see why," he said, pressing me down onto the bed.

I grumbled, but his hands felt fine, and I figured it was just as well to let him think he was in charge. (He did only *think* that, right?) His mouth was on mine, then on my neck, his hands were under my shirt, then tugging and pulling on my pants. I felt his teeth pierce my throat, felt the dizzying sensation of being taken, being used, as he sipped my cool blood. His hands were on my ass, pulling me toward him, and then he was sliding into me, and that was that, the fight was over. Or at least on hold.

We rocked together for a fine time, and I counted my orgasms like fireworks going off in my brain: one, two, three!

(Elizabeth, my own, my queen, my . . . bride.)

"Get used to that one," I panted, meeting his thrusts with my hips, trying not to hear the laughter in his head.

He bit me on the other side of my throat, and I thought, we're going to have to change the sheets. Stupid undead lovemaking!

He stiffened over me and then rolled away, stifling a yawn. "There, now. Don't you feel better?"

"Loads. So about the wedding—"

"The ceremony we have no use for?"

Poof. All gone, afterglow. "Shut *up*! Some moldy old book written by dead guys tells you we're married, and that's good enough for you?"

"Are we discussing the Book of the Dead, or the"—he made a terrible face, like he was trying to spit out a mouse, and then coughed it out—"Bible?"

"Very funny!" Though I was impressed; even a year ago, he could never have said Bible. Maybe I was rubbing off on him? He was certainly rubbing off on me; I'd since found out the *Wall Street Journal* made splendid kindling. "Look, I'd just like you to say, just once, just this one time, I'd like to hear that you're happy we're getting married."

"I am happy," he yawned, "and we *are* married."

And around and around we went. I wasn't stupid. I was aware that to the vampires, the Book of the Dead *was* a bible of sorts, and if it said we were consorts and coregents, then it was a done deal.

But I was a different sort of vampire. I'd managed (I think) to hang on to my humanity. A little, anyway. And I wanted a real wedding. With cake, even if I couldn't eat it. And flowers. And Sinclair slipping a ring on my finger and looking at me like I was the only woman in the universe for him. A ring to match the gorgeous gold engagement band clustered with diamonds and rubies, wholly unique and utterly beautiful and *proof that I was his*. And me looking understated yet devastating in a smashingly simple wedding gown, looking scrumptious and gorgeous for him. Looking *bridal*. And him looking dark and sinister and frightening to everyone except me. Him *smiling* at me, not that nasty-nice grin he used on everyone else.

And we'd be a normal couple. A nice, normal couple who could start a—start a—

"I just wish we could have a baby," I fretted, twisting my ring around and around on my finger.

"We have been over this before," he said with barely concealed distaste.

We had. Or I had. Don't get me wrong; I wasn't one of those whiny women (on the subject of drooling infants, anyway), but it was like once I knew I could never have one (and once my rotten stepmother, the Ant, *did* have one), it was all I could think about.

No baby for Betsy and Sinclair. Not ever. I'd even tried to adopt a ghost once, but once I fixed her problem, she vanished, and that was that. I had no plans to put my heart on the chopping block again.

I sat up in bed much too fast, slipped, and hit the floor with a thud. "Don't you want a baby, Sinclair?"

"We have been over this before," he repeated, still not looking at me. "The Book of the Dead says the queen can have a child with a living man."

"Fuck the Book of the Dead! I want our baby, Sinclair, yours and mine!"

"I cannot give you one," he said quietly, and left me to go back to his desk. He sat down, squinted at some paperwork, and was immediately engrossed.

Right. He couldn't. He was dead. We could never be real parents. Which is why I wanted (stop me if you've heard this before) *a real wedding*. With flowers and booze and cake and dresses and tuxes.

And my family and friends looking at us and thinking, *now there's a couple that will make it, there's a couple that was meant to be*. And Marc having a date, and Jessica not being sick anymore. And my baby brother not crying once, and my stepmother getting along with everybody and not looking tacky.

And our other roommate werewolf, Antonia, not having a million bitchy remarks about "monkey rituals" and George the Fiend—I mean Garrett—not showing us how he can eat with his feet. And Cathie not whispering in my ear and making me giggle at inappropriate moments.

And my folks not fighting, and peace being declared in the Middle East just before the fireworks (and doves) went up in the backyard, and someone discovering that chocolate cured cancer.

Was that so much to ask?

Chapter 2

ake that rag off," my best friend rasped. "It makes you look like a dead crack whore."

"Not a *dead* one," my roommate, Marc, mock-gasped. "How positively blech-o."

"It's not that bad," I said doubtfully, twirling before the mirror. But Jess was right. Nordic pale when alive, I was positively ghastly when dead, and a pure white gown made me look like—it must be said—a corpse bride.

"I think it looks very pretty," Laura, my half sister, said loyally. Of course, Laura thought everything was very pretty. *Laura* was very pretty. She was also the devil's daughter, but that was a story for another time.

The five of us—Marc, Jessica, Laura, Cathie, and I—were at Rush's Bridal, an überexclusive bridal shop that had been around for years, that you could only get in by appointment, that had provided Mrs. Hubert Humphrey and her bridesmaids with their gowns. (The thank-you note was framed in the shop.)

Thanks to Jessica's pull, I hadn't needed an appointment. But I didn't like stores like this. It wasn't like a Macy's . . . you couldn't go back in the racks and browse. You told the attendant what you wanted, and they fetched (arf!) various costly gowns for you to try on.

I found this frustrating, because I didn't *know* what I wanted. Sure, I'd been flipping through *Minnesota Bride* since seventh grade, but that was when I had a rosy complexion. And a pulse. And no money. But all that had changed.

"I'm sure we'll find something just perfect for you," the attendant, whose name I kept forgetting, purred, as she had me strip to my paisley panties. I didn't care. Jessica had seen me naked about a zillion times (once, naked and crying in a closet), Laura was family, and Marc was gay. Oh, and Cathie was dead. Deader than me, even. A ghost.

"So how's the blushing bridegroom?" Marc asked, surreptitiously trying to take Jessica's pulse. She slapped him away like she would an annoying wasp.

"Grumpy," I said, as more attendants with armfuls of tulle appeared. "I swear. I was completely prepared to become Bridezilla—"

"We were, too," Cathie muttered.

"—but nobody warned me Sinclair would get all bitchy."

"Not pure white," Jessica said tiredly. "It washes her out. How about an Alexia with black trim?"

"No black," I said firmly. "At a vampire wedding? Are you low on your meds?"

Marc frowned. "Actually, yes."

"Never mind," I sighed. "There's lots of shades of white. Cream, latte, ecru, ivory, magnolia, seashell—"

"You don't have to wear white," Laura piped up, curled up like a cat in a velvet armchair. Her sunny blond hair was pulled back in a severe bun. She was dressed in a sloppy blue T-shirt and cutoffs. Bare legs, flip-flops. She still looked better than I was going to look on The Day, and it was taking all my willpower not to locate a shotgun from somewhere in that bridal shop's secret back room and shoot her in the head. Not to kill her, of course. Just to make her face slightly less symmetrical. "In fact, it's inappropriate for you to wear white."

"Virgin," I sneered.

"Vampire," Laura retorted. "You could wear blue. Or red! Red would bring out your eyes."

"Stop! You're all killing me with your weirdness."

"What's the budget on this thing, anyway?" Cathie asked, drifting close to the ceiling, inspecting the chandeliers, the gorgeous accessories, the beautifully dressed yet understated attendants (who were ignoring all the vampire talk, as good attendants did), the utter lack of a price tag on anything.

"Mmmm mmmm," I muttered.

"What?" Cathie and Jessica asked in unison.

"Cathie was just asking about the budget." One of the yuckier perks of being queen of the dead? I alone could see and hear ghosts. And they could see and hear me. And bug me. Any time. Day or night. Naked or fully clothed.

But even for a ghost, Cathie was special. As we all know, most ghosts hang around because they have unfinished business. Once they finished their business, poof! Off into the wild blue whatever. (God knows *I'd* never had that privilege.) And who could blame them? If it were me, I'd beat feet off this mortal plane the minute I could.

But even after I'd fixed Cathie's little serial killer problem, she hung around. She even ran defense between the ghosts and me. Sort of like a celestial executive assistant.

"So?" Marc asked.

"Don't look at . . . me," Jessica gasped. Marc's lips thinned, and we all looked away. "Gravy train's . . . over."

"Would your friend like some water?" a new attendant said, swooping in out of nowhere.

"Got any chemo?" Jess asked tiredly.

"It's, um, three million," I said, desperate to change the subject. I couldn't look at Jessica, so I looked at my feet instead. My toenails were in dire need of filing and polishing. As they always were—no matter what I did to them, they always returned to the same state they'd been in the night I died.

"Three *million*?" Cathie screamed in my ear, making me flinch. The attendants probably thought I was epileptic. "What, rubles? Pesos? Yen?"

"Three million *dollars*?" Marc goggled. "For a party?"

All the women glared at him. Men! A wedding wasn't "just a party." A *party* was "just a party." This would be the most important day of my—our—lives.

Still. I was sort of amazed to find Sinclair had dumped three mill into my checking account. I didn't even bother asking him how he'd pulled it off.

"What the *hell* will you spend three million on?" Cathie shrieked.

"Cake, of course."

"Talking to Cathie?" Laura asked.

"Yeah. Cake—" I continued.

"Cathie, you should go to your king," Laura suggested.

"King?" Cathie asked in my head.

"She means Jesus," I said.

"This haunting isn't very becoming," my sister continued doggedly.

"Tell your goody-goody sister to cram it," Cathie said.

"She says thanks for the advice," I said.

"Just think of all the charitable contributions you could make with that money," Laura gently chided me, "and still have a perfectly lovely ceremony." (Have I mentioned that the devil's daughter was raised by ministers?)

"There's the cake," I continued.

"What, a cake the size of a Lamborghini?" Cathie asked.

"Gown, bridesmaids' gowns, reception, food—"

"That you can't eat!" Marc groaned.

"Honeymoon expenses, liquor for the open bar, caterers, waiters, waitresses—"

"A church to buy from the Catholics."

The others were used to my one-sided conversations with Cathie, but Marc was still shaking his head in that "women are fucknuts" way that all males master by age three.

"None of these are working," I told the attendants. I wasn't referring to the dresses, either. "And my friend is tired. I think we'll have to try another time."

"I'm fine," Jessica rasped.

"Shut up," Marc said.

"You don't look exactly well," Laura fretted. "Aren't you supposed to go back to the hospital soon?"

"Shut up, white girl."

"If I ever said 'shut up, black girl,' you would land on me like the wrath of the devil herself." Laura paused. "And I ought to know."

"Stay out of my shit, white girl."

"If you're ill, you should be in the hospital."

"Cancer isn't contagious, white girl."

"It's very selfish of you to give Betsy something else to worry about right now."

"Who's talking to you, white girl? Not her. Not me. Don't you have a soup kitchen to toil in? Or a planet to take over?"

Laura gasped. I groaned. Jessica was in an ugly mood, but that was no reason to bring up The Thing We Didn't Talk About: namely, that the devil's daughter was fated to take over the world.

Before the debate could rage further, the attendant cut in. "But your wedding is only a few months away. That doesn't leave us much—"

"Cram it," I snapped, noticing the gray pallor under Jessica's normally shining skin. "Laura, you're right. We're out of here."

Chapter 3

But all that stuff at the bridal shop happened months ago, and I was only thinking of my friends because I was all alone. Worse: all alone at a double funeral.

My father and his wife were dead.

I had no idea how to feel about that. I'd never liked the Ant— my stepmother—a brassy, gauche woman who lied like fish sucked water, a woman who had shoved my mother out of her marriage and shattered my conception of happily ever after at age thirteen.

And my father had never had a clue what to do with me. Caught between the daily wars waged between the Ant and me, and my mom and the Ant, and the Ant and him ("Send her *away*, dear, and do it *right now*"), he stayed out of it altogether. He loved me, but he was weak. He'd always been weak. And my coming back from the dead horrified him.

And she had never loved me, or even liked me.

But that was all right, because I had never liked her, either. My return from the dead hadn't improved our relationship one bit. In fact, the only thing that had accomplished *that* trick was the birth of my half brother, BabyJon, who was mercifully absent from the funeral.

Everybody was absent. Jessica was in the hospital undergoing chemo, and her boyfriend, Detective Nick Berry, only left her side to eat and occasionally arrest a bad guy.

In a horrifying coincidence, the funeral was taking place where my own funeral had been. Would have, except I'd come back from the dead and gotten the hell out of there. I was not at all pleased to find myself back, either.

When I'd died, more than a year ago, I'd gotten a look at the embalming room but hadn't exactly lingered to sightsee. Thus, I—we—were sitting in a room I'd never seen. Sober dark walls, lots of plush folding chairs, my dad and the Ant's pictures blown up to poster size at the front of the room. There weren't coffins, of course. Nothing that might open. The bodies had been burned beyond recognition.

"—a pillar of the community, and Mr. and Mrs. Taylor were active in several charitable causes—"

Yeah, sure. The Ant (short for Antonia) was about as charitably minded as that little nutty guy in charge of North Korea. She threw my dad's money at various causes so she could run the fund-raising parties and pretend she was the prom queen again. One of those women who peaked in high school. It had always amazed me that my father hadn't seen that.

I looked around the room of mostly strangers (and not many of them, either, despite the two of them being "pillars of the community") and swallowed hard. Nobody was sitting on either side of me. How could they? I was here by myself.

Tina, Sinclair's major domo, had gone on a diplomatic trip to Europe, to make sure everybody over there was still planning to play nice with everybody over here. The European faction of vampires had finally come to visit a few months ago, murder and mayhem ensued, and then they got the hell out of town. Me? I thought that was fine. Out of sight, out of mind . . . that was practically the Taylor family motto. Sinclair the worrywart? Not so much.

Since Sinclair and I were wrapping up wedding arrangements, Tina had agreed to go. Since Tina was never very far from Sinclair, a solo trip for her was sort of unheard of. But her exact last words as she left the house were, "What could possibly go wrong in two weeks?"

Famous friggin' last words.

Chapter 4

I stared at the poster-sized picture of Antonia Taylor, the Ant, which was grinning at me. *Right* at me. I swear, the eyes in her picture followed me whenever I moved. It was on an easel, beside my dad's picture.

I recognized my dad's pic—it had been taken by the Minneapolis Chamber of Commerce when he and the Ant won some useless award that he bought her. The Ant's photo was from Glamour Shots. You know the kind: smokey-eyed, with long fingernails and teased hair.

"—truly found happiness in their later years—"

Barf. I didn't know whether to just roll my eyes or to laugh. Given the circumstances, I did neither.

Sinclair had disappeared a day after Tina left the country. I assumed he was still sulking about our constant bickering and had decided to avoid the thing that was Bridezilla. And in truth, I was a little glad to get a break myself. I wanted to love the bum, not fantasize about staking him. And I missed our lovemaking. Our . . . everything. I was just as sorry he was gone as I was relieved.

Not to mention, I was too proud to call his cell and tell him what had happened to my dad and his wife. That would be like asking him for help. He'd be back on his own, without me calling him, the fuckhead. Any day now. Any minute.

There weren't any windows in the room, which was a shame as it was a gorgeous summer day in Minnesota, the kind of day that makes you forget all about winter. Big, fluffy marshmallow clouds and a beautiful blue sky, more suited to picnicking than funerals.

It was kind of weird. If the occasion called for a double funeral, wouldn't it also call for thunderstorms? The day I died was
cloudy and spitting snow. Plus I'd gotten fired. And my birthday
party had been canceled. It had all been properly disastrous.

"—truly a tragedy we mortals cannot comprehend—"

At last, the minister had gotten something right. Not only could
I not comprehend it, I couldn't shake the feeling it was a sick practical joke. That the Ant was using her fake funeral as an excuse to
break into my house and steal my shoes. Again. That Dad was on
the links, chortling over the good one he'd put over on us. Not
dead in a stupid, senseless car accident. Dad had stomped on the
accelerator instead of the brake and plowed into the back of a
parked garbage truck. Immovable force meets crunchable object.
Finis for Dad and the Ant.

The other Antonia I knew, a pseudo-werewolf, had vanished
with her mate, George—er, Garrett, the day after Sinclair had left.
That didn't surprise me. Although Antonia couldn't turn into a
wolf during the full moon (causing ridicule among her pack, and
eventually driving her to us), she was still a werewolf bred and
born, and had a werewolf's natural need to roam.

She'd been complaining of splitting headaches right before
she left (rather than change, she could see the future, but it wasn't
always clear, and the visions weren't always welcome). She'd
been, if possible, bitchier than usual, while entirely close-
mouthed about what might really be bothering her. Garrett was the
only one who could stand her when she was like this.

A word about Garrett. Nostro, the old vampire king—the one
Sinclair and I had killed—had liked to starve newly risen vampires. And when that happened, they turned feral. Worse than
feral . . . animals—scrambling about on all fours and never showering or anything. They were like rabid, flesh-eating pit bulls.
Two-hundred-pound, rabid, flesh-eating pit bulls.

Laura and Sinclair and Tina had insisted I stake the lot of
them. I'd refused—they were victims and couldn't help their unholy craving for human flesh. And I'd been vindicated, I think.
By drinking my blood (yurrgh!), or my sister's blood (better, but
still yucky), Garrett (known back then as George) had recovered
his humanity. Even better, he had become capable of love with
Antonia.

So Garrett seemed fine now. But I didn't know enough about
Fiends, or vampires (shit, I'd only been one for little more than a
year) to try another experiment, and so a cute loyal vamp named

Alice cared for the other Fiends, and Antonia and Garrett kept each other out of my hair.

Maybe someday soon, I'd ask Laura if she'd let another Fiend suck her blood, but now was definitely not the time.

All the cars driving by outside (stupid Vamp hearing!) were distracting me from the insipid service preached by a man who clearly had never met my dad or his second wife.

Once again I was struck by the fact that, no matter what rotten thing happened, no matter how earthshaking events became, life (and undeath) went on. People still drove to and from work. Drove to the movies. Drove to doctors, airports, schools. Hopefully none of *them* were getting the accelerator mixed up with the brake.

I stifled a sneeze against the overwhelming scent of too many flowers (Chrysanthemums, ugh! Not to mention, the Ant hated 'em), embalming fluid (from one of the back rooms, not Dad and the Ant), and too much aftershave.

If nobody else was going to say it, I would: being a vampire was not all it was cracked up to be. Even though it was 7:00 p.m., I had sunglasses on for multiple reasons. One, because the lights, dim as they were, made me squint. Two, if I caught the gaze of an unmarried man, or an unhappily married man, he'd more than likely slobber all over me until I coldcocked him. Stupid vampire mojo.

Most annoying, one of my few blood relatives (I had three: my mother, my ailing grandfather, and my half sister), Laura, wasn't there either. She hadn't known my father at all, had only recently met her birth mother, the Ant (the devil had possessed the Ant long enough to get her pregnant and then decided childbirth was worse than hell), and so busied herself with interesting logistics like the wake and the burial arrangements.

Cathie the ghost had also disappeared—just for a while, she told me nervously. Not to heaven, or wherever spirits vamoosed to. Her whole life she'd never been on a plane, never left the state of Minnesota. So she had decided to see the world, and why not? It wasn't like she needed a passport. And she knew she was welcome back here anytime.

"—perhaps this is the Lord's way of telling us to get yearly driver's exams over the age of fifty—"

I smoothed my black Versace suit and peeped down at my black Prada pumps. Both very sensible, very dignified, the former was a gift from Sinclair, the latter a Christmas present from Jessica four years ago. If you get the good stuff and take care of it, it'll last forever.

Just thinking of Jessica made me want to cry—which made me feel like shit. I was sitting through a double funeral totally dry-eyed, but the thought of my cancer-riddled best friend was enough to make me sob. Thank goodness Marc, an MD for a Minneapolis emergency ward, was taking care of her.

I mean, *had* been taking care of her. Once he made sure Jessica was squared away, Marc had disappeared, too. That was more alarming than anything else, funerals included: Marc Spangler did not have a life. He didn't date. He didn't sport fuck. His life was the hospital and hanging around vampires.

I'd been calling his cell for days and kept getting voice mail or, worse, no signal at all. It was like he'd gone to Mars.

"—the comfort of many years of mutual love and affection—"

Oh, fucking blow me. Mutual credit lines and many years of the Ant seducing my dad and then begging for a fur coat. He'd married her for lust, and she'd married him for his money. And on and on and on, and never mind the cost to my mother's heart, or soul, and never mind that it had taken Mom the better part of a decade to pick up the pieces.

And thinking about the good Dr. Taylor (doctorate in history, specialty: the Civil War; subspecialty: the Battle at Antietam), my mom wasn't here, either. I knew she and my dad hadn't been on good terms for years, and I knew she cordially loathed the Ant (and believe me, the feeling was sooo mutual), but I thought she might come so I'd have a hand to hold.

Her reply to an invitation to the funeral was to quirk a white eyebrow and throw some Kehlog Albren my way: " 'Sometimes the best of friends can't attend each other's funerals.' And your father and I were not the best of friends, dear, to say the least."

In other words: *Nuts to you, sugar bear.*

But she was helping in her own way, taking care of BabyJon. I'd go see them after. Only BabyJon's sweet powder smell and toothless (well, semitoothless; he had three by now), drooly smile could cheer me up right now.

I sighed, thinking of the empty mansion waiting for me. Even my cat, Giselle, had gone on walkabout. Normally I didn't care. Or notice. But it was scary staying in the big place by myself. I wished Sinclair would come home. I wished I wasn't still so mad at him I couldn't call him. Most of all, I wished—

"The interment will be at Carlson Memorial Cemetery," the minister was saying. "For those of you who wish to follow the deceased, please put on your headlights."

—that this was over.

I stood and smoothed my black dress, checked my black pumps and matching hose. Perfect, from head to toe. I looked exactly like a smartly dressed, yet grief-stricken, daughter. I wasn't going to follow my dead father to Carlson Memorial, though, and never mind appearances. *My* headstone was there, too.

I followed the mourners out, thinking I was the last, only to stop and wheel around at a whispered, "Your Majesty?"

I recognized her at once. Any vampire would. I was even supposed to be afraid of her (every vampire was). Except I wasn't. "Do not, do *not* blow my cover," I hissed to Marjorie, who looked like a librarian (she was) but was also an eight-hundred-year-old vampire.

She was dressed in sensible brown shoes (blech), a navy blue skirt, and a ruffled cream blouse. Her brown hair was streaked with gray, and her pale face was played up with just the right amount of makeup. "Forgive my intrusion, Majesty."

"What are you doing at a funeral home, anyway? There's probably a whole back room full of Bibles in this place."

Marjorie grimaced at "Bibles," but readily answered. "I read about the accident in the paper and came to pay my respects, Majesty. I regret the deaths of your father and mother."

"She was *not* my mother," I corrected out of years of habit. "But thanks. That's why you're lurking? To pay your respects?"

"Well, I could hardly sit through the service."

I almost giggled at the image of ancient Marjorie, probably the oldest vamp on the planet, cowering in the vestibule with both hands clamped over her ears, lest she hear a stray "Jesus" or "the Lord works in mysterious ways."

I, if I may be immodest for a brief moment, could hear any religious epithet, prayer, or Christmas carol. It was a perk of being the vampire queen.

"If you need anything, you will please call on me," she insisted.

Oh, sure, Marjorie. I'd love to go to the warehouse district and hang around in the vamp library, checking out thousand-year-old dusty tomes and being more depressed than I already am. I avoided that place like most vamps avoided churches. Even in life, I'd never been a fan of libraries.

Luckily, Marjorie took care of all that tedious stuff for Sinclair and me. And even more luckily, she had zero interest in grabbing power. She'd lived through three or four kings (I think . . . I was vague on bloodsucker history) and had been content to putter among her stacks while they wreaked their reigns of terror. She had outlasted them all. I wondered idly if she would outlast me and Sinclair. Would she even remember us, two thousand years from now?

As stiff as she was, I had to admit it was nice to see her. At least somebody had bothered to show up, even if it was a vampire.

"Are you going to the cemetery?"

And see my own grave again? Not a chance in hell. But all I said out loud was, "There's nothing for me there."

Marjorie seemed to understand and bowed slightly as I turned on my (elegant) heel and left.

Chapter 5

I had heard the car turn in the drive, of course (sometimes I could hear a cricket from a mile away), but took my time walking to the door and listening to the increasingly frantic hammering.

Finally, after growing weary of my passive aggressiveness, I opened my front door and immediately went for the kill. "Thanks for all the support at the funeral, *Mom*. Really helpful. Why, with you there I didn't feel like an orphan or anything! Having a shoulder to lean on and all was such a comfort."

My mother brushed by me, BabyCrap™ (an established property of BabyJon™) in tow. She smelled like burped-up milk. She was wearing a blue sweater (in summertime!) and plum-colored slacks, with black flats. Her mop of curls was even more a mess than usual.

"By the way," I said cheerfully, "you look like dried up hell."

She ignored that. "A funeral service is no place for an infant," she panted, struggling to manage all the paraphernalia. It was amazing . . . the kid wasn't even a year old, and he had more possessions than I did.

Mom thrust BabyJon at me and I bounced him in my arms, then kissed the top of his head. I might have been pissed at her, but damn, I was glad to see *him*.

"You missed a helluva party," I said dryly.

"No doubt." Mom puffed white curls off her forehead. "Your father was all about parties. That's why he was foolish enough to ingest a magnum of champagne and then go joyriding into the back of a garbage truck with your stepmother."

Hey, they needed a break from all the selfless charity work. I paused, gauged what I was thinking, and then shelved it. *Nope. Too soon for jokes.* They'd only been in their graves for half an hour. Maybe by tomorrow . . .

"How are you holding up, dear?"

"Like you care!"

She scowled at me, and I almost giggled. Hadn't I seen that scowl enough times in my own mirror? But I remained a stone. "You've had a difficult day . . ."

"And you'd know this how?"

"But my day hasn't exactly been a day at the zoo, either. So answer my question, young lady, or you'll find you're not too big to spank." This was laughable, since I could break my mom's arm by breathing on it.

"Well?"

"I forgot the question," I admitted.

"How was the funeral?"

"Besides my entire support system, present company included, abandoning me in my most dire time of need?"

"I think *your* death was your most dire time of need," she corrected me. "And the only ones who abandoned you then are underground now."

This was true, but I was in no mood for logic. "And you didn't even say good-bye. I know you didn't like them, but Jesus!"

And why were we screaming at each other in the foyer? Maybe I was still too mad to make nicey-nice hostess, even to Mom, whom I usually adored. How could I not adore someone who welcomed her daughter back from the dead with open arms?

"Someone had to watch your son," she replied sharply. "And it's not as though you have no friends. Where is everybody, anyway?"

"The question of the day," I muttered. No way was I telling her Sinclair and I were fighting—she liked him, if possible, more than she liked me. And she'd worry herself sick about Jessica. And she didn't know Marc or Laura that well, or the others at all.

Then the full impact of her words hit me like a hammer upside the head. "Someone had to watch my *what?*"

"Jon."

"What?"

She pointed at my half brother, as if I'd forgotten I was holding him in my arms. In fact, I had. "Your son. The reading of the will? Yesterday? Remember?"

"You know full well I wasn't there. My nails were a mess, and it's not like the Ant was going to let Dad leave me a damned thing. So I gave myself a manicure in Wine Cordial."

My mother sighed, the way she used to sigh when I told her my middle school term project was due later in the morning, and I hadn't even started yet. "In the event of their deaths, you're his legal guardian. They're dead. So guess what?"

"But—but—" BabyJon cooed and wriggled and looked far too happy with the circumstances. I couldn't decide whether to be thrilled or appalled. I settled on appalled. "But I didn't want a baby like *this*."

"Like what?"

"Like—you know. Via the vehicle of death."

Mom frowned. "What was that again?"

"I mean, I wanted my own baby. Mine and Sinclair's baby."

"Well, you've got this one," she said, completely unmoved by my panic.

"But—"

"And you certainly have the means to bring him up properly."

"But—"

"Although I wonder . . . will he get his days and nights confused, living with you two as parents?"

"*That's* the burning question on your mind? Because I can think of a few dozen other slightly more pressing ones!"

"Dear, don't scream. My hearing is fine."

"I'm not ready!"

"You're still screaming. And no one ever is, dear." She coughed. "Take it from me."

"I can't do it!"

"We all say that in the beginning."

"But I really *really* can't!"

"We all say that, too. Well, the first twenty years, anyway."

I thrust him toward her, like I was offering her a platter of hors d'ouevres. "*You* take him!"

"My dear, I am almost sixty years old."

"Sixty years young," I offered wildly.

Mom shot me a black look. "My child-rearing days are over. You, on the other hand, are eternally young, have a support system, a rich best friend, a fine soon-to-be-husband, legal guardianship, and a blood tie."

"And on *that* basis I'm the new mom?"

"Congratulations," she said, pushing the baby back toward my face. His great, blue googley eyes widened at me, as his mouth formed a drool-tinged O. "It's a boy. And now, I have to go."

"You're *leaving?*" I nearly shrieked.

"I'm supposed to visit your grandfather in the hospice this afternoon. You remember your grandfather, dear? Lest you accuse others of neglect."

"I can't believe you're leaving me like this! I have three words for you, Mother—state-funded nursing home. Do you hear me? STATE-FUNDED NURSING HOME!!!" I yelled after her, just as BabyJon yarked milk all over my beautiful black designer suit.

Chapter 6

The kitchen phone rang, and I ran toward it, stopping to plop BabyJon in his port-a-crib (a subsidiary of BabyCrap™) on the way, where he promptly flopped over on his back and went to sleep. Yeah, well, dead parents were exhausting for everybody.

I gave thanks for all the junk we'd bought when he'd been born, hoping to have occasional chances to babysit. *Babysit*, not raise him to adulthood! But because of my precautions, we had diapers, cribs, formula, bottles, baby blankets, and onesies up the wazoo.

It was funny, the Ant had only warmed up to me when she saw how much BabyJon liked me. As a newborn, he screamed almost constantly from colic (or perhaps rage at the decor of his nursery) and only shut up when I held him. Once the Ant saw that, I was the number one babysitter.

Sinclair had not been pleased. But I wasn't going to think about Sinclair, except how much I was about to *yell* at him when I got him on the phone.

The thought of surprising Sinclair with this kid, I have to admit, gave me a certain perverse pleasure. It salved the terror I felt at the sudden responsibility.

I skidded across the floor and snatched the phone in the middle of the sixth ring. "Hello? Sinclair? You bum! Where are you? Hello?"

"—can't—cell—"

"Who is this?"

"—too far—can't—hear"

I could barely make out the words through the thick static. "Who! Is! This!"

"—worry—message—country—"

"Marc? Is that you?"

"—no other way—don't—okay—"

"Tina?"

"—back—time—"

"Dad? If you're calling from beyond the grave, I'm going to be very upset," I threatened.

There wasn't even a click. Just a dead line.

I sat down at the table, deliberately forgetting about all the times the bunch of us had sat around making smoothies or inventing absurd drinks (e.g., The Queen Betsy: one ounce amaretto, two ounces orange juice, three ounces cranberry juice, seven ounces of champagne, and let me tell you, it was heaven in a martini glass).

I thought: *Everybody's gone. Everybody.*

I thought: *How could they do this to me?*

Okay, Jessica had an excuse. Battling cancer via chemo was a dandy way to get out of social obligations. And Detective Berry— well, I didn't especially want him around. He had known, once upon a time, that I had died and come back to life. I had drunk his blood, once upon a time, and it had gone badly. Sinclair had fixed it by making Nick forget. The last thing I needed was for him to be at the same funeral home he'd come to two Aprils ago for *my* funeral.

No, it was good for Nick to be at Jessica's side when he wasn't foiling killers and petty thieves.

Same with Tina. When she left to check on the European vampires, she had no idea this was going to happen. No, I couldn't blame her, either.

But Marc? He of all people didn't have a life, and he picks now to disappear? To not call, or return calls?

Mom? (Like she couldn't have gotten someone else to watch BabyJon?)

Sinclair? The guy who knew friggin' *everything* didn't show up for the double funeral?

Laura? She rebelled against her mom, the devil, by being the most churchgoing, God-fearing person you ever saw (when she wasn't killing serial killers or beating the shit out of vampires), but she couldn't be bothered to go to a family funeral?

Cathie the ghost, on a fucking world tour?

Antonia? Garrett? Okay, I hadn't known them very long, but they did live in my (Jessica's) house rent-free. I'd taken her in when her Pack wanted nothing to do with her. When the other werewolves were scared shitless of her. And Garrett? I'd saved him from staking multiple times. But they took off on me, too.

What the *fuck* excuse did any of them have? They were supposed to be my friends, my fiancé, my family, my roommates. So why was I rattling around in this big-ass mansion by myself? Except for BabyJon, snoring in the corner? Shit, nobody even sent me flowers!

It wasn't fair. And don't tell me life isn't fair, either. Like a vampire doesn't know *that?*

Chapter 7

Oh, Your Majesty!" Tina gasped, sounding tinny and distressed on the other end of the line. "I'm so dreadfully sorry! My deepest condolences. Oh, your poor parents! Your poor family! I remember when I lost mine, and it's still as fresh as it was—"

"Me time, Tina, got it?"

"Majesty, how may I serve?"

I puffed a sigh of relief. Some things, in this last crazy week, hadn't changed. Tina had always treated me like a queen, and anyone Sinclair loved, she served with everything she had. In fact, she'd had a bit of a crush on me when we first met, until I took care of our little misunderstanding ("I'm straight as a ruler, honey") and since then our relationship had been kind of complicated: sovereign/servant/friend/assistant. She was still overseas, but at least she was answering her fucking phone.

"How is the king taking it?"

"That's just it. He's not."

"I am sure he will comfort you in his own way," she soothed. "You know as well as I that a taciturn man can be difficult even during the—"

"Tina, did you forget English when you went to France? He's not taking it because he's gone. Vamoosed. Poof. Buh-bye."

"But—where?"

"Like I know? We haven't, um, been getting along lately, and he went off a bit ago—"

"And you've been too proud to call him."

I said nothing. Nothing!

"Majesty? Are you still on the line?"

"You know Goddamned well I am," I snapped, taking evil pleasure in her groan at the G-word.

"I will call him," she said, sounding cheered to have something to do. "I will request he come to your side at once. Whatever . . . difficulties you two are having, surely deaths in the family will supersede other considerations."

"They'd better, if he ever wants to get laid anytime in the next five hundred years," I threatened, but felt better. Tina was here for me (sort of) and on the case. She wouldn't be trapped in France forever.

Sinclair would turn up. Marc would reappear from whatever dimension he had slipped into. Antonia would get over her snit-fit and come home, dragging Garrett behind her on a leash. Jessica's chemo would triumph over the cancer, and she'd sprint home, bossing us around as was her wont. My life (such as it was) would be normal again.

"How is everyone else taking it?"

"Well, that's the thing." I perched on the counter, got comfy, and explained where everyone was. Or where I thought they were, anyway.

Afterward there was a long, awkward silence on Tina's end, which I broke with a faux-cheerful, "Weird, huh?"

"Rat fuck," Tina muttered, and I nearly toppled off the counter. Tina, ancient bloodsucking thing that she was (she'd made Sinclair, and he was, like, seventy!), had the manners of an Elizabethan lady and almost never swore. She was perfectly proper at all times.

"Mother fuck," she continued. "Conspirational bastard shit-stains."

"Uh, Tina, I think someone else just got on the line—"

"They're all gone? All of them?"

"Duh, that's what I just—"

"For how long?"

I looked at my watch, which was stupid, as it didn't show the date. "Almost a week now."

"I'm calling the king."

"Right, I got that the first time. Fine, call him, but he'd better not show up without flowers. And possibly diamonds. Or some Beverly Feldmans! Yeah, the red and gold flats would be perfect—"

"My queen, you will not leave that house. You will—"

"Huh? What are you talking about?" Long pause. "Tina?"

Nothing. Dead line. Again.

I shrugged and hung up the phone. If the French couldn't get their act together—ever—to win a war, how could they be expected to keep the phone lines open?

A mystery for another day. For now I had to figure out a feeding schedule for my new (groan) son, visit Jess (she'd want all the gory funeral details), and leave yet another message for Marc. A busy evening, and not even nine o'clock yet.

Chapter 8

Y ou look like hot death," I informed my best friend cheerfully.

"Go to hell," she snapped back, then coughed. Her normally gorgeous dark skin was more grayish than ebony, and her eyes were bloodshot. But she sounded a helluva lot better than she did three days ago. They'd finally quit the chemo, so she could get better.

The horrible thing about chemotherapy, of course, is that it is poison, working by killing both cancerous and normal cells. Jessica said the cancer didn't bug her hardly at all, except for making her tired. It was the cure that fucked her up severely: vomiting, constant nausea, weight loss (and if anyone on the planet didn't need to lose weight, it was scrawny Jess). How fucked up was that, I ask you? In a hundred years, doctors will be laughing their asses off at how we, the century-old savages, "cured" cancer. I mean, why not just break out the leeches?

"The moment you barf, I am so out of here." I plopped down in the chair beside her bed and got comfy, BabyJon snuggled against my shoulder.

"I haven't barfed since suppertime, and that's because it was Salisbury Steak night."

"Who could blame you?"

"How go the wedding plans?"

"They sort of screeched to a halt," I admitted. *When you all abandoned me.*

"What? Bets, you've got to pick a dress! You've got to settle on the flowers—the florist is going out of her mind! You've got to meet with the caterer for the final tasting! You've—"

"I will, I will. There's lots of time."

"There's two weeks. Isn't Eric helping you at all?"

"He's gone. Still sulking."

"Oh, Betsy!" she practically yelled, then coughed again. "Will you just call him and apologize?"

"Me?" I yelped, loud enough to stir BabyJon, who immediately settled back to sleep. "I didn't do a damned thing. He's the one who left in a huff. Stupid runaway groom."

"He'll be back," she predicted. "He can't stay away. He can't leave you, there's no such thing for him. You're in his system like a virus."

"Thanks. That's so romantic, I may cry."

"Well, don't cry. Nick was in here a while ago all teary and junk."

"Big bad Detective Nick Berry, catcher of serial killers?"

"To be fair, you and Laura and Cathie caught the killer."

"Right, but he helped. I mean, he came to the house and warned us."

"He made me promise not to die," she said, folding her arms behind her head and looking supremely satisfied. "And I made him promise. So that's all settled."

"Can I borrow that emesis basin?" I asked politely.

"Cram it, O vampire queen. Nobody barfs but me, it's the new rule."

I grinned, but couldn't help feeling the smallest twinge of jealousy. Which was completely stupid. But . . . Nick had originally been interested in yours truly. And I'd thought he'd asked Jessica out as a way to get closer to me. In fact, that had been utter wishful thinking on my part.

I was wildly happy for Jessica, but couldn't help feel a little miffed that Nick had recovered from his unholy lust for me so quickly. Which was also stupid: the whole reason Sinclair had made him forget our blood sharing was to *make* him forget. Not to mention, I had the sexiest, smartest vampire in the world on *my* hook.

When he was talking to me, that is.

"What's with the kid?"

"You won't even believe it."

Jessica covered her eyes. "Don't even tell me. You're his legal guardian."

"Got it in one."

She looked up. "Why so glum? You've wanted a baby since you came back from the dead."

"But not like *this*! I mean, gross. Garbage trucks and inciner-ated birth parents? Yech."

"Well, there's plenty of room in the mansion for a baby. And you're crazy about him. And he pretty much only tolerates you. So it all worked out." She paused. "I'm sorry. That came out wrong."

"S'okay. It's always nice when someone else puts their foot in their mouth. I get tired of it sometimes."

"Really?" she asked sweetly. "It's hard to tell."

"Shut up and die."

"See? You just did it!"

I didn't answer. Instead, I jiggled BabyJon to wake him up. Since I was conked out during the day, and *alone*, if he cried dur-ing the day he was shit out of luck. This was going to be a noctur-nal baby, by God.

"Better start interviewing day nannies," Jessica observed.

"There's usually a hundred people hanging around the house," I complained. "We need one more? And how can we hide all our weird goings-on from her? Or him?"

"How about a vampire nanny?"

I was silent. The thought hadn't occurred to me. Then: "No good. Any vampire would need to sleep during the day."

"But Marc, me, Cathie, and Antonia are usually around during the day."

I was silent. She had enough problems without knowing that everyone had disappeared on me.

"Maybe a really old vampire? You know Sinclair can stay awake most of the day. Find some seventy-year-old bloodsucker for the job."

"Oh, sure, what a great honor. 'Hey, ancient vampire, mind changing the shitty diapers of my half brother? And don't forget to burp him before his nappy-nap. Also, don't suck his sweet, new, baby blood.' "

"Blabbb," BabyJon agreed. He turned his head and smiled sweetly at Jessica. He really was getting cute. When he was born, he looked like a pissed-off plucked chicken. Now he'd filled out with sweetly plump arms and legs, a rounded belly, and a sunny grin. His hair was a dark thatch that stood up in all directions. Jes-sica grinned back; she couldn't help it.

"He's definitely growing on me," she said.

"Like a foot fungus."

Jessica's door whooshed open, and the night nurse stood there.

Luckily for me, it was a man. "I'm sorry, miss, but visiting hours were over an hour ago."

I slid my sunglasses down my nose and said, "Get lost. I can stay as long as I like."

"These aren't the droids you're looking for," Jessica added, giggling.

Like a badly maintained robot, the nurse swung around and walked stiffly away.

I propped my feet up on Jessica's bed and got comfy. BabyJon squirmed and, to divert him, I plopped him on her bed. He wriggled for a moment, then flopped over and popped his thumb in his mouth, his deep blue eyes never leaving my face.

"So, dish. How was the funeral?"

"Gruesome. And filled with lies."

"So, like the Ant was in life?"

I laughed for the first time in two days. God, I loved her. That chemo was going to work. Or I would *not* be responsible for my actions.

Chapter 9

The phone rang (at 1 a.m.!), and I lunged for it. "Sinclair? Hello? You rat bastard, where the hell have you—?"

"Is this the head of Antonia's den?" a deep male voice asked.

I was flummoxed. It was a week for weird phone calls, barfing best friends, and fucked-up funerals.

"Which Antonia?"

"The only Antonia. Tall, slender, dark hair, dark eyes, werewolf who can't Change?"

"Oh, the live one! Yeah, this is her, um, den."

"Explain yourself."

I was having major trouble following the conversation. "Explain what?"

"She has not checked in this month. As her pro tem Pack leader, you are responsible."

"Responsible for what?"

"Her safety."

"What's a pro tem what's-it?"

"Do not play the fool, vampire."

"Who's playing? And how'd you know I was a—I mean, who are you calling a vampire?"

"I gave Antonia leave to den with you under strict conditions. You are breaking those conditions."

"What conditions are you—?"

"Produce her at once, or suffer the consequences."

"*Produce* her? She's not a manufactured good! Who *is* this?"

"You know who this is."

"Dude: I totally completely do not."

"Your attempts to act an idiot will not sway me from my course."

"Who's acting?" I cried. "Who are you, and what the *hell* are you talking about?"

There was a long pause, punctuated by heavy breathing. Great. A prank call from a pervert. "Very well," the deep voice growled. *Really* growled; I could feel the hairs on the back of my neck trying to stand up. "Be it on your head and suffer the consequences."

Click.

Story of my life, this week.

I stared at the now-dead phone, then threw it at the wall hard enough for it to shatter into a dozen pieces.

Chapter 10

The next evening, after feeding BabyJon his 10 p.m. bottle, burping him, and plopping him into the playpen in the kitchen, I took the new phone out of the box (thank goodness for twenty-four-hour Walgreens).

I had literally just hooked up, and hung up, the phone when it rang, making me jump right out of my skin. I snatched up the new receiver.

"What freak is calling me now?"

"Only I, Your Majesty."

"Tina! You sound tinny. Still in France?"

"Still. And worse: I have been unable to raise the king."

Raise him at poker? was my wild thought. "What?" I asked, my word of the week.

"He has never, in seventy-some years, not returned a call, or a letter, or a telegram, or a fax."

"Well. He was pretty grumpy when he left."

"Grumpy." Tina let out a most unladylike snort, almost as startling as when she was swearing like—well, me. "I dislike this. I dislike this extremely. I will be returning on the next flight."

"But what about the European vamp—"

"Hang them. Hang them all. This is much more distressing. Besides, there's not much to do here. After the show you put on a few months ago, they're quite terrified of you."

I smirked and buffed my nails on my purple tank top. It was all the sweeter because it was true: they'd seen me pray, and that had been enough for them.

"On the next flight? How are you gonna pull *that* off? Isn't it, like, a twenty-hour flight? Some of it during daylight hours?"

"I'll travel the traditional way, of course. In a coffin in the cargo hold. Our people here will forge a death certificate and other appropriate paperwork."

I shuddered and gave thanks, once again, that I was the queen, and not a run-of-the-mill vampire. Don't get me wrong; I'd prefer to be alive. But if I had to be dead . . . "Tina, that sucks."

"Recent circumstances are highly suspect. The king would not leave you for so long—"

"It's only been a few days—"

"—nor would he ignore my messages. Something is wrong."

"He doesn't want to wear the navy blue tux I picked out?" I guessed.

"Majesty. This is serious."

I shrugged, forgetting she couldn't see me. "If you say so."

"Until I return, do not answer the door. You will not try to contact anyone who has gone missing. You will not answer the phone unless the caller ID tells you it is me." Her subservient tone was long gone; this was a general thinking fast and issuing orders. "Your Majesty, do you understand me?"

"Uh, sure. Simmer."

"I will simmer," she hissed, "when I get a few heads on sticks. And the devil pity the rat fuck who gets in my way."

"Yeesh."

"Heads. On. Sticks."

"I got it the first time."

On that happy note, she hung up.

Chapter 11

I broke one of the rules less than twenty-four hours later. I blamed sleep deprivation. Despite my efforts over the last three days, BabyJon still had the whole "stay awake at nighttime" thing a little mixed up. (But then, so did I.)

Small wonder. The Ant, Satan rest her soul, had stuck him with night nannies all the time, and they had encouraged him to sleep so they could goof off.

I groped for the bedside phone, forgetting to check the caller ID. "Mmph . . . lo?"

"—can—hear—"

For a change, I actually identified the crackling voice. "Marc! Where the *hell* are you?"

"—can't—make—drop—"

"Are you hurt? Are you in trouble?"

"—trouble—fucked—death"

"Oh my God!" I screamed, instantly snapping all the way awake. I glanced at the bedside clock; four-thirty in the afternoon. In his port-a-crib, BabyJon snored away. "You *are* in trouble! Can you get to a computer? Can you send me an e-mail? Why aren't you answering *my* e-mails? Tell me where you are, and I'll come get you!" *With a baby in tow*, I neglected to add.

"—can't—worry—trouble—"

"Where are you?" I hollered.

"—dusk—dark—come—"

"I'll come, I'll come! Where *are* you?"

"—see—stars—"

"Marc?"

"—worried—"

"Marc?!" I was yelling into a dead line.

That was it. That was *it*. I threw back the covers of my lonely bed, trying not to realize that things were getting mighty fucking weird (and failing), and got dressed with amazing speed.

I plucked a sleepy, wet, yawning BabyJon from his crib, changed him with vampiric speed (he seemed surprised, yet amused), grabbed the diaper bag and some formula, and headed for the bedroom door to beat feet for Minneapolis General, Oncology Ward. I was breaking rule number two, and I didn't give a tin fuck. Not for the rules of ordinary man was I, the dreaded vampire queen. No indeed! I was—

My computer beeped. Rather, Sinclair's computer beeped (what did *I* need a computer in the bedroom for? We only had, like, nine offices). The thing hadn't made a peep in days, so for a long moment, all I did was stare. It beeped again, and I lunged for it, ignoring BabyJon's squawk, and saw the YOU'VE GOT MAIL icon pop up.

I clicked on it (Sinclair had set the thing up so I could use it whenever I wanted), hoping. He knew it was in our bedroom, he knew I'd hear the chime wherever I was in the house, ergo it had to be from—

My sister, Laura.

Grumbling under my breath, I read the e-mail.

Betsy,
I'm dreadfully sorry I was unable to attend the funeral of your father and my mother. I was, as you know, occupied with the arrangements for the wake and the burial, as well as helping your mother with the baby, but deeply regret my unavoidable absence. I do hope we can get together soon. Please call me if you need anything, or if you run into trouble.
God bless,
Your loving sister,
Laura
"And they that know thy name will put their trust in thee: for thou, Lord, hast not forsaken them that seek thee." (Psalms 9:10)

"Yeah, yeah, yeah," I said aloud. "Verrrry helpful." But I was all talk. At least someone hadn't forgotten me, left the country, or disappeared. Or gotten cancer.

Or if you run into trouble? What did that mean? It was almost like she knew things were getting weirder by the second. Which of course she couldn't. We hadn't even spoken until the day before the funeral, and that was all Ant stuff, not Jessica and Marc and Sinclair and Antonia and Garrett stuff.

I shoved the thought out of my head. Of all the people I had to worry about, Laura was so *not* one of them. Even if she was, according to the Book of the Dead, fated to take over the world. She was a good kid

(when she wasn't killing vampires pretty much effortlessly)

with a steady head and a kind heart

(when she wasn't killing serial killers),

and she was the definitive good girl

(even if she was the devil's own).

So there. Dammit.

I said it out loud, just to cement the idea into my head. "So there. Dammit!"

"Blurrgghh," BabyJon agreed, kicking his footie pajama feet into my hip bones.

"Ready for a trip, baby brother?"

"Yurrgghh!"

"Right. Onward, and all of that."

Chapter 12

I was so used to pouring out my troubles to Jessica—I'd been doing it since seventh grade—that I was actually shocked to find a bunch of doctors and nurses clustered around her bed. I couldn't even see her, much less talk to her. Not to mention, usually there was just one nurse, and that was only if it was time for a new bag of death.

Nick was standing off to one side, watching with his jaw clenched so tight I could see the muscles in his cheek jumping.

He saw me and said dully, "They're doing another round of chemo. She's something of a nine-day wonder. *Everyone's* been invited."

"But—" Shocked, I shifted BabyJon to my other shoulder, for once praying he wouldn't wake up. "But she just had a round of it!"

"It's a hard cancer to kill."

"But—but—I have to tell her . . . um, stuff." *Careful,* I said to myself. Nick's poor scrambled brains didn't need any more clues that things weren't normal at the House O' Vampires. "I mean, I came to talk to her."

"Well, you can't." Clearly distracted, he ran his hands through his thick blond hair. Even though his black suit was rumpled and he had a ketchup stain on his navy blue shirt, he looked like a million bucks: swimmer's build, long legs, sharp, Norwegian features—cheekbones you could shave with!—and ice blue eyes. Before I'd died, he'd been the closest thing to a boyfriend I'd had for years. And we hadn't been that close, frankly. Friendly, not friends.

See, the Fiends had attacked me outside of Kahn's Mongolian Barbeque (this was long before I knew what a Fiend was). And like a good citizen, I reported the assault to the police. Nick had helped me look through mug shots, and we'd shared a Milky Way. That was it. The big romance. It was only after I rose from the dead (after getting creamed by a Pontiac Aztec) that I put two and two together.

Not that Nick knew any of this, and not that I had any plans to enlighten the good detective.

"They're not letting anybody talk to her," he was saying, bringing me back to the present with a yank. "But I want to talk to you."

My heart instantly went out to him. Sure, I loved Jessica as much as I loved Sinclair and Manolo Blahniks. But she and Nick had gotten pretty tight over the last few months. This couldn't be easy for him, either.

"Sure, Nicky, honey." I took his elbow and led him out into the hall. "What's on your mind?"

"In here," he said, gesturing to another room. I stepped in after him and saw it was an empty patient's room. "Put the baby on the bed."

Somewhat puzzled, I did so. BabyJon never twitched, bless him. Maybe Nick needed a hug? Maybe—oh God no—he was going to make a pass at me? Maybe he *was* only going out with Jessica because he couldn't have me! Oh my God! Like things couldn't get worse! Should I let him? Should I knock him out? Should I kill him and tell Jessica he got hit by a bus?

I turned to him and began, "Nick, listen, I don't think you're in your right—"

I stopped talking as I realized something cold and hard was pressed under my chin.

His nine millimeter Sig Sauer. (There were advantages to growing up with a mother who was an expert in small arms.)

"You're not going out with Jessica to get to me, are you?" I managed, so totally shocked that he had drawn his police-issued firearm and tucked it under my chin before I had time to realize that I couldn't move, much less slap the gun away. I was more shocked by the look in his eyes: flat rage.

"Betsy. I like you a lot. Even before you died, I liked you. But if you let Jessica die of this thing, I will shoot you in the face. I'll empty the whole clip between your pretty green eyes. I don't know much about vampires, but I bet it'll be tough for you to grow your brain back. Such as it is."

My jaw sagged in shock; the gun never wavered. "You—you *knew*?" Once Jessica got over the new chemo round, I was going to kill her! "And what's that supposed to mean, 'such as it—'"

"Of course I knew," he said impatiently. "I've known since that taxi driver gave his report—you remember. About a gorgeous blond woman who chased off a vampire and picked his car up with two fingers?"

"But—but—but—"

"Why didn't I say anything? Because you all took such great pains to keep it from me. If Jessica had wanted me to know, she would have told me. And I was content to wait. And then this—this *thing* happened to her. And that was the end of the waiting. So in case you missed it the first time: if you sit by and let this happen, I will make you regret the day you ever met me."

"Already regretting," I gurgled, since he was digging the barrel of his gun pretty tightly into my chin. "I already asked her if I could turn her."

"Then what the *fuck* are you waiting for? For her to vomit until she dies like Karen Carpenter? For her to be more miserable? For her to rupture the lining of her throat? For the chemo to kill more healthy cells?"

"Owwwww!" I complained, because boy, he was really grinding the Sig into my chin. "I'm not waiting for anything, Detective Demento. She said no. And that was that."

"So? You're stronger, faster than us. You can make us believe something . . . or forget." I should have been super pissed, but instead I was embarrassed and my heart actually flipped over in my chest. Because he sounded bitter, so bitter.

He leaned forward until our eyes were about four inches apart. Mine were wide, I knew, with amazement. His were slits of blue fire. "I thought I was going crazy, you know? Kept dreaming about you for months. Dreaming about you biting me and me . . . liking . . . it. Needing it."

"I didn't know," I said faintly. "I was newborn. Still am. I didn't know what I was doing to you. I'd have given anything to fix it, but I didn't know how. An older vampire fixed it."

"I *know* who fixed it," he informed me. "I dream about him, too. Dream about blowing his fucking mind-meddling head-peeping brains out. Dream about setting him on fire. Most nights I'm afraid to close my eyes."

"Nick, I'm sorr—"

"Know who fixed that? Your best friend. The one currently

engaged in the business of dying. Your hellhound bastard lover fixed me, honey, and you're going to fix *her.*"

I thought about taking the gun away. I could probably do it. Probably. Too bad I had the nasty feeling his finger was white on the trigger. I'd survived arrows to the chest, and a stake to the chest, and even a bullet to the chest. But a Sig Sauer clip to the brain? I had no idea. And I had no plans to find out. The week had been weird enough without getting shot, thanks very much.

And who would take care of BabyJon, if I were left with half a head? *I need to write a will,* I thought crazily. *Can I do that, now that I'm dead? Maybe Marjorie can help. But who do I trust to watch BabyJon—*

"I'm waiting," he whispered.

"Nick, you've gone seriously nuts, you know?"

"What can I say?" he replied, almost cheerfully. "I'm in love."

"Uh-huh." I thought about mojoing him, except I had my damned sunglasses on. I doubted he'd give me the second I needed to take them off. "Listen, Nick, I already told you twice, I can't—"

He cut me off, smiling. "Are we clear, Betsy? Honey? Deadly sweetheart with a killer figure and long legs and green eyes to get lost in? *Are we clear?*"

"I hear you, Detective. But it's her choice. Not mine. And not yours. So get that peashooter off of me before I make you eat it."

He grinned entirely without humor, but pulled the gun down and holstered it. His eyes were still flat. "Nice seeing you again, Betsy," he said cheerfully, and actually held the door for me as I picked up BabyJon and scuttled out. I didn't know which was scarier: the flat rage or the fake (or was it fake?) recovery.

What was going on with everybody?

Chapter 13

All the way home, I was practically gasping for breath. Which, as I didn't need to breathe, made me dizzy. So I held my breath for five minutes, trying to calm down. It worked. A little.

Nick knew? A Minneapolis detective *knew* I was a vampire, that my runaway groom was a vampire? How many other cops knew? Even if he was the only one (and one was waaay too many), what if he found out about Antonia the werewolf, assuming the walkabout wench ever came back? And Garrett? And if Jessica got worse or—oh God please no—died, what was he going to do? What the fuck was I going to do?

Mojoing him was out. Sinclair's clearly hadn't taken. Or had taken for a while and then worn off. But why? Sinclair was a pretty damned powerful vampire—old, and the king besides.

I took a yellow light way too fast, remembered BabyJon trapped—I mean strapped—in the car seat behind me, and slowed to a reasonable speed.

Why had Sinclair's "you are getting very sleepy" routine worn off? He could make people forget their own mothers. Was it because—it couldn't be. Naw. That was idiocy and worse, ego.

But . . . well, I couldn't shake the idea that because the long-prophesied queen of the vampires (*moi*) had gotten to Nick first, Sinclair never had a chance. That he maybe fixed it for a while, but my power was too strong, and eventually Nick remembered.

Naw. That was too conceited, even for me.

Although it was pretty much the only thing that made sense, unless Nick had been lying about Jess not telling him. And I knew in my dead heart that Jessica would set herself on fire before telling my secrets.

Sure, the Book of the Dead prophesied that I would be the strongest, coolest, most badass vampire in a thousand years, but I still had trouble actually grasping it, you know? Shit, sixteen months ago I was a secretary dreading her thirtieth birthday. But the Book had been right about everything else. So why not this?

Which meant, maybe the way to fix this was to mojo Nick myself.

Except I wasn't sure I dared. For one thing, he would be ready for that—for me.

For another, I wasn't keen on mind-raping my best friend's boyfriend.

And for another, what right did I have to wipe anybody's brain, even if it was dangerous not to? I wasn't God. I was just me, Betsy, onetime secretary and part-time vampire and soon-to-be married woman.

I screeched into my driveway, decamped with BabyJon, hustled through the front door and up the stairs to his nursery. Changed him, fed him, burped him, all the while trying to figure out what to do about Nick. And Jessica. And Sinclair. And Antonia. And—

The door chimes rang, and I leapt out of the rocking chair, gaining another gasping burp from my brother. I plopped him into the crib (it was 6:30 p.m.—time for his midafternoon nap) and hustled down the stairs.

Yippee! Who would it be? Did Garrett eat his key again so they couldn't get to it? Had Sinclair sent flowers? Was Nick waiting on the porch with a twelve gauge shotgun? Was it my mom? (I would consider listening to an apology.) Had Marc escaped the clutches of whatever madman had snatched him from his shift at the EW? Had Tina's coffin been rolled in from the airport? And would I have to sign for it? Was Laura stopping by with her usual sweetness to offer condolences and offer to take BabyJon off my hands?

Who cared? It was somebody, by God. I wasn't going to be rattling around the house by myself a minute longer, and that was cause for a *Hallelujah brother!*

I yanked the door open, a cry of welcome (or "Holster that sidearm, Nick") on my lips. I had just enough time to register the gleam of a wedding ring, as a fist the size of both of mine smashed into my face, knocking me back into the foyer.

Chapter 14

Ouch, dammit!" I yelped, skidding on my back like a bug and coming to a teeth-rattling stop against the parlor door. I was splayed in a most undignified way, luckily wearing walking shorts and not a miniskirt. And my jaw hurt like a bitch. So did my head, from where it had banged into the door. I responded to the indignity in the usual way. "Ouch. Dammit!"

While I was swearing, several people had come in (uninvited!), and all of them were looking down at me.

Wedding Ring Asshole crouched, blinked big yellow owl eyes at me, and said, "So it's true. You're a vampire. No mortal would be breathing after that one."

"Who's breathing?" I bitched. I started to sit up, but Wedding Ring Asshole quickly stood, planted his foot in the middle of my chest, and kept me flat on my back.

"Oh, now. That's just plain rude. I mean, rud*er*."

"You have much to answer for," he informed me. He was a fabulous looking fellow, I'll give the asshat that much. Tall, really tall. Brown hair and gold eyes. Not light brown, not hazel. Gold, like old coins. Not like an owl, more like . . . a lynx? A lion? Whatever. He was as powerfully built as Sinclair, and easily as tall. And I hadn't been laid in—

Never mind. Focus, Betsy! "Get your foot off my tits right now." *Nobody puts his foot on my tits.* It's a good rule to live by.

"After we talk."

"Oh, dude. You are so picking the wrong week to fuck with me."

"Produce my Pack member at once," W.R.A. demanded.

In response, I grabbed his ankle and twisted his foot all the way around. A hundred eighty degrees! Or would that be three sixty? Either way, he howled—an actual howl, like a dog!—and fell backward, losing his balance as his pulverized ankle collapsed under his weight. I flipped to my feet (well, more like staggered, but the important thing is, I was standing), momentarily triumphant.

I say momentarily because this did not make the other ones—four? five?—happy at all. I'm guessing this, because they all jumped on me at once. Unlike what happens in a karate movie, these guys didn't take turns. Nope, it was dog-pile time, with me on the bottom. (Did that make me the dog? Oh, never mind.)

I jerked my face to the side, just as a fist slammed through the floorboards where my head had been. "Wait. *Wait!*" I screamed.

Three fists (from two different people!) paused in midair, as I pulled my legs up, yanked off my saddle shoes (vintage, 1956, eBay, $296.26), and threw them into a corner.

"Okay," I said. "Go."

I blocked (barely) another fist, catching it on my crossed forearms à la Uma Thurman in *Kill Bill* (either one). I had zero martial arts training, but by God, I'd remember anything Uma did.

Fighting these guys was like dodging bullets: I could do it, but I sure as shit had to pay attention. They were fast. They were unbelievably fast. Old vampire fast. And their smell. Their iron-rich smell. It was tough work, fighting them off and trying not to bite them at the same time.

I clawed my way back to the top of the pile through sheer force of will and, oh yeah, almost forgot, super human strength and reflexes. Not that these guys were too shabby in the area of paranormal abilities, either. Bums.

I managed to duck a few more punches and deal a few of my own, took a bite—a bite!—to the shoulder from one of them, and responded with a knee in the groin and a fist in the belly, so deep I thought I touched the guy's spine.

I took another punch to the nose (ow!) from a tank-top wearing brunette (the buzz cut was not for everyone, but it looked fabulous on her) and retaliated by stomping on the gal's ankle, smirking at the crunch, and the shriek.

I shouldn't have been smiling, I should have been pissed. Okay, I was pissed. But at least I was doing something instead of waiting for the phone to ring. If I couldn't squabble with Sinclair or bitch to Jessica, a knock-down, drag-out fight in my foyer was the next best thing.

Wedding Ring Asshole was coming for me again, and I watched in amazement as he limped, limped less, and, by the time he reached me, wasn't limping at all. I was so busy gaping I nearly forgot to duck as that ham-sized fist looped toward my head again.

Nearly. Instead I sidestepped the punch and shoved the guy so hard into the wall that the plaster (or whatever old walls are made out of) cracked all the way up to the ceiling.

Note to self: do not mention all the household repairs to Jessica until she is back on her feet.

The effect was so much fun I grabbed him by the hair and threw him into the wall again. Wheee!

"Don't hurt my daddy!" someone shrieked, and I was horrified to see a girl of about six standing to the side, white faced. How had I missed her? Besides the fact that the adults had all converged on me at once, like IRS agents on a small business owner?

"Are you people all crazy?" I cried. "You brought a *little girl* to a fistfight?"

I was so shocked that I didn't move fast enough to avoid the bullets: one to my heart, two to my left lung.

"Jeannie, no!" Wedding Ring Asshole howled, as I went down and down and down and down . . .

Chapter 15

I opened my eyes to see a ring of faces around me. Since none of them were the faces I wanted so desperately to see, I responded in the usual way: by yelling. "Gah!"

"I think we'd better take you to the hospital," a curly haired blond woman I hadn't noticed before said. Since her hands reeked of gunpowder, and I could smell the leather of her holster (fat lot of good it did me to notice that now), I had an idea who to thank for my perforated heart. "Can you walk?"

"I think she should stay put. How would we explain this? We're fifteen hundred miles from home. I'm not sure how many of the locals would be sympathetic."

"Well, I think—"

"I think you psychos better get the hell out of my house!" I then spat blood in a fine cloud that they all stared at. Nauseating, yet weirdly pretty. *Focus, Betsy.*

I tried to sit up but, weirdly, they all had their hands on my chest, even the kid. I shrugged them off (gently, for the kid's sake) and sat up. "Owwww, my heart." I furtively felt my tits. "And my lung! You bums barge in, attack the hostess, then *shoot her* in front of a child?"

"I'm no child," the child said, blinking her gold eyes at me. It reminded me of a cute little owl, and I chomped on my lip so I wouldn't smile at her. "I'm the next Pack leader." She extended a small, chubby hand. "My name's Lara."

"So pleased to meet you, darling. Nice handshake. Now get out and take your psycho guardians with you."

"I don't think you should stand," Wedding Ring Asshole worried.

"You weren't too worried about my health five minutes ago," I snapped. "And I don't think you should keep your hands on me for another half second." I climbed unsteadily to my feet. The room tilted, then steadied. Luckily I'd fed a couple of days ago—another queen perk. All vampires had to feed every day. 'Cept me. I'd snacked on a homeless guy on the way home, then picked him up (literally), ran the eleven blocks to the nearest hospital (in three minutes), and dumped him at the ER for some blankets, TLC, and hot food.

Anyway, the most-helpful drunken darling had helped me more than he knew. I heard three clinks as the bullets worked their way out of my body and fell to the wooden floor. I ignored them (must be a Tuesday!), but the other five stared at the misshapen bullets, then at me, then at the bullets.

"Out, out, *out!*" I reiterated, since they all seemed slow. Or hard of hearing. Or both.

"Truce?" W.R.A. asked, smiling warmly.

Ooooh, great grin. I ignored the twinge that brought to my nether regions and crowed, "Oh ho! Now that your tiny brains have processed the fact that I'm fairly unkillable and you couldn't beat me—or shoot me—into submission, you're all Peace Talk Central. Well, fu—" I remembered the kid. "Well, forget you."

"We just wanted to talk," one of them had the unbelievable audacity to begin, but I stomped all over that one right away.

"You all suck at talking without punching." I listened hard, but there wasn't a sound from BabyJon's room. Thank God. He'd slept through the ruckus—and the gunshots! Or he'd crawled into the laundry chute. Either way: quiet as a little baby mouse. "I mean it, ass—uh, arrogant intruders. You don't want to see my bad side."

"It gets worse than this?" one of them teased, a real cutie, with blond hair, green eyes, and a Schwarzenegger build. He was the only one who looked genuinely friendly. He was wearing faded blue jeans, beat-up sneakers, and a T-shirt that read "Martha Rules." He rubbed his chest and added, "You pack a pretty good punch, blondie. Ever think of taking up the circus life as the strong man?"

"Ever think of introducing yourselves before you mug a lady?"

"I'm Derik," the good-looking blond said, "and this is my Pack leader, Michael Wyndham." The dark-haired guy with the impressive smile and yellow eyes nodded at me. "And our alpha female, Jeannie." The curly haired shooter also nodded. "And Brendan, and Cain, and Lara—Michael and Jeannie's daughter."

All the ridiculously good-looking people nodded at me, the soul of politeness, almost like they hadn't been trying to kill me five minutes ago. And they were as amazing looking as any vampire, except they were the picture of robust, superhuman health, with blooming complexions and deep tans.

My mouth was watering just looking at them. God, they smelled so *good*. Ripe and lush, like grapes on the vine. Except for the blond gun-toter. She smelled . . . could this be right? Ordinary?

"We came looking for Antonia," Jeannie said, not taking her hand off the butt of her thirty-eight. I quickly revised "ordinary" into "gun-wielding psychobitch."

"Oh. Duh. Werewolves, right?"

"We did tell you we were coming," Michael reminded me.

"No, you dumped a totally cryptic conversation on me without even telling me your *name*, and then you hung up."

"I told you she wouldn't get it," Jeannie sighed. She snapped her holster closed, zipped her hoodie (in late June!), and I felt a little better as the gun was hidden away. Bullets couldn't kill me, but they ruined my clothes and stung like crazy.

"Antonia wouldn't have moved in with her without explaining . . . um . . . okay, it's possible my logic where Antonia's concerned is a little faulty." Michael sighed and added something puzzling while shrugging. "Rogues."

Derik smirked, Jeannie rolled her eyes, and the other three remained stone-faced, but Michael had the grace to look abashed. "I, um, like we were saying, I thought Antonia would have explained things to you. I thought you were ignoring instructions and—"

"Hello? You're her—what's it? Pack leader?"

"So she *did* tell you."

"And you never noticed that Antonia wouldn't say shit if she had a mouthful?"

"Point," Derik said cheerfully.

"I'm not the boss of her, dildo breath, just like you prob'ly weren't."

"What's a dil—" the kid began, but she shut up at a warning glance from her mother. I cringed; I'd forgotten all about her again. I reminded myself that it was their own fault for bringing a child here. *Yeah! All on them.*

I cleared my throat, which, since I had no saliva, was more of a harsh bark than anything else. Two of them jumped, and Jeannie's hand strayed toward her gun again. "Anyway. Antonia. She grew up with you bums, right? She's only been here for a few months, but she *grew up* with you bums, *right*?"

"I sense culture clash," Derik piped up. He really did look like he was enjoying himself, and it was hard not to smile back at him. He gave off friendliness like a teenage girl gave off hair spray fumes. He was like a big . . . well, puppy. "Werewolves punch first and ask questions later."

"How totally fascinating and yet not interesting to me at all."

"Unlike vampires, who never ever do anything bad," he continued, still madly cheerful.

I said nothing.

"But you stood up to our Pack and fought. So we're more inclined to listen to you now."

"Yawn," I said, since actual yawning probably wouldn't have shut them up. "So like I was saying, Antonia comes, she goes, she conquers, she bitches, she moans, she eats all the raw hamburger out of the fridge. That's what she does, that's all she does, and we sure don't get into discussions about you guys—she's made it mondo-clear that Pack business isn't any of our business." *Drives my fiancé crazy*, I thought but didn't say. "She's a ship passing in the night. She and Garrett take off *all* the time. I'm not her damned keeper. I'm her—" Uh. Friend? Ally? Thorn? Fellow bitch? Yeah, that one sounded right . . .

"Point," Derik repeated, still smiling at me. "Man, you are cute. If I wasn't married—"

"To a sorceress who'd turn her husband inside out if she saw him right now," Jeannie piped up. "I knew we should have brought her."

"She's eight months pregnant, for God's sake!"

"Still, we could have used her to fight a single vampire. This one is powerful. We could have lost someone."

I barely stopped myself from saying something stupid like, "A single vampire? Try the *queen* of the vampires, you furry nitwits!" But it was a near thing. How was it that I was constantly either denying queen-hood or embracing it?

"Can we focus, please?" I demanded, as much of myself as of

them. "From what I'm gathering, Antonia missed checking in with you guys. So what?"

"So, we'd better sit down, don't you think? It sounds like we've got some catching up to do."

I nearly wept. "You're not going to leave, are you?"

"Not without Antonia," the kid piped up. She had a look on her face that was absolutely identical to the look on the gun-toting blonde's. If it hadn't been so weird, it would have been funny. "You didn't take her, I guess. Right?"

"Take her? Shit, I didn't even ask her to move in. She just did. Story of my life," I added in a mumble.

"Then we'd better talk," Michael said. "It seems we have a mutual problem."

"Can't we talk with you guys on the other side of the door? Or the state?"

None of them answered me. *Hell. Worth a shot.*

"Why'd you shoot me, anyway?" I asked the blonde.

"Because you were winning," she answered cheerfully.

"Swell. Last chance to leave."

They didn't move.

I thought about it, and they watched me think about it. Except for Derik and Jeannie, they all looked way too uneasy, shifting their weight and fidgeting like kids. From punching to looking freaked out in . . . what? Ten minutes? What was up with these weirdos?

"I thought you guys didn't believe in vampires," I said in a lame attempt to stall for time. At least, Antonia had said as much, way back when she'd first moved in.

"Recent events have changed our minds," the brunette—Cain—said dryly. And what kind of a name was *Cain* for a five-foot-nothing, buzz-cut brunette with a sharp fox-like face and smoothly muscled arms?

Then badass buzz-cut looked down and actually fidgeted like a little kid who needed to pee. What the hell? There were more of them than me, even if I (sort of) won the fight. Or did I? Anyway, I was outnumbered and outgunned (all my shotguns were in the gun safe in the basement). So what was their problem?

I remembered something Antonia had once said—that vampires had no scent. It took her a long time to get used to Sinclair, Tina, and me being able to sneak up on her. Obviously, my lack of scent was giving the werewolves the heebies. Ha, ha, *ha!*

I badly wanted to give the slaphappy bunch the heave-ho, but couldn't. For one thing, I was curious to hear what they were about.

For another, I was too damned lonely to send them away.

For another, Antonia and Garrett *had* gone missing. These guys might have some light to shed.

"Kitchen's that way," I said, pointing. "Anybody want a smoothie?"

Chapter 16

I darted up the stairs, praying the werewolves wouldn't get into trouble while unsupervised, checked on BabyJon (still snoring away), then ran back down and led the werewolves and Jeannie into the kitchen just in time to grab the phone as it rang.

"S'up?"

"Betsy? It's Laura. Listen, I wanted to talk to you about—"

"Not now," I said, and hung up. I felt bad, but not too bad. She'd been one of the bums to disappear on me in a time of need, after all. And that was weirdly convenient, wasn't it? That Antonia and Garrett and Marc and Sinclair should all disappear right around the time my dad died and my half sister made herself scarce?

Naw. Crazy. But . . . weird.

Naw.

Weird.

Naw! Dammit, naw!

Great. Lonely, and now paranoid. *Oh, and surrounded by werewolves. Let's not forget that!*

"Let's see," I said, peering into the fridge. "We've got strawberries, bananas, and peaches. Also ice, for smoothies. Oh, and Antonia's left half a raw T-bone." I sniffed. "Smells fine. Prob'ly good for another day or two."

"We'll pass on the fruit."

"I could also," I added doubtfully, "defrost some hamburger for you guys."

"We're fine. Let's get down to business."

"I'm not fine. I'm thirsty as hell." I gave them all a big, toothy grin, enjoying the mutual flinch. "So it's smoothie time."

"I'd like a smoothie," Lara piped up. "Banana, please."

"Coming right up." Now it was my turn to flinch; how many times had I heard that phrase from Marc in this very kitchen as he played bartender? How many strawberry smoothies had I fixed for Sinclair? How many times had he brought me upstairs and poured said smoothie all over my—

"Banana, please!" she repeated.

I shook myself. "Sorry. Drifted off for a moment. Peel these, will you?" I said, handing Lara some bananas.

Michael cleared his throat, while his kid (cub? puppy? whelp?) stripped three bananas and tossed the skins into the sink. "So, ah. Antonia didn't check in. And she checks in at 10:00 a.m. EST on the twentieth of the month. So when she didn't, you can imagine our—"

The rest was drowned out as I hit "puree." I left it on for a nice long time, ignoring the way it felt like a thunderstorm in my head (stupid advanced vampire hearing). It was worth it just to drown out the arrogant, gorgeous asshat.

Wait. Did I say gorgeous? Sinclair, where the hell did you go?

Via gestures, I directed Lara to the glasses, and she brought me two. She really was the cutest thing, and I smiled at her, then dropped the grin when she didn't smile back. This was a kid older than her years, that was for damned sure. What had she said? That she was the future Pack leader? That was a lot to pile onto a— what? Seven-year-old? Eight?

A perfect miniature amalgam of her mom and her dad: his eyes, her face, their attitudes. She'd be scary as shit when she hit adolescence. Or possibly the fourth grade.

I shut off the blender, filled Lara's glass to the brim, then heard Michael droning, "—natural for us to jump to the conclusion that nefarious creatures of the night had—"

And on goes the blender again. I took my time with my own smoothie, but eventually I couldn't liquefy the fruit and ice any more and had to shut it off.

"—the fight," he finished.

Jesus! Couldn't this guy take a hint? How did Jeannie stand it? How did any of them? Luckily, I was not that kind of leader.

I was no kind of leader.

"Yeah, well, you were wrong, wrong, wrong." I took a large gulp of my smoothie. "Which I'm betting is a common thing with you people."

" 'You people'?" the strawberry blond—the guy they called

Brendan—demanded. He was about a head shorter than Michael, with the aforementioned shoulder-length strawberry blond hair, the usual-to-werewolves sculpted muscles (at least, the werewolves I'd seen), lean build, chiseled good looks, big gorgeous eyes (a kind of gold/brown in his case). They almost seemed to glow from within. *Luminous.* That was the word. "What's that supposed to mean?"

Were there no fugly werewolves? Fat ones? Nearsighted, squinty-eyed ones?

"I *said*, what's that supposed to mean?"

Mild-mannered ones?

"You carnivorous ravenous creatures of the full moon," I said sweetly. "Carrying off babies, biting people and turning them into fellow ravenous creatures of the full moon, attacking large-breasted women wearing tight T-shirts." I hailed him with the smoothie. "You know. '*You* people.'"

"Ugh!" Derik said, looking genuinely revolted. Looking, in fact, a lot like Antonia when she had told me what he was about to say. "Omnivores taste awful. Trust me. We don't eat you."

"And it's not the measles," Cain (again: What kind of name was that for a woman?) barked. Literally. "You can't catch it. We're two different species, you highlighted dimwit."

"Like them?" I asked, pleased, while I patted my bangs back into place. "And if we're two different species, you want to explain her?"

Lara coughed out some banana smoothie as I pointed at her.

"Uh," was all Derik got out.

"I mean, there are no zebra-tigers, right? No gorilla-giraffes? Porcupine-platypi?"

"It's . . . complicated," Michael grumped.

"Nothing you could possibly understand," Cain snarled.

"Cain."

Cain sat down and shut her mouth. *Hah!* I looked at Michael with a smidge more respect. Guy hadn't even raised his voice, and Cain was looking like a whipped hound. Really, he was a lot like Sinclair in many ways, and it was a damned shame he was m—

Stop that, Betsy.

"—mean to offend you in your own home."

"No, you certainly wouldn't want to offend me. That's coming through loud and clear, Fist Boy."

"Pack Leader Fist Boy," Brendan corrected, fixing me with a glare he probably thought was menacing. He'd never dealt with a hysterical Marc when he couldn't find a clean scrub shirt. Or Laura when she was late for church. Or Garrett when he ran out of yarn before he finished a sweater.

Or Sinclair, for that matter, at any time. My guy had only to look this pup dead in the eye, and the kid (couldn't have been a werewolf hair over twenty-two) would be his slave as long as Sinclair wanted.

As a matter of fact, *I* could probably make this kid my slave.

I actually thought about it while one of them babbled about something or other. But in the end I decided to play it carefully. They already knew I was quick and strong. That was two things too many for strangers to know about me. There was plenty of time to turn on the charm, if I needed to.

"—where they might be?"

"Who?"

"Antonia and Garrett, you twit!"

"Brendan."

Puppy Boy sat down and shut his piehole.

"So?" Michael prompted.

"What?"

Michael ran both hands through his brown hair, mussing it to no end. "So. Where. Do. You. Think. Antonia. And. Her. Friend. Are?"

"I. Have. No. Idea. That's. The. Whole. Problem."

Lara giggled. Or gurgled; she had another mouthful of smoothie. I drained the rest of mine in two gulps and got up to head for the counter.

"Not the blender again, vampire, we're begging you." Cain said it with touching, horrified sincerity; Brendan managed to look equal parts sneery and weary.

That's vampire queen, I thought. But I took pity on them. Their hearing was probably as good as mine.

Maybe better. I narrowed my eyes at them while I rinsed my glass without looking, then accidentally broke it on the faucet head. I assessed their strength, their tone, their differences from Antonia.

Antonia, who was strong but not a shape-shifter.

Antonia, who could see the future but at a horrible cost to herself, and the one she loved.

I couldn't imagine what was worse: being considered a freak by, well, other freaks, or having horrible visions that were never, ever wrong.

Is that why she was gone? Had she seen something awful
*(Please God, nothing bad about Sinclair or Marc or Jessica
okay, God? I'll owe you a big one, God, in Jesus' name, amen.)*
and vamoosed, taking her own personal Fiend with her?

No way. Antonia was a lot of things, but she'd never run for
cover. And if she did run for cover, which she'd never do, she
wouldn't do it without warning me first. After all, I was her—what
was it? Pack leader pro tem?

"You know," I said, sitting across from Michael, "Antonia was
pretty tight-lipped about you guys."

Silence.

"She didn't talk a lot about Pack stuff." In fact, I was trying to
remember a single damned thing I knew about the Pack. And I
was coming up pretty close to blank. And not just because I usually tuned Antonia out five or ten seconds into her rant du jour.
Well, yeah, that was probably the main reason, but, bottom
line . . . "She just didn't."

"She didn't talk to me about vampire stuff," Michael volunteered. "Every month it was the same thing. Everything okay?
Yes. Need anything? No. Any messages you want me to pass
along? No. Anything you want to tell me about? *Hell*, no."

We all sat in silence for a few seconds. I don't know about
them, but I was thinking that I was damned fortunate Antonia was
able to juggle her loyalties so well. From the look on Wyndham's
face, he was thinking the same thing, or close to it.

I crossed my legs and stared at my black socks. *Must remember to get my saddle shoes out of the foyer.* "She must have explained when she moved in. Didn't she?" I looked up and beheld
identical puzzled expressions. "I mean, she said she had to get
permission from you, and I thought it was extremely weird that a
grown woman had to 'get permission' to live with us, but when I
said that, all she said was that my face was extremely weird and to
shut the hell up."

Wyndham and his peeps nodded. Michael added, "She had little to say about you even when she moved to the Midwest. 'I found
my destiny,' she says, 'and it's with the king and the queen of the
vampires. Yes, they're real,' she says."

"Don't feel bad about not believing," I told him. "I didn't believe in werewolves until Antonia showed up. And, uh, didn't
change into a wolf."

" 'I'm not coming back,' she says—this was her way of asking permission. 'So sell my house and cut me a check. And don't give me any shit, or I'll foresee your death and forget to mention it.'"

I had to admit, it had the ring of authenticity.

"She agreed to check in every month," Michael said, "and that was the end of it. Until, of course, we didn't hear from her. Now. Tell me, Betsy. What is a Fiend? And where can we find the one that killed our Pack member?"

Chapter 17

Whoa, whoa, *whoa*!" I said, wishing I wasn't doing this all by myself. "Let's not jump to any conclusions, my eager little pups. Garrett would eat his own balls before he'd ever hurt Antonia, and he'd never, *never* kill her."

Derik shuddered and covered his eyes. "Must you use phrases that I'll never get out of my head? 'Eat his own balls'? Who *says* that?"

"Not to mention, it's hard to believe," Cain added.

"Believe? Why is that so hard? Now all of a sudden you're big vampire and Fiend experts?"

"Vampires aren't accident-prone?" Jeannie asked, and to her credit, it sounded like an honest question.

"Well, I am," I admitted. "But not Garrett."

"You can explain about Fiends?"

"Sure."

"There are no taboos against discussing such things with outsiders?"

"I dunno." Wyndham couldn't hide his surprise, so I borrowed a phrase from his pal Derik. "I think it's that culture clash thing again. If it'll keep you from pulling Garrett's legs off, I'll answer any question you like."

"That's a *good* thing, Chief," Derik said. "Stop looking like you're expecting the other shoe to drop—on your head."

"For a ruthless despot of the undead, you're awfully charming," Michael said, and no one in the room was surprised when Jeannie's fist slipped. But he got his breath back in no time at all.

Lara asked—and received—permission to use the bathroom.

Jeannie got up to accompany her. And I used the kid's absence to explain about Fiends, about Nostro and his sick-ass psycho games, about Garrett's slow recovery, about all the progress he made and how much he and Antonia loved—

"So by your own admission, this creature was subhuman only six months ago?"

"I don't know if sub—"

"Subsisting on buckets of blood, running around on all fours, and howling at the moon?"

"Physician, howl thyself," I pointed out.

"And he couldn't even talk?" Michael persisted.

"I don't know about *couldn't*. *Didn't* talk would be more accurate. But see, after he drank my blood and the dev—and my sister's, he got better. And you guys—you just don't know. I mean, the way he feels about Antonia. She's his everything. He'd ki—uh, he'd die for her."

"And she for him, I s'pose?"

"Well, it's hard to imagine Antonia getting all mushy and stuff, but yeah, I imagine she'd—" Too late, I saw the trap Michael had set for me. I shot to my feet and started to pace. "You guys, Garrett did not kill Antonia and then take off for parts unknown. There's no way. *No* way."

"Mmmm," Wyndham said.

"Hmmm," Derik added, also apparently unconvinced.

"You don't see me with my knickers in a knot, asking you if your Pack member killed *my* guy and then took off. Did I show up, fists flying, jumping to conclusions? No." I smirked to see the Wyndhams looking uncomfortable. Except for Brendon, who glared at me.

"We've been over this," Michael said, mildly enough.

"Yeah, but now that your kid's gone, you can apologize for being totally out-of-control, foaming, slavering assholes who hit first and asked questions later."

He drummed his fingers on the table for a few seconds, and then, after a long, difficult moment (difficult for him, not for me) he said, "I apologize."

"Okay. It's totally conceivable that Antonia saw the future and got the hell out of here and that Garrett tried to stop her and so she—she—I dunno, gave him a bath in holy water and then left town on the first Amtrak headed east. That could totally happen, but I'm not getting all suspicious and paranoid, right? So there's no reason for you guys to stay beady-eyed."

"Are there any other unusual goings-on?" Michael asked, leaning forward. "Anything mysterious? Something that might lead us to answers?"

"Everything's fine," I lied. I cocked my head; I could hear BabyJon asking for a bottle. Loudly. "And you'll have to excuse me a minute; my brother needs me."

I moved past them, and Wyndham's hand shot out and closed over my forearm. I saw the whole thing and had plenty of time to avoid him. But I didn't. His hand was really warm. I could actually feel his heartbeat through his fingers.

And he smelled—have I mentioned how frigging *delicious* these guys smelled? No wonder Garrett found Antonia irresistible. It sure wasn't her personality.

Michael's hand squeezed my arm. He was so cute, thinking he was actually holding me in place. "Betsy, really. *Is* there anything going on?"

I smiled. "Michael, you worry too much, anybody tell you? I said everything's fine, now didn't I? So don't sweat it."

On my way to the nursery, from one room and a hallway away, I heard Michael's very distinct order to Derik.

Chapter 18

Derik bounded beside me on the stairs like a big blond puppy. "It's nothing personal," he said cheerfully, keeping pace with me as I climbed the eighty zillion stairs to the nursery. "But we can't tell if you're lying or not—that whole 'no scent' thing—and it's driving the chief out of his head."

"I'll bet." I was a smidge—just a smidge—sympathetic. To go your whole life being able to tell if everyone around you was lying or not, that had to come in handy. One of the few things Antonia had mentioned was that her Pack hardly ever bothered with lying . . . there was absolutely no point.

And then to run into me, someone who could say she was a short, genius brunette and still smell fine (or not smell, as the case was), that had to be frustrating.

"So I, the most charming and handsome werewolf in all the land—"

"Should I throw up here on the stairs? Or try to wait until I can find a garbage can?"

"—will catch you off-guard with my witticism and charisma."

"And don't forget your sexy Martha Stewart T-shirt."

"Hey, hey. Don't diss my girl Martha. She could kick your fine undead ass with one homemade seashell napkin holder behind her back."

"Derik, you're seriously bent, you know that?"

He ignored me. "And then I, fearless Pack member, shall swoop down on the truth like a crow on a grub."

"Did you just call me a worm?"

"I did not," he said, following me into the nursery. "I called you a grub. Big difference. Huge!"

I laughed; I couldn't help it. The big doof probably *was* the most charming werewolf in all the land. "Dude, you really are the—eh?"

I had reached the crib, bent over, plucked BabyJon out. And was surprised to be alone. I turned and Derik was—there was no other word for it—he was cowering beside the nursery door.

"What's going on?" I asked, completely startled to see the six-foot-plus blond huddling in terror.

"I was gonna ask you the same thing. Jesus!" He forced himself to straighten, shook himself all over, then cupped his elbows in his palms. It almost looked like—it looked like the big strong badass werewolf was hugging himself for comfort. But *that* couldn't be right. "Every hair on my body is trying to jump ship right now. Least that's what it feels like. I've got the *worst* fucking case of the creeps. I—what's that?"

"This is my baby brother." BabyJon wasn't crying or anything. I had slung him over one of my hips, and he was just looking at Derik, patiently waiting for his bottle. What a sweetie. Orphaned, and hungry. And not crying! "Isn't he the cutest?"

"Keep him away from me," Derik ordered, actually backing out of the room. Guess he wasn't fond of babies. "It feels like thirteen o'clock in here."

"Derik, what the hell's gotten into you?" I followed him out into the hall, genuinely puzzled. If Michael had sent his Good Guy WereCop after me to try to fish for more info, this was a weird way to go about it. "You're acting all—"

"Don't do that!" Both Derik's hands shot out, palms up. He was—warding me off? No way. I had it wrong. I was misreading werewolf body language, or whatever. "I might have to bite you. And not in a nice way, get it? So just—*aaaaiiieeeeee!*"

He said *aaaaiiieeeeee* because at that moment he fell down the stairs. All the way down. And with my hands full of BabyJon, I had no chance to catch him. So I just stared, cringing at some of the thuds and wincing at some of Derik's more colorful language as he plummeted to the bottom.

I sighed. Then I put BabyJon back in his crib, ignoring his surprised squawk, shut the nursery door, and started down the stairs.

There was no way they were going to believe Derik fell down the stairs—all the stairs—without assistance. I assumed there was going to be another fight. Best to get it over with.

Too bad, really. Just when I thought we'd established a little trust.

Chapter 19

Well, thanks for stopping by," I said again, and it was even more lame than the first time I said it.

Derik, upon his quick recovery, had done some fast talking to save me from another werewolf beat-down, and now they were all leaving. And not being very subtle about wanting to get the hell out of my house, either. If I hadn't felt so anxious, I would have been amused.

Derik limped past me, which was a big improvement, because he'd broken both legs when he'd hit bottom. These guys regenerated as fast as Sinclair and me ... maybe faster. Must be their iron-rich, high-in-protein diet. Mmm ... their yummy, yummy diet. I was drooling just watching them file past. How had I never noticed how delicious Antonia was?

Easy. When Antonia was around, Sinclair had also been around, and his blood was just fine. More than fine. We'd actually incorporated blood-sharing into our lovemaking and now, like a Pavlovian dog (or George on the *Seinfeld* episode when he equated salted cured meats with sex), all I had to do was get a whiff of someone's delicious blood and also find myself horny as hell. Which wasn't exactly—

"Why are you looking at me like that?" Derik asked, massaging his knee.

"Uh. No reason. Thanks again for visiting. And good luck picking up Antonia's scent." I'd offered to show them her and Garrett's room, let them get a whiff of the sheets or whatever, and they'd all looked at me as if I'd lost my mind.

I guess I was picturing a scene right out of a cop movie: baying bloodhounds sniffing sheets or a dirty sweater and then howling off into the night, hot on the trail. Apparently real life was different. And werewolves weren't bloodhounds.

Which was a shame, because bloodhounds were really cute.

"Crazy fucking vampire," Jeannie muttered, so softly she probably assumed I hadn't heard her.

"Don't forget your parting gifts!" I cried, sending Lara after them with a helpful shove.

"Thanks for your hospitality," Michael said without the teensiest bit of irony. We shook hands as the others filed past. He squeezed. I squeezed. He squeezed harder. So did I. I figured anybody else's hands would have been crushed to bloody powder by now. "We'll be doing some checking around town and will keep you posted," he added, slightly out of breath from our *mano a bimbo*.

"And I'll call you"—I held up the card with his cell phone number on it—"if I hear anything from either of them."

"Thanks. Have a good night."

"You, too. Bye, Derik. Cain. Brendon. Lara. Jeannie. Michael."

"Betsy," Jeannie said, "I want to make clear that I only shot you because—"

I shut the door. And since it was a big heavy door about two hundred years old, it cut her off with a solid *BOOM*!

Did I think they had anything to do with everything that was going on? No. I really didn't. Werewolves weren't exactly famous for lying or subversiveness. I seriously doubted they'd—what? Snatched Antonia back, staked Garrett, then shown up at my house and staged a pretend fight, all the while playing like they had no idea where Antonia and Garrett were?

Vampires would pull that sneaky shit in a cold minute. The Wyndham bunch? Naw.

Probably naw. Their appearance today was still an awful coincidence.

It was either a really really good thing that the werewolves were in town right now, or a really really bad thing. Too bad I had no idea which it was.

I took the stairs two at a time, plucked a fuming BabyJon out of his crib, fixed a fresh bottle (he liked 'em cold, and we kept a supply in the small fridge in his room), and let the poor starving tyke have at it. While I was walking with him back to the kitchen, I wondered about Derik's extreme reaction to my half brother.

Hadn't he said that his wife was pregnant? Maybe babies freaked him out.

I cuddled BabyJon closer into my side and kissed the top of his fuzzy dark head. "Guess he'd better get over that in a hurry," I told him. "Unless he likes sleeping on the sorceress's couch."

The phone rang as I got near the swinging door, and I grimaced. What fresh hell was this?

Chapter 20

Majesty?"

"Tina? Hey, finally! Great to hear from you!" From anybody without fur, frankly. "What's going on?"

"Nothing good, Majesty, I assure you." She made a sound that from anyone but Tina would have come off sounding like a snort. "Are you well?"

"Oh, sure. A bunch of werewolves stopped by to pick a fight, but—"

"You mean they broke in?" Tina interrupted. Since she never interrupted, I assumed she had to be fairly shocked. Then I remembered her strict instructions, most (or all? I couldn't remember all of them, to be honest) of which I'd broken since we last spoke.

Lucky for me she was half a continent, plus an ocean, away. She could only scold; she couldn't strangle.

"Well, no. They didn't break, exactly. They, um, knocked."

"And you *let* them *in?*"

"Like I said. Knocked. Then, the fight. Which I won, so don't worry." I decided not to mention Jeannie "Quick Draw" Wyndham. Tina hated it when I got shot. "Turns out they thought we were being sneaky, because Antonia hasn't checked in with them."

"Um."

"But I convinced them that we hadn't done away with her or anything, using my Kissinger-like powers of diplomacy."

"Um-hum."

"Now we're buddies!" I tried to put as much enthusiasm as I could into that lie. I mean line. "Isn't that great? Even as we speak, they're scouring the town, looking for the hair of Antonia's chinny-chin-chin. Wait, that was the pigs, right? That line made no sense, then. Let me think of—"

"Majesty! I must beg you to—"

"I know, I know. I've been answering the phone and the door. It's all gone horribly, horribly wrong, and all because I didn't listen to you." I slung BabyJon over my shoulder to burp him, tossing the now-empty bottle in the general direction of the sink. "If only I had listened." BabyJon yawned, and I knew how he felt. The lecture loometh.

"Majesty, I do not wish to alarm you—"

"Then don't."

"But I fear the king may be dead."

"See, that? I find that alarming." I whacked BabyJon a little too hard, because he groaned—then belched. I plunked him into the port-a-crib so I could pace.

"I'm sorry, Majesty, but it is the only conclusion that fits the data."

"What the hell makes you think that?"

"He would have answered me by now, Majesty. In seventy-some years, he has never *not* answered me. We have a code we use for emergencies, and the other one, no matter what is happening in his or her life, the other one must answer. And he has not."

"He blew off your super secret vampire code?"

"I realize that infantile jokes are your way of dealing with serious issues, but with all due respect, Majesty, now is not the time."

"Noted," I said, chastened.

"He is not sulking, as you think. He is not hiding. He is not shirking his duties as your groom. And more—"

"What? There's more? What?"

"He would never abandon the queen," she said quietly. "No matter how silly he thought the wedding rituals. Someone has him. Or someone has killed him."

"What—what are we going to do?"

I heard a thud and realized that Tina, from eighty zillion miles away, had punched a wall. "I. Will do. Nothing!" Another thud. She was pounding the wall like Rocky Balboa worked a punching bag. "I cannot get back to you. There are riots in France, and all flights are canceled until further notice."

"Riots?"

"Surely you saw on CNN—never mind."

"Oh, the riots! Right, right. The riots. Those pesky French riots."

She ignored my lame-ass attempt to pretend I was up on current events. "I cannot even charter a private plane. To go by boat would take too long. I am trapped here, Majesty. And you are alone."

"Tina, it's—" *Okay*, I had been about to say, and who was I kidding? Tina, one of the smartest people I'd ever met, thought Sinclair was dead. *Ergo*, he . . . wasn't.

I would take refuge in my stubbornness. She was wrong, wrong, wrong and also needed a deep conditioning treatment. I wouldn't let the panic take hold. I wouldn't. It couldn't have me. The panic would have to find someone else to bug; *I* wasn't going to play ball. Sinclair wasn't dead. Or even in danger.

Tina was wrong. This one time, in a matter that was as important to her as it was to me, this one time she had screwed up. Who knew why? The stress of being away from home? The hassle of going through Customs via coffin? The important thing was, she was stressed out and jumping to conclusions. Because the alternative was totally beyond my grasp. I couldn't imagine a world without Sinclair in it. And wasn't that silly? Two years ago, I hadn't even known the guy existed.

"Tina, stop hitting that wall. You're going to hurt yourself."

"I did," she said dully. "I broke most of the fingers in my left hand."

"Jeez, what are you punching, cement?"

"Yes."

"Well, stop. Focus on getting back."

"But the rioters—the roads are closed, or barricaded. No one can get in or out. I cannot help you, my queen, I am stuck in this place." "Place" came out like "placcccccce" because Tina hissed it as opposed to saying it like a person who wasn't half crazy with guilt and grief.

More riots in France! Perfect timing. So typical of France not to consider *my* needs before passing martial law.

"I know it seems tough, but they'll eventually let planes out, they've got to. For one thing, FedEx can't get there. People need their overnight packages, Tina! They want their Sephora and their cheese. The French people won't stand for it, trust me, the airports won't be closed for long. Or at least get out of the country and take a plane from a country that *isn't* rioting in the streets."

"That is . . . excellent advice, Majesty." I could hear the sur-

prise in her voice, but couldn't blame her. It was weird enough
Tina hadn't thought of it. Weirder that I had. It showed how upset
she really was. And how convinced she was that Sinclair was
dead, how rattled her conclusions had made her. "I will start at
once. With your permission, I will not waste your time with phone
calls unless I have news to report."

"That's fine, Tina."

"And, Majesty?"

"Yeah?"

"Consider now following my advice. Do not answer the
phone, do not answer the door. I doubt whoever ki—"

"Don't say it!"

"—I doubt whoever detained His Majesty will be content only
with him."

"That's better. *Detained.* Yep, that's the word of the day, all
right. Listen, be careful."

"You took the words," she said, "right out of my mouth." And
without so much as a "See ya later, gator," she hung up.

Chapter 21

He is not dead.

He is not dead.

He is not dead, because if he was? I'd kill him.

But I had to face facts. Sinclair wasn't sulking. For one thing, it wasn't his style. He liked to engage, not withdraw. For another, as silly as he thought the wedding stuff was? He'd never stick me with all of the prep less than two weeks before the big day.

Well, he might stick me with it, but he wouldn't out-and-out disappear on me. Even when I thought I hated him, he'd been impossible to get rid of. Now, when we loved each other, he'd made himself scarce? Not likely.

Tina was half right: someone had snatched him. But who? And how come? And where the heck was he?

I glanced over and saw BabyJon had tired of playing with his soft blocks and toppled over on his side, one thumb corking his mouth shut. He watched me with sleepy blue eyes as I paced, as I grumbled and thought and chewed my nails and prowled back and forth.

Finally I sat down at the kitchen table, folded my hands, looked at my folded hands, and thought: *this is not a coincidence.*

I thought: *Sinclair and Marc and Antonia and Garrett and Cathie and Tina and Jessica and Nick and a double funeral and Laura and my mom? All those people either missing or deliberately absenting themselves from my life? And now, of all times? The week my dad and the Ant died? Two weeks before I married the king of the vampires? Granted, I remember wishing everyone would leave me alone for a few days, but this was ridiculous.*

I thought: *Who killed my father and my stepmother? Because this was all just a little too neat, you know? Too neat by a damn shot.*

Didn't they know they were fucking with the queen of the vampires? (Whoever "they" were?) Didn't they know what I—we—could do to them?

Sure they did. They just didn't care. They didn't think I was a threat; no vampire had ever thought I was a threat. They only believed me as I was killing them. And even then, the rumor spread that Sinclair had really done it. Even the European faction had taken a damn year to pay their respects.

And who was I kidding, calling myself a vampire queen? If I didn't believe the Book of the Dead said Sinclair and I were married, how could I believe it about anything else? *Can't have it both ways, Bets,* as Jessica might have said.

So who had seen my weakness, and acted?

And what the blue hell was I going to do about it?

This was, of course, assuming it was all about me.

I almost laughed. Of course this was all about me! Just not in a good way.

I picked up the phone, dialed my mom's number, and waited for her to answer. "Mom? Listen, I need a favor. The shit's hitting the fan over here, and I don't think it's safe for BabyJon. Can you take him for a couple of days?

"Mom?

"Hello?"

Chapter 22

Just what do you think you're doing, young lady?"

I stared at my mom, whose white curls were straggly in her wrath. She'd roared right over to the mansion in her Honda to kick my ass. I was just having trouble figuring out . . .

"You want to know why I'm so angry?"

"Not really."

"I'll tell you why. You are responsible for this infant." She pointed a nonmanicured index finger at BabyJon, who yawned. "You. Not me. Not your sister."

"Did Laura talk to—"

"You. And at the first sign of trouble—"

"The first?" I yelped.

"—you come running to me to kiss your boo-boos and make everything all better. Well, I can't, Betsy. You're a grown woman, and it's about time you started acting like one."

I looked at my mother, Dr. "Suburbs" Taylor, with real irritation. I hadn't felt this close to smacking her since I was fourteen and she'd caught me with her credit cards at the Burnsville Mall (she knew what that shoe sale meant to me!).

I was a grown woman, and it was about time I started acting like one, eh? Well, let's see. Let's think about all the things this grown woman did that Dr. Taylor, safe in her book stacks, had no clue ever happened.

There was the overthrowing of not one, but two vampire psychopaths. There was the tracking down and dispatching of the serial killer (though technically Laura got the kill claim on that one). There was taking on the responsibility of governing the vampire nation, whatever the hell that was. The tension of the European faction finally visiting, and solving *that* subsequent murder. And the zombie in my attic who showed up from God knows where, God knows why, which I had to kill. By myself.

Oh! And let's not forget about the pack of werewolves who showed up trying to tear my head off!

All right, to be fair, it wasn't her fault she didn't know about any of the above. I had made a conscious choice to leave her out of the vampire side of things, a choice wholeheartedly endorsed by Sinclair and Tina.

But the stuff she knew about was bad enough: the tension of the wedding, not to mention the funerals. Oh! And suddenly being the guardian of a baby. Almost forgot that one! And if she was vague on the details of my vampiric lifestyle, she at least knew the basics: I had died, I had come back, and my life was infinitely more complicated as a result. Oh, and my *father* had just *died*.

Ah, but the broad had a few more left. "Really, Betsy. At the first sign of trouble, your impulse is to dump your problems on someone else. You've got to grow up."

"Are you taking him for the next two days, or aren't you?"

My chilly tone must have startled her, because she actually paused for a few seconds, then said, a tad on the meek side, "Of course I'll take him. Laura promised to give me a hand. I just wanted you to know—to realize what you—I just don't want you to get in the habit of—"

Yawn. I had no time for this. I handed her BabyJon, snug in his carrier (the base was on the front porch, where Mom would pluck it and then strap it onto her backseat), and the diaper bag with the BabyCrap™. "Thank you. Good-bye."

Mom hesitated, glanced down at the baby, then hurriedly looked back up at me. But not so fast I didn't see the flash of distaste cross her features.

Ah-ha. And duh. Should have guessed that one. "I appreciate that babysitting the living embodiment of your late ex-husband's faithlessness can't be easy, but I'm not exactly having a fun week, either, Mother."

"I—I know, Betsy, it's just that—"

"I have work to do, Mother."

"What kind of work?"

"Just a pedicure. You know. The usual thing since I died and came back as a vampire. Thanks for helping me out of yet another frivolous jam."

"Betsy—if I spoke without thinking—"

I picked up the phone and stared at her. She clutched the car seat to her, then grimaced and eased up on her grip. BabyJon just watched her. So did I.

"Betsy, is there something you want to talk about?"

"Not anymore." I started to dial Minneapolis General. "If you'll excuse me, I need to call the oncology ward. You know, my best friend's new digs? Boy, talk about frivolous! You should hear her bitching about all the puking the chemo makes her do. Maybe I should send you over for a pep talk."

"I went and put my foot in it, then," Mom said, sounding so much more like her old, supportive self that I almost weakened. "And not only was I unfair, but I've got lousy timing, is that it? Well, you're right and I'm sorry. Other than—this—" She frowned down at the baby. "Is there another way I can help?"

"Don't be silly, Mom. I know how hard you're working this month, what with your department *not* teaching courses all summer."

"Fair enough." She started for the foyer. "When you're ready to listen to me grovel, I'll be glad to do so. For now, dear, please call me if you need anything else. And yes, I'm aware of the irony of encouraging you to call me after this argument."

"Good thing I don't have to point it out, then!" I yelled after her.

While I waited to be connected to Jessica's room, I pondered the odd series of events that led to my mother babysitting her dead rival's youngest child. I hadn't wanted to call Mom—I wasn't entirely insensitive. On that topic, anyway. And I hadn't been able to reach Laura . . . most likely because she was busy calling my mom. It sounded like they'd already had at least one conversation today, topic: BabyJon.

But it just wasn't safe around here for BabyJon right now. Shit, it wasn't safe for *me*. I'd take a lot of chances with my own safety, no problem.

But not BabyJon's, possibly the only baby, ever, who was going to be really mine.

Chapter 23

Some jerk of a male nurse wouldn't connect me (why oh why didn't my vampire mojo work over phone lines?), so I disobeyed Tina (hey, it was that kind of week), hopped in one of Sinclair's Volkswagens (my Ford was in the shop—it needed a new starter), and was at Minneapolis General in fifteen minutes. (One of the blessings of being undead? I never faced rush hour anymore.)

Sure, at 10:00 p.m. it was way past visiting hours, like I gave a rat fuck. Even when I was alive, I wouldn't have cared. Because I, Betsy Taylor, was . . . an ex-model!

The key to not getting kicked out of a given restricted area is to stride briskly and look like you have every right to be there. (I learned this my first week as a model . . . in fact, I got backstage passes to Aerosmith that way.) Being tall helped, too. And pretty.

Look, I've never made a secret of the fact that I was genetically blessed. To ignore said blessings would be like a great painter throwing away her brushes. Or Jessica not using any of her money just because she inherited it from her scumbag father. Why make life harder by not using what you had?

Anyway, I was striding down the hall toward Jessica's room, having made it past reception to the elevator bank, past several nurse's stations, and I was about thirty feet away from being home—

"Excuse me? Visiting hours are over."

I turned and smiled. Visiting Hour Enforcer smiled back. *My* smile broadened when I noticed the lack of wedding ring on Nurse Guy's finger. He was a cutie, too—about five ten, curly black hair cut short, flawless dark skin the color of expensive coffee. Big, gorgeous dark eyes, the whites almost bluish with health. He smelled like cotton candy and French fries. Two of my favorites!

So we were grinning at each other like a couple of idiots, when I remembered I had a mission, and he remembered the same.

"Listen, sorry to be a dick, but visiting hours were over a while ago. But if you want to leave your phone number, I could call you when we're back up for guests."

I laughed at his audacity. T. Starr, R.N., his name tag read. "I'm getting married in a few days, T. Starr," I replied. "But that's the nicest offer I've had all week."

"Nuts!" he said, snapping his fingers. "Guess my horoscope was wrong this morning."

"Stick with the comics," I advised him, then took off my sunglasses. I blinked painfully at the fluorescents, then caught his gaze and said, "I've got special privileges, T. Starr."

"Yup."

"I can come and go no matter how late it is."

"Yep, you sure can."

"Tell the charge nurse, will you?"

"I am the charge nurse."

Finally, a break. "Well, spread the news, T. Starr. Betsy Taylor. Unlimited visiting privileges."

"Yup, you can come and go whenever you want, everybody knows."

"And you have a very nice evening."

"No phone number?" I heard him ask mournfully, and I snickered. Even deep in the thrall of sinister vampire mojo, he was still trying to score. T. Starr was gonna go far.

I pushed open the door to Jessica's room, ignoring the soft sigh of the hydraulic hinges (or whatever made big doors wheeze like that), and stepped inside just in time to hear some pompous asshole say, "—really a very rare form of blood cancer. A fascinating case study, really."

"No thanks," Jessica said. Sighed, really . . . her normally strident tone of voice was running at about 15 percent.

"But if my colleagues could read about your case in *J.A.M.A.*, they might be able to help others with your condition."

I knew from my two-year stint as a medical secretary that *J.A.M.A.* was the *Journal of the American Medical Association*. *J.A.M.A.*, along with the *Lancet*, were two of the biggies for docs to publish the weird and unusual.

"No thanks."

"Really, Miss Watkins, you're being a little selfish, don't you think?"

A doctor couldn't write up a patient without his or her permission.

"Miss Watkins, don't you think?"

But they were supposed to ask. Not nag. Not guilt-trip.

I opened my mouth to leap to Jessica's rescue, when the bathroom door slammed open and Detective Nick Berry snarled, "The lady said *no,* asshole. Take a walk."

I was actually glad to see him, but had to wonder . . . when did he sleep? Or work? For that matter, how'd he keep getting up here?

"Detective Berry, it would be a pity to ban you from the floor. Your visits seem to have a positive effect on my patient."

"No . . ." Jessica's voice was a thread. I could tell it hurt to talk. "Don't do that . . . maybe I could do the . . . the thing . . ."

"Forget it, baby," Nick told her.

"Yeah," I said. I tried to slam the door behind me, but the damned thing just slid slowly shut on those whispery hinges. "Forget it, baby."

From the way the men jumped (Jessica, obviously, didn't have the strength), I realized they hadn't known I was in the room.

And the dickhead bullying my best friend? When he wasn't flushed red to the eyebrows, he was probably almost normal-looking. Mussed brown hair, cut short. About my height, with bluish-green eyes and a truly heroic nose. Slump-shouldered and too thin for his height. Bony wrists sticking out of the lab coat. A full-on, grown-up geek. And let's not forget about that spectacular blush! I couldn't tell if he was embarrassed or angry. I was hoping for embarrassed.

"Hey, shitstain, ever hear that no means no?"

"What are you people doing here after visiting hours?" B. McGill, M.D., Oncology, sputtered.

"Kicking your ass." I crossed the room in a hurry—Nick had his gun out of his holster, guess I'd startled him, too—and picked B. McGill up. By his throat.

I won't lie. It felt gooooood.

"Don't. Bully. My friend. Ever. Ever! Again." Each word was punctuated by a teeth-rattling shake. B. McGill's eyes were starting to roll like dice.

"Let go, Betsy, he's mine."

"Back off, Nick. I'm *starving*."

"Awwww." Jessica smiled. "I hate it when Mom and Dad fight."

"I can't let you commit felony assault on him, even if he's the biggest dick on the ward."

"Nick? Sweetie? You couldn't stop me with a flamethrower."

"Rrraaggle," B. McGill managed.

"Betsy. There are days when I almost don't hate you, so don't make me shoot you."

"Oh, go ahead and shoot!" I snapped. "The way my week's going? You think I'm scared of your thirty-eight?" And what happened to his Sig? How many guns did the guy have, anyway?

"Kids, kids," Jessica said.

"Gragggle."

"Put him down! Now!"

"Make me."

"Gggkkkk!"

"Kids?"

I heard the click as Nick cocked his gun. I could hear the bullet tumble into the chamber. The barrel looked really big. That was *fine*. Finally, a foe I could grapple with, a problem I could confront head-on. *Misplaced aggression,* Sinclair whispered in my head, which was irritating. For an undead (possibly all-the-way dead) runaway groom, he had sure made himself at home in my brain.

"Kids, Dr. McGill is out cold."

I looked. Nick looked. She was right. His head was lolling, and he was drooling on my wrist. Well, shit. That was no fun at all. I dropped him, and he hit the tile and splayed in a most unflattering way. Nick put his gun away.

We glared at each other across Jessica's bed.

"Pull that again, and I *will* arrest you."

"Draw down on me again and I *will* eat you."

"Again," he sneered. He poured Jessica a cup of water and fixed the bed so she was sitting up. He guarded her like a pissed off mama cat, while she drank it all down.

"Oh, like it was such fun for me, too, that first time! Get it through your head, lamebrain, I was a brand-new dead girl! I didn't even know I was a vampire until my teeth came out. I went to you for help, remember?"

"Help?" he nearly shrieked.

"How could I know what chomping you would do?"

"You didn't think biting me on the neck and drinking my blood would be problematic?"

Wince. *Score one for Nick. Never mind.* "In case it's escaped your notice, I'm one of the good guys! I kill bad vampires and stop serial killers and—and—" I was going blank. What other good things had I done? Surely there were at least a few more . . .

"Of course you stop killers, why do you think I've been feeding you information for the last eighteen months? Because I'm soooo in love with you?"

"That was the prevailing theory," I admitted, feeling vain and stupid at the same time. "Of course, I'm revising it rapidly. So you, uh, don't love me, yeah, I'm getting that."

"Not fucking likely, you blond leech on legs. I dream about locking you up in a sunny cell."

Jessica said nothing. And I kept my face perfectly straight. So Nick didn't know everything about me. Thank goodness! He probably thought a cross or holy water would hurt me. Excellent.

"You know something, Nick? I'm glad you don't like me. Because you're a self-absorbed, overreacting, testosterone-filled, gun-toting dipshit."

"Will you two cut the shit?" Jess demanded. "I'm having a real crummy day. Night. Whatever."

"He started it."

"You started it."

"I'm ending it! I will turn this hospital bed around right now if you two don't knock it off. And before you ask, Bets, I didn't clue him in as to what you are."

"Of course you didn't." Jess looked ghastly and had lost more weight. Trouble was, she didn't have that much to lose in the first place. Five pounds from her was, like, 10 percent of her body weight. Or whatever. "Sinclair's mojo wore off. Nick and I already discussed that."

"Yeah," she said. "You know, when I'm out of this bed, we're going to have to find a way for everybody to play nice."

I grimaced. And Nick looked like someone had placed a scorpion on his tongue.

I stepped over the unconscious asshole, gently put a finger on Jessica's chin, looked at her neck, then turned her head and looked at her other side. Then I looked at her wrists.

Clean as a whistle. I'd check her thighs, next (wasn't looking forward to that wrestling match), and then her—

"Don't bother," Nick grumped. "I already looked."

"Yeah, and here I thought we were going to get sweaty, and it was just another exam. What are you guys looking for?"

"There's a lot of weird stuff happening all at the same time," I replied. "I thought it was kind of interesting that you had a big-ass relapse around the time everybody started disappearing."

"No bites," Nick told me. "Not even a scratch."

"So this is just bad timing?"

"Luckily for you."

"Oh, put *both* your guns away," I snapped. "Nobody's impressed."

"I am," Jess said cheerfully. "In fact, it's turning me on like you wouldn't believe."

"I'm outta here."

"Wait! You said everybody was disappearing? Who?"

"I'll tell you the whole story after."

"After what?" I heard Nick ask as the door started to wheeze shut behind me.

"After it's all over," Jessica sulked. "She keeps me out of the cool stuff until it's too late to have any fun of my own."

"Humph," Nick replied.

I couldn't believe, all this time, that I thought he'd been on my side! That he'd liked me. Here it was all a lie, he hated my guts and fed me info just to get creeps off the street. Not caring, I assumed, if I got hurt or even killed in the process.

Jeez, he'd made a special trip to my house to tell me all about the serial killer Laura went to town on! He must have known I wouldn't have known about him, avoiding the news as I did.

What a manipulative bastard! He'd been pulling all our strings for so long, I didn't—

Whoa. What?

I wheeled around, marched back to the room, shoved the door open, waited patiently for it to actually *be* open, then rushed in and grabbed Nick's head in my hands before he could turn, much less find his gun.

"Betsy! What the hell do you think you're—"

I ignored her. "Nick."

"Yes."

"You have to tell the truth, Nick."

"Yes, I do."

"Are you responsible for Sinclair's disappearance?"

"I wish."

"Do you know who is?"

"No. But good luck to them."

I thought for a second, never breaking eye contact. "Do you have any advice?"

"Go back to the beginning. Find them. Kill them."

"Go back to the beginning?"

"Who else is gone?"

"Marc. Cathie-the-ghost. Tina. My father and his wife. Antonia. Garrett."

"Then it's personal. You already know who's doing it. Go back to the beginning."

I stared at him thoughtfully. He was dreaming with his eyes open, looking not at me but through me, past me. "I'm sorry for what I did, Nick, and for what I did just now. You'll remember everything . . . in five seconds."

"Great," Jessica snapped. "Leave me to deal with the fallout."

"Sorry, hon. Catch you later."

"Let me guess!" she hollered. Wow, water had certainly perked her up. "After you go back to the beginning!"

Well, yeah.

Chapter 24

What did it mean? I wasn't a detective, God knew. And the people around me usually did the thinking. That was how I liked it. I liked that Tina and Sinclair dealt with most of the shit. I liked that another vampire looked after the other Fiends, that two other vampires looked after my nightclub, Scratch. Shit, Jessica had even hired someone to feed my cat. My time was spent reading, snacking, fucking, wedding planning, playing bartender in the kitchen with my friends, and occasionally vanquishing evil . . . again, with help.

The answering machine in the kitchen was blinking. I scowled at it, then pressed Play.

"Hi, Betsy. Michael Wyndham. We're coming up empty. Completely cold trail. The Pack members in the area haven't seen either of them. We're still looking. Call me if you find anything."

"Hi, hon. It's Mom. The baby is doing fine. I thought you might want to know. Laura's here, if you need either of us. So . . . talk to you soon?"

My, my. Weren't those two getting thick as thieves?

"Hi, Betsy, it's Marc. Man, I hope you get this. Anyway, call me right away." He left a phone number—not his own cell phone—with an unfamiliar area code.

"Hello, Jessica. It's Don. Listen, I set up that new tax shelter for you, I just need you to sign some paperwork. I can come over to your place whenever you like. We can shelter a good seven figures, and as you say, you'd rather give it to charity than the government. Your wish is this CPA's command. Call me."

Ah, Don Freeman, the sexiest accountant on the planet. When

he'd first come to the house (he was always bringing things for Jess to sign, and nobody expected a mega-millionaire to come to them), I'd mistaken him for a Minnesota Viking. Shoulders out to *here*.

"Betsy, why the hell haven't you called me back? It's Marc again. Listen, call me. I'm starting to worry."

He was starting to worry? He sounded fine, not dead at all. And not under duress. I leapt for the phone, played his first message back again, and punched in the number.

"Pirate's Cove Resort, Little Cayman."

"Uh, yeah. I'm looking for Dr. Marc Spangler? He left this number?"

"I think he's still scuba diving."

Scuba diving?

"Can you hold on, while I check?"

"Take your time," I managed through gritted teeth.

There was a clunk as someone put the phone down.

He was on *vacation!* Oh, I would kill him. I'd eat him alive and then cut him into a thousand tiny pieces and then set each piece on fire. Then I'd force the ashes to watch reruns of *Survivor*, Season 4. Then I'd—

"Hello?" Marc panted. "Betsy? Is that you?"

"Sorry to interrupt your scuba-ing," I said coldly.

"Oh, that was this morning. I've been hanging around the bar waiting for you to call back. Listen, I've been trying to reach you for days."

"Yes, I know! What's going on? Are you really in the Bahamas?"

"The Caymans," he corrected, "and yeah. But this is the getaway of all getaways. Cell phones are dicey, and so is their Internet connection. We just had a wicked bad storm come through here, which didn't help. Scuba diving's been for shit ever since."

"But what are you doing there?"

"Boning my brains out," he said, sounding way too cheerful. "You know David Ketterling? The cute new pediatrics fellow?"

I had a vague memory of Marc burbling about the new guy at the hospital, but had paid it no mind at the time, since Marc, as we all knew, had no life beyond . . . well, us.

"Well," he bubbled on, "we both had our four-day stretch at the same time, and his grandma owns this resort, so on the spur of the moment—"

"You left the country with a total stranger."

"It was more romantic in my head," he admitted.

"Marc, I've been worried to *death!*"

"I'm sorry, Betsy. I told you, it was spur of the moment. And I've been trying to call since we got here. David was the one who suggested we use the lodge landlines. I can't believe I didn't think of that three days ago."

"Guess you had other things on your mind."

"And in my mouth," he said cheerfully.

"Thanks for that grotesque little mental image."

"Homophobia rearing its ugly head?"

"Honey, if Jessica was telling me about Nick's body parts in her mouth, I'd have totally the same reaction."

"Hey, is she around? Let me talk to her. David's dad is a king shit oncologist in New York. He had a few ideas."

"Um . . ." The temptation to pour all my troubles over the phone line like smelly oil was almost too much. He could be back here this time tomorrow. I wouldn't be by myself. He was a doctor, he was smart, he was funny, we were good buds. He could help me. He *would* help me.

And the only thing it would cost him would be his first vacation in years. His first romantic getaway in five years.

I opened my mouth. Marc to the rescue!

My mouth wasn't paying attention to my brain, because what came out was, "She's out stocking up on tea and cream. I'll tell her about your new boy-toy, though."

"He's a *man*-toy, and don't you forget it, blondie. Listen, I'll be back on Sunday. How goeth the wedding plans?"

"Wha? Oh. Everything's fine. I found a dress, and of course Sinclair has about forty tuxes already." Two lies and one truth. "Listen, I'm glad you're okay. I was—I was worried."

"Oh, who'd do anything to me? When you'd give 'em the smackdown?"

Who indeed. But at least they couldn't get to you, Marc.

"So I'll see you in a couple of days, okay? Call me at this number if you need anything."

"Oh, please. Everything's fine. Have fun. Give what's-his-face a dry peck on the cheek from me."

"No romance in your soul," he teased. "None at all."

He hung up.

And then it was just me. Again.

Chapter 25

Go back to the beginning.
Whoever was pulling all the crap, they are not afraid of me.

What did it mean? Or was I kidding myself, trying to play detective? Maybe this shit was all random. I mean, I was a vampire. My friends were ghosts, vampires, werewolves, millionaires, ER docs. Why wouldn't weird shit happen all of a sudden? Weird shit did happen all of a sudden. Just not to everyone, and not all at once. Usually.

I looked at my watch. Almost eleven o'clock. Too late to call Mom back. Not that I was in the mood. But the werewolves were probably still up and around.

I punched in Wyndham's cell number, and he picked up immediately.

"Yes, Betsy?"

"How'd you know it was me?"

"Caller ID, dear. What can I do for you? Have you heard from our wayward lambs?"

"No, I was just returning your call. Wait a minute. My name wouldn't show up on your—"

"No, but your landlady's does. And she's in the hospital right now, yes? Unlikely to be phoning me." There was a pause, and then he added, "We did our research, dear."

"You did?" I said, mildly creeped out.

"We've looked into a few more things since our arrival here. It simply will not do to underestimate you again." He laughed, a rich, deep chuckle.

In the background, I could hear, "Is that Betsy? Let me talk to her."

"Stop that, you're married." Then, louder, "Betsy? Are you there?"

"Of course I'm here," I grumbled. "Where the hell else would I be?"

"As I said in my message, the trail is cold. I think you may have to prepare yourself for the worst."

"I've been doing that since I woke up dead," I lied, trying to sound tougher than I felt.

"Uh-huh. But there is a somewhat larger problem we'll have to deal with."

"Fabulous. Hit me."

"The full moon, dear. It's in two days."

"What?"

"The. Full. Moon. We. Will. Get. Hairy."

"Cut that out. Sorry. The werewolf I lived—*live*—with doesn't do that."

"Right. But the rest of us will, except Jeannie, who's human, and Lara, who's too young."

Dimly, I heard, "Come on! Lemmee talk to her."

"Shut up, or I'm calling your wife. Betsy? Are you there?"

"Yes," I said, my patience stretched almost beyond endurance. "So you'll have to leave town?"

"Not at all. We'll stay."

"You think the good people of Minneapolis won't notice werewolves running around on Nicollet Avenue?"

"Give us a little credit, Betsy. In fact, we might be able to find Antonia and her mate on all fours. Our senses are much, much keener when we run with the moon."

"Well, do that. Run along with the moon. Have fun. Keep me posted."

"I have a favor to ask."

"Of course you do."

"Would it be all right if my wife and cub stayed with you during the first night of the full moon? This is a strange city, and I prefer not to leave them unguarded while my Pack members and I go hunting."

Dimly in the background: "I don't need a damned babysitter, Michael!"

"Uh, maybe you better run that one by the little woman first."

"I will pretend," he chuckled, "you didn't just call her that. May we impose?"

I sighed. *I don't get these people.* "Sure. Be nice to have some company. But Michael?"

"Yes?"

"Tell her to leave the gun at home."

"Well, she'll keep it holstered," he said, sounding almost shocked.

"When should I expect you?"

"Two days, maybe sooner. We'll call before coming by."

"Oh, I can't wait. I'm all atingle," I muttered, hanging up.

Derik was right. Definitely a cultural thing.

Chapter 26

I think this is a sign from God," my half sister, Laura, told me after she took a sip of her orange pekoe.

I managed not to groan out loud. She'd swung by for tea, showing up about twenty minutes after I woke up (being the queen, I usually woke up around 4:00 p.m. or so, and could go outside without being sautéed).

As usual, she was indecently beautiful: about my height, with long buttercup-blond hair caught up in a sensible ponytail. No makeup. Tan capris and a faded blue oxford shirt. Navy blue Keds, one black sock and one navy blue sock. Big, gorgeous blue eyes framed by lashes that you usually only saw on little boys.

I'd given serious thought to not inviting her to my wedding, because, bottom line, she looked better on her worst day than I did on my best. Fortunately, I quickly came to my senses. Well. Six or seven days later, anyway.

"Really, I think God is trying to tell you something," the daughter of the devil went on. (Have I mentioned? She rebelled against her mother, the Lady of Lies, by being a faithful churchgoer.) "You should take it as a sign. I was praying over it just last night."

"Laura, what the hell are you talking about?"

She frowned. "Don't talk like that. I'm saying that perhaps your wedding to the king of the vampires wasn't meant to be. He could have picked any other time to leave you, but he chose now?"

"That's the thing, Laura." I ignored my own tea. I was ragingly, crazily thirsty, and I didn't give a damn. "I don't think he left me. I think someone snatched him."

"But why? Why would someone do that? No, I think you

should cancel your wedding and be thankful he didn't decide to pull this nonsense after you'd been married a hundred years. By then, you'd have been emotionally committed."

"Laura, he didn't run out on me. Even Tina agrees."

"Oh, her." Laura waved Sinclair's most loyal friend away with her unmanicured hand. "Another vampire. What do you expect her to say? You're always complaining that she's more loyal to him than you."

That was true, I had confided that to Laura. I never dreamed she'd toss it back in my face, though. And it was getting real hard to hold on to my temper. "She's worried about him. So am I."

"She's a vampire. She lies."

"I'm a vampire."

"Yes, well. I know you're doing the best you can."

"When you said you wanted to come over to help me figure out what to do, this was your big plan?"

"I'm helping," she said, reaching for my hand. I snatched it away. "You need friends now, Betsy. Besides your mother and a sick Jessica, I'm the only one left who really cares about you."

"Laura. Darling? You're so full of shit your eyes are brown."

She stiffened. "Don't talk like that."

"Then cut the shit. Jeez! Did you really come to my house—"

"Jessica's house."

"—to encourage me to forget about the man I love? Who's either dead or captured? To blow off Tina, who spends all her time trying to make our lives as comfortable and murder-free as she can?"

"God doesn't want you to throw in with the minions of Satan," she sniffed. "Don't ignore the signs."

"What the hell do you know about God, you murdering psychotic spawn of Satan?"

She was on her feet. So was I. "Don't talk to me like that!" she shrilled, our faces only inches apart.

"Or what? You'll give me shitty, insensitive advice?"

"It's not my fault that creature tricked our father, birthed me, then went back to Hell!"

"Well, it's not my fault I'm a vampire who fell in love with a vampire!"

"You can control who you live and—and fornicate with. *I* can't control my bloodline."

I felt my eyes bulge. "Are we really playing Who's The Biggest Sinner?"

"You chose to throw your lot in with him," she went on. "I didn't choose what happened to me."

"Oh ho! The prude is rearing her ugly head. It's not the wedding that's bugging you, it's the living in sin."

"It's a sign," she repeated stubbornly. "You're blind not to see it."

A chilling thought occurred to me. "Laura? Honey? Did you snatch my fiancé? Did you stick him with that light-show sword of yours?"

"I did *not*."

"I've seen your temper tantrums before, Laura, so don't get up too high on that horse. People usually die when you get pissed."

"They do not! Not real people, anyway. And you're one to talk, you have to drink blood to keep walking around. You—and your kind—are abominations!"

"At least our socks match!"

"That's it!" She threw up her hands. "I'm leaving. I might have known you would spurn perfectly good advice."

"Spurn this," I said, and gave her the finger.

She looked like she'd found a minnow in her cereal, which was probably close to the expression on my own face. She turned, and I grabbed her shoulder and shoved her across the kitchen. She bounced off the wall, hit the floor, but was back on her feet in half a second. Just in time for me to grab her by the throat and slam her against the wall.

That's when I noticed the bright light just below my left eye. Her sword. She could call it up simply by force of will. It was made of Hellfire, and turned vampires into towers of flame, and then ash. Where it went when she wasn't using it, even she didn't know.

"Let go," she grated.

"Put it away," I snapped back.

"Let *go*."

"Put it *away*."

The light from her sword—if my eyes could have watered, they would have. They would have been streaming by now. As it was, I couldn't see out of that eye at all.

"You're not leaving until you tell me what you did."

"Put me down or I'll—"

"What? Kill me? Like you killed Sinclair?"

"I didn't kill him! I wouldn't do that to you!"

"No, you just suggested I leave him forever."

"For your sake!"

"No, for yours. It's hard to pretend to be Miss Goody Goody of the universe if your sister is the queen of the vampires, isn't it?"

"You know what you're doing is wrong."

"Says the girl with a temper-powered sword."

"I don't mean to lose my temper."

"Did you lose your temper with Sinclair?"

"No!"

"How about Antonia and Garrett? You nearly beat Garrett to death once. Did he piss you off again? Did you dispatch him with your handy-dandy sword, get rid of Antonia, and then lie yourself black in the face?"

"I don't lie!"

Ah. There we go. Her eyes were shifting from blue to poison green. Her blond hair was growing red streaks. She was losing her temper. She wasn't Laura, daughter of a pastor. She was the Devil's Own, and she was in my kitchen with a weapon that could kill me.

Excellent. "Fess up, Red. What'd you do?"

"I did *nothing*. Let me go or I'll—"

"Kill me?"

"Let me go," she hissed. "Let me go or I'll kill you, and never mind if I'm sorry after."

"Are you really going to stick me with that thing? Kill your only sister? Orphan BabyJon . . . twice in one week?"

"All that and more if you don't let me go now let me go *let go* of me right now, Vampire Queen, right now!"

"What'd you do, Laura?"

"Let go of me!" she screamed, and behind me, the window over the sink shattered.

"Whoa. New trick. Nice one, devil's daughter. Any other new stuff you want to share with the class?"

She was silent for a long moment, and I suddenly felt silly, hoisting my little sister by the neck a good foot off the ground, trying to avoid the sword pointing at my eye. Was this what happened when things went wrong all at once? You couldn't trust *anybody*?

"I see what you're doing. It won't work. Put me down, please."

Her eyes were blue again, the red fading to blond. The sword disappeared in a flash. No, it didn't work. If she had done something, it likely would have come out when she was her other self, her darker self. When she was in a temper, she lost her mind. She wasn't sly, like her mother. Just red-rage pissed. Too pissed to lie.

But now she was calm again. Careful again. Now she could lie. I put her down.

"Really, Betsy," she fumed, straightening out her mussed shirt. "What would Jesus do?"

"Turn you into loaves and fishes?"

"I've had about enough of your blasphemy." She started for the door, puffing her bangs out of her face as she stomped past me.

"You're a lot more interesting when you're pissed!" I yelled after her.

"Go to hell! And I mean that as a literal invitation."

"Where do you think I am right now?" I cried, but the slamming of the front door (damn, she must have really booked down that long foyer) was my only answer.

Chapter 27

I didn't want to do it. In fact, I could think of about a thousand things I'd rather do, including having a root canal without anesthesia.

I resisted it as long as I could. Well, I resisted it for about ten minutes after I had the idea. But this could be considered "the beginning."

It was also right around the time Nick would have realized I was a vampire, and that we had stomped all over his brain with big black boots. But Nick wasn't the only one we'd vampire mojoed and regretted it, after.

One phone call to Tina, who was in the middle of trying to cross the border into Switzerland, was all it took. This was a surprise. Not that she had the info. Frankly, I had no idea Switzerland was anywhere near France.

"Isn't that, like, way farther north? Like by Greenland?"

"My queen, how may I be of service?" Tina replied, sounding harassed.

"I need Jon Delk's home address."

Long pause.

"Tina? Stupid cell phones . . ."

"My queen, what good would that information do you? As you have promised not to leave the house until I return."

"Every day is another pint of Sinclair's blood, Tina, assuming he's still alive at all." I could actually feel her wince through the phone. "Delk's old job was killing vampires, and he hates Sinclair more than anyone I know. It's worth paying a visit to the family farm, don't you think?"

Another pause, this one shorter. Then: "Bring Laura."

"Sure," I lied. Damn. I was getting good at lying through my fangs. I'd make it up to Tina once she got back.

"And please call me the minute you find out anything," Tina was saying. "Or don't find out anything. It's an excellent idea, Majesty. I just wish I was there to run the errand for you."

"You've got your hands full already, Sunshine. Now hit me with the address, please."

"I've text-messaged it to your phone while we've been talking."

"Sneaky and efficient. That's my girl."

"Majesty, it's kind of you to pretend I'm actually being of assistance."

"Stop that," I ordered. "There's no point in beating yourself up. You had an important job to do, and you did it. Who could have predicted all this?"

"Someone," she said, "my age with my IQ."

"Whoever did this took him out from under my nose. Did all this shit right in front of me, and I didn't even notice. Whatever's happened . . . well, it's on me, that's all. Not you."

"Kind," she replied, "but untrue. Take all care, Majesty. How I adore thee."

"What?"

"N-nothing."

Awkward!

As we hung up, I found myself wondering about the mysterious Tina. How had she turned into a vampire? Who had done it, and why, and where were they now? I had no answers here, only her unabashed devotion. In fact, the only person I knew less about was my recently vamoosed fiancé.

How was it that these two vampires, who seemed to care so much about me, had remained so mysterious about their pasts?

Well, wondering wasn't getting me any closer to finding Sinclair. After some digging (I was always misplacing the damned thing), I found my cell in the bottom of an old Louis Vuitton purse Jessica had bought me for my twenty-first birthday.

I noted not only the address but precise directions (I knew Tina would make sure she could track down a Blade Warrior if necessary), and got ready to make the long drive to the Delk family farm.

Chapter 28

Jon Delk's parents lived in a St. Paul suburb, but lately he was spending a lot of time at his grandparents' farm in Burlington, North Dakota. I made the fourteen-hour drive in nine hours, mostly because I didn't have to stop to pee or eat, and because I went ninety on the interstate almost the whole way. I was pulled over three times, all three times by single male state troopers. Didn't get a ticket once.

It was the next evening—I'd had to get a motel room just before sunrise, but was on the move again by 5:00 p.m. the next afternoon.

Long gone were the Minnesota cornfields I was used to; out here, close to the Canadian border, it was all wheat fields and sloughs. Got kind of monotonous after a while. At least cornfields were an interesting color.

I pulled into the mile-long drive and shut off the engine (I'd picked Sinclair's banana yellow Ferrari for this drive . . . ninety felt like fifty), staring at the neat, large cream-colored farmhouse with not a little trepidation. I wasn't at all looking forward to what was coming next.

For one thing, it was late—for farmers, anyway. Ten o'clock at night. For another, Delk and I had not exactly parted on good terms. Specifically, he found out we'd stomped around inside his head and was not at all pleased. He expressed this by shooting me. (It was astonishing how often this sort of thing happened.) Then he'd stomped out, and we hadn't seen him since.

Making him a pretty good suspect for all the weird goings-on.

I stumbled up the gravel driveway, regretting my choice of

footwear. I was wearing lavender kitten heels to go with my cream linen shorts and matching cardigan (sure, it was eighty degrees outside, but I felt cold almost constantly).

I went up the well-lit porch steps, inhaling myriad typical farm odors on my way: manure, wheat, animals, rosebushes, the exhaust from Sinclair's car. There were about a zillion crickets in the back field—or at least, that's what it sounded like.

I knocked on the porch door and was instantly distracted when a shirtless Delk answered.

"Betsy?" he gaped.

Farm Boy was *built*. Too young for me (not yet drinking age), blond, nice shoulders, fabbo six-pack. Tan, really tan. Blond hair almost white from being out in the sun all day. He smelled like soap and healthy young man. His hair was damp from a recent shower.

"What are you doing here?"

"Huh?"

His blue eyes went flinty, and he squinted past me, trying to see past the porch light into the dark driveway. "You didn't bring anyone with you, did you?"

"I came by myself."

"Well, I'm not inviting you in." He crossed his (muscular, tanned) arms across his (ripped, tanned) chest and glared.

I opened the screen door and pushed my way past him, gently. "Old wives' tale," I said. "Got any iced tea?"

Chapter 29

My grandparents are asleep upstairs," he said, keeping the crossbow pointed in my general direction, while I dropped six sugar cubes into my tea. "Twitch in their direction, and I won't take the arrow out."

"I tremble and obey. Got any lemon?"

"Yes, and you can't have any."

"Crybaby." I took a sip, then dropped in two more cubes. Delk knew that a stake (or wooden arrow) to the heart wouldn't kill me like it would any other vampire . . . but until he pulled it out, I'd do an excellent impersonation of a dead girl. "Don't worry, I grabbed a snack on the way." From that pig of a Sleep E-Z Motel front desk guy who'd actually *goosed* me while I signed the register. I'd nearly bitten his fingers off. Settled instead for hauling him behind the registration desk and helping myself to a pint.

Delk shifted in his chair, the arrow point never wavering. "What do you want?"

"Oh, the usual. World peace, a pair of Christian Louboutin heels, a perfect wedding."

He tried not to wince, and I pretended not to notice. "Still marrying King Psycho, huh?"

That remains to be seen. Did you kill him, Delk? " 'Fraid so," I replied with a cheerfulness I sure didn't feel.

"What do you want?"

"Info."

"So take a community ed course."

"I don't want to learn how to throw clay, Delk. Some extremely weird things are going on in St. Paul. I was wondering if there was anything you wanted to tell me."

"Why don't you just mind-fuck me and get it over with?" he sneered, but the tip of the crossbow shook.

"Why don't you just answer me?" I deliberately looked away. I didn't want to take a chance on even accidentally mojoing him. The poor kid had been screwed over enough by me and mine. "People are getting hurt. Some of them are victims. My dad's dead. My stepmother's dead, and I'm BabyJon's new mommy. Vampires have gone missing, and people are acting weird. Jessica's trying not to barf out all her guts from chemo."

Delk's jaw dropped in what I hoped was unfeigned surprise. "Jesus Christ!"

"Something's going on. And . . . well, I couldn't help wondering."

"You think I killed your parents?"

"She wasn't my mother," I said automatically.

"I didn't have anything against your dad and your stepmother. I never even *met* them. And you thought I—"

"Well. You and I didn't exactly part on good terms."

He snorted and leaned back, and the crossbow dipped until it wasn't quite pointing at my chest anymore. "You mean when I found out that I'd written a book about you—*your* Goddamned biography!—and then Sinclair and Tina made me forget all about it, all to protect the precious vampire nation? Except for some reason this book, which I don't remember writing, ended up getting submitted to a publisher and is a fall title? A fall *fiction* title?"

"Well, yeah," I admitted. "But anything sounds bad when you say it like that."

"I take it Sinclair is gone, too?"

"Yeah."

"Well. I didn't do it. I doubt any of us did. The Blade Warriors disbanded."

I giggled, the way I always did when I heard the name of their kiddie club.

"Knock it off. My point is, I haven't talked to any of them since Anya and Tina broke up. You know about that."

"I also know that we were kind of friends once, and then I let Sinclair and Tina do something I knew was wrong, and then we weren't anything."

"Do you blame me?" he asked quietly, setting the crossbow

between the sugar bowl and the cream. You had to admire your North Dakota farms . . . good food, sturdy furniture, checkered tablecloths, crossbows.

"No! *Heck*, no. I never blamed you. I'd have done the same thing. Possibly discharging a few firearms before I left town."

He smiled. "Yeah, I bet. But I've been here helping out with the farm since I last saw you. Grandpa has plenty of help for harvest, so I'll probably finish my senior year at the U this fall. I miss the Cities."

"I bet dorm living isn't your cup of crossbow, either."

He laughed and looked about sixteen instead of twenty. "After the shit *I've* seen? And done? I'd probably strangle my roommate before orientation was over."

"Well, we've got plenty of room at the mansion. You're welcome to crash there until you find a place of your own."

He just looked at me. Now it was my turn to shift uncomfortably. "Look," I continued, "I'm not saying it wouldn't be awkward or anything—"

"Awkward?"

"—but bottom line, we fucked you over, and that was wrong. And I let them do it because I've got responsibilities that I didn't have when I was alive. That doesn't make it right. We owe you one. A big one. You can live with us as long as you like."

"I'm sure Sinclair and Tina would love that."

"They owe you a big one, too."

He chuckled and helped himself to a swig of my tea. "Argh! There's less sugar in a Coke. You'd really let me stay with you?"

"Sure. Hey, it'd be a pleasant change for me to *invite* a guest to move in. Usually they just . . . move in."

"How do you know I'm not lying? Maybe I got the drop on Sinclair and Tina and threw your dad down the stairs—I'm sorry about your folks, by the way."

"Thanks, but Tina's alive and well, and my dad died in a car accident."

"Maybe I'm just a really really good actor."

"Well. That's why I didn't call. I wanted to talk to you in person. Watch your face. Your eyes."

He swallowed hard. "Oh."

"You're slick, Delk, but I'm the vampire queen."

He fiddled with the yellow tablecloth for a moment, trying not to stare at me. "I think that's the first time I've heard you refer to yourself that way."

"Yeah, well, it's been a super fun week. And by 'super fun' I mean 'horrible and endless.'"

"Well," he said with the air of a person who had suddenly made up his mind, "I don't know about staying with you. But I'll come back with you and help."

Part of me leapt at the idea. And part of me wanted to cover my eyes and groan. I had figured this meeting would go one of three ways.

One: Delk would throw things, aim weapons at my head, chase me away like I was a rabid coyote. Two: Delk would instantly let bygones be bygones and offer to come back and help (more on that in a minute). Three: some weird combination of one and two.

Once again, I was madly tempted to take him up on his offer, and once again, I wasn't going to allow myself the luxury. For one thing, I had *no* idea what was going on or how dangerous things could get. Delk, although adept at killing vampires *with the Blade Warriors backing him up,* was still little more than a kid. For another, it was no secret to me that Delk had a bit of a crush. Leading him on wasn't an option.

Finally, I didn't drive all the way out here to drag him into my troubles. After what we'd done to him, he didn't owe us a thing.

"After what we did to you, you don't owe us a thing."

"I wasn't thinking 'we' and 'us.' I just want to help *you* out."

"Touching, yet mildly creepy. Nothing's changed, Delk. Once I track Sinclair down, I'm still marrying his sorry ass."

"And the rest of him as well, presumably. Look, Betsy, I—I've missed you. And I consider us even."

"Oh. Even as in, 'Hey, you mind-fucked me, but then I shot you in the chest, so let's start fresh' even?"

"Anything sounds bad," he teased, "when you put it that way."

"You're sweet," I said, and I meant it. Once upon a time, I'd thought Delk's crush was cute. Now it just made me tired. I made a mental note: once I'd fixed the current disaster, *however* it shook out, I was going to fix Delk up with someone nice.

Laura?

No, no.

Hmmm.

"—no trouble to come back to the Cities with you."

"You're sweet," I said again, "but it's my mess to clean up, not yours. But think about what I said. About this fall." I drained my tea and finished. "Now, if I expect to make some time before the sun comes up, I'd better book. Sorry to barge in on you like this."

"Wait, wait." Delk grabbed a Post-it and scribbled on it, then stuck it to my arm. "That's my cell. Call me and I can be in the Cities in less than a day."

"Thanks," I said, not mentioning that Tina had extensive files on various ways to track him down. I pulled it off my arm and stuck it in my pocket. "I'll treasure it always."

"Say hi to Jessica and Marc for me."

"Sure. Thanks for not staking me the minute I knocked on your door."

"Aww. You're too cute to stake."

All of a sudden I was in a big hurry to leave. I was afraid I'd weaken and tell him to come back with me—I was so tired of being by myself. And I felt guilty about his crush. He'd forgiven me pretty quickly for what I still considered to be an unforgivable act. Was that my fault? I'd never led him on deliberately. I didn't think.

"Want to hear something funny?" he asked, getting up to walk me to the door.

"Absolutely."

"I wrote the publishing house. The one that's publishing *Undead and Unwed?* I pretended to be a reviewer, and they sent me an ARC."

"ARC?"

"Advanced reader's copy. Of my book. It's kind of cute. It's told in first person. You know—you're telling your own story."

Suddenly the front door was about a hundred miles away. Guilt was washing over me like a tsunami. "Oh?" I managed, trying not to gallop the rest of the way to the door.

"Yeah."

"Delk, I'm—"

"I know." He looked at me thoughtfully. I tried not to look at his nipples. "I guess if you're going to be the queen, you have to be the queen."

Whatever that meant. "Yep, that's about right."

"But I hope you'll remember that you were human first, and for a lot longer."

"I try to." Finally, a pure truth. "Every day, I try to. It's sort of what drives the other vampires batshit."

He grinned. "Well then! An even better reason to keep it up."

"Thanks for the tea."

"Thanks for having the courtesy to come and see me yourself."

He held the door open for me. We stood there, fairly awkwardly, while I tried to think of something to say. I didn't dare kiss him, not even a buss on the cheek. Shaking hands seemed kind of overly formal, given all we had been through. Not doing anything at all would be rude.

"Fuck it," I said, and grabbed him and gave him a resounding kiss on each cheek, real smackers. "There. Bye."

"Hey, if it turns out Sinclair is dead—"

"Stop."

"Too soon for jokes?"

"Just a bit." I started down the steps. "Behave yourself. Maybe I'll see you in September."

"More like probably," he said cheerfully. He let the porch door slam behind him and leaned on the railing. "It'd be worth it just to irritate the piss out of your runaway groom."

"You're not staring at my ass as I walk away, are you?"

"Of course I am!"

I grinned in spite of myself and shot him the finger over my right shoulder. He waved as I started the car and put it in gear, and I flashed my high beams in response.

Cross another suspect off my list. But I felt slightly better for coming. And I made a promise to myself. Two promises. I would fix Delk up, and no matter what it took, I'd make sure he got the credit for Undead and Unwed, as well as the royalties.

How? I had no idea. But it was the least I could do.

Chapter 30

I can't believe you're babysitting me."

"Hey, you didn't have to come."

"Uh-huh. Rattling around that mausoleum you live in was a much better plan."

"Mom, can I have some more paper?"

Jeannie and Lara Wyndham and I were back at the bridal shop. Tonight was the first night of the full moon. My wedding was in four days.

Denial? Was that why I was here? Pretending everything was fine and I really was getting married next week? Well, yeah. Besides, if Sinclair did show up (or if I was ever able to figure out where he was), I had no plans to walk down the aisle naked.

Given that I'd been planning my wedding since the seventh grade, it was slightly insane that I'd left the dress for so late. Not only did it have to be The Dress, but at this stage of the game it needed to require few if any alterations.

The florist was taken care of, ditto the reception menu. The justice of the peace was booked—he was a friend of my mom's. The RSVPs had all come in long before Sinclair had disappeared. It was a small civil ceremony, so there'd be no rehearsal. No bridesmaids, either, though I'd picked out designer suits for my girlfriends to wear, all Vera Wangs, all jewel colors.

Speaking of jewel colors, Lara was lying on the floor, drawing with Crayola Sparkly Markers. Jeannie was slumped in one of the armchairs, staring at the ceiling. And, what came as a pleasant surprise, she wasn't armed. And I was trying not to remember the last time I'd been at the bridal shop, when things had been almost normal.

"How was your wedding?" I asked, waiting for the clerk to haul out some dresses.

She snorted. "I didn't have one. The day I met Michael I got knocked up with this one." She nodded at her daughter. "As far as werewolves are concerned, that was the wedding."

"Really?" I was interested in spite of my own problems. "I'm kind of in the same boat. We've got this thing called The Book of the Dead, which foretold—uh—me. And my fiancé, Sinclair. So he always figured we were married, too. Even when I couldn't stand him, he assumed we were hitched."

"Aggravating."

"Say it twice. Anyway, the last thing he wanted was a real wedding with a dress and a caterer and a cake we can't eat."

"Oh. And now he's gone?"

"Yeah."

Jeannie was probably a lousy poker player. I was grateful she was too tactful to suggest Sinclair hadn't been kidnapped. She looked at me, bit her lip, and then went back to staring at the ceiling.

"I hope we get this cleared up sooner rather than later," she fretted, shifting in her seat. Her shoulder-length hair, normally curly, was bordering on frizzy, thanks to the humidity, and she shoved a wad of it behind one ear and crossed her legs. "I haven't seen my son in a week."

"Oh? How many kids do you have?"

"Lara here, and my son, Aaron. He'll be two next month." She sighed. "Obviously this trip was too dangerous for a toddler."

"Uh." I glanced at Lara, reassuring myself she was engrossed and paying no attention. "Not to tell you your business, but I think it's too dangerous for anybody under thirty."

She smiled thinly. "Lara will be the next Pack leader. The more she knows about the world before she has to take over, the better."

"Yeah, but—not much time to just be a kid, huh?"

Jeannie said nothing. But I could tell she didn't like it. *What must it be like,* I wondered, *to be a human in the middle of a bunch of werewolves? In love with your husband and glad enough to have kids with him, but caught up in a society with completely different rules?*

I could so totally relate.

"So even though you have a little boy, Lara will—?"

"The mantle's passed down by birth order, not gender."

"How refreshing!" And I meant it. Men usually got all the breaks.

"Yeah. But I see where you're going with all this. And yeah, I wish I could protect Lara from—well, everything. But a werewolf cub isn't like a human child. Even a half/half, like my daughter. They're bolder than we are, and faster, more pragmatic and . . . well, crueler, in some ways. From the day she was born she was different than any human baby. I swear, she was born without the fear gene."

"Fear is a gene?"

"You want to get into it, blondie?" she demanded, but she was smiling. "Because we'll go, if you want to go."

"Don't call me blondie, fuzzball."

"Mom, you worry too much," Lara said from the floor, drawing what appeared to be a field of upside-down mushrooms on fire.

"That's my prerogative."

"What's—"

"It means that as your mom, I retain the right to worry about you pretty much until the day I die."

"Oh, yay," the kid muttered, then giggled when Jeannie nudged her rump with the toe of her sandal.

"So your husband and his buds are running around on all fours in the middle of St. Paul right about now?"

Jeannie shrugged. This was obviously old stuff to her. I couldn't help but admire her. She'd adjusted to her extreme lifestyle change a lot better than I had. Of course, she'd had a few more years to deal with it.

"I wish *I* was on all fours right now," Lara said.

I looked a question at Jeannie, who replied, "Puberty, usually."

"Oh, *that* sounds like a fun time."

She grinned and opened her mouth, but before she could elaborate . . .

"Ah, Ms. Taylor! So nice to see you again."

"Yeah, hi, uh—"

"Misty, Sherri, and I will be heading out for a quick bite, but you're our only appointment this evening. Christopher is in the back, selecting some gowns we think will superbly suit your height and complexion."

"Superb," I said.

"Mega superb," Jeannie added.

"We've got some lovely things in from Saison Blanche, Nicole Miller, Vera Wang, and Signature."

"Terrific. But you know, time's kind of an issue for me."

"And not wanting to be here is kind of an issue for my mom," Lara added, ignoring another toe-poke from her mother.

"Can't I just go in the back and sort of look around? It'd go a lot faster, don't you think?"

"I'm afraid that's against policy, Ms. Taylor. But we're willing to stay as late as necessary this evening to be sure you find the perfect gown."

Jeannie groaned. I couldn't blame her. If I were in her shoes, I'd probably be bored out of my mind, too. In fact, I was sort of amazed that—

(Beth)

"Sorry, what?"

Jeannie glanced at me. "What?"

"What'd you say?"

"Nothing out loud. But I was thinking all sorts of nasty things." She grinned. "What? Vampires can read minds?"

"No." Not entirely true. I could read Sinclair's mind when we were making love. In fact, it was just as well we were fated to rule for a thousand years, because he had *ruined* sex for me with anybody else.

Wait a minute! The Book of the Dead *said* we were fated to rule for a thousand years. There wasn't anything in there about Sinclair being killed before we even got officially hitched.

Why hadn't I thought of that before?

I was so excited I wanted to run out of the bridal shop and—and—well, I wasn't sure what I wanted to do, but I sure didn't want to sit there a moment longer. I—

"Here we are, Ms. Taylor." Christopher emerged from a side hall, where I knew he'd hung three or four gowns in a dressing room for me to try on. It was good timing, since the other three clerks had just left.

Concealing my excitement, I slowly got to my feet, sauntered over to Christopher, gripped him by the elbow, and murmured, "Take us to *all* the dresses."

He wheeled around like a reprogrammed robot and started

marching toward the back. Snickering, Jeannie rose and followed, and Lara followed her.

Now we were getting somewhere. That's right, everything was coming up Betsy!

Chapter 31

The salon had, at rough count, three thousand gowns in the back. I could eliminate some right off the bat. No meringue dresses. Nothing with too many beads—I hated shiny. Nothing strapless— I'd freeze my ass off. Nothing with a long train—I'd trip and make a fool of myself, guaranteed. No mermaid styles—the clingy gown that flared out from the knees.

And none of that new slutty style, either—the kind that looked like a traditional dress from the back, but from the front the skirt split just below crotch level and showed miles of leg. Not that my legs weren't fabulous. But this was a wedding . . . some decorum was called for.

I was looking for a nice, creamy ivory. Pure white was too harsh with my undead complexion. Even off-white was a little too much.

Lara went back to coloring, and Jeannie paced around the back like a caged cat. I would occasionally emerge for a thumbs-up or -down.

"No."

"Uh-uh," Lara said, glancing up from her new drawing.

"Doesn't suit you," Jeannie said when I emerged again.

"Mom's right."

And again . . . "Nope."

"Too billowy."

And again. "Your tits are just about popping out. Now, if that's the look you're going for . . ."

And again. "You're lost in all those ruffles."

"Buried," Lara agreed.

"What about some color?" Jeannie asked. Her voice was muffled, as she was pretty far in the back.

"No, I want traditional, yet fabulous."

"I don't mean all red or all blue. But how about this?" Jeannie emerged holding a cream-colored gown with a plunging-yet-not-slutty bodice, cap sleeves, an A-line style with a simple skirt that fell straight to the floor. Small red silk stars and flowers were embroidered all over the skirt and bodice.

I stared. Lara stared. Then Jeannie looked at the price tag and stared. "Fuck a duck," she said. "Never mind."

"Hold it!"

And that's how the alpha female of the Wyndham werewolves found my wedding gown.

Chapter 32

It fit you perfectly." Jeannie still couldn't get over it. We had just gotten back to the mansion. "Didn't you say you're getting married in a few days? You really lucked out. Whoever heard of an off-the-rack wedding dress that didn't need alterations?"

"Proof that it's The Gown For Me. Thanks again. If you hadn't found it, I never would have thought to ask for such a thing."

"No need to thank me, my motives were purely selfish. That's three hours of my life I didn't have to waste in that taffeta hellhole. Lara, go find your bag and get ready for bed." She turned to me. "We grabbed one of the bedrooms on the third floor, is that all right?"

"Sure. There's plenty of room up there." I glanced at my watch. Nine o'clock. I was giving serious thought to flipping through The Book of the Dead. But I was also afraid. The last time I'd tried such a stunt, I'd turned into a truly awful bitch for the better part of the evening. Hurt my friends. Hurt Sinclair. It had taken me a long, long time to forgive myself.

And there was Jeannie and Lara to think about. Michael hadn't left them in my care so I could attack them after reading the wrong chapter in the vampire bible.

Worse: the Book didn't have an index, or even a table of contents. There was no way to look anything up. I'd have to flip through it—skim as much as possible—and hope I stumbled across something helpful.

On the upside? The Book was never wrong. It had successfully predicted me, Sinclair, my powers, and come to think of it—

"My baby," I said out loud, ignoring Jeannie's curious look.

How did it go? "And the Queene shalt noe a living childe, and he shalt be hers by a living man." Yeah. That was more or less it. When Sinclair had told me at the time, it had depressed the hell out of him. He assumed it meant I'd get knocked up by someone else. But I "knew" a living child who was mine by another man . . . my father.

So The Book of the Dead had been right about a baby. It also foretold that Sinclair and I were supposed to be the king and queen for a thousand years. Did that mean I could quit worrying? That everything would work itself out?

(Beth)

"What?"

"Betsy?"

"What?"

"Your purse is ringing."

I glanced at the table where we habitually tossed our purses, wallets, and keys. Jeannie was right. My purse was ringing. I opened it and grabbed my cell.

"Hello?"

"Hey, it's me. Whoa, you actually answered your cell!"

"Hi, Jess, and yes I did. What's up?"

"I was wondering how the dress shopping went."

"Awesomely."

"I'm pretty sure that's not a word."

"Who cares? I found it."

"Great! It's still cream, right? You stayed away from the pure whites?"

"Yeah, and—"

"Great. Come on over to the hospital, will you? I've got something for you."

"You mean right now?"

"No, I mean next month. Yeah, now."

I glanced at my guests, who I assumed were more interested in going to bed than running around the oncology ward at this hour. I covered the bottom half of the phone. "Do you guys mind if I run out for a bit?"

"No," Jeannie yawned. Lara was already sleepwalking toward the stairs, a toothbrush clenched in one fist.

"Okay, Jess," I said. "I'll be there in twenty minutes."

If this is an ambush so Nick can shoot me in the head," I announced, walking into her room, "I'm going to be very upset."

"He went home to crash in a proper bed for a couple of hours. I practically had to call Security to get him out of here."

"Well. He's worried about you, the fascist."

"He'll get over this latest, uh, wrinkle." Jessica didn't look—or sound—at all sure of herself. In fact, she looked generally ghastly. The new round of chemo was not being kind. And as I'd said, Jessica couldn't afford to lose any weight. But she was smiling and had an expression on her face I knew well: Jessica had a secret.

"You mean the whole mind-rape thing? He *hates* me. And Sinclair."

Jess didn't bother denying it; we'd been friends for too long to take refuge in false comfort. "But he loves me. We'll figure something out. First things first. I've got your wedding present."

She opened the drawer to her right and took out a shoe box wrapped in heavy white paper and topped with a pale blue bow.

I smiled in anticipation. Jessica was rich and had great taste. Even better, she knew what I liked. I plucked off the bow and stuck it to her forehead, ripped off the gorgeous paper, and flipped the lid off the box.

And stared. Inside the box were a pair of Filippa Scott Rosie bridal shoes in the exact shade of my dress (the cream-colored part, that was). I knew she hadn't bought them for less than four hundred bucks. I also knew they were handmade with duchesse satin, with a padded foot bed that meant even with three-inch heels, they'd be comfortable. And the slim bow across the front was just the right touch.

"Oh my God," I said.

"I know," Jessica said smugly, reclining in her hospital bed like a goddess being fed grapes.

"They're perfect."

"I know."

I burst into tears.

"Whoa. Hey!" Jess shot upright, then gagged, and for a minute I thought she'd barf on me while I wept into the shoe box. We both struggled to control ourselves, but only Jessica won the battle. "This really wasn't the reaction I was going for."

I cried harder.

"Betsy, what's wrong? Is it Nick? We'll figure something out. We're going to have to. But I don't think he'd really try to hurt you."

"It's Nick," I sobbed, hiding my face with the box. "It's every-thing."

"What everything?"

So I told her.

Chapter 33

Wow."

"I know," I sniffed.

"*Wow.*"

"I know."

"Why didn't you—never mind. I know why you didn't say anything." She propped her chin in her palm and stared past me. "This stinks to high heaven."

"Yeah. I don't know what to do."

"Well, he's not dead." She said this with such authority that I instantly cheered up. "No chance. No chance."

"Why? He's *not* immortal."

"Why? Because he's Sink-Lair, that's why! You think he's easy to kill? You think you wouldn't *know* if your king was dead? He's stuck somewhere. Some asshole snatched him, and you've gotta figure out who."

"That's what I've been trying to do."

"Yeah, so you said. It's not the werewolves, it's not Delk. It's not Laura. It's—what did you say Nick told you? To go back to the beginning?"

"Yeah."

"So when did things start to get weird?"

I thought about it. I took my time, and Jessica let me. It wasn't the fight we'd had over the wedding announcements. Sinclair and I fought all the time. What was the first really weird thing to—

"The double funeral," I said at last. "That's when I realized things were mondo-bizarro. It was like one day everything was the way it's been the last couple of years, and the next, I was alone.

You were sick. Dad and the Ant were dead. Tina was in Europe. Mark had disappeared. Laura and Mom blew off the funeral. Antonia and Garrett had vamoosed."

"You think your dad and the Ant weren't killed by accident?"

"Who'd want to get rid of them? I've been so busy I haven't had time to feel sad. If someone was trying to hurt me, that's not really the way to do it. I guess that makes me a bad daughter, but—"

"But your dad was a pud," Jessica said bluntly, "and that's the end of it."

"I'm wondering if there might be some answers in the Book of the—"

"You stay away from that thing," she ordered. "You going psycho-bitch isn't going to help anything."

I sighed and slumped back. "I suppose."

"Tina called it right. This whole thing reeks like last week's sushi. I wish you would have told me earlier."

"You've got more important things to worry about."

"Oh, what's more important than my best friend?" she asked irritably.

"Your life," I replied. "Focus on getting better."

"Well, today was the last day of chemo. So I ought to be able to come to the wedding without heaving all over my suit. If I have to be dragged in on a stretcher and propped up like Hannibal Lecter, I'll be there," she vowed.

"Revolting," I said. "Yet comforting."

Chapter 34

I dragged myself into the silent house. The third floor was dark; I assumed Lara and Jeannie had hit the sheets. But this wasn't the week to make assumptions, so I tiptoed up to the third floor and found them in the second bedroom I checked. They were both conked and both snoring. I shut the door and snuck back downstairs.

I kicked off my pumps, tossed my keys in the general direction of the foyer table, then went into the library and sat down across from the Book of the Dead.

The nasty thing was on a mahogany book stand by the fireplace, open to God knew what page. I stared at it and tried to make a decision. *Any* decision.

"You might as well," a horrifyingly familiar voice said from across the room. "You can't screw this up any worse."

I looked over, and there she was: Laura's mother, the devil, seated behind the desk.

"Fabulous," I muttered.

"So nice to see you, too, dear." Satan looked a lot like Lena Olin: long brown hair streaked with silver. Calm expression, beautiful gray suit, classic gold earrings (in the shape of angel wings!), black stockings, and . . . I peeked under the desk. And groaned silently. She was wearing fourteen-thousand-dollar Manolo Blahnik black alligator boots. "Like them?" She rotated her left foot around her ankle. "I'm sure we could work something out."

"Get lost."

"Now, Betsy. You need me. After all, you're not using that

teeny, tiny brain of yours. In fact, you haven't been since this whole thing started."

"And what do you know about it? Scratch that: go away." I wasn't the brightest bulb in the chandelier, but I knew that the devil never gave up anything for free. I was crazy even to be talking to her.

"Oh, Betsy. Don't you know? I can help you. I *want* to help you. Him?" She jerked a thumb toward the ceiling. "Not so much. You think He cares about you now that you're a vampire?"

"I think you lie like old people fart."

"I've never lied to *you*, dear."

I had to admit that was true. Not that I was going to say so out loud.

"It distresses me to see my daughter's sister so upset. So alone in the world. Beset from all sides."

"Really."

"I'll help you, dear. All you need do is ask."

"How about if I ask you to toddle off back to Hell?"

Lena Olin made a *tt'tt!* noise and shook her head sorrowfully, as if at a disobedient daughter. "Why make things so much more difficult? You know I can help you."

"I know nothing's free with you, Lena Olin."

"Let me help you. I'm *dying* to help you. He's still alive, you know. It's not too late . . . yet."

That hurt. A lot. I closed my eyes and chewed on my tongue so I wouldn't say something that would cost me my soul.

"I'll be glad to lend a hand. Because once you have your lover back, you'll stop thinking the worst of my poor Laura. I dislike it when the two of you argue."

I grunted.

"All you need to do is ignore Him and pray to me."

I nearly fell out of my chair. "Pray to *you*?"

"Well, why not? You've seen the state of His world, right?" she said with a gesture. "Your best friend fighting for her life? Your father dead in a senseless accident? Your brother orphaned? You alone in your time of greatest need? And let's not even talk about all the children He does away with every hour of every day. Who knows how long BabyJon has under His regime? Pray to *me*, dear. At least I'm not crazy."

"That's tempting," I said. "Really tempting."

She smiled and smoothed her hair. "We try."

"Well, try this. Take your satanic, designer-shoe-wearing ass right out the door, willya?"

The devil frowned. "Betsy, this is a chance that may never come again."

"Bullshit! You show up whenever I'm in a jam, but I'm not dumb enough to think you care about me. You're *the devil*, for crying out loud! Your reputation is *horrible!* Now get lost!"

She stood. It seemed to take a long time. It seemed like she was ten feet tall. "Enjoy the funerals, dear. Because without my help, there will be more. And say hello to my dear one when you see her again."

I opened my mouth to say something snappy, but I was alone in the room.

Chapter 35

It took me about ten minutes to stop shaking. It had never been so hard to tell Lena no. Sure, my soul would sizzle in the bowels of Hell for eternity, but on the other hand, I was going to live for at least another thousand years. I wouldn't have to worry about Hell for a long time.

And I believed her when she said she could help me. She wouldn't have shown up here if she couldn't help me. Even now, I was tempted to yell for her, call her back, make a deal . . .

Had she said *funerals*, as in plural?

The desk extension rang, and I nearly jumped out the window. What now? I snatched up the receiver. "Hello?"

"Betsy? It's Mom."

"Hi, Mom. You're up late."

"BabyJon had a late nap," she said ruefully. "But I don't have anything scheduled for tomorrow, so we can sleep late."

"That's good."

"So . . . how are you?"

"Not so good," I admitted. "Things are kind of a mess." *And I deeply, deeply covet Satan's footwear.*

"I'm sorry," she said at once. "I can relate to what you're saying, hon, make no mistake. Do you believe the funeral announcement didn't come out until yesterday? I could have sworn I made the newspaper's deadline, but they said I missed it by twenty-four hours."

"What? You mean Dad and the Ant's funeral?"

"Isn't that stupid? My point is, I've been a bit of a scatterbrain since the accident. And I know I made things harder for you at exactly the wrong time. My only excuse is . . . I don't really know. It's not like I was still in love with your father. I guess I wasn't ready to say good-bye forever. Not so soon after *you* died, anyway."

"I didn't think about it that way," I said. "I guess I shouldn't have been such a jerk."

"Your father died, dear. You were entitled."

"Well, I wasn't there by myself. So how did Dad's coworkers know to be there?"

"Oh, I'd called your dad's secretary—Lorraine?—the day I heard about the accident. And I guess she called the others. And you know your stepmother wasn't averse to using Lorraine for her charity work. That's how her friends knew to come. And of course, I had called you myself."

"Yeah, I remember." Something was bumping my brain like a minnow nudging a weed. It was great that my mom had called, great that she had apologized, great that we were patching things up. Why, then, did I feel so weird? Sort of sick to my stomach and excited at the same time? I was filled with a kind of happy dread, if there was such a thing.

"I thought I'd bring the baby to see Jessica tomorrow," Mom was saying.

I barely heard her. *Start at the beginning. The funeral was the beginning. There was no announcement. So the only people there, would have been people who* knew . . . *who knew* . . .

"I'll visit during afternoon hours if you'd like to join us . . ."

"MARJORIE!" I shouted and heard the receiver crunch as I squeezed it too hard.

Chapter 36

Jeannie and Lara were still conked, and thank goodness. With zero traffic and a lead foot, I made it to the Minneapolis warehouse district in record time, my knuckles white on the steering wheel. I had to be very careful not to bend it out of shape, or even pull it off.

It had been so thoughtful of Marjorie to pay her respects at my father's funeral. Marjorie, in fact, seemed to enjoy being helpful in all sorts of ways. Marjorie, the eight-hundred-year-old vampire who disdained politics.

Why had she come? To see how I was bearing up under all the pressure she was bringing? To try to get a whiff of my pain? To throw me off her scent?

I didn't know. But I was going to find out.

I pulled up outside a dilapidated warehouse, which I knew was beautiful and spacious inside, filled with thousands of books and state-of-the-art computers. Marjorie's digs. Her lair. *Fucking she-spider.*

I didn't bother knocking, just shoved the big double doors open and stomped inside. Like all important confrontations in my life, this one was anticlimactic. Marjorie was nowhere to be found.

The place looked the way it usually did . . . lots of low lighting, comfortable chairs, benches. Lots of conference tables and chairs. Row after row of computers. Quiet as a grave (really!), and smelling like reams and reams of old paper. Oh, and dust. And Pledge!

Well, a case of Pledge wasn't going to stop *me*. It wasn't even going to slow me down. I'd—

(Elizabeth)

"Eric?" I whispered. That tiny voice in the back of my brain, previously so faint I couldn't make out who it was, or even what it was saying, was now quite a bit clearer.

I sniffed. Stupid Lemon Pledge, I wasn't getting anything but—I sniffed harder. Ah! There we go. Yep. Sinclair had been here. Was maybe still here. I stiffened like an English setter on point, then followed the scent through several doorways and down two flights of stairs into a dank basement.

My heels didn't make a sound on the carpeted stairs, which was fine with me, as I was busy trying to look in fifteen directions at once. Had Sinclair really been one town over the entire time? And where was she keeping him, that I could barely hear him? What had she done to him?

The place didn't *look* like a torture chamber. It looked like what it was: an old library, well-maintained, with plenty of money for books and computers. Heck, plenty of money for fluorescent lights as opposed to, say, torches sticking out of the wall.

I finished with the stairs and slid open the huge door in front of me—down there, at least, the place looked like a warehouse. The door rattled past me, and the smell of mildew and sweat assaulted my delicate, queenish nostrils.

The first thing I saw was Antonia in a spacious cage, the kind they used to cage Dr. Lecter in *The Silence of the Lambs*. She was shaking the bars, and I remembered how claustrophobic she was. Her dark hair was matted with sweat, and her face was pale; she stank to high heaven, and her clothes were filthy. Her big eyes rolled toward me, like an animal in a killing pen, and she greeted me with a shrieked, "Get me *out!*"

Then I saw the coffins. Two of them, chained shut and draped with . . . were those *rosaries?* Yes. Dozens, covering almost every inch of the top of the coffins.

(Elizabeth)

I ran to the one nearest me and stripped the rosaries away, then yanked at the chains until they tore and bent in my hands. I didn't know how Marjorie had placed them—wearing asbestos gloves, maybe? I didn't care. I just had to get him out and face whatever hunger and crosses had done to him.

"Me first, me first, me firrrrsssssstttt!"

I flipped the top off the coffin and bit back a scream. Sinclair, yes. Incredibly wizened, incredibly old. Shrunken. Dried out. His lips were drawn back so his fangs were prominent. He looked a thousand years old. He looked dead.

"Oh my God!" I cried. "Oh, Sinclair! Tell me what to do! How can I—"

"Did your mother never teach you to call before dropping by? Oh, I'm prepared to validate your parking whenever you wish. How clever of you to park right out in the open like that."

I spun so fast I nearly went sprawling. Marjorie was descending the last of the steps; I'd been so caught up in freeing Sinclair I'd never heard her.

"You *cunt*."

"You infant."

"Why?" I had to yell to be heard over Antonia's howls of rage. She was unusually bitchy during the full moon during the best of times . . . which this certainly was not. "Why did you do this?"

"You made it necessary."

I wanted to cry. I wanted to scream. I wanted to punch her sly face in. "What the hell does that even mean?"

She stepped into the room, looking neat and trim in her tweed suit and sensible shoes. "He can't keep you in line. Case in point, your monthly newspaper column. Your autobiography, the fall fiction offering! You live your life openly—everyone around you knows your true nature. You collect people instead of living a solitary life. This is incredibly dangerous, to all you claim to rule. You left me no choice."

"You don't agree with the way I live my life, and so you do *this?*"

"As I said, you forced me to."

"Oh, right. Kidnapping, false imprisonment, torture. Blame *me*."

She shrugged. "Unlike you, I do what must be done. Unlike him, I'm not besotted with your dubious charms. By keeping Sinclair under my control, I'll be able to keep you under control. Because someone has to take charge. And you clearly aren't up to it."

"But—but—"

"I have him. I'll keep him. And I'll kill him the moment you don't do as I say."

"But I am the queen!"

"You're a fluke. An accident. And now, you'll be my tool."

She followed my glance into the open coffin. Sinclair was still doing his impersonation of a wizened mummy. "I knew he wouldn't go along with my idea. So I needed him to come and see me. He brought these two—unexpected, but I could deal with them." She glared at Antonia, who was making an ungodly amount of noise rattling her bars.

"But why would he come see you so quickly?"

Her eyes narrowed. "Because I had information for him. Information is power; libraries are full of power. I can change records, reveal deaths, make up new ones, transfer ownership. I can change the facts, change history, if I like. I can grow my own power base and even presume to be queen myself someday, if I like. Eventually, I can discard you on the rubbish heap of rumor and misinformation. Betsy Taylor was no queen—she was a pretender, or a prophet, or whatever I'd like to make her. Who, exactly, will dispute the facts with me? The only vampires old enough to know better are in Europe. Would they argue if you die? If Sinclair did?"

I was trying to follow all this. "What information did you tell him you had?"

"I told him your engagement ring was cursed."

"And he *fell* for that?"

"Of course. Because it is."

"Aw, say it isn't so." I examined my diamond and ruby ring. "Cursed how?"

"Did you ever read *The Monkey's Paw?*"

"In high school."

"What a pleasant surprise. Here I thought I'd have to show you the picture book. Well, as in that story, your ring grants wishes. But always at a cost. You see, the stones were stolen from an Egyptian tomb. They followed quite a path before they got to me. I split them up and spread their pieces around the world. For research purposes.

"One actually made it back to me here years ago, set in a beautiful antique ring. I buried it far enough away where it couldn't hurt me, but where I could still find it if I thought it might come in handy. And so it did, when Sinclair actually came to me a few months ago and asked me if I knew of any special jewelry he could give you for engagement purposes!" She laughed. "He actually paid me a quarter of a million dollars for it. I couldn't wait to see what you wished for."

A thousand thoughts were whirling through my brain. The zombie, who showed up without explanation three months ago. Tina and Sinclair had tried, and failed, to figure out why it had come. They hadn't even known zombies existed. A total mystery, unsolved until now. But hadn't I wished for a real challenge when the Europeans were in town? A way to prove to myself that I was worthy of my title?

I had wished for everyone to go away and leave me alone—I had never felt more isolated than this past week.

And I had wished for a baby of my own. And then my father . . . and the Ant . . .

"Oh God," I moaned. I was fairly certain I was going to pass out. *I* had killed my father! *My father!* (And the Ant.)

"So, seeing the new opportunity the ring afforded, I then breathlessly contacted the king and told him I had done more research on the stones and found out unpleasant facts. Naturally he came on the run." She frowned at the other coffin. "With company."

I figured Antonia must have had a last-minute psychic flash and either accompanied Sinclair, or followed him. And Garrett had followed her. What a cluster-fuck.

"Apparently she tried to talk him out of coming, but of course Sinclair is sensitive to vampire courtesy, and my great age. And came anyway. And so here we are."

"You bitch."

"Yes, yes. Now. Let's discuss my first orders to you."

I dove at her. Well, the wall, as she neatly sidestepped. "Don't be tiresome," she snapped. "You won't best me. Sinclair is incapacitated, and without him by your side, you are a nothing. A typo. No one has been able to harm me for over five hundred years. You—ow."

I had punched her in the back and felt her ribs splinter. But fast as a snake, she'd gotten a grip on my arm and thrown me into the wall. I felt my nose break as it made brisk contact with the concrete.

I spun and slapped her so hard she staggered sideways, and I managed to avoid her elbow. I was going to kill this bitch *twice*. Not because she was a duplicitous cow. Not because she was trying to hurt and manipulate me. I was going to kill her for what she had done to him.

I heard a crunch as my knee broke, and I hobbled sideways, swiping at her with my good leg. With a grunt she went down, but before I could blink she was back on her feet, hoisting her sensible librarian skirt up and kicking me in the same knee that was still trying to grow back.

I shrieked and flung myself at her. I was bigger and managed to force her to the floor, then shrieked louder as her fist explored my spleen. I rolled away, fairly certain I was going to puke, then felt her on my back as she slammed my head against the wall.

"This is foolish," she said in my ear. "All you need do is fall in line, and we can get down to the business of governing the vampire nation properly."

I whipped my head back, smiling at the crunch of her nose breaking. I jerked an elbow back, but only caught air. I felt her hands on me, and she pushed, hard. My teeth broke as I hit the concrete again.

Hmm. Getting the shit kicked out of me was no fun at all. I bit back a howl as she twisted an arm so hard, it broke in two places.

(Elizabeth, get away.)

Shut up, Sinclair. I turned just in time to catch a librarian fist in the face, and there went more teeth. I coughed up blood and spat it right in her face.

"Oh, dear! Not . . . *blood*." She laughed at me and licked her lips, her fangs appearing like needles springing from her gums. I slapped her again, and she shook it off, then punched me in the gut. I bent, gagging, and she grabbed my head and twisted.

I just managed to get an arm up before she broke my neck, and we moved around the basement in a flailing dance. Then she stomped on my foot with her sensible soles, and I felt a few more bones break and lost my balance. I went down, and she was right on top of me.

She had both hands around my neck and was squeezing and yanking my head up and down. The squeezing didn't bother me so much (I didn't need the breath) but every time she slammed my head into the floor I heard another fracture. It sounded like someone was crunching ice in my ear. It hurt, *and* it was annoying.

Slam. Slam. Slam. I brought my legs up to wrap them around her neck, but she simply leaned forward and fractured my skull again. And things were getting a little dark in here. I didn't think it was the ambiance. Nope, she was killing me. I'd been stumbling around like an idiot since Sinclair disappeared, had the clue in front of me the whole time,

(Go back to the beginning.)

finally figured out who the bad guy was, and for my trouble? She was kicking my ass sideways. It hurt like hell and was fairly humiliating.

"And to think—I thought—you'd be—reasonable." Bitch wasn't even out of breath! Each pause was punctuated by another head slam. I was getting killed by a scrawny suit-wearing woman with graying hair. And sensible shoes!

Black roses were blooming in front of my eyes, and all of a sudden things hurt less. Hmm. Stakes hadn't killed me, and neither had bullets. But if an older vampire did enough damage (particularly to my head), if an older vampire pretty much tore my freaking head off, it seemed that would do the trick. Fine way to find out.

It was all right, though. It really was. I'd been floundering around in the dark for so long, it seemed appropriate that things were going dark for real. She was right; I was no queen. Look how easy she'd led me by the nose, and for how long. Heck, she'd been able to fool Sinclair!

(Elizabeth, get away. Run!)

Easy for *him* to say; he was napping in a nice comfy coffin.

No, it was probably for the best. My dad was dead, practically by my own hand. I'd probably have screwed up BabyJon beyond repair. Antonia had apparently gone completely nuts from the stress of being locked up most of the week. God knew what state poor Garrett was in. Jessica was a goner—you only had to look at the weight dropping off her to see it. And Sinclair—

If this bitch killed me, he was dead meat.

If this bitch killed me, there was no stopping her from hurting anyone she liked. My family. My friends. Sinclair.

The back of my head was sticky with blood; it was running down my face. I had a hundred broken bones; three of my ribs were gone. Not broken. Gone. Blood was draining from me. I had never been so . . .

hungry?

. . . in my life. Never. I needed to drink, and I couldn't. I needed to live, and I wouldn't. But Marjorie had power and energy to spare; the most I'd been able to inflict on her were defense wounds.

Marjorie had power and energy to spare.

Marjorie.

I reached for her. Not with my hands. Not with my teeth. With my mind. Even as everything faded to black I could sense her energy, her strength, and I grabbed for it like a fat kid grabs for pie. And just like a fat kid, my chubby mental fingers crushed her tinfoil skin, and my chubby mental eyes gleamed at the crumbling, steaming crust.

"*Unh,*" I heard her grunt. She let go of me, her head tossing in confusion. Something had a hold of her and wasn't letting go. I rolled over to see who it was.

There was no one else there. But that didn't matter, because just seeing her like this was making me feel a bit stronger. The black blooms vanished, and I could see again. Her limbs thrashed as the chubby, pie-loving child inside of me poked at her to see what kind of fruit filling was inside.

Mmmmm. Blood pie.

Without touching her, I began to drink.

She screamed and fell to her knees.

No one else is doing it, I realized with more alacrity as the blood rushed into my system. *Just the Queen. The Queen of the Fucking Vampires.* Her *Queen. And her Queen requires her goddamn, fucking obedience. She has something, I need it, it's mine.*

Mine!

The darling pie-loving child was gone now. I split her open with my mind, grabbed for her, and pulled *everything* she had into me.

Her suit emptied—the blood first, then the shriveling muscles, then the flaying bits of dried skin, and then the billions of splinters of bone.

By the time I was done, I was standing tall over a librarian's suit, a librarian's sensible shoes, and about twenty grams of dust. I felt absolutely fine.

In fact, I had never felt fucking better in my life.

Chapter 37

Power slammed through me, and I screamed. Well, not so much screamed as roared. I felt energy running through my spine like a waterfall; the overload of *good* was becoming worse than the beating. I staggered away from Marjorie's remains and nearly fell into Sinclair's coffin. I grabbed him and *poured* some of the new strength I had into him; it was either get rid of it or blow up.

Even as he stirred, grew younger, grew strong, sat up, it wasn't enough, I was still going to blow.

I stumbled away from Sinclair, kicked Marjorie's things (and probably a bit of old Marjorie, too, poor thing) out of the way, and reached for Antonia through the bars and *poured* more of it into her.

I was not entirely sure what I was doing and yet wasn't even shocked when Antonia screamed again, a scream that turned into a howl. She dropped to all fours, sprouted dark brown fur, and then an enraged werewolf was howling at the ceiling and tearing at the bars with her teeth.

No fair! I thought. *You're not supposed to be allowed to do that. Rule breaker!*

"Elizabeth!" Someone was shaking me. "Elizabeth! Whatever you're doing, *stop it!* It's too much, you're—"

Through blurred vision I saw Antonia-the-wolf tear through the bars with her teeth and wondered vaguely what the hell a werewolf's teeth were made of. *Titanium?* In no time at all she'd torn or pulled a big enough hole through the bars and wormed through, then attacked the other coffin with desperate savagery. The rosaries flew off, and she started to rip at the chains.

Getting some of my mind back, I began to help her. Well, by began I mean I flipped the coffin lid open as though the chains weren't there, stuck my hands inside, and poured everything I had onto the shriveled thing inside.

In a few seconds, Garrett was sitting up and looking around.

"Wow, I feel terrific! Um. What the hell just happened?" he asked, sounding quite un-Garrett-like.

Whoever had tried to shake me before—that would be Sinclair, right? Sure, I could see him now, it was Sinclair.

Hey, he looks good! I made him all right. That's nice. Now if I could just do something about this force inside of me that feels like it wants to split my skin . . .

"Elizabeth!" His eyes were wide with awe and fear. "Elizabeth, what are you doing?"

And I was still burning up, still exploding, there was still too much of whatever I had taken from Marjorie in me, on me, all over me, around me.

I had an idea, but I knew I only had a few moments of conscious thought left. So I leaned into Sinclair, making him wince with the touch, and whispered my instructions into his ear.

He nodded. "Yes, my queen."

"Hurry," I finished, and then I collapsed to the ground, wreathed in flames.

Chapter 38

"—maybe we should—"

"—so glad to see all of—"

"—doctor wouldn't do any—"

"—hurt bad?"

I opened my eyes and bit back a shriek. Sinclair, Marc, Tina, and Garrett were all bending over me. I chased them all back with big arm motions and sat up. I saw at once we were in the hospital.

But had we gotten here in time?

"Where is she?" I managed. Then Sinclair's mouth was on mine, his arms were around me, and I sort of forgot about all the madness of the evening for a minute.

"Wait, wait!" I fended him off and looked around. We were in the right room, I thought. But they all looked alike. "Did it work? Where is she?"

"It's so wonderful to see you're all right, Your Majesty!"

I smiled as I turned to Tina. "When did you two get here?"

"I got home an hour ago," she said, the circles under her eyes even darker than usual. "Marc had just shown up, and then Sinclair called. Um. Why is Antonia a wolf?"

"You wouldn't believe it if I told you."

"Elizabeth did it, right after she destroyed Marjorie. And nearly killed herself for her trouble." Sinclair turned to me—well, really, he turned *on* me, like a wolverine. "Did you not hear me telling you to stay away?" he demanded, shaking me like a cheap Christmas present.

"Oh, stuff it in your socks, Sinclair. Like I was going to leave you in the clutches of the librarian from Hell. What a *bitch*."

"You're sure you're okay?" Marc, being the doctor he was, began to prod my body.

"I—think so." I felt all right. Almost normal. Normal for me, I meant. Gone was the frantic surge of energy I'd feared would consume me.

And from the way they were looking at me, they all knew it. Their expressions were equal parts awe and fear.

But *what* about . . .

"Well, I have to say, I haven't felt this good in quite some time," Garrett said cheerfully. Since he usually spoke in monosyllables, this was going to take some getting used to. "Although I'm not sure what Antonia will say when she's back on two feet tomorrow morning."

"Yeesh, don't give me something new to worry about. By the way, did you notice if the two guests in our house were still there? Are they okay?"

"Jeannie and Lara are fine," Marc said. He was dressed in a shirt studded with big purple flowers, muddy khaki shorts, and sandals. "I made their acquaintance a bit abruptly in the bathroom; but we sorted it out as Tina arrived. After Sinclair called, it was clear the danger was pretty much over, so they opted to stay in the mansion."

"Great. Now that we've accounted for everyone EXCEPT the person we came for, *can someone please tell me where my best friend is!?!*"

This got a couple of them smiling. Which got me steaming even hotter. Finally, Marc piped up. "Well, we got you here, and your boyfriend did what you told him to do. He dumped you right on top of Jessica, who until then was resting comfortably. By then, you weren't in flames anymore—but you were still giving off tons of heat and sweat. Seeing you roll back and forth on top of Jessica in her bed—well, I'll tell you. I almost turned heterosexual."

"But the bed's empty now! Did it work? Is she okay?"

"Better than okay," Tina said, smiling. She was flushed at Marc's description, but she managed to motion to the hallway. "After Detective Berry's initial shock, he saw what we were doing for Jessica and kept you on top of her. Once she was—once you were both okay—well, Jessica and Nick wanted to find some privacy, and we were all in the room, and you still looked like you needed the bed, and so—"

My jaw dropped in appalled outrage. "She's out *getting some?*"

"In a word," Tina began.

"Yeppers," Marc finished.

"Why that—that—"

"They're still somewhere in the hospital," Sinclair gently corrected me.

As if on cue, Jessica and Nick burst into the room (well, burst through the slowly opening door), giggling and leaning on each other. She was still in her wrinkled hospital gown, and his shirt was decidedly untucked from his pants. No socks. No shoes.

"Well, that was—" She saw all of us waiting for her and clammed up.

"Short?" Marc volunteered.

I knew the moment I saw her that it was gone. For good. She looked beautiful.

I stared. We all stared. Finally, Marc cleared his throat and said, "How are you feeling, Jessica?"

Beaming, she pulled away from Nick and spread her arms wide. "I feel *great*. But I'm super-duper hungry. Anybody have a candy bar in their pocket? Or possibly a steak?"

Finally, she turned to me, still grinning like a fool. "Bets, you look like shit. What happened?"

Chapter 39

Sinclair carried me up to bed the moment we got home, which was silly because I could walk perfectly well. I was pretty sure. Actually, given that it was only about 1:00 a.m. I was awfully tired.

The last thing I felt before I conked off was him pulling my engagement ring off my finger. I hope he threw it into the nearest sewer. Boy, was I going to give him a piece of my mind when I . . .

I sat up. The bedside clock said 5:30 p.m. Sinclair was at his desk, scribbling on papers, but looked up and was at my side in half a second.

"Elizabeth—"

"Dead."

"—are you—"

"You are so *dead.*"

"—all right?"

"You gave me a *used* engagement ring?" I yelped.

He looked pained as he sat down beside me. "Antique."

"Used."

"As you like. I am very sorry."

I slumped back against the pillows and slapped a hand over my eyes. "You couldn't have known. Friendly helpful Marjorie, right?"

"I thought a ring set with stones that had belonged to a queen would be a fitting gift."

"Zombie. Dead dad. Dead stepmother. Well, the dead step-mother might actually not be so bad . . . but then YOU almost died!"

"I am very sorry."

I removed my hand and looked at him. His fierce dark gaze was boring into me, and his hands were trembling. "Oh, hey. Like I said. You couldn't have known. You got rid of it, right?"

"I did. I—"

"Never mind. I don't care if I never see the thing again, and I sure don't want to know what you did with it. Also, we're going to Tiffany's to pick out a new one, right?"

"If you wish."

"You look like hell."

"I was . . . terrified for you. I was certain she would kill you. And I was useless. Worse than useless. I could hear what was happening but could not help. I—"

"Come here," I said. "Have I mentioned I missed you like crazy?"

"Not that I recall."

"Well, I have. Missed you like crazy, I mean." I was tugging at his shirt, and buttons were flying all over the place. "Place just isn't the same without you. And hey! Next time the Big Bad lures you out of the house, maybe you could leave a note?"

"Or even text-message you," he agreed solemnly. I was frantic to get his clothes off, frantic to touch him, feel him, taste him. I heard cloth tear as I got his shirt off, broke his belt buckle, tore at his pants.

I gripped his hips with my knees and knelt down to have a bite or two. Or three. Oh boy, oh boy, oh boy!

"Oh boy," he groaned.

It was so fucking fine to have him in my house, my bed. It was everything I'd missed and then some. It was a dream come true.

(For me as well, my own.)

And oh, it was so good to feel him against me, his hands on me. I pulled at him until we were both sitting up, me still on top, and we kissed hungrily, as if we couldn't get enough air. Or enough of each other. He pushed and I went over . . .

. . . and then I pushed, and I was back on top again.

Mine, I thought.

Yours, he agreed.

I straddled him to get closer, to take him inside of me, and rode him with great delight, staring at the ceiling while his fingers dug into my hip bones. He nipped at my fingers, and I swooped down to kiss him again.

Oh, Sinclair.

Elizabeth. My own, my queen, my dread queen.

Wait a minute. Are we—?

I beg you. Do not destroy the moment with a rude gesture or thought.

But we're—

Yes.

You can—

Yes.

I love you.

Yes. Oh, yes. Right . . .

. . . there.

Chapter 40

Here comes the bride," I hummed, slipping into my shoes. "All dressed in white. (And red.) Here comes the bride, back from the dead. (Again.)"

"That song blows." Jessica leaned over my shoulder to freshen her lipstick with my mirror. "And don't get me started on your singing voice."

"Cured your cancer and all I get is grief."

"Hey, I didn't *make* you cure me. By the way, is it just me or is everyone still *freaked out* about what you did the other night?"

"Yeah, well. I'm not exactly sure what it is I did."

"Neither are Sinclair or Tina. That's why it's driving them nuts."

"Not to mention Michael and the others," Antonia piped up, coming into the dressing room without knocking, as was her habit. "They're gonna walk soft around you for a while. Heh. Oh, and bimbo? Next time you've got two dead guys in coffins and me in a cage, lively and ready to kick ass, let *me* out first! I could have helped you with that rotten monkey Marjorie."

"I'll keep it in mind."

"Least now I know what the fuss is all about," she muttered, waving away Jessica's offer of a mascara wand. "Running around as a wolf is *fun*." She fussed with her lapels and managed only to hopelessly rumple her ruby jacket. "But you know? I haven't had a vision since the one indicating Sinclair shouldn't go to Marjorie's alone. I wonder if I can still see the future."

"Well," I said, feeling uncomfortable, "if you can't, and you miss it, I'm sorry. I didn't—"

"Can it, Betsy. I'm not bitching. Just wondering."

"Will you hold still?" Jessica demanded. Her suit, a twin to Antonia's, was sapphire blue. "You're all rumpled."

"And you're all annoying, but I'm putting up with that shit, aren't I? I'm here in the middle of monkey rituals, aren't I?"

"Shut up," I said warmly.

Tina rapped on the door, then poked her head inside. "It's almost time, Majesty. My! You're breathtaking."

"It's true," I said modestly. Tina was in the same Vera Wang suit as Jessica and Antonia, except hers was buttercup yellow. With Tina's teeny frame and big dark eyes, and cascades of blond hair, it worked.

Everything worked. It was my day, and everything worked.

I sighed happily and applied more blush. "Hey, did Sinclair talk to you about the new job?"

"What new job?" Jessica asked.

"We need a new librarian," I told my reflection, and grinned. "The last one came down with a slight case of death."

"I have many responsibilities here in the mansion," Tina said. "I will have to consider this very carefully."

"Crissake, when don't you consider everything very carefully?" Antonia yawned and—I wasn't sure how she did this without moving—rumpled her suit jacket again.

"But the chance to get my hands on all those tomes . . ." Tina was practically drooling. "The opportunity for pure research alone makes it a tempting prize."

"Yeah, yeah. Tempting. Betsy, lighten up with the Peach Parfait or you'll be all slutted out."

"Here, let *me*." Jessica snatched the blusher from my hands and grabbed a tissue with the other hand. She rubbed my cheeks, and for an awful moment I thought she was going to spit on the Kleenex.

"Hmm," Tina said. That was all, just, "Hmm."

"How can you screw up blush?" Jessica was bitching. "You make it look like you're blushing. Then you stop."

"Hmm."

"Will all of you bitches just leave me alone?" I cried.

"The warning cry of the Raptor Bridal Bird," Antonia snickered.

"Look how snotty you got since you found out you are able to turn into a wolf."

"And when your boyfriend remembered how to read. Oh, and that he has a master's in math."

"That's it!" Tina cried, startling all of us into shutting up. "You never feed, Majesty, compared to us you never feed. So you're always hungry. Always. You think that's how it's supposed to be. For you, hunger is as much a state of the mind as it is of the body. So when Marjorie was killing you, your instinct wasn't to reach with your teeth. It was to *reach with your mind!*"

She was on her feet, screeching that last.

Antonia stared. I stared. Jessica corrected my blush.

"Um. Excuse me," she muttered, smoothing her skirt.

My mom poked her head in the room. "Are you ready?"

"Yeah," Antonia replied.

"I think she was talking to me," I said.

"Oh, yeah, like it's all about you."

"Today it is. Let's do it!"

You may kiss the bride," Judge Summit informed us, and Sinclair was too glad to comply. He'd done a remarkable job of concealing his boredom during the brief ceremony, though his dark eyes had gleamed at the sight of me in my gown.

The guests (all the usual suspects, plus the Wyndhams) clapped politely and, as we went back down the aisle, tossed little paper hearts instead of rice.

"They're throwing paper hearts? At vampires?" Sinclair bitched.

"Oh, hush up and try to enjoy the moment."

But why didn't you tell me you thought there'd be a problem with Sinclair going to see Marjorie?" I asked while the others devoured the chocolate cake (with raspberry filling!) and I tried not to drool. Too bad solid food made me barf.

"She dealt with the problem directly," Michael explained. "She teamed up with the alpha male and tried to support him. Going to you would have been . . ."

"Useless?" I offered.

"Unnecessary," Antonia corrected me, but her cheeks were red. She had underestimated how much I could help, and who could blame her? I wouldn't have thought I could do much, either.

At least not until today.

"Culture clash," Derik said cheerfully, wolfing down his second slice of cake. "Antonia has spent too much time with you vampires. A true werewolf would have sought to put together the largest pack possible."

"Yeah, well, a true werewolf can kiss my ass," Antonia offered.

"You are a true werewolf," Michael pointed out. "You always have been."

"Come on, Pack leader. Don't deny there'll be some at home who will finally decide I'm actually worthy of the secret handshake."

Michael said nothing, but Derik broke the tension by showering Antonia in cake crumbs.

"Anyway," Tina put in, batting a few wayward crumbs out of her hair, "everything worked out fine that day, thanks to Her Majesty. Now people will know better than to ask you, Eric, when they need help." She delivered this last line with a nasty, but still friendly, smile.

"I will pretend my feelings aren't lacerated," Sinclair said dryly. His hand was resting on my shoulder. In fact, since I'd rescued him, he was always touching me somewhere or other. Not that I minded in the slightest. I was also loving the fact that we were spending most of our evenings trying to hurt each other during lovemaking.

I glanced down at my new rings. Traditional wedding band and engagement ring. Platinum bands (Sinclair had the twin), one carat diamond setting. *Not* used. *Not* cursed.

And Sinclair had taken the news that he was BabyJon's new daddy with remarkable calm. I suspected he still felt tremendous guilt over giving me the cursed ring in the first place. So it was only fair that he would help me raise this kid for the next seventeen or eighteen years.

"So where are you guys off to?" Laura asked. We'd made up just before the wedding, and she had apologized. I'd told her that dear old Mom had dropped by from Hell, and she'd been horrified. She'd suited up in her Vera Wang (emerald green, the color of her eyes when she was eeeeevil). We were fine again. For now.

"New York City," Sinclair replied. The one aspect of the wedding he'd actually taken an interest in was planning the honeymoon. "And I thank you for taking the baby while we're gone."

"Oh, it's my pleasure," Laura gushed.

"We're leaving him behind?" I cried. "But he'll miss us! Me."

"Sorry, my wife. On that I draw the line. Babies and honeymoons do not mix."

"Fascist," I muttered, but I didn't put any real heat into it. In three days I'd gone from lonely and frightened to surrounded by friends, family, and new allies. And Jessica was all better! "You wait until later."

"I dream of later," he murmured back.

I laughed and squeezed his hand. Poor guy, he was holding up pretty well under all the nuttiness. Werewolves, a queen with mondo weird new powers, his privacy shattered by hordes, all who wanted to talk to me. Don't even get me started on BabyJon. So I knew he was looking forward to ditching the group as much as I was, but he didn't know what I'd gotten him for a wedding gift.

Spray-on gourmet flavors. I had bought him Turkey, Gravy, Raspberry, Hash Browns, and Baked Alaska.

I could hardly wait to squirt them all over him. And I'd never been to the Big Apple. I planned to take a great big bite.

"—my own."

"What?"

"I said, come along for a moment, my own. I have something to show you . . . upstairs."

I glanced at our guests. They had broken off into small groups and were chatting about this and that.

"Race you," I whispered, and chased him all the way to our bedroom.

A Letter to My Readers

First of all, thank you, dear reader. It's standard to refer to you as "dear," but you really are dear to me, and I'll tell you why. Thanks to you, I've gone from the excitement of never knowing when the power will be shut off (during a party? when my folks are over? during my kid's science experiment?) to the staid, dull lifestyle of one who can actually pay her utility bills. Because of my readers, I never go to a book signing unless I'm sporting (a) designer shoes or (b) a pedicure. Because of my readers, I've gotten to research mermaids, ghosts, psychics, manta rays, the Caymans, Florida, Cape Cod, Monterey Bay, Texas, zombies (Texas zombies?), vampires, were-anythings, Alaska, royal lineage, Martha Stewart, bellinis vs. mimosas, bed-and-breakfasts, wax fangs, and why nobody starts smoking at age thirty-five.

I've also learned how to write an ongoing series versus a stand-alone single-title novel.

Which brings us to *Undead and Uneasy*.

If you've been with me since the beginning, since *Undead and Unwed*, bless you. Your patience is about to be rewarded, I think. If you're new to the series, you've come along just in time: as one of the weird sisters in *Hercules* said, "It's gonna be big."

Everything in the Undead universe has been leading to this book (say it with me: poor Betsy!). Yes, there has been a method to my madness. The support group she has so carefully, if unconsciously, been building around herself, that I've been building for her, is about to disappear. Everything she thought she knew about the undead? Totally wrong. Marriage? Life? Death? It's all, like her favorite book and movie, *Gone With the Wind*.

That's not to say we won't have some fun along the way . . . Those of you who've been with me before know that the Undead universe is always a good time. It's just . . . we're not all going to make it out alive. And I'm sorry. I know that sucks. But it's just . . . it's just how life is sometimes. And death.

So, dear reader, thank you for coming along for the ride. Thank you for *staying* along for the ride. You won't be sorry, I'm pretty sure. And if you are? Well, I can write fast or I can write long, but I can't do both. This is the long version, so what say we give it a try?

So let's get going, shall we? As Betsy might say, "Pipe down and listen up, asshat."

Undead and Unworthy

For my dear husband, who remains undaunted.

Acknowledgments

How about that dedication, huh? (I know, I know. It's so gauche to pat yourself on the back . . . and in the section where you're supposed to be thanking other people!)

It's like that old saying, "May you live in interesting times," which sounds nice if you don't sit down and think 'er over, but which is really kind of horrifying.

And I'm not leading up to anything here. That dedication wasn't a dig at my husband, who's only the funniest, smartest, and coolest guy in the—in the—ever. Okay? Ever. I know people twice his age who are half as smart.

Hmm. That was more flattering when we were twenty.

Well, bottom line, he's awesome, and I'm lucky, but I had to use that dedication, because it made me think "that was just like that dedication about interesting times," and I always wished I could think up a vague dedication, something a little more interesting than "To Spot, the greatest Dalmatian ever!!!!!!" and then I did, and so there you go.

And I know what you're thinking: "I didn't shoplift this MJD book for mush, for schmaltz, for a bunch of ooooh-I-love-him-so-much crapola. I shoplifted it for sarcasm and a lightweight plot!" And you'll have that, I promise. It's just that I don't always give credit where credit is due, is all. And I wanted to be sure to do that this time.

Which brings me to other family members. As always, they are relentlessly funny and knee-weakeningly supportive. As always, I don't usually notice at the time, but end up absurdly grateful after the fact.

Thanks to my children, who make being a full-time writer easy, because they're so darned low maintenance. Just last month I walked in on my mother showing my youngest where I'd dedicated a book to him, and it was a beautiful scene. "See? That's about you. That's you, honey, on a page with a first American print run of six figures, which will of course be increased at no hesitation if there is sufficient public demand, so give this to your teacher and talk it up at show and tell, all right?"

And my son was all, "That's nice, I'd like a pear now."

Well, okay, not really. I mean, his reaction was real. Pretty much verbatim. That stuff my mom said was made up after the second "you." Although she is very supportive. Hand-sells lots of my books. You know that strange woman who walks right up to you and starts chatting about her stupid kid, who you've never met and never want to meet, but who apparently writes (yawn), and you buy her kid's dumb book so you don't hurt her feelings, because, even if she's lightly medicated, she's really nice? That's my mom.

And the tall guy lurking in the background ready to defend her honor—seriously, he will *kick* your *ass* if you look at her sideways. He's as quick to get down and rumble now as he was in his twenties. In his own disturbing way, also supportive.

The other child they had, who will correct booksellers if she spots my books spine-side out in stacks, instead of cover side out? My sister. (Booksellers, beware.)

There's a bunch of other nutwads in the family tree who deserve mentioning, I mean, we haven't even *touched* on the in-laws yet, and that's a whole other family tree of monkeys. But I'm starting to get bored, and if I am, you've gotta be snoring. Or close to it.

Anyway, thanks, everybody. For everything.

Author's Note

This book takes place two months after the events of *Undead and Uneasy* and *Dead Over Heels*. Also cops, like pharmacists, are weird. They can't help it. It's a hazard of their occupation. It's also why they're cool.

Finally, my father was a valuable resource for this book; he's an encyclopedia of guns and ammo. Any mistakes are mine, not his.

A Note to the Reader

This book, book seven of the Undead series (book *seven*! Jesus!), is the beginning of a new story arc. You probably noticed a change in the cover design (if you're reading the American version, that is), among other things, and that is indicative of the new direction I'm taking the series in.

Just as the first six books in the series were their own story arc, so the next three books will be an arc . . . think of this book as the first of a trilogy within a series.

My point being, if you get to the end, you needn't fear . . . there's more to come. Unless you're not a Betsy fan, in which case . . . be afraid. Be very afraid.

—MaryJanice Davidson
Minneapolis, MN
Winter 2008

The Queene hath dominion over all the dead, and they shalt take from her, as she takes from them, and she shalt noe them, and they her, for that is what it is to be Queene.

and

The Queene shalt see oceans of blood, and despair.

—THE BOOK OF THE DEAD

Frivolous: Unworthy of serious attention; trivial: *a frivolous novel.*

—THE AMERICAN HERITAGE
DICTIONARY OF THE ENGLISH LANGUAGE,
FOURTH EDITION

I would rather go to any extreme than suffer anything that is **unworthy** of my reputation, or of that of my crown.

—ELIZABETH I (1533–1603)

Out of me **unworthy** and unknown
The vibrations of deathless music.
—"ANNE RUTLEDGE," BY EDGAR LEE MASTERS
(1869–1950)

Chapter 1

Bored, I crossed the carpet in five steps, climbed up on Sinclair's desk, and kissed him. My left knee dislodged the phone, which hit the floor with a muffled thump and instantly started making that annoying *eee-eee-eee* sound. My right skidded on a fax Sinclair had gotten from some bank.

Surprised, but always up for a nooner (or whatever vampires called sex at 7:30 at night), my husband kissed me back with enthusiasm. Meanwhile, due to the aforementioned knee-skidding, I slammed into him so hard, his chair hit the wall with enough force to put a crack in the wallpaper. More work for the handyman.

He yanked, and my (cashmere! argh) sweater tore down the middle. He shoved, and my skirt (Ann Taylor) went up. He pulled, and my panties (Target) went who knew where? And I was pretty busy tugging and pulling at his suit (try as I might, I could not get the king of the vampires to *not* wear a suit), so the cloth was flying.

He did that sweep-the-top-of-the-desk thing you see in movies and plopped me on my back. He reached down, and I said, "Not the shoes!" so he left them alone (although I noticed the eye roll and made a mental note to bitch about it later).

He tugged, pulled, and entered. It hurt a little, because normally I needed more than sixteen seconds of foreplay, but it was also pretty fucking great (literally!).

I wrapped my legs around his waist, so I could admire my sequined leopard-print pumps (don't even ask me what they cost). Then I grinned up at him, I couldn't help it, and he smiled back, his dark eyes narrow with lust. It was so awesome to be a newlywed. And I was almost done with my thank-you notes!

I let my head fall back, enjoying the feel of him, the smell of him, his hands on my waist, his dick filling me up, his mouth on my neck, kissing, licking, then biting.

Then my dead stepmother said, "This is all your fault, Betsy, and I'm not going anywhere until you fix it."

To which I replied, "Aaaaah! Aaaaah! AAAAAAHHHH-HHH!"

Sinclair jerked like I'd turned into sunshine and spoke for the first time since I swept into his office. "Elizabeth, what's wrong? Am I hurting you?"

"Aaaaaaaaaaaaahhhhhhhhhhh!"

From my vantage point, my dead stepmother was upside down, which somehow made it all the more terrible, because, contrary to popular belief, you *can't* turn a frown upside down.

"You can fuss all you want, but you've got responsibilities, and don't think I don't know it." She shook her head at me, and in death, as in life, her overly coiffed pineapple-blond hair didn't move. She was wearing a fuchsia skirt, a low-cut sky blue blouse, black nylons, and fuchsia pumps. Also, too much makeup. It practically hurt to look at her. "So you better get to work."

"Aaaaaaaaaaahhhhhhhhhh!"

Sinclair pulled out and started frantically feeling me. "Where are you hurt?"

"The Ant! The Ant!"

"You—what?"

Before I could elaborate (and where to begin?), I heard thundering footsteps, and then Marc slammed into the closed office door. His scent was unmistakeable—antiseptic and dried blood.

I heard him back off and grab for the doorknob, and then he was standing in the doorway. "Betsy, are you—oh my God!" He went red so fast I was afraid he was going to have a stroke. "I'm sorry, jeez, I thought that was a bad 'aaaaahhhh,' not a sex 'aaaaahhh.'"

More footsteps, and then my best friend, Jessica, was saying, "What's wrong? Is she okay?" She was so skinny and short, I couldn't see her behind Marc.

"The Ant is here!" I yowled, as Sinclair assembled the rags of his suit, picked me up off the desk, and shoved me behind him. I don't know why he bothered; Marc was gay *and* a doctor, and so couldn't care less if I was mostly naked. And Jessica had seen me naked about a million times. "Here, right now!"

"Your stepmother's in this room?" I still couldn't see her, but

Jessica's tone managed to convey the sheer horror I felt at the prospect of being haunted by the Ant.

"Where *else* would I be?" the Ant, the late Antonia Taylor, said reasonably. She was tapping her Payless-clad foot and nibbling her lower lip. "What I'd like to know is, where's your father?"

"Yeah, that's all this scene is missing," I fumed. "If only my dead dad were here, too."

Chapter 2

After Marc decided a Valium drip probably wouldn't work on a vampire, he brought me a stiff drink instead. Could he even tap a vein? I was over a year dead, after all. Would an IV take? Someday I was going to have to sit down and figure all this shit out. Someday when I wasn't plagued by ghosts, serial killers, wedding planning, rogue werewolves, mysterious vampires bursting in on me, and diaper changing.

It was sweet of Marc to bring me a gin and tonic (which I loathed, but he didn't know that), but I was so rattled I drank it off in one gulp, and it could have been paint thinner, for all I knew.

"Is she still here?" he whispered.

"Of course I'm still here," my dead stepmother snapped. "I told you, I'm not going anywhere."

"I'm the only one who can hear you," I shrilled, "so just shut up!"

"Bring her another drink," Sinclair muttered. We were still in his office, but Jessica had kindly brought robes to cover our shredded clothes. "Bring her three."

"I don't need booze, I need to get rid of you know what."

"Very funny," the Ant grumped.

She and my father had been killed in a gruesome, stupid car accident a couple of months ago. Where she had been since her death, and why she had shown up now, I didn't know. There were so many things about being the vampire queen I didn't know! And I didn't *want* to know.

But I was going to have to find out, because the ghosts never, ever went away, until I solved their little problems for them.

And where *was* my dead dad, anyway? I sighed. Noncon-frontational in life as well as in death.

"What do you want?"

"I *told* you. To fix this."

"Fix *what*?"

"*You* know."

"This is so weird," Marc murmured to Jessica, forgetting, as usual, about superior vamp hearing. "She's having a conversation with the chair."

"She is not. Quiet so I can hear."

"I *don't* know," I said to the chair—uh, the Ant. "I really, really don't. Please tell me."

"Stop playing games."

"I'm *not*!" I almost screamed. Then I felt Sinclair's soothing hands on my shoulders and sagged into him. Like our honeymoon hadn't been stressful enough, what with all the dead kids and Jessica and her boyfriend crashing it and all. This was a hundred times worse.

"If you could just—" I began, when the office door crashed open, nearly smashing into Marc, who yelped and jumped aside.

A bloody, stinking horror was framed in the doorway, then darted right at me like a goblin in a fairy tale. Since I was a tad keyed up from the Ant popping in, my reflexes were in excellent shape. I slugged the thing—it was a man, a big, bearish, shambling man—so hard I knocked him halfway across the office. He hit the carpet so hard, buttons popped off his shirt, which looked about ready for the ragbag anyway.

He was on his feet in a flash and looked wildly from Sinclair to me and back again. And he was—there was something familiar about him. Something I couldn't put my finger on.

Sinclair and I started toward him in unison, and he backed up, pivoted, and *dived* out the second story window.

"What the blue hell—?" I began.

The office door crashed open, and I felt like clutching my heart. I couldn't stand many more of these shocks to my system.

Garrett, the Fiend formerly known as George, stood in the doorway, panting. Since he was seventy-some years old and didn't need to breathe, I knew at once something was seriously wrong.

What fresh hell was this?

"They're awake," he gasped. "And they want to kill you."

"Who?" Sinclair, Jessica, Marc, and I asked in unison. It could be anyone. The guys who delivered pizza from Green Mill. Other vampires. The Ant's book club. Werewolves. Zombies. And, of course, the uninvited guest who'd jumped out the window. So many enemies, so little—

"The other Fiends. I've been feeding them my blood, and they're pissed."

"You've what, and they're what?" I asked, horrified.

Garrett couldn't look at me—never a good sign. "They—they sort of 'woke up,' and now they want to kill you."

"It's this lifestyle you lead," the Ant said smugly. "These things are bound to happen."

"Oh, shut up!" I barked. I actually had to clutch my head; which problem to tackle first? "You couldn't have crashed into the office tomorrow? Or yesterday?"

"You'd better sit down and tell us everything," Sinclair said, reminding me he was the vampire king. "The queen has just been attacked . . . and now you come bearing tales of murder." Bam. Decision made. We'd deal with what Garrett had done first.

So take that, dead stepmother.

Chapter 3

Like I wasn't dreading the coming winter already. These days I was always cold, even on the hottest day in July; November was going to suck rocks. What I wanted to do was adjust to married life, set up house (well, the house had been set up for more than a year, thanks to Jessica and her big bucks, but I was still finding places for our wedding gifts), finish writing thank-you notes (yawn), and settle down to the job of raising BabyJon, my half brother and legal ward. (You remember, the whole my dad and the Ant being dead thing.)

Yep, yep. Everything was normal. I was a newlywed and would-be parent. Nothing wrong or weird here. Nope.

"—felt responsible," Garrett was yakking, which in itself was hard to get used to. He'd gone from slobbering Fiend to monosyllabic boyfriend (Antonia-the-werewolf's stud . . . more on that later) to verbose old vampire. The fact that he *looked* about twenty-three didn't fool anybody. "So I began visiting them. It didn't seem right that I was back to myself while they were— were—well. You know."

Fine time for his newfound vocabulary to fail him! But we knew. The old king—the one I'd killed to take the crown—liked to torture newly risen vampires by refusing to let them feed. After a few months of this treatment, they went crazy. Worse than crazy— feral. Forgot everything they ever knew, or could know, about being human. Think dangerous, rabid wolves, wearing L.L. Bean.

Sinclair and his major domo, Tina, had asked me again and again to stake the Fiends through the heart.

But I couldn't. It'd be like stomping puppies. Bloodthirsty, feral, dangerous puppies, yes, but still—puppies. Had I made the puppies? No. Was any of it the puppies' fault? Nope. Was I going to kill—worse yet, order to kill, wouldn't even have to get my hands dirty—innocent puppies, no matter how many buckets of blood they drank a day?

No.

And now the puppies were going to eat out my soft human heart. You'd think I'd have learned the essential Rule of the Undead by now: cuddly undead are still undead.

"How come nobody tried feeding them their own blood before?" Marc asked. "Why the buckets of animal blood?"

"They're too dangerous to be allowed to hunt. They'll kill anyone they can find."

"Yeesh."

"I don't think we have time for a recap," Garrett said, nervously cocking his head to one side. "Recap," that was very good; man, he was sharp! Picking up slang like no tomorrow. To think, six months ago he couldn't even purl, much less knit.

"But Garrett fed them his blood. 'Live' blood—so to speak. So, how come nobody tried that before?"

"Nobody," Sinclair said, the corners of his mouth drawing down, "cares to get near them. No offense, Garrett."

"None taken, my king," he said stiffly, not looking at my husband.

And there it was. The Fiends were the untouchables, the unwashed. In a society built of nonhumans, of monsters, these guys were considered a level below that. A good trick, if you sat down and thought it over.

I smacked my forehead with the palm of my hand. "I *knew* I recognized that guy! He's one of the Fiends? Jesus, he's really out?"

"Did somebody break a window?" Tina asked, walking into the office with what appeared to be a ream of paperwork waiting for Sinclair's signature. Privately, my husband was the king of the vampires; publicly, he owned several companies, tracts of land, and office buildings and was ridiculously wealthy. Half mine now, under Minnesota law. I think. Or—wait. Were we a community property state or—I guess I'd blocked out most of my mom and dad's divorce—

"Garrett brought the Fiends back to life like some kind of moody 1920s Frankenstein, and now they're on their way here to kill Betsy," Marc said in one breath, looking pleased at his ability to spit out several words without passing out. Of all the nights for him not to be on call at the ER! There'd be no shaking him off our heels tonight. Normally, we tried to keep the respirating roommates out of vampire biz, for their own safety if nothing else.

"They're what? Who's here to *what*?" Tina's jaw sagged; papers fluttered. She was a doll of a woman with waist-length blond hair and enormous pansy eyes. She looked delicious in knee-length shirtdresses and nonprescription glasses she didn't need. She was wearing both, in navy and tortoiseshell. "Why are you all standing around? Why—"

"Also, the Ant has started haunting me."

"I was wondering when you'd remember I existed," the wretched woman snapped.

"Did you remember to pick up tampons?" Jessica asked, and now the *men* looked appalled. That was a good question, actually. I sure didn't need them anymore, ergo Tina didn't. Jessica's cycle had been all over the place since the cancer. Did Antonia—any female werewolf, for that matter—need them? The ghost definitely didn't.

And what did it say about my life that I was living (again) with two women named Antonia? Most people went their entire lives without running into an Antonia. When one of them died, I figured I was home freaking free! Really, it was all—

"Majesty, will you focus!"

"Huh? Why?"

Sinclair actually laughed out loud while Tina stomped a tiny foot. "Angry vampires are on their way here to kill you."

"It's hard to get worked up," I said truthfully as my husband bit back another laugh, "when the Ant is breathing over my shoulder. So to speak. And it's not exactly the first time unwelcome guests have been on the way." I turned to Jessica. "Remember homecoming 1996?"

She shuddered. "I never thought you'd get the Dewar's out of the curtains."

"But I guess we'll just have to—"

Bam! Ka-Bam! BAM! BAM! BAM!

"*What* the—?" Jessica wondered.

"That would be hordes of the ravenous undead, kicking in the front door," Tina said, dropping the rest of the paperwork and whipping off her glasses. I waited for her to do a Wonder Woman twirl (Wonder Vamp!), but she just looked alert and ready to flee.

Sinclair sighed, looking greatly put upon. But men who have interrupted sex tend to get that look. "Shall we flee, or fight?"

Tina glanced at Jessica, who glared. "Ah. Flee, I think. At least until we know more about this particular threat."

"Don't run off on my account," Jessica warned. But of course, that's exactly why we were choosing flight over fight. We couldn't risk Marc and Jessica's lives until we knew more about what was going on. "I mean it, you guys."

Sinclair ignored her. "Very well. Let's take the tunnel."

Tunnel? We were taking a tunnel? We had the king, the queen, Tina, a former Fiend—the odds were okay, I thought. But Tina had an excellent point—we had a couple of humans to watch out for, too.

Tina led the way to one of the many doors leading to the basement, and I had to jog to keep up. "What? We have a tunnel?"

"Betsy, come *on!*" Marc said, grabbing an elbow and giving such a yank I nearly fell down the stairs.

"Not without me, you're not," the Ant said triumphantly, and marched (Marched? Couldn't she float?) behind me just as the door closed, leaving all of us in pure darkness.

Chapter 4

Well. Not *pure*. I could see fine, as could Garrett, Tina, and Sinclair. But from the moans and whimpers coming from farther down the stairs, the humans were having more trouble.

"Stop that sniveling, Marc Spangler, or I'll de-testicle you," Jessica snapped. When she was scared, she got pissed. Man, you should have seen her the day she got a false positive on an EPT. We were buying new dishes for days.

"I can't see a fucking thing," he snarled back. There was an abrupt silence, a—I know how this sounds, but I could hear it—a flailing, and then a rattle of thumps, followed by moans of pain.

"Getting eaten alive by the Fiends can't be worse than this," Marc groaned from the floor. Ouch. He must have fallen at least ten steps. Onto cement.

"Be careful," Tina said.

"Thanks. At least someone cares."

"You could have broken your ankle on the way down and slowed our escape."

"I hate vampires," he replied. "So much."

I eased past Jessica on the stairs, went to Marc, and picked him up. "This is so romantic," he cooed, modestly kicking his unbroken foot.

"Shut up, or I'll use you for Fiend chum."

"Why," Jessica demanded, "have we decamped to the basement?"

"And why haven't we turned any lights on?" I asked.

"Tina, take Jessica's hand. Elizabeth, keep carrying Marc."

Sinclair groaned softly in the dark, as if he couldn't believe he'd said such a thing. "Everyone else, follow me."

It took a long time. The basement was as long as the house, which was a mansion on Summit Avenue. And we had to wander around various tables and chairs, in and out of mysterious rooms—I could count on one hand how often I'd been down here since we moved a couple of years ago. I had never liked it, not even—especially even—when Garrett was living down there, knitting afghans and learning to crochet.

The journey wasn't improved by the occasional yelps, as Jessica stubbed a toe or cracked an elbow. Marc just snuggled deeper into my arms (ridiculous—he had thirty pounds of muscle on me) and waited patiently for me to make him safe.

Story of my life, since I'd died.

Chapter 5

We could hear faint crashings from upstairs; the Fiends, making a mess because they couldn't find us. Chewing on my drapes; defecating on my carpet, ripping up my graphic novels in their bloodthirsty rage. But surely they could follow their noses?

That's when Sinclair stopped walking and began tapping his knuckles on what looked like a solid cement wall.

"I don't think you should do that," I said nervously. "They might hear."

"Over the sound of their own nonsense? Doubtful."

I opened my mouth to object again (quietly) when the solid cement wall suddenly swung wide to the left, revealing a narrow, dimly lit (with fluorescents, blinking on one by one even as we stared) tunnel.

"Tunnel?" I asked, peering.

"Tunnel," Marc confirmed, peering with me. His grip tightened around my neck. "Did this come with the house, or did you put it in after?"

Good fucking question, which, I couldn't help notice, my husband didn't bother to answer.

"The lights and heat are motion activated." Sinclair turned to me, smiling with all his sharp teeth. "Usually, in our case, heat activation would do little good. After you, my queen."

Wondering what else about the Vampiric Mansion of Mystery I didn't know, I went.

Chapter 6

I'm tired," I whined after we'd been walking for a hundred years.

"It's only a bit farther," my lying bastard husband said.

"You keep *saying* that, and we keep not *being* there."

"I keep *dreaming* about divorce and not *being* divorced."

"Oh, very nice!" I raged, running to catch up with them, ignoring Marc's yelps as he was jolted in my arms. "Married not even a season, and you're looking for the door, *such* a typical guy, I knew you—hey!"

I had been lifted easily, effortlessly. "Now shush, Your Majesty," Tina said, shifting my and Marc's combined weight with no effort. "And we really are almost there."

"This," Marc announced over the distinctive gagging noise of Jessica stifling laughter, "is too much. My masculinity could stand being carried by Betsy, but—"

"The gay guy has concerns about masculinity?" Jessica managed, then broke down completely.

"I'm gay, not a eunuch. Have you ever seen me in drag? Or even mascara? I'm a regular guy in every way—"

"Except you like to put your penis in weird places," I said primly.

"Can we please have one midnight getaway without having to talk about Marc's penis?" Tina asked, aggrieved.

We all shut up as we navigated another set of stairs . . . and then another. I'd been living here for months and months, and *nobody had told me about the secret vampire escape tunnel*.

I remembered that Sinclair had steered Jessica toward this house when we had to upgrade. Back in the days when I thought I hated him. And here I thought it had been because he was a history buff and liked old houses!

"I've never been bored, and scared, at the same time," Marc commented.

"What do you want me to do with that information?" Tina asked.

"Just put us down," he grumbled, and Tina did, hard enough to rattle my teeth. Marc and I groaned in unison.

Sinclair pressed another button, another wall raised, and I suddenly could hear flowing water. He walked out into what must have looked like pure darkness to the others, except I could hear his heels clanking on the boards of the dock. He sounded like a sheriff from the Old West.

"We walked all the way to the Mississippi?" Marc goggled.

"What 'we'?" Jessica asked. "And it was, what? Seven, eight whole blocks?"

We heard Sinclair start up the Evinrude, and as he hit the lights Jessica and Marc cheered.

"Get the rope, will you, darling?" he asked casually, as if he didn't look, at that moment, like the coolest guy in the universe.

The dock was a memory a few seconds later, and when Sinclair opened 'er up, I decided I wasn't mad anymore and allowed him to put his arm around me.

Chapter 7

All right, Garrett," my husband said about half an hour later. I had no idea where we were, but we were out of the Fiends' reach, at least for now. He'd powered down the motor, and we were floating between a couple of islands. City lights were visible, but far off. I'd always sucked at geography; the lights could have been St. Paul or Minneapolis for all I knew. "Suppose you tell us everything."

I realized that during our tunnel getaway and subsequent penis discussion, Garrett hadn't said word one. And at some point, the Ant had disappeared. Thank goodness for small etcetera.

Garrett, a slim, tall blond with hair almost as long as Marc's, was sitting low in the bow, staring at his hands.

"Garrett? Helloooo? Time, if you didn't notice by the whole Fiends breaking down the door and the tunnel escape, is not on our side."

"I am shamed," he said at last, still staring at his hands. "I feel ashamed."

"Well," Marc said reasonably, swiveling around in one of the captain's chairs, "what'd you do?"

He looked up at me, the moonlight bouncing off his face and making his eyes seem to gleam. "You should kill me, dread queen. Right now."

"Blech! I mean, uh, no way, Garrett, you're one of the family." The giant extended family I neither wanted nor asked for. To think, three years ago I was living in a two-bedroom in Apple Valley, bitching because I hadn't had a date in over a month. My biggest problem had been fixing the copy machine at my day job—management *would* try to fuck with the machines, and often there was no hope afterward. "Besides, if I didn't kill you when you were a Fiend, I'm sure not going to now and risk your girl-friend's wrath." Antonia-the-werewolf was a high octane bitch when she was in a *good* mood. I never, never wanted to see her when she was really mad.

"Antonia," Garrett said, almost sighed. "As you know, my mate has to leave me. Often, she leaves. More so, now that you changed her."

We nodded, like we'd been cued. We did know this. Antonia had to pop over to Cape Cod now and again—the seat of werewolf power, pardon me while I snigger—and tend to pack business. We assumed she didn't take Garrett, because traveling with a vampire could get tricky.

Also, up until two months ago, she was a werewolf who had never changed during the full moon. I had done something to her, something we all still didn't like to talk about, and now she *did* change. The meetings on Cape Cod had increased as a result, but those of us in the manse weren't talking about it.

"I stay," he continued, "because I'm afraid."

"Of what?" Jessica asked.

"The world," he replied simply. "The last time I went out in the world, I was captured and bound like a slave."

Thank you, Marjorie, you kidnapping fuck, may you roast in Hell for a zillion billion years.

"The time before that, I was killed. The monster got me. I don't go out in the world anymore."

It occurred to me (it was going to be a night of discovering things that had been under my nose) that except for going after An-tonia last summer (and getting captured, as he put it, and bound like a slave), I couldn't remember the last time he had left the mansion.

I imagined he fed on Antonia, but such things were none of my business, so I didn't ask. As long as he wasn't hurting innocent people, I had no interest in where he was getting his liquid diet.

"An agoraphobic vampire?" Marc asked, and I could tell he was trying very, very hard not to laugh.

"It's more common than you might think," Tina said, pacing the small deck. She was so light on her feet, the boat didn't even rock. "Particularly when the vampire in question had a bad death."

"Uh, excuse me, but don't you guys have to kill somebody for them to come back? Aren't all vampires, by definition, murder victims? They all sound like bad deaths to me."

"Point," Jessica said, actually sticking her left index finger in the air to mark the point.

"So, didn't you guys all have bad deaths? Except for Betsy?"

"Call me the day after *you* get run over by an Aztec, and then we'll talk," I grumbled.

"We are not here to discuss such things with—with guests," Sinclair said, correcting himself so smoothly Tina and I were probably the only ones who knew he'd been about to say "outsiders" or "humans." "And you were telling us about Antonia."

"Other than my mate, I have no peers. All of you, even the humans, are smarter than I."

"What 'even'?" Marc said. "I'm a doctor."

Jessica put a soothing hand on Marc's arm. "Garrett, don't be so hard on yourself. You've been out of it for, what? Sixty, seventy years? Crack a few modern history books, you'll be up to speed in no time."

Garrett waited patiently until Jessica was finished. "It is not my place to befriend a queen, or a king. So when Antonia leaves me, I am lonely."

I was beginning to see where this was going. Oh, it'd be a lovely children's book: *Garrett the Fiend Finds Friends!*

"And it seemed to me that I was—that I was the way I am now—because the good queen and the devil's daughter allowed me to feed off them. I thought perhaps if I gave my old comrades my blood . . ."

Okay. This is a little embarrassing to explain, so I'm just gonna plunge in and get it over with. See, I *had* let Garrett feed from me, ages ago. And as a sort of punishment, I'd ordered the devil's daughter to do the same thing.

The devil's daughter being my half sister, Laura.

(I know. Bear with me.)

See, the Ant was possessed by the devil years back, only she was so fucking nasty nobody noticed. And the devil didn't care for child rearing, so she dumped Laura and took off back to Hell. Laura was adopted by (seriously, don't laugh) a minister and his wife.

How do you rebel against the evilest nastiest yuckiest entity in the universe (who looks like Lena Olin and has an amazing shoe collection)?

You go to church. You teach Sunday school. You don't touch a drop of booze until your twenty-first birthday.

And you conceal a hateful, murderous temper. Laura was going to blow one of these days, but I just didn't have time to worry about it right now. Among other things, I had slavering Fiends on my tail and thank-you cards to finish.

"So I began to visit them and let them feed off me."

"Eh?"

"Pay attention, Elizabeth."

"They didn't try to puree you or anything?" Marc asked.

Garrett shook his head. "Even though I had . . . changed, they still knew me as one of them. They would never have hurt me. Or so I thought, until tonight. And I felt . . . bad. To see them. I had everything, and they were drinking buckets of cow blood."

I was suddenly interested in studying my feet. I wouldn't have credited Garrett with a guilty conscience. But then, I scarcely thought about him at all.

"I was not sure what would happen, but I kept trying. I had found so much happiness in—"

"Your agoraphobia," Marc prompted.

"—in my new life, I felt it cost me nothing but blood to try to help my old friends. And Antonia is generous with her blood. She regenerates quickly, as is part of her superior genetic heritage."

"Superior genetic—" Tina began, equal parts outraged and interested (until a very short time ago, neither she nor Sinclair believed in werewolves), but Sinclair shook his head, and she shut up without another word. God, I'd love to learn that trick. I'd only use it for fighting evil, though.

"It worked. My friends were helped by my blood. The effect wasn't all at once. It took many visits. It was—was—"

"Accumulative?" Jessica and Marc asked in unison.

Garrett nodded.

"But they weren't really friends, right?" I asked anxiously. "You guys didn't even know each other in life, right? Once in a while, ole Nostril would take it in his teeny brain and toss another one of you into the snake pit and that was about it. Right?"

"We were prisoners together," Garrett said quietly, "for decades."

"Right, right, got that, sorry." I was so embarrassed I couldn't look at him. So I went back to studying my toes. "So, you had good intentions, right?"

"Exactly so, my queen," he said eagerly. "I only wished—"

"And in your loneliness and self-exile, you put the queen's life in danger," Sinclair said coldly. "You put her friends in danger, and my friend." I noticed he didn't include himself in the pack. "I should have ignored Elizabeth's soft heart and staked you myself."

I heard Tina flip open the seat on the stern (you could sit on it, but it held life jackets and things . . . sort of like a padded cedar chest), rummage around, and produce—ack!—a stake. The boat that had everything!

Garrett sank to his knees. "All you say is true, bold king," he said to the deck.

"Marc, Jessica, step to the back. You don't want to get splashed."

"Now wait just a fucking minute!" I slapped the stake out of Tina's hand so hard she nearly plunged overboard. (And what other nasty implements of death were in that chest?)

I marched over and hauled Garrett to his feet. The book rocked alarmingly, then steadied. "This is a monarchy, right, Sinclair? And if the Book of the Dead is right, *I* outrank *you*. I was *born* the queen; you had to fuck me to get your crown."

And oh, boy, I still got pissed if I thought that one over too carefully.

"So I'll be the one to say who gets staked." I shook Garrett, who drooped at the end of my arm. "Stand up straight! Defend yourself! Be a man of the early twentieth century, for God's sake—ignorant yet sure of your superiority." (We were sure he'd been killed in the thirties or forties.)

"Ever the graceful hostess," Sinclair commented.

"Besides, smart guy, you didn't even notice that every time Antonia left town, Garrett was leaving the house and feeding other vampires. Too busy looking for new companies to buy?"

"Touché," Tina muttered, not looking happy about it. Watching over the estate, including the Fiend farm, was part of her job, but she knew I preferred to yell at Sinclair rather than her.

"So, Garrett, where were we? What's the rest of the story?"

"My plan worked," he continued miserably. "Too well, I fear . . . my comrades wanted to know where they were, what had happened to them. Unlike me, they were—were displeased to find themselves—"

"Stuck on an abandoned farm full of animal blood?" Jessica suggested.

"Exactly so. I tried to emphasize the queen's goodness in letting them live, tried to explain that she had set us free by killing our jailor, but they only became more enraged. Essentially, they could not understand—"

"Why you and not them?" Marc asked.

"What?" I cried. "So this is *my* fault?"

"Looks like," Jessica replied.

"They were so angry," Garrett said dolefully.

"Angry? After you saved them? Ungrateful brutes. Besides, with Nostro dead, what's to be mad about?" Marc asked.

"Ah, let me count the ways," Sinclair purred. And he did just that, ticking the points off on his long, slender fingers. "They are angry because they are old vampires with no real power. Deprived of live blood for so long, like Garrett, they will never have real power. They are angry about, as they see it, being dumped on a farm, and never mind that it was for the public's safety."

"But it was!" I cried.

"The vampire queen puts vampires first, my dearest. As I have repeatedly told you. Next—"

"I don't wanna hear any more," I groaned.

"—they are angry that a new queen has been in power for two years and done nothing to help them—"

"Nothing! I stopped you from killing them about nine times!"

"—angry that the new queen knows she could have 'cured' them at any time (case in point, the happily married, articulate Garrett), and, finally, extremely angry that they've been given silly nicknames."

"That wasn't the queen," Tina said loyally. "That was Alice."

"Alice is dead," Garrett said.

"Happy, Skippy, Trippy, Sandy, Benny, Clara, and Jane killed her?" I said, horrified.

"I tried to stop them, but they are many, and I am one. I only barely escaped myself. Alice . . ." He looked away, out over the water. "Died cursing me."

"And then you led them straight to the queen."

Garrett shivered. "I had not—thought of that. My only thought was to return to safety. One of them followed me. He must have picked up the queen's scent—from my clothes, I think—and—"

"Blown past you, beat you to the mansion. You fell for the oldest trick in the book," Marc said, not unkindly. "Leading the bad guys to the good guys."

"I am a coward. I was afraid to be alone, and now I have endangered you all."

"Well, now, uh, that's a little harder to defend," I admitted, "but you didn't set out to do bad."

Sinclair made a disgusted sound and threw his hands up in the air. "Elizabeth, really!"

"If I went around killing everyone who made a mistake, I'd be pretty damned lonely," I snapped back. I actually patted the trembling Garrett. "Nobody's going to kill you, Garrett."

"Well, maybe some of his old friends," Jessica said helpfully.

"Yeah," I sighed. "There's that. Ideas?"

Chapter 8

We (Sinclair) decided to go to the farm to check out the scene of the crime. We (Sinclair) figured it was best to see if things were as bad as Garrett intimated. And no one was in a rush to get back to the mansion.

Nostro had, once upon a time, owned this property, and I had been, once upon a time, a prisoner here. And getting here had taken no time at all . . . once Tina's cell got a signal, she made a call, Sinclair docked the boat at some teeny marina, and an empty, idling SUV was waiting for us.

"It's good to be the king," Marc murmured in my ear, as we all climbed in, making me giggle.

Under no circumstances would Jessica and Marc allow themselves to be dumped somewhere safe. The argument got so heated that Sinclair pulled over on a quiet corner of Minnetonka (at this hour, every corner in Minnetonka was quiet) so we could disembark onto the sidewalk and discuss (read: shriek) it without endangering nearby traffic.

It was only when I saw Sinclair gliding behind Jessica when I realized (a) she couldn't hear him, and (b) what his plan was.

"Don't you *dare* knock her unconscious!"

"I wasn't going to!" Marc yelled back, flinching away from me.

"Or him, either," I added, noticing Tina sidling up to Marc.

"It would have been for their own safety," El Sneako grumbled.

"We're perfectly safe," Marc said, but then, he would. He loved all things vampire. Given that he'd been about to hurl himself from a tall building to escape his boring life when I met him, I couldn't entirely blame him. "We've got the king and queen of the vampires with us and, a, um, shell of a vampire to bring up the rear."

For Garrett had been no good at all since we got off the boat. He shivered, he shook, he tried to curl up. It was obvious that, since we weren't going to kill him, being outside made him miserable. For the first time I noticed how torn his clothing was, though his injuries had healed. Old, Sinclair had said, and that was certainly true. But not powerful. Never powerful. There had been a time after I brought him home like a stray when we thought . . . but no.

Old, but not powerful. Poor guy.

As we grumpily climbed back into the SUV, I wondered again about power. What, exactly, made a vampire powerful? Not age, certainly (I was two!), or at least, not *just* age. I had been told that, like me, Sinclair had risen strong. Most vampires went through a ten-year phase where they'd do anything for blood and couldn't remember their own names.

Was determination a factor? Anger, hate, vanity? Hmm, that last could explain my meteoric rise to power . . .

"We're here," Sinclair said abruptly, braking hard enough to make my seat belt lock (force of habit; no real reason to wear the thing these days). "And you two will *stay here*. I mean it, Marc. Jessica. Remain *in this vehicle*, or I will be cross."

"Excuse me, captain my captain," Marc said, "but do you know how many horror movies start out like this?"

"We probably shouldn't split up," Jessica agreed. "Besides, if you really thought the Fiends were still here, you'd never have let us come. You'd have clocked Betsy, too, if it had come to that."

Sinclair muttered something that the chime of the "door open" light drowned out; sounded like "wretched woman." We all solemnly clambered out with him, knowing that even if Marc and Jess had won a victory, it was nothing to celebrate.

Chapter 9

We were okay until we found Alice's body. Sure, there had been an obvious fight, the fence had been torn open in several places, there were splashes of blood on the ground, but . . . really, I was okay until we found her head.

While Marc supported Jessica as she threw up in the chokecherry bushes (he was pale, but had seen so much death as a doctor, even this couldn't make him sick) and I swayed dizzily on my feet,

(don't faint don't faint don't faint QUEENS DON'T FAINT!)

Tina and Sinclair prowled the area like vampiric bloodhounds, finding arms, legs, both halves of a torso.

"This is maybe a dumb question," Marc began, smoothing Jessica's tight black cap of curls and letting her lean on his shoulder.

(don't faint don't faint don't faint)

Tina shook her head. "There's no chance of regeneration. Absolutely none. Frankly, I'd be amazed if the queen could handle this kind of punishment. My queen?" Her voice sharpened. "Are you all right?"

"Of course she's all right," Sinclair said, squatting to examine another body part. "Queens don't faint."

"Damn right! Look, Alice is obviously dead. What are you poking around for?"

"Oh, this and that," he said vaguely. "I'm a little puzzled by the condition of the corpse."

"I was thinking that exact thing," Tina added.

"What are you talking about?" I asked, but they were ignoring me and having their own conversation.

"Did you call—"

"Already done, my king."

"Excellent."

"Ah, and a mysterious van of vampires will show up and dispose of all the evidence," Jessica managed, wiping her mouth.

"More or less."

"I think we should go back now, can we please go back home now?"

Sinclair looked at Garrett with obvious distaste. "What makes you think it's safe?"

"I-I don't think they'd stay. Not if they couldn't find . . . her."

Okay, so Garrett wasn't exactly being the stand-up guy you read about in romance novels. But I felt sorry for him—it couldn't have been much fun getting the crap stomped out of him by half a dozen pissed off vampires, vampires he'd tried to *help*, and then come home to tell Sinclair what he'd done.

Sinclair didn't understand about fear, how it ate your guts, and how nobody came off like they did in the movies. He'd claimed, on occasion, to have feared for my safety, but frankly, I doubted it.

"Even if they are still there, it's our home, and a bunch of jerkoff vampires aren't keeping me out of it. I mean, you explained that to me once already, Sinclair. How we're not worthy of our crowns if our people can't find us."

"Yay, Queen Betsy," Jessica said.

"But they're sure as shit keeping you two out of it," Marc teased.

"Boo, Queen Betsy."

The argument raged all the way back home.

Chapter 10

Marc and Jessica's apparent casual attitude toward death was partly my fault. Make that totally. I'd saved their butts so many times (from suicide, murder, cancer) they just naturally felt impervious around me.

It didn't help that none of us were talking about it in any real detail. See, I'd always been different from other vampires. So different than even Tina (the oldest vampire I hadn't killed; she had made Sinclair way back when) didn't know much about me, or what I could do.

I had, completely by accident, cured Jessica's cancer and killed an eight-hundred-year-old vampire librarian. And I'd done it without laying a finger on the librarian. I just sort of—*pulled* her into me. What was left wouldn't have filled an urn.

That didn't bother Sinclair or Tina especially, since I'd saved Sinclair at the time. What *did* bother them was that I had no idea how I'd done it and had been unable to do so again. Not that I'd tried. *God*, no. I figured somebody would have to die for me to try out my nifty new power. Pass.

Sinclair had been spending some time in the library perusing the Book of the Dead. He thought I didn't know. But I understood his puzzlement, and I knew he was being careful.

Read that thing too long—written on human skin with blood by a centuries-dead insane vampire—and you went crazy. Upside was, it was always right. Downside, there was no index or table of contents. You just opened it and took your chances that you'd actually read something, y'know, useful.

Worst of all, it always came back to me. It had been set on fire and thrown into the Mississippi River (on two separate occasions!). It always showed up wherever I was. Fucking creepy thing that I didn't dare read and couldn't get rid of.

Or tell Sinclair I knew he was reading it. How could I bring that up without mentioning Jessica's cure, or what I did to Marjorie?

And don't even get me started on what I did to the Ant and my dad. I'd wished for a baby, and I got one—because they had been killed. It wasn't my fault, it was a Monkey's Paw situation. I'd been wearing a cursed engagement ring at the time. One gruesome car accident later, and I was the sole guardian of my half brother, BabyJon.

Thank God he'd been spending the weekend with the devil's daughter and didn't get ripped to pieces by the Fiends!

(I can't believe I just said that. This, this is what my life had become.)

What was worse, that my distant dad and bitchy stepmother were dead, or that I didn't feel too broken up about it? Let's face it, he'd never been there for me, and she was a stiff-haired nightmare.

Who, last I checked, had been *haunting* me. Maybe I'd get lucky—maybe instead of an actual ghost, that vision of her was just a hallucination, the onset of permanent brain damage.

I sighed as we pulled into the driveway. *I should be so lucky,* I told myself.

Chapter 11

This is an inopportune time," my husband pointed out as I knocked on the door at 1001 Tyler Street, a small, neatly kept gray and white house.

"No shit," I muttered. The mansion had been trashed; it was the next evening, and Jessica had called in an army of fixer-uppers. Even now, after sunset, they were still working on the house. No sign of the Fiends, and Tina had promised to get Marc and Jess into the tunnel at the first sign of trouble. She even thoughtfully provided flashlights by the entrance to the mansion basement. Even better: Marc's ankle was much better. No break, thank God.

"Then why are we here?" Sinclair asked, looking around the tidy suburban neighborhood. Inver Grove Heights was famous for their tidy suburban neighborhoods.

"Because he's been incarcerated for months, and this is the first time I've seen him since I got married."

"And . . . ?"

"I want my bigoted, angry, dying grandfather to meet my dead husband. Now slap on a smile and feel the family joy!"

Sinclair managed a friendly grimace, as the lady who ran the hospice ushered us in. It wasn't really a hospice; she was a registered nurse who owned the house, and she had three patients, including my grandpa. She could give meds and change dressings, and knew when to haul in an MD.

In return she made a reasonable living and managed not to smother my grandpa with a pillow. For their part, they were living in an actual home and not dying in an impersonal hospital ward.

"Get lost," my beloved maternal relative said warmly.

"Hi, Grandpa. Just dropped by—"

"Did you bring me a Bud?"

"—to say hi and tell you I got married."

He squinted at me with watery blue eyes. His hair was lush and entirely white—it thrived on Budweiser. His eyebrows looked like angry albino caterpillars. He was in his wheelchair by the window, dressed in sweatpants and a blue checked flannel shirt, feet sockless in the heel-less slippers.

He didn't need a wheelchair, but Mr. Mueller in the next room had one, and my grandpa broke every plate he could find until Nurse Jenkins relented and ordered one for him. Mueller also had a colostomy bag, but my grandpa graciously decided not to go after that as well.

Next to the Ant, and maybe the devil, he was the most evil person I'd ever known. Come to think of it, most of the male influences I'd had growing up had either been—

"Your mom still fat?"

"She's at the perfect weight for her height and age, you bony smelly man!" I snapped. Great, a new record. I'd been in the same room with him for eight seconds, and already I was screaming. "It's a miracle she isn't a sociopath, raised by a rotten old man like you!"

"Hello," Sinclair said. "I'm Eric Sinclair, Elizabeth's husband."

Gramps scowled at the vampire king. "You look part Indian. You got any Injun in you, boy?"

"It's possible," Sinclair said mildly, as I moaned and chewed on a throw pillow. "I never knew my biological father."

I spit out some feathers and stared at him. "You never knew your father?"

"He could be part black!" my darling, dying relative howled. "He could be—he could be Catholic!"

"I believe I may be Californian," Sinclair added helpfully.

"*Anyway*, I got married, this is the guy, nice to see you again, don't drop dead anytime soon, because I couldn't handle another funeral this year, good-bye."

"Yup," Grandpa said, smacking his teeth (he still had them all . . . a chronic drinker and smoker with gorgeous hair and perfect teeth). "Hope that witch is having a good time screwing the devil in Hell."

"I don't think the devil swings that way," I said truthfully. I had finally remembered the one reason I hadn't wrung the old buzzard's neck twenty years ago.

Sinclair cleared his throat. I prayed he wasn't eyeing my grandpa and trying to figure out which one of the two of them was older. "Oh, you knew the, ah, late Mrs. Taylor?"

"Knew her? Beat the shit out of her."

"How sweet."

"Twat stole my girl's husband." A cat wandered near, and Grandpa kicked it away, sending his slipper flying. Sinclair snatched it out of the air and courteously handed it back. "She had to go down."

"Go . . . down?"

"Fistfight. The Halloween I was fifteen. The cops came," I sighed reminiscently, "and everything."

"Bitch went to her grave with fewer teeth than I have," my warm, friendly grandfather cackled.

"You engaged in a physical fight with a woman?"

"Slut should have kept her legs closed round a married man. 'Course," he added, looking at me, "your father always was a worthless bastard."

"As I recall, he got a fist in the face that night as well."

"And woulda got a boot in the ass! If the cops hadn't cuffed me by then."

"The arresting officer gave me a Charms Blo-Pop," I reminisced, "and took me over to stay with my mom. She got to read the police report." I stooped and kissed his wrinkled forehead. And handed him the Cub grocery bag, which was full of cans of Bud.

Chapter 12

Who's here?" I asked, yawning as I strolled into the kitchen. Sinclair, once done laughing, had been in a rush to get back to the manse, for which I could not blame him. He'd snuck into the library to read the Book of the Dead, and I'd come to the kitchen to pretend I didn't know, and also for a smoothie.

"Here, what? *Here* here?" Marc was yawning, too, and scratching his ribs; he smelled like cotton balls, antiseptic, and was wearing last night's scrubs. His hair, shaved nearly bald when I met him, was now shoulder length, dark, and fell into his eyes a lot. It was a wonder how he examined anyone at the hospital. "I hate your creepy vampire superpowers."

"Liar."

"It's Nick," Jessica announced, shutting the fridge and turning around, a pomegranate (a pomegranate! She ate 'em like oranges, I swear to God) in her left hand.

"Oh."

I'd probably better leave. I had recently discovered that Detective Nick Berry, who was in love with my best friend, hated me. And not "hate" like "I hate boogers." Hated me like plague. Hated me like famine. The fact that I deserved it didn't make things any easier. "You guys have a date?"

"No," she said cryptically, which made me want to strangle her. When Jess didn't want to cough up, you could stick a gun in her ear, and she'd laugh at you. Must be from growing up rich. Sinclair was the same way. Stick a gun in *my* ear, and I'd talk until your pants fell down.

Then: "How's your grandpa?"

"Still worried that your blackness will infect me."

"That's the plan. First you, then all the other blondes, and then on to brunettes and redheads. Once we have the womenfolk, all the babies will come out black, too. We all voted on the plan at the last Black Conspirators meeting." Ignoring Marc's choking, she added, "Bet Sinclair had a good laugh."

"To put it mildly. He was all soft and nostalgic at first, talking about how it was nice to have live in-laws, but my grandpa wiped the smile off his face soon enough. But never mind that. What's Nick doing here?"

"Meh," the Cryptic One replied.

"He's a carpenter by night? Not that we need one anymore; that gang you hired did a pretty good job." And they did. Except for the smell of sawned wood and fresh paint, you'd think nothing had happened.

"Yeah, thanks, Jessica. What do we owe you?" Now that I was married to a rich guy, I could say something like that and not have Jessica burst into derisive laughter. But as usual she just waved a hand: don't worry about it. I was so used to her money I hardly noticed it was there. Shit, *she* hardly knew it was there. But she was never obnoxious about it, seeing it as something permanent and unchangeable, like her skin color and taste in music.

"So," I continued, "not to go on and on about something—"

"You?" Marc asked.

"Never," Jessica declared.

I scowled at them both. "What *is* Nick doing here?"

"What do you care?" Marc asked, plucking an apple out of the basket on the counter and taking a wet bite. "He'd rather see you dead than in last year's Blahniks."

I shuddered and wiped masticated apple off my cheek. "That was mean. Even for you."

"Obviously," Marc continued, shaking his hair out of his eyes (and into Jessica's pomegranate), "he and the richest woman in the state—"

"Richest *person*," Jessica corrected gently.

"—have a hot sloppy date. FYI, girlfriend, you're aware he's using you for your money, right?"

"His grandpa was one of the Deeres."

We gaped at her. This was a tidbit we hadn't heard before.

"Shut . . . *up!*" Marc nearly screamed.

"Nuh-uh." Jessica popped another pomegranate seed into her mouth and tried not to look smug. She sucked at it, as usual.

"As in the John Deere tractor company?" I advanced cautiously. (As in, anyone who wanted a tractor, trailer, thresher, or combine usually bought 'em from the John Deere Company.)

"Yup. He's got money falling out of his butt."

"Yum," Marc said absently.

I tried to speak for a couple of seconds and finally choked out, "Why didn't you tell us?"

"Why would I? What difference does it make if he's got a seven figure trust fund?"

"Well, it certainly makes him a more attractive man," Marc blurted before he could stop himself. "Also, money makes a guy's dick huge."

"Go fuck yourself," she said congenially enough.

"If only I could," he mourned. "It'd be the only way I'd get any, that's for sure."

The thing is, as exasperated as Marc and I were to be the last ones in on this incredibly juicy gossip (me more than him, probably, I mean, we *were* best friends), Jessica really meant what she said. She wouldn't know what difference it made, and wouldn't care.

It occurred to me that Sinclair had probably found this out ages ago and had also neglected to tell me. Must be a rich guy thing. Excuse me. Rich *person*. Not to mention, definitely the week for me to find out shit I should already have known.

"I'll get the door," I said gloomily, because I knew neither of them could hear Nick coming up the walk, and also because I decided the quickest way to find out why he was here was to let him in. As I started to leave the kitchen I nearly ran into my husband.

"I'm getting the door," I explained, trying to sidestep him.

He resisted, which made it like trying to sidestep a barn. "I'll accompany you."

I stared up at him. He must have died clean shaven. At least, I never saw him shaving, and there weren't any shaving—what was the word? accoutrements?—in his bathroom. God, he was gorgeous. Gorgeous and distant, like the sunrise he could never see. There were times I looked into that perfect, impassive face and wondered what he was thinking. Sometimes I was truly mystified: Out of all the vampires in all the world, why'd he want me?

We were still sidestepping each other in the hallway. "Why d'you want to come with me?"

"I'm unable to be outside of the goddess-like presence that is you?"

I heard Marc making vomiting noises as the kitchen door swung shut behind us. "No, seriously." Except with Sinclair, I never knew when he *was* serious.

"I miss you, and I want to be with you?"

"Come on."

"I am coming," he said, falling into step behind me.

"Yeah, this stopped being cute about five seconds ago."

"If only," my husband sighed.

"Sinclair, what the hell is up?"

"You have a meeting with Detective Berry, who has in the past threatened you with a firearm, and thus I will be in attendance as well. That is all."

"That is *all*?"

"Oh. Also, if he points a firearm anywhere near you, I shall pull off his arms and stuff them down his throat."

He said *that* just as I was swinging the front door open. "You will not! Jessica will be impossible to live with! (More impossible.)" Then: "Wait a damned minute! You knew about Nick coming to see me before I did, even if he tried to kill me?"

"Of course."

"You prick."

Nick, all annoying blond good looks and broad shoulders, smirked at us. For the first time, I noticed he dressed pretty damned well on a cop's salary. That was an Armani hanging off his swimmer's shoulders, if I wasn't mistaken.

"Did I come at a bad time?" he asked, grinning, and it took all I had not to slam the door in his stupid, rich, cop face.

Chapter 13

I should explain that before I died, Nick and I had been almost friends. When I'd been attacked by the Fiends outside Kahn's Mongolian Barbecue (the heavy garlic I'd used had saved my life; the Fiends had nibbled and fled instead of really going to town on my gizzard), he'd been the cop to take my report. We'd occasionally shared a candy bar and, if not friends, had at least been friendly.

Then I'd risen from the dead and, completely unaware of my undead sex appeal, left Nick panting after me. Sinclair had to mind-wipe him, including the part about me dying.

Trouble was, it wore off. Or my mind-wipe had been stronger than the king's. Either way, we found out a couple months ago that he knew what we were, knew what we did, knew what we had done to *him*, and pretty much hated us.

So out of guilt, I usually try to be super nice and accommodating whenever he came around.

Except, of course, right now.

"Nobody's having *any* meeting until you two *jerks* tell me when you set this up!"

Nick arched his brows at my husband. "You didn't tell her?"

"I was hoping," he said stiffly, "she would be out shoe shopping."

"Well, the joke's on you, *asshat*! Ha! I went shoe shopping last week! So there!" I jerked my pointing finger away from my husband and jabbed it at Nick, who flinched. "So talk! Are you here to kill me?" (Man, the number of times I had to ask this question in a month . . .)

"No, my captain said I couldn't, unless I could prove in court you were a vampire."

I nearly fell down in the foyer. "What?" I gasped, barely hanging on to the doorknob.

"Kidding. Come sit down before you stroke out." Nick pushed past us and, like robots, we followed him into one of the parlors.

Chapter 14

So!" he said with faux brightness. "Set up a meeting with your wife, which you didn't share with your wife. I love open marriages, don't you?"

Since I'd been having some doubts in that area myself, all I could do was scowl at Sinclair while smiling at Nick, which gave me an instant migraine. "How can I help you, Nick? Did you want to see Jess? Oh, wait—" I should offer him a drink. But what *did* he drink? Was it Sprite, or Coke? Wait. *I* drank Coke. I—

"Detective Berry," Tina said demurely. She entered, eyes lowered, and offered him a tray on which were a tall glass full of Sprite, another glass full of ice, a silver ice picker-upper, a small bowl of sliced lemons and limes, and a big, thick, cloth napkin. Also, there was—

"My queen," she said in a soft voice, gaze on the carpet. I took the iced Coke (with a wedge of lime, just the way I liked it), and Tina managed to somehow glide away while not looking at anyone, yet giving the impression of instant service, should anyone need a refill. This, I had since learned, was the height of vampiric etiquette. It's tough to do the vampire mojo and work your will on the poor human if you're not looking them in the eye.

I thirstily slurped my Coke, amazed all over again at Tina's unflagging efficiency. Super secretary, maid, waitress, Sinclair's right hand, and she'd been loyal to me from the moment the vampires threw me into Nostro's pit of despair. I couldn't help but admire her, but I never forgot the basic fact: her loyalty, always, was to Sinclair first. Her loyalty to me was because I was *his wife*.

The day I forgot that might be a short damn day.

"Good service around here," Nick said, slurping his Sprite and chewing enthusiastically on his lemon wedge.

"Oh, like you're not used to it at the Deere family compound," I snapped, chomping into my own lime slice. Yerrgh, sour! Even for a lime. I reached into my left pocket and pulled out a Cherry Blo-Pop. Unwrapped it, dipped it in the Coke, then contentedly sucked the Coke off the Pop.

"How disgusting," Sinclair commented.

"Which? That I'm slowly getting addicted to suckers, or that Nick comes from the Deeres?"

"Finally bothered to find out about someone besides yourself, huh?"

"Jam it up your ass!" I snarled, a not auspicious beginning to our meeting. And why were we meeting? He hated me, I was scared of him (but not for the reasons he thought), and Sinclair would just as soon he dropped dead (he took a dim view of cops shoving their service revolvers into his wife's face). "On the way out the door!"

"Hmm." Nick checked his watch. "Four minutes . . . a new record for us. Actually, Betsy, as I explained to the king of all suckheads over there, I need your help in tracking down a bad guy."

"You—me? Tracking down a—what?"

"English really is your second language, isn't it? And your suckhead is here because he's got this nutty idea that I'm going to try to shoot you in the face. Maybe twice!" he added cheerfully, slurping the last of his Sprite.

"Have a seat, Detective Berry." Sinclair looked up at me and patted his lap, and I ignored the tug between my legs because a meeting with a homicide detective while curled up in the arms of the vampire king would not be the severe business mien I was hoping for. Bad enough I was wearing faded blue sweatpants and a sweatshirt that read EVERYTHING YOU'VE HEARD IS TRUE.

Instead, I plopped on the couch across from Nick (ignoring the plume of dust I accidentally raised), parallel to Sinclair.

"What's up, boys?" I asked, sniffing my Coke glass.

"Murder, of course." Crunch, slurp. He was really going to town on those lemons. "Check it."

He spun open several folders, and suddenly there were (gag) autopsy photos all over the Victorian-era mahogany coffee table. Thankfully, none were of children, but in all other ways they were different: race, sex, age, hairstyle.

"And how can the house of Sinclair help the Minneapolis Homicide Department?"

I opened my mouth (momentarily forgetting the lollipop; the thing almost fell on the floor), but decided I kind of liked that. House of Sinclair. Like House of Pancakes! Without so much syrup.

"Guess what all these guys (and gals) have in common?"

"They all need a set and shampoo," I said, examining one photo and putting it down with a grimace. I wiped my fingers on my sweatpants, as if the picture had actually been dirty.

A year ago, I'd be sprinting from the room and vomiting. That was before Nostro, and Marjorie, and Alice, to name just a few. The guy who said "the more things change, the more things stay the same" had a major frigging head injury. Because I, Betsy, the vampire queen, am here to tell you that the more things change, the more things *change*.

"Close," Nick said, still looking abnormally cheery, "but no Kewpie doll for you, blondie."

Sinclair was also examining the photos. "They certainly weren't killed by vampires."

"True."

"Do we have to do the guessing thing?" I whined. "Just tell us."

"They all had records."

"Like, prison records?"

"Like, they were all thieves, rapists, killers."

No wonder he was so happy. Cops loved it when bad guys got killed.

"This is how you spend your evenings?" the Ant said behind my left shoulder, causing me to yelp and spill my ice all over Nick. "Looking at disgusting pictures? This is worse than when you were modeling for the Target catalog."

"Go *away*. I'm working."

"Gaaahhh," Nick gah'd, frantically scraping ice out of his crotch. "What's gotten into you, blondie?"

"Private family business," Sinclair said smoothly.

"My dead stepmother is haunting me," I snapped. "Now get lost, Antonia!"

"Oh, that." Nick looked unimpressed. "You see dead people. Jess told me all about it."

"Well, that's super. Remind me to strangle her when I see her again."

"Touch her," Nick said pleasantly, "and I'll empty my nine into your nose."

"Children," Sinclair warned. "It seems the late Mrs. Taylor has a gift in death, as in life, of getting on my wife's nerves and distracting us from our point."

"Just like your wife!"

"Shut up," I insisted. "Tell us what you want, or get lost. Or both."

"Fine," the Ant huffed, and vanished.

Well! That was unexpected, and welcome.

"Guess what else all these guys have in common," Nick said, rattling my empty Coke glass. Tina appeared from nowhere, refilled it, and glided away. He absently handed the glass to me, and I didn't know whether to be flattered he'd noticed I needed a refill, or annoyed he was treating the brilliant Tina like she was a waitress. "Go on. Guess. You'll never guess."

"Since we'll never guess," Sinclair said, "why don't you just tell us?"

"Just *one* teensy guess?"

"Niiiiiick," I whined.

"Um. Ah. Hmm. They were all killed by a rogue cop or cops?" Sinclair inquired innocently.

We both stared at him.

"Goddammit," Nick cursed. He ignored, or didn't notice, Sinclair's flinch. "You gotta tell me how you knew that. I know for a fact there's no suckheads on the force."

"No, but there are sources available to the suckheads. As you well know, Detective Berry, nothing leaks more quickly or messily than a police station."

"So cops are tracking down bad guys and executing them?" I stared at the pictures. Gunshot wounds, all of them.

"The ones we can't put away legally, yeah. This guy." Dave tapped the photo of a pale, brown-eyed man who looked extremely pissed off, either because or in spite of the bullet wound over his left eye. "This guy was a burglar, and worse. He'd rape whoever was asleep in the house—we think he was getting the security codes from someone inside the security company, but he, uh, died before we could prove anything."

"Charming," Sinclair said coldly.

"Anyway, after the rape, he'd take everything out he could carry. We know he did it seven or eight times, but couldn't ever prove it. No ID. No prints. No semen. Nothing. Then—bam. He shows up deader than hell."

"And your problem with this is . . . ?" Sinclair's dark brows arched.

"Because the cops are good guys," I said before Nick could reply. "I mean, it sucks if they can't catch a rapist, jeez, you won't hear me argue that, but we have *laws*. We have *rules*. The good guys can't all of a sudden throw the Constitution out the window and strap down and shoot people."

I looked at Sinclair and Nick, who had identically blank looks on their faces. "Well. They *can't.*"

"As it is, I agree with the psycho vampire queen. Which brings me here."

"Why does the house of Sinclair have to clean up your mess?" my husband asked quietly.

"It's like your wife said. We make various promises and pledges when we get our badges—I won't bore a sociopath like you with them—but what it boils down to is, we follow the law. And boys and girls, Sherri's boy Nicky loves the law."

"Don't you have a special team or task force or whatever working on this?"

"Yeah. I'm it."

"You? Just one guy? I mean, I know you're good at your job, Nick, but—"

"Well, let's say I have some influence with the captain." Nick mimed driving a tractor.

"No doubt. And, could it be, the police do not necessarily wish for these people to be caught?"

"It could be," he admitted. "But they're gonna get caught. 'Cause I've got a secret weapon." He pointed at me.

"What makes you think—oh, shit, never mind, you know I'll do it."

"That's true." Nick smirked. "I did know it."

Chapter 15

You should let him solve his own problem," Sinclair said in a low voice, as Nick let himself out. "He's playing on your misplaced guilt."

"Misplaced? We *raped* his *brain*. And lied about it. To his face. For over a year."

He shrugged. He'd been a vampire too long; his conscience went right out the window sometimes.

"Have you ever considered—"

"Yes."

"Don't be a wiseass. Have you ever thought that the guy hates us and knows how to kill us, but hasn't?"

"I credit Jessica with that more than Detective Berry's good sense."

"Point," I conceded. "And yeah, it's a little obnoxious that he came over all expecting me to say yes right away—"

"Also, you're flattered."

"I am not! Okay, a little. Listen, this is our chance to win him back!"

"And why," he sighed, rubbing my shoulders, while I tried not to purr and lean into him, "would we want to do that?"

"Listen. Oooh, don't stop. The whole reason you pushed Jess to go out with him was because you wanted a source in the police department." I paused. "Another source, I mean. That reminds me. You've been keeping secrets. More than usual, I mean."

"Oh?" he said silkily, tightening his grip. My collarbones groaned under the pressure. Or maybe that was me groaning.

"Because there are one or two things I would like to discuss with you as well, if you're opening that door."

"Ahhhh . . . well, that's, um—" Fortunately, I was saved by the sound of splintering wood, and then Nick skidded down the foyer, his face a mask of blood.

"Face us, false queen!"

"Oboy," I said, nearly tripping as Sinclair grabbed me and thrust me behind his back. "That doesn't sound good."

Chapter 16

They streamed in, stepping smoothly over Nick's unconscious body. They moved like cats and had the hungry, feral look of same. At least, as far as I could tell from peeking over Sinclair's shoulder; I kept trying to elbow him out of the way, and he kept jamming me behind him.

"Uh, hi. You'd be, um, Garrett's friends, right?"

Happy, Skippy, Trippy, Sandy, Benny, Clara, and Jane glared at me as one. Somewhere, they'd clothed themselves—probably at the farm, I was seeing an awful lot of flannel—but still had the rank smell of the unwashed. They were all too thin, even bony. Their hair was varying colors and degrees of snarled.

"Well," I plunged, "I'm sorry I wasn't here when you stopped by the other night—"

They weren't moving. Perhaps I was dazzling them with my ineptitude. It had happened before.

"But at least this gives me a chance to, um, explain and even, um, apologize—"

"Do *not* apologize to them," Sinclair snarled. "One such as you should not even speak to them."

"Shush! He's cranky," I explained, "no blood tonight, you know how it is."

"We know exactly how it is," Clara said.

"Oh. Right." Awkward. What was interesting wasn't their reaction so much as Sinclair's. He wasn't angry so much as—as—*offended*, that was the word. Their presence offended him. I guess the Fiends were the vampire untouchables.

"Anyway, the thing is, it has been a *crazy* couple of years. For me, I mean. First there was the whole 'you are the queen' thing, which I was so *not* prepared for. And, I might point out, a lot of people were telling me to kill all you guys when Nostro—when you ate Nostro—but I didn't. In fact, I *saved* you."

"For imprisonment and slow starvation."

"I'm *getting* to that." I lowered my voice. "Okay, so then there was a serial killer—more than one, come to think of it—and then my half sister turned up, who was the daughter of the devil. The devil! I mean, please!"

"Yes, please," one of them said. "Let us end this."

"But I'm not finished! And then—before then, actually—all these ghosts started showing up looking for favors, like in that movie? Never mind, you didn't see that movie."

One of them was rubbing her temples. I sped up the This Is My Life portion of our program. "Then my friend got sick, lethally sick, and I had this wedding to plan, and all these werewolves showed up, and my dad and step mom died because I wanted a baby, and I had to kill a librarian, and it was just—just a crazy, crazy time. I mean, totally nuts."

"So. Essentially," Sandy—or was it Benny?—said, "you forgot about us."

"Well."

"Do not," Sinclair said through gritted teeth.

"Kinda," I admitted. "But I had all these really good reasons! I—yeek!" Sinclair had shoved me into the curtains as seven enraged vampires launched themselves at me.

Chapter 17

It's hard to even describe the fight. With enhanced strength, speed, and reflexes, everything happened so fast, and then it was all over but the bandaging.

The first one that got near Sinclair dropped, and so did the next one. One got past him and got a good grip on my hair (must have been a female killed in the 1920s . . . that was the hair-pulling era, right?), but I brought my head forward in a blur of coolness and broke her nose with a satisfying crunch. The blow made me stagger, and I wiped her blood off my forehead . . . sluggish, nasty dark stuff.

And the screaming! All the screaming! Wait. Only one person was screaming. *Marc* was screaming.

I shoved Hair Puller at the fireplace, peripherally noticing the ceramic tiles rain down on her stupid face as she hit the floor. Then I ran toward the shrieking Marc, who was on his back fighting off flashing fangs and teeth (Clara? Benny? It was going so quickly I couldn't tell).

Before I could get to them, Tina leaned over them, grabbed Clara/Benny *by the hair* and yanked him (ah, a guy, I saw it now) off Marc. She had something long and shiny in her other hand, and I recognized it, as she swung the Wusthof butcher knife (Jessica's pride and joy, she had a whole collection in the butler's pantry, and they were wicked sharp), hard enough to decapitate Benny. His headless body fell with a thump, and Marc scrambled back on his hands, so the thing wouldn't fall on him.

Tina had dropped the head and was turning to see who else she could decapitate, when a wooden spoon burst through her chest.

"This?" the Ant demanded. "This is how you spend your time? Squabbling with people who don't bathe?"

"Not . . . *now*!" I ran to Tina, nearly tripping over the body of a Fiend Sinclair had killed, and yanked the serving spoon out of her heart. Then I grabbed her head and screamed into her eyes, which had begun to gloss over. "Don't you *dare* die on me, you efficient bitch, don't you *dare*!"

"I—I'm fine. I'm all right, my queen." We both looked down. The wooden serving spoon, about nine inches long, was now ash. I had turned it to ash. And Tina was all right.

No, I didn't know how.

And then the door was slamming, the other Fiends were gone, and the fight was over.

Chapter 18

We'd killed two of them: Sinclair had killed Trippy; Tina had killed Benny. Marc was wounded, bleeding like the proverbial stuck pig, but it looked mostly superficial. Jessica, who had been keeping a terrified Garrett from fleeing down the tunnel, drove Marc to the ER. Marc's last delirious comment was, "Will I become a vampire now? Cool!"

By then, the rest of the Fiends had fled, and Nick had regained consciousness. "Yeah, that'll show 'em," he said groggily, as he caromed from one wall to another, trying to stagger out the door. It looked like he had a broken nose, but I hoped that was the worst of it. We offered to call an ambulance, but he tagged along with Jessica, who I knew would tell him the whole story.

Sinclair carried Tina upstairs to the hot tub room, dunked her in (over her protests; we were pretty sure I'd cured the wound), and, after ten minutes, let her out.

About the water thing: for some reason, when vampires are grievously hurt, water speeds up the healing process. I had no idea why. Maybe because our undead bodies didn't have much moisture? I didn't know. So much of being a vampire was like magic to me. And not the cool kind, either.

Tina shook the wet hair out of her eyes and grinned at me. "Two down. Five to go."

"You were nuts, launching yourself at that guy."

"You and the king had your hands full," she said dryly. I handed her a robe, and she snuggled into it. Not a mark on her, thank God.

"But you were stabbed with wood," Sinclair said, looking ashen. "I saw it."

Tina looked at me, and I winked. So she shrugged and said to the king, "It must have missed my heart."

Oooooh, she's actually lying to the king of the vamps! Somebody write down the date and time. And I had to admit, it was nice to be the one keeping secrets for a change.

"But I *saw*—"

"Come on," I sighed. "Let's make smoothies. Or something."

Chapter 19

We visited Marc later that night. Sure, two o'clock in the morning isn't considered optimum visiting hours, but this wasn't the first late-night trip to this hospital for me. Or even the tenth. I knew who to sidestep, who to put the vampire mojo on, and who didn't give a tin shit if Bin Laden was on the floor, as long as he or she could snag an extra hour of sleep in the on-call room.

"Disgusting," Marc informed me cheerily from his bed, as he played with the tilt settings and television remote control at once. "This hospital's about as secure as the men's rooms in the Target Center. But thanks for coming to see me so fast."

"After my second smoothie, you were all I could think about."

"Tell the truth," he said soberly. "My hair looks awful, doesn't it?"

"Well . . ." If he considered most of the hair on the right, which was clotted with blood and hopelessly snarled to be awful, then . . . "At least you've got your health. Oh, wait."

"Aren't you funny." He stretched out his bandaged arms and looked at them. After being stitched up (fifteen stitches in his left arm, twenty-six in his right, thirty-one in his right leg, eighteen in the muscle just below his right nipple, seven stitches to the left of his belly button), he'd been admitted for overnight observation. "It looked worse than it was, in case you were wondering."

"Actually, I was wondering if you could pull the blanket up a little more."

"Oh." Marc was still staring down at himself, but had yet to notice he was naked.

"I'll, uh, just do that." I bustled around the bed, trying to make myself useful.

He looked pleased. "Now I'm tucked in!"

For the first time I realized his green-eyed gaze was a little cloudy. I peered closer. So did he. Our faces were about an inch apart but, again, Marc didn't seem to think this was at all unusual.

"Jeez," I said, so close my breath (if I had any) would have fogged his glasses (if he wore them). "How much medication are you on?"

"Well, let's see. I had some Valium at the house, and some more on the way to the hospital. (I offered some to Nick, but he said no thanks.) Then in the ER, the intern said—"

"You know what? It doesn't matter. As long as you're okay is all."

"Oh, sure! I'm great! You know, for someone who was trying to kill me, he mostly just knocked me down and got me dirty. I mean, did you *see* those guys? Covered with mud!"

"Yeah, that's annoying." I fought not to roll my eyes or sneak a peek at the clock on the wall.

"I think he wanted to kill you and was mostly trying to get me out of his way. I'll be sore and itchy for ages, and I'll have spec-*tacular* bruising, and maybe a couple of really butch scars, but that's the extent of it. I feel pretty lucky."

"I'm—I'm glad, Marc." He *had* been lucky, but I was mostly too tormented by guilt. And hunger pangs. I was so thirsty, and the smells generated by the hospital were making me drool. As the queen, I didn't have to feed every night like all the other vampires, and sometimes I made the mistake of pushing it. It had been at least four days. "Also, don't come back."

He absently cracked his knuckles; they sounded like Rice Crispies. "Yep, after tonight it'll be smooth—what?"

"You can't come back until we take care of this Fiend situation."

"Take care of the situation? You're talking like it's a termite infestation!"

"If only," I muttered. "Look, I feel crummy that you got hurt, but you *were* lucky, and I'm not enough of a twit to put you right back in danger."

He blinked at me slowly, like an owl, and I could tell he was trying to muster an argument. After a long silence he said, "But we have the Super Secret Vampire Tunnels to escape to."

"Yeah, except every one of the Fiends is faster than you and

Jess, and what if they cut you off next time? What if Sinclair and I, God forbid, aren't even home next time?"

"But we can—"

"Marc, I'm sorry, I guess I didn't realize . . . you think this is a debate. It's not. You *could* run to the tunnels, Sinclair and I *might* be able to protect you, the Fiends might come back *but* not try to hurt you . . . whatever, man. Too many maybes for me—you're out."

"But Betsy . . ." His eyes filled, and he shook his head savagely, making the tears fly. Then he was glaring at me with wet cheeks. "That's my *home*, same as it is yours. Where can I go?"

"Yeah, about that." Marc wasn't seeing anyone right now (he'd had a fling a month or so ago, but otherwise was something of a dateless wonder), and no family—at least, none he would ever live with ever again. "Where do you want to go? You pick the place, and Sinclair will pay for it. Sinclair and I," I corrected, since technically it was now my fortune, too.

"I don't want to pick anything," Marc began, still pissed, but then I could see the possible advantages of the situation begin to trickle past the fog of drugs. "Uh. Anywhere I want?"

"Anywhere. Until we fix this. The day the Fiends pack it up and go home"—Yeah, sure, that's how this would end—"is the day you move back in."

An expression of vague alarm crossed his features. "But what if the Fiends stay out of sight for, I dunno, two years? Before they make their move? Are you going to keep me out of my home for *years*?"

"It won't come to that." And try as I might, I just couldn't picture it. Not to be all egotistical or anything, but I couldn't imagine the Fiends could do much of anything until they'd settled with me. Laying back in the buckwheat for a couple of years was definitely not their style. "It absolutely won't. But right now it's too dangerous for you. Of course it's your home, and the day the Fiends are taken care of is the day you come back. But until then . . ."

I tucked another blanket around Marc and left him sleepily murmuring, "The Radisson? No. The Millennium? No. Sofitel? I know! The Grand! Will they do turndown service for me . . . ?"

Chapter 20

As Marc's door was wheezing shut behind me, I heard Jessica trotting toward me. I was able to pick up the sound of her footsteps over everyone else's in the hall (granted, at this hour, there weren't many, but still—my very own stupid pet trick!) and turned in time for her to wave to get my attention.

It seemed to take a very long time for her to get to me. Sinclair and I had talked about this phenomenon once or twice, after making love. It was starting to seem more and more natural, taking advantage of my vampiric senses and all. In the beginning, they either overwhelmed me (especially when I was hungry) or I had to sit still and make a conscious effort to hear, to smell, to whatever outside the range of normal human activity. Now I could probably pick Sinclair or Jess or Mom out of a Metrodome crowd.

Now her mouth was moving, verrrry slooooowly. I squinted at her and then yelped when she pinched me.

"Sorry, but you had a very goofy look on your face. How is he? Is he sleeping?"

"He's a little out of it."

"Oh." She stared at the closed door as if she had suddenly developed X-ray vision and could, y'know, actually see what was happening on the other side. "Do you think I should go in? It's so late. Think he'd be mad if I didn't come in tonight? I don't think he'd be mad. And I'll see him tomorrow. I'll bring him some Bruegger's for breakfast. Let's walk. Can we walk? Come on."

I didn't say a word, just fell into step beside her. It wasn't hard to figure out why she was nervous—she had, after all, spent many days in this very hospital as a terminal patient. That'd take the shine off your night, even if the other events hadn't.

I cut through her nervous chatter as we headed to the hospital parking ramp. "Actually, you could help me out *and* radically reduce your trips to the hospital."

"Sing it."

"Well, we're putting Marc up somewhere nice, sort of as a treat, you know? I mean, he's been through a *lot*. He was finally starting to date again but he had that bad breakup last month . . . and he's been picking up so many extra shifts . . . and he really got torn up tonight."

"Yeah," Jessica said slowly, "I guess you could say he's had a crummy few weeks."

"Right!" She was falling for it! The puny human had no hope whatsoever of overcoming the mightiness that was me, Betsy, vampire queen and recovering Miss Congeniality. "So maybe you could go with him, wherever he picks, and sort of settle him in, you know? Make sure he's got everything he needs, and—"

Jessica had stopped walking, which was awkward, as I didn't immediately notice, and I have long legs and walk fast, so I had to walk all the way back across the skyway if I wanted to keep participating in the conversation. Which, judging by her thunderous expression, I did not.

"Betsy. Oh my God. How—"

—did I know that was just what Marc needed? How could we best help him get settled? How did I manage to say the right thing time and time again?

Naw. I knew the tone and I knew it wasn't going to be good.

"—fucking dumb do you think I am?"

"You mean, on a sliding scale, or—"

"You've gotten rid of one human, and now you're trying to ditch the other."

"Oh, say, hey now! I think 'ditch' is a little—ow."

She had jammed her index finger into the middle of my chest and now poked to emphasize her words. With each poke a cloud-colored fingernail jabbed me. It was like being pricked over and over again with the world's dullest needle. We'd had so many fights like this, I practically had scars there. "I'm. Not. Going. Anywhere. Besides, it's my house! You can't kick me out of—"

"Also, Sinclair wants to buy it from you. I mean, we want to buy it. The house. We totally do. Together. It's not just him alone. *We* want to." Because that's what married couples did, right? Bought real estate together and drank each other's dark, dead blood?

"Oh, I'll just *bet* you do." She pulled her small, sleek head back, like a snake getting ready to bite. It was silly, kind of: I was a foot taller, I was thirty pounds heavier, I had legions of the Undead at my command (sorta) and vampiric strength, and I was scared to death of her. I tried not to cower as she ranted, "Well, you can't have it! For one thing, it's not for sale, and for another, it's my house!"

"Jessica, we almost lost you this summer, and—"

"Betsy, even if you couldn't cure cancer, I wouldn't be afraid of the Fiends. But hey! Since you can? I can't say I'm worried about something as silly as a few bites."

We started walking again, only she was stomping toward the elevator, and I was doing the Igor Shuffle ("Yes, master, right away, master, I am not an animal, master.") right behind her. "A few bites? That's like calling the cost of the War on Terror a few dollars. And I know you're not afraid, it's not about you being afraid, it's about taking the sensible precaution of being elsewhere when the bad guys come back, doy!"

She snorted and jabbed the elevator button. "Listen to you. 'Sensible precautions.'"

"And don't forget the 'doy.' Jess, how many scary movies have we seen where the heroine does something really dumb like hang around in a hallway when she knows the bad guys are, like, a room away?"

"'Bout a zillion," she acknowledged.

"We got off *real* lucky this time—Marc with a few scratches, and you not even hurt—and I think it's completely nuts to push it. So how about you don't be an asshole about it and just stay with Marc until we kill all the bad guys?"

"Oh, someone's being an asshole," she agreed, practically leaping into the elevator in her agitation, "but it's not this girl."

I leaned against the wall and closed my eyes. Mostly against the awful fluorescents in the elevators; there were about eight too many. "I knew you were gonna be like this."

"But you had to open your yap anyway."

I squinted at her. "Don't come crying to me when a Fiend tears your head off."

She smiled a little, and I knew that was partly because she thought she had won the argument. She hadn't, but she was forcing me to do something I really, really, really didn't want to do.

I was gonna tell on her.

Chapter 21

I nearly walked through the Ant on my way from the bathroom to the bed, and neither of us were very happy about the near miss.

"Must you ignore everyone's personal boundaries?"

"Yeeeeeggghh! Stop *doing* that, you disgusting horrible dead wretch!"

Sinclair, all the way across the room, looked guilty and bent down to untie his other Kenneth Cole, as opposed to just yanking it off and tossing it in the general direction of the closet.

"You might think about what would happen to me if you got your silly self killed."

"Yeah, I should have realized what a terrible thing that would be, Ant. *For you.*" I ran the six steps from the bathroom, jumping into the middle of the bed, so nothing hiding under it could grab my feet. "And I wasn't talking to you," I added to my husband, "but it's nice to see you treating your shoes with more respect."

The Ant was looking in our direction with rabid suspicion. Which, since she'd been heavily Botox'd before her death, came across as slightly raised eyebrows and rapidly blinking eyes. "What are you two doing? You're not going to bed *now*?"

"We've been up all night, you pineapple-colored idiot." Pineapple referring to her hair, which was stiff and yellow. "Dawn's about an hour away."

"Well, in that time you could be—"

"Having nasty sex with my husband. Nasty," I added, ignoring Sinclair as he picked up a pillow, calmly pressed it over his face, and barked laughter into it. "With, um, probes and things. We like to role-play. I'm the alien, and he's the helpless probed human. Now get lost, because it's going to get messy in here."

Ah! It worked. She'd popped out while I was horrifying her with lurid descriptions of my imaginary sex life. I wish she'd just tell me what she wanted and go back to Hell already.

"Thank"—I searched for a word that wouldn't make Sinclair cringe—"goodness she's gone."

"Help, help, I'm being probed!" The pillow sailed at my head, and I knocked it away, trying not to grin. Beside me, Sinclair tried his best to look horrified. "If only I didn't feel a sick, wrong sexual attraction to these alien invaders. If only I had listened to my mother's warnings about loose alien women!"

"Pal, you are so not getting any tonight."

"If only," he continued dolefully, "they didn't keep telling me to turn my head and cough."

That was it; I lost it. I shrieked and laughed and kicked at the covers until the bed looked like what I told the Ant we'd be up to.

"That was slightly . . . hysterical."

"Hey, it's been a long night."

"Indeed it has, my darling alien intruder." Sinclair yanked the remaining sheets and blankets off the bed and threw them to the floor with a theatrical flourish. Then he pounced on me while sheets billowed all over the place.

He kissed me for a wonderfully long time, then pulled back and cocked an eyebrow. "Want to see my probe?"

Chapter 22

The next evening started off nice and quiet. Marc wasn't around, of course, Garrett was probably still cowering in the basement, and I didn't look too hard for Jessica.

Almost as soon as I'd gotten up, Tina and Sinclair had left for the library. This made sense, as the former librarian, Marjorie, had kept extensive files on every vampire she knew of, heard of, or could track down.

Information, as far as the late, unmourned Marjorie believed, had been power.

They had politely asked if I wanted to come, pretending I'd actually be of use to a couple of near geniuses trapped in a warehouse disguised as a library. They probably thought hours of research on computers and—and whatever you did research on would be a good time, poor morons. Of course I'd said no.

But even if I'd lost all my cool points and was a hopeless, helpless virgin weirdo geek who *wanted* to spend half the night in a vampire library, I couldn't.

I, after all, had serious work to do for the Minneapolis Police Department. Make that Homicide Department. Yeah, that's right, we vampire queens are in constant demand all over the place for—

"Are you actually going to get in my car?" Nick Berry demanded, shaking his keys at me. "Or just keep staring off into space like that? Because it is fuckin' creepy, Betsy, you look like the Exlax is about to kick in."

"Huh? Oh. That was mean. And I'm *coming*, don't *nag*."

"I'm a grown man," he forced out through gritted teeth, "and we don't nag."

"You were! You *were* nagging!"

"Betsy, I swear to God, if you don't shut your fucking yap and get in the car, I'm going to pull out my gun and blow your—"

"Ha! You said 'blow.' "

The gun had cleared the holster. Hmm, Nick was a short-tempered fellow these days. "I'm gonna count to ten. One. Seven. Nine. T—"

"Hold it right there!"

We both jumped like we'd been caught doing something nasty, and looked. Jessica the Terrible was stomping down the porch and across the driveway toward us.

Quick as thought, Mr. Gun was back in his house, Mr. Holster.

"Hi, babe, I thought you were sleeping."

"Oh, Jess. I didn't know you were up."

"Well?" She stopped, slightly out of breath. She must have sprinted when she figured out Nick was here. "Which is it? I'm in bed asleep because I have a human boyfriend, or I'm wide awake because my best friend is a vampire?"

"Uh—"

"You're so great," Nick said warmly. "It's both."

Man, I could never pull that off.

"You sneaky lying sack of shit."

Apparently Nick couldn't, either.

"You're sneaking off with him to—well, I don't know what, but I don't like it. And you!" She rounded on Nick, jabbing with the dreaded index finger (which was now painted eggplant). "I know damn well you don't like being alone with Betsy anymore. So what are you up to?"

He didn't tell her?

"You didn't tell her?" I tried to hide my delight at Nick's look of consternation . . . and the fact that it bummed me out, hearing Nick was scared to be alone with me. At least I wasn't the only one who was scared to death of Pissed Off Jessica—hell, he was *armed*, and he looked ready to sidle around the corner and hide. "That's awful. Why wouldn't you tell her?"

"Because she'll jump to the conclusion that I'm trying to get you killed," he snapped.

"Yeah, she's funny that way."

"What? Get killed? Why might you get killed? Betsy, you can't go off doing something dangerous with Nick, when those disgusting Fiends could be back any minute and try to finish what—" Then she shut her mouth with a snap.

Nick and I looked at each other, then at Jessica. I felt sorry for her. She really did try to keep Nick out of the vampire stuff, telling him only what she absolutely thought he needed to know.

And of course, she didn't get into the gory details of Nick's terror and hatred of me, just made the occasional reference to it. She was a good dancer. And it was too bad she had to dance at all. I mean, more than the normal amount any best friend does when balancing a lifelong friendship with a new love affair.

"Why don't we get in the car," I suggested, "and Jess goes back in the house, and the three of us pretend the last forty-five seconds never happened."

"Deal."

"Deal."

Nick started up his SedanMobile as I waved to Jess, who was back on the porch and anxiously waving back.

"Betsy! Let's go!"

"Your car," I told him, gingerly climbing into the front seat, "smells like ass."

Chapter 23

Man, that was bad. We coulda handled that one better. A lot better."

"What are you talking about, 'we'? I'm not the one who completely screwed that one up. Hey, Jess gets full disclosure from me, pal."

"Oh fucking bullshit," he snapped, almost running down a squirrel. He turned onto Grand Avenue, where he'd have better luck with hapless pedestrians. "You told me yourself after that—after that business around your wedding that you kept her out of the vampire stuff."

"After I cured her terminal illness, you mean? Is that what you're referring to?" My voice was so sugary it would have given a diabetic an instant attack. I normally wouldn't bring it up, especially since I had no idea how I'd done it, but hey, Nick was bigger than me, and smarter. And armed. And he hated me. "Sure, Sinclair and I keep her out of it—keep her out in the sense of actually, physically keeping her out of it. But I still *tell* her everything."

"Nnmph," he grunted. Then, "Put on your seat belt."

"Please. Would you really give a gold-plated crap if I was launched screaming through your windshield?"

"State law."

Oh. Right. I, the Minnesota law-abiding vampire queen, obediently buckled up.

"She's got enough to worry about," he finally (lamely) said.

"You big liar! You're using me to ramp your solve rate, and I might get hideously mangled or killed. *That's* what you don't want her to 'worry' about."

"Ramp my solve rate?" He slid over two streets and merged onto I-94. "Betsy, stop watching *NYPD Blue* reruns."

"I don't! On purpose."

He groaned. "Please don't explain that."

"But Marc has a big crush on Sipowicz, and he's always hoping to see the man's butt again, and I can't help it if every time I go into the TV room or his room or one of the parlors, he's playing the DVDs."

"Well, if you're so damn sure I'm up to no good, how come you're here?"

"You know why."

"Enlighten me."

"Stop it."

"C'mon, I'm serious."

I stared at him. He stared back with his blank cop's face. Truth? Lie? Somewhere in between? I bet he could take a polygraph and never, what was the cop phrase? Never bounce a needle.

"I'm here to prove to you that I'm no danger to you, that we could be friends if you didn't shrivel with horror at the thought, that vampires can be good guys, too." I said it all in a rush, and it came out sounding like my drunken Marilyn Monroe impersonation.

"Yeah, you're going to have to slow that one down and run it by me again."

"I'm. Here. To. Prove. That. I'm. No. Danger. And. We. Can. Be. Friends. If. You. Didn't. Shrivel."

"That's okay, I think I can piece together the rest. Trouble is, blondie, why should I ever believe anything you tell me, ever again?"

"Oh, jeez!" I threw my hands up in the air. "How long are you going to hold that one thing against us? I've told you and told you, I was a new vampire and didn't know the rules!"

"Yeah, so you fucking mind-raped me."

I noticed that, like me, he tended to swear more when he was nervous or mad.

"Anything sounds bad when you say it like that," I conceded sulkily, staring out the passenger window.

He made a sound that might have been a snort, or a muffled laugh. When I looked, he had his cop face back on.

"So where are we going?"

"What a tactful, yet subtle way to change the subject."

"Fine. Don't tell me. Keep being the biggest, most gigantickest asshole—"

"Gigantickest?" he said, delighted. "Are you using word-a-day toilet paper again? Okay, okay, don't pout. And don't enlighten me about vampire toilet habits, I don't think I could stand it. I've managed to run down a couple of leads and thought I'd bring my favorite dead enforcer with me to see what's what."

"I thought you said your vigilante killer was a cop? Or cops, plural?"

"I did."

"So how can we check on them without, I dunno, scaring them? Tipping them off?"

"Very carefully. I've been running down when the murders took place—best as the M.E. can tell us, anyway—with the duty logs of the ones I think might be capable of something like this."

"Oh." That was really smart. And just laced with common sense. Exactly why I never would have thought of it. God, I'd be the *worst* police officer. I knew that about myself, had always known it, which was why it was kind of a thrill to be in a police car (the front seat, anyway), helping solve murders. Well. Coming along for the ride while someone else solved murders. "Huh. Okay."

"Do you know much about guns, Betsy?" He indicated his service piece. "If you're ever in a situation where you need to shoot a guy to save my ass, could you do it?"

"Wait. Do you hate me now because I'm a ruthless vampire who has killed before, or do you hate me because I'm a careless dimwit who can't be trusted with this power?"

"You mean, right now? Right this minute, why do I hate you?" he asked in a voice that was almost—so close!—teasing. "Do I have to choose? God, so many choices . . ."

"I don't have a lot of use for handguns," I said after a glance at the pistol at his waist. "Mostly I know about shotguns from goose hunting with my mom, and rifles for target practice."

"The professor hunts?"

"The professor can shoot the eye out of a squirrel at two hundred yards. I'll tell you who knows a ton about guns—Tina. She's an expert. You should get with her sometime."

"No thanks," he said curtly, and just like that, our fragile whatever it was came to an end.

Chapter 24

Nick dropped me off at about two-thirty in the morning, not remotely discouraged, although it looked to me like his leads hadn't panned out. At least he was being (relatively) friendly again, so I didn't say anything to wreck it. I just waved good-bye and trudged into the mansion.

Where a grim Sinclair and a fretful Jessica were waiting for me.

"Whaaaat?" I whined, moodily pulling off my Herrera boots. "What'd I do? I didn't do it. I'm pretty sure it was Marc. No, wait. Cathie!" Cathie, the ghost-gone-walkabout, who I could actually use to help me with the aunt. She was usually convenient for blame. Of course, if she'd been there, I never would have gotten away with it.

She'd been killed by a serial killer (who was later killed by my sister, Laura, who had a spectacular temper tantrum in the killer's basement) and, even after his death, had hung around being my ghostly secretary of sorts. If ghosts showed up needing help, Cathie would try to help them herself . . . and only if she couldn't would she then let the ghost bother me. Plus, she was super funny and nice. I missed having her around. Even more so now that the Ant was pestering me.

"Sinclair told me," Jessica said without preamble.

"About what?" I asked, totally at a loss. Man, I'd have to drink some blood soon. I was getting dumber by the hour.

"About Nick's little murder project," she said grimly, and I winced.

"That wasn't nice," I said to Sinclair, the reproach quite clear in my tone.

" 'Nice' is the least of my concerns, or interests. He is trying to get you killed, or at least cares not if you're hurt. If I could tell his superior without jeopardizing our secret, I would."

"You'd tattle to his boss! Oooh, that's *really* mean." I walked into the parlor and carefully flopped down onto a fainting couch, which someone had probably lugged over on the *Mayflower.*

"I'll deal with him later," she swore, and I almost felt sorry for the guy. "I just wanted to make sure you got back all right."

"Sure I did. Heck, it didn't even pan out. It was an evening of driving around, basically. Feel bad for *him,* he was the one trapped in a car with me." In fact, a couple of times he had rolled his window down and hung out his head like a dog, screaming into the wind. Heh.

"And I," Sinclair said, "wished to attempt to convince you, once again, to leave police matters to the police. We have other things to attend to."

"Oh, like I would have been any help to you and Tina tonight."

Sinclair lifted his left shoulder up about half a centimeter, which, for him, was the same as a shrug of agreement.

"Like I said, it was one big safe boring evening. No problems. And," I added, looking around the small, peach-colored parlor, "I assume the Fiends haven't been back?"

"No, thank God."

"Did you and Tina learn anything?"

"Oh, this and that," Sinclair said vaguely, which either meant (a) he had gobs of tidbits he didn't want to spill in front of Jessica, (b) he had nothing, or (c) he had plenty, but didn't want to worry me.

"So. Let's go to bed?"

"Do that," Jessica muttered, turning around like a soldier doing an about-face and marching out of the parlor. "I've got to call Nick."

"Very, very mean," I told my husband, as I followed him up the stairs. "Ratting Nick out like third graders squealing about who stole the chocolate milk. Nice!"

Sinclair shrugged again. I pulled our bedroom door shut and jumped on his back.

"Ah?" he managed, looking around for his suit hanger.

"I'm *starving,*" I purred into his left ear.

The hanger, which he had just picked up, went sailing over our right shoulders. Then he reached back, got my coat in a fist, and yanked me off of him, *over* him, and flopped me onto the bed.

"Then let's eat," he said, and fell upon me like a scary fairy-tale monster, only a whole lot sexier and, let's face it, better dressed.

Chapter 25

The sun fell down the next night, but I'd been awake for about an hour by the time it was full dark. Still wasn't taking my increasing resilience to sunlight for granted, and still not trying to rub it in to Tina and Sinclair who were, after all, much older than I was.

I knew it was a real treat to be able to go for a walk outside in the late afternoon. I'd paid for it, though, thanks to the Faustian bargain that was the Book of the Dead. (Sinclair lost a bet once when he didn't think I knew what *Faustian* meant; but there's more than one way for a girl to Google a cat.)

I got dressed, then remembered what I'd forgotten last night. Amazing what good sex and half a pint of vampire king blood could do to jog your memory.

I flopped onto the bed, picked up the bedside phone, and dialed Nick.

"Homicide, Detective Berry."

"This is the woman," I purred in my throatiest voice, "who is going to make all of your dreams come true."

"Aunt Marian?"

"Gross!" I nearly dropped the phone. "Nick, that's disgusting!"

"So is your sexy voice. You sound like Patrick Warburton with a head cold. What's on your microscopic mind?"

"I forgot to tell you something last night."

"Of course you did. You're a dimwit."

"It's something that will make you extremely happy," I wheedled.

"You're moving, and you can't remember your forwarding address."

"You wish."

"The mailman left a hand grenade in your slot?"

"Do you want me to tell you, or do I have to listen to more dumb comments?"

"They are not dumb. So. What is it?"

"Nothing much. A cadre of old vampires is ticked at me, has already tried to kill me once, and won't stop until I'm dead or they are, and there's, like, twenty of them and only one of me. Also, we're out of milk."

"Really?" Nick sounded like he'd won the lottery. "You wouldn't tease me, would you?"

"I swear on every one of Marc's stitches that it's true. Not a drop of milk in the whole house."

"Marc's stitches—hmm. Interesting that Jessica hasn't mentioned any of *this*. You'd better tell me."

So I gave him the whole story, thinking, *You only think Jessica's in hot water, you poor bastard.* She must not have reached him last night. He had no idea the storm was about to break over his head.

"Uh-huh." I'd assume he was taking notes, only Nick never wrote anything down. Not like the cops on TV, that was for sure. "Uh-hmm. And you don't know where they are?"

"Not yet, but Sinclair and Tina are doing hours of drudgery research to figure that out."

"And Marc's at the General?" he asked, using the slang we used for the local hospital.

"Yeah, but he'll get out today. They ended up keeping him for a couple of nights, but not because anything wrong popped up. I think it was probably because he's big-time popular on the staff. But we're moving him to The Grand Hotel tonight."

"Where he'll stay indefinitely."

"Yeah, and the thing is, Jessica won't go. I mean, flat-out refuses."

"Yeah?"

"Yeah. Sic her!"

"Doesn't she have, I don't know, a fucking Swiss chalet or something? Some other property besides the mansion where she can stay?"

"No, she doesn't care for Europe unless it's Tuscany, but surely you've got a chalet up your sleeve, John Deere Boy."

"Well, she doesn't have to stay there," he said grimly. "Not in Vampire Central."

"Yeah, so sock it to her." I didn't mention that Jessica wasn't staying at the mansion because she had nowhere else to go. He knew why she was staying, too, but didn't want to admit it, at least out loud. "Go tell her who's boss, by God."

"Oh, shut up," he said, and clicked off his phone.

Chapter 26

My semi-good deed done for the day, I rolled over, thumbed off my phone, dropped it on the bedside table (Sinclair was already bitching about the marks my phone and keys were leaving on various antiques around the house), and examined my feet.

There were advantages to being a vampire. I had refused to admit that for a long time and, even now, wasn't very happy when forced to make such an admission. The strength thing, and the speed. The hearing, of course.

More than once I'd been grateful for all three, usually while some psycho was trying to kill me. (Although if I hadn't been undead in the first place, said psycho would not have been trying to kill me, but screw it.)

And, although there were far more drawbacks than advantages to being queen, that had its high points, too.

But there were plenty of disads to being dead. One of the many was, you couldn't change your looks. I mean, you could, but whatever you did—paint your fingernails, cut your hair, curl your eyelashes—was undone when you rose the next night. I had no idea why, just like I didn't know how we could walk around with a heart rate of seven, or how we didn't need to breathe more than a couple of times an hour.

Thus, I always—*always*—needed a pedicure. (Thank God I had died only a few days after a cut and highlights!) It was depressing and a fact of life (or death, if you will), but there it was.

No time to mope. (Well. There was always time to mope. But I wasn't in the mood tonight.) I decided to do a quick one, myself, and twenty minutes later I was admiring my pink, newly smooth feet, and the wiggling toes with their coat of "Bitterness," which was actually a lovely soft gray.

Energized with the gorgeousness of my feet, I darted into the bathroom, rummaged around in the counter under the sink, and extracted a box of Crimson Tide, a wash-in/wash-out hair color. Stayed in for up to twelve shampoos. If you were alive, anyway.

When I got out of the shower, I couldn't help grinning at myself in the mirror. My hair was a dark, unnatural red; the shade made my skin paler than usual and my eyes seem green (they tended to fluctuate between blue and green, depending on what I was wearing and the quality of the light). And the box only cost twelve bucks. Since I'd be blond again tomorrow night, it wasn't worth going to the salon and dropping a hundred bucks for a custom dye job.

I dried off and got dressed, then opened my bedroom door, briefly wondered where my husband was (Sinclair only had to rest on occasion and, likely after sex, had waited until I conked out and then gone to the library or the fax machine or the local Kinko's to make color copies of something—wait, he had Tina to do that), furtively checked for unwanted ghosts, then bounded down the steps.

I could hear the fight long before I got to the kitchen door.

Chapter 27

I can't believe you're staying! You *know*, and you're fucking *staying!*"

"Well, what about you, white boy?" Hmm. Jessica must be mega-pissed . . . "white boy" and "white girl" tended to come out only when she was furious, or scared. "You somehow forgot to mention that you're using my best friend to help you look good for the chief."

Wait. What?

"Not to mention, you expect her to take bullets for you if things get nasty. Slip your mind?"

"I'm not taking bullets for anyone," I announced, pushing open the door, "unless it's Beverly Feldman."

"Stay out of this, Betsy."

"Yeah, fuck off, blondie."

Sinclair's head came up with a jerk (he'd been seated at the counter, pretending to read the *Journal*), and he opened his mouth to hiss or roar something, but I overrode him with a breezy, "And a verrrrrry pleasant good evening to all of you, too."

The pleasantness of my greeting appeared to take the wind out of everyone's sails, not just his. I poured myself half the pitcher of orange juice and sat my ass down just like I belonged there.

It could be tricky, busting in on a fight. There was the "oh my God, I'm so sorry you didn't see me, I'll just scuttle back out the way I came" method, always popular with roommates of the female persuasion.

And there was my "hey, you're doing this in a public place—sort of, our kitchen—and you're fighting about me, so guess what? I'm staying" method, which I normally didn't have the nerve to try.

Jessica was eyeballing my head. "Nice hair."

"Thanks."

"It's very," Sinclair said carefully, "bright."

"Felt like a change."

"Mmmm. Detective Berry," Sinclair tried again, in a much calmer tone, but no less frightening, if you knew him, which we all did, "please do not speak to my wife that way in her own home."

"It's my girlfriend's home," Nick said, sounding sulky, but at least he was quieting down, too.

"Yes, so you delight in reminding me, and as I said earlier, I would be delighted to purchase the place from her at a fair market price. She could then move in with you, or not, as she liked, and as you liked, and several of your so-called problems would be over."

Nick had nothing to say to that, of course, and why would he? Sinclair was only telling the truth. In fact, I could see on Nick's face how very, very badly he wanted that option for Jessica.

Too bad he'd have about as much luck making her do anything she didn't want as I'd had in the past. Put it this way: I'd had more luck persuading the Ant not to wear so much polyester.

In fact, the only way he could maybe get her to leave would be if she moved—

Abruptly, Nick was on one knee. This startled Jessica, who kept her finger pointed at the space where his chest had been two seconds earlier. "I don't like you talking like—what the hell are you doing?"

He looked up at her soulfully, grabbed the hand that wasn't stabbing the air above him, and clutched it to his chest. "Jessica, will you marry me?"

"What?"

"Or at least move in with me? Right now?"

"*Très* romantic," Sinclair muttered, and I winked at him. I noticed his green teacup was empty, rose, and poured him a fresh cup, ignoring his raised eyebrows. It was possible I had never done such a thing before. Damn, I was in a good mood tonight! It could only mean doom was on the way. Doom, or the Ant.

"How sweet of you to ask." She yanked her hand out of Nick's no doubt sweaty grip. "And I'm only being half sarcastic when I say that, because you *do* think you're protecting me. But what a rotten way to begin living together or being engaged—so you can move me out of my best friend's house."

"*It's your house!*"

"That's true," I said, guzzling more juice. "It is."

"And you," he said, rounding on me. Definitely should have stayed out of this one. "Jessica's in mortal fucking danger— again! And this one is one hundred percent at your door, Oh Great Queen of the Suckheads!"

"You quit it," Jessica ordered, as the three of us pretended he wasn't one hundred percent right. "You were chortling over the possibility of the Fiends eating my friend—except if those things take out Sinclair and Betsy—"

"Actually," I said, "we prefer 'Betsy and Sinclair.' "

"We certainly do not."

"—just what do you think they'll do to the rest of us?"

"Force us to buy time-shares in Cabo San Lucas," Tina suggested in a low voice, passing the local newspapers to Sinclair. I stifled a snicker.

"If they take out Sinclair and Betsy, who's gonna be safe?" Jessica asked. "Don't you get it, white boy? Half the time, those two walking wood ticks are the only thing between us and the *real* monsters."

"That was wonderful," Tina said, scuttling in with her head down, as if Nick and Jess were throwing frying pans in addition to words, "except for walking wood ticks. Good morning, Majesties. Good morning, Detective. Jessica."

They ignored her. Nick was still on his knees, but at least Jessica had stopped pointing at air. "Yeah, but you have to admit, most of the stuff they 'save' us from wouldn't be threatening us if not for *them* in the first place."

Oooh, ouch, good one. I certainly had no comeback.

"Yeah, well, with rank comes responsibility. Or is it with great power comes—anyway, that's what happens when you decide to shack up with dead monarchs, or even just a friend, something I knew long before Betsy and I were shacking up *here*, my come-lately lover." That was as close, normally, as Jess would come to "good point, you're right." "I remind you that she's been on the scene a lot longer than you have."

"You think I don't know that?"

"And that I *wouldn't* be on the scene if it hadn't been for her," she continued quietly. "I'd be a month dead by now. But she saved my life. Better: my appendix grew back, and so did my tonsils, and I've never felt better."

"Say *what*?" I asked, choking on my juice. Tina had frozen in the act of handing several faxes to Sinclair. And he just looked at me with those dark, expressionless eyes and said nothing. "Stuff that got cut out of you grew back?"

"Of course I'm grateful to her, she's alive, isn't she?" he snapped. "She's walking around not arrested, right? I didn't mention her secret to any of the thirty-some *Pioneer Press* reporters I know. Did I?"

"Yikes. Thanks." Reporters? Arrested? Man, I was getting an awful lot of new information to process at once. Time for more juice.

"You haven't done any of those things, because you don't want me to *dump* your sorry ass, not out of gratitude to Betsy."

Oh, and the quarterback scores!

Nick slowly got up off the floor, brushed off his knees, and turned to me. "You know this is your fault."

"I do know. I'm sorry, Nick. I tried to make her leave."

"I can make her leave," Sinclair said pleasantly, watching Nick.

"No, no," I said, pouring the rest of the pitcher into my glass and draining it in three gulps. Other liquids didn't kill the thirst for blood—nothing but, well, *blood* could do that—but they helped a little. The household was used to watching me go through a gallon of juice at breakfast. Though breakfast tended to be at ten o'clock at night these days. "Nobody's gonna make Jessica do anything, I think we got that established in the seventh grade. And Nick's right. The Fiends thing—it's my fault. I just—I just sort of forgot about them for a while."

"Typical," Guess Who sneered.

I could feel my good mood draining away, sort of like the OJ out of the pitcher. Because I made this mess, I made it happen—or allowed, through inaction, it to happen. I felt shitty about it, but it was way beyond late for that. Feeling shitty wasn't going to solve the problem. Probably more people dying would, and I absolutely hated that.

The really awful thing was, the thought of the deaths to come didn't depress me so much as it made me tired.

Chapter 28

Officer, I would like to report a crime. Several crimes."

Ah, the perfect touch to destroy the last of my good mood. I sighed and rested my forehead on the counter. "He's a detective, you dimwit; note the plain clothes and the holster. And he can't hear you."

"What?" Nick said.

"Never mind that," the Ant snapped. She was standing in the middle of the stove. *That* was surprising. Usually the ghosts behaved like they were still alive and tried not to walk through things unless they absolutely had to—say, through a door that was shut (because, natch, they couldn't grasp the knob). The center burners came up to the bottom button on her too-tight lime green blouse. It clashed awfully with her bright yellow hair and made her skin look positively greenish. "Tell him about how you're keeping me prisoner."

My head snapped up so quickly I nearly overturned my chair. "I am not! You're here of your own free will, Antonia, and the sooner you figure that out the happier I'll be."

"Make that all of us," Jessica added. "Get lost, Mrs. Taylor."

"You should tell the help not to speak to me," she said triumphantly, thrilled that someone else was acknowledging her presence.

"You know damned well that's Jessica!"

"Is that bigoted bitch slamming me from beyond the grave? Where is she?"

"What difference does it make?" I sighed. "You can't touch her."

"No, but I can throw things through her. Make me feel better, anyway." She darted to one of the tables, snatched up a plate, and hurled it toward the fridge. Where it fluttered to the ground, since, to save on dish washing, we tended to use paper plates for breakfast.

"Stop that, and she's in the *stove*, okay? The stove!"

"What the fuck is going on?"

"Betsy's dead stepmother is haunting her," Jessica told him.

"Oh, that's—" Nick threw his hands up in the air and walked around in a tight little circle.

"The last straw?" Sinclair suggested. "I quite agree. So snatch up your girlfriend and flee for your lives."

"That's it," Jessica said. "I just doubled your rent."

"Everything in the whole world sucks." I rested my chin in my hand and stared past Sinclair's shoulder at the window over the sink. "Every. Single. Thing."

"A pity," Sinclair replied. "And you were in such a charming mood, too. Although a little warning would be appreciated the next time you do something drastic to your hair."

"Oh, it'll be blond again tomorrow, who cares? What was I thinking, when I said I could do this job? I must have been out of my mind!"

"That's the spirit," Nick said, instantly cheering up.

"Stop that," Sinclair and Jessica ordered in unison. They looked at each other in surprise, almost laughed, and then Jessica continued. "You're doing the best you can. Nobody expects more."

"Ha!" I pointed to her boyfriend. "He does."

"And I can't be the only one," Nick added.

"Well, what's she supposed to do, smart guy? By all means, enlighten all of us. How would *you* help run the vampire kingdom?"

"I'd start," he replied sweetly, "by rounding up all my 'subjects' and blowing their faces off."

Sinclair snorted. "Then let us say, for the sake of argument, that you were the king, and you did that. I'm sure you can see the consequences."

I could feel the confidence I'd gained after defeating Marjorie draining out of me. Whatever I'd done to Marjorie had been, like most of the great events of my life/death, both a fluke and dumb luck. I was lucky to be alive (ahem), and it was nuts to read any more into it than that.

"I'm guessing I can't abdicate," I said to Tina.

She looked more than a little taken aback. "Ah . . . no."

"That's quite enough," my husband said coolly. "You've let this silly little man rattle you and for no good reason."

"Yeah, but the Fiend thing really is my fault."

"And none of mine?"

"Hey, yeah!" Nick said. "It's *both* your faults!"

Sinclair ignored him. "I knew, as you did, that they were out there in Minnetonka. I chose, as you did, to do nothing."

"Yeah, but if I'd done like you wanted, they'd all be dead, and we wouldn't be in this mess."

"And if wishes were horses, beggars would ride."

"What?"

"An old saying of my mother's."

"Very old," Tina said, almost—but not quite!—smiling.

"Elizabeth, it's far too late to play the 'what if' game. We have a situation. We are dealing with it. The opinions of the occasional passing human are of no import. I am the king, you are the queen, so shall it be forever."

"Or, at least," Jessica added, "for a thousand years."

"Passing human?" Nick asked.

"I noticed you put yourself first." I slid my empty glass over to him. "Pour me something, will you? Something. Anything."

"Why don't you snack on Detective Berry?" Tina suggested. "That would make us all feel better."

"You assholes stay away from me," Nick warned, backing up until his butt hit the kitchen door.

"Then do not," my husband said, "let us keep you."

Chapter 29

Well, that was—"

"Can you believe the nerve of that guy?" Jessica bitched, plunking down in the chair opposite Sinclair. "Asking me to marry him just so I'd move."

"Perhaps it was the right question under the wrong circumstances," Sinclair suggested, which I thought was an elegant way of looking at it.

"And perhaps he's losing his damn mind."

"There is always that," he admitted.

"Are we all going to pretend that he didn't make some really good points?" I demanded.

"Oh, right," Jess replied. "I forgot: this is all about *you*."

"Well, it kind of is," I grumbled, chastened.

"When you are older," my husband said, folding up his newspaper (I don't know *why* he didn't read them online), "you will see the futility of second-guessing yourself and wasting time with it."

"Great. I can't fucking wait. Hey, when I'm older, do you think I'll turn into an emotionless robot like someone we all—"

"Betsy!" The kitchen door swung open, and Nick stuck his head inside. "There's a vampire here to see you. I think she's a vampire. She fucking stinks, man."

"Great. A new subject to disappoint! Let's go see her, so I can let her down right away."

"Can someone let me off of the pity train now?" Jessica asked, getting up and following me. "This is my stop."

I thought I heard Sinclair snicker, but when I glanced at him, he was as smooth-faced as usual. And, thank God, the Ant wasn't following us. Perhaps she'd popped out again. I'd hope it was permanent, except I wasn't *that* dumb.

"Thank you, Detective Berry, you would make a fine butler. Now run along."

"Like I want to stay?" he retorted, falling into step beside us. I wondered who the new vamp was. Maybe a straggler of sorts who had just heard about the new king and queen. Now and again a vampire from the middle of nowhere would show up to pay tribute (gag). "Besides, I gotta get back to work."

"He did," I whispered to Jessica, "get here really quick. He must have hung up and rushed right over. That's pretty sweet, doncha think?"

"Hey, that's right! *You* called him and told him about the Fiends!"

Oh, shit.

Jessica was shaking her head. "The things I'm gonna do to you when we have a little privacy—I think it's time to pour vinegar on your Jimmy Choos again."

"No!" I practically screamed, beyond horrified. "Once was enough!"

"Obviously not, since I've done it twice."

I'd probably put up a psychological block the size of the Great Wall.

"Anyway, here she is," Nick was saying. "I put her in the, uh, other parlor." He meant the one that was the least presentable of the four we had. Or was it five? Anyway, the wallpaper was faded and even torn in some places; the rugs were worn. And it smelled musty, like old books in an attic. We hardly ever spent any time in there. In a mansion this size, it was no trouble to ignore the less comfortable rooms and stick with the ones you liked. "She, uh, really stinks pretty bad."

"Maybe she got caught out late and had to pop into the sewer," Tina suggested. "That's happened to me a time or two."

"I'll see you later," Nick said, giving Jessica a noisy smack on the lips.

"To be continued," she warned him, but at least she kissed him back.

"Hello," Sinclair said. "I am King Sinclair, and this is Queen Elizabeth."

The vampire, who had been huddled by the fireplace, turned to face us. "I know who you both are."

Tina took one look, shrieked, "Clara the Fiend!" and launched herself at the smaller, smellier vampire.

Chapter 30

Which was unbelievably startling, to say the least. Before I could move, or think, or react in any way, Sinclair's hand shot out almost faster than I could track, and he caught Tina by the back of her sweater. He held her in midair, her short legs kicking back and forth.

Clara the Fiend had backed into the nearest corner and was pressing herself into it as if she could shove herself through the wall and disappear. Given Tina's sudden viciousness, I could hardly blame her. "Please, I came alone! Please, I just want to talk!"

"Eric, put me *down*." Tina was practically spitting. And she'd used his first name . . . oooh, he was in trouble now. "Put me down right now so I can—and you! You get out of my master's house, you wretch! You pathetic creeping *thing*, you disgust us all, and you insult their majesties with your very presence! How dare you come to their home! Get out, before I kill you!"

"Tina, it's okay—" Jessica started.

"Oh, Jesus." Nick had his gun out and was standing in front of Jessica. The gun barrel kept wavering between Clara and Tina.

I couldn't blame him. I'd never seen Tina so out-of-control furious. I mean, *I* was scared of her, and I knew that under ninety-nine-point-nine percent of the circumstances, she not only wouldn't hurt me, she'd give her life to save me. Even Sinclair, much bigger and stronger, had to hang on to her with both hands. "Jesus, Jesus, these are the guys that clocked me in the nose the other day. These are the Fiends?"

"They are," Sinclair replied, turning pale at the reference to

God's son. "Tina, calm yourself. She appears to have come in peace."

"And she'll leave in pieces!"

"Good one," Jessica piped up from behind Nick, "if a bit clichéd."

"Out, out *now*, you vile bitch! You *get out of our house!*"

"Holy shit," Jessica muttered. "I have no idea which one to be more scared of."

"Makes two of us," I whispered back. Maybe somebody should slap her? It always worked in the movies. And after you clocked them, they always said, "Thanks, I needed that."

I didn't really see Tina saying anything of the sort, so I reached up—Sinclair had hoisted Tina pretty high—and grabbed a flailing fist. "Tina, relax. If Clara tries anything, you can kill her all over the place."

The mad frenetic kicking stopped. "You swear it? Swear it on your crown," she ordered, then instantly changed her mind. "No: swear it on the king."

"I swear on my husband's testicles that if Clara tries even one sneaky thing, you can play soccer with her head."

Tina abruptly stopped struggling. Sinclair, just as abruptly, set her down. He didn't seem particularly concerned for his genitals, despite my promise. Maybe he thought this would all end up okay. I sure as hell didn't know that for sure.

Chapter 31

All right," he said to the huddled, smelly vampire. (Nick was right: she reeked.) "Suppose you tell us why you're here, Clara."

"That's not my name," she said. "My name is Stephanie Connor. Thank you for seeing me, dread king."

I heard a commotion and turned to see Nick trying to haul a very reluctant Jessica out of the room. She kept yanking her hand out of his and hissing at him to hush up, she wanted to hear.

"Detective Berry, perhaps you could escort Jessica somewhere safer?" Sinclair asked, soooo politely, so I knew he was really sticking the knife in. "Anywhere outside of Ramsey County would be preferable."

"Dread king, may I—?"

"Nick, let me *go*."

"It's a little chaotic right now," I told Cl—uh, Stephanie. "Give us a minute." I turned to Jess. "You know I'll tell you all about it later. Why don't you am-scray for now?"

Giving me an "I'll deal with you later" glare, Jessica allowed herself to be herded out. Nick shot me a look, too, one I found startling: pure gratitude.

Tina was panting and patting her hair back into place. Thank goodness she'd worn a ponytail. I hated to think of the masses of blond hair flying all over the place. "Would you," she managed through gritted teeth, "like a refreshment?"

Cl—uh, Stephanie looked shocked, like it was a trap. The trap of the Coca-Cola products. Ah, I'd fallen into that sweet, sweet trap a time or two myself. "Uh, no. No thank you, ma'am."

"My name is Tina." Still forcing the words out through teeth ground so tightly, I could hear them rasping against each other. "I am the adjutant to their majesties."

Adj-u-*what*? Was that, like, a super secretary or something? I was pretty sure I'd never heard that word out loud before. Maybe I'd read it, but it was spelled completely differently. I made a mental note to ask about it later. Sinclair would know. He knew pretty much everything.

"Why don't you come out of the corner," I said, crossing the room and offering my hand, "and have a seat? Oh, and unless this is a trap, thanks for coming out to see us all peacefully and stuff."

Sinclair had stiffened when I'd moved toward Stephanie, but relaxed when all she did was meekly follow me and look down at one of the couches. "I'm . . . dirty. I'll stand, if that won't, um, offend." Another nervous glance at Tina, who was examining the rips in her sweater. I tried, and failed, not to raise my eyebrows: she'd been struggling so hard to get away from Sinclair she'd torn the seams out from under both arms. And wool was *tough*. Cripes.

"No, please, take a seat. A little dirt won't kill anyone." Oh, shit, I said kill. Reminding her of what the Fiends had tried to do to us. "Um, I mean hurt anyone." Oh, shit! "Um, just sit the hell down, okay?"

She sat on the far, far edge, looking like she wanted to leap away at any second. And I could see why she smelled—her clothes were filthy, and the mingled odor of dirt, dog poop, and blood came off her.

I wondered where they were sleeping during the day. They had no money or resources unless they killed or robbed or both.

In the past, when a vampire came back to him- or herself, they could go to the library in Minneapolis and find out who they were, if they owned property, if they still had a bank account . . . like that. And Marjorie, the dead betrayer, would give them a hand. It occurred to me that we needed a new system in place . . . like two months ago. Because right now, a vampire who wasn't an out of control newborn had few options. Just feed and hide, feed and hide.

While you live in luxury on Summit Avenue.

I shoved that thought away, hard.

"Now," Sinclair was saying, "what brings you to us, Ms. Connor?"

She picked at the knees of her torn, stained jeans. "I, uh, thought maybe we could talk." She had a mild southern accent—Virginia, maybe? Missouri? Not a drawl, but almost. Of course, anyone who sounded like they weren't from the set of *Fargo* or *Drop Dead Gorgeous* sounded southern or eastern to me. "About our, um, problem."

"Do you represent the interest of your companions, or only your own?"

She blinked at that one, then seemed to decode it in her mind. "Oh. Um, I'm here by myself. I mean, the others don't know I've come."

I listened hard for the sounds of ambush, but could only hear the usual household noise. Then I yowled as the furnace kicked on, which sounded at the moment like a jet plane taking off from inside my skull.

Startled, everyone twitched or looked in my direction. "Sorry," I said. "I just remembered that *30 Rock* is a rerun this week."

Stephanie looked more confused than before, but that was all right. I noticed neither Sinclair nor Tina took a seat, so I did—straight across from our visitor. "You came by yourself," I said, "that seems pretty obvious now. Sorry about Tina jumping on you like that. She had a flashback to the Civil War." I ignored Sinclair's snort. "So what's on your mind?"

"And why should we think anything you say is the truth?"

I shot a look at Sinclair—that sounded a little too much like Nick to suit me.

"I don't—I can't *prove* I'm telling the truth," she said, a little desperately. "I guess the others could be parked a mile away, and this is step one in some elaborate, I dunno, plan? But it's not. We're—we're not well organized."

"You looked pretty organized when you hurt our friends," I said mildly. "They had to go to the hospital." A minor exaggeration—once Nick's nosebleed had cleared up, he'd been fine. It was a measure of his contempt for our lifestyle that he hadn't thought twice about strange vampires punching him in the face and then attacking us. It was only when I'd given him the gory Fiend details that he had realized exactly what had happened—and what it meant for Jessica. "We were pretty bummed about that."

"Well. The others are—they're mad at you."

"But not you," Sinclair said, soooo silkily.

"I am. I mean, I was. How could you—I dunno." She had an interesting way of speaking . . . not slowly, exactly, and maybe it was the accent. But it was almost like she was searching for each word and found it almost every time, in the unused corners of her mind. I reminded myself that last week she'd been batshit crazy. No idea who she was, where she was, what she was.

"Did you guys sort of 'wake up' all at once, then?"

Stephanie looked, if possible, even more uncomfortable. Clearly not a subject she wanted to discuss. Too bad.

"Well, each time Garrett came we felt—I dunno, better? We felt *more*. And then, a few days ago, it was like—like I'd been asleep for a long time, only now, right now I *knew*, I remembered I was Stephanie. I don't . . ." She shook her head. "I don't know who killed me. And I couldn't tell you where I grew up, or the name of my first boyfriend, or even where I went to middle school. I remember some things—my first job out of high school, and the name of the man I almost married, but—mostly I remember the blood. Drinking all of that . . . that dead blood. For years and years and years." She cleared her throat and worked her jaws like she wanted to spit, but didn't dare.

I glanced at Sinclair and Tina, then took the plunge. "The thing is, Stephanie, it was kind of our only option."

"Once we took killing you off the table," Sinclair said pleasantly.

"I didn't want to kill you guys, but I couldn't set you free, either."

"Why?"

"Oh, boy." I thought about the best way to explain this. "Stephanie, you have no idea how scary you guys were." Was *scary* the right word? I probably shouldn't have told her that. Fuck it. "The few times you got out, you ripped people just to *pieces*. There was no way we could let you have live blood. You would have killed the donor every time."

"Oh. Yes, I see that now." Except she sounded like she didn't, not exactly. "I should go now."

"You don't believe me," I said.

Her eyes betrayed her emotion: trapped. I had seen through her lie, and now all she could imagine was that she was in fantastic trouble.

"Stephanie, I'm not saying I've treated you and the others

perfectly. I think I had the right idea when I began to feed Garrett, regardless of the danger. And I think Garrett had the right idea, when he began to feed all of you. I'm glad—"

"Glad?!"

"Yes, glad, Tina, that he did so. And I hope you and the others can forgive me, and see that I really did start the awakening for all of you. Just not fast enough, or well enough. I can do better, if you give me the chance."

I warned Sinclair, with a look, from saying a word. Stephanie was plainly trying to digest what I had told her. For all I knew, she was still trying to understand some of the words. Or maybe she had one of those 1970s game shows playing in a loop in her mind ("Things you kill. Things you maim. Things you wish you could drink instead of blood! YES, YOU'VE WON THE *$64,000 PYRAMID!*").

"Thank you, Your Majesty," she finally said. "I have to get back. The others will miss me. They'd kill me if they knew I was here."

"Then why *are* you here?" Tina asked.

"To find out more. To learn if what the others say is true."

"What do the others say?"

"That we are the queen's wolves, bred for her wars, and the foreshadow of what the world will become under her reign."

We all took that in for a moment. It was so horrible, so preposterous . . . I didn't know whether to laugh or cry.

"Perhaps you could educate your colleagues," Sinclair suggested, "as to the true nature of this queen."

"Well, I would try to talk to them, but it wouldn't work." Stephanie shrugged. "And I couldn't try too hard, or they might kill *me*."

I was trying not to gape at her, and failing. In my efforts to apologize and see her point of view, I had missed how fearful she still was . . . and how undependable an ally she would be.

"You have overstayed your welcome," Sinclair said, which felt a bit harsh to me, but I had no idea how to correct him.

"All right, but . . ." She licked her lips. "I am afraid we will come back soon."

"Not if you obey your queen," Tina pointed out.

"I cannot stop them."

"If you cannot stop them," Sinclair pointed out, "then you cannot help us. And if you cannot help us, we cannot let you go back."

I stared at Sinclair, trying to see where this logic train was going to end. *Nowhere happy*, I told myself.

"We cannot let you stay here, any more easily than we can let you go back. The effort to watch over you securely, combined with the potential costs if we fail, lead to only one solution. Tina," he ended calmly, "kill her."

Chapter 32

No no no no no no *no!*" Only just in time did I leap from my seat and jump in front of the cringing Stephanie, who had shoved herself so far back she had nearly disappeared into the couch.

Tina slammed into me hard enough to make me stagger— she'd launched herself the moment Sinclair got "kill" out of his mouth. Like she'd been ready the whole time. Like she was waiting for it.

"Bad, Tina! Down!"

"Elizabeth, do not—"

"Keep her away from me!" Stephanie squealed, scrambling off the couch.

I managed to grab Tina by the shoulders and hold her at arm's length. At least she wasn't trying to kick me. "You guys, you guys! We are not killing her, she came in peace, and she's leaving the same way."

"Like hell," Tina managed through gritted teeth.

"Don't listen to her! You can go. Good-bye, Stephanie. I'm sorry about what happened to you."

"Do not," Tina snarled, "apologize. To that thing."

Meanwhile Stephanie was halfway out the door. "Thank-youforseeingmegoodbye."

I let go of Tina, and we all listened to the rapidly retreating footfalls.

"Soft," was my husband's verdict. "Much too soft. Even now. Hmm."

"And you're too hard," I shot back with my own judgment. That's right—two could play the judge-and-jury game! "And too stupid. And don't be siccing Tina on people, like she's your own personal pit bull!"

"But I am," she replied at the exact moment Sinclair said, "But she is."

" 'Kill her,' my God! Haven't you ever heard of a flag of truce? These Fiends are growing. Maybe they can grow emotions beyond hate and fear. Maybe they can become . . . like Garrett. Like us. Why is that so hard for you two to see?"

They'd flinched when I'd broken the commandment, but now they were both giving me that *look*.

"There will come a time when you will regret having let her leave," my bloodthirsty psycho husband said.

Tina was shaking her head. "You should have let me kill her, Majesty. If for no other reason than the audacity she showed in coming here, soliciting an apology, and giving nothing in return! Not even an offer to *try* to lift a finger to stop the others."

"She'll remember I was nice to her."

"Mercy," Sinclair lectured, "is a poor weapon."

I stared at him. Sometimes—many times—I didn't know him. At all. "It's the only one I'm using right now."

"*You* don't have to use a weapon at all," Tina pointed out. "I would take care of these problems for you."

I think what finally made me snap was seeing Tina degrade herself—describe herself as nothing but a deadly vessel, when I knew she was so much more. Or maybe I was just pissed at my fucking arrogant husband.

"The only problem I have," I hissed, "is a couple of subjects who don't think I have what it takes to be queen! Perhaps if they'd sit down, shut up, and listen to her, they'd learn something!"

Yuck, did I just refer to myself in the third person? Even weirder, Tina looked embarrassed beyond belief, and quickly sat down. Sinclair also sat down, much more slowly, with an odd expression on his face—a cross between outrage and pride.

Well. Now what?

"So." I started to pace. "Let's figure this out. Where are the Fiends staying during the day?"

"I would be more interested in how and where they are feeding," Sinclair said. "I would ask Detective Berry to look for any unusual homicides, but he is not our friend at the moment. His loyalty is solely with Jessica. Perhaps another source can help us."

"He'd look for vampire attacks in two seconds, regardless of how he feels about you, me, and Tina."

I was about to elaborate, when the front door was slammed open and an all-too-familiar voice greeted us with, "What the *hell* is going on? I leave this shitheap for three days, and the fuckin' Fiends are loose, my boyfriend's practically catatonic, and the smelliest bitch I've ever fuckin' seen practically ran me down on the porch! Not to mention I nearly got into a fender bender with the devil who looks like Miss Fuckin' February! Jesus fucking Christ, what the hell is going on?"

Antonia the werewolf was home.

"Oh, gosh, Antonia, you know you shouldn't talk like that."

As well as the devil's daughter.

Chapter 33

Two ridiculously beautiful women hurried into the parlor, and I sighed. I often felt like the homely judge at a swimsuit competition; all the women in our house were just so pretty.

Antonia Wolfton, current werewolf and former psychic, was a lean, tall brunette (almost as tall as me), with striking dark eyes and the palest, softest skin I'd ever seen on someone alive. She was like a foulmouthed milkmaid.

The waves of her hair crashed and bounced halfway down her back. Her lips were rosebud pink, and when her hair was pulled back by a red ribbon, as it was now, she looked like Snow White.

"I thought you were gonna get the fucking driveway fixed," she griped. "And what'd you do to my boy toy while I was gone, you rotten bitch?"

I didn't laugh—barely—but then, I was used to it. For Antonia, that was a downright warm greeting. It was just so *weird*, those excellent good looks, that amazing figure, that perfect mouth . . . and then the *words* that kept coming out over and over again. It was as if God had fused a swimsuit model with a teamster.

"Oh, now, stop it," the devil's daughter (really!) said with gentle reproach. "The driveway's not that bad, and I'm sure Sinclair and Betsy have lots more important things on their minds." Laura Goodman (don't laugh) looked like, as Antonia had put it once, "a dirty old man's wet dream," with long, butterscotch blond hair, big blue eyes, and long strong limbs. Her nose was a sculpted delight, her mouth wide and generous.

She had never had a pimple.

I think I mentioned before that Laura had a unique way of rebelling against her mother. When your mother was the devil, *the* devil, there wasn't much you could do for rebellion; after all, how do you rebel against the embodiment of evil?

You go to church. You teach Sunday school. You volunteer for soup kitchens. You are kind to children and small animals. You constantly watch your language. You pray.

That's how.

"What are you guys doing here?"

"Ha!" Antonia brayed. "I knew you'd play dumb. Actually, you can't *not* play dumb, huh, Bets? My boyfriend called, and he's a gibbering wreck. Something about his 'foul behavior' and 'base betrayal' and how there can be no forgiveness 'n' shit, then I got bored, so I kind of tuned him out."

"And yet," Sinclair said dryly, "here you are."

"Shit, yeah. Apparently everything's going to hell around here. You dummies *need* me."

"You don't especially need me," Laura said, almost apologetically. "But I got worried when you canceled our lunch." From anyone else, that would have sounded reproachful. Laura was too tenderhearted to pull something like that, even though it hadn't been one lunch I'd blown off, it had been two. "I apologize for dropping by without calling, but I was beginning to worry."

There was a method to my madness, and I wasn't at all happy to see my sister here. Bottom line? I didn't want her anywhere near the Fiends, especially since we didn't know when they'd come calling again. Part of the reason they'd gotten better so quickly was because they had drunk a combination of my blood . . . and hers.

It wouldn't be understating the point to say I wished she'd leave the state until this was all straightened out. I was just too chickenshit to tell her.

"It's been really crazy around here," I managed.

" 'Really crazy'?" Antonia sneered. "Oh, okay. That's not the Betsy play-it-down machine getting into gear, is it?"

"My gosh," Tina said mildly, "what happened to your arm?"

"Oh. That." Antonia gleefully rolled up her sleeve and displayed her disgusting injury to all of us. What I hadn't noticed turned out to be a hideous blackish red bruise running from her wrist to past her elbow. "Jumped from one of the bluffs and miscalculated the distance."

"Antonia, you've got to take better care of yourself," I scolded.

"You're not used to changing into a wolf, and besides, last night wasn't even the full moon . . . what are you doing jumping off bluffs?"

"Quickest way to get where I wanna go. Anyway, tomorrow night is the full moon, and then we'll have fun fun fun." She was positively gleeful, and I couldn't blame her.

"One of these days you'll miscalculate and break your rotten little neck."

This was true, despite Antonia's glare. See, when she first came to us, Antonia was a very special kind of werewolf. She was born into the pack, had a werewolf mom and dad, but had never changed. Never become a wolf during the full moon.

Instead, she could see the future. It wasn't always clear, and sometimes only after the fact could we figure out exactly what she'd been trying to warn us against. (Like most supernatural abilities, it sounded better on paper than the real deal.) But she was never wrong—just oblique.

Until Marjorie the librarian came along—in addition to giving me a cursed engagement ring and snatching my groom, she'd locked up Antonia as well—and Garrett. Do you have any idea how claustrophobic werewolves are? They dealt with enclosed spaces the way I did with knockoffs. Just a bad, bad situation all around.

Anyway, while I was busy killing Marjorie and soaking up all her evil energy, I let Antonia have a blast of it (most of the rest I saved to revive Sinclair and cure Jessica's cancer). It was the first time she had ever changed into a wolf, and she'd been enjoying it ever since.

As I said, she had lived her whole life among werewolves while being unable to change into a wolf herself. Now she saw herself as complete, and didn't seem to mind the loss of her psychic abilities as a trade-off.

But, as Laura pointed out, she was taking too many risks. Nothing we would say would talk her out of it, either; she thought she was invincible even when she wasn't in wolf form.

"So what'd you dimwits do to my boy toy?" she demanded, rolling down her sleeve. I noticed for the first time that she was wearing one of my oxford shirts, and stifled a groan. Antonia had the table manners of Boss Hog. Assuming I ever got the blouse back, I'd probably have to chuck it. "He's practically fetal with wretchedness."

"You could tell that over the phone?" Sinclair asked, amused.

"Enhanced senses," she sneered, staring him straight in the eye—the height of rudeness for a werewolf. "Way better than anything a dead guy can do."

"It's really none of my business," Laura said, fiddling with a lock of her hair and looking at the assembly of personalities in the room, "but something certainly seems to be going on. Are you all right?"

"As rain," I said heartily.

Antonia and Laura stared at me.

"Well." I coughed. "There have been a *few* things going on . . ."

Chapter 34

We ended up sitting down in the kitchen and telling the girls everything. If for no other reason than they had to be warned—Antonia lived there most of the time, after all, and Laura was famous for the pop-in.

Antonia's face got darker; Laura's became more concerned. When I finished (after frequent interruptions from the love of my life and his personal pit bull), there was a long silence, broken by Antonia bawling, "Garrett! Get your ass up here!"

"But you could have been killed!" Laura said, rubbing her ear as Antonia disappeared in the direction of the basement. "Why didn't you call me?"

"It would be unsafe to have you near such dangerous vampires at this time," Sinclair said bluntly.

"What? I could help," she said, hurt.

I glared at Subtle Boy. "Honey, it's not personal. It's just—the Fiends are like this because of my blood *and* your blood."

"But you're the one who made me—"

"I know, I know. Like I said, it's not personal. But I can't take a chance of one of them attacking you, getting a mouthful, and getting even more dangerous. And, no offense, sometimes your temper gets the better of you." To put it very freaking mildly.

"It does not!"

"Hon. It so totally does."

"That was one time!"

"Are you talking about the time you beat the shit out of Garrett, or the time you killed the serial killer?"

Laura's mouth thinned, but before she could reply, Garrett

came skidding into the kitchen on his back, as if someone was using him to play shuffleboard. We heard footfalls, and then Antonia slapped the door open.

"It's one thing to want to help your comrades in arms," she told him as he climbed slowly to his feet. "But something else to put your friends in danger and then hide from what you've done. Literally hide—have you even been out of the basement since you called me?"

"No," Garrett said.

"And you're living under her roof! Calling for me to come save you, calling from *her* phone! You made this mess, Garrett, and much as I love you, you'll fix it, or I'll pull all your limbs off."

"It's not his fault." Sure, she'd been saying things I had secretly been thinking, but I could have cried at the expression on poor Garrett's face. He was trying to shake the long hair out of his face, and was too ashamed to look at any of us. "He didn't know what would happen. He's only been speaking English for two damn months!"

"It is my fault," he said dully, looking at the floor.

Antonia's tone gentled about a fraction, and she bent to help him to his feet. "I know we have different backgrounds—and the age thing—I'm not stupid, I *know* we're different. Shit, we're not even the same species; needless to say we weren't brought up the same way. But I can't be with someone who puts his friends in danger and then hides to save himself."

"The Fiends are my responsibility and no one else's," I said, resisting the urge to step between Antonia and Garrett. "This isn't a debate we're having, okay? The Fiends are my problem. How they got on the radar is irrelevant. Does everyone understand that?"

This, as I knew it would, put Antonia in a major bind. A creature of pack leaders and strict hierarchies, when she was under this roof, I was her pack leader pro tem. She could tease me, mouth off, borrow my clothes without asking (though she knew better than to touch my shoes), and give me untold rations of shit, but it was very, very difficult for her to out-and-out cross me.

In a strange way I knew I could count on Antonia's obedience and support more than anyone else's in the room. Of course, I had no power over the devil's daughter, except her willingness to please a sister.

Tina obeyed me in superficial matters (while you're up could you get me a glass of orange juice? Could you show Officer Berry the door? Could you hit Sinclair over the head with the fax machine?), but on matters like this, her allegiance was clearly to Sinclair.

I had zero power over Sinclair.

"If you're taking responsibility, I guess it's none of my business," Antonia said with a shrug. "But holler next time one of them comes calling. Might be fun. As for you . . ." She pointed to Garrett, and he followed her, slump-shouldered, toward the basement door.

"I hope she isn't too hard on him," Laura worried.

"Ha," I said sourly. Already I could hear things crashing. "She'll be hard on him. But at least they'll kiss and make up."

"You think?"

"Who else could stand to be with either one of them?"

"Point," my sister conceded, and we both laughed.

I asked after BabyJon, whom Laura had been watching, before dropping him off at my mother's for the day.

"She'll be underwhelmed," she pointed out diplomatically, when I suggested BabyJon might need to stay there longer.

"Laura, I know she thought her baby-rearing days were long over—"

"And don't forget BabyJon is a constant reminder of her late ex-husband's infidelity."

"—and I respect that. But she still loves BabyJon, kind of, and she won't want him harmed. If we laid it out for her, told her he could either stay here and maybe get nibbled by Fiends, or stay with her and spit up on her Civil War bullet collection, you know which one she'd pick. But please don't tell her why BabyJon needs to stay. She'll just worry."

"I'll come up with something," Laura promised at once. God, she was so low maintenance. When she wasn't in the grip of a simmering, murderous rage. "It wouldn't be such a big deal, but I think your mother is still taking your father's death kind of hard. Harder than—I mean, hard."

Laura had corrected herself because she'd been about to say "harder than you," which was nothing but the truth. I'd been fairly indifferent about my dad in life and wasn't sure how I felt about him dying. It was even partly my *fault* he was dead and I wasn't sure how I felt.

When *I* had died and come back as a vampire, he'd essentially told me to stay away. Seemed only fair that I return the favor . . . to seem like I didn't care if he was gone forever. But then, that sounded so cold and mean, I couldn't stand it. He was my *father.*

"Which reminds me," I sighed, slumping in my seat, "you won't even guess who's been hanging around."

"Umm . . . Detective Berry?"

"Well, yeah, but also my stepmother . . . and your birth mother."

Laura had been polishing an apple on her immaculate buttercup yellow wool blazer, but stopped. "She's haunting you?"

"Yeppers."

"What does she need you to do?"

"That's the super fun part. She won't tell me."

Laura shook her head; gorgeous blond strands flew about her face and then settled perfectly. "That does it. I can no longer stay away from your house for more than a week. I miss too much!"

"It's not always like this," I sighed.

"In fact, I'm going to stick to you like cow poop on a Furragrammo."

"It's Fair-uh-gahm-oh . . . and don't even say it!" I begged, but it turned out she wasn't exaggerating.

Chapter 35

"I still don't understand why Midwestern Barbie is along for the ride," Detective Nick whined as we pulled onto the highway.

"One of the three of us in this horrid little car has my sister's best interests at heart. One of them isn't you," Laura said sweetly, "and the other isn't her."

I forced a cough. "Any luck with that, um, errand Jessica asked you to run?" After some discussion, Tina, Sinclair, and I had agreed Jessica was the best person to ask Nick to keep an eye out for unusual murders.

"You mean have your runaway pets mangled any citizens? Not that we can tell. Yet. And again, if I didn't make this clear: nice one, doorknob."

"I *said* I was sorry," I grumped, slumping against the backseat. (Yes, he'd dumped me in the back—at least it was a plain car and not a cruiser.)

"You stop picking on her," Laura ordered. "She's doing the best she can. Although when she shuts out family members it only makes things—"

"I'm sitting right behind you. I can, sorry to say, hear everything. Where are we going, anyway?"

"Got a tip that our bad guys might be meeting down here."

"Wait, 'bad guys' the Fiends? Or—"

"No, my bad guys, dummy. I hate to break this to you for the twentieth time, but it's not always about you, Betsy."

I disagreed, but let it pass. "And a fellow cop showing up isn't going to scare the alleged bad guys away?"

"We think they're actually contracting out—giving the info to one of their perps, a guy (or gal) they can count on to pull the trigger. Do a few of those, and the triggerman disappears."

"So . . . wait. You think they aren't just killing bad guys, they're getting other bad guys to kill bad guys, and then killing *those* bad guys?" Laura sounded truly horrified, but I had to admit it was fiendishly logical.

"Hey, I know it sounds bad, but our stats look great. Crime's down across the board almost eighteen percent."

"Nick Berry!"

"I know, I know." He slumped against the steering wheel. Luckily he'd gotten off the highway and we were at a red light. "We gotta put a stop to it. Tell me something I wasn't the first to figure out. Why do you think the chief's been riding my ass?"

"The entire force should be out on this, not just you," Laura continued, snug in her cocoon of moral superiority. "It dishonors all of you. Your chief should understand that."

"The last thing we need is the papers getting ahold of this tidbit. So it's on the down low for now."

"You worry too much about the papers. Also, nobody says *down low* anymore," I announced.

Nick sighed. "Bad enough you have to come along. Next time," he said, catching my gaze in the rearview mirror, "Pollyanna stays home."

I shrugged. "See if *you* can make her."

We were in a fairly beat-up Minneapolis neighborhood, one of those places that might have been pretty a few decades ago, but had suffered from a few too many absentee landlords, and not quite enough good jobs.

Nick parked, and we all got out. The street was dimly lit, and clumps of teenagers and twenty-somethings stood out like mushrooms sprouting on various corners. We got a few looks, but nobody came over—or appeared to recognize Nick as a cop.

The storefronts were all empty, some with windows soaped over. The sidewalks were a mess; paper, beer bottles, and cigarette butts all over the place. If I hadn't been dead (or with the devil's daughter), I never would have gotten out of the car.

At least it wasn't too cold out yet; it was nearly seventy degrees, not too shabby for nighttime in September. It was funny; I'd always had contempt for California and Florida transplants who bitched about how cold the weather got in my home state. Shoot, I used to wear shorts in February and sneer at the whiners.

That was all over with, now. *O, irony, you are a harsh mis-*

tress. I actually had a pair of gloves in my Burberry handbag . . . how was *that* for wimpy?

"I've just got a tag number," Nick was saying, "but I don't know if it ties in to—"

I didn't hear the rest, because I was distracted by rapidly approaching footfalls and turned just in time to get slammed off my feet. The chilly sidewalk rushed up to smack into my back, and I cracked my head hard enough to see black roses.

Then someone with truly awful breath was yanking me off the ground by my purse strap, which, to my amazement, held. I had no idea if I was mad or glad. It *had* been a gift from Jessica. It was my only designer handbag. But then, if it had snapped free, I wouldn't have a stranger's hands around my neck right now. Decisions, decisions.

"Leave her alone!" Laura shrieked, while around her, teens fled. "Let her down! Detective Berry! Do something!"

"Freeze?" he suggested.

Bad Breath Boy and I were spinning around on the sidewalk in a tight little dance, and the stench of fresh, drying, and old blood was making me nuts.

"A Fiend," I managed, trying to break his grip—he was much taller, much broader. "It's a Fiend, don't get too close." Here? Now? What the *fuck*? Had they followed me from the house? Worse, had they followed Laura? That could be extremely awful.

"I could shoot it, but might kill Betsy by mistake. Ah, well," Nick said cheerfully, and I could hear him unsnap his holster. "A risk I'm willing—hey!"

There was a blinding light, like someone was holding a bolt of lightning, and then the light swung through both of us. It didn't do a thing to me but make me blink furiously.

But the effect was devastating on the Fiend, who didn't so much burst into flame as burst into ash. This was actually really weird for a vampire—unlike in the movies, where most vampires, when killed, just laid there, dead forever.

Not this one; he was a puddle of ash inside filthy clothes. Oddly, there was no smell, and no real flash of heat, just that blinding, gorgeous light. This made sense, as it wasn't *real* heat that had demolished the Fiend.

I coughed explosively, spitting dead Fiend out of my mouth and wiping it out of my eyes.

"Holy shit!" Nick said from the sidewalk where Laura had shoved him. "What the hell did you do?"

"*Hell* being the right word," I muttered, straightening out the kinks in my back, groaning and spitting. I was pretty sure Nick didn't know Laura was the spawn of Satan, so I kept the explanation brief, yet truthful. "That's her hellfire sword."

"You said that like 'that's her third cup of coffee.' "

"You know how some girls get pearls for their sweet sixteen? Laura's mom gave her weapons made of hellfire."

"You guys never tell me anything. I should have guessed your sister would be a freak like you," he bitched, climbing to his feet—only to get kicked over on his back by Laura, who was still holding her sword made of light.

"Now, Laura," I started, trying to swallow my nervousness.

"She was in trouble, and you just *stood* there," my sweet, good-natured, murderously dangerous sister hissed. "She might have been hurt or killed! Protect and serve, my ass!"

Uh-oh. She'd said *ass* instead of butt. Really mad, then.

"That was a Fiend! She said that was a Fiend! You *led us down here*, and a Fiend jumped her! Did you plan it? Do you have something up your sleeve besides catching rogue cops?" She jammed her sword under his chin, and his eyes watered at the light. It was pure bluff; her sword only disrupted unnatural magic: vampires, werewolves, spells. And only when she wanted them to, which is why it didn't work on me.

But Nick didn't know that.

"Get that thing out of my face," he snarled, not quite daring to bat it aside. "Think I would have brought a damn witness if I was trying to eighty-six your sister? Or are you as dumb as you look?"

"Stop it, that's enough, just—quit!" I gently pulled my sister away. "Laura, put that thing away before half the street sees it."

Laura sullenly complied, sheathing her sword into . . . well, nothing, as far as I could tell. Nobody knew where her weapons went when she wasn't wreaking havoc with them.

"And you!" Nick, climbing to his feet, nearly fell over when I rounded on him. "She makes a good point, you know. A Fiend just *happens* to burst out of nowhere and try to kill me, and you just stand there?"

"What the fuck do I know about killing vampires? My bullets won't kill you. I don't think." The truth was, we didn't know. His bullets *had* killed a vampire . . . once. On my honeymoon, no less. "Why would they kill that thing? Do you think we have a police training course on arresting the undead? Do you think I've got Fiend Hunter tattooed on my forehead?"

"No, you've got Brutal Imbecile tattooed on your forehead," Laura interrupted.

"When I want your opinion, Barbie, I'll pull the string on your back."

"Give it a try," she snarled. "See how many fingers you pull back."

"You wanna go, Barbie? Because we'll go."

"Shut up!" I howled. "I'm not a queen, I'm not a wife, I'm not a big sister, I'm a WWF referee! Sorry, Nick. This expedition is *over*. Everyone get in the car *right now!*"

Meekly, they did. This was more like it—Eric and Tina never did a damned thing I asked them to. But first, Nick carefully eased my purse off my shoulder . . . I guessed he was going to try to get some fingerprints off it. We sure couldn't print the pile of ash on the sidewalk. I warned him not to use any of my credit cards and to leave the strawberry Blo-Pops alone. Sometimes I went through a dozen a day. It helped keep the blood craving down.

"Heir to the John Deere fortune, remember? I've got more money than *you* do, honey."

"Good. Then you can bring me to Wendy's," I commanded, all queen-like. "Being the victim of assault and battery gives me a craving for a chocolate shake."

Chapter 36

That is strange," Sinclair admitted. After Wendy's, we'd ended up going back to the mansion and telling him and Tina what had happened. It was the first night of the full moon; Antonia was running around somewhere on all fours. Garrett had probably gone with her.

Jessica was visiting Marc at his new digs at The Grand, and I hoped he'd be able to come home soon. Things weren't the same without him. Besides, people disappearing out of our house brought back bad memories of last summer, when I was all alone.

Shoot, I even missed BabyJon's shitty diapers.

"Which part is strange?" Nick said dryly, bringing me back to my consideration of Sinclair's comment. "The part about my receiving a call and being sent to a bad neighborhood on what might have been a phony tip? The part where a Fiend just *happened* to run into us? Or the part where your wife's sister pulled a fucking flame brand out of thin air and killed said Fiend, before threatening to do the same thing to me?"

Hearing that Laura had threatened the officer didn't seem to perturb Sinclair one bit. "You say the chief is the one who gave you this assignment?"

"Yeah. And don't go there, pal, he's a stand-up guy."

"Oh, Nick." I shook my head sorrowfully. "Nobody says 'don't go there' anymore. Seriously. I'm so embarrassed for you right now. More so than usual, even."

He ignored me. "The chief's a year away from forced retirement—it's no time for him to fuck up a perfect record. It'd be the closest thing to suicide—this guy's job means *everything* to him. That's why Chief Hamlin wants these rogue cops caught, but he doesn't want to trash the police department's rep at the same time. Hell, he's the one who figured out the pattern—and the killings have been going on less than a month."

"I would think the reputation of his house would be the least of his problems," Tina ventured.

"Yeah? Come on, they're *still* making jokes about the LAPD, and how many years ago was Rodney King?"

"Some might say," I said carefully, "that there've been one or two incidents in that department since the King videotape."

Laura beamed at me. "You're right, Betsy. Some police departments deserve the reputations they have."

I shrugged under Nick's withering stare. "I don't have a problem with cops," I said apologetically. "But I've been known to channel Jessica's point of view, from time to time."

"Getting back to the issue at hand," Sinclair suggested, "I wonder why this Fiend came alone. Did any of you get a look at which one it was?"

"Skippy," I said immediately.

"Skippy?" Nick asked, incredulous. "Friggin' Frankenstein was named Skippy? He was almost seven feet tall!"

I was embarrassed to hear the nickname repeated; what had at first sounded fun now seemed stupid, careless, and immature. Worse, nobody'd ever know the dead guy's real name now. The least I could have done when they came by was ask their real names. Mistake number 1,429 in what was turning into a shitty week.

"I am in your debt, Ms. Goodman, for the assistance you rendered my wife."

Laura blushed to her eyebrows. "Oh, no, Eric, it's fine. We're family. I'm just happy *I* was there to help." She sharpened her words by narrowing her eyes at Nick.

"Hey, hey," he protested. "The whole thing happened in about two seconds. I could have got a shot off, but I might have blown a hole in your pretty wife's head. I mean, I could have lived with it, but—"

Sinclair silenced him with a wave of his kingly hand, which I could tell irritated Nick to no end.

"So what are you going to tell your boss? The chief?"

"That I couldn't find the tag, but I'll go back and look again."

"Alone," Sinclair said. We all noticed it wasn't a request. "You will go back and look again alone."

"You think I want those two PMS poster babies along for the ride? Ha!"

"Then allow me to escort you out," Tina said politely, getting up from the table.

"I'll see my own damned self out. In fact, I'm gonna start hanging out at The Grand instead of this house of freaks."

"The door can stick a bit," Tina yawned. "Make sure you pull it shut all the way behind you."

"Me-yow," I smirked as the door swung fully shut a few moments later.

Tina's bored expression vanished, nearly startling me into a yelp. "Curious."

"I was thinking the same thing."

"What?" I resisted the urge to yank my hair out by the double handful. "Oh, God, what now?"

"He insists the queen assist him in a delicate matter. He seems determined to put her in harm's way. He has made no secret of his contempt for and fear of her. And now, tonight—a Fiend happens to show up."

"You're not thinking—wait. What *are* you thinking?"

"But Nick couldn't be the rogue killer," Laura said—and thank goodness someone else was catching on. "He's the one killing all the bad guys, *and* he tells us all about it, and brings Betsy in to help him? You're saying it's an elaborate trap so he can kill her?"

"No way." I was shaking my head, though it did make a sneaky amount of sense. "He wouldn't dare."

"He does seem to dislike you a lot," my sister said thoughtfully.

"Yeah, but you guys are forgetting the Jessica factor. He wouldn't dare risk their relationship just to get me. I don't think he'd risk *anything* if it meant Jessica would toss him like hot vomit."

"An appealing image," Tina said, stifling a giggle. "But I still suggest we take a closer look at the good detective. A pity the body was essentially vaporized; I would love to have gotten his fingerprints."

"Why?"

"Knowing who they used to be would be helpful, I'm sure. If nothing else, Detective Nick could see if they had priors, when they were born—like that."

"Sorry," Laura said. "That's the trouble when hellfire meets vampire. Poof!"

"Yeah, it's cool, but then you've got dead vampire in your hair for hours. But Nick might have some luck with my purse. I'd better get that back from him, the crumb bum. Which reminds me, if the festivities are over for the night, I'm gonna shower."

"And I," Sinclair said, rising, "shall assist you."

He chased me all the way to our room.

Chapter 37

Sinclair was as good as his word; he soaped my back, washed my hair for me, and pretty soon we were groaning and biting each other under the pounding water. Sex in the shower didn't always work for people, but I was a tall girl.

And while he pushed, pushed, pushed into me, I watched the blood from my bite trickle down his back and swirl down the drain. Then the universe went away for a few seconds, while my orgasm took over my brain. Thank God Sinclair had a good grip, or I would have gone down like a sawed Sequoia.

We were relaxing in the second or third afterglow—we'd gone from the shower to the bed, and the sheets had completed the job of drying us—and I was grinning like a monkey. Sure, there were still problems, but now we were thinking about solutions. Maybe we were turning a corner on this. Maybe we—

From far below us, the front door boomed open, and I heard the very distinctive sound of Antonia's growl, followed by Tina's shrieked, "Majesties!"

"It never ends," I moaned, reaching for a robe. Sinclair had slipped into a pair of pants and was already out the door. "It never ends!"

I beat him to the foyer, but only because he had too much dignity to vault the banister and bypass the stairs. Ha! Score one for—aggh! I had nearly skidded in the blood.

Antonia was in her werewolf form—I glanced at the bigass clock at the far end of the hall and saw that dawn was still at least ten minutes away.

She had dragged a dead Fiend in with her.

"Um. Good dog?"

Garrett was shivering behind her. He clearly hadn't cared for the night's fun-filled activities, but knew he looked bad enough already in his lover's eyes.

I felt sorry for him. Anybody who says good guys never get scared and do stupid things has watched too many action movies. Yeah, he'd shown the less noble half of the human condition these past few days, but I could never forget what he'd gone through, and how far he'd come.

The man had never asked to become a vampire, or a Fiend, or anything else. He just woke up one day in a world full of pain, and wondered why. Just like the other Fiends.

I couldn't even look to myself as a better example of how to act. Any poise I had, I was sure, was a function of my ignorance of what I truly faced as queen. To put it more bluntly, I was so clueless about the magnitude of my new job, I was too dumb to be scared.

Antonia was sitting on her haunches, seeming to laugh at us with her wide mouth and eight zillion teeth. Her coat was the color of her hair, rich and dark. Interestingly, she had a white splotch on her chest, roughly diamond shaped. The splotch had a dark red smudge on it, and blood still trickled down her panting tongue.

Tina was examining the dead (again) Fiend. "This one appears to be the one Betsy named Sandy."

He was a large man, built like a farmer with thick shoulders and long, powerful legs. Not as tall as Skippy, but still formidable. Shirtless, with ripped jeans. No shoes or socks. His feet were filthy; God knew how long he'd been running around like that.

His throat had been torn out. Among other things.

"She found his scent in the garbage pile out back—the stuff the contractors left after they fixed the house," Garrett said. "We've followed it all night. She caught him alone and—well. You can see."

"Sure can."

Okay, there was another corpse in my foyer, and that was, under any circumstances, bad. But Marc and Jessica were out, and untouched by this. So I was at a total loss as to how to react: Great job? Naughty werewolf? Thanks? Don't run off ever again on a murderous rampage, or I'll kick your ass? Murder bad? Murder good?

I finally settled on concern for my friend. "For crying out loud, Antonia! You could have been killed! Bad, bad werewolf!" I was towering over her, shaking my finger (but not getting it too close to all those teeth). "This is the sort of thing that can get you killed, and then where would Garrett be without you? You were really sweet to try and solve our problem, but I don't want you going off alone like that ever again!"

Bored, Antonia licked blood from her left paw.

"I mean it!"

The werewolf yawned.

"If you have more to add to your lecture," Sinclair said, his lips twitching, "you had better hurry. I estimate the sun will be up in less than five minutes."

"Dammit!" While I could withstand sunlight, the coming of dawn was still a narcoleptic trigger for me. Worse so than for other vampires; apparently, this was part of the price of being queen.

I tried to end my lecture quickly, but Sinclair had been (unintentionally, I'm sure!) mistaken: sunrise was in less than ten seconds.

"There she goes," Tina commented, as the floor rushed up to my face and everything went dark.

Chapter 38

$\mathcal{S}$omeone had considerately carried me up to bed (I prayed it was Sinclair), and I woke up with a large Post-it stuck to my forehead.

I snatched it away and read: *Developments! Come down as soon as you get rid of your horrible vampire breath. Also, your mom wants to know how long she's going to be stuck with BabyJon; I guess he's teething again.*

Oh, goody. Jessica was back. And my poor baby brother! He drooled like a beast when he popped a new tooth; I'd seen him soak an entire quilt. He was impossibly cute most of the time, with his shock of black hair, amazing blue eyes, and sweetly chubby limbs, but I could hardly bear to look at him when he was slobbering his way through the tooth of the week.

I couldn't help it; I grinned, picturing my mother's horror at watching BabyJon soak one of her antique quilts.

I hopped out of bed, shrugged out of yesterday's outfit, and brushed my teeth and hair. Then I changed into gray leggings, a dark blue PROPERTY OF RENFEST sweatshirt, and black flats—no socks. Then I hurried downstairs to the kitchen.

"—took him down so easy," Antonia was bragging. "Look! Not a mark on me."

"Anymore," Sinclair corrected her politely. "You don't fool *me*, dear."

"Okay, maybe El Fiendo got in a few good ones, I admit it. But I'm all healed up and *he's* roasting in hell. That puts it in the win column for me."

"It was foolish of the two of you to go after him by yourselves. You might have run into all of them."

All of them—I wondered how many were left. Jeez, even when I knew they were running around pissed at me, I couldn't keep track of them.

"Hey, think I'm gonna sit around on my ass while the fuckin' Fiends pop up without warning whenever they want? Who needs the pressure? Besides, I hate pop-ins. I hate this whole stupid situation." Except she appeared to be thriving on it.

"So where *is* the dead guy who was in our foyer?" I asked, gratefully accepting a glass of grapefruit juice from Tina. It wasn't nearly as good for me as Sinclair's blood, but I'd had enough from my husband to keep me going for a while. "Not that I mind that he's gone."

"The body," Sinclair said carefully, knowing how I felt about such icky things, "is in the basement, in the walk-in freezer."

I shuddered, and juice slopped over the rim of my glass. Among other things, when the mansion had been modernized thirty years ago, the old owners had put in a giant freezer for entertaining. Luckily, we kept it empty. Most of the time.

"We don't know if we will need access to the body again," Tina said apologetically. "I staked it after you fell asleep, just to be sure."

"Do we know his real name?" I wasn't expecting a good answer here, but I had to ask.

I got a pleasant surprise from Tina. "Nick was here, and printed him. He's going to run it through privately—"

"Why privately?"

Antonia gave me a "you poor dumb bitch" look, as Tina patiently explained, "What if the dead man was born in 1910? And he looks like a man in his late thirties? That might bring up questions we would find awkward to answer."

"Does Nick have enough juice to run prints—twice—without anybody else finding out?"

"We will see."

I had to be happy with that. I knew dick about police procedural. But if he was getting secret assignments from the chief, he probably had some clout.

"Thank you for your assistance, Antonia," Sinclair said over my musings. "We are grateful."

"Why do you think I beat feet to get back here from the Cape? You guys'd sit around and talk it to death. You need a werewolf to get shit done."

"Are all werewolves as insufferable as you are?" I asked sweetly, "or are you a genetic anomaly?"

Before she could answer, I looked around and said, "Hey, where's Laura? I'd think she'd want to be in on all this stuff now that she knows what's going on."

"She called while you were sleeping; she's teaching her church youth group tonight," Tina said with a barely repressed shudder.

"Okay, how about Jess? She left me a sticky note."

"You just missed her; she went to Detective Berry's house, complaining bitterly that it had been 'ages and ages' since they'd had some alone time."

"Why didn't she just go with him?"

"Oh, it's kind of dumb. She doesn't like to be stuck at anybody's house without a getaway car. It's one of her things. But it's great that she gets to see him tonight . . . he must have the night off."

Tina was opening her laptop. "Yes, yes, the poor deprived things. Let them stay gone for a month."

I was unwrapping a blue raspberry Blo-Pop. "Tina," I said reproachfully, then popped it into my mouth and sucked enthusiastically.

"Sorry, Majesty, you know I'm fond of Jessica. It's *him* I can't stand. And if he deliberately places you in harm's way once more, I may not be responsible for my actions."

"You shush. Just check your e-mail."

"Actually," she said, not looking up, "I'm checking Nick's e-mail."

I nearly gagged on the sucker. "Boo! Unless you've got a warrant. And vampires can't get warrants, I bet." I paused. "Can we?"

"You're so adorably naive, I may vomit," my husband said from behind the *Washington Post*.

"And you're so—" My cell phone chirped "Living Dead Girl" and I snatched at it. I was sure it was my mom, bitching about baby duty. But there was no way BabyJon was coming back here until we— "Hi, Mom?"

"It's Jessica!" I winced and held the phone away from my ear. "You've got to come, quick! All of you! Nick's gone, but the Fiends have been here!"

"Whoa, whoa, calm down." I was trying to take my own advice and not hyperventilate. "How d'you know the Fiends took him?"

"Who *else* would break in and attack him? Please, please come right now! There's blood all over the place!"

"But—but—" I was so panicked I couldn't think, much less speak. "But why did they take Nick?"

"Because," Tina said, not looking up from her laptop, "the fingerprints came back. Forensics notified him by e-mail, but he hasn't actually gotten this message yet, so they had to move fast. And so will we."

"What? Why?"

"The Fiend's name was Edward Hamlin."

Hamlin? Why did I know that name? So much had been happening in a short time, I—

"Nick has been working on a little project for Police Chief Hamlin," Tina added, helping me out.

"We're coming!" I shrieked into the cell, then snapped it shut so hard I broke it.

Chapter 39

Nick lived in a great-looking bachelor pad in Minneapolis, overlooking the Mississippi River. The view was terrific, which made up for the fact that the yard was the size of a Post-it note, and just as yellow.

I'd never been there—luckily, Tina's laptop was stuffed with all sorts of interesting tidbits, including addresses she had no business knowing. She had MapQuested it, and here we all were.

Jessica had the place wide open for us, and I could see it was full of rich-guy toys: an extra truck, skis, a snowmobile, a Jetski. And that was just the garage. The house itself was brick, with dark green trim and a short, crack-free driveway.

Inside, the place was a complete shambles—we could practically follow the progress of the fight by observing the broken furniture and shattered glassware. He clearly hadn't gotten to his gun, which was too bad for him. I couldn't blame him—he'd been relaxing at home, getting ready for a date with Jessica, with no way of knowing his boss, the chief of police, had fed him to the wolves—almost literally.

Jessica was waiting for us in the living room, which looked like a bomb had detonated from beneath the carpet. He might not have had his gun, but he'd put up a helluva fight. It made me remember why I'd liked him a couple of years ago.

"Ballsy bastard," was Antonia's comment.

FALSE QUEEN was written on the biggest wall, the one without any windows. Sinclair leaned close, sniffed, then reported quietly, "Detective Berry's blood."

"But not so much that he's dead, right?" Jessica begged. "Not enough to kill him, right?"

Sinclair put an arm around my trembling friend. "No, dear one. Not nearly enough."

"She cannot go," Tina said firmly.

"Indeed, no."

"What are you two talking about?" I tried to keep my voice low and authoritative, when it wanted to go high and squeaky.

Tina shook her head, but Sinclair came right out with it. "This is an ancient challenge among vampires—"

"So how do Fiends who have been out of it for six decades know anything about it?" I asked, trying not to sound hysterical.

"It's important to keep in mind they are remembering more and more every day—and in fact may have lied to us about what they *do* remember, at any rate." Sinclair glanced at the bloody letters again. "Regardless of how they know, they know. Such a step is usually taken to settle a grudge or, occasionally, determine ability to rule. This message means that if you value your crown, you will rescue Nick and defeat the Fiends."

"But how would I even know where to—"

"He'll be where it began for *them*," Garrett said quietly. I jumped; he hadn't said a word since we'd left the mansion.

"Nostro's house," Tina added.

"Well, then, I'm outta here!"

Cue huge squabble fest. Not even Jessica was sure I should go, and, needless to say, Tina and Sinclair weren't keen on the idea at all. Antonia was practically foaming at the mouth to come with me; she'd had a taste of Fiend already and didn't mind getting wet. I had a momentary flash—thank goodness Laura had her youth group tonight; she'd just be one more person trying to stop me.

Don't get me wrong, I sure as shit didn't want to go. I predicted a messy death and Nick's curses being the last thing I ever heard in this life. But, like it (I didn't) or not, *I was the queen*. Did I think a hideous mistake had been made somewhere along the way? You bet. Was I going to welsh out of my obligation? Never in life. (Or death, I s'pose.)

The rules were, I go alone. So, I go alone. Besides, the Fiends would spot the others, and then they'd play kickball with Nick's head. How could I face my best friend if I got her lover killed 'cause I was too chickenshit to show up alone?

"—absolutely out of the question—"

"—but she's the only one who—"

"—can't leave Nick to—"

"—not open for discussion, as far as I am concerned—"

"—her responsibility—"

"—not going to let her essentially commit suicide—"

The argument was escalating in both intensity and volume (I noticed no one was much interested in *my* opinion), and there was no time, Goddammit, no time at all.

"Shut up, shut up, *shut the fuck up!* We have no time, don't you get it? Now I'm *going*."

"Not at all," Sinclair said calmly.

"Tradition dictates she do exactly that," Tina said reluctantly, correcting her sovereign for maybe the fourth time in eighty years—a real toughie for her, since she wasn't too keen on me going in the first place.

"They'll kill you!" Jessica cried.

"Yes," Garrett said. "They will."

"The fuck they will! They can't take the king and queen *and* a fellow Fiend *and* me. We'll eat 'em for dinner! Let's go! Right now!" And I noticed an odd thing; all the fine hairs on Antonia's arms were standing straight up. If she'd been in her wolf form, she'd be bristling all over.

"We had practically the same group the first time the Fiends came, and we ran away," Jessica said. "What's changed?"

"A challenge written in your lover's blood," Sinclair said, kindly enough.

"Come on, you chickenshits!" Antonia barked. "We can take those fuckers."

"Maybe. And then Nick will be fish food," Tina said, biting her lip.

"My alpha's not going alone, and that's how it is!"

"Shut up, Antonia, all of you shut up! Just—shut up!" My head was pounding, like it was going to split down the middle of my forehead; I was clutching my temples and wondering why it was so damned hot in here. It seemed like the heat was battering at me, trying to get in, and all at once I dropped my hands and let it, let it all in, let it burn me alive.

Instantly, the room went quiet, a quiet broken by the thuds of my friend's bodies hitting the floor. I stood over them, shocked. Knelt quickly and found Jessica's pulse, realized Tina and Sinclair were as alive as they could be, just unconscious. Antonia, too, was out cold—and so was Garrett. I was the only one still standing.

And I felt like a million bucks. I felt like I could jump across the Mississippi. And I loved the sudden peace and quiet—I could finally hear myself think. I felt almost—what was the word? *Euphoric.* Yeah. I felt—I felt an awful lot like the way I'd felt when I'd sucked Marjorie dry, only not so frenzied and out of control.

I'd done it again! The chill in my bones subsided as I realized I had not killed anyone this time. In fact, they were safe and sleeping and, did I mention, *safe?* How did that work? Was it something I could control? If I didn't, what did?

I had no more time to think about it. If any of my friends woke up while I was still here, the trick I'd pulled (can I call it a "trick"?) would have been for nothing. Knowing exactly where I had to go, I got the hell out of there, casting a last guilty look at my unconscious husband.

No sex tonight, that was for sure.

Chapter 40

After borrowing (okay, stealing) Sinclair's Lexus SUV, I made the trip in less than half an hour. Nostro's old digs were a combination of farm and what Jessica called a McMansion. Most of the houses in the neighborhood, while in the low seven-figure range, still looked a lot alike. They came with your standard pool, your standard half-acre backyard, your standard ballroom.

For an extra five figures, you could get either a gazebo, or a chicken coop. "Wholesome country living with the convenience of city living," that's what the brochure said. I knew, because my dad and the Ant had lived in one. It had been left to BabyJon, along with all their dough and the condo in Florida; some lawyer I'd only met once was keeping everything in a trust for him.

The McMansion was brown, with cream-colored fake shutters (what exactly was the point of shutters that didn't open or close, anyway?) and a big, crimson-colored front door. The walkway and patio were brick; the grass was starting to get a little shaggy. There was a tall hedge that went around the side of the house that I could see, and a few baby trees in the front yard. In a hundred years they'd be gorgeous elms. It was weird to think that I might be around to actually see that.

I brazenly parked on the front lawn (yeah, that's right, the queen of the vampires is here!), giving thanks that the nearest neighbor was on the other side of the lake.

I walked up the sidewalk and knocked on Nostro's front door, remembering the last time I'd been dragged through this very door. I'd been a vampire for about two days, no idea what was going on (as opposed to, you know, now), and almost before I knew it, people were bowing and calling me queen. It had been more bizarre than senior prom.

Nobody answered, so I tried the knob—unlocked. Ah, a welcoming killer mob. Good times.

I knew my way around a little, but proceeded cautiously. Frankly, tracking them in the bland-smelling house was pretty easy—even from a floor away I could smell their reek.

I passed a sitting room, a library, a bathroom, two bedrooms, and an office on the way. Unlike our mansion, the McMansion had much larger rooms (older houses tended to have tons of little rooms).

In fact, the place seemed too big and rather empty; there was dust on a lot of the tables and countertops. Of course, Alice had been the only one staying here . . . before she was killed and dismembered, the poor girl . . .

There weren't any paintings or pictures on the walls and, weirder, no books. No books anywhere. The bookcases held wine bottles and lamps that looked old-fashioned but operated on electricity. No magazines, even.

At least all the lights were on, which made the whole thing seem less scary—I don't know why. I sure as shit knew that things went bump in the night even *with* all the lights on.

The carpet was so thick in each room that my footsteps made no noise, but I didn't much care, because I wasn't trying to sneak in. Instead I walked straight into the upstairs living room and was greeted with, "Who the hell invited you, blondie?"

Chapter 41

I blinked, more than a little surprised. Mostly at the fact that there was an *upstairs* living room; I'd never seen that before. Just more proof of Nostro's essential nuttiness. And I'd had more pleasant greetings. Shoot, the IRS guy had been nicer.

Focus, Betsy!

A bloody and battered Nick was slumped in a dining room chair. There was a row of floor-to-ceiling windows behind him and, weirdly, three of them were open. There was quite the breeze whipping through the room—I guess the Fiends, used to living outside, didn't much notice the cold.

Then I remembered that they'd been kept outside all year round, like dogs you didn't mind having around but didn't want to spend much time with, either.

They ripped up anything they got near; it's not like they were aware enough to sleep in beds, or even on a carpeted floor. You're acting like they were POWs and you were a Viet Cong!

Nick wasn't tied to the chair or anything—why would they? But he sure was pissed.

"Well, uh, they sort of did," I answered, gesturing to the Fiends. "Invited me, I mean."

"You just *had* to come and save the day, didn't you?"

"Alone," one of the Fiends said—it was Stephanie, and she wasn't bothering to hide her surprise. "She came alone."

"Of course I came! What, you think I'd stop for cocktails instead?" The Fiends stared at me, unblinking, while I bragged, "You have no idea who you're dealing with." Okay, to be fair to them, *I* had no idea who they were dealing with. "You think you can get what you want by grabbing my friend—"

"I'm not your friend," Nick whined.

"Fine, you grabbed my best friend's boyfriend, and now you think you're going to get what you want. But you don't even know what you want, do you?"

The Fiends looked at each other, while Nick, looking thoroughly disgusted to be there, rolled his eyes.

I examined them as closely as I could without making it obvious I was staring. Happy, Jane, and Clara looked a little better—something in the eyes, I guess. They didn't seem as savage or as confused.

Wonder of wonders, although they didn't appear to have showered, they were at least wearing clean clothes. It occurred to me that the bedrooms in the McMansion probably still had dressers with clothes in them. And these guys had eventually fed enough, or remembered enough, to realize that.

Jane had long, dirty blond hair—it hung halfway down her back in greasy strings. Her mouth was a thin line, and her fingernails were filthy, but, incongruously with the rest of her, she had bright blue eyes, definitely her best feature.

Clara and Happy also had long hair but of course Happy, being a guy, towered over them both. He was one of those fellas who are so big they slump to try to look smaller, which only drew attention to his sheer bulk.

Happy had the tip-tilted eyes of an Asian American and would have been pretty good looking, if not for the hate-filled expression on his face. His jeans and shirt were clean, but he needed to wash the dried blood off his chin.

I wondered if anything was driving the Fiends now *besides* hate for me.

"Look, guys, let's talk about this. I think there's been enough killing, don't you?"

"No," Happy said.

"Because this could get a lot worse, you know. Before it gets better."

"It will never be better," Clara—also known as Stephanie, but I wasn't going to let on—said sadly. "I thought maybe—" She cut herself off, and I knew why. Even now, she couldn't let on to what she had been up to earlier. She was as much a prisoner as Nick. "Not ever."

"Then what's your goal?"

"You must pay for what you've done," Jane said.

"Pay as in kill? I didn't kill you, I didn't make you vampires and starve you—I tried to *help* you. You know what your problem is? The one you really want to hurt is dead. Nostro's out of your reach, and you can't fucking stand it."

"Stated with Kissingerian diplomacy," Nick snarked.

"Quiet, Chair Boy. Look, I'll apologize again, okay?"

"No," Happy said.

"Then what do you want? You want to go back in time? Because that's the only way to—wait." I thought for a second. And then another one.

I thought about Jessica, and how much she loved Nick. I thought about these Fiends, and the lives they had before they became my subjects—yes, my subjects. And even if the old king, Nostro, had done this to them, I was still responsible for them.

So what would a queen do, for her subjects? What kind of queen did I want to be?

"Okay. Let Nick go, and I'll stay, and you can have at me."

The three Fiends glanced at each other.

"Maim, kill, fold, spindle, mutilate. Whatever. Just let Nick go."

"You offer yourself in his place?" Stephanie/Clara seemed genuinely shocked by the offer.

"Yup."

"This is not a trick?"

"Uh, I don't think so."

"You are not setting a trap?"

I lifted my bare hands. "If this were a trap, wouldn't I have sprung it by now? I'm here alone. I'm not here to trick you. I don't want to kill you. I want you to get better. If the only way you can get better is to deal with me alone, then this is your chance. So what the hell are you waiting for?"

Happy moved in and sniffed the air around me. "You are serious."

I made an effort not to lean away from him; yeesh, he stank. "Yes."

"It may be painful."

"It might be." I tried not to shake. I tried to sound brave. I guess I didn't, though, because he almost smiled.

"We give you no guarantees," he warned. "We may come after your friend here, anyway, after you're gone."

I thought of Sinclair. "My friend," I sighed, "will be the least of your problems, if you kill me."

"We are afraid of no one. Not even our queen."

I shrugged. "Obviously not."

Happy looked over his stooped shoulders at the other two. They gave no sign, but he seemed to understand them anyway.

"We accept. Your friend can go."

"No fucking way!"

The four of us stared at Nick.

"Oh no you don't," he hollered, white-faced with blood loss. "You don't get to save me, no way, uh-uh. They kill me, and you feel like shit for, what is it? A thousand years? *That's* the way it's supposed to be. You're supposed to live with failure, not be the hero. Hear that? You're not the hero, Betsy Taylor! So hit the bricks! Get lost! Crawl back into your mansion basement and hide again!"

"He does not want to go," Happy observed after a short silence.

"Yeah, no shit."

"Are you sure you wish to take his place?"

"I'm having second thoughts," I admitted grimly.

"Perhaps he is not the friend to her we thought he was," Stephanie told the others.

"Damn right we're not friends!" Nick hollered.

"Will you stop screaming? And no," I sighed. "We used to be, sort of, but no, not anymore. But the offer still stands. Let him go, and I'll stick around, and we'll see what we'll see."

"I have doubts," Stephanie told her comrades. Aha! I silently congratulated myself for stopping Sinclair and Tina from killing her.

"What d'you mean?" Jane asked. Happy looked like he was wondering the same thing. Both of them had a little suspicion in their eyes, and I prayed Stephanie would be careful with her next words, so she wouldn't give herself away.

"She is not what we expected." Stephanie circled me and Nick. "Nothing about her. Not her friends, not those she calls her friends but are not—" She stopped and sniffed Nick, who made a batting motion at her with his hands, like he was shooing away a fly. "She is not the queen we thought. She is not smart, or powerful, or terrifying. Not like a real queen."

"More like a commoner," Happy added.

"Thanks?" I called out.

"She might help us," Stephanie added.

"How?" Jane asked, shaking tangled hair out of her face. "If she is not like a real queen, what can she give us?"

"We could start with your names," I suggested, still hoping to avoid hostilities. "I'd like to know them."

My request confused them, until Stephanie cleared her throat. "My name is Stephanie," she told me, as if for the first time.

Happy licked his lips. His tongue was weirdly long. "Richard," he finally said.

"Jane," the third one said.

Huh, I told myself. *Jane's name is actually Jane! What are the chances?*

Chapter 42

I took a shallow breath and let it out. Okay. Things were going—if not exactly well, at least it wasn't the disaster on wheels I'd been envisioning five minutes ago. Names were a good start. Now to keep the lines of communication open.

"Stephanie. Richard. Jane. I . . . well, I can't say it's wonderful to meet all of you, just like I know you weren't exactly thrilled about meeting me. But I can say I'm glad I've learned who you really are. I, uh, felt bad about the silly nicknames."

"You did?" Jane asked, open skepticism in her voice.

"Well, sure. See, I—"

"Don't be fooled!" Nick warned them. "She's got this annoying weird charm thing going on. It's hideous. Like head lice. Everything she touches turns to shit."

"Would that include Jessica?" I snapped.

"Well," he snarled, "she didn't have cancer before she moved in with you and a bunch of other mutant bloodsucking freaks."

I didn't even want to respond to that. Emotionally exhausted, I sat on the arm of the couch next to him and waited to see what the Fiends would do.

And for the first time, I noticed Nick was bleeding—from the inside of his elbows, his neck. There were more serious cuts up and down his arms—from the fight at his house, I assumed. Maybe he'd rolled on some of the broken glass on the carpet? Maybe he'd—

Oh, God, his neck. They'd—they'd fed on him while waiting for me. His skin must still be crawling.

I imagine he felt raped and suddenly couldn't look at him.

"We have to deal with this one before we do anything else," Richard said, hauling Nick out of the chair. "They don't care for each other, so he's officially become useless."

"Useless?" Nick yelped, outraged.

"Hey, a minute ago you were ready to die just to make me feel like shit for the next thousand years. Now you're all mystified because you might be executed?"

"We should kill him," Richard decided.

"What about the queen?" Stephanie asked, looking around nervously as if the queen's guard was going to burst out of the walls at any moment. Ha! If only. I could use a last-minute rescue. Dammit, why, *why* wasn't my life more like a movie?

Richard squinted at me, and I got a decidedly distrustful vibe from him. "We should kill her anyway."

Then I got a stroke of real luck. Nick tried to pull away from Richard and briefly succeeded, separating himself for a bare second from his supernaturally strong grasp. Quick as thought, I stood up, snatched Nick by the back of his neck and the seat of his pants, and tossed him out the bank of windows.

"You biiiiiiiitch," he yowled all the way down. Then, thank God, I heard him cursing as he thrashed around in the hedges.

"She lies!" Jane shrieked, and came at me.

Chapter 43

God, I was *so sick* of people just launching themselves at me without warning. Big-time rude, not to mention hell on my nerves. I backpedaled like mad, physically and verbally.

"I didn't do anything to—"

Her fist was a blur, and I took a teeth-rattling punch in the mouth, which wasn't fun at all, and threw an elbow into Richard's throat before he could do the same.

I chastised myself immediately: I was fighting like a human, but Fiends didn't need to breathe. He did cough and grab his throat, which I figured was good enough, so I turned my back on him, seized Jane by the hair, and spun her across the room.

Richard recovered faster than I expected. He delivered a blow to my right kidney, which *hurt*—oh, man, getting punched in the back was no fun at all—and then delivered a roundhouse kick to my left kidney, which hurt even more.

"You told us you would not try to trick us!" he seethed, hurting me some more with his fists. Kick, kick. Stomp. Best I could tell, Richard was apparently quite the kickboxing champion in his former life. "You swore!"

"I said," I gasped between blows, "that after Nick left . . . ooof . . . I would let you have at me. Feels like . . . ow, ow, oh God *ow*! . . . I'm keeping my end of the bargain. Shame . . . aggh! . . . you couldn't keep yours."

"My end of the bargain," he hissed in my ear, "is to survive. That's all you taught me to do."

The fire inside me kindled, and I felt a surge of power, as something made Richard stagger back. It didn't knock him unconscious, much less kill him, but it did give me enough space to get up and straighten myself to my full height.

And yes, I was still wearing my Marc Jacobs heels, which helped.

"Maybe you're not as good a student as you think." I couldn't help the disdain in my voice, though normally I tried not to sound like such a snob. What was wrong with this man? His queen had spared his life from the wrath of her husband, offered an apology, reached her hand out in friendship—and he had slapped it down?

What was wrong with him? *Who the fuck did he think he was?!*

My blood ran super-hot again, and he shrieked as if I had struck him. Again, he seemed too strong to suffer worse than a blow—or maybe the fact that he shared my blood spared him from the worst I had to offer—but it didn't matter. His kickboxing career was over.

"On your knees!" I snarled at him. When he didn't move, I ignited my blood again—yes, I think I was controlling it now, at least somewhat—and *made* him get down. And I won't lie. I wouldn't deny it felt good to see him submit. To make him submit.

I turned long enough to ensure that Stephanie and Jane were not coming at me—they weren't, since they, too, were on their knees—and then I gave Richard my full attention again.

Nick's chair had been upturned in the fracas; I reached down and snapped a leg off the bottom. "You and I will come to terms of peace," I suggested, "or you will die." A dim thought that this wasn't exactly the best way to enforce peace was immediately shoved to the back of my brain.

Richard's body was beaten, but his eyes were still full of defiance and distrust. "I see your true colors. No peace, my queen."

"My true colors. My true colors!" I felt my fangs spring from my gums and resisted the urge to bite him on the face. I raised the stake and brought it down faster than he could possibly move . . .

. . . right into his throat.

I don't know what made me miss his heart. Maybe it was poor aim—swinging a stake in lavender pumps is harder than it looks. Maybe the part of me that wanted him dead wasn't as strong as the part of me that just wanted him to shut the hell up.

Pulling the bloody stake from his throat, I turned to the others, who were still (willingly) on their knees. His body made a soft thump on the plush carpet behind me. Yes, he'd be out of action for hours. "And now, what to do with you two," I said grimly, hands on hips. Richard's black blood dripped slowly onto my—oh no!—Ann Taylor linen pants. I quickly rearranged the stake.

"I, um, think we should let her go," Stephanie managed with her head down.

"Perhaps there can be . . . forgiveness," Jane said, also not looking up.

"Maybe," I agreed. "I guess that'th up to each of you."

"What?"

"Never mind." This was no time to let the Fiends know that I lisped whenever my fangs came out. It wouldn't exactly strike terror in their heart of hearts.

I could hear the squeal of brakes outside the windows, familiar voices, the front door opening, and pounding footfalls.

"In the thort time we have left alone together," I suggested, "you two thould probably do everything you can to look ath— *as*—unthreatening as you possibly can." Thank God, my fangs were retracting. I was still pretty thirsty, but it would appear that the energy I'd gotten from my family, as well as from Richard, were keeping the worst of the pangs away. "Because if you think *I'm* bad? You should see my husband in action."

They swarmed into the room like a pack of wolverines. I relaxed, smiled at the first face I saw, and felt some of the fire leave my blood.

"Don't you bitches touch—oh." Antonia skidded to a halt, then nearly went sprawling, as Sinclair almost ran her down. "Oomph! Um, we're here to save you."

"Go save Nick," I suggested. "He's in the bushes on this side of the house."

"*You will pay for*—oh," Sinclair said, straightening as he took in the three prostrate forms around me. The others piled in behind him and did the same. "Hmm."

"Yeah, so, thanks for showing up, but I took care of things. Pretty much. Of course, in the last week you guys whittled down their numbers for me. That was," I decided, "a big help."

Tina and Antonia each nodded. Garrett, hiding behind Antonia, swallowed with what looked like a mixture of relief and lingering fear. He tried a shy smile, and I smiled back.

"Stake 'em all!" Nick hollered, limping through the doorway and waving his arms like the Winter Carnival grand marshal. "Betsy, too!"

Jessica rushed to Nick, clearly relieved that he was unharmed (well, it was possible he had a sprained ankle, and that was a helluva scratch on his forehead . . . and he seemed to be favoring the ribs on his left side . . .).

"Agreed," Sinclair said, sighing at the three Fiends. "Well, not agreed about my wife. But the others must die now. In fact, it is long overdue."

"As you wish." Tina pulled out a thin mahogany stake from somewhere within her navy blue wool sweater and skirt set (truly frightening efficiency), and stepped forward.

"Forget it!" I said, holding up my hands. "We are going to be magnanimous in victory."

"Magnanimous equals pussy," Antonia commented.

"Again?" Tina whined. "We're going to let them live again?"

"Elizabeth, they are too dangerous to simply—"

"I didn't say we were going to set them free. They'll have to earn their freedom." I turned to the three Fiends—well, okay, the two that were conscious. "You had a grievance with me. You should have stuck with *me*. Had all seven of you done that, seven of you might be alive now. I'd like it if you three, at least, stayed alive. It's up to you."

"What—" Stephanie swallowed, then tried again. "What do we have to do?"

"You guys can be the queen's personal bodyguards and doers of annoying chores. Or I can leave the room, right now, and my husband and friends will chat with you. A *lot*. Until you have cavernous facial wounds." I tilted my head toward the exit and not coincidentally to the people who would stay behind. "Your choice."

"Pick the stake," Nick suggested, wiping streaks of blood from his face. God, that made me even hungrier. And wouldn't he just *shit*? "You don't want to spend the next thousand years doing that twit's dirty work." He turned to me. "You almost killed me, you numb fucking twat! Again!"

"I did not! I saved you."

"You threw me out a fucking window!" Nick was actually going purple with rage.

I tried to hide my amazement. Unlike occurs in the movies, Nick clearly hadn't suddenly forgiven me and been warmed by my selfless act. We weren't going to ride off into the sunset together (so to speak) and get Blizzards from Dairy Queen.

Frankly, I didn't get it. In the movies, when the heroine did something heroic and cool, everybody loved her at the end. Okay, I didn't *really* expect life to be like the movies . . . uh. That was maybe a lie.

"You are a menace, and if I could make it stick, I'd throw your ass in jail for the next hundred years."

"Nicholas J. Berry!" Jessica gasped. "What is the *matter* with you?"

"With me? You should have seen this psycho bitch in action."

"That is *enough*," she snarled, hands on scrawny hips. "When are you going to get it through your head that Betsy isn't the cause of all your problems?"

I was frantically trying to signal to Jessica, making a slashing motion across my throat, the universal gesture for "shush!" Although it made me sad, I felt Nick's rage was a perfectly appropriate reaction to the evening's festivities. I appreciated Jessica sticking up for me—she always stuck up for me—but she didn't have all the facts.

He had been attacked. Again. Violated by vampires . . . again. I was amazed he hadn't gone fetal in the hedges.

"How many times do I have to say it," Jessica was saying. "How many times do you have to *see* it? She's a good guy!"

"No, Jess, it's okay, he—"

"She drinks blood, because she's dead," he said, spitting on the floor—spitting blood, I might add, and I was ashamed, because my fangs were out again. I didn't dare speak anymore; I didn't want him to know I wanted to drink and drink and drink. "She's a killer, and you know it."

"I love her, she's the sister I never got, and *you* know *that*."

"Ah, perhaps we could, ah, step into another room and discuss, ah, the new terms for surrender," Tina said, because even the Fiends looked uncomfortable to be witnessing the lovers' quarrel.

"Or maybe you could talk about this later, when everybody's calmed down," I tried.

"Don't make me choose," Jessica warned, ignoring us. For her, the only person in the room was Nick.

"I'm not making you choose. *I'm* choosing. We're done." He wiped his face again, and we all pretended not to notice how his hand shook and how he couldn't look at her.

"That's right," Jessica replied coolly. "We are."

And just like that—it was over. *They* were over. We could all practically hear the snap.

Chapter 44

Stephanie and Jane were sullen, but agreeable—apparently being the doers of the queen's scut work was more appealing than being staked.

I gave them permission to live on Nostro's property (by vampire law, when you killed a vampire all his stuff came to you, so technically, it was my property), and they agreed to be at my beck and call, as it were.

I'd probably put at least one of them to work in my nightclub, Scratch. Another vampire property that had come to me by law—long story. Actually, that wasn't true. I had killed another badass vampire, and her property went to me about the time her soul went shrieking into Hell.

Unlike their lives before, the Fiends wouldn't just frolic in the moonlight like undead puppies, but they'd live and read and watch TV like real people . . . which should be fun, since for all I knew Jane and Stephanie had no idea what a TV was.

They could feed on each other—if they were comfortable with that—or they could snack on bad guys. We would help them figure out who it was all right to bite and who was off-limits. Yep, they could make new lives for themselves, be almost like normal people.

Unless I needed them, of course. Then they'd come on the run, or I'd know the reason why. Shit, with all the bad guys popping out of the woodwork these days, I *needed* bodyguards.

Of course, we weren't going to just leave them to their own devices . . . Sinclair and I would have to think about who could keep an eye on them, maybe even live in the McMansion with them. For now, they were cowed enough by recent events that I felt safe leaving them there for the next few nights.

"That was pretty anticlimactic," Antonia bitched on our way out.

"What can I say? It can't be bloody revenge and near-death experiences every day."

"You're about to have a near-death experience," Sinclair promised grimly as we climbed into his Lexus (I noticed Nick's truck was also there and deduced they'd grabbed it when they woke up at his house after I'd put the whammy on them). "Specifically, you will never, ever sucker punch me like that again and run off into mortal danger."

"I didn't do it on purpose." Not quite a lie.

"Irrelevant."

"I'm not getting laid tonight, am I?"

"Probably not."

I batted my eyes. "What if I let you punish me?"

He paused, and his step actually faltered; I imagine he was thinking about my drawer full of scarves and our four-poster bed. Then he straightened up and went back to being Sir Pissypants. "Do not change the subject. You must promise to never, ever—"

"I won't!" Strangely, I felt my blood start to heat up again. *And I won't do that again, either. At least not right now.* Who knew if my friends could take it again? Besides, I really had no right to their—their life essence, maybe? Whatever it was that I could feed on without touching them. It wasn't mine. And I wasn't a thief.

With that in mind, I struggled to hold my temper, something I wasn't especially good at. "Sinclair, enough with the promises to stay safe and hidden from the world. It didn't suit me when I was alive, and I certainly can't comply now."

"I will not tolerate—"

"Are you listening, schmuck? You almost *died* this summer. Had I acted then like you wanted me to act this time, what would have happened? You'd be a pile of fucking ash, and you'd still be full of shit!"

"Aw, that's romantic," Antonia piped up.

"Damn right it is." I turned back to my idiot husband. "I love your arrogant ass, numbnuts, and I'm not going through something like this summer ever again. Besides, there are going to be times when we'll have to deal with problems alone . . . I mean, jeez. If *I* can figure that out, you can, too. You're just going to have to get used to the idea."

He sighed, and I could tell he wanted to smile at me but was forcing himself to remain stone-faced. The better to intimidate you with, my dear. Too bad it didn't work on me. Never had. "I love your arrogant ass as well, my own, but I meant every word I said, and you will mind me, Elizabeth. In this one thing, you will mind me."

"Fuck you, lover. I'm the queen, and I'll do as I please."

"I am the husband, and you will do as you're told."

"Hi, I'm Betsy. Nice to meet you."

"Do not sass me."

"Do not piss me off."

He stomped his foot. Actually stomped it (clad in a Kenneth Cole loafer), like a kid having a tantrum. I managed not to laugh. Just barely. "This argument is over!"

I stomped my heel, nearly staggering—damned vampire strength! If I ruined these pumps I'd never forgive myself. "You're fucking right it is. Go suck on a turnip."

Chapter 45

We got out of the car, still not talking to each other. Even more awkward, Jessica and Nick had tagged along in his truck—I would have thought he'd had enough of me for a lifetime, but there wasn't room in Sinclair's SUV for me, Sinclair, Antonia, Garrett, *and* Jessica. Is there anything worse than being trapped in a car immediately after you've just broken up with your boyfriend? Eeesh.

Worst of all, the Ant was waiting for me on the porch, knockoff-clad toe tapping impatiently. "It's not over yet," she warned.

"Tell me about it," I snarled. "It'll never be over, until you cough up why you're sticking around." I walked through her, shivering (it was like walking through a curtain of freezing water) and opened our front door. "Why can't you go to hell like any other—"

Suddenly I was shoved so hard, I smacked into the wall and fell down. The impact forced a shower of plaster to rain down on me. There was the deafening boom of a pistol being fired several times over my head. We were trapped in the doorway like ants in a straw—nobody had any room.

"That girl," a new voice said, "had amazing reflexes. I haven't missed a shot in forty-six years."

"Chief Hamlin?" Nick asked, horrified.

I slowly sat up. The Minneapolis police chief, less than a year from retirement, was standing at the end of the foyer, smoke curling up from the barrel of his pistol. He was a tall, gray-haired man in a neat dark blue suit, with wrinkles cutting deeply into his face, kind blue eyes, and a smoking gun.

"My father told me about you over three weeks ago," he said to (ulp) me. "How you left him for dead on that God-awful farm."

"Wh-what are you—?"

"I was just a boy when he disappeared—and died the first time, best I can tell. By the time he came back years later—last month, in fact—I was a police chief."

"But I don't understand why you—"

He was staring at me with exhausted eyes. "You were all he could think of. He was the gentlest man I'd ever known, and all he could think of was hurting people. Hurting you."

"So you set him to work," Nick said shakily. "You sicced him on perps we couldn't put away. Pretended to figure out the pattern—which I bought, because you've got a great rep as a detective. Gave your dad cold guns, so we wouldn't think it was a vampire."

"But these guys had a caretaker at the farm/mansion place." I was having a terrible time puzzling this out. "She never noticed your dad kept slipping off the property?"

"Silly boy. They killed her a month ago."

That explained why Tina and Sinclair couldn't puzzle out Alice's remains. They hadn't been fresh. And it was entirely possible they *had* known and kept the info to themselves. It would be typical behavior. I bit the inside of my cheeks, so I wouldn't start shrieking at them.

Secrets, secrets. Cripes. My life was stuffed with them.

"Jeez, jeez," Nick was saying, his hand on his hip. I could see his fingers wanted to pluck at a gun he wasn't wearing. "Your only mistake was sending him to me when you gave me the fake tags to check."

Chief Hamlin shook his head. "I didn't send him. He had been following your Betsy. And when he saw her on the street—"

"He snapped, and—" I almost said, "My sister killed him," but rapidly rephrased. I didn't want *any* of this fallout to poison Laura's life. "I killed him. But you didn't count on Nick getting his fingerprints off my purse strap. Once he had that info, it wouldn't have taken long until he knocked on your door."

The chief's lip trembled. "He was my father. He would not have hurt me."

I shook my head. "Oh, man, you're so wrong. Like, the earth is flat kind of wrong. I don't even know how to explain it to you. You don't understand what he had become."

"He was my father," the chief repeated. It was clear he was

trying to convince himself, more than anyone else. "Back—mirac-
ulously—from the dead. And only I could help him." He shuddered at whatever memories of his father he had and looked past
my shoulder. "A shame about your friend. I've never seen anyone
move that fast in my life."

I didn't dare turn to find out whom he was talking about.
"She'll be okay," I said bravely, hoping that was true. "And you
won't get a second chance."

"No," he said politely. "She won't be okay. I used twenty-two
longs, you see. But you're right about me. I won't get a second
chance. I have only the one gun, you see—and by my count, one
bullet left. I figured I'd never get the chance to reload, given the
size of your entourage." He looked down at his gun. "I wish I had
hit you and finished what my father started. I'll have to settle for
hurting you. I hope your friend was important to you. Very, very
important."

I still refused to turn around. Tears began to well in my eyes.
"You're going to regret what you've done, asshole."

"No, I'm not. I have no intention of letting you turn me into
what my father was."

Then he tucked the barrel under his chin and pulled the trigger.

Nobody tried to stop him. In fact, before his body hit the floor,
I was already turning to find out who had taken the bullets meant
for me.

Chapter 46

I first realized who it was when I saw the cascade of black waves blowing in the chill Minnesota wind—our front door was still open. The body lying face-down beneath that hair did not move.

Tina was lifting one pale hand, checking for a pulse. Garrett was holding the other.

"Why isn't she getting up?" I asked, rushing to Tina's side. "What kind of bullets were these? Were they silver?"

"They didn't have to be silver," Tina guessed as she examined Antonia's body. She knew more about guns than anyone I'd ever met. "Twenty-two longs, as he said, quite perfect for the job. They ricocheted around her skull but didn't exit. That particular ammunition lowers the innocent bystander rate. He may have expected civilians—or perhaps Detective Berry—to be near you when he shot you."

"But she's a werewolf!" I shook Sinclair's comforting hand off my shoulder.

Tina looked up at me, eyes almost black with sympathy. "Her brains are all over the floor, Majesty. There will be no coming back from this."

I barely noticed Garrett get up and slip out of view.

"But she—she's Antonia!" Foulmouthed and smart and strong and invulnerable. And alive—always so vibrantly, shockingly alive. "She can't be—I mean, shot? It's such a mundane way for someone like her to—"

"No." Jessica staggered as if the shock was going to knock her on her ass, and Nick steadied her. "No, she can't be. You're wrong. She's not."

And the worst part was— "She jumped in front of me. She— saved me."

"Everybody saves you," Nick said neutrally. He tried to slip his arm around a sobbing Jessica, but she knocked it away.

Then we heard the splintering crash come from the stairwell.

I stood, trembling at the subsequent silence, and peered into the foyer. I choked back a sob at what Garrett had done to himself.

The regretful Fiend-turned-vampire had kicked the banister off a stretch of curved stairs in the foyer, leaving a dozen or so of the rails exposed and pointing up like spears. Then he had climbed to the second floor to a spot overlooking the stairs and swan dived onto the rails, which had gone through him like teeth.

"See?" the Ant said sadly as we stared down at the second body of a friend in less than a minute. "I warned you."

"Yeah, well." I wiped my face. "You could have been a lot more specific."

"I didn't know exactly. But I had a feeling. This stuff is pretty inevitable around you."

"Please go away."

"Yes, I think so. You wouldn't believe how depressing all this is. Good-bye, for now." And like that, she was gone.

"We'll take care of the bodies," my husband told me quietly.

Jessica kicked the wall and wiped tears from her cheeks. "Take care of the bodies? Just like that? It's not that easy, Eric. You can't just snap your fingers and make vampire minions clean up the crap. Not this time. What about Chief Hamlin? How are we going to explain *that*?"

"Don't worry about it," Nick said, clearly uncomfortable. "I can fix that."

"You can fix that," I spat. "Like you helped us fix things with the Fiends. Like you wanted me to fix your problems. You're going to fix this."

Sensing my lack of faith, he coughed and softened his tone. "Yeah. I can. I promise. Um, Betsy. You've had a rough—I mean, maybe you should, uh, go lie down."

"I agree," Sinclair said, too quickly. "Elizabeth, let us handle this for you."

I wanted to leave. God help me, I wanted to run away from this house and never, ever come back.

But I'd settle for fleeing to my bedroom and dropping the mess in my husband's lap. And the cop who hated me.

"It was all just so—so stupid," I said. *And preventable*, my conscience whispered. *If only you'd been paying attention to business . . .*

I trudged up the stairs. Nobody went with me, which suited me fine.

Chapter 47

Sinclair came upstairs hours later and cuddled me into his side. I sighed, and he stroked my shoulder and then kissed that same shoulder. I closed my eyes and breathed in his scent . . . warm, clean cotton. And dried blood, of course. Mustn't forget that. Not ever.

"She died well."

"I don't give a fuck. I want her back. I want her *here*."

"As do I, Elizabeth. But I will honor her memory forever, for the sacrifice she made. It might have been your brains all over the foyer."

"Well, what if it was? Why should I be alive and Antonia be so much cooling meat?"

"I do not know, dear one. But I am fervently glad it worked out the way it did, for all I was fond of Antonia."

I mulled that one over for a minute or two while Sinclair sat up, slipped off my shoes, and rubbed my feet. I wiggled my toes against his palms and almost smiled. Then felt bad for thinking it'd be okay to smile, even for a second.

"I just don't get it," I said at last.

"Get it?"

"When stuff this awful happens, you're supposed to learn something. Look Both Ways Before You Cross The Street. Be Kind To Children And Small Animals. Something. Jeez, anything. But there was all this death, all this waste, and for what?"

Sinclair was quiet for so long I assumed I'd stumped him, a rare and wonderful thing. But he was just trying to figure out how to break it to me. Should have known.

"It is that to be queen," he said at last. "There will be times when you will see an ocean of blood and despair. So it says in the Book of the Dead, and so it shall be, dear wife."

"You suck at cheering me up. You're not telling me there's gonna be worse days than *this*?" To say I was appalled would be putting it mildly. "What else did that rotten Book of the Dead tell you?"

He paused for a long time. Then: "Elizabeth, I can promise nothing, save that I will always be by your side."

I noticed he didn't answer the question. "Oceans of blood," I said.

"Possibly. Yes."

"We'll just see about that."

"Elizabeth, if you'll forgive a pun, do not bite off more than you can chew."

"That's been the story of my life since I woke up in that funeral home wearing the Ant's shoes. Oceans of blood? Shit on that. Shit all *over* that."

I had no idea what I was going to do, or how. But I was going to work *real* hard to make sure my friends and I never had to go through a week like this again.

This was going to sound dumb, but the empty crib in the next room was practically calling my name. I had to stop fobbing my brother on other people.

I wondered if the Ant ever visited him.

Chapter 48

It was a day later; Garrett had been respectfully buried. Sinclair owned several farms and lots of land; what with Alice's remains, among others, we were starting quite the little private cemetery out on Route 19. It was awful and interesting at the same time.

The police chief's body had been found in his home, dead from an apparent suicide. Many cops went on record saying he had been deeply depressed about retiring but had rejected counseling.

Deeply depressed. Yeah. They didn't know the half of it.

"I have to tell Antonia's pack leader what happened. They deserve to know what happened to her, how she died. How she—how wonderful she was. I got the impression her pack never appreciated her, didn't you guys?"

They all nodded. Sure, we knew. Her ability to tell the future (and not turn into a wolf) had given all the other werewolves the creeps. They had been happy to see her go. And when I had "fixed" her, the fact that she hadn't rushed back home meant so much to me. She chose to stick it out with me.

I'd never get the chance to thank her. As far as a recall, I don't think I ever thanked her for anything.

My chest hitched once . . . twice . . . then settled. No, I was done crying for a while.

"Anyway, I want them all to know how she saved me. Hopefully they can guide us in how to treat . . . what's left of her."

Poor Antonia was in our basement freezer until I learned more about werewolf rituals for their dead. I wasn't looking forward to telling the boss werewolf that I'd gotten his pack member killed

(Michael Wyndham had a wicked temper and a terrifying left cross), but it was something that had to be done.

Jessica didn't say anything, just poured herself another cup of tea. I'd told her my plan the night before in a lame attempt to distract her from breaking up with Nick. I felt tremendously guilty that she'd picked me over him. Of course, I would have felt a lot worse if she'd gone the other way.

Maybe someday they could patch things up. I'd see if I could do something about that. He'd been hurt and scared and said things he didn't mean. I had tried to explain it to Jessica last night, but had no idea if she really heard me. Maybe . . . in time . . .

But maybe it was for the best if they *never* got back together. It would sure cut down on the vampire attacks he had to endure . . . the price of admission when you hung out with the people in Monster Mansion. And I truly didn't know how much more Nick could endure. He seemed like a rubber band, stretched almost—but not quite—to the breaking point.

I shook my head, then noticed Marc was shaking his head. "I spend one Goddamn week in a hotel and then *this*." He was feeling as guilty as I was; he was convinced he could have done something for Antonia if he'd been here.

"Mathematically," Tina began gently, "given the age and abilities of our opponents, we got off rather lightly. And Garrett made his own choice. I—"

"That's enough," I said coldly, and Tina shut up.

"When?" my husband asked, mildly enough. "I'll need to clear my schedule."

"Tomorrow."

"As you wish."

"I'll come with, if you like," Laura offered. She'd been agog all evening, listening to our tale of the awful events of the night earlier. "It's not trouble at all."

I was glad she had missed it (yay, church youth group!), to be honest. No telling what the body count would have been if she'd lost her temper. Or where the chief's bullets might have gone if he'd known who had really killed dear old dad. Just the thought of it gave me the willies.

In fact, it was safe to say that her temper was hanging over my head like a friggin' broadsword. Someday I was going to have to really sit down and figure out just what the deal was with the devil's daughter.

But not today. Not even this month. I was just so fucking tired.

"I'd be glad to come," my sister was continuing, eager to help. "I've got a Toys for Tots meeting, but it's no problem to postpone—"

"No, I need you to stay here and hold down the fort. And Tina—Richard, Stephanie, and Jane need looking after. Move them here while we're out of town, if that helps. Or *you* can move out to the McMansion until we get back. It's just temporary, until we can figure out something more permanent."

Tina nodded and jotted a note to herself on the notepad she always kept nearby. "As you wish, Majesty."

"I'll keep BabyJon for you," Laura volunteered.

I smiled at my sister and shook my head, then turned to my husband. "Actually, I'd like to bring him to the Cape with us, if you don't mind. I've been spending too much time fobbing him off on other people, which is no good. I'm the only mother he's got now."

Sinclair tried to hide the wince (not a baby guy, my husband), but nodded. "As you like, Elizabeth. I do agree, we should probably get used to the idea of being"—he didn't quite gag on the word—"*parents*."

"A fine thing, my son being brought up by vampires," the Ant said.

"I suppose you're coming, too."

"Of course," my dead stepmother said, amused.

"That reminds me," I told my puzzled friends. "I figured it out. Why the Ant's here."

"To find a cure for bad dye jobs?" Jessica joked.

"Not hardly. See, she lived for making me miserable, she got off on setting my dad against his only kid, she loved irritating me in a thousand small ways."

"You make it sound as if that was my only purpose in life," the Ant sniffed.

"It was."

"What was?" Jessica asked.

I kept forgetting no one could hear her or see her but me. Lucky, lucky me. "Never mind. Point is, she's not done yet," I finished. "Not near done. So she's not going anywhere. She can't."

"Believe me, I've tried," she said sourly.

"So we're stuck with her indefinitely."

"That's right!" the Ant said triumphantly. "No more Mrs. Nice Guy!"

Exactly. Things were going to be very, very different from now on.

But the Ant didn't know me. Not the new me, the me that forced Fiends to their knees and broke necks and cured cancer. She was going to have her hands full.

For that matter, *anyone* who got in my way, who hurt my friends, who tried to stop me from making the world better, was going to have their hands full.

They didn't know this queen. Not like I did.

Epilogue

Y ou again."

"Me again," I agreed, plonking the six-pack of Budweiser into my grandpa's lap. He let out a yelp and gave me a look like he'd like to burn me alive. I'm sure if he'd had a can of gasoline and a box of matches, he would have tried.

He slipped a can free, popped the top, took a greedy swig, then let out a satisfied belch. "Ahhhh. You're not entirely useless."

"Aw, Grandpa. That gets me right here."

He grunted and almost smiled—almost. "Where's the new guy? The Injun you married?"

"It's Native American, you old jerk."

"Oh, fuck me and spare me that PC crap."

I could see we weren't going to get anywhere unless I worked around to my topic of conversation a lot faster.

"To answer, he's looking after his business and junk like that." Truth was, I had no interest in involving myself in Sinclair's business affairs. One, it would have bored me near to death. Two, he'd been making himself rich for decades. He sure didn't need any help from me.

I settled myself into the chair across from the bed. He was in his wheelchair (the one he didn't need) by the window. It had been full dark for half an hour.

"So what's on your brain, Betsy?"

"I distinctly remember you telling me on several occasions that I didn't have one," I teased gently.

"Yeah, well, you never come over without a purpose. Introducing the new guy. Telling me about that twat and your dad when they died. So what do you want? There's a *Sandford and Son* marathon starting in twenty minutes."

"How d'you do it?"

"Do *what?*" he said impatiently, then slurped up more beer.

"Kill people. And then not worry about it." I was speaking with a world war veteran, a man awarded the Bronze Star. Fourth highest award in the armed forces. It was hanging on the wall above my head.

His platoon had run into some bad luck, had been in the wrong place at the wrong time . . . a not unusual occurrence in wartime, I was sure. Grandpa had grabbed his Lee Enfield sniper rifle, found scant cover, and picked off Germans one by one while his buddies were scrambling to get away. As sergeant, he had *ordered* them to get away.

He took four bullets: two in his left arm, one just above his right knee, and one had clipped off his left earlobe. Two of his men had dragged him away, as he protested bitterly that he was just fine, *fine, Goddammit, let go, you jackasses, I've got work to do!*

I had work to do, too.

Meanwhile, my grandpa had finished the beer (barf . . . words could not describe how much I hated the taste of beer) and was holding an unopened can in his left hand. "Kill people? Izzat what you said? And then not worry about it?"

"Yeah."

"What happened, idiot?"

I shook my head. "It's a really long story, and I come off pretty bad in it."

Grandpa shrugged, instantly losing interest in what brought me here, what had happened to make me ask that question. As Margaret Mitchell wrote about Scarlett O'Hara, he could not long endure any conversation that wasn't about him.

"It was wartime," he said at last. "They were the bad guys. It wasn't like it is now. Things were a little more black and white back then. They were killing every Jew they could find. I think those little black beanie things the men wear are pretty stupid, but it's no reason to pick 'em off like Goddamned mosquitoes."

I had to admit, I was surprised. Among other things, my darling maternal grandfather was a major bigot. I found it distinctly interesting that he'd fought because he saw a minority in trouble.

He was staring out the window now, and I had the very strong impression that if I spoke to him before he'd gotten all of it out, he'd clam up and take it to the grave.

The secret.

"Yup, they were doing terrible things," he mused. "And we were fools to wait until after Pearl Harbor to kick some ass. But once we were there, we were *there*. We did the work, and we didn't bitch about our feelings the whole time, either. God, I hate that 'tell me how that makes you feel' touchy-feely bullshit."

I nodded. I knew that, too.

"And when my guys got in a tight spot—why, I looked out for 'em just like they'd been looking out for me. I just kept that in my mind. Keeping my guys alive and sending as many of the bad guys to Hell that I could. That's all I thought about."

He looked straight at me, his eyes—my eyes—green and gleaming. "And then I never thought about it again. What for? Dead's dead, honey. You don't know that by now, I wash my hands of you."

"Thanks for the tolerance and acceptance," I said dryly. Thinking, *there's a trick or two I could tell you about death, Grandpa. Things you never, ever dreamed of. Things that would turn your hair white, if it wasn't already.*

But of course I wouldn't.

"What it comes down to is this, Betsy: you do what you need to, and then you haul ass out of there. Every single time."

"And never think of it again."

He nodded and popped the second Bud. "I didn't say it was an easy road. Shit, I lost plenty of my own fellas over there. I still miss Leary, that Irish fuck. But he died for a reason—a good one. Maybe the best one—kicking ass to keep the bullies out of the sandbox." He was looking at me almost sideways, a sly look. "So whether you killed somebody or someone got killed 'cause a you—oh, I can see it all over your face, girl, aren't you my own flesh and blood? Just . . . never think of it again. Life's messy, honey."

So's death, I thought, and turned the conversation to other things.

Dead and Loving It

Acknowledgments

Thanks to my husband, who amuses the kids when I'm on deadline and thinks it's swell when I ignore the family for days to finish a story. (Hmm. That could be more a reflection on me than him, but never mind.)

Thanks also to my editor, Cindy, who asked me, when I was trying to figure out what to write for this collection, "How is George doing?"

Asked and answered, bay-bee!

Santa Claws

Chapter 1

Alec Kilcurt, laird of Kilcurt Holding and the most powerful werewolf in Europe, stomped through the snow and slush and wished he were anywhere, anywhere but here.

He stopped and stood obediently with the rest of the herd, waiting for the light to change. Snow was spitting down on him with malice he could almost feel. It did nothing for his mood. He disliked leaving his home for any reason, but being called to America to pay homage to The Wonderful Child was a bit much.

And now he was shamed; his duty had never seemed a chore before. He admired and respected the pack leaders, Michael and Jeannie Wyndham. Michael was a good man and a fine leader; his wife was a crack shot cutie; and their baby, Lara, was adorable. Because the cooing, drooling infant was likely to be his next pack leader, Alec's presence—the presence of every country's werewolf head—had been required for both political and practical reasons. The pack was some three hundred thousand werewolves strong; unity was both a desire and a necessity.

Unfortunately, visiting the Wyndhams in their happy home just exacerbated his own loneliness. He'd been searching for a mate for years, but had . . . how did the humans put it? Never found the right girl. He thought it was funny that human women complained their men didn't commit. An unattached werewolf male was likely to want to move in after the first date. What was a man, after all, without a mate, without cubs?

Nothing, that's what. Meeting baby Lara, aka The Wonderful Child, was a great relief; pack leaders without heirs made everyone nervous. Seeing Michael's happiness, on the other hand, was a torture.

Now his duty was done, and thank God. His plane left Boston tonight, and nothing was keeping him from it.

Faugh! More snow! And not likely to be much better, even when he got home. Really, there was nothing to look forward to until spring. Others of his kind might enjoy romping through the slush on all fours, but here was one furry laird who hated getting his feet wet.

And Boston! Gray, drizzly, dreary Boston, which smelled like damp wool and exhaust. He felt like pulling his scarf over his nose to muffle the smells of

(peaches, ripe peaches)

unwashed masses and

(peaches)

He stopped suddenly and felt a one-two punch as the couple walking behind him slammed into his back. He barely felt it; he hardly heard their complaints. He spun, pushed past them, and walked back, nostrils flaring, trying to catch that elusive

jangleJANGLEjangleJANGLEjangle

intoxicating

jangleJANGLEjangleJANGLEjangle

utterly wonderful scent.

He stiffened, not unlike a dog on point. There. The street corner. Red suit trimmed with white. White-gloved hand shaking that annoying bell. Belly shaking like a bowlful of jelly. The glorious smell was coming from Santa Claus.

jangleJANGLEjangleJANGLEjangle

He charged across the street without looking, ignoring the blaring horns, the shriek of airbrakes. The closer he got, the better Santa smelled.

jangleJANGLEjan—

"Jeez, there's no rush," Santa said in a startled contralto, pulling down her beard to squint up at him. Her eyes were the color of Godiva milk chocolate. Her cheeks were blooded, kissed by the wind. Her nose was snub. Adorable. He felt like kissing it. "I mean, the bucket and I aren't going anywhere."

"Nuh," he said, or something like it.

"You really should forget that whole 'pedestrians have the right of way' attitude when you're in this town . . . errr . . . everything okay?"

He had been looming over her, drinking her in. Now he jerked back. "Fine. Everything's fine. Have dinner with me."

"It's ten o'clock in the morning." She blinked up at him. A stray snowflake spiraled down, landed on her nose, and melted.

"Then lunch."

The woman looked down at herself, as if making sure that, yes, she was dressed in the least-flattering outfit a woman could wear. "Are you feeling okay?" she asked at last.

"Never better." It was the truth. This was rapidly turning into the best day ever. He had visions of spending the rest of the day rolling around on Egyptian cotton sheets with Santa. "Lunch."

She peered at him with adorable suspicion. "Is that a question? Is this your first day out of the institution?"

Right, right, she was human. Be polite. "Lunch. Please. Now."

She burst out laughing, putting a hand on her large belly to keep from falling into the street. As if he'd let that happen. "I'm sorry," she gasped, "but the absurdity of this . . . you . . . and . . . it just hit me all at once." She cut her gaze away from his to smile at the woman who had just tucked a dollar into her bucket. "Merry Christmas, ma'am, and thank you."

Now that he was no longer gazing into her eyes, he felt much colder and realized his feet were wet. *Faugh!*

"I can't have lunch now," she said kindly, looking back at him. "I can't leave my spot until noon."

"Not even if you made lots of money before then?"

"Not even if the *real* Santa came along to relieve me."

"Noon, then."

"Well. All right." She smiled up at him with timid liking. "You'll be sorry. Wait until you see me out of this Santa outfit." The spasm of lust nearly toppled him into the gutter. "I'm not at all cute," she finished with charming idiocy.

"Noon," he said again and then pulled his roll from his coat pocket. He plucked the money clip off the wad and dropped the eight thousand dollars or so into her bucket. "I'll be back."

"If that was Monopoly money," she hollered after him, "lunch is *off*!"

Chapter 2

Giselle Smith watched the visitor from Planet Hunk stride away. When he'd rushed up to her, she had nearly dropped her bell. There she was, jangling for charity, and then Hunk Man was *right there*. She couldn't believe the speed at which he'd moved.

His hair was a deep, true auburn. His eyes were a funny kind of brown, so light they were nearly gold. His nose was a blade, and his mouth—oooh, his mouth! A girl could stare at it and think . . . oh, all sorts of things. He was tall, too; she had to crane her neck to look at him. Over six feet, for sure. Shoulders like a swimmer. Knee-length black wool coat, probably worth a grand at least. Black gloves covering big hands; the guy looked like he could palm a basketball, no problem.

He had come charging across the street to, of all things, ask her to lunch. And to give her thousands—thousands!—of dollars.

Her, Giselle Smith. Boring brown hair, dirt-colored eyes. Too short and definitely too heavy. The most interesting thing about her was her name—which people always got wrong anyway.

Obviously a serial killer, she thought sadly. *Well, we'll have lunch in a public place where I can scream my head off if he starts sharpening his knives.*

It was too bad. He was really something. What the hell could a guy like that want from a nobody like her?

+ + +

Alec watched the woman (he was still angry at himself for not getting her name . . . or giving his, for that matter) from halfway down the block. His spot was excellent: he could see her perfectly and, better, he was downwind.

He thought about their conversation and cursed himself again. He'd babbled like a moron, ordered her to lunch, stared at her like she was Little Red Riding Hood. Yes, like Little Red . . . *hmmmmm.*

He wrenched his mind from that delectable mental image

(the better to eat you with, my dear . . . eat you all . . . up!)

and concentrated on thinking about what an idiot he had been. It was a miracle the woman had said yes. It was a miracle she hadn't hit him over the head with her bell. He had to be very careful at lunch; it was imperative she not spook. He thanked God he was weeks away from his Change; if he'd caught her scent any closer to the full moon, he'd have scared the pants off her. Literally.

God, she was so *adorable.* Look at her, shaking her little bell for all she was worth. Many people stopped (pulled in, no doubt, by her allure) and threw money in her bucket. As they should! They should give her gold bullion, they should lay roses at her feet, they—

He pushed away from the wall, appalled; someone hadn't put money in! An expensively dressed man in his late thirties had used the bucket to make change and went on his merry way.

Alec got moving. In no time, he had closed the distance and flanked the man, snaked out a hand, and pulled him into a handy alley.

"Wha-aaaggh!"

"This is cashmere," Alec said, his hand fisting in the man's coat.

"Let go of me," the man squeaked, reeking of stale piss—the smell of fear. "Or I'll yell rape!"

"Your shoes," Alec continued, undaunted, "are from Gerbard in London and didna cost you less than eight hundred pounds." Only Samuel Gerbard used that kind of supple leather when making his footwear; the smell was distinctive. "And that's a Coach briefcase."

"Gggglllkkkk!"

Perhaps he was holding the man a little too firmly. Alec released his grip. "The point is, you c'n stand to share a little this holiday season."

"Wha?"

"Go back," he growled, "and put money. In. The bucket."

He let go. The man fled. In the right direction—toward his Santa sweetie.

A minute later, Alec was back at his post. He checked his watch for the thirtieth time in the last half hour. Ninety minutes to go. An eternity.

An eternity later, at 11:57, he realized the skulking teenagers were ready to make their move. The three of them had been casing the block for the last fifteen minutes, had been watching his lunch date much too closely. It was the bucket, of course; they wanted lunch money . . . or the eight grand he'd dropped in. It would be laughable, except one of them smelled like gun oil, which meant Alec had to take some care.

Their path took them right past him; he reached out and slammed the one with the gun into the side of the building. The boy—a child in his late teens—flopped bonelessly to the sidewalk.

His friends were a little slow to catch on, but they finally turned when they nearly tripped over their unconscious leader. And then they saw Alec, standing over the unconscious punk, smiling. Well, showing them all his teeth, anyway. "Take somebody else's bucket," he said. Oh, wait, that was the wrong message entirely. "Don't take anybody's bucket," he called after them, but it was too late. They were running away.

He looked at his watch again. It was noon!

Chapter 3

It's Giselle," she said to Hunka Hunka Burnin' Love. "Giselle Smith. And you're . . . ?"

"Alec Kilcurt. You have a lovely name."

"Yeah, thanks. About that. The never-ending compliments. What is your deal? Now that I'm out of costume, you can see I'm nothing special."

He laughed at her.

She frowned but continued. "Too short, too heavy—"

He laughed harder.

"—but you keep complimenting me, and I'm waiting for the other shoe to drop. You're a census-taker, right? A salesman? You want to sell me a fridge. A timeshare. A kidney. Stop laughing!"

He finally sobered up, although the occasional snort escaped. He snapped his fingers, and the glorious redhead at the next table, who'd been studying him while pretending to powder her nose, gave him her full attention. Her eyelashes fluttered. She licked her red, glistening lips.

Alec held out his hand, and after a puzzled moment, the redhead placed her compact in his palm.

"Obliged," he said carelessly. Then he snapped it open and showed it to Giselle. "This is what my people call a mirror," he said in his ultra-cool Scottish brogue. "Y' should spend more time looking in one."

"I know what a mirror is, you goob," she snapped. "Too damn well. Stop shaking that thing at me, or you won't get anything nice for Christmas." She nudged the bag at her foot that held her Santa costume. "I've got friends in high places."

"Are you getting angry with me?" he asked, delighted. He handed the compact back to the redhead with barely a glance.

"Yes, a little. You don't have to look so happy about it."

"Sorry. It's just . . . I'm a lot bigger than you are."

"And almost as smart," she said brightly.

"Most women find me a little intimidating." He smiled at her. Giselle felt her stomach tighten and then roll over lazily. God, what a grin. "In my . . . family . . . we treasure women who speak their minds."

"Then you've won the lottery today, pal. And you never answered my question. What are you up to?"

He reached out, and his big hand closed over her small, cold one. His thumb burrowed into her palm and stroked it. Her stomach did another slow roll, one she felt distinctly lower. "Why, I'm seducing you, of course," he murmured.

Multiple internal alarms went off. "Who *are* you?" she said, almost gasped.

"No one special. Just a lord looking for his lady."

"Oh, you've got a title, too? Well, of course you do. That's the way this day is going."

"It's Laird Kilcurt."

"But your name is Kilcurt. Isn't your title supposed to be completely different? Like Alec Kilcurt, laird of Toll House? Or something?"

He laughed. "Something. But my family does things a little differently. Too bad . . . I like the idea of being laird of chocolate chips."

The waiter came, refreshed their drinks, and put down the two dozen oysters she'd ordered. She pulled her hand away, not without major reluctance. She figured this was her first and last date with the man, so she'd ordered recklessly. He'd probably flip out when the bill came. He probably spent all his money on clothes and, given his trim waistline, only ate porridge once a day.

Wrong again. He nodded approvingly at the ridiculous size of her appetizer. He was leaning back in his chair, studying her. He had, if it was possible, gotten even better looking since morning. The expensive coat was off, revealing a splendid build showcased to perfection in a dark gray suit. His brogue, she noticed, came and went, depending on the topic of conversation.

"You haven't lived in Scotland your entire life," she observed, sucking down her second daiquiri. Normally not a big drinker, she felt the need for booze today.

"No. My family often had business on Cape Cod, so I spent a lot of time in Massachusetts. And I went to Harvard for graduate school. I've probably lived in America as many years as I've lived in Scotland."

Titled, gorgeous, rich, smart. Was she on *Candid Camera*, or what? "That makes sense . . . I noticed your accent comes and goes. I mean, sometimes it's really faint, and sometimes it's pretty heavy."

"It's heavy," he replied, "when I'm tired. Or angry. Or . . . excited."

"Okay, that's *it*," she said, slamming down her glass. "Who *are* you? What do you want with me? I made eighteen thousand dollars last year. I'm poor, plain, cursed with childbearing hips— and ass—and I'm prospect-less. What the hell are you doing with me?"

His eyes went narrow. "I'll have to find the people who convinced you of such things. And have a long chat with them."

"Answer the question, Groundskeeper Willie, or I'm out of here."

He looked puzzled at her pop culture reference, but he shrugged and answered easily enough. "I'm planning to spend the day getting you into my bed. And I'm thinking about marrying you. *That's* what I'm doing with you, my charming little chocolate treat."

She felt her mouth pop open and felt her face get red. If this was a joke, it was a pretty mean one. If he was serious, he was out of his fucking mind. She seized on the one thing she could safely question. "Chocolate treat?"

"Your eyes are the color of really good chocolate . . . Godiva milk, I think. And your hair looks like fudge sauce. Rich and dark. It contrasts nicely with your pale, pale skin. Your rosy cheeks are the . . . cherry on top."

She downed the rest of her drink in two monster gulps.

Chapter 4

I'm sorry," she groaned. Sweaty strands of hair clung limply to her face and temples.

"It's all right lass."

"I'm so sorry."

"Don't fret. I've been puked on before."

She groaned again, this time in complete humiliation. She hadn't thrown up near him. Hadn't thrown up around him. Had actually barfed *on* him. On *him*!

"You promised to kill me," she reminded him hoarsely. The elevator doors slid open, and he scooped her easily into his arms and carried her down the hallway. "Don't forget."

His chest rumbled as he choked down a laugh. "Now, I didna promise to kill you, sweetheart. Just to take you up to my room so you c'n get your strength back."

"I'll be all right once I get off my feet," she lied. Death was coming for her! She could feel its icy grip on the back of her neck. Or was that the ice from her third—fourth?—daiquiri? "Just need to get off my feet," she said again.

"Sweetie, you're off them."

"Oh shut up. What do you know?" she said crossly, getting more and more dizzy as the ceiling tiles raced by. "And slow down. And kill me!"

"Usually ladies wait until the second date before begging me for death," he said, straight-faced. He paused outside a door, shifted his weight, and somehow managed to produce the card key, unlock the door, and sweep her inside without putting her down.

Two hotel maids and a woman in a red business suit were

waiting for them. Giselle had a vague memory of the woman in red examining her while the sound of running water went on and on in the next room. She kept fuzzing . . . that was the only way to describe it. One moment things would be crystal clear—too sharp, too loud—and the next she could barely hear them for their mumbling. It was annoying, and she told them so. Repeatedly.

"—lukewarm bath will make all the difference—"

"—just got so sick, it's verra worrisome—"

"—mild food poisoning—"

"—she'll be okay in no—"

"—close to your Change for it to be a problem?"

"—canceled my flight earlier so she can—"

"—push fluids—"

She reached up blindly. What's-his-name

(Alec? Alex?)

caught her hand and held it tightly. "What is it, sweetie? D'you want something to drink?"

"No, I want you to STOP YELLING! How can I quietly expire if you keep screaming?"

"We'll try t'keep it down."

"An' don't humor me, either," she mumbled. "Oh, now, what's this happy crappy?" Because now she was being undressed and helped off the bed. "Look, stop this! Isn't there an ice bucket or a hammer or something in here? All you have to do is hit me in the head *really hard,* and my problems will be over."

"You'll feel better in twenty-four hours!" the woman in red screamed.

"Jesus, do I have to get out the hand puppets so you people understand? Not so loud! And I'll be dead—*dead*—in twenty-four hours, thank you very much, and—where are we going?"

The bathroom. Specifically, the bathtub. She started to protest that a change of temperature in her state would kill her, but the lukewarm water felt so blissful she stopped in mid-squawk.

And that was all. For a very long time.

+ + +

Giselle woke up and knew two things at once: 1) she would burst if she didn't get to a bathroom within seconds and 2) she was ravenous.

She stumbled through the darkness into the bathroom, availed herself of the facilities for what felt like half a day, and brushed her teeth with the new toothbrush she found on the counter.

While she swished and gargled and spat, the day's humiliating events came back to her. Working the bell, meeting Alec, being wined and dined—and God, he'd been *flirting* with her!—then throwing up on him *(groan)* and the table tipping away from her.

Everything after that was, as they say, a blur. Mercifully so. She wondered where Alec was. She wondered where *she* was.

She stepped back into the hotel room—Alec's hotel room—and stole to the window. She saw an astonishing view of the New England Aquarium and, beyond that, Boston harbor. It was very late—after midnight but well before dawn; the sky was utterly black, but there was little traffic moving.

So she was on the wharf, then. Probably the Longwharf Marriott. She'd often wondered, walking by, what it would be like to stay there with someone glorious.

Well, now she knew.

She turned to look for the light and saw Alec for the first time. He was sitting in the chair by the door, watching her. His eyes gleamed at her from the near dark.

She screamed and would have fallen out the window if it had been open. As it was, she rapped her head a good one on the glass.

"Yes, a typical date in nearly every respect," he said by way of greeting.

"And a good evening to you, too, dammit!"

"Morning, actually."

"You scared the *crap* out of me." When she'd first seen him—it was a trick of the light, obviously—but his eyes had . . . well, had seemed to gleam in the dark, the way a cat's did at night. Very off-putting, to say the least. "Your eyes—Jesus!"

"The better to see you with, my dear. And it's Alec."

"Very funny." She leaned against the radiator, panting from the adrenaline rush. "Never do that again."

"Sorry." He swallowed a chuckle. "I was watching you sleep. When you got up and made such a determined beeline to the bathroom, I was afraid to do anything that might slow you down. Were you sick again, sweetie?"

"Uh, no. And about this afternoon—"

"When you—er—gifted me with your daiquiris and oysters and swordfish and hash browns and *tarte tatin?*"

"Let's never speak of it again," she said determinedly.

He laughed, delighted; stood in such an abrupt movement if she'd blinked she'd have missed it; and crossed the room. In another moment, he was holding her hands. "I'm so glad t'see you're better," he said with such obvious sincerity she smiled—for the first time in hours, it seemed. "I was worried." Except in his charming brogue, it came out *sae glad tae see yerrr betterrrrrr. Ai wooz worried.*

"I'm pretty damned glad to be feeling better myself. God, I've never been so sick! I guess I'd be a terrible alcoholic," she confessed.

"It wasna the alcohol. The doctor said it was food poisoning. I'fact, this hotel is full . . . quite a few guests of the restaurant suffered from the oysters and are resting up because of it."

She thought she ought to pull her hands out of his grip, but she couldn't bring herself to take the step. His hands around hers were warm—almost hot—and looking up into his unbelievable face was just too good right now. "What doctor? Was she the lady in the red dress? I remember someone in red who wouldn't stop with the shrieking . . ."

Alec's lips quirked in a smile. "Dr. Madison is a verra soft-spoken woman, actually. You were just sensitive to noise while you were sick. I called her when you—uh—"

"Remember. We're not speaking of it."

"—became indisposed," he finished delicately, but he wouldn't quit smiling. "She helped me take care of you."

"Oh." Touched, she squeezed his hands. "Thanks, Alec. I guess I was a lucky girl to be out with you."

"Lucky?" The smile dropped away. "It was my fault you got sick, so the least I could—"

"Your fault? Held me down and shoveled in the oysters, did you?" she said dryly. "Hardly. In case you haven't noticed the inordinate size of my ass, I'm a girl with a healthy appetite. I got so incredibly sick because I ate so incredibly much."

He squeezed her fingers in response. She had a sudden sense of crushing power held in check. "I adore your ass." *Ai adorrrre yuir arse.* Was she crazy, or was his brogue getting thicker by the second? What had he said? That it came out when he was angry or . . .

Or . . .

She snatched her hands out of his grip. "Paws off, monkey boy. Time for me to get the hell out of here."

"I'd prefer it if you didn't call me that," he said, mildly enough. "It's quite an insult where I come from."

"They've got a real mad-on against monkeys in Scotland, eh? Whatever. Gotta go now, it's been fun, buh-bye."

"Can't go." He folded his arms across his chest and smirked at her. "Your clothes were quite ruined in the incident-that-shall-ne'er-be-named."

For the first time, she realized she was wearing a flannel nightgown. It had a demure lace collar that scratched her chin, and the hem fell about three inches past her toes. *How could she not have noticed this before?* She'd just used the bathroom, for God's sake. Sure, she'd had to pee so bad nothing else had registered, but . . . she made a quick grab and found she *was* wearing her old panties beneath the gown. Whew!

His eyebrows arched while she groped herself, but he wisely said nothing. "The doctor said you needed rest and quiet until you—er—purged your—"

"Oh, Christ."

"Anyway." He turned brisk. "I had the staff send up something for you to sleep in."

Any thoughts he was embarked on sinister seduction fled as she fingered the gray flannel. She felt like an extra on *Little House on the Prairie.* "Thanks." She smiled in spite of herself. "Flannel?"

He shrugged. "It's cold where I come from. I wanted you to be comfortable."

"And I am," she assured him with a straight face. "But I would be more comfortable if I got the hell out of a stranger's hotel room."

"Stranger?" He grinned at her, all devil and mischief. "After all we've been through today? Shame!"

She laughed; she couldn't help it. Quick as thought, his hand came up and caught one of her curls. He pulled it and watched it spring back. Uck. "Sorry."

"Don't, now."

"No, really . . . I know, I look like Bozo the Clown on mescaline. If Bozo didn't have red hair. And was really short. And was a woman. You should see it in the summer . . . giant fuzzball! Hide your children!"

He was eyeballing her hair. "I'd like to see it in the summer."

"Okey-dokey," she said, humoring him, "and *I* would love to see my uniform. I can wear my Santa suit on the subway home."

"At two o'clock in the morning? Alone?" He sounded mortally offended. "I think not. Besides—" His voice became sly. "Aren't you hungry?"

Hungry! Oh, God, no one in the history of Santa bellin' for

bucks had ever been this hungry. She actually swayed on her feet at the thought of eating.

"That's my girl. Let's call room service. Anything you want."

"I'll have to get my wallet—"

He frowned forbiddingly. "Do not get your wallet."

"Fine. We'll fight about it later. Where's the menu? God, I could eat a *cow*."

"I know the feeling."

She ordered a steak *au jus,* rare, with mashed potatoes and gravy, broccoli, and half a loaf of wild rice bread. "This is going to be really expensive," she warned him. "Are you sure I can't . . . ?"

"Quite sure. It's such a relief to be with a woman who eats." He sat beside her on the bed and sighed. "I'll never understand the American custom of starvation. You're the richest country in the world, and the women don't eat."

"Hey, not guilty. As you can see by the size of my ass."

"Tempting. Let's see how well you do with your dinner first."

She glanced uncertainly at him and caught his low-lidded look. It seemed incredible, but the man was actually turned on at the thought of her nontoned ass. His words hadn't been enough to convince her, but his thickening brogue was telling.

It was all very strange. Not to mention marvelous. And oh-so-slightly alarming.

Chapter 5

She did very well. Polished it all off and then ordered ice cream. He watched in pure delight. And thanked God again he was nowhere near his Change.

Keeping his hands—and mouth!—to himself was beginning to be a sore task. It hadn't been a problem when she'd been so miserably ill, but she was obviously feeling better . . . he could hardly talk to her; his tongue felt thick in his mouth. She was just so—just so adorable—alive and sexy and fragrant. When he'd tugged on one of her glossy curls, it had taken nearly everything he had to keep from plunging both hands in her hair and taking her mouth.

He'd been wild with worry for her and hadn't left her side for a moment since she threw up her lunch on his shoes. He was going to see that chef's head on a pike—or his name on a termination slip—before the sun set again.

"That's better," she sighed, patting her mouth with a napkin. It was a lovely mouth; wide-lipped and generous. When she smiled, her upper lip formed a sorceress's bow. He had to concentrate very hard on *not* sucking that lip into his mouth. "Now about my imminent departure. Not that you haven't been a perfect gentleman. Because you have. Yes, indeedy! But, bottom line, I haven't known you for twenty hours." She stood and began pacing. "So I'm definitely not sleeping in your hotel room. Anymore, I mean."

"S'dona sleep," he teased, catching her hand and pulling her toward him. Her dark gaze caught him, held him. A line appeared between her eyebrows as she frowned. He kissed the line.

"Now listen here, Grabby McGee . . . ah!"

He kissed the sweet slope of her neck and was lost. He might not have been, had she not instinctively leaned into the caress of his mouth. He reached up, found the soft splendor of her hair, and caught her mouth with his. She smelled like surprise and vanilla-bean ice cream.

"Oh, God," she said, almost groaned, into his mouth. "You're like a dream. The best dream I ever had."

"I was thinking the same thing."

"What? I'm sorry, your accent—" She giggled and kissed his chin. "It's so thick I can barely understand you. Which, by the way, I'll take as a compliment to my own massive sexiness."

"Y'should. Stay with me."

"I can't." She was wriggling—regretfully, but still wriggling—out of his grasp. Trying, anyway. He had no trouble whatsoever keeping her in the circle of his arms. "I'm sorry. I'd love to. I can't. Leggo."

"But you must." He found her breast—not easy, given its encasement in sensible gray flannel—and cupped it in his palm. The firm, warm weight made his head swim. "You're for me and I'm for you, lovely Giselle. Besides, I'm not going to let you leave."

"*What?*"

"Besides, what if you heave?"

"Oh. I thought—look, I feel fine. I don't think I'll be sick again."

"But what if y'are? I promised Dr. Madison I'd look after you for the next twenty-four hours. It's only been about six."

"But I feel fine."

"But I promised."

"Well . . . if you promised . . . and if it's doctor's orders . . ." She was weakening. She wanted to be persuaded. So he'd persuade her, by God.

Chapter 6

One minute they were having a (reasonably) civilized conversation, and the next his hands were everywhere. Her nightclothes were tugged, pulled, and finally torn off her. His weight bore her back on the bed.

"Alec!" Surprise made her voice squeakier than usual. "For crying out loud, I feel like I'm caught in an exercise machine—yeek!" "Yeek" because his head was suddenly, shockingly between her breasts, his long fingers were circling one of her nipples and then tugging impatiently on the bud. Heat shot through her like a comet. And speaking of comets, what the hell was *that* pressing against her leg?

"I don't think this is what the doctor had in mind—" she began again.

"Giselle, my own, my sweet, I would do nearly anything you asked." He was having this conversation with her cleavage. "But will you please stop talking for just a minute?"

"Forget it. I reserve the right to chat if you've reserved the right to rip up my nice new nightgown," she informed the top of his head. And her old panties. Well, at least it wasn't laundry day. No granny underpants on her, thank you very much!

She was striving to sound coolly logical and matter-of-fact, but his mouth was busy nibbling and kissing and licking; it was too damned wonderful. Distracting! She meant distracting. She ought to kick him in the 'nads. Why *wasn't* she kicking him in the 'nads? Or at least screaming for help?

Because he wouldn't hurt her. Because he wanted her with a clear, hungry passion no man had ever shown her. Because she had a crush on him the size of Australia. Because if she screamed he might stop.

"Uh . . . help?" she said weakly, a moment before he rose up and his mouth was on hers. He smelled clean and masculine; his lips were warm and firm and insistent. His tongue traced her lower lip and then thrust into her mouth. Claimed it. His groin was pressing against hers, and she could feel his . . . er . . . pulse.

She tore her mouth from his, not without serious regret. If he kissed her like *that* again, it was all over. Good-bye, good-girl rep. Hello, new life as a slut puppy. "Condoms!" she shouted into his startled face. "I'll bet you a hundred bucks you don't have any."

"Of course I don't," he said indignantly. He was—*ack!*—shrugging out of his shirt. His chest was tanned (in December!) and lightly furred with black hair. She actually moved to see if his chest hair was as crisp as it looked but then pulled her hands back and clenched them into fists. "I didna come here to mate. Have sex, I mean. I'm here on business. I never thought—"

"Yeah, well, that's a problem, Buckaroo Banzai, because I didn't exactly line my bra with prophylactics, either. Which means looky but no nooky. In fact," she added on a mutter, "we shouldn't even looky."

"But you're on the pill—ow, dammit!"

She'd formed a fist and smacked him between the eyes. The only way he would have known she was taking birth control pills is if he had gone through her purse while she was sick; she'd stopped at the pharmacy on the way to work and picked up her prescription.

"We had to," he said, as if reading her mind. He rubbed the red spot on his forehead, which was rapidly fading. "Dr. Madison was concerned we'd have to take you to the hospital. She needed to know if you were taking any medication."

"A likely story," she grumbled, but it sounded plausible, so she didn't follow up with a headbutt. Not that she'd ever done one in her life, but how hard could it be? "And it's the minipill, Mr. Knows-So-Much. Besides, I'm not worried about getting pregnant—"

"You should be," he teased. Except she doubted he was really teasing.

"I'm worried about catching something. Without condoms, our options are—thank God—limited. Saran Wrap and a rubber band? Forget it. For all I know you could be crawling with disease. I could be taking my life in my hands if I let you bone me!"

"*Bone* you? Crawling—" He got up off her—*weep!*—and started to pace, shirtless and with an interesting bulge beneath his belt buckle. She struggled to keep her gaze on his face. Well, his shoulders, at least. "First of all, my family—we don't—that is to say, I've never been sick a day in my life, and no one I know has ever had—er—problems in that area. Second, I know for a fact *you're* disease free."

"How?" she asked curiously. He was right, of course, but how'd he know?

"It's hard to—never mind. And third . . . third . . ." He laughed unwillingly and ran a hand through his hair. It stuck up in all directions, but instead of looking silly, it only made him look immensely likeable. Adorably rumpled. "Giselle, you're unlike any woman I've ever known. You—" He shook his head. "There's just something about you. I can't put it into words. Come back to Scotland with me."

She'd been busily arranging the covers over herself, though it was a bit late for modesty, and looked up. "What? Scotland? You mean, like a visit?"

". . . sure. A visit." He grinned. "Starting tomorrow, and ending never."

"Yeah, yeah. Look, if you still feel like this tomorrow . . . later today, I mean . . . I could leave you my phone number." *And never hear from you again, most likely.*

"We need Santas in Scotland," he said seriously. "It can be a verra lonesome place."

"Oh, come on!" She started to get the giggles and laughed harder when he pounced on her like a big cat. A good trick, as he'd been standing several feet away from the bed. The man was in great shape, no doubt about it. "Now, cut it out . . . get off, now! I told you, no condoms, no nooky."

"What if I could prove I wasn't—er—how did you put it? Crawling with disease?"

"Prove it how?" she asked suspiciously. Part of her couldn't believe they were having this discussion. The last time she'd had sex had been . . . uh . . . what year was it? Anyway, the point was, this was *so* unlike her.

Well, why not? Why not jump without looking for once in her ridiculously dull life? The most interesting thing about her was her name . . . Mama Smith had been Jane Smith, of all the rotten jokes, and wanted her kid to be remembered. It didn't work. Short, plump women with brown hair and brown eyes weren't exactly noticed on the street.

Until today.

"Okay," she said slowly, "and back off a minute. Let me think." She pinched his nipple, hard. He yelped and reared back. "That's better. Okay, if you can prove you're disease free, I'll stay the night with you." She forced herself to meet his gaze. Her face was so red she was sure her head was going to explode, like that poor schmuck in *Scanners*. "I'll do anything you want until the sun comes up. You've got my word on it. And a Smith never goes back on her word. This Smith, anyway," she finished in a mutter.

He looked at her, wide-eyed. Then he turned so quickly—snake-quick, it was uncanny—and grabbed for the telephone.

"Wait a minute, who are you calling?" she asked, alarmed. She hadn't thought he could prove a damn thing at two o'clock in the morning. "If it's some buddy in Scotland who's gonna back you up—"

"I'm calling Massachusetts General Hospital," he said, grinning widely. "Good enough? Dr. Madison has staff privileges there. She's been looking after my family for years and years. She'll tell you all about my medical history if you like."

He put the phone on speaker so she could hear the hospital operator. Dr. Madison was paged and soon came to the phone.

"How are you feeling, dear?" she asked. She also had an accent, this one the clipped intonation of a blue-blooded Bostonian. "I had a terrible time calming down Alec while you were ill."

"I'm—ack!"

"No idle chit-chat," Alec said in her ear and ran a finger all the way down her spine.

She turned and slapped his hand away and then grabbed for the receiver so Alec wouldn't hear the rest of the conversation. "I'm fine, much better . . . listen, does Alec have any STDs that I, as a potential—*ack!*—sexual partner should know about?"

"STDs? You mean like AIDS or—oh dear—"

Giselle held the phone away, the better not to be deafened by the woman's shriek of laughter. A few seconds later, Doc Madison had it under control. "Sorry about that. I give you my word as a physician and a lady, Alec has never been sick a day in his life. Nor any of his family. They're a . . . a healthy lot." Another chuckle. "Why do I have the feeling I'll be seeing more of you, dear?"

"Beats the hell out of me. Okay, then, tha—" That was as far as she got before Alec was tossing the phone across the room and her back on the bed.

Chapter 7

Ah . . ."

"Don't be afraid."

"I think this is an excellent time to be afraid. For one thing, a) you're a lot bigger than I am, and b) I'm pretty sure you'll tackle me before I get to the door."

"A) you're right, and b) you're right. You're welcome t'try, though." His eyes gleamed. "I like to play chase."

Oh, Jesus. She slid from the bed, and he was right behind her. "Now, now," he said, almost purred, "a promise is a promise. Right, Giselle sweetie?"

Odd, the way he said that . . . like it was one word: *Gisellesweetie.* She liked it. Liked him. And a good thing, too, because they were about to get down to it. "You're right. I gave my wor*mmmphhh!*" His mouth was on hers, he was pulling her toward him, and she went up on her tiptoes. His tongue was in her mouth, jabbing and darting, and she could actually *feel* that between her legs. One of his hands was on the back of her neck, holding her firmly to him. The other arm was around her waist—luckily, he had long arms.

He broke the kiss—with difficulty, she was delighted to see. As for herself, she was panting as if she'd just run a marathon. And as elated as if she'd just won one. "Now," he said, almost gasped. "You said anything. That you'd do anything. Until the sun came up."

"Yes." It was hard to breathe. Black excitement swamped her. A promise *was* a promise, dammit, and she had his personal physician's word that he wasn't sick. More, she trusted him implicitly. She had been handed a fantasy on a plate, and she meant to take full advantage. After tonight, she'd never see him again. But by God, she had tonight. "Yes, anything. Anything you want."

"Ooooh, verra good," he crooned, almost growled. He sank to the bed and pulled her down with him—and kept pushing her down until she was on her knees, facing him. "Unbuckle my belt. Please," he added with a wolfish grin.

She did, with fingers that were clumsy and stupid. She finally pulled the belt free and wordlessly handed it to him. He tossed it in a corner. "Since you're keeping your promise—so far—we likely won't be needing *that*." She gulped—what the *hell* had she gotten herself into? "Now. My slacks, love. All the way off."

She did so, and then, when asked, relieved him of his boxers. It was too dark in the room to see their color—navy blue? puce?— but by their slippery feel she guessed they were made of silk. No flannel for *him*.

"Now," he breathed. "Kiss me."

She understood him perfectly, kissed the head of his cock, and then rubbed her cheek against him like a cat. He smelled warm and musky and undeniably male. He was also quite thick; she had difficulty closing her fingers around him. "Again," he groaned, "kiss me again, Giselle sweetie."

She did so, tasting the saltiness of pre-come. She licked it off and then licked up and down the length of him. She could feel his bristly pubic hairs tickling her chin on the down stroke. His hand came up and caught and fisted a handful of her curls. "Now," he growled, "open your mouth. Wide." His voice was so gritty she could hardly understand him, but it didn't take a rocket scientist to understand what he wanted—needed. Then he was filling her mouth, her throat. He withdrew in time for her to take a breath and then was in her mouth again. His hips were pistoning toward her face, and she realized he was *fucking* her *mouth*. While part of her was wildly excited, her practical side reminded her that although she could count the number of blow jobs she had given on one hand, she was definitely *not* a swallower.

His other hand had found her breasts, and he was kneading, squeezing. The sensation of his hands on her and his cock in her mouth was as exciting as it was overwhelming. She tried to pull back, but his grip tightened and then she felt him start to throb. Shockingly, suddenly, her mouth was flooded with musky saltiness and she reared back, but he had a grip like iron. In a second, he had pulled free of her but clapped a hand over her mouth.

"Swallow," he murmured in her ear. "All of it. Right down." *Aoull oof it. Ret daeown.*

She did. "Bastard!" she cried, making a fist and smacking him on the thigh. "A little warning next time, all right?"

"I promise," he said solemnly. "The next time I'm about to come in your mouth, I'll give ye ample warning. Ouch!"

"I've never done that before."

He was rubbing his thigh where she'd pinched him, hard. "I could tell."

Incredibly, pierced vanity was now warring with outraged propriety. "Well, *hell,* I'm not exactly known as Slut Girl around here, and besides, I didn't exactly plan—"

He stopped her with a kiss. "You were wonderful," he said warmly. He nuzzled her nose for a moment. "And I'm verra sorry if I startled ye. But I needed ye t'do that for me. Now I can touch you wi' a clear head. Now the fun can *really* start."

"You're still a bastard," she said sulkily. She could still taste him in her mouth, her throat. "You didn't have to make me—"

His smile flashed in the dark. "Well enough. But now it's y'turn, sweetie."

Her irritation lessened as he eased her back on the bed and knelt between her legs, and disappeared entirely as she realized he was going to be as good as his word.

It seemed as though he spent hours between her thighs: kissing, nibbling, sucking, and licking—ah, God, the licking. Lots of it, slow and steady; the man never got tired. In no time, her clit was enthusiastically throbbing, and that's when he started paying special, extended, loving attention to the little button Giselle hardly thought of unless she was enjoying the evening with Mr. Shaky.

His tongue darted and stroked. She could feel its warm, wet length sliding and slipping between her throbbing lips. She felt him sucking on her clit with a single-minded enthusiasm that was as exciting as it was astonishing.

After a while she was squirming all over the bed, trying to get away from the delectable torture of his mouth. He wouldn't— he—he never stopped, never got tired, just kept at her, at her, at her. Lick lick lick and suck suck suck and even small, tender bites. She could feel herself getting drenched and would have blushed if she hadn't been so close to shrieking. She'd start to feel her orgasm approach, and he'd somehow know and back off. Instead of giving her the last few flicks of his tongue to push her over the brink, he'd move to her inner labia and gently suck them until she was no longer close to coming, or his tongue would delve inside her—so deeply!—leaving her clit bereft.

"Oh, *God,* y'smell so damned good!" After that breathless declaration, he buried his face between her legs and commenced tormenting her anew. His hands spread her thighs so wide her knees were almost parallel, baring her fleshy mound for his hungry mouth. He started licking her in long, slow, agonizing slurps, from bottom to top, over and over and over. Her back bowed, and she was certain she was about to lose her mind if she didn't come *now.*

So she squirmed and wriggled, and when she made progress getting away from him, he simply grasped her thighs and pulled her back to his mouth. This went on for about seventeen years, until he tired of playing with her, sucked her clit into his mouth, and slipped two fingers inside her. The feeling of his warm lips on her and his long fingers in her was exquisite, brilliant. His fingers moved, stroked, and pushed hard inside her, pressure that was just short of discomfort, pressure that was amazing, mind-boggling. His lips had closed over her clit while his tongue flicked back and forth with dizzying rapidity. Her orgasm crashed over her like a wave, and she shrieked at the ceiling.

When he came up to lie beside her, she was still shaking. "Better?"

"Oh my *God.* Do you have a license to do that? You ought to be against the law." She reached out and did what she had longed to do an hour ago: gently stroked his chest hair and then followed a path down to his groin. She found him thick, hard, and ready for her. He sucked in breath when she gently closed her fingers around him. "By the way," she added cheerfully, if breathlessly, "I'm on to you. There's no way you're an ordinary guy. Not that I mind."

He stiffened, though whether it was from what she had said or what her fingers were doing, she couldn't tell. She was squeezing and releasing, squeezing and releasing. Her other hand slipped lower until she was cradling his testicles in her palm, testing their warm weight. "You've got a butterfly's touch, Giselle sweetie," he said, almost groaned.

She almost giggled. She'd never pictured her plump self as something so light and delicate as a butterfly. Alec was no doubt mumbling nonsense because all the blood had left his head some time ago and gone significantly southward.

She slipped her hand up, down, up, down, with excruciating slowness, with all the care he had shown her a few moments ago. She wasn't terribly experienced, but she *was* well read. She'd been buying Emma Holly's books for years. "That's why you shouldn't mess with a bookworm," she whispered in Alec's ear. "We know some pretty good stuff." He didn't answer her, but because she had brought her palm across his slippery tip and circled, circled, circled while her other hand stroked, she didn't expect him to.

She had meant to keep playing with him as long as she could draw it out, but he suddenly jerked away from her and kneed her thighs apart. He was terse, silent, but oh, how his hands were shaking. "Shouldn't you buy me dinner first? Again, I mea— *eeeeeEEEEEEEEEEE!*" He entered her with one brutal thrust, all the way, all at once. She was slick and more than ready for him, but it was startling—a little frightening, even—all the same.

He started to drive himself into her.

She squirmed beneath him, felt her eyes roll back in her head . . . ah, Jesus, this was almost too much! Almost. "Alec."

His hips were shoving against hers, his eyes were tightly closed; his mouth was a narrow line.

"Alec."

"Sorry," he muttered. "M'sorry. Wait. I'll be—nice again. In a minute."

"Alec."

"I can't—stop. Just yet. S-Sorry. So sorry." His hands were on her shoulders, pinning her down, keeping her in place for him. His sex was rearing between her legs, into her, out of her. Digging, shoving, filling her.

"Alec. If you do it a little faster, I'll be able to come again."

That got his attention; his eyes opened wide. And then he smiled, a grin of pure male satisfaction. And he obliged. She heard the headboard start slamming against the wall and didn't give a tin shit. She wriggled for a moment until he let go of her shoulders and then brought her arms around him and her legs up. She started doing a little pumping of her own. Their bellies clapped together, a lustful, urgent beat.

His eyes rolled back. "Ah, *Jesus!*" His mouth found hers, and he kissed her savagely, biting her mouth, her lips. Then he abruptly pulled back, as if aware he was nearing a line he wasn't ready to cross with her—absurd, given what they were engaged in. His head dropped, and she could feel his face pressing against the hollow between her neck and shoulder. There was a sharp pain as he bit her.

He's marking me, she thought. She heard a purring tear as he tore the sheets. *He's making me his own.* That thought—so complicated, so strange, and so completely marvelous—spun her into orgasm.

He stiffened over her as she cried out and his grip tightened—painful for a split second—and then he relaxed. "Do that again," he growled in her ear and then bit her earlobe.

"I can't," she gasped, almost groaned. And still he was busy, still he was fucking her with long, fast strokes.

"Yes."

"I—can't!" Pump, pump, pump, and her neck stung where he had bitten her. As if sensing her thought, he bent to her and licked the bite and then kissed her mouth.

"I need to feel your sweet little cave tightening around me again," he said into her mouth. "I must insist."

"I'm done. Please, I can't anymore. Please, Alec—" Oh, but her body was betraying her. She was arching her back to better meet his thrusts, and she could feel that now-familiar tightening between her thighs, the feeling that told her she *would* do it again, thank you very much. "Alec, please stop, please, I can't. Stop! St—" Then it was singing through her, *tearing* through her, and this one made the other two seem like mild tickling in comparison. This one was the biggest thing to ever happen to her.

She felt him stiffen above her again, but, oh, Christ, he wasn't done, he was still thrusting. He seized her knees and pushed them wide, spreading her, making her wider for him. She screamed in pleasure and despair; more of this was sure to kill her. It'd be the best death ever, but it'd still be death.

"More," he muttered in her ear.

". . . can't."

"Can. Will."

She reached down, stroked his ass, felt, groped . . . and then shoved her finger inside him, right up his ass, as far as she could. At the same time, she clenched around him

(thank you, Kegel exercise)

and was gratified to hear his hoarse shout. Then he was pulsing inside her and throwing his head back and roaring at the ceiling. The headboard gave one more loud THUMP! and was quiet.

She sobbed for breath, and he soothed her with gentle strokes and small kisses. "Shhhh, sweetie, you're all right. I just don't think *I* am. Shhhh."

"That was—that—"

"Easy. Shush, now. Get your breath back."

As the ripples from her last, titanic orgasm faded, she realized she was still throbbing. She still wanted him. She was a bookworm cursed with the body of a slut.

"That was—mmbelievable. 'Mazing." Oh, great, she was babbling like a cheerleader after her fifth beer. She tried again. "Unbelievable. Amazing. I'm sure you hear this all the time, but that was the best *ever.* I don't mean for me. I mean in the history of lovemaking."

He was kissing her forehead, her mouth, her cheeks. "For me, also. And I don't hear it all the time. I haven't been with a lady in almost a year."

She nearly fell off the bed. "What? *Why?* You're so—I mean, the overall package is just—and then what you can do in the bedroom—what the hell have you been waiting for? Did you lose a bet?"

"I did not. Who," he said. "Who the hell have I been waiting for. That's the question." He bent and nuzzled her cleavage. "God, I could get lost in you. So easily. Which means I have to kill you or marry you."

"Har, har. And get your nose out of there, it tickles." She could feel his cock on her thigh, very warm, and reached out. "Jesus! You're hard again!"

"Sorry," he said dryly. "I can't much help it if you've got the sweetest cunt. Not to mention some *very* talented fingers."

"No, I mean . . . uh. I don't know what I mean." Their gaze met. Her eyes had long ago adjusted to the dark; she could see him quite well. "Do you want to keep going?"

He smiled slowly; it was like an extra spoonful of sugar being stirred into really good coffee. "Do you?"

"That's not really relevant," she said tartly. His eyebrows arched. "A promise is a promise, remember?"

"What I like about you—one of the things—is that you're not done. With me." His hand slid down the soft mound of her belly and cupped her between her legs. Then he gently parted her, and his fingers slid up inside her. She sucked in breath and moved with his hand. "You haven't closed off," he murmured into her mouth, "the way a lady will when she's had enough." She could hear herself whimpering softly as his fingers slid in and out and around, as he got slick with their juices. "Of course, you have other qualities, very fine ones." His voice held a teasing note. "But I wouldn't have guessed at this one while I was wooing you over lunch."

"Wooing me?" she gasped. "Is that what you were doing?"

"What I was *doing* was concentrating on not bending you over the nearest table and taking you until my knees gave out. I'm amazed I was able to talk to you at all—ah, God, that's sweet, Giselle. Those sounds you make in the back of your throat make me forget everything. Come down here."

He pulled her until she was kneeling before the bed. She could feel him behind her, holding her around the waist, then stroking her buttocks and kneading the plump flush. "I could bite you here about a hundred times," he muttered.

"Better not if you want to save room for breakfast." She yelped as his kneading inched toward pinching. "Easy, Alec. I have to sit on that later."

He swallowed a laugh. "Sorry. But Giselle sweetie, you do have the most luscious ass." Then his hands moved lower until he was holding her open with his fingers. She could feel herself—everything in her—straining toward him, silently begging for him. "Oh, God, Alec . . ."

"I like that, Giselle. I like hearing you groan my name." He eased into her, inch by delicious inch. She leaned forward and braced her arms on the bed. "Now, if y'don't mind, I'd like to hear you scream it." He thrust, hard.

He stroked, and his hands were everywhere . . . running up and down her back, cupping her breasts, stroking her nipples . . . and then roughly pulling them between his fingers, as if he instinctively knew when she wanted him to be sweet and when she wanted—needed—him to be rough. She screamed his name, begged him to stop screwing around and *do her, dammit.* He laughed in pure delight, laughed while she writhed and groaned and shoved back at him. Then his strokes pushed her into orgasm, and he abruptly quit laughing and gasped instead.

She realized the sun had come up a while ago. Well, who gave a rat's ass? She couldn't believe the man's stamina. She couldn't believe *her* stamina.

"Getting tired?" he panted in her ear. He was still crouched behind her, still filling her the way no man ever had. When he braced himself and thrust, she swore she could feel his cock in her throat. "Giselle? All right?"

"Yes, I'm tired, I'm exhausted, you big dolt, and don't you dare stop."

He chuckled, and she could feel his fingers dancing along the length of her spine. Then his hand came around and found her clit. He stroked the throbbing bud with his thumb and said, "I wish my mouth was there right now. Later, it will be," and that was enough, that tipped her into another orgasm.

She felt his grip tighten on her. "Oh, God, that's so sweet," he groaned. "Has anyone told you? When you come, your muscles lock." He shuddered behind her as he at last found his release. "*All* your muscles."

She giggled weakly and rested her head on the bed. Three times . . . or was that the fourth? The man wasn't human. Thank *God* she was on the pill.

He stood, then picked her up, and cradled her in his arms as if she were a child. "You'll sleep now," he said, laying her in the bed and covering her. "And so will I . . . you've worn me out, m'lady." Then, incongruously, "Do you have a passport?"

"No," she said drowsily.

"Hmm. I'll have to fix that. Can't come to Scotland without one of those."

"You still want me to come?" She blushed, remembering how they'd spent the last five hours. "To Scotland, I mean?"

"Of course." He was arranging the covers over himself, pulling her into his embrace, and wrapping his long legs around hers. She was instantly warm and sinfully comfortable. The throbbing between her thighs had finally quit. *It quit because you're numb, you twit. He's fucked you numb. And it was just fine.* "I said I did, didn't I?"

"Well . . ." She yawned against his shoulder. "That was before I gave up the goods, so to speak."

"Giselle, darling." He kissed the top of her head. "I've never known a woman so smart and so silly at the same time. You're coming to Scotland. To put it another way, I'm not leaving without you."

"Bossy putz," she muttered. Then she squinched her eyes shut as he turned on the bedside light. "Aggh! I think my retinas just fused!"

She could hear him swallow a laugh. "Sorry, love. I just wanted to get a good look at your neck." She felt him push her hair back and gently touch the bite. "A bite's a serious thing . . . I'm really sorry if I hurt you. You know that, right, Giselle?"

"Don't worry about it. At the risk of making you more arrogant than you already are—though how that's possible I just can't imagine—I loved it. Hardly even hurt."

"Oh." She could hear the unmistakable relief in his tone. "I'm glad t'hear it. I don't have an explanation except . . . I don't want you to think I go around biting just anybody. I just . . . lost myself in you."

"That, and you wanted to mark me," she added drowsily. Ah, even with that obnoxious light on, she was going to be able to get to sleep quite nicely. Take that, bedside lamp! "It's all right. I don't mind wearing your mark for a while."

"*What* did you say?"

"Marked me."

"What?"

"Arked-may E-may! Jesus, for a guy with heightened senses, you're really slow."

"*What?*"

"Don't yell, I'm right here. I forgot werewolves were so touchy."

"Oh my *God.*"

"Steady, pal." Concerned, she sat up. He looked like he was going to pass out. "Hey, it's okay. I said it was, right? You marked me so another werewolf won't take it into his head to jump me. Theoretically, they'll see your mark and steer clear. Or lose their minds and decide, of all things, to fight for me. Ha! Like that'd happen."

She saw him lurch into the chair—sitting down before he fell down. Very wise. "You know? About me?"

"Sure. Not right away," she added comfortingly, because he looked so shattered. "Took me a while to figure it out. But come on, you're a little too quick and too strong for a guy in his—what? Early thirties?"

"Thirty-one," he said absently.

"Plus, your stamina between the sheets was—was really something." Was she blushing? After what they had just shared? *You're obviously overtired. Go to sleep, Giselle.* "I've never met one—a werewolf—but my mom used to work for Lucius Wyndham."

He was staring at her with the most priceless look of astonishment on his face. "*Your mother worked for the former pack leader?*"

"Will you *stop* with the yelling? Yes, she managed his stables for him. 'Course, he couldn't come near any of his horses without them going crazy trying to get away from him. He finally had to tell her the truth, because she thought he'd abused them and was getting ready to sic the ASPCA on him.

"Well, of course he wasn't hurting them. It's just instinctive for horses to stay the hell away from werewolves. So he told her, and proved it to her, and she liked the horses, and liked him, and stayed on. 'Til she married my dad and moved to Boston. But she'd seen a lot by then. My mom," Giselle added with satisfaction, "tells the *best* bedtime stories. I figured you out a little while ago. I said so . . . remember?"

He was shaking his head, his mouth hanging open. "I just can't—all night I've been trying to figure out if I should just kidnap you t'Scotland and tell you the truth over there—"

"Typical werewolf courtship," she sneered. "You guys really need to work on the romance thing."

"Or try to explain it to you tomorrow. Later today, I mean. Or wait until we knew each other better—but you knew!"

"Yup."

"And you didn't say anything!"

"It didn't seem polite since you didn't bring it up." She blushed harder, like that was possible. "Besides, we . . . had other things on our minds."

He burst into laughter—great, roaring laughs that made her ears ring. "Giselle sweet, you're for me, and I'm *definitely* for you. I knew it the moment I smelled you. Ripe peaches in the middle of all those street smells and slush. The only Santa who was ovulating." He pounced on the bed and pulled her into his arms, kissing her everywhere he could.

"Jeez, cut it out!" She was laughing and trying to fend him off. "Can't we do this later? We ordinary humans get *tired* after making love all night."

"There's nothing ordinary about you, sweetie."

"Oh, come on. You can't tell me that on that whole street, where there were probably a couple hundred people, the only one ovulating was me?"

"No, I can't tell you that." He kissed her on the mouth. "What I can tell you is that the only woman *for me* was ovulating."

"Oh. Sleep now?" she added helpful, groping for the bedside lamp.

He shut off the light for her. "Scotland?"

"Yes."

"Forever?"

"Nope. Sorry, my parents are from here. I have friends here, too. A life I made before I ever laid eyes on you, pretty boy. And, hello? Courtship, anybody? It'd be nice to date a little before we got married."

He mock-sighed. "Humans, oh, Lord help me. A house in Boston, then, but at least half the year at my family home. After," he sighed again, "an appropriately lengthy courtship."

"Done."

"Naked courtship?" he asked hopefully.

She laughed. "We'll work out the details. Doesn't really matter, though. Wither thou goest, I will go. And all that."

"And all that," he said, and kissed her smiling mouth.

Monster Love

Author's Note

The events of this story take place in February of 2006, following the events of *Undead and Unreturnable.*

Also, I have changed Chicago's Chinatown to suit my needs. It's a wonderful city, but I just couldn't leave it alone. That's a failing in me, not the city of Chicago.

I did the same thing, again, with Summit Avenue in St. Paul. A lovely city. Just couldn't leave it be. Sorry.

*"We shall find no fiend in hell can match
the fury of a disappointed woman."*

—COLLEY CIBBER, Love's Last Shift, *Act 2*

*"Like a fiend in a cloud
With howling woe,
After night I do crowd,
And with night will go."*

—WILLIAM BLAKE, *from Poetical Sketches*

*"Don't threaten me with love, baby.
Let's just go walking in the rain."*

—BILLIE HOLIDAY

Prologue

*From the private papers of Richard Will,
Ten Beacon Hill, Boston, Massachusetts*

Becoming a vampire was the best thing that ever happened to me. The very, very best. Which is why I don't understand all the literature, how the vampires are usually these moody fellows who rue the day they ever got bitten, who pray for some illiterate European to plant a stake through their ribs. Rue the day? If the mob hadn't torched my killer the next night, I'd have kissed his feet. I'd even have kissed his behind!

"After all, what else was there for me? Take over the farm when my father died? *No, thank you.* Farming is back-breaking work for very little reward and even less respect. And I could hardly endure being in the same room with my father, much less work for him the rest of my life. (Punch first and punch second, that was my dear departed papa's motto.)

"Lie about my age to join the army and get my head blown off? (All so sixty years later we can ignore the Holocaust and pretend the Germans are good guys?) But back then, if you didn't fight you were a coward. Of course, two wars later, the young men were *encouraged* to go to Canada, to avoid responsibilities to their country. If they fought, and lived, their reward was to be spit upon at the airport. It just goes to prove, nothing changes faster than the mind of an American.

"No, life wasn't exactly a bowl of fresh peaches. I was in a box, and each side of the box was equally insurmountable. I wasn't the only one, but I was the only one who noticed the shape and size of the prison. I was always different from my chums. At least, I think I was . . . it was a long time ago, and don't we always think we're different?

"So when Darak—that was his name, or at least the name he gave me—bought me a drink, then two, then ten, I didn't turn him down. What did I care if a stranger wanted to help me forget about the box? I was big—twenty-three years working on a farm made for a big boy—and if he wanted to get inappropriate, I was sure I could handle it.

"Yes, there was homosexuality in the forties. People like to pretend it's a modern invention, which always makes me laugh. Anyway, I figured Darak wanted to see what I had inside my drawers, but I had no intention of showing him—what men did with other men was none of my concern. Of course, my drawers weren't what held his interest at all.

"I'd been supremely confident I could toss Darak through a window if I needed to, which just goes to show I was something of a naive moron when I was a boy. Darak took what he needed from me, and never mind pretty words or even asking permission. He stopped my heart and left me on a filthy floor to breathe my last. The last thing I remember was a rat scampering across my face, how the tail felt, dragging across my mouth.

"I woke up two nights later. It was dark and close, but in a stroke of luck, I hadn't been buried yet. I didn't know it then, but the town's only mill had blown up and there were forty bodies to be interred. Plus they'd cornered Darak and set him on fire. Yes, things had been positively hopping in the small town of Millidgeville, pop. 232 (actually 191 now). They were in no rush to get me in the ground. They had more important things to worry about.

"I was thirstier than I had ever been in my life. And strong . . . I meant only to pop open the door to the coffin and ended up ripping it off the hinges. I lurched out of the coffin and realized instantly where I was. And I knew what Darak was . . . I'd read Bram Stoker as a teenager. But even through the mad haze of my unnatural—or so it seemed to me then—thirst and the disbelief of my death, the main thing I remember is the relief. I was dead. I was free. I silently blessed Darak and went to find someone to eat.

"Being a vampire is *wonderful.* The strength, the speed, the liquid diet . . . all solidly in the plus column. The minuses—no sunbathing (so?), sensitivity to light (sunglasses fixed that nicely), no real relationships other than those of a transitory nature (call girls!)—are bearable.

"I miss women, though. That's probably the worst of it. No more sunsets? Phaugh. I saw plenty of them on the farm. But I haven't had a girlfriend since . . . er . . . what year is it? Never mind.

"I can't be with a mortal woman, for obvious reasons. She'd never understand what I was, what I needed. I'd constantly fear hurting her—I can lift a car over my head, so being with a mortal woman is not unlike being with a china doll. And being dead hasn't affected my sex drive one bit. I was a young man of lusty appetite, and while I still look young, my appetite has increased exponentially with my age.

"I've only met six other vampires in my life. Of the six, four were women, and let me tell you, they were complete and unrepentant monsters. They ate children. *Children!* I killed two, but the other two got away. I could have gone after them, but I had to get the child to a hospital and—well, I wouldn't have wished their company on my fiercest enemy, much less welcomed them to the marriage bed.

"Yes, I'm lonely. Another price to pay for the eternal life and the liquid diet. But I'm young for a vampire—not even close to a hundred yet. Things are bound to look up. And even if they don't, my patience—like my thirst—is infinite."

Chapter 1

A monkey. *A fucking monkey!*

Janet Lupo practically threw her invitation at the goon guarding the doors to the reception hall. Bad enough that one of the most eligible werewolves in the pack—the world!—was now off the market, but he'd taken a pure human to mate. Not that there was anything wrong with that. Humans were okay. If you liked sloths.

She stomped toward her table, noticing with bitter satisfaction the way people jumped out of her path. Pack members walked clear when she was in a *good* mood. Which, at the moment, she was not.

Bad enough to be outnumbered a thousand to one by the humans, but to marry one? And fuck one and get it pregnant and join the PTA and . . .

The mind reeled.

Janet had nothing against humans as a species. In fact, she greatly admired their rapaciousness. *Homo sapiens* never passed up prey, not even if they were stuffed—not even if they didn't eat meat! They'd kill each other over *shoes,* for God's sake. They had fought wars over shiny metals and rocks. Janet had never understood why a diamond was worth killing over but a pink topaz was hardly worth sweating about. Humans had fought wars over the possession of gold, but iron ferrite, which looked *exactly the same,* was worthless.

And when humans started killing, watch out. Whether it was "Free the Holy Land from the infidels!" or "Cotton and Slave's Rights!" or "Down with Capitalism!" or whatever was worth mass genocide, when humans went to war, your only chance was to get out of the way and keep your head down.

But marry one? Marry someone slower and weaker? Much, much weaker? Someone with no pack instincts, someone who only lived for themselves? It'd be—it'd be like a human marrying a bear. A small, sleepy bear who hardly ever moved. Fucking creepy, is what it was.

And there was Alec, sitting at the head table and smirking like he'd won the lottery! And his mate—uh, wife—sitting next to him. She was cute enough if you liked chubby, which the boys in the pack did. A bony wife wasn't such a great mother when food was scarce. Not that food *was* scarce these days, but thousands of years of genetic conditioning died hard. Besides, who wanted to squash their body down onto a bundle of sticks?

Okay, there wasn't anything wrong with her looks. Her looks were fine. So was her smell—like peaches packed in fresh snow. And the bimbo knew what she was getting into—her old lady had worked for Old Man Wyndham, way back in the day—so the whole family had experience keeping secrets. But to call a sloth a sloth, the new Mrs. Kilcurt was not pack. She wasn't family. And she would never be, no matter how many cubs Alec got on her.

Jesus! First the pack leader—Michael—knocked up a human, and now Alec Kilcurt. Didn't any of her fellow werewolves marry *werewolves* anymore?

"Dance, Jane?"

"I'd rather eat my own eyeballs," she said moodily, not even looking to see who asked. Why was she going to her table, anyway? The reception wasn't mandatory. Neither was the wedding. She'd just gone to be polite. And the time for that was done.

She turned on her heel and marched out. The goon at the door obligingly held it open. Which was just as well, 'cuz otherwise she'd have kicked it down.

+ + +

Janet vastly preferred Boston in the spring, and as cities went, Boston was not awful. Parts of it—the harbor, the aquarium— were actually kind of cool.

Thinking of the New England Aquarium—all those fish, lobsters, squid, and sharks—made her stomach growl. She'd been too annoyed to eat lunch, and when she had walked out of the reception, she had also walked out on her supper.

She turned onto a side street, taking a shortcut to Legal Sea

Foods, a restaurant that did not suck. She'd have a big bowl of clam chowder some raw oysters, a steak, and a lobster. And maybe something for dessert. And a drink. Maybe three.

A scent caught her attention, forcing a split-second decision. She turned onto another street, one much less crowded, curious to see if the men were going to keep following her.

They were. She hadn't seen their faces, just caught their scents as they swung around to follow her on Park Street. They smelled like desperation and stale coffee grounds. She was well dressed and probably looked prosperous to them. Prime pickings.

She turned again, this time down a deserted alley. If the two would-be robbers thought they were keeping her from supper, they were out of their teeny, tiny minds. She could easily outrun them, but that would mean kicking off her high heels. The stupid pinchy shoes cost almost thirty bucks! She wasn't leaving them in a Boston alley. If push came to shove, she'd bounce her stalkers off the bricks. Possibly more than once, the mood she was in.

"Halt, gentlemen."

Janet jumped. A man was standing at the end of the alley, and she hadn't known he was there until he spoke up. She hadn't smelled him, even though he was upwind. When was the last time *that* had happened?

He was tall—over six feet—and well built for someone who wasn't pack. His shoulders were broad, and he definitely had the look of a man used to working with his hands. He had blond hair the color of wheat, and his eyes—even from fifteen feet away she could see their vivid color—were Mediterranean blue. He was wearing all black—dress slacks, a shirt open at the throat, and a duster that went almost all the way to his heels. And—what's this now? He was squinting in the poor light of the alley and slipping on a pair of sunglasses. *Sunglasses*—how weird was *that,* at ten-thirty at night?

"I have business with the young lady," Weirdo continued, walking toward them. His hands were open, relaxed. She knew he wasn't carrying a weapon. He moved with the grace of a dancer; if she hadn't been so fucking hungry, she might have liked to watch him prance around. "Much kinder business, I think, than you two. So be on your way, all right?" Then, in a lower voice, "Don't be afraid, miss. I won't hurt you. Hardly at all."

"Stand aside, four eyes," she snapped, and with barely a glance, she stiff-armed him into the side of the building and hurried past. She had no time for would-be muggers and less for

Mr. Sunglasses-at-Night. Let the three of them fight it out. She had a date with a dead lobster.

Behind her, Sunglasses yelped in surprise. There was a flat smack as he hit the wall and then slid down. She'd tossed him a little harder than she meant—*oopsie*—and then the other two jumped him, and she was out of the alley.

She could see the restaurant up ahead. Just a few more steps, and she could order. Just a few more . . .

She stopped.

Don't you dare!

Turned.

C'mon, enough already! They're human . . . it's none of your business.

She started back toward the alley. Sunglasses was a weirdo, but he was vulnerable to attack because of what she had done. Yeah, they were human, but it was one thing to mind your own business and another to turn your back on a mess you helped make.

You moron! Who knows when you'll get to eat now?

"Fuck off, inner voice," she said aloud. People thought the outer Janet was a bitch; God forbid they should ever meet the inner Janet.

She stepped into the alley to help and was just in time to see the second mugger crumple to the filthy street. The first was half in and half out of the dumpster. And Sunglasses was hurrying, hurrying toward her, licking the blood off his knuckles. "As I was saying before you tossed me against the wall, I have business with you, miss. And where on earth do you work out?"

She was so surprised she let him put his hands on her shoulders, let him draw her close. He smiled at her, and even in the poorly lit alley, she could see the light gleaming on his teeth. His very long canines. His fangs, to be perfectly blunt. He had fangs, and it wasn't even close to the full moon.

"What the hell are *you*?" She put a hand to his chest to keep him from pulling her closer. His heart beat once. Then nothing.

He blinked at her. "What? Usually the lady in question is halfway to fainting by now. To answer your question, I'm the son of a farmer. That's all."

"My ass," she said rudely. "I came back to give you a hand—"

"How sweet."

"—but you're fine, and I'm hungry."

"What a coincidence," he murmured. He tapped a sharp canine

with his tongue. Beneath her palm, his heart beat again. "My, you're exceedingly beautiful. I suppose your beaux tell you that all the time."

"Beaux? Who the hell talks like that? And you're full of shit," she informed him. Beautiful? Shyeah. She wasn't petite, and she wasn't tall—just somewhere in the middle. Average height, average weight, average hair color—not quite blond and not quite brown—average nose, mouth, and chin. She could see her average eyes reflected in his sunglasses. "And you'd better let go before I hit you so hard, you'll spend the rest of the night throwing up your teeth."

He blinked again and then smiled. "Forgive the obvious question, but aren't you a little nervous? It's dark . . . and you're quite alone with me. Why, I might do anything to you." He licked his lower lip thoughtfully. "Anything at all."

"This is really, really boring, fuck-o," she informed him. "Leggo."

"I decline."

She brought her foot down on his and felt his toes squish through the dress shoe. Then she knocked him away from her with a right cross. This time, when he went down, he stayed down.

Twenty minutes later, she was happily slurping the first of a dozen oysters on ice.

Chapter 2

He knew he was lurking like a villain in a bad melodrama, but he couldn't help it. He had to catch her when she came out of the restaurant. So he was reduced to watching her through the restaurant window from across the street.

Richard rubbed his jaw thoughtfully. It didn't hurt anymore, but if he'd been mortal, it likely would have shattered from the force of the woman's punch. She hit like a Teamster. And swore like one, too.

She was stunning, really very stunning, with those cider-colored eyes and that unique hair. Her crowning glory was shoulder length, wavy, and made up of several colors: gold, auburn, chestnut . . . even a few strands of silver. The silky strands gleamed beneath the streetlight and made him itch to touch them, to see if they were as soft as they looked.

She had been fearless in the near dark of the alley, and he'd become utterly besotted. He had to see her again, take her in his arms again, hear her say "fuck" again.

Ah! After a five-course meal, here she came. And look! She had spotted him instantly and was now stomping across the street toward him. Her small hands were balled into fists, and her lush mouth was curled in a snarl.

"Fuck-o, you don't learn too quick, do you?"

"You're marvelous," he said, smiling at her. Few people were on the street at this hour, but the ones who were around caught the tension in the air and did a quick fade. Most mortals had zero protective coloring, but something about the proximity of a vampire put their wind up, even if they weren't consciously aware of it. "Just charming, really."

She snorted delicately. "I see you're heavily medicated, on top of everything else. Get lost, before I belt you in the chops again."

"You came all the way over here to tell me to go away?"

A frown wrinkle appeared on her perfect, creamy forehead. "Yeah, I did. Don't read anything into it. So blow, okay?"

"Richard Will."

"What?"

"My name is Richard Will." He held out his hand, hoping she wouldn't be startled by his long fingers. Most people—women—were.

"Yeah? Well, Dick, I don't trust people with two first names." She stared at his outstretched hand and then crossed her arms over her chest.

He let his hand drop. "And you are . . . ?"

"Tired of this conversation."

"Is that your first name or your last?"

Her lips curled into an unwitting smile. "Very funny. You never answered my question."

"Which one?"

"What are you? Your heart . . ." She started to reach for him but then stopped. "Let's just say you should get your ass to a doctor, pronto."

"You know what I am." He bent toward her and was thrilled when she didn't back off. "In your heart, you know."

"Dick, as my family will tell you, I don't *have* a heart."

He rested his palm against her chest, feeling the rapid beat. "Such a lie, dearest."

She knocked his hand away and sounded gratifyingly breathless when she said, "Don't call me that."

"I have no choice, dearest, as you never told me your name."

"It's Janet."

"Janet . . . ?"

"Smith," she said rudely, and he chuckled. Then he laughed, a full-blown guffaw that sent more stragglers hurrying away. "What the hell's so funny?"

"Don't you see? We simply must get married. Richard and Janet . . . Dick and Jane!"

She gaped at him for a long moment and then, reluctantly, joined him in laughter.

+ + +

"So you don't like the new wife?"

Janet moodily stirred her coffee. It was after midnight, and they were the only couple in the coffee shop. "It's not that I have a personal problem with her. She's just . . . not our kind, is all."

"She's Polish?"

She snorted a laugh through her nose. "Nothing like that . . . I'm not *that* big a bitch. It's hard to explain. And you wouldn't believe me anyway."

He grinned, flashing his fangs. "Try me."

"No way, José. I want to hear about *you*. I didn't know there were such things as vampires. Assuming you're not some pathetic schmuck who filed his teeth to get the girls."

He considered lifting her, in her chair, over his head, but decided against it. Among other things, it was unnecessary. She knew what he was, oh yes. She had felt his heart. And he had felt hers. "I didn't know there were such things either, until I woke up dead."

She leaned forward, which gave him an excellent view of creamy cleavage in her wine-colored dress. "How old are you?"

"Not so old, for a vampire. Not even a hundred yet. And as it's not polite to ask a lady her age—"

"Thirty-six."

Perfect. Giggling girlhood was left behind, she was closing in on her sexual peak, and the best was still ahead. He tried very hard not to drool.

"I'm the old maid of the family," she was saying. "Most of my friends have teenagers already."

"You have plenty of time."

She brightened. "See, that's what I always say! Just because we're trapped in this damned youth-obsessed society doesn't mean we have to do *everything* in our twenties. What's the fucking rush?"

"Exactly. That's what I—"

"Except my family thinks totally differently," she said, her shoulders slumping. "They're very *in-the-now*, if you know what I mean. Sometimes there's . . . there's fights and stuff, and you never know if today's your last day on Earth. There's lots of pressure to make every single day count, to cram *everything* you can, as often as you can. Nobody really stops and smells the fuckin' roses where I come from, you know?"

"That's fairly typical of . . . of people." He'd almost said "of mortals," but no need to push things. As it was, he had a hard time believing this conversation was taking place. She'd insulted him, pounded him, knew what he was, and was now having coffee with him. Amazing! "If your life span is so brief—what? seventy years or so?—well, of course you want to make every minute count."

"My family's life span is even shorter," she said moodily.

"Ah. Dangerous neighborhood?"

"To put it mildly. Although it's better since . . . well, it's better now, and I just hope it lasts."

"Which is why you can take care of yourself so well."

She cracked her knuckles, which made the lone counterman cringe. "Bet your ass."

"Indeed I would not." He stirred his coffee. He could drink it, though all it would do was make him thirstier. Instead, he played with it; he enjoyed the ritual of cream and sugar. "How long are you in town?"

She shrugged. "Long as I want. The wedding's over, so we'll probably hang out for a couple days, then head back to our homes."

"And home for you is . . . ?"

"None of your fucking business. Don't get me wrong, Dick, you seem pleasant enough for a bloodsucking fiend of the undead—"

"Thank you."

"—but I'm not opening up to you with all my vitals, no matter how good-looking and charming you are."

"So my powers of attraction aren't completely lost on you," he teased.

She ignored the interruption. "And if you don't like it, you can stop dicking around with your coffee and get the hell gone."

"I cannot decide," he said after a long pause, during which he guiltily put down his spoon, "if you're the most refreshing person I've ever met, or the most irritating."

"Go with irritating," she suggested. "That's what my family does." She glanced at her watch, a cheap thing that probably told time about as well as a carrot. "I gotta go. It's really late, even for me." She laughed at that for some reason.

He leaned forward and picked up her warm little hand. Her palm was chubby, with a strong life line. Her nails were brutally short and unpolished. "I must see you again. Actually, I would prefer to spirit you away to my—"

"Creaky, musty, damp castle?"

"—condo on Beacon Hill, but you're quite a strong young lady and I seriously doubt I could do so without attracting attention. So I must persuade you."

"Damned right, chum." She jerked her hand out of his grasp. "Try anything, and—"

"I'll vomit my teeth, or be split down the middle, or my head will be twisted around so far I'll be able to see my own backside." She giggled. "Yes, yes, I quite understand. Have dinner with me tomorrow night."

"Don't you mean 'let me watch you eat while I play with my drink'?"

"Something like that, yes."

"Why?" she asked suspiciously.

"Because," he said simply, "I've decided. You're refreshing because you're irritating. Do you know how long it's been since I've had a nice conversation with a lady?"

She stared at him. "You think this has been a nice conversation?"

"Nicer than 'Help, eeeeeek, stay away you horrible thing, no, no, noooooooooo, oh, God, please don't kill me!' I can't tell you how many times I've had *that* conversation."

"Serves you right for being a walking wood tick," she said. "Dinner, huh? On you?"

"Of course." *Possibly on you,* he thought, suddenly dizzy with a vision of licking red wine off her stomach.

"Mmmm. All right. I'll admit, it's nice to be myself with a guy and not have him be such a fucking Nancy boy whenever I say something the least bit—"

"Fucking obscene?"

She giggled again. "But you gotta tell me all about waking up dead and what it's like to be on a liquid diet. And how come my family didn't know about you and your kind?"

"Why would your family know about my kind?"

"We're pretty far-flung. There's not much going on on the planet we *don't* know about. So you'll feed me, and we'll talk. Deal, Dick?"

"Deal . . . Jane."

"I find out you've got a dog named Spot, and dinner's off," she warned.

Chapter 3

The phone rang, that shrill "pay attention to me!" sound she hated. She groaned, rolled over, groped for the phone, and knocked it off the hook. She relaxed into the blessed silence, which was broken by a tinny sound.

"Hello? Jane?"

She burrowed under the covers.

"Jane? Are you there? Janet. Hello??"

She cursed her werewolf hearing. Tinny and faint the voice might be, but it was also unmistakable. "What?"

"Pick up the phone," the voice coming through the telephone squawked. "I want to be sure you're getting all this."

"Can't. Too tired."

"It's six o'clock at night, for God's sake. Pick up the phone!"

She muttered something foul and obeyed the caller. "Whoever the hell this is, you'd better be on fire."

"It's Moira, and I practically am . . . the high today was eighty-two. In May!"

"Moira."

"You should see what the humidity did to my hair."

"Moira."

"I look like a blond cotton swab."

"Moira! This is fascinating, but you sure as shit better not be calling me to babble about your for-Christ's-sake *hair*. What do you want?"

"It's not what I want," Moira went on in her irritatingly cheer- ful voice. "It's Michael. The big boss wants to see you on the Cape, pronto."

Finally, the silly bitch had Jane's attention. Her eyes opened wide, and she sat straight up in bed. "Michael Wyndham? Wants to see me? How come?" And on the heels of that, a panicked thought: *What'd I do?* And resentment: *Come, girl, good dog, here's a treat for the good doggie.*

"Mine is not to reason why, girly . . . and neither is yours. I suggest you get your ass out here yesterday."

Jane groaned. "Aw, fuck a duck!"

"I'll pass."

"I've got a date. Today." She squinted at her watch. "Tonight, I mean."

"You *do?*" Moira sounded—rightfully so—completely astonished. She modified her tone, too late. "I mean, of course you do. Sure. It's only natural, a . . . a lively and . . . er . . . opinionated young lady like yourself. With a date on a Saturday night. Yep."

"Cut the shit. You're embarrassing both of us." *Young lady.* Right. Moira was at least ten years younger, half Jane's size (and weight), and twice the brains. Calling Moira a silly bitch was only half right. "Fuck! I don't need this now. You don't have *any* idea what it's about?"

"Um . . ."

"Come on, Moira, you and the boss are practically littermates. Spill."

"Let's just say that in his newfound happiness with mate and cub, our fearless leader thinks it's high time you settled down—"

"No, no, *no!*"

"—and he's met *just* the right fella for you," she continued brightly. "He's sure you'll hit it off."

"Doesn't the head of the pack have anything better to do than fix me up on yet another stupid blind date?" She could hear plastic cracking and forced her fingers to loosen around the receiver.

"Apparently not. Now tell the truth; the last one wasn't so bad."

"He cried like a third-grade girl when I beat him to the kill."

"Well, you *did* hog all the rabbits yourself. *Tsk, tsk.*"

"Figures," Jane grumbled, swinging her legs over and resting her feet on the floor. "The first halfway decent guy I meet in forever, and the boss wants me to blow him off to meet some new dildo."

"Sorry," Moira said, sounding anything but. "I'll leave the dildo part out when I tell Michael you're on the way. And now, having imparted my message, I'd say something like 'have a nice day,' except I know you—"

"Hate that shit. Bye." She hung up and resisted the urge to throw the phone against the wall. Fuck. Fuck fuck!

She'd been so excited about dinner with Dick, she'd had a hard time getting to sleep. She'd finally dozed off near dawn . . . and slept the entire day away. Now she had to beat feet for the Cape of all places . . . fuck!

She did throw the phone. But it didn't make her feel any better, not even when it shattered spectacularly against the wall.

+ + +

She was tapping her foot on the curb, waiting for the slothlike doorman to hail her a cab. She could hail her own damned cab, thanks very much, but when in Rome, do what the sheep do. Or something like that.

She'd packed like a madwoman, and it showed—she could see the corner of her dress sticking out of the suitcase. *Aarrggh!* Fifty-nine ninety-nine at Sears, and she'd probably never get to wear it again. Like clothes shopping wasn't an unending horror anyway—now she'd have to go *again*.

And Dick. She felt really bad about up and leaving town. He'd think she stood him up. Like *that* would happen. He was ridiculously good-looking but, even more important, she could talk to him. Not be herself—not completely—but close.

Shit, she couldn't even be herself with the pack; they'd written her off as an old maid a decade ago. Pack members mated young, dropped kids young, and died young. And she didn't want kids, which, among her people, made her *El Freako Supremo*.

Getting knocked up—assuming your mate could get you pregnant without getting his bad self hurt—was one thing, but then you were a slumlord to a fetus for ten endless months. At least the humans only had to suffer for nine. Even worse, you puffed up like a blowfish and ate everything in sight, then squeezed out a kid during hours of blood and pain . . . *blurgh.*

And afterward! Just the thought of having to tote around a nose-miner who cried and screamed and puked and shit—and that was just the first week!—was enough to curl her hair. She hadn't liked kids even when she was one. The feeling had been mutually—and heartily—returned. She'd felt that way at eighteen, twenty-three, thirty, thirty-four. Sure, kids were necessary—for other people. Janet preferred to sleep late, wear clothes that hadn't been puked on, and not watch her language.

"Where to, ma'am?" the doorman asked, breaking her anti-infant reverie. He was ineffectually flapping a hand at the occasional cab. She could have hailed four on her own by now. Shit, she could have *jogged* to the airport by now.

"Logan," she practically snapped. It wasn't Door Boy's fault she'd been ordered to leave town, but the big boss wasn't here for her to take her anger out on him. "Quick as you can."

She thought about leaving a note for Dick and reluctantly decided against it. Better find out what Boss Man Michael wanted first. And if it wasn't life and death, she'd let him have it. Who gave a rat's ass if he was the pack leader? She had a life. Well, before yesterday she really hadn't, but *he* didn't know that. It was his privilege to snap his fingers and have any one of them come at a dead run, but it was hers not to like it.

She observed the doorman shivering and realized the sun had nearly set, and the temperature had dropped a good ten degrees. Still, it wasn't *that* cold. And why did the kid look like he was ready to drop a steaming load into his trousers? She was irritated, but not at him . . . surely he knew that.

God, the reek the kid was giving off! Like mothballs dipped in gasoline. His fear—his terror—burned her nose. It put her wind up, and she cupped her elbows, shivering. From grumpy to edgy in less than five seconds . . . a new record!

The ball dropped, and she understood a half second too late. She was spun around and had time to take in burning blue eyes before there was a walloping pain in her jaw and Dick turned off the lights. And everything else.

Chapter 4

He didn't care. He really didn't. She was fine, and if she wasn't, who cared? He hadn't hurt her. Not really.

He checked on her for the eleventh time in sixty minutes and was relieved to see the bruise on the underside of her jaw had faded to a mere shadow. Guilt rolled off his shoulders like a boulder.

To save time and steps—if he left he'd just be in here five minutes later—he sat down in the chair beside the bed. He cupped his chin in his hand, leaned forward, and watched her sleep.

Jane scowled, even in the throes of unconsciousness. It would have made him smile if he hadn't felt so angry and betrayed.

Betrayed? All right, tell the truth and shame the devil . . . yes. *Betrayed!* And angry and sick at heart and *furious* with the little twit tied to his bed. Most of his anger was directed at himself, it was true, but he had a nice helping saved for Miss Jane.

She'd fooled him; that was all. A simple thing, but unforgivable. She made him believe she accepted the monster, when in fact she most assuredly had not. The duplicitous wretch agreed to join him for dinner to placate him and then made arrangements to slink out of town like a thief. If he hadn't shown up early to escort her to dinner, she would have disappeared and he might never have known what had become of her. He would have wasted years of his life worrying about her fate.

Instead, he'd taken in the situation at a glance and acted accordingly. Well, all right, that was a rather large lie. He had panicked—all he could think of was to get her home, stop her from leaving him. Leaving *town*, rather. And in his panic, he'd smacked her when he only meant to tap her. The one bit of luck was that it had happened too quickly for the lone witness—the doorman—to see much more than a swirl of cloth. Dusk and speed were his friends, even if Jane was not.

And that was the rub of it. He'd allowed himself to forget, for one evening, that he was the monster in the fairy tales. He had forgotten there could be no relationship with a woman other than the most carnal type. He wouldn't have vampire women, and mortal women wouldn't have him. Well, that was fine. That was just fine.

He was a monster, and he was done pretending otherwise.

But Jane would pay for making him forget. She'd pay for making him think, however briefly, that he was a man first and a beast second.

Chapter 5

Jane groaned and tried to roll over. The phone was ringing. It would be Moira, telling her to get her ass to the Cape. She couldn't see Dick tonight. She had to answer the phone and tell Moira to go fuck herself, and then—

Wait.

That had already happened. So why was she still in bed?

She opened her eyes and tried to sit up. Three alarming facts registered immediately on her brain: 1) she couldn't sit up, and 2) she was tied to a bed. She was, in fact, 3) tied down in the same room with an annoyed vampire. And not a prayer of room service.

"Ohhhhhh, you *idiot!*" she howled. If she could have slapped her hand over her eyes, she would have. If she could have slapped *him,* she would have. As it was, her ankles and arms were spread wide and tied to each poster of the bed. "Do you have any idea of the trouble you've landed me in, numb nuts?"

Dick, sitting in the chair next to the bed, blinked at her. He did that a lot . . . a long, slow, thoughtful blink when he was taken by surprise. It was like a stall for time or something. She thought it was kind of cute yesterday. "I shouldn't have expected maidenly protestations," he said after a long pause.

"You *should* expect a fractured skull, you undead idiot! What the *fuck* am I doing tied to your bed? *Is* it your bed? It damn well better be your bed! If I'm in some strange dead guy's bed, your ass is grass!"

He brought a hand up to his chin . . . and then got up and

abruptly left. She used the chance to yank at her bonds—no good. They were soft, like cloth, but amazingly strong. Were her bonds lined with bubble gum or what?

She strained to hear and, very faintly, could hear muffled laughter coming from about thirty feet away. Dick had trotted out to the hall to have a giggle at her expense—fucking great.

The door was thrown open a moment later, and when Dick returned, he was stone-faced. "Sorry about that. I thought I left something on the stove. Now where were we?"

She kicked out at him. The bonds let her leg leave the bed, but not by much. "We were talking about how you're going to die a painful and horrible death—again! What the hell have you trussed me up with?"

The left side of his mouth twitched. "It's elastic lined with titanium wire. It won't hurt you if you pull on it, but it's impossible to break. Even I have trouble breaking it, and I'm quite a bit stronger than you are."

Wanna bet, Dead Man Walking? "Do you have any idea— *aarrgh!* I'm supposed to be meeting my boss right this minute! What time is it?"

"About two A.M."

"*Aaaarrrgggghhh!* Jerk! I'm five hours late!"

"Another date?" he asked silkily.

"No, Deaf and Undead, I *told* you. My boss called—well, *he* didn't call, one of his lackeys did—and told me to get to the office, pronto. And when he says jump, we *leap,* dude. I didn't have time to leave you a note, but I would have come back!"

"Sure you would have."

Jane was so annoyed, she felt like biting herself. Instead, she yanked impotently on her bonds again. "Yes I would have, dill-hole!"

"Your boss calls you on a weekend, and you must drop everything and race to his side? Really, Janet. I was expecting a better story than that."

She snarled at him. If he made her much madder, she'd start barking at the goddamned ceiling. "Jesus, to think I was actually looking forward to seeing you! And this is how you take rejection . . . pervert!"

Something flashed in his eyes then. Way down deep. She was suddenly reminded of the lake back home she used to do laps in. The blue water was pretty and inviting, but the lake was spring-fed and freezing cold, even in July. You didn't know how cold it was until you committed yourself and jumped. Then you were stuck, and you got moving or you froze.

"So you admit you rejected me?"

"No, doorknob! I told you the truth. You can believe it, or you can go fuck yourself."

"Is there a third choice?"

"Yes . . . untie me so I can make a phone call!"

"I decline."

"You can't just keep me here like a . . . a . . . ." She practically spat the word. "Like a *pet* or something."

"Can't I?"

Suddenly he was standing over her, casually unbuttoning his shirt and sliding it off his shoulders. Her eyes widened until they felt like they were practically bulging. "What the hell are you doing?"

"You're a bright girl. You'll figure it out in a minute."

"Don't you *dare!*"

"I dare much, now that my heart—" He cut himself off abruptly, and she heard the click of his teeth coming together. What the hell was going *on* with this guy?

Off came the trousers, the socks, the underwear. Nude, Dick was exceedingly yummy . . . long legs, broad shoulders, and a tasty flat stomach that made her think about hot fudge sauce and whipped cream. His chest was lightly furred with blond hair two shades darker than the hair on his head. His muscle definition was excellent, and she had a sudden, maddening urge to touch him to see if his skin was as smooth as it looked. It would be, she thought, like velvet encased in steel. Or marble . . . he was quite pale.

He reached out and flipped off the light . . . *click.* She consciously dilated her pupils and could see him again, a pale blur in the dark. A blur with glittering blue eyes.

She felt his cool hand on her thigh and then his fingers were nimbly unbuttoning her dress. She kicked out again, to no avail. He popped open the clasp on her bra—stupid front clasps!—and with odd care, gently tore her panties down the middle. She hissed at him. Twelve bucks at Victoria's Secret! The bitch's secret was that she marked up her underwear by six hundred percent!

"You are an asshole," she said clearly.

"True enough." He pulled her panties free, spread her dress wide, and then pushed her bra out of the way. "Umm. Very nice."

"Go fuck yourself, perv."

"I'd rather not . . . besides, *you're* here, so why should I have to? We have hours until sunrise." He chuckled. It sounded like cold water flowing over black rocks. "And Jane . . . I'm sooooo hungry. I've been waiting and waiting for you to wake up."

"I hope I poison you. I hope you choke until your lungs explode. I hope my blood burns your windpipe. I hope—"

"I get the gist. *I* hope the next time you agree to spend the evening with me, you keep your word." Then he was on her so suddenly she didn't have time to pull in air for a gasp. She braced herself as best she could for his brutal entry, for teeth and blood and pain. *Oh, when I get out of here I'm going to use your vertebrae for dice. See if I don't. And I won't cry, either. So there.*

His mouth skimmed her jaw, and she felt him lick her jugular and nibble gently at the tender flesh. His cool hand closed over her breast, pressed against her warm flesh, and she felt her nipple harden against his palm. Then he was kissing her throat, the middle of her chest, and her stomach. She felt his thumbs on her cunt, spreading her wide, and she felt his tongue snake inside her. The shock of it nearly bent her up off the bed. His mouth was cool but quickly warmed, and she flinched back, thinking of his sharp canines.

But there was nothing to fear—or there was, but she quickly forgot it as waves of heat started from her crotch and radiated upward. His tongue was flicking in and out of her little tunnel, stabbing her clit, and then he pulled back and licked . . . excruciatingly slow licks that made her shake. She gritted her teeth as hard as she could and locked away the sounds she wanted to make. So he wasn't being a hard guy—fine. This still wasn't her idea. It still wasn't any different from smacking her around or shoving her up against a dirty alley wall or—or—

He stopped. He pulled back. She started to relax but then felt the sharp sting as his teeth broke the skin over her femoral artery. She gasped—she couldn't help it—and tried to jerk away, but his hands held her fast.

His fingers smoothed the soft pelt between her thighs and then he was parting her lips again and stroking her throbbing clit. One of his fingers dipped inside her while his thumb pressed gentle circles around her increasingly slick flesh. Meanwhile, his mouth was busy on her inner thigh, and she could hear soft sucking.

This went on and on . . . she quickly lost track of time. She was screaming inside. Whenever she started to get close, he somehow knew and his fingers would still or pull away entirely. His mouth *never* stopped. Then he'd resume again, careful not to push her over the edge. After a while she still wasn't making any sounds, but the bed shook with her trembling.

At last he was sated. He pulled back and then bent to her and gave her a long, leisurely lick. "Ummm. You're so wet. I love that. And you taste *soooo* good. Everywhere, it seems. Your blood is really rich. What on earth have you been eating?"

She ground her teeth at him for answer. She felt his pelvis settle over hers, heard him chuckle. "Your rage could set the room on fire—better than being cold, I think?"

She didn't dignify that with an answer. Besides, if she opened her mouth—what might she say? She was horribly afraid she might ask—beg—to be fucked. Hard. For a long, long time. Her cunt throbbed. Her thigh throbbed. It wasn't pain; it was sheer yearning. She had never needed to come so badly.

When she felt him start to enter her, it took every ounce, every drop of her willpower not to strain to meet him. She resisted by listing his many odious offenses inside her head.

That part of him was warm. And hard, and huge. His cock was parting her slowly and gently, and she had a quick thought: *He has to be gentle . . . he wasn't a few times before, and he hurt his partner. That's how he knows to tongue fuck first.* But that thought spiraled away into confusion as he shoved, and she felt him slam into her. She made a sound, some small sound, and his mouth was instantly on hers. She could taste her lust, and her blood, and then he was whispering into her mouth, "I couldn't help that, I'm sorry— am I hurting you?" His hands were fisting in her hair, he was groaning and thrusting, and her breath was coming in harsh gasps.

"Please," she groaned. "Please—" *Don't stop. Don't ever stop. Harder. More. Faster. Please. Please. Please.*

He groaned, too. "I wanted to hurt you but not like . . . I'll make it up to you, my own—" She heard him grind his teeth . . . and then he stopped so suddenly he was rigid with the strain of it. She was afraid to move, to breathe, but it didn't matter. He did the unthinkable anyway—slowly pulled out of her. She closed her eyes and whimpered as he went, hating herself for it even as she knew she could have done nothing to quell the sound.

"Jane. Tell the truth, love. Am I hurting you?" She felt his hand caress her cheek and opened her eyes. His teeth were set so hard his jaw trembled. Here was a perfect opportunity for revenge. And she couldn't do it.

"Twice," she whispered.

He bent closer and dropped a kiss to her shoulder. "What?"

"Twice. This is my second time. Ever. In my life."

"You—*what?*" She could have laughed at his horrified expression if she hadn't been ready to claw his eyes out for not letting her come. "Oh, Christ! I had no—I thought you—you seemed so tough I was sure—"

Tough? Sure. Real tough. She'd grown a shell around her soul the night she lost her virginity. The night she, in her ardor, broke her lover's back. It had happened on the last day of her freshmen year in college, and her then-boyfriend, as far as she knew, was still in a wheelchair. It was the first and last time she'd chosen someone who wasn't pack. It was, in fact, the last time she'd chosen anyone, until tonight. And she hasn't exactly chosen this, had she?

"You can't say *Christ,*" she whispered. "You're a vampire."

"One of the many myths," he whispered back. He stroked her hair. She could feel his cock on her leg, throbbing impatiently. *It* didn't give a fuck if she was hurt or not. It had business to get back to. And so did she. "Jane, why did you try to run away from me?"

"I didn't, dimwad. I told you the truth."

"Hmm."

"Now will you *please* finish and untie me?"

"Pick one."

She nearly screamed. "What?"

"Pick one." He tapped her clit with a teasing finger. "And I'll do it." He kissed her again. He ducked down and licked her nipple and then sucked, hard. In their bonds, her hands curled into fists. "Whichever one. I'll do it. Thoroughly."

"I hate you," she nearly sobbed.

"I know."

"Finish."

"Oh, thank God." In an instant he was pushing his way inside her again, and for a half second, she understood why he had been concerned—the friction was delightful, *so* delightful, it was just this side of pain. Then he was pumping his hips against hers, and it became more than delightful; it was exquisite.

"Kiss me back," he said into her mouth. "Give me your tongue."

Half-blind from the swamping pleasure, she did so. He sucked on it in time with his thrusts, and she could hear someone making high, whimpering noises and realized with amazement it was *her* making those silly bitch sounds. The bed thumped in time with their fucking and then he tore his mouth from hers. "Now," he hissed in her ear, "come now." Then he pinched her nipple, hard, and that spun her into the most powerful orgasm of her life. She could actually feel the spasms ripple through her uterus, and the world got dark and fuzzy around the edges for a few moments. Above her he stiffened, and for a moment his grip was painful. "God, my God, Jane!" Then he shuddered all over, and he relaxed as she felt him spurt deeply inside her.

She dozed for a few minutes—it had been a stressful few days. She came all the way awake when she realized he was stroking her lower lip with his thumb. "Get the fuck off me *now*."

"Ah, you're back. I thought you were being uncharacteristically quiet."

"Off. Now. Hate you. Kill you."

He burst out laughing, which did nothing for her temper. She strained mightily and managed to roll him off her. "I'm sorry, love, it's rude to laugh. But most women in your position would be fetal with shock, sobbing into the bedspread. All *you* can think about is how to get your teeth into me."

"And how you might taste," she added silkily.

"Umm . . . well, there are ways to answer *that* question . . ."

"Anything you put in my mouth, you're gonna lose."

He sighed. "I suppose it was too good to last. Pity we're only compatible in bed."

"Compatible in—you *raped* me, asswipe! Do you have any idea what my family is going to *do* to you? What *I'm* going to do to you?"

"I did rape you." He tweaked one of her nipples. "At first."

She blushed with shame. He saw it, and it moved him whereas her death threats did not. "No, you're right—I forced you. None of this was your idea. You're still tied up, for heaven's sake. You don't have anything to feel guilty about."

She was, absurdly, grateful for the lie. Not that she had any intention of showing it. "I feel very guilty that I didn't break your neck in that alley when I had the chance. *Now let me go!*"

"Sorry, Jane. You had your chance to be free, and you chose to stay."

"I did *not*—"

"So stay you will, and just like this, until . . ."

"Oh, what, *what?* Christ, you're driving me crazy!"

". . . until you agree to be my wife."

Long silence, broken by, "You're on drugs."

"Only if you are. Is that why your blood is so rich? God, it was like wine. I don't think I've ever felt better," he said giddily. "I had planned to fuck you and eat you and turn you out into the street in the wee hours of the morning without so much as an 'I'll call you,' but now I'll never, never let you go. You're a rare jewel, Jane. An emerald, a ruby."

"I'm tied to the bed next to a crazy person," she mused aloud. Thinking, *Never drank from a werewolf before, eh, buddy? Interesting. If you become addicted to me, that could be useful.* "And as far as being your wife—you've probably heard this from all your *other* rape victims, but I'd rather be dead."

"Undead," he said brightly. "Well, we've got time for that. You're still in your prime. Although I have no intention of becoming a widower in forty or fifty years."

"What?"

"Oh, I won't insist upon it right away, but probably within the next ten years or so, I'll definitely have to turn you into a vampire."

An undead werewolf? What's next, Frankenstein's Monster coming over for dinner? "You're out of your fucking mind."

"Apparently so," he said cheerfully, kissed her, and left her.

Chapter 6

Richard knocked modestly—absurd, given what he had just done to her—and opened the door. She was staring at the ceiling and didn't look at him when he came in. He nibbled his lower lip and tried to distract himself from the sight of the lovely Janet, spread-eagled on his bed. It was amazing—he'd just spent over an hour with her, but he could have taken her right this minute. And again. And then again.

He was carrying a tray full of savories. She smelled it and sat up as much as her bonds would allow. "Feeding time at the zoo," Jane said moodily. The spot on her thigh where he'd fed from her was purpling. He stifled an urge to kiss it and beg her forgiveness. *She lied,* he reminded himself. *And you're the monster.*

"Oh, hush. No one in a zoo eats so well. See? Lobster bisque, biscuits, a steak, and milk. And if you eat everything, chocolate ice cream."

"That's a ridiculous amount of food," she said, staring at the tray.

"I've seen you eat, my love. I'm going to let you out of your bonds, but before you hit me over the head with the tray and flee for the hills, I should explain that there are no fewer than three bolted doors—all English oak—between you and the street. You'd never get through them all before being caught. And you must be starving. Surely it's more prudent to eat and plot revenge, right?"

She drummed her fingers on the bedspread and stared up at him. Her eyes went narrow and flinty, but at last she said, "I'm starving."

"Eat, and then a hot bath . . . sound good?"

"And then what?"

"And then agree to be my wife."

"Don't," she practically snarled, "start with that again, dick-lick."

"Ah, a blushingly modest bride, how refreshing. I can see you're contemplating homicide—try not to spill the soup."

He set the tray down on the table and unsnapped her ankle bonds. Then he seized the footboard and tugged the bed away from the wall. She could have done the same thing herself, but she couldn't help but be impressed—not bad for an undead monkey. He walked to the headboard, reached behind it, and in a few seconds had her wrists freed. She was off the bed in a bound, pulled off the shreds of her clothes and let them flutter to the floor, and then made a beeline for the tray.

"I brought you a robe—"

"Who cares?" she said with a mouthful of biscuit. "You've already seen me naked."

"Uh—" *You're gorgeous. You're distracting. If you prance around in that sweet little body you'll have your hands full. You have soup on your chin.* "As you wish."

He sat down across from her and watched her eat. She ate like a machine, seeming to take no enjoyment from the meal. *Refueling, the better to kick my ass. Well, so be it.* He deserved that, and more. And he was a fast healer. Let her do her worst. "Why did you break our date?" he asked abruptly and surprised even himself—he had no idea he was going to say such a thing until it was done.

She grunted irritably. "We've been over this."

"Jane . . ." Again, he had no idea what would come out of his mouth, but he plunged ahead anyway. "Jane, if you tell the truth, I'll unlock those three doors and walk you back to your hotel. Just admit that you were afraid of me, that you were only pretending to accept what I am, and—"

Her gaze locked on his like a laser. "My name is Janet Lupo," she said coldly. "I'm not afraid of any man. And. I. Don't. Lie."

He actually felt the chill coming off her. Absurd! She was half his size, even if she had twice the mouth. Her gaze was odd, almost hypnotic. With difficulty, he broke her challenging stare. "Well," he said at last, "perhaps you can understand why I have difficulty believing that your 'boss' would insist on your free time, and why you would have to drop everything and rush to meet him at a moment's notice."

"Pack rules."

"Beg pardon?"

"Pack . . . rules . . . dumb . . . fuck. Am I stuttering? I'm a werewolf. My boss is the head werewolf."

He laughed and then ducked as her soup bowl sailed over his head. "Oh, come now, Janet! Because you know I am a vampire, you've decided I'll believe you're a werewolf? I'm *that* gullible? There's no such thing, and you know it well."

"Says the bloodsucker!"

He was still chuckling. "Nice try."

"If you could think about something besides your dick for five seconds, you'd see it makes sense. My strength, my speed . . ."

"All well within the range for *Homo sapiens* . . . albeit the high end."

"You've been dead too long, Dick. The average *homo loser* can barely lift the remote control. My rich blood? That's from a diet high in protein. *Raw* protein, during the full moon."

"Ah, the full moon. It's a few days away, but I suppose I had better take care when—"

She slammed her fork down; the table trembled and then was still. "The full moon is eight days away. And when it comes, you're going to get a big fucking surprise. Your little oak doors won't hold me then. I'll be out of here—possibly eating your head on my way out the door—and you'll realize you fucked up, bad. You'll know I was telling the truth the whole time, but you couldn't see past your stupid injured male pride. I'll be gone forever, and you'll have the next hundred years to realize what an asshole you were."

She was so convincing, he actually panicked for a moment. To add drama to her little speech, she stopped eating, walked to the bed, got under the covers, and faced away from him the rest of the night. She never said another word, or looked at him, not even when he tempted her with a brimming bowl of frozen custard.

Chapter 7

He was right. The doors—this one, anyway—were oak. Thick and heavy, with the hinges on the outside where she couldn't get at them. She threw her shoulder a few times—okay, thirty—into the door, but it barely rocked in its frame. "Fucking Brit wood," she mumbled, rubbing her aching shoulder.

She'd prowled around her cage for the last couple hours. It was a gorgeous room with plush, wine-colored carpet, a soft queen-sized bed with about a zillion pillows, and a truly glorious attached bathroom (free of all razors and other sharp things, she was sorry to note). But as far as Janet was concerned, if you couldn't leave, it might as well have a cement floor and bars on the window.

She went through the bureau and found several robes in her size, in various materials. No real clothes. No television, either, but several books. She saw some classics—Shakespeare, Mark Twain, and Tolstoy—as well as—too funny!—the entire collected works of Stephen King. She supposed she might stand half a chance if she threw *Hamlet* at Dick as hard as she could. She'd gotten the drop on him before in the alley, but she wondered if it was possible now. He didn't believe she was a werewolf, the stupid dickhead, but he'd be careful. He thought she was one of the monkeys, but he respected her anyway. If he wasn't such a fuckstick, she could have really liked him.

She wondered what the pack was thinking—what boss man Michael was thinking. Probably that she'd been run over by a train or something. Death was about the only acceptable reason for skipping a meeting with the big dog. Interestingly, that thought—she'd unwillingly disobeyed a command from her pack leader—brought no anxiety. In fact, it was kind of nice, knowing Michael wanted her on the Cape, and here she was, still in Boston.

If only Dick hadn't been such a beast. If only he hadn't been so *nice* about being such a beast—he might have wanted to really hurt her, but he sucked at it. She remembered him pulling out of her when he thought he was too big for her . . . remembered the excellent food, and the large quantities of it. The absurd marriage proposal. Absurd because . . . well, just because.

If he wasn't such a dick, she could start to like him. But nobody—fucking *nobody*—snatched Janet Lupo from the street, tied her down like a dog, and did whatever he wanted. He'd pay. She would have to wait for her chance, but it would eventually present itself. And then he'd better watch out for his guts, because she meant to have them on the floor.

+ + +

The smell of eggs basted in butter woke her up. Before she could open her eyes, she realized Dick was under the blankets with her. Then she felt his mouth on her neck and felt brief pain as his fangs broke the skin. She tried to push him away, but he pinned her down and held her to the bed while he drank. She had no leverage and could only lie beneath him while he took from her.

"You piece of shit," she said directly into his ear.

He laughed against her throat. "That's the problem, Jane m'love. If you screamed or fainted or cried, I'd have no interest in you—I'd want to be rid of you as quickly as possible. But you're fearless, and furious, and it works on me like an aphrodisiac. Which is why you *have* to be my wife."

"I'd rather eat my own heart."

He licked the bite mark on her neck and then nuzzled the tender spot. "That's a rather disturbing visual. Did you sleep well? I admit I was astonished you weren't lying in wait ready to strangle me with the sash from one of your robes."

"I'd rather wait until you dropped your guard. Then you'll be sorry," she said with total confidence.

He rested his forehead against hers. "God, you're delightful."

"I'm going to skin you alive, you fucking undead monkey. Then I'm going to set your skin on fire. Then I'm going to roast your skinless body over the fire I made with your skin."

"And so ladylike, too! Umm . . ." His cool mouth closed over one of her nipples, and she brought her fist down on top of his head, hard. Then she yelped when he bit her. "Sorry," he said, rubbing the top of his head. "That was you, not me. You hit me so hard my teeth nearly clacked together."

"Just you wait," she said ominously.

He kissed her wrist, her pulse point, and then the crook of her elbow. She balled a fist and got ready to sock him again.

"Jane, as delightful as last night was—for me, anyway—I'd rather not tie you up again." She punched him square in the face, a poor blow with her lack of leverage, but his head rocked back, which was gratifying. He went on as if nothing had happened. "So let's make a deal, you and I. I won't tie you up, and you won't fight me. As of now," he amended.

"You won't tie me up?" she asked suspiciously. "But I have to let you fuck me?"

He looked pained. "Yes, you have to let me fuck you."

She pretended to think it over, but it was an easy decision. She could stand almost anything but being tied down. It went against her very nature and made her want to bite somebody. "Okay. I won't punch, and you won't get out the elastic bubble gum."

"And you'll kiss me back."

"Forget it."

"All right, then, I will do all the kissing for both of us." He smiled at her, put a hand on the back of her neck, and pulled her to him.

"What, I can't eat first? This deal blows."

"Later, Jane. I'm begging you." His mouth was slightly warm, and his tongue slipped past her teeth to stroke her own tongue. She felt his hand cup one of her breasts, testing the weight of it, and then his thumb was rubbing her nipple.

She wriggled, pushing more of her breast into his palm. "So the quicker you get off, the quicker I can have eggs?"

He sighed. "You're really killing the mood here."

"What mood? I'm a prisoner, for fuck's sake. And I'm hungry," she whined.

"Oh, for—" But he let go of her and she bounded off the bed. She wolfed down her breakfast—eggs, six strips of bacon, four pieces of toast, and two glasses of milk—in five minutes while he laid on the bed and watched her with his fingers laced behind his head and a mildly disbelieving look on his face. She got up, wiped her mouth with a napkin, tossed it over her shoulder, and climbed back into bed.

"All right, then," she said, infinitely more cheerful.

He smiled at her. "All right, then." He reached out, took her hand, and led her to the bathroom.

Ten minutes later, they were in his giant bathtub and the floor was soaked. Her legs were spread wide and resting on each rim of the tub, and she was gripping the sides so tightly her knuckles ached. Richard was beneath the water, nuzzling and tonguing and fingering her cunt. He'd been down there for five minutes, and she was about ready to lose her fucking mind.

Now his tongue was inside her, and one of his fingers was worming into her ass. She'd never been interested in assplay—the idea had always grossed her out—but the sensation of his long finger sliding up inside her while his tongue darted and stabbed and licked her cunt made her throb. She had no control over her reflexes, she simply started to thrust her hips at his face. Her muffled groans (for her teeth were tightly clenched) bounced off the bathroom tile.

He rose, water dripping down his marble-white skin, and grinned at her. He pulled her up to him and growled, "*Now* you'll kiss me."

She did, without hesitation. He sucked her tongue into his mouth as he pushed her thighs wide, as he took himself in hand and rubbed his cock against her sopping cunt. She moaned into his mouth and strained toward him. He tore his mouth from hers, sought her neck, and she felt him bite her just as his cock thrust inside her. The combination of sensations—slight pain, swamping pleasure—made her come so hard she bucked against him, and another gallon of water sloshed over the side of the tub.

"Ummmm," he said against her throat. "Oh, that's very good. I could do this all day."

"Better . . . not . . ." she managed. "It'll kill me."

He laughed and leaned back. She was still spread up against the sloping end of the tub; they were connected only by his cock. He ran his hands over her soapy breasts, smiling as she groaned again. "Oh, you *are* going to marry me," he said huskily. "Believe it."

"Why don't you . . . stop talking . . . and finish fucking?"

He grinned, flashing fangs, and obliged. When he finished, she was indecently satisfied, and there were only a few inches of water left in the tub.

✦   ✦   ✦

Later, he brought a second breakfast. "After that half an hour," he explained, "even *I* could eat a few more eggs."

"Not bad for a dead guy," she said casually, pretending she wasn't still throbbing. The man had a fiendish touch between the sheets—or in the tub—and that was a fact. "I'm sure the ladies like you all right, when you're not being such a jerkoff."

He didn't answer, but just sat down across from her and watched her eat. After a few minutes, he started drumming his fingers on the table.

"Yeah, *that's* not gonna get annoying. The kidnapping and the fucking I can take, but not the nervous tics. Cut it out."

"Why only twice?"

"What?"

He was nibbling thoughtfully on his lower lip and watching her. "Why was last night only your second time? You're in your thirties. You should have had hundreds of experiences by now. It can't be a dislike for the act itself—you're sexy, responsive, and open to new experiences. So what's the explanation?"

Her mouth was suddenly dry—weird!—and she gulped some juice. "None of your goddamned business."

"Did he hurt you? Because if he did, I'd be delighted to track him down for you and teach him a richly deserved—"

"Am I speaking a language you don't know? I said it was none of your business." Her hand was shaking. She put down the juice glass with a bang and hid her hands under the table. "And even if it was, I don't want to talk about it. Especially with you."

His eyes were narrow, thoughtful. "Ah . . . *you* hurt *him*. And felt needless guilt ever since—Jane, for heaven's sake. Whatever you did, it was an accident. You didn't mean it."

"Are you deaf? I said I *don't want to talk about it!*" The glass zoomed at his head; he ducked, and it slammed into the far wall. Orange juice and broken glass sprayed everywhere.

"All right," he said calmly. "We won't talk about it."

Her hands weren't the only thing shaking. She grabbed her elbows and squeezed; she clenched her teeth to stop them from chattering. She was morbidly afraid she might puke, and soon.

He got up from his chair, came to her, and scooped her up as if she was a child. For a wonder, she didn't try to pull his eyeballs out of his head. "You're tired," he soothed. "You've had a rotten week. Why don't you take a nap?"

"Why don't you go fuck yourself?"

"Can't we do both?"

She chuckled unwillingly.

Chapter 8

Two nights before the full moon, and she was actually torn.

Torn! It was almost like she was dreading her impending escape. Which only proved a steady diet of rich food and amazing sex lowered IQ points.

Every day, he asked her to tell him the truth, promising to let her go if she did. And every day, she told him the truth . . . a lie would have choked her. She hadn't broken their date by choice. She had wanted to see him again. And she almost didn't hate him.

That one she kept to herself.

He hadn't tied her up since that first night. And she hadn't tried to attack him. Another example of her quickly lowering IQ. When they were between the sheets (or in the bathtub, or on the floor in front of the fireplace), the last thing on her mind was leaving. But far more disturbing, when they weren't between the sheets, the last thing on her mind was leaving.

And it wasn't that she was thinking with her pussy instead of her brain. Well, it wasn't *just* that. Because to be perfectly honest, what exactly, was she going back to? To be at Mikey's beck and call? To hang out with a group of people who disapproved of her and then go home to her lonely bed? The pack didn't much want her, and she sure as shit didn't want someone who wasn't pack, someone who was fragile—who would break if she really let loose.

Dick fit the bill admirably, and he approved of her—to the hilt! He thought everything she did and said was swell. She could have farted on him, and he would have rhapsodized about it. In fact, she did . . . after a particularly strenuous sexual marathon and when she was relaxing in his embrace. Relaxing a little too well, in fact—she really cut one. Quick as thought, she pulled the blankets over Dick's head, trapping him with the noxious odor. Cursing, he finally freed himself and then they both laughed until they cried.

She rolled over on her back and stared at the ceiling. It was getting rapidly dark in the bedroom; the sun would be down in a few more minutes. She'd adjusted nicely to his schedule and now slept her days away. Frankly, she preferred his schedule—she'd never been much of an early riser.

He'd be here any minute. Any minute. She felt a tightening in her stomach and was disgusted with herself. Just thinking about him—about his long fingers and his mouth and his tongue and his cock—was making her wet. Some prisoner. Now she had Stockholm Syndrome. Except it was more like Bimbo Hypnotized by Bad Guy's Huge Cock Syndrome.

And then later he would bring amazing food, and they'd talk about everything and anything. And he'd read to her—they were halfway through *Salem's Lot,* which he seemed to think was a comedy—while she paced. She liked books but couldn't stand to sit still for the hours and hours required to read one. Or they'd wrestle, and once she'd thrown the leftover apple pie at him and they'd had a food fight that ruined the drapes.

Jane sighed. If it was *just* his dick, it wouldn't be so bad. She could always buy a vibrator. No, it was *Dick.* She really, really liked him, more than any guy she'd ever known, and she knew a lot of fellas. And she was having a helluva time remembering she was a prisoner. In fact, she didn't think Dick remembered much, either.

+ + +

Her vision doubled, trebled . . . and then her knees buckled. Luckily, she was bent over the footboard, so she had some support.

Dick let go of her waist and pulled her back onto the bed. "That was . . . sweaty." Panting lightly, he flopped over on the pillows. "Jane, your stamina knows no bounds. Look at me; I'm actually out of breath. And I don't even need to breathe."

"My stamina? Look who's talking. We've been at it since—holy shit, the sun's gonna be up in another hour. You'd better beat feet back to the coffin, old man."

He snorted. "It's a bed, not a coffin. It's one of the guest beds, in fact. *You're* in my coffin, so to speak."

"So why don't you sleep here?"

"I've been thinking about it." He propped himself up on one elbow, bent to kiss her shoulder, and then said, "More and more, actually. In the beginning, I dared not leave myself at your mercy, but now I wonder."

"What the hell are you talking about? You take longer to say something than anyone I've ever met."

He didn't smile at her bitching like he usually did. "I'd be quite helpless, Janet. If you, ah, decided to be angry, there's nothing I could do until the sun went down. And the tables in here are all made out of wood . . . so are the chairs. It wouldn't be difficult for someone with your determination to fashion a rudimentary stake."

She'd never thought of that. She couldn't believe she'd never thought of that. "Oh." She mulled it over for a minute and then said, "Well, I don't especially want to stake you in the guts."

"The guts I wouldn't mind so much. How about the heart?"

She rolled over and rested her chin on his chest. "There either. I dunno, you're okay. When you're not being a total shit. Stay, go, I don't give a fuck."

"Well, I can hardly turn down such a warm invitation." Still, he glanced nervously at the table in the corner before climbing under the covers. "Ah, well, here goes nothing. Climb in next to me."

"I have chicken grease under my nails," she pointed out.

"So we'll take a nice hot shower together later tonight."

"Sounds like, a date." She snuggled in next to him and rested her head on his shoulder. His body was still slightly warm from their earlier exertions and, as she pressed closer to him, remained that way.

"Ahhhhh," he sighed. "You're better than my electric blanket."

"That's the nicest thing anyone's ever said to me. You should write for fuckin' soap operas," she grumbled, but inside she was glowing. He was trusting her with his life. He knew he was easy prey, and he was going to sleep anyway. It spoke volumes about his true feelings for her . . . and her status as his "prisoner."

Well, shit, she thought, drifting into sleep. Her palm rested over his heart, which beat once or twice every minute. *Maybe there's hope for us after all.*

Chapter 9

Richard woke, as he had for the last several decades, just as the sun slipped past the horizon line. He felt Jane's head resting on his shoulder and smiled. A wonderful way to start the evening. And he was *warm,* so delightfully warm. She was better than a hot tub. He'd have to do something really nice for her for not killing him. Like . . . let her go?

He couldn't. He knew it was the right thing to do, knew he had no business keeping her as a sort of mid-sized boy toy, but every time he thought of his condo emptied of her refreshing presence, he wanted to shiver. Hell, he wanted to go for a walk in the sunshine.

He couldn't even pretend it was about revenge anymore. Even if she had lied, they were square after that first night. No, he was keeping her because he was a selfish monster and he couldn't bear to let her go. To be brutally honest, he was thrilled she was sticking to her story, because it gave him the perfect excuse to keep her.

The fact that he wasn't pinned to the bed via a table leg through his rib cage spoke well of her feelings for him. He was as hopeful as he'd been in—what year *was* it? She had her chance for vengeance and hadn't taken it. And he doubted his lovely Jane was in the habit of passing up a chance to avenge herself. Was it possible she'd forgiven him? That was too unrealistic to believe, but perhaps there was hope. Perhaps—

"No! No, God, no . . . aw, jeez, Bobby!"

She was screaming. Screaming in her sleep. He was so startled he nearly jumped off the bed. Never had he heard his Janet so terrified, and so young. She sounded like a teenager.

"I didn't—Bobby, don't move, I'll get an ambulance, oh, God, don't die, please don't die!"

She was clawing at him in her sleep. He caught her hands and squeezed. "Jane, love. It's a dream. It's not real." *Anymore,* he added silently. His chest and throat felt tight. Whatever had happened, it had been horrible. Awful enough to scare her away from lovemaking for years and years.

Her eyes flew open. He was shocked to see them filling and then her tears spilled over and ran down her cheeks. "I didn't mean to," she sobbed.

"Of course you didn't."

"They told me it wasn't a good idea—that monkeys are fragile—but I didn't listen." She made a small fist and thumped it against his chest. "Why didn't I listen? Oh, we were having such fun—it didn't even hurt, and I thought it was supposed to hurt the first time. And then I started to come and I wrapped my legs around his waist and squeezed and—and—"

"Janet, it was an accident." *Monkeys?* Odd slang—he had never been able to keep up with it. Had she broken the boy's ribs? Had they been in a precarious position and fallen, and perhaps the boy had . . . ? Well, whatever had happened, he was thoroughly certain of one thing. "You didn't mean to hurt him, Jane. You never would have hurt him. You've got to let this go." He was stroking her back while he soothed her, and she finally relaxed against him. He added jokingly, hoping to see a scowl, "Besides, you don't need to worry about such things with me. You could set me on fire while you were having your way with me, and I'd be fine the next day. Before you ask, though, I'm really not into that."

She jerked up on one elbow and stared at him. Her eyes were smudged with tears, bloodshot, and enormous. He thought she'd never looked so pretty. "That's right," she said slowly. "I was thinking about that last night and you . . . I can't hurt you. You can take whatever I dish out."

"And have been," he added, "for several days now. See, look!" He showed her his arm where, in her agitation, she'd clawed off ribbons of skin. It was nearly healed.

Oddly, she was still staring at him as if she'd never seen him before. "I don't know why I didn't think of it before, Dick."

"You've had other things on your mind. Now, that's enough crying over a fifteen-year-old accident you couldn't help," he said briskly, hoping she agreed. He couldn't bear to see her cry. He rolled out of bed and stood up, casting about for a way to distract her. "How about sushi and maybe some vegetable tempura for breakfast?"

She perked up immediately. "I like raw fish," she said. "I like steak tartare, too, but I like it better with steak, not hamburger."

"Sounds like we have lunch figured out, too, m'love."

"But first we have to shower," she said, almost shyly.

He laughed, bent to her, picked her up, and kissed her. "Yes indeed. You are *filthy*. And so am I. I foresee lots of scrubbing in our future."

"Fucking pervert," she snorted, and he cheered inwardly, knowing she was back to herself.

+ + +

For the second night in a row, Richard woke up warm and content. He had made up his mind as dawn broke in the wee hours of the morning, as Janet cuddled up to him and snored softly in his ear. Today they would go out. He'd take her shopping and buy her a ridiculous amount of clothes. Clothes, lingerie, priceless paintings, pounds of steak tartare—whatever she wanted. He knew in his heart she wouldn't run away from him, and it was past time he let her out of his bedroom. She had been admirably patient, and it was time for a reward.

He stretched. He didn't really need to—he always woke energized and hungry and raring to go—but he enjoyed the sensation. Yes, they would go shopping, she would bully the sales clerks, and it would be delightful. Then back to his place for a light lunch and some energetic lovemaking, and possibly a nap, or more of *Salem's Lot*. Yes, it was all—

Where the hell was Janet?

He'd been groping absently for her while he'd been thinking, but she wasn't in his bed, and the bathroom light was off. He could hear her on the floor, gasping in—pain? Was that pain?

In the second before he looked, it seemed like every malady mortals were prone to raced through his brain. She had appendicitis. He'd knocked her up (it was supposed to be impossible, but who really knew?) and she was having a miscarriage. She was having a heart attack. A brain embolism. A kidney shutdown. God help him, he was as afraid to look as he was afraid not to.

He looked. Janet was on her knees beside the bed, panting harshly, and her back—it almost looked like the knobs of her spine were *moving*. Her hair was hanging in her face in sweaty tangles, and her nails were sunk into the carpet. His feet hit the floor with a double thud, and he reached for her. "Janet, I'm getting a doctor. I'll be right—"

A low, ripping growl froze his hand in mid-reach. And then—so fast, it was so quick, he blinked and it was done—she sprouted hair, her nose turned into a long snout, her eyes went wild, and she was leaping for the door.

She bounced off it, but he was alarmed to see it actually shudder in its frame. She coiled and leapt again. And again. He remained sitting on the bed—he was afraid if he stood he would fall—and stared at her. Janet was a dun-colored wolf with silver streaks running down her back. Her eyes were the same color as when she was a biped, but now they were glittery and homicidal. He remembered how she paced when he read, how she couldn't seem to sit still for long, and realized that in this form she was claustrophobic.

Chunks of the door were leaping off the frame and falling to the carpet each time her body hit the door, but at this rate it would take at least ten minutes and she was likely to damage herself. He got up and walked to the door on legs stiff with shock, fumbled with the lock, dropped his key twice (all the while dodging her small wolf's body—she never stopped, she completely ignored him, he doubted he was even a cipher to her now), and finally swung open the door.

He ran after her to do it again, and again. Then she spotted the bank of windows facing west and lunged toward them. He dived and managed to catch her back left leg just as she was coiling for a leap that would take her through the window. She spun, and he had a dizzying glimpse of what looked like a thousand sharp teeth as she growled.

"We're three stories up," he panted, clutching her while at the same time trying not to break her leg. "You'll never survive the fall. Well, you might but—Janet, don't go!"

She snapped at his fingers. Wrathful growls bubbled up out of her without pause or breath.

"Please don't leave! I was wrong and you were right—God, you were so right, I was a blind fool not to see it. *Please* don't leave me."

She snapped again, her jaws closing about a centimeter from his flesh. A warning. Probably her last warning.

"I can't bear it without you. I swear I can't. I thought I was content before, but it was a lie, everything was a lie, even why I was keeping you was a lie—"

His grip was slipping. He talked faster.

"—but you were right, and you never lied, not once, not even to get away, and Janet, I will spend the rest of your life making it up to you—"

She was almost free, and he was afraid if he let go to get a better grip, he wouldn't be fast enough.

"—but please . . . don't . . . go!"

She went.

He lay on the floor in his study a very long time. It seemed too much work to get up, find the broom, and start sweeping up the broken glass. He owned the building anyway, so who cared? Who cared about anything?

He couldn't believe she was gone. He couldn't believe he— who prided himself on possessing at least a modicum of intelligence—had let this happen.

My name is Janet Lupo.

Had done such things, and to such a woman.

I'm not afraid of any man, and I don't lie.

What had he been thinking?

My name is Janet Lupo.

How could he have been so blind?

My name is Janet Lupo.

So stupid and arrogant?

The full moon is eight days away. And when it comes, you're going to get a big fucking surprise.

Oh, if there was a God this was a fine joke indeed. He had finally found the one woman he could spend eternity with . . .

Your little oak doors won't hold me then.

. . . and he had kidnapped her and raped her and kept her and ignored her when she spoke the truth.

You'll realize you fucked up, bad.

He'd demanded she admit to being afraid of him, and when she wouldn't, he assumed it was a lie.

You'll know I was telling the truth the whole time, but you couldn't see past your stupid injured male pride.

His stupid injured male pride.

I'll be gone forever, and you'll have the next hundred years to realize what an asshole you were.

He would have cried, but he had no tears.

Chapter 10

Three days later

J ane rolled over and stretched. Then shrieked in anger as she fell three feet and hit the cement with a *smack.* She'd curled up on the base of the statue in Park Square, promptly gone to sleep, and then forgotten about the drop when she woke up. *Why don't I ever remember this shit until it's too late?* she thought, rubbing her skinned elbow.

She was pleasantly tired and would be for the next couple of days. It was always like that when she chased the moon. She also felt very new, almost husked out. Purified. Whatever.

She stood and shivered. Step one: find clothes. Spring in Boston was like spring in Siberia.

She marched up to an early morning commuter, a business-man obviously cutting through the park to get to the subway. He stared at her appreciatively as she approached, but she had eyes only for his cashmere topcoat. "How—" was all he had time for before she belted him in the jaw and mugged him.

She had made her choice as a wolf and would carry it out as a woman. She didn't have to wake up in the park, naked and alone. Or yesterday, in an alley. Or the night before that, beneath the docks by the harbor—ugh. She didn't think she'd ever get the smell out of her hair.

There were only a hundred safe houses in Boston, as well as acres and acres of woods owned by pack members. She could have romped there and woken to clean clothes and a hearty break-fast. But as a wolf, she had avoided all those places and her kind. The beast knew what she wanted. Now it was time to get it.

Of course, she didn't know where Dick lived exactly. It's not

like she scribbled down the address with her paw on her way out
the window. Luckily, there were ways and ways. She might not
have a super nose like some of her kind, but the day she couldn't
sniff up her own backtrail to a den was the day she'd jump off a
fucking bridge.

It didn't take long, but her feet were freezing by the time she
got there. Dick lived in a dignified brownstone condo that was
probably built the year the *Mayflower* landed. She shifted her
weight back and forth, stuck her hands in her stolen pockets, and
looked up at his window. The glass hadn't been replaced; there
was a large piece of cardboard taped into the frame instead. Guess
it took time to order that fancy old-fashioned stuff. Except for the
rumble of an early morning delivery truck, the street was quiet.

"'Scuse me. D'you live here?"

She looked. The delivery boy was holding three brimming
grocery bags, and looking glum. "Yeah. Why?"

"Well, thank God. 'Cause I've been making deliveries for two
weeks, but the last couple days nobody ever takes the food in, and
it goes bad or gets swiped, and it's just a waste, is all."

Ah, so that's where all the sumptuous feasts came from! Dick
had the food delivered and cooked the meals for her. *Yum.* "I was
gone for a while," she told him, "but now I'm back."

"Who are you?"

"I'm the owner's fiancée." She shook her head. It sounded just
as weird out loud as it did in her head. "Do I have to sign something?"

"No. He's got an account with us."

"Then get lost."

"Nice!" He set down the bags, slouched back to his truck, and
pulled into traffic without looking, in typical Boston fashion.
Which was good, because it wouldn't do for him to watch her
break into the house.

"Well, shit." That had been considerably easier said than
done! Dick's front door wouldn't budge, and she was reluctant to
break more of that expensive glass. He might not be so thrilled she
came back. She had a vague memory of him grabbing her and
begging her not to go, but it was more like a dream. She didn't
trust her wolf-brain to factually interpret human emotions.

She smacked herself on the forehead. Dummy! Why was she
trying to see him in the *daytime*? Even if she got in, he wouldn't
exactly be a thrilling conversationalist. He'd be holed up in his
bedroom, dead to the world—literally. Until then, she might as

well chat with a rock. Still, it would have been nice to swipe some clothes.

Oh, well. The coat was plenty warm enough, and she didn't give a fuck how many people stared at her feet. At least she was in a big city instead of some rinky-dink small town. The yokels always loved something new to gawp at. She just had to kill another ten hours until the sun set. Thank God for the Barnes & Noble café.

Chapter 11

Richard slumped in the chair beside the fireplace. He'd been sitting in this room every evening since Jane had left. It had been the last place he'd seen her.

He was starving, and he didn't care. He deserved to go hungry. And the thought of leaving—of perhaps missing her if she came back—was unbearable. What if she was hurt? What if she needed something and he was out assuaging his thirst?

Who are you kidding? She's gone, fool. You did everything but toss her out the window yourself.

True enough. Still, he waited. It was the only thing he could do. He'd never insult her by trying to find her and convince her to return. Return to what? An unnatural existence with a monster? And what in the world could he ever say to her? "Janet, dear, sorry about kidnapping you and raping you and keeping you and all but calling you a liar to your face, kiss-kiss, let's go home." As the lady herself might say, "In a fuckin' pig's eye."

"Dick! Stop with the fucking sulking and open the front door!"

Oh, Christ, now his inner voice sounded like *her.* Bad enough he was starving, but it appeared he was slowly going insane as well.

"You son of a bitch! You piece of shit! I trot my ass all the way back down here—twice!—and you keep me standing out here on this freezing sidewalk?"

He buried his face in his hands. How he missed her!

"I am going to rip your heart out and pin it to the bedroom wall with a swizzle stick! I'm going to yank the fixtures out of that

stupid bathroom you're so proud of and shove them up your ass!"
Wham! Wham! Wham! "Now let me in before I lose my temper!"

That's no inner voice, Richard. I ought to know . . . I'm *your inner voice.*

He jumped up so quickly his head actually banged into the ceiling. He barely felt it. He clawed for the doorway, raced through it and down the hall, down three flights of stairs, fumbled for the bolts and locks, and flung the door open.

Janet stood on his front step, flushed and out of breath. Her little fists were red from the cold and from banging his door. She was wearing a man's overcoat roughly six sizes too big for her, and three large grocery bags were at her feet. She was scowling. "Well, *finally.* Don't sulk on my time, all right, pal?" She stomped past him.

Like a zombie, he picked up the groceries and then slowly turned and followed her. She shrugged out of the coat and headed straight for their—for his room. He watched her naked form sway back and forth as she went up the stairs like she owned them. "Food," she said over her shoulder on her way up. "I could eat a cow. In fact, I think I did, night before last."

By the time he brought her tray to the bedroom, she had showered and toweled off. She strolled out of the bathroom and sniffed appreciatively. "Oooh, yeah, that's the stuff. I could eat *two* steaks."

"They're both for you," he said automatically. "Why . . . how . . . why . . . ?"

"You sounded a lot brighter when you thought I was a liar." She brushed past him and jumped for the bed, landing in the middle, lolling like a queen, and favoring him with a smirk. "Ah, the mileage I'm gonna get out of this. Let's start with your whole smug speech about how just because you're a vampire, there's no such thing as werewolves. That sound like a good place to you?"

"Janet—"

"Or we could touch on why it's not a good idea to kidnap people when they're on their way to an important meeting."

"Janet—"

"Or we could go into all the times you asked me to tell the truth, and I did, and then you didn't believe me, and then you—"

He fell to his knees beside the bed. He had to grit his teeth for a few seconds to keep his jaw from trembling. "Janet, why are you here? Why aren't you with your family?" His voice was rising, but he was helpless to stop it. "Why didn't you head for the road and keep going? Why are you back?"

She frowned. "You're taking the fun all out of this. I've been looking forward to it for days. I need to see some major ass groveling, pal."

He didn't speak.

She sighed. "What, I gotta get out the hand puppets? You haven't figured it out? Dick, *you're* my family now. I never want to go back there. Cape Cod in the summer—yech! Tourists cluttering up the roads, the beaches, and the mall—and you get in trouble if you eat them. Can't even take a little bite to discourage them from coming back—"

"Janet."

"I'm serious! Anyway, if I stay with you, I don't have to go back. I didn't realize how unhappy I was with them until I fell in with you. I'm not pack anymore, I'm yours. I mean—if you want."

"Is this a joke?" he almost whispered. "Is it a trick to get even? Because while I wouldn't blame you—"

"Oh, hey, I'm a bitch, but I'm not, like, a sociopath! That'd be a rotten thing to do. I love you, you stupid fuck. I'm not going anywhere. Except, of course, for a few days a month. Think you can put up with that, you undead dope?"

"I've been waiting almost a hundred years to hear those words. Well, not those exact words." He reached out and pulled her down onto his lap. They sat on the floor while she cuddled into him like a bad-tempered doll. "Oh, Janet. I missed you so much. And I was such a fool."

"Yeah, a real arrogant asshole."

"Yes."

"Completely unreasonable and jerkish."

"And then some."

"And you're really, *really* sorry."

"So unbelievably sorry."

"And totally unworthy of me."

"In a thousand ways."

"And you're gonna buy lots of food and get a house in the country so I don't have to hunt in the city."

"The refrigerator is full, and I already have a house in the Berkshires."

"Then that's all right," she said, sounding quite satisfied. She stretched out her legs and wiggled her toes. "Um . . . the steaks are getting cold."

"So am I."

She giggled and turned so she was straddling him and then

hooked her ankles behind his waist and kissed him on the mouth. Slowly, she cupped the back of his neck and brought his mouth to her throat. "Hungry?" she purred.

He thought he would have a seizure. She had come back—she loved him—she would stay—and now she was freely offering him her blood. Soon the Palestinians and the Israelis would make peace, and Janet would willingly enroll in charm school.

He sank his fangs into her throat without hesitation—he couldn't have held back if he tried. He could feel her breasts pressing against his chest while her blood warmed him from the inside out. She was wriggling against him—now her fingers were at his zipper—now her warm little hand was inside his trousers, clasping him, stroking him. He groaned against her throat.

"You *did* miss me!" She shoved him back and he was happy enough to lie down for her. He stopped feeding and licked the bite mark. Her glorious breasts were jiggling in his face, and he couldn't recall ever being happier, not once in his long, long life.

She seized his cock with delightful firmness and raised herself above him. His arms went around her waist as he guided her to him.

Entering her was like slipping into luxurious oil. Her head tipped back, and she said "Ummmmm . . . that's good. I missed that," to the ceiling.

He stroked her breasts, running his fingers over her firm nipples, marveling at the softness of her skin in contrast with her strength and stamina. She'd jumped three stories, and there wasn't a mark on her—and he was certainly looking! Not a bruise, not a scratch. She healed almost as quickly as he did.

"You're gorgeous," he said.

"You're just saying that to get laid," she teased.

"In case you haven't noticed, I *am* getting laid."

She snorted and then began to rock back and forth. He noticed an odd, sudden reticence about her and wondered about it—then suddenly realized she had likely been on top when she crippled her first lover.

"For heaven's sakes," he said with mock disgust, "can't you go any faster than that? Any harder? I'm about to fall asleep down here."

She was so astonished she nearly fell off him. Then she made the connection and smirked. "Okey-dokey, dead guy. Here we go."

They ruined the carpet. They didn't care. Toward the end, she was screaming at the ceiling and he could feel his spine cracking—and didn't care. Her legs were around his waist in a crushing grip, her arms around his neck, cutting off his air—and he wanted more. He told her so, insisted on it, demanded it, and then bit her ear. He could actually feel the temperature change within her as she reached orgasm, felt her uterus tightening around his shaft. That was enough to tip him dizzily over the edge.

They weren't able to speak for several minutes until Janet finally managed, "Oh, cripes, I think that should be against the law."

"It probably is, in at least three states."

"My supper's cold," she complained, making no move to stand up and get the tray.

"So I've got a microwave. Why did I even cook it? I doubt you'd have minded it raw. A werewolf," he mused, stroking her thigh. "Even after I saw the truth with my own eyes, I could hardly believe it."

"That's because you're kind of a dumb-ass sometimes."

"I have to take this from a foul-mouthed tart like you?"

She pounced on him and nibbled his throat. "I'm *your* foul-mouthed tart, so there."

"Excellent." He kissed her nose. "So . . . how do you feel about being an undead werewolf?"

She groaned. "Let's talk about it in ten years, all right? Let me get used to the idea of not being pack anymore first."

"It's a date. Will they come after you?"

"I have no idea. No one's ever voluntarily left before. I doubt the boss would really mind—he's softened up since he got hitched—but I s'pose I should tell them I'm not dead."

"Tomorrow."

"Yeah. Tomorrow."

"We've made our own pack, Jane. We're two monsters who do as they like, when they like. Everyone else had best stay out of our way."

"Ooooh, God, I love it when you talk like that . . ."

"How about when I do this?" He leaned down and nibbled on her impudent nipple, running his tongue over the velvety bumps of her areola.

"Oh, God."

"Or this?" He sucked hard and nipped her very, very lightly.

"Ummmmm . . ."

"I love you."

"Ummmm. Me, too. Don't stop."

He laughed and bent to her warm, lush flesh. "Not for a hundred years, at least."

"We'll figure something out."

Epilogue

*From the private papers of Richard Will,
Ten Beacon Hill, Boston, Massachusetts*

I'm in love! No entries of late—too busy. Too much to do just to keep up with my lovely monster. She's everything I ever wanted and, even better, I appear to be everything she ever wanted.

"No more time to write today—we're breaking in a new chef. He's used to catering large office functions, so he should be able to keep Janet satisfied.

"I suppose I'll give up this journal very soon. I realize now I wrote in it as a way to stave off my loneliness. No need for such distracting tricks any longer.

"Must go—my bride has just playfully tossed a marble bust at my head to get my attention. I think I'll chase her down and spank her."

There's No Such Thing as a Werewolf

Chapter 1

As any werewolf knows, smells and emotions and even raised voices have colors and texture. And as any blind werewolf knows (not that there were any besides him to the best of his knowledge), you could take those smells and emotions and conversations and do a pretty good job of seeing. Not a great job, comparably speaking, but enough to get around. Enough to have a solid sense of the world.

"But I can't be pregnant," Mrs. Dane was saying. "There's just no way."

"There's at least one way."

"But I'm infertile! The clinic said!"

"Accidents happen," he said cheerfully. He knew she was stunned but pleased. And as soon as the shock wore off, she'd be ecstatic. He could have told her that her fallopian tubes had managed to unblock themselves over the years, but that would raise awkward questions. After all, he was just her G.P. He wasn't treating her for infertility.

"I'd say you're"—*Thirty-nine and a half days along*—"about six weeks pregnant. I'm going to write you a scrip for some prenatal vitamins, and I want you to take two a day. And the usual blandishments, of course—ease off alcohol, don't smoke; blah-blah-blah. You know all this." Mrs. Dane was an OB nurse.

"Yeah, but . . . I never thought I'd *need* it."

He heard her weight shift as she leaned forward and was ready for it when she flung her chubby arms around him in a strangler's grip. "Thanks so much!" she whispered fiercely. "Thank you!"

"Mrs. Dane, I didn't do anything." He gently extricated himself from her grip. "Go home and thank your husband."

"Oh, I'm sorry." Now she was brighter in his mind's eye, glowing with embarrassment. "I read somewhere that blind people don't like it when their balance is thrown off."

"Don't worry about it. You couldn't throw off my balance," *Not without a truck.* "Don't forget to fill this on the way home," he added. He could write perfectly well, which was to say, his prescriptions didn't look any less legible than a seeing doctor's.

"Right. Right!" She bounded off the table, nearly careened into the closed door, and left without her clothes. The gown flapped once as the door closed behind her.

"I don't think they'll let you in the pharmacy dressed like that," he called after her.

✦ ✦ ✦

"I'm just saying you should think about it," his nurse, Barb Robinson, argued. "I hate the thought of you going home to an empty house every night. And it would—you know. Be helpful."

"Put a harness around a dog and expect it to lead me around all day?" He tried not to sound as aghast as he felt. "That's awful!"

"Drake, be reasonable. You get around fine, but you're not a kid anymore."

"Meaning since I'm looking at the big four-o it's time to check out nursing home brochures?"

Barb's scent shifted—it had been lemony and intense before, because while she was embarrassed to broach the subject, she was also determined. Now, as she got annoyed, it intensified until she damned near smelled like mouthwash.

"Very funny," she snapped. "Pride's one thing. Your safety is another. For crying out loud, you don't even use your cane most of the time."

"Will it get you off my back if I start lugging the stick around?"

"Yes," she said promptly.

Oh, for God's sake. "Fine. You may now refer to me as Dr. Stick."

"It's just that I don't want you to get hurt, is all," she persisted. "You bugged *me* about moving to a safer neighborhood."

"Repeatedly?"

"Oh, hush up. And you'd better get going—isn't tonight another one of your big nights out?"

You could say that. "It is indeed."

"Well . . . maybe you should take it easy. You look kind of worn out today."

"I was up late," he said shortly. "Give me the damned cane."

He heard her rummaging around beneath the counter and then she tapped the floor in front of him. He snatched it out of her hand. "There, satisfied?"

"For now."

"Also, you're fired."

"Ha!"

"Maybe next time." He obediently started tapping his way to the front door, though he knew perfectly well it was eight feet and nine inches away. "See you Monday."

"And think about the dog!" she yelled after him.

"Not likely," he muttered under his breath.

Chapter 2

The small gang—two boys and one girl, not one of them out of their teens—followed him off the subway. Typical thugs—they needed reinforcements to rob a blind man. He led them down Milk Street and let them get close.

"Just so you know," he said, turning, "in about half an hour the moon will be up. So this is a very, very bad idea. I mean"—they rushed him, and his stick caught the first one in the throat—"it's a bad idea in general. There are only about a thousand"—his elbow clocked down on the skull of the second—"more respectable ways to make a living." He hesitated with the girl and nearly got his cheek sliced open for his trouble. He pulled his head back, heard the whisper of steel slide past his face, and then grabbed her wrist and pulled, checking his force at the last moment. She flew past him, smacked into the brick wall, and then flopped to the ground like a puppet with her strings cut. "Seriously," he told the dazed, semiconscious youths. "You should think about it. And what are *you* up to?"

"Nothing," the other werewolf said cheerfully. "Just came down to see if you needed a hand. Christ, when was the last time these three had a bath?"

"About two weeks ago."

"How's it going, Drake?"

"It's going like it always does," he said carefully. He had known Wade when they were younger, but it paid to be careful around pack.

He held out his hand and felt it engulfed by the younger man, who smelled like wood smoke and fried trout. Drake was a large man, but Wade had three inches and twenty pounds on him. If he wasn't such a pussycat, he'd be terrifying. "Still keeping to your place in the country?"

"Sure. This city is fucking rank, man. I only came in to stock up. The day got away from me."

"Try not to eat any of the populace."

"Yuck! Have you seen what *they* eat? I wouldn't chew a monkey on a bet."

"That's not nice," Drake said mildly.

"Yeah, yeah, pardon my un-fucking PC behavior. Humans, okay, and never mind what they originated from. No, really! They should be *proud* to be shaved apes."

"*Tsk.*"

"Hey, I'm glad I ran into you—you should head out to the Cape, say hi to the boss and Moira and those guys. Did you hear Moira got hitched?"

"I did, yes. To a monkey, right?"

"Yeah, well . . ." Wade stretched; Drake could hear his tendons creaking and lengthening. Their Change was very close. Luckily, adolescence was far behind them both; they would stay well in control. "The new alpha gal, Jeannie, she heard about—uh—she noticed that none of the pack—uh—"

"Was cursed with a devastating handicap?" he asked pleasantly. He tapped his cane for emphasis.

Wade coughed. "Anyway, she hit the fucking roof when Michael told her the score, and they pissed and moaned about it for, like, a damn month, during which time our fearless leader was so *not* getting laid. Finally Michael said it wasn't an automatic; it would be up to the parents. They both had to agree."

Drake was silent. For the pack, this was forward thinking indeed. Handicaps were so rare they were nearly unheard of, and when a pack member was born blind or deaf or whatever, it had been tradition since time out of mind that the sire killed the cub. The dam was usually too weak from whelping but was almost always in agreement.

His sire, however, had died in Challenge before his birth, and his mother had wanted him. She had hidden him away at the time so the well-meaning pack leader, Michael's father, couldn't find him and kill him. She had raised him defiantly and heartlessly—absolutely no quarter given or asked.

Drake had eventually left the pack on his own, made his way to Boston, and made a life among humans. Here, at least, he could hold his own. Humans didn't care about Challenges. They didn't even *know* about them.

"Well, maybe I will pay them a visit," he lied. "It's been a long time." Michael hadn't even been pack leader when he'd left . . . Moira had been a precocious brat, one of the few who'd tried to talk him out of leaving.

No. Done was done.

"A long time?" Wade was saying. "Yeah, like about twenty years. It's a little different now. Michael's a modern dude. No one will fuck with you."

"Thanks for passing on the news. But I didn't leave because I was afraid of being fucked with."

"You did win all your Challenges," Wade admitted.

"I left because I was never allowed to be myself."

"You think you're allowed that *here*? In Monkey Central?"

He shrugged. Loneliness was such a central factor of his life, he barely recognized it anymore. "It doesn't matter."

"Well, think it over. I know Jeannie'd like to meet you. If nothing else, to be proved right. She lives for that shit." This was said in a tone of grudging admiration.

"We'll see."

Drake heard Wade inhale and stretch again. "Fine, be a stubborn ass, *I* don't care. Better beat feet out of here. Gonna be a long one. Last night of the full moon."

"Happy trails," he said dryly. "Again, try not to eat anyone."

"Again," the larger man said, loping off, "don't make me puke. Company coming."

"Yes, I—" He nearly fell down, right there in the alley. "I know."

"Jeez," the girl said, coming closer. She glanced over her shoulder at the rapidly retreating Wade and then turned and glared at the unconscious gang. "You gigantic losers!"

Everything was suddenly very bright, very sharp. The exhalations of the would-be attackers, Wade's retreating footsteps, the girl's perfume—L'Occitane Green Tea.

He could *see* her.

Not sense her, not get an idea of where she was and how she felt by her voice. *See* her. Everything around her was shades of gray, but she stood out like a beacon.

She was tall, for a woman—her jaw was up to his shoulder. And her hair was that light, sunny color he assumed people meant when they said blond. Her eyes were an odd color . . . not blue like ice was blue, and not purple like people had described irises . . . somewhere in between.

Her hair was brutally short and so were her nails. She was wearing six earrings in her left ear and eight in her right. She had a nose ring and a hoop through her left eyebrow, and her shirt was short enough to show off her belly button ring. Her stomach was sweetly rounded, and she was wearing shorts so brief they were practically denim panties. Her black tights were strategically ripped, showing flashes of creamy skin. Her tennis shoes (what color was that? red? orange?) were loosely tied with laces that weren't any color at all.

"Are you all right, guy? I'm really sorry if they tried anything. I told them to cut the shit. I didn't think they, y'know, meant it."

He gaped at her.

"Oh, sorry," she said, glancing at the cane. "I didn't realize. Do you need me to walk you somewhere? Did they hurt you?"

"I can see you!"

"Ooooookey-dokey." She took a cautious step backward. "Listen, I've got stuff to do tonight—last chance. D'you need me to call you a cab or something?"

"Holy Mary Mother of God!"

"So no. Well, 'bye." She turned, and, frozen, he watched her walk away. Her butt was flat, and she hitched up her shorts, which gaped around her waist. He couldn't begin to imagine her age—twenty-two? twenty-five? He had at least fifteen years on her.

He heard a crack and dropped the cane—he'd been gripping it too hard and it had split down the middle. Why could he see her? Why now? Was it a function of the full moon? If so, why hadn't it ever happened before? Who was she? And where was she going in such a hurry?

The clouds skudded past the moon, and suddenly it felt like he had twice as many teeth.

Chapter 3

Crescent stood on the rooftop and stared down at the street. It wasn't so far. One measly story. Shoot, people fell that far all the time and survived . . . mostly . . . and besides, she wasn't a regular person. Probably.

If she was ever going to fly, now was the time.

She put her hands on the ledge and started to boost herself up when she felt a sharp tug on the back of her shorts and went flying backward. She hit the gravel rooftop, and all the breath whooshed out of her lungs. She laid there and gasped like a fish out of water, and when she was able, she rolled over on her knees.

The largest wolf she had ever seen was sitting three feet away. She was too startled to be frightened. And it wasn't growling or baring his teeth, but just staring at her in the moonlight.

A dog she could almost understand, even here, in the middle of the city. But a wolf? Where had it come from? Did it escape from a zoo? And how did it get up on the roof? Could wolves climb fire escapes? *Was* there a fire escape?

If she spread her fingers as wide as she could, its paws were just about that size. And its head was almost twice as wide as hers, with deep, almost intelligent brown eyes. Its fur was a rich, chocolate brown shot with silver strands, and when the breeze ruffled its pelt, the wolf looked noble, almost kingly.

"What'd you do *that* for?" she asked it. "If I want an animal biting my butt, I'll start dating again."

It stared at her.

"All the better to see you with, my dear," she muttered. "Now you stay here. I have to do something." She got up, brushed the dust off her knees, and started for the ledge. She got about a step and a half when she heard a warning growl behind her. She threw up her hands and spun around. "Jeez, what *are* you? Why are you picking on me? And why do you care? Look, I won't get hurt. I can fly. I mean, I'm pretty sure. And if I'm wrong—but I don't think I am—it's only one story."

Nope. The wolf wasn't buying it.

"Well, hell," she said, and sat down cross-legged.

It had been a long day and a longer night. Almost before she knew it, she was tipping over sideways. The gravel was probably cutting her cheek, but it felt like the softest of down pillows.

She slept.

Chapter 4

She was stiff and freezing, and someone was shaking her by the shoulder. What the hell had happened to her cot?

She opened her eyes to see a man down on one knee beside her. And, hello! *Not bad* for an old guy. He looked to be in his mid-thirties and had great dark eyes, brown hair touched with gray, and smile lines bracketing his mouth. His shoulders, in the dark suit and greatcoat he wore, were impossibly broad. His thighs were almost as big around as her waist, and he was crouching over her like a dark angel. It was a little disturbing, but kind of cool.

"Good morning," he said. His voice was deep, pleasant. He probably worked in radio. "Are you all right?"

"Sure," she said, but she groaned when she sat up. "I can't believe I fell asleep up here." She brushed gravel off her cheek and looked around. The wolf was gone, thank goodness. "Oh, shit! I never got to—never mind."

"What are you doing up here?"

"Mind your own beeswax," she said. "You can go now."

"You don't seem suicidal," he commented.

"I'm not!"

"Then why are you up on a roof?"

"You'll laugh at me."

"Doubtful."

"Also, it's none of your business."

"Well," he said pleasantly, "I'm not leaving you up here by yourself. So you might as well tell me."

"Dammit!" What was going on? First the gang decided to be

dumb (dumber than usual, anyway), then a weird-ass giant wolf tormented her, and now *this* guy. God hated her is what it was. "Fine, I'll tell. I'm pretty sure I can fly. I've felt I could all my life. It sort of—runs in my family. Except my family's all dead, so I never really knew *for sure* for sure, y'know? So anyway, last night I finally screwed up the courage to try, but I couldn't because— never mind, you'll think I'm a nut-job. More so than now, I mean. Anyway, that's why I'm up here. Not to die. To fly."

"Mmmm." He put a big hand on her face and peered at her pupils. "Well, you're not on drugs. That's something."

"I quit doing drugs when I was seventeen," she snapped and batted his hand away. "I've been clean for ages."

"And you're not terminally ill," he finished.

"How d'you know *that*?"

"I'm a doctor. It's my job to know."

"What, did you do a blood test in my sleep?"

He ignored that. "What's your name?"

"Why do you care?"

He looked at her soberly. "I care."

Weird. But cool. Okay, fine. "It's Crescent."

"That's it?"

"No, I have a last name, but I'm not telling."

"Why? Are you a fugitive?"

"I wish. It's just that everybody laughs. You'll laugh."

He raised his hand, palm out. "I promise I won't laugh."

"It's Muhn."

"Crescent Moon?"

"The h," she said with as much dignity as she could, "is silent."

"That's all right," he told her. "My last name is Dragon."

"Doctor Dragon?"

"Doctor Drake Dragon."

"Oh dear." She giggled. "We're both cartoons."

"You realize, of course, that we must get married." He said this with a perfectly straight face, which made her laugh harder.

"It's just too good a story to tell our grandchildren," she agreed. "But first I have to do this. So good-bye."

"Come down and have breakfast with me instead," he coaxed.

Interestingly, she was tempted. He really was a stone fox. And she hadn't been on a date in . . . let's see, she had been able to legally drink for three years, and there was that guy who took her to the rave right after . . .

Wait a minute.

"Wait a minute!" God, she was slow this morning. "You're the blind guy from the alley!" Except he didn't *seem* blind. He'd checked her pupils, for crying out loud.

"Yes," he confirmed.

"You don't seem very blind."

He hesitated and then said again, "Have breakfast with me."

"Why?"

"You might as well. I'm not going to let you jump."

She sighed. "Well. I am hungry." *And I can ditch this guy after I cadge a free meal off him.* "Okay. Lead on, MacDuff."

Chapter 5

He offered her his arm when they were at street level, and her smell shifted to amusement—ripe oranges. After a moment, she grasped it.

"Cripes, I can't even get my fingers around your bicep. D'you work out, like, nine times a day?"

"No. But I like to keep in shape."

"Y'know, we don't have to go anywhere fancy," she said. "We could just get a cup of coffee."

"You're underweight for your height. We'll get a proper meal."

"Bossy," she coughed into her fist.

He smiled. "Yes." It was all he could do not to gape at her like a schoolboy. He had no idea why he could see her, but the effect hadn't worn off with daylight . . . she was like a flame in a street of shadows. "I'm afraid it runs in my family."

"Can I ask you something? How come you don't use a dog? And where's your cane? Didn't you have one last night?"

"I get around pretty well," he said, avoiding her question. "I've been blind all my life. It's all I know."

"Oh. Well, like I said, you don't seem blind."

He shrugged. Humans always told him that.

✦   ✦   ✦

Over a breakfast of three pancakes, six pieces of toast, and two cups of coffee (hers), and a bowl of oatmeal (his), they talked.

"Don't you want some ham or bacon? Please, order whatever you like. I can assure you I'm good for it."

She shuddered. "No, thanks. I'm a vegetarian."

"Oh." Hmm. That could be interesting. "You know, that's really not the best diet for an omnivore."

"Dude, I'm not chomping on dead flesh, and that's the end of it."

"Drake," he corrected.

She mopped up syrup with the last pancake. "Yeah, whatever. Can I get more coffee?"

"Of course." He signaled the waitress and then asked, "Why are you so thin?"

"Why do you ask so many questions?"

"I'm interested in you," he said simply.

"Uh-huh. Dude, you're, like, twice my age."

Yes, that was annoying. But it couldn't be helped. "Stop calling me dude. And it's probably not twice. I'll be forty this year."

"Oh." She seemed surprised. "You look younger. I'm twenty-four."

"You look younger, too. If I may ask, where are you staying?"

"There's a shelter on Beacon Street," she said without a trace of embarrassment. "I lost my job—the economy, you know—and couldn't make rent, so I've been bouncing around a bit."

"Is that how you fell in with the little gang that attacked me?"

"I didn't know they were going to do that," she said earnestly. "I thought it was just talk."

"I believe you. What about your family?"

"Don't have one."

"I'm sorry."

"It's all right. I never really knew them. Like you—I guess—being by myself, it's all I know."

"Why don't you stay with me for a while? I have a big house in Cambridge, and there's plenty of room for a guest."

She snorted into her coffee cup. "Right. Go home with the strange guy who showed up out of nowhere, who says he's blind but doesn't trip over anything. Not *too* creepy."

"What's the worst that could happen?"

"You could kill me in my sleep."

He tried not to show offense. "That's ridiculous. In your *sleep*? I would never."

She laughed at him. "Oh, okay, so, we've established you won't kill me in my sleep. *That's* promising."

"The homeless shelter is preferable to my home?"

"Well . . . no offense, dude . . . Drake, I mean . . . but put yourself in my shoes."

"I understand. But consider this, you could have pancakes every morning," he coaxed, "and all the coffee you could drink. Until you get back on your feet."

She shook her head but look tempted. "Jeez, I can't believe I'm even considering this. If this was a horror movie, I'd be yelling at the screen, 'Don't do it, you dumb bitch!'"

"That's nice. I would really enjoy your company. I live a . . . solitary life. It would be nice to have a—a friend over."

She stared at him for a long moment. "Well. I have to admit, it's the nicest offer I've gotten all year. But here's the thing. I'm getting these 'take the poor waif home and take care of her' vibes from you, but I'm not sure you get it. My family died when I was a toddler, and I left the foster home when I was ten. I've been on my own a long time. I can take care of myself."

"Of course."

"And the thing is, there's nothing I'll—uh—do for you. You know. To stay at your house."

"No, I wouldn't expect you to." And, fortunately, she was a good two weeks from ovulation. He'd be nowhere near his Change then. It could be problematic when a roommate's cycle coincided with a male werewolf's, but he didn't have to worry about that, at least. "There aren't any strings, Crescent."

"Well." She finished her coffee. "I can't believe I'm saying this. But we'll try it. For a while."

"All right, then." He smiled at her, and she smiled back. He'd never seen a smile before. Hers made him dizzy.

Chapter 6

They walked in, and she was instantly dazzled—like the big Colonial house hadn't been impressive enough on the *outside.* "Wow! How many windows do you *have*?"

"I have no idea."

"Right. Sorry. It's so bright in here!" She was staring; she couldn't help it. Her first, jumbled impression was lots of light, a soaring living room ceiling, a loft, and lots of hardwood flooring. "You don't even need to turn on any lights during the day. Not that you would."

He was hanging his greatcoat in the closet. "I like to feel the sun on my face," he said simply.

"Did anyone ever tell you, you live in a pink house?"

"A few have mentioned it." He shrugged. "What do I care?"

She laughed. "I s'pose. It's just sort of funny. I mean, you're this big, super-masculine guy, and your house is the color of raw salmon. It's a little weird."

He smiled. It was disconcerting—like he was looking *right* at her. But of course he wasn't. He probably knew she was standing by the door because of her voice. "Super-masculine?"

"Dude, you're about the biggest, boldest guy I've ever met."

"Thank you. And stop calling me dude."

He was the sharpest "handicapped" person she'd ever seen. He paid for breakfast with cash . . . and she noticed the twenty dollar bills were folded into triangles and the ten was a rectangle. Of course . . . it made perfect sense. He couldn't see the denominations, and the bills would all feel the same. Did he get them that way from the bank? Or did he have a helper to fold his money? Maybe she could fold his dough to earn her keep . . .

But it was just so weird, because he always seemed to know where she was—he caught her before she started to trip on the curb, for God's sake.

"Why don't I show you to your room?"

"Yeah," she said, kicking off her sneakers and following him. "Why don't you?"

She expected a simple guest room with a utilitarian twin bed and an empty bureau. Instead, he escorted her to paradise. The bed, a mahogany four-poster, was against the window, and sunlight was splashed all over the Shaker quilt. Through the open door on the opposite side of the room she could see a gleaming bathroom with tiles the color of the sea, and the bureau beside her was almost as tall as she was.

"Uh . . . you sure you don't have a cot in the basement or something?" she asked nervously. The room was so clean, so beautiful, she was afraid to move lest she destroy it all. "Or maybe a blanket I could spread out on the kitchen floor?"

"Nonsense. This is your room now, for as long as you like. I'll leave you to get settled." And abruptly, he was gone.

"Get settled?" she asked the empty room. "How?" She hadn't wanted him to see the shelter, so she had no extra clothes. Well, she'd sneak out tonight and go get them. And she'd find Moran and his little gang of retards and give them a piece of her mind. Imagine, trying to rob a *blind* guy.

She wandered back out to the living room and eyed the loft. Hmmm . . .

She noiselessly climbed the stairs and had time to notice the loft was actually an office—desk, computer with big-ass speakers, bookshelves—before she clambered up on the railing. This would be even easier—this was only one story. Less, actually. Just a few feet. Piece of cake. If she couldn't fly here, she couldn't fly anywhere.

"Something for lunch?" Drake called from the kitchen. Good, he was a couple rooms away.

"I'm still stuffed from breakfast," she called back and dived off the railing.

She flopped over in mid-air, had time to notice the living room doing a one-eighty around her, and then she fell into Drake's arms.

"Wow!" she gasped. "How'd you do that? You were, like, fifty feet away!"

"Will you *stop* that?" he snapped. "Stop climbing things and leaping off of them before you give me a heart attack."

"But how'd you know I—"

"Promise, Crescent. As long as you're in this house, no more crazy jumps."

"But I won't be hurt," she explained earnestly, resisting the urge to snuggle into his arms. He was holding her like she weighed as much as a bag of feathers, like it was nothing. And the way he was scowling down at her—it should have been scary, but instead, she wanted to smooth out the frown lines with her fingertips. "Really! I'm sure I can do it."

"Not in my house," he said firmly. "Now promise."

"Or what?" She wasn't being sarcastic. She was curious.

"Or I won't put you down."

Now she did smooth out the frown line over his eyebrow. Weirdly—but nicely—he leaned down and nuzzled her nose. She felt her nipples tighten and fought the urge to squirm in his arms.

"You're just going to carry me around all day?" she teased.

He smiled down at her. "It wouldn't be much of a hardship."

"Okay, okay. I promise. No more jumping off stuff in your house." *But I can't promise I won't jump anywhere else . . .*

"All right, then." He set her on her feet and gave her a warning smack on the ass that stung like hell—

"Hey!"

—and walked back to the kitchen.

Chapter 7

He heard her as she tiptoed past his room. Actually, he heard her when she opened her eyes and sat up in bed. He knew from her smell she hadn't slept, and he made sure he didn't, either.

When she stole out of his house like a thief in reverse, he was right behind her.

✦ ✦ ✦

Bags were always in short supply at the shelter, so she just gathered a few changes of clothes to her chest and stole back outside. Unfortunately, she caught Maria's eye on the way out. Well, it couldn't be helped. The woman gobbled speed like it was Tic-Tacs, and she never slept.

Crescent crept down the alley behind the shelter, thinking she still had time to catch the Red Line back to the bus stop near Drake's house, when she heard running footsteps and turned to see the Asshole Brigade.

"New crib?" Maria asked. She was one of those women who always smiled—who smiled when you knew they were screaming inside. "New man?"

"Yes, and no, and mind your own business."

"Hold up, Cress." That was Nick Moran, the leader of the incredibly lame group. "You got something for us?"

"It's Cres-*ent*, and no, I sure don't. What's wrong with you?" She shifted her weight and clutched her clothes a little tighter. She did *not* want to let these three put her in the middle of their nasty little circle. Her gut almost always led her right—why else was she staying with a stranger?—and maybe it did this time, too.

Maybe when she fell in with these idiots, they didn't really know how bad it could get. Her gut was good, but it couldn't foresee the future. "Robbing a blind guy? Trying to, anyway. You couldn't even pull *that* off."

"Shut up," Nick said roughly. He was a tall, cadaverously thin man with the bare beginnings of a mustache and a scar that bisected his left cheek. "We had it under control."

"Sure you did. 'Bye."

Jimmy, the other schmuck, clawed at her elbow and managed to grab it. "Whyn't you take us to his place?" he asked. His tone was reasonable, but she wasn't fooled. "Cute piece of ass like you, bet you've already got a key."

As a matter of fact, she did. As a further matter of fact, she certainly wasn't going to let *them* have it. "Forget it," she said, trying to pull away. "Fuck off, you three, before I lose my temper. I can't believe I ever felt sorry for you."

"Sorry for us?" Nick echoed, his expression darkening. "Be sorry for you. Because when we get done, you won't be so pretty no more."

"It's *any* more. For God's sake, Nick, you went to private school before your folks kicked you out."

Nick blushed—he hated being reminded he hadn't been born to the streets—but Maria's smile widened, if that was possible. Crescent observed that the woman had a nodding acquaintance at best with toothpaste. "We can do this the easy way—" she began.

"Oh, spare me your thug clichés." Crescent was more annoyed than frightened, which she supposed was something. She'd been a moron to come back here by herself—and for what? So Drake wouldn't see the shelter? Who cared what he thought? Big, overprotective dope. And she wasn't going to be winning any college bowls, either, unless she starting relying a little more heavily on instinct and less on pride.

Jimmy's other hand—the one not squeezing her elbow—darted forward like a pale spider and grabbed her nipple. Then he started to pinch. Hard. Crescent could drop her clothes all over the filthy alley floor, or she could stand there.

She stood there. Never in a thousand years would she show these three how much he was hurting her. "Cut the shit," she said through gritted teeth. "You think acting like bullying assholes is going to change my mind about you?" She looked at Nick, waiting for him to call off his dog.

Jimmy was giggling, Maria was grinning, and Crescent's eyes

were watering. She had just decided to drop her clothes and kick Jimmy in the 'nads when Jimmy was flying away from her—*literally* flying. He sailed through the air and crumpled to the street a good ten feet away.

She had a glimpse of big hands cupping the curve of Maria's skull, and Nick's, and then there was a *klonk* as their heads banged together. It sounded awfully like the time she dropped a cantaloupe on the floor.

And then Drake was towering over her, scowling, as usual.

"Have I mentioned," she said, gaping up at him, "that for a blind guy, you get around pretty good?"

"Once or twice." He pushed her crossed arms down, carefully raised her T-shirt, then eased her bra cup down so he could examine her nipple. This was startling, and quite nice. She reminded herself that he was a doctor, and hers was probably one of about six thousand nipples he saw in a year.

"It's pretty red," he said after a long moment. He was leaning so close, she could feel his breath on the swollen peak, and she shifted her weight again. Suddenly her shorts felt too tight, in a pleasantly irritating way. "But I don't think it'll bruise."

"How—" Her mouth was suddenly very dry, and she coughed. "How do you know it's red?"

He didn't answer her. Instead, he smoothed her hair away from her eyes. "If you steal out of my house in the middle of the night again," he said, quite pleasantly, "I'll beat you."

"No you won't."

He sighed. "No. I won't."

"Drake, seriously. Why d'you care?"

He sighed again. "I care." Then he pulled her up on her tiptoes and kissed her with bruising strength.

She dropped her clothes. *Fuck it.*

Kissing Drake—well, being kissed by Drake—was an entirely novel experience. For one thing, the man didn't have an ounce of flab anywhere. For another, she had the distinct impression he could snap her spine like kindling. But this thought was as exciting as it was slightly scary.

He pulled away, and she stumbled forward. "Oh, no, don't stop," she gasped. "Kiss me some more—I'm not dizzy enough."

"I can't," he said, and she was delighted to see his breaths, too, were coming hard. "I don't want to take you in the alley like a—come on."

He grabbed her hand, hauled her out of the alley until they

were under the streetlights, and flagged a cab. He practically threw her inside, then slammed the door and tersely told the driver his address.

"My clothes," she said, staring out the back window. "And after all the stupid trouble I went to . . ."

"I'll buy you a Gap store," he replied and didn't let go of her hand until the cab pulled into his driveway.

Drake fumbled for his wallet, then grabbed a bunch of cash and threw it at the driver, dragging her out in the same instant. She heard the driver's gasp of surprise and appreciation and then he was pulling out of the driveway and, in typical Boston driver fashion, pulling into traffic without looking.

She jumped into Drake's arms. He held her easily, his hands cupping her bottom, and she nibbled his lower lip. "I think you tipped him 'bout a thousand percent," she teased.

"Ask me if I give a fuck," he growled back, reaching up and tearing her shirt from the neck down.

Chapter 8

They didn't make it to the bedroom. They didn't even make it to the front steps. Instead, he took her in the lilac bushes, and to the end of her days, she would associate that scent with Drake's urgency.

"This is insane," she panted, helping him tear out of his coat, his shirt, his pants. "We don't even know each other."

"I know you."

"Yeah, yeah, that's what they all say." Except she felt as if she knew him, too. Independent and proud and kind and gentle, but a hard man when he had to be. A velvet fist when circumstances demanded it.

He tore off her panties and then gently parted her. She was slippery, and he groaned when his fingers slid through her, into her, and while his fingers were busy stroking and parting the slick folds between her legs, his thumb was on her clit, gently rubbing, and his lips were on her sore nipple, licking and kissing.

"Later," she groaned. Oh, Christ, had she ever wanted anyone this badly? Had anyone? "Later for that stuff. Fuck me, before I go out of my mind."

He left her nipple after one last kiss, caught her hand and brought it between them, and she curled her fingers around his enormous length. He throbbed beneath her touch, and she could feel his slippery tip. She ran her thumb over it, and he shuddered in her arms.

"Now?"

"Yes."

"You're so small, I don't want to—"

"Yes." She wriggled beneath him and licked her lower lip. "I'm small and you're big, and it's going to hurt just right. Now stop talking and . . . fuck . . . me."

He obliged, parting her and surging forward, filling her up, forcing her to open for him. And still he came forward, pushing, thrusting, until she thought she would soon feel him in the back of her throat.

He withdrew, and in the waning light of the moon, she could see the sweat on his brow, the way his eyes were shining, almost glinting. Then he surged forward, *shoved* forward, and she wrapped her legs around his waist and shrieked into the night air.

They rocked together in the dirt, and when she put her hands on his hard, taut ass, she could feel the muscles flexing as he worked over her, as he thrust and withdrew and pushed and surged. She opened her mouth for another yell—it was too sweetly divine to keep quiet—when his hand clamped over her mouth. She writhed in silence beneath him and, several seconds later, heard the couple walk by on the sidewalk a bare ten yards away.

"They'll hear you," he murmured in her ear, his voice so thick it was nearly unrecognizable. "They'll come over here and see me fucking you in my side yard."

The thought was so blackly exciting she came at once, actually felt herself get wetter. He groaned in her ear and then bit her earlobe.

It went on like that for some time—she would never be able to guess how long they went at each other in the lilac bushes. Every once in a while his phenomenal hearing would pick up something and he'd cover her mouth again, without missing a stroke. But when he finally came, his shout was a roar that made her ears ring.

"Oh, Christ," he gasped, collapsing over her.

"If anybody heard *that,* you'll have some explaining to do, Doctor." She tried to sound saucy, but mostly, she just wheezed.

"Umm." He was kissing the side of her neck—wet, snuffly kisses that made her shiver and press closer to him. "Don't leave in the middle of the night anymore."

"All right, then. Think we can make it inside without showing the neighbors our bare butts?"

"We're about to find out."

Chapter 9

I think I got something caught on your belly button ring," he said later, simply because it was much too soon to ask her to be his mate and he had to say *something*.

"What can I say? Life with me is a constant adventure." She yawned and flopped over on her back. "And may I add, *not* bad for an old guy. Seriously. You must take, like, super Geritol, because . . ."

"Thank you so much," he said wryly. They were in his bed, watching the stars through the skylight. "I was just about to compliment you on being adequate in bed despite an obvious lack of experience."

She smacked him on the bicep. "Hey! And . . . ow . . . that was like slapping a rock. FYI, dude, I've got gobs of experience. There was that time in the movie theater . . . um . . . and once during a snowball fight a boy fell down on top of me . . ."

"Stop it, you're embarrassing yourself."

"Drake, what *is* it with you?" she asked abruptly. Her scent shift warned him—from playful soap bubbles to fresh green leaves—even if her tone hadn't. "Seriously. I mean, you swoop down on me all Knight in Shining Armani—which is nice, if weird—and you don't ask for anything at all, and you're super nice, but you must want something. I mean, here we are, and you haven't kicked me out, which frankly, most men—"

"Spare me your knowledge of most men."

"Okay, okay. But seriously. What's your deal?"

"It's a double deal," he said after a long pause. "And either one will, as you might say, freak you out in the extreme."

"Oh, dude, I'd never say anything so lame . . . well, why don't you try one, see how that goes."

"Uh . . ."

"Come on, come on! Then I'll tell you something about me. Something nobody else knows."

"You mean besides the fact that you have smelly feet?"

"Draaaaaaaaaaaaake!"

"All right, don't yowl. Okay. Well. Here it is, then."

She propped her chin up on her fist and waited.

He coughed.

She kept waiting.

"Well. Ah. You see, it's difficult to just—you know—blurt it out like this—"

"Are you hoping I'll die of old age so you won't have to say it?"

"Fine, *fine,*" he practically snapped. "I'm a werewolf."

Silence.

"I know," he continued, easing a hand over her thigh and, emboldened when she didn't run screaming from the room, patting her tentatively. "It's startling, but you don't have to be afraid, because I'd never hurt you or eat you—ah, that is to say, outside the bedroom I would never eat you, and—"

"Oh, Christ! That!" She batted his hand away. "I knew about *that*! You were supposed to tell me something I didn't know."

He actually shook his head to check his hearing. No, there was her heartbeat, *lub-dub, lub-dub,* and her breaths, and the hum of electricity, and the cool clink of the freezer making an ice cube. Everything was working fine. "What?"

She lunged upward, hopped off the bed, and started pacing back and forth. Moonlight splashed her as she stomped—an enraged goddess etched in cream. "Well, what else would it be? You're super-strong, super-fast, you're blind but you get around better than I do . . . plus, you're a *doctor,* for God's sake. How could you be such a good doctor without, I dunno, super everything else? It was either that or I figured you were an alien. But after just now—the bushes, you know—I figured you probably weren't an alien. Besides, this wolf stops me from throwing myself off the roof and then you just *happen* to show up a few hours later?"

He blinked at her. "Oh. I must say, this is very anticlimactic."

"Serves you right for assuming I was a dumb-ass."

"I did not! No one's ever guessed before. And I've had . . ."

ah . . . lady friends who have hung around quite a bit longer than you have."

"Oh, that." She waved away "lady friends who have hung around." "Well, that's the thing about me—the secret thing—I was gonna tell you. I can tell things about people. That's why I came home with you. I didn't just think you wouldn't hurt me; I *knew* you wouldn't. It's like I can get into a person's head and tell exactly what they're feeling."

"Empathic, hmm? That's interesting. Well, Crescent, for heaven's sake, why do you keep giving that gang of yours a second chance?"

"I think they might be a little crazy," she replied matter-of-factly. "When we meet up, they never *feel* like they're going to hurt me. Then they get mad, and . . . anyway, obviously my radar isn't one hundred percent right all the time. Close enough for jazz, though."

"And this fixation with flying?"

"Dude, I totally can! I know it! *You* just have to stop getting in the way when I jump off things."

Empathy . . . flight fixation . . . and her build, small and speedy . . . but surprisingly heavy for her height . . . could it be? He had assumed they were legend. Rather like werewolves. "Crescent," he said abruptly, "have you ever had an X ray?"

Startled by the abrupt subject change, she blinked at him like a blond doe. "Uh . . . not in the last few hours."

"And you never knew your family?"

"Nope."

"Hmmm."

"Have I mentioned you're sexy when you go all 'pondering physician-esque'?"

"No," he said, pouncing on her and bearing her back on the bed like a cat with a new toy. "You haven't. Please elaborate."

She did.

Chapter 10

Drake. Seriously. How many T-shirts do you think I need?"

"But they're *so* versatile," the Gap saleswoman piped up.

"Not to mention fragile," Drake whispered in her ear, and was gratified to see her blush.

"You go away," she ordered the woman, smiling. "You're helping him spend way too much money as it is. And you—put that down. Khaki—yech."

"But this is the Gap," the saleswoman said ("Ask me how to save 15%" was emblazoned in hysterical red ink on her lapel button), obediently retreating.

"What, so *I* have to wear the uniform, too? Keep going."

"I'm offering you any woman's dream," he said, "and you're still making mischief."

"A) Chauvinist much? Any woman's dream? Shopping at Faneuil Hall? And B) put those *down*. I already picked out pants."

"You'll need more than two pairs."

"Not according to some," she said, arching an eyebrow.

"Hmm," he said, advancing on her, momentarily slowed by a whirl of khaki as she threw the pants at him.

"Forget it, pal. Neither the time nor the place. Excuse me," she added, bumping into a silver, headless mannequin. "Oh, gross! I hate when I think they're people."

"That's some empathy you've got at work there," he commented.

"Off my case, Dr. Furball. What, you never ever made a mistake?"

He thought hard. "Nothing springs to mind."

She let out a yelp of anger, and he could tell she was sorry she had nothing in her arms to toss at him any longer. "Dude, I hate to point this out, but you can't see. You must have screwed up something. Clashing tie, maybe?"

He tossed her a blouse the color of her eyes and said in a low voice, although the saleswoman was across the store, "*Homo saps* are more handicapped than I, dear."

"Oh, sure, the one-eyed man in the country of the blind and all that."

"Essentially."

"We're not that bad."

He shrugged. "I can smell an iron deficiency. I can hear a heart murmur without a stethoscope."

"Well, *I* can tell this blouse doesn't go with those pants, so put it right back on the rack, pal. God, aren't you bored? These are all for me, and I'm just about bored out of my tits."

He grinned. "Thanks for the visual. I'll make a note to catalog order for you from now on."

"Well, *thank* you. Not that you need to keep buying me clothes."

Want to bet?

"I suppose taking you to Anne Klein to look at dresses would be a complete waste of time?"

"Barf out! Jeez, look how late it's getting! The sun's actually gone down. God, how long have we been doing this?"

"Since supper. Stop complaining. We're almost done."

"Well, I'd like to see you make me," she said pertly.

"Done and done. If you're quite—" He paused suddenly. Was that a whiff of pack? Sure it was. Hmm, two in one week. It wasn't often he ran into one a year. That was interesting. Now what to do about it?

"Dick, I swear to fucking God, if you don't stop bitching I'm going to pull out your eyeballs and shove them down your pants." The voice was strident, loud, and female.

"That could be fun," a low-pitched male voice he didn't recognize said cheerfully. "And who's bitching? I just got up. What are we doing here? I didn't know you liked the Gap, m'dear."

"I fucking well hate it, and you damned know it. But they're having a sale, and I can stock up. I fucking hate shopping!"

"A woman after my own heart," Crescent muttered, holding up a sleeveless sweater the color of mucous.

Drake moved to get a closer look. Was that . . . ? No. It

couldn't be. And with a man? No. It had been too many years; he was mistaken. Still, no one else he knew packed that many "fuck"s into everyday language.

He stepped around the stack of red miniskirts. "Janet Lupo?"

She dropped the pile of clothing and stared at him with her jaw sprung wide. Despite her completely flabbergasted expression, he could see she looked good—great, in fact. Very healthy, almost glowing, with a vitality about her that had been lacking in the girl he'd once known. No, wait, that wasn't vitality—she was *smiling,* that's what threw him off.

Interestingly, he had no sense of the man with her except as a bundle of formidable power. No real scent, but pale, really very pale and tall. Blond, with a swimmer's build, and—

"Fuck a duck," Janet said.

"Hello, Janet. It's nice to—"

Drake had an impression of blurred motion and then he went sailing through the windowfront and bounced onto the cobblestones. Broken glass rained down everywhere.

Chapter 11

Crescent worked very hard on not shrieking. It wasn't easy. There they'd been, minding their own business, when this bitch came out of nowhere and threw Drake through a window—*through* the damn window!—and now the two of them were rolling in the street like a couple of alley cats—or wolves, probably, wolves would be more accurate. The place was emptying pretty quick as the stampede started, and Drake was down, was on his back, and—

"Get *off*!" Crescent leapt forward, but a brick fell on her shoulder and yanked her back.

"I wouldn't," the blond hottie said mildly. He was a yummy one, all right, and towered over her almost as much as Drake did. Skinny drink of water, though. She observed that the brick was his hand. Strong drink of water, too. "I think it's a family thing. Better let them—ow."

She'd never hit anyone in the face before, and she was disappointed. Blondie just sort of shook it off and rubbed his jaw. "Now don't *you* start. There's only one woman permitted to smack me around, and she's currently rolling in a mud puddle with your friend."

Show him your necklace.

Obeying the inner voice that was never, ever wrong (but which didn't speak up nearly often enough), she fumbled for one of the three necklaces around her neck, broke the chain, and thrust it at him. To her amazement, he stumbled backward and threw a hand over his face. Just like in the movies!

"Now you're just being mean," he said reprovingly, groping for her. "Put that cross away before you hurt someone. Like me!"

She ignored him, turned her back, stuffed the cross down her shirt, grabbed the cow around the waist, and pulled. "Get *off*," she huffed. Grabbing her lover's attacker was not unlike trying to stop an army tank—the woman absolutely did not budge. But she shrugged—nearly dislodging Crescent—and punched Drake in the eye for good measure.

"Your monkey's bothering me," she told him, and punched him again.

"Crescent, *don't*," Drake said sharply. There was a rill of blood trickling down his chin, but other than that he looked unharmed. Anybody else would be spurting blood from about six different arteries after sailing through a plate-glass window. Thank goodness for werewolf constitution! "Get back. Get out of the way. Don't worry about me."

"Yeah, short stuff." Bam! Another punch. "He'll be just fine. Why don't you go get a Frappuccino?"

She ignored them and stubbornly tugged again.

"Crescent, *get away from here*. In a minute I'm going to forget to be a gentleman—Goddammit, Janet, if you hit my jaw again I'll put you over my knee!"

"It's a date, gorgeous."

"Oh no you don't!" Crescent tried a new grip and pulled harder. "Nobody's getting spanked but me."

"Really?" Hottie said from behind her.

"I said get off him!" She suddenly felt her forearm clutched in an unbelievably strong grip and then she was sailing over the woman's head, only to hit the sidewalk ass-first. The shock went all the way up her spine, and she yelped.

"Unwise," Drake said, shrugging out of his coat.

"Oh, please. Nothing personal, Blind Man's Bluff, but you're fucked. Can't have anybody ratting me out to Mikie Boss Man, so sorry, sit still and die now, okay?"

"I'll pass. And I have no idea what you're talking about."

"Really, Janet. Can't you two solve this a little more amicably than introducing death into the equation?"

"Pipe down, Dick. No one hit your buzzer."

Crescent bounced up from the pavement. All three of them looked surprised to see her still in the game. "I *said*," she growled, "keep your hands off my man, bitch!" Then she punched the cow in the jaw.

This was infinitely more gratifying than when she'd hit El Hottie. The woman rolled away from Drake like a bowling ball and slammed up against the Gap's front door, cupping her hands beneath her chin to catch the blood, and Crescent felt the shock of the blow race all the way up to her shoulder.

The woman spit a tooth into her palm. "Hey, that actually hurt, you little cunt!"

"Now *that's* interesting," El Hottie said approvingly. He was the most detached man she'd ever met. What a weirdo! "You don't smell like a meat-eater."

"Crescent!" Drake was utterly shocked. It was almost worth getting jumped just to see the look on his face. "How did you manage that?"

"Do we have to talk about it now? Or do I have to keep kicking the shit out of what's-her-cow?"

"Hey, hey," she said warningly. "Watch the language."

"You have a problem with *cow*? You put your hands on him again, I'll kick your ass up so high people will think you have a second head. *Cow.*"

"Says the midget." But the woman's lips were twitching—like Drake's did when he was amused and trying not to show it.

"For heaven's sake, Janet," Drake was saying, limping over to her and helping her out of the dirt. "What's the problem? I haven't seen you in—what? Fifteen years? And you attack me?"

"I don't suppose we could talk about this over a drink," Hottie commented. He grinned, and Crescent nearly screamed. He had about a thousand teeth, and they all looked very sharp. "So to speak."

+ + +

"So now we're sort of . . . uh . . . in love and stuff. And I'm not going back," Janet added defiantly.

"You don't have to sell me on the advantages of going rogue," Drake said.

"What, so, you'd get in trouble with your boss? The what-d'you-call him? Pack leader?" Crescent dumped a third packet of sugar into her coffee. "What's he care?"

"He probably wouldn't," Janet replied. "But it's not worth it to me. The risk, I mean. He could order me to stay on the Cape and I—I would have to obey, or disobey."

They were sitting in the corner of the Starbucks on Park Street, speaking in low voices. Although Crescent wasn't sure why they bothered. This was Boston, after all. Nobody gave a shit.

"Well, you don't have to worry about me. You're only the

second pack member I've run into in the last year. And even if I were to run into Michael—which isn't likely—I certainly wouldn't mention you."

"Well, thanks. I guess I shouldn't have. Uh." Janet coughed. "You know. Kicked the shit out of you without asking questions first."

"That's all right," Drake said kindly, ignoring Crescent's and Richard's snickers.

"You might think about moving," Crescent suggested. "If your boss and all his lackey werewolves live on the Cape. I mean, you're only ninety miles away. If you lived in—I dunno, Argentina? That would be better."

"Our home is here," Janet said stubbornly. "Besides, we're all over the world. Might as well stake out a small claim and defend it here as well as anywhere else."

Crescent noticed the hottie—Richard—hadn't touched his frozen coffee. "Aren't you thirsty?"

"Yes."

"So what's your story, Blondie?" Janet asked. "Getting smacked by you was like getting smacked by a two-by-four. What do you have for bone marrow, steel ball bearings?"

"Well, I think I—"

"—might be part fey."

Richard's eyebrows arched. "Really? I thought your kind died out years ago."

"It's fairy, not fey, and most of us have—at least, I've never been able to find anybody else like me, and Drake, how the hell did you know that? I never got around to telling you!"

"I guessed yesterday, and when you smacked Janet, I knew for sure."

"Whoa, back up." Janet put her palms out like a traffic cop. "You're a fairy? Like Tinkerbell? With wings and shit?"

"Do you see any wings?" she snapped.

"Jeez, nobody told me fairies had such rotten tempers."

"She's just mad because I figured it out," Drake said with annoying smugness. "She was saving it for a surprise."

"You're so insufferable!"

"Yes."

"It runs in the family," Janet added with a grin. "The men especially. *So* annoying."

"Oh, yes," Richard said. "*Male* werewolves are the annoying ones."

"You shut up. Listen, I always heard fairies were these little delicate things. You hit me like a bulldozer."

"Dense bones," Drake said.

"Difficult to break," Richard added. "I ran into one of your kind about seventy years ago, and he nearly killed me. He was quite old even then, dear, so don't get your hopes up. I'm sure he's dust by now."

"Oh."

"Don't sound so disappointed. He was a nasty old man."

"This explains your fixation with flying," Drake said, thinking out loud.

"Dense bones *and* she can fly?" Janet snorted into her Caramel Mocha Frappucchino. "Yeah, that makes sense."

"You ever see an airplane take off?" Crescent asked. "You look at it and wonder how something that heavy can ever get off the earth . . . and then it goes . . . and you're left on the ground."

"Well, of course you can't fly with all those accessories." Whip-quick, Richard flicked his spoon at his whipped cream and a dollop appeared as if by magic on the end of Janet's nose. "But you knew that."

"What?"

"Dammit, Dick! Quit throwing whipped cream on me. You *know* I hate that."

"What?" Crescent nearly yelled.

Richard looked startled. "All your piercings. You probably set off metal detectors in airports. And of course your kind can't tolerate certain metals."

Drake's eyes nearly bulged out of his head. Crescent knew exactly how he felt. How had she never thought of this before?

"What are you guys talking about? Drake, you look like you just crapped your pants."

"I—um—I want to fly, but I can't. But I never made the connection—"

"What are you guys talking about?"

"Fairies have a legendary fear of metal, especially iron," Richard explained. "In Crescent's case, I would guess that translates into being unable to get off the—what are you doing?"

Tearing out all her goddamned earrings and rings, that's what she was doing. Between her ears, nose, and belly button, she had more than a dozen.

"I guess we're done talking," Janet commented when Crescent stood up so quickly her chair fell over.

"There's a back door behind the second coffee machine," Drake said, "but I'm not sure now is the appropriate—Crescent?"

She ran for the door, and it was right where he told her it would be. She was through it in a flash and bounding up one, two, three flights of stairs, and praise all the gods, the door to the roof was propped open. And then she was out in the open.

She dove off the roof. At the last moment, she closed her eyes—she'd been disappointed too many times not to feel a twinge of anxiety. She knew she wouldn't break any bones, but landing hurt all the same.

Except she wasn't landing.

She cracked open one eye and saw Janet, Richard, and Drake standing on the roof, looking at her. Except they were upside down.

Correction: *She* was upside down. In midair.

"There we go," Richard said cheerfully. "Problem solved."

"Uh." She could feel the grin split her face. "Can somebody reach my foot? I have no idea how to get down."

Chapter 12

N ow, it's none of my business," Janet began with, for her, heartening tentativeness.

"Oh, here we go."

"She's a little young for you, don't you think?"

"I have to take relationship advice from a woman who hangs out with a dead guy?"

"Figured it out, did you?"

"Took me a while. He doesn't really have a scent, you know? In fact, he smells more like you than anything else."

They were back at Drake's house, and the sun would be up soon. Crescent's feet hadn't touched the ground in three hours. Richard was amusing himself by bouncing her off the roof to see how high she would go. His personal best was sixteen feet. Drake and Janet were sitting cross-legged near the edge of the roof, watching.

"She's one of a kind."

"No shit. But she's a little—uh—that is to say—you think she's in it for the long haul?"

Crescent shrieked with joy as Richard bounced her on the balls of her feet and she shot into the air again.

"I have no idea," he said.

"It's just—you know, I didn't really know what I was missing until Dick kidnapped me—"

"What?"

"Long story. Anyway, you're a pretty good guy. I mean, I always liked you. It'd be nice if you could finally settle down."

"Why, Janet, I never dreamed this tender side of you existed."

"Shut the fuck up."

"And it's kind of you not to mention my grossly debilitating handicap."

"What? Oh, that. I'm not being *nice*. I just keep forgetting. I mean, you don't act like a blind guy."

"How exactly does a blind guy act?"

"How the hell should I know? So anyway, back to Blondie. You just, like, saw her and knew? Well, I know you didn't *see* her . . ."

"Actually," he said suddenly, "I did. See her, I mean. I can."

"For real? Not just make a picture from how she smells?"

"For real."

"Well." Janet rested her chin on her knees for a moment. "I don't know dick about fairies. Except I remember this story from when I was a kid—you remember Sarah Storyteller? Michael's grandma?"

"Sure. She used to read to all of us on the grounds, under those trees by the pond."

"Right. Well, there was this one story—about fairies? They were little and invisible. They'd only appear if you caught them. And if you caught them, they'd grant wishes. So maybe Crescent appeared to you. You know, maybe that's why you can see her."

"Or maybe," he said slowly, "she granted my wish."

"Well, sure. That, too. I mean, whatever."

"There's that tender side again. My, Richard has been *quite* the good influence."

"Oh, shut up. So what are you going to do?"

He sighed and shifted his weight. "Hope she flies back to me, I suppose."

"Lame."

"Mature."

"I kicked your ass all over Faneuil Hall, you know."

"Then my girl kicked *your* ass."

"Oh shut up."

+   +   +

Janet and Richard left, but Crescent refused. He'd tried to explain why she should go, but she wasn't having it. "What, is this that dumb 'if you love something let it go, if it comes back blah-blah-blah' thing? Because that sucks. You said I could stay as long as I wanted, you welsher."

He tried to disguise his joy. "Crescent, there's something you should know—"

"Later. God, I'm *starving*. Listen, I'm going to run up ahead and see if those guys are serving breakfast yet."

"It's four o'clock in the morning."

"I *know*, that's why I want to *check*. Be right back."

He shook his head as she hurried away, and then he realized they were quite close to the shelter where she'd been living. Maybe it was foolish to be concerned—she was a tough one to hurt, after all—but he decided to catch up with her anyway.

That was the last rational thought he had for a while. Stupid, really—the punk shaking Crescent like a maraca looked far worse for the wear. An obvious beta type—he needed to be led and, in abandonment, he couldn't take care of himself. He certainly wasn't worth getting worked up over. He supposed Nick and what's-her-name had gone on to greener pastures . . . or easier marks.

"Jimmy, you idiot," Crescent was saying, prying his fingers off her arm, "will you give it up? Grabbing me is not going to fix your life. Now buzz off."

"It's all your fault," Jimmy was insisting. "Nick and Maria took off because of you."

"My ass! They took off because you can't walk ten feet down here anymore without tripping over a cop. Too bad they didn't bring you with, huh, Jimbo?"

Jimmy's eyes flashed murky murder, and Drake moved quickly, spinning him away from Crescent. "Just once I'd like to take a walk with you without being assaulted," he muttered, carefully examining her arm.

"What can I say? I've got a dark past. He's harmless. Let's go eat."

He ignored her. Then he whirled and grabbed Jimmy by the throat, lifting him in the air as easily as a mother picked up her toddler.

"Did you really," he began. He was so angry, it was hard to talk. He wanted to growl and bite. "Did you *really* think you could put your hands on my mate and live to see the sun come up?"

"Whoa!" Crescent said, tugging on his arm. Before them, the punk squeaked and kicked, his face turning an interesting shade of purple. "Let go, Drake. He's just an asshole."

He was shaking the man—really just an overgrown boy, but surely old enough to know better—like a dog shakes a rag doll. "Did you really?" he said again. "*Did* you?"

"Drake! You are freaking me out, dude!"

You're a doctor.

She'll have bruises. He actually marked her—marked her with his filthy hands!

But you're a doctor.

"Drake, will you put him down already? He's already passed out, for Christ's sake. And I really don't want to finish the day at the Cop Shop."

He growled and then flung the man away. They both watched the unconscious tough sail through the air and hit the street like a sack of sand. Jimmy groaned but didn't regain consciousness.

"Jeez, overprotective much?" But she was smiling. "Remind me to never tell you about my years on the streets."

"You *will* tell me."

"Later. After that vein in your forehead isn't throbbing. Yuck, by the way."

"He touched you. He should never have done that."

"Yes, and I think he gets that now! Your mate?" she added, teasing. "Is that what I am?"

He put his arms around her. "Yes. That's what you are."

"Well, all right. Let's go eat."

"If I have to look at another pancake, I may well vomit."

"Dude, it's fine. I'll get waffles," she added with a wicked grin, and stretched up and kissed him.

"I have to tell you something. No waffles. I've put this off long enough—"

"What, no waffles, like, *ever*?"

"Crescent . . . this may be hard to believe—"

She kissed him again. "Your intolerance of starchy foods?"

"Be serious. I'm talking about—"

"The fact that you can see me?"

He blinked. "Well . . . yes. You're not surprised?"

"Of course not." She smiled at him, and he swore he could almost see her glowing. "I granted your wish. Apparently, it's what we do."

"News to me! What exactly did I wish for? To have you in my life, or to see you?"

"I don't know, but it's kind of nice that you got it all in one package, isn't it?"

He supposed it was.

A Fiend in Need

Prologue

Bev Jones took a deep breath and stepped out onto the roof. She'd snuck to Chicago's Chinatown on her lunch break because she wanted to die with the smell of fresh potstickers in her nose.

She walked slowly to the edge of the roof and peeked over. The winter wind ruffled her short, dark hair, but for a miracle, it was almost a nice day—nice for Chicago, anyway.

It was a typically busy Friday afternoon . . . the Friday before Valentine's Day, in fact. And if she had to spend one more Valentine's Day alone—or worse, with only the company of her psychiatrist—she would kill herself.

People said that a lot, but Bev never said anything she didn't mean. And so here she was.

She put her hands flat on the ledge and got ready to boost herself up. Given that she was wearing snow pants and a down-stuffed parka, it might take a while—say, her entire lunch break. Ah, well. If nothing else, she was mildly curious to find out if there was an afterlife. Would there be potstickers and noodle nests in the afterlife? She didn't—

"Bev! Hey! Wait up!"

She started—the last thing she'd expected on a rooftop was to hear someone calling her name—and turned around. And instantly assumed she'd gone crazy: there was a woman running toward her, a woman who—whoop!—just jumped *over* the Chinese arch separating the two buildings. And now—was she?—she was! She was hurrying right over to Bev.

"Thanks for waiting," the strange woman who could jump like

a grasshopper said. "I was running a little behind this morning and was worried I'd miss you."

"Miss me?" Bev gasped. Holy crow, it was like *Touched by an Angel!* "You mean you're here to—to save me?"

The woman—a tall, lean brunette with striking dark eyes and the palest, softest-looking skin—blinked in surprise. Bev had never seen such skin before; maybe the grasshopper/angel was also an Irish milkmaid.

Then she laughed. It wasn't, Bev thought a little sullenly, a very nice laugh.

"*Save* you? Save *you?*" Again, the laugh. The woman actually leaned on the ledge so she wouldn't fall down. "Honey, you're such a dope you actually showed up for work the day you planned to kill yourself."

"How did you—?"

"I mean, of all days to call in sick to your dreary, hated job, don't you think today's the day? And you know damn well the fall won't kill you. What is it, like two stories? If you *really* wanted to ice yourself, why not use the shotgun you keep in your closet? Or one of those Japanese sushi knifes you saved up six months for, really do the job right?"

"I—I—"

"No, you have this stupid idea in your head that swarms of people will gather on the street below, and some good-looking Chicago P.D. monkey will coax you down and fall in love with you. Among other things, you watch too much television."

Bev stared. She was mad, and getting madder, but the grasshopper/angel/demon had said nothing that wasn't true. Hearing it out loud made her feel like a real pigeon turd. It was more than attention, right? Wasn't it?

"*Save* you! You don't want to be saved! You want a date for next week! Ha!"

"That's it," Bev snapped. "I'm jumping."

"Oh, stop it, you are not." The brunette pulled her away from the edge with a casual strength that nearly sent Bev sprawling onto the blacktop.

"I am, too!" She managed to wrench her arm free, nearly dislocated her own shoulder in the process. The stranger was fiendishly strong. "I—I'm clinically depressed, and I can't take it anymore."

"You're mad about not getting the promotion, not having a date, and your mom forgetting your birthday."

"Who *are* you?"

"My name's Antonia. And the reason I'm here is to tell you the fall won't kill you. In fact, it'll break your neck and you'll be a quad in a monkey hospital for the rest of your life. It'll wreck your mom—her insurance company won't cover you because you've been out of the house too long, and *your* insurance sucks. She'll spend the rest of her life in debt and visiting you, and you think you'll be able to get a date from a Shriner's bed? Bottom line, you think your life is in the shitter now? Go ahead and jump. You'll see the shit fly."

"But how do you know?" Not, "that isn't true" or "you're on drugs." Antonia had the creepy ring of truth in everything she said. Even weirder, Bev had never met someone as obnoxious as she was beautiful. She was like the swimsuit ad model from the ninth gate of hell. "How did you know to come here?"

"I just did."

"And why do you keep saying 'monkey'?"

"Because," Antonia sniffed, "you're descended from apes."

"Well, you are, too!"

"No, I'm descended from *canis lupus*. A much more impressive mammal to have in your family tree, in case you didn't know. Which none of you seem to."

"But you're not here to save me?" Bev was having a little trouble following the conversation. She tried to give herself some credit; it had been a surreal five minutes.

"Shit, no! What do I care if another monkey offs herself? There's too many of you anyway. Go ahead and jump, ruin your mother's life, I don't give a shit."

"Then why were you running across rooftops to stop me?"

"None of your damned business," she snapped.

"There has to be a reason."

"Look, are you going to jump or not?"

"That depends. Are you going to tell me why you came?"

The brunette rubbed her temples. "Okay, okay. Anything to shorten this conversation. I see the future, all right?"

"Like a psychic?" Bev gasped.

"Nothing that lame. I see what's going to happen. And, file this away, I'm never wrong. But the thing is, when people don't do what I tell them, when they ignore my advice and sort of plunge ahead on their own, I get the *worst* migraines."

"So you're here . . . to stop yourself from getting a headache."

"Hey," Antonia said defensively. "They're really bad headaches."

"And you're descended from *canis*—from wolves?"

"Duh, yes! Do we have to have this talk all over again?"

"So you're, like—" It was stupid, but Bev made herself say it anyway. "A werewolf?"

"You've heard this before, right? 'Duh, yes.' "

"But—but you just sort of blurted it out! You can't go around just telling monk—people that you're a werewolf."

"Why not?"

"Well—you just can't is why not."

She shrugged. "Who are *you* going to tell? Who'd even believe you?"

Bev pictured herself explaining that she didn't jump because a woman claiming to be a werewolf told her the future (after jumping over a roof) and saw Antonia had a point.

"Nobody'd believe *me,* either," she added, almost as if (ludicrous thought!) she was trying to make Bev feel better.

"Why's that?"

"I don't Change."

"You mean you don't—" Bev groped in the air, trying to find the words. "You don't get furry and howl at the moon and steal babies?"

"Babies! Monkey babies? Ugh! Do you have any idea how *awful* you guys taste? I'd rather eat shit than an omnivore."

Bev, stuck in a job she hated, was nevertheless finding her background in social work quite handy about now. There was a pattern to Antonia's outbursts. In fact, the snarkier and louder she got, the more painful the subject under discussion was.

She tried again. "So what you're saying is, you never turn into a wolf. Never. But you're a werewolf."

Antonia's lips nearly disappeared, she was pressing them together so tightly. "Yss," she mumbled. "Tht's trr."

"But then . . . how do you know you're—"

"Because my mom's a werewolf, okay? And her dam, and her dam, and her dam, going back about eighty generations, okay? I'm a right line descendant of the She Wolf Rayet, and my dad being a monkey doesn't change that. I am so a werewolf, I am, I am, I am!" She smacked her fist on the ledge for emphasis, and Bev was astounded to see a chunk of concrete fly off in the distance.

"Well, okay," she said, trying to soothe the younger woman. "Nobody said you weren't, all right?"

"*You* did," she sniffled.

"No, I just questioned the logic of running around blurting it out to monkeys. Dammit! Now you've got me using that odious word."

"Sorry," she said, but she seemed to be cheering up. "It's a sore spot, I admit. There are lots of hybrids in the pack—my alpha sired one, for Rayet's sake. They can all Change. Everybody can Change but me. And monkeys."

"So did they—did your friends kick—ask you to leave? Because you don't, uh, do the Change?"

"You mean, did my pack boot my ass because I'm a freak?" She smiled a little. "No. I came west because I—I saw something."

"Was it me?" Bev asked eagerly.

"*No,* it wasn't you, greedy monkey. The whole world doesn't revolve around *you.* Giving you the 4-1-1 was sort of a side trip. I'm really on my way to Minneapolis."

"What's in Minneapolis?"

"That's enough sharing with strangers for one day," she said, kindly enough. "Because we both know you aren't going to jump, why don't you come down?"

"I'll come down after you tell me why we're going to Minneapolis."

"We're?"

"Sure! I'll be your cool sidekick. We'll have adventures and—"

"Stop. Go ahead and jump."

"Awwwww, come on, Antonia," she whined. "It's just the thing I need."

"It's the last thing *I* need. And I don't bargain with monkeys on Chicago rooftops, okay?"

"Okay, okay, calm down. Just tell me why you're going and then I'll climb down. Otherwise, if you leave, you don't know if I'll jump or not."

"You won't—"

"Just think, you could be minding your own business—"

"It's what I should have done this morning, by Rayet!"

"—when bam! Giant killer migraine. All because you didn't hang around and finish a conversation." Bev slowly shook her head. "Tsk, tsk."

Antonia scowled down at her. Bev pushed her reddish blond bangs out of her eyes so she could see if the woman was going to dart off over the rooftops to avoid communicating.

"Okay," she said at last. "I'll tell you why I'm going and then you climb down and go back to your life and stop with the goofing around on rooftops."

"Deal," she said promptly. "So why are you going to Minnesota?"

"Well . . . the pack lets me hang around because I'm full of useful little tidbits, you know?"

"I can imagine," Bev said, impressed.

"But the problem is, I think some of them are, um, scared of me. And the ones who aren't scared don't like me."

"I can imag—uh, go on."

"So there's the mate thing."

"You mean, finding a husband?"

"Yeah. It's a real drive among us, because compared to you guys, there aren't hardly any of us. And the thing is, nobody wants to be my mate. They don't know if their children will, um, be like me. And it's not like I haven't tried to be nice to guys, right? Even though, if I fooled a guy into mating with me I wouldn't have much respect for him. But still. It doesn't matter if I'm nice or awful. Nobody wants to take a chance on a deformed cub."

"Oh." Bev's heart broke a little for the beautiful woman leaning against the ledge. *If someone that thin and that pretty can't get married, there's no hope for the rest of us,* she thought grimly. "So maybe you'll meet someone in Minneapolis?"

"Well, all my—my visions, I guess you'd call them. All my pictures of the future—and it really is like there's some sort of divine camera in my head, and the pictures she takes are never wrong—anyway, they were always about somebody else. Michael, your future wife is going to be on the third floor of your building on such and such a day. Derik, you have to go save the world. Mom, if you go out driving in this weather you won't come back. But they're never about me, you know?"

"Sure."

"So, I'm twenty-five, right? That's old to be an unmated female. And there isn't a werewolf in Massachusetts—maybe the whole world—who wants me to bear his cubs. So I sat down last week and thought and thought. I was trying to *make* a vision happen, which I'd never tried before."

"And it worked?"

"Duh, it worked. I'm here, aren't I?"

"Oh, you're back," Bev said. "Good; it's harder when I feel sorry for you."

"Save your pity, monkey. Anyway, this thought pops into my head: If you help the queen, you'll get what you need."

"And?"

"And that's it. Well, almost it . . . an address popped into my head right after. So off I go."

"To help the queen and get what you need," Bev repeated thoughtfully.

"Yup."

"Why aren't you flying? Or is it so you can occasionally stop and help a monkey stop doing something silly?"

"Don't flatter yourself. Fly? Stick myself in a tin can that hurtles through space at a zillion miles an hour, a thousand miles up on the air? Breathing recycled monkey farts and choking down peanuts?" Antonia shuddered. "No no no no no no no."

"Werewolves are claustrophic?" Bev guessed.

"And the monkey gets a prize!" Antonia patted her, mussing her short red curls. "Good, good monkey!"

Bev knocked her hand away. "Stop that. I can't help not being as evolved as you are."

"That's true," Antonia said cheerfully. "You can't."

"Is that your big problem with humans? We can't leap tall buildings in a single bound?"

"Not hardly. Although, that's a good one."

"So what else?"

"This wasn't part of our deal."

"Yes, but . . ." Bev smiled at her, and Antonia actually blanched. "You're dying to tell me. You can't *wait* to tell me. So . . . tell me."

"Okay, you asked for it. Not only are you not evolved—which, granted, you can't help—but you're the most rapacious, bloodthirsty species the planet has ever seen. You go to war over money, religion, land, and drugs. If there isn't a war on, you make up a reason to have one. You kill when you're not hungry, and you kill when you're fat and don't need it. And you *stink*."

"We stink?"

"You reek. It's awful! You don't take enough showers, and when you do shower, you slop nine kinds of perfumed soap, body powders, scented shampoos, and aftershave or perfume all over yourselves. I had to take the subway once in Boston—never again! I had to get off after one stop—*after* I threw up."

"I don't think all of us stink," Bev said carefully. "I think your sense of smell is developed to such a high degree that it seems like—"

"No. You all stink."

"Oh. Well, sorry about that. Thanks for answering my questions."

"Thanks for not jumping—I'm almost out of Advil."

"It was nice meeting you." Bev stuck out her hand. After an awkward moment, Antonia shook it, and Bev tried not to wince at the bone-crushing power in the woman's grip. "Good luck with the queen."

"Good luck with your life. You might try ratting your boss out to the IRS. He hasn't paid taxes in five years. That could put a little excitement in your life—he's a big fish and the feds would love to get him on that, if nothing else."

Her boss? Which boss? She couldn't mean . . . not the big guy. He had fingers in too many pies for her to count. Besides, she was just a worker bee in one of many hives.

"This is Chicago," she explained to the werewolf. "Things are different here."

"But you could change that," Antonia said, climbing up on the ledge. She balanced easily for a moment, her long coat flapping in the wind. "And they have programs, the police do. They could give you a new name, a new life. Something more interesting than contemplating rooftops, anyway."

"Yes," she said dryly, "but there's always the chance that he could have me killed."

"Sounds exciting, doesn't it?" Antonia said, and jumped. She landed on her feet in a perfect little crouch; Bev was instantly jealous. More than jealous. Sure, it was easy for the gorgeous werewolf to give career advice. It was slightly more difficult for the little people, thanks very much.

But the niggling thought
(*sounds exciting, doesn't it?*)
wouldn't go away.

Chapter 1

Antonia paused and then knocked at the door of 607 Summit Avenue. Mansions, of course, were nothing she wasn't used to, but she had never seen an entire street of them. And this one—across from the governor's mansion, no less—was nearly the grandest of them all.

It was white, except for enormous black shutters. Three floors that she could see from the front. Wraparound porch deep enough for couches and several rocking chairs. A detached garage as big as most people's starter homes.

Well, a queen lives here, she reminded herself. *Of course it's going to be grand. What did you expect, a tent?*

Still, it was weird. She had no idea American monkeys had started electing royals.

She didn't bother to knock again; she could hear someone coming. The door was pulled open—the small, skinny woman had to struggle with it—and then Antonia was face-to-face with a beautiful woman (yawn . . . they were a dime a dozen on the Cape) with skin the color of good coffee. Her eyes were also dark and tip-tilted at the ends, giving her a regal (daresay queenlike?) air. She had cheekbones you could cut yourself on.

"Are you the queen?" Antonia asked. Dumb question; of *course* she was the queen, who else could be? The woman was born to be on the one dollar bill.

At least this one didn't stink too badly—she'd had a shower that night and, even better, hadn't drowned herself in nine kinds of powders, soaps, perfumes, and deodorants.

"I'm here to help you," she continued when the woman didn't say anything. "I'm Antonia Wolfton, from the Cape Cod Pack."

The queen blinked at her, a slow-lidded, thoughtful blink, and then said, "You'd better come with me." She turned, and Antonia followed her through an enormous entryway, down several hallways (the place smelled strongly of old wood, old wool, and Pledge), and into the largest kitchen she'd ever seen. Several people were sitting on stools, which were grouped around a long, industrial counter, bar-style.

"Guys," the queen announced, "this is Antonia Wolfton, from the Cape Cod Pack. Hold onto your panties: She's here to help us."

One of them, a leggy blonde dressed in linen pants and a sleeveless white blouse, looked up from her tea. Actually, they all looked up. But it was the blonde Antonia couldn't look away from.

And there was something going on here, wasn't there? It wasn't just the group, almost unnaturally still. And it wasn't their smell—though they'd obviously gone easy on the fake scents and heavy on good, old-fashioned showers—their scents, that was it, she almost had it, could almost taste the problem, the—

She heard someone coming down the stairs and then the door about fifteen feet away swung open and a man walked in.

Well. Not walked. Loped, really. He was tall and lean, with a swimmer's build—narrow hips and broad shoulders. Shirtless, with a fine fuzz of dark hair starting at the top of his ribs and disappearing into his jeans. He had shoulder-length, golden brown hair—sunny hair, as her pack leader's daughter would have said—and mud-colored eyes. When he looked at her with those eyes, she had the distinct sensation of falling.

"Oh, it's you," she said faintly. Those eyes . . . they weren't intelligent. They were just this side of savage. Oh, she liked those eyes. She just needed to fatten him up some; he was far too thin. "How's it going, Garrett?"

"What?" the blonde said, spilling her tea. "What did you say?"

"Garrett Shea, right?" Antonia asked. "I—saw a picture of you."

"What?" someone else said, someone with a profound bass voice, someone not to be ignored, but she couldn't stop looking at Garrett.

Which was a good thing, because Garrett Shea picked that moment to leap at her. Really leap, too. He covered the distance between them in half a heartbeat, tackling her so hard she slammed back into the wall.

He was sitting on her chest, ignoring the pandemonium that had just erupted. His long hair swung down into his face, almost touching hers. His hands were on her shoulders.

And . . . he didn't smell! He had *no scent at all.* Not "he recently showered and took it easy on the Mennen"—no scent. Zero scent. He smelled like a piece of paper. She had never, in her quarter-century of life, ever smelled a person who—

That's how he got the drop on her! He could get the drop on any werewolf, and what the hell was he, anyway?

"You're not pack," she told him, trying to get a breath.

"Garrett Shea?" he asked.

"Right," she groaned. "Get off." He was leaning in, his upper lip curling back from his teeth, and she didn't know whether to be alarmed, afraid, pissed, or aroused. It was so damned confusing she just laid on the tile like a squashed bug.

"Shea?" he said again, almost into her neck.

"Now. Get off now."

"George!" someone shrieked, a drilling sound like a bad visit to the dentist. "Get the hell off her right this minute!"

"—swear I didn't know, she just said she was here to help and I thought you guys would get a kick out of—"

"Sir, if you'll grab a hand, and I'll grab a hand—"

"We'll be too slow."

"Shea?" Garrett asked her again. His befuddled expression had entirely disappeared, leaving a look of sharp concern in its place.

Too bad; she had her legs up now, her feet resting on his belly, and she kicked out, hard, and was extremely satisfied to see him sail over the counter and crash into the tiles behind it.

She flipped to her feet, making the dark-skinned woman flinch, and grinned as Shea slowly pulled himself up behind the counter.

"Are we going to do this now, or should we put it on our schedules for later? Because either way works for me. Actually, right now works for me."

"Jesus," the blonde said, making everyone *but* the dark-skinned woman flinch. "How many teeth do you *have*?"

Oh. Her smile. Monkey etiquette, monkey etiquette! Her palm shot up, covering her mouth. "Enough to get the job done, I s'pose. Who are you?"

"Introductions," the bass voice said, and it belonged to a terrifying-looking man, tall and dark, a man who did not suffer fools lightly, a man who would just as soon eat you as listen to you whine. Oh, she could like this man. "They are long overdue."

Chapter 2

The tall dark man was the king of the vampires: Sinclair. The tall blond woman was the queen: Betsy (har!). The black woman was their monkey-servant/friend/watcher-type: Jessica. Garrett was a "Fiend" named "George." The shorter brunette woman was an ordinary vampire, their servant, like a beta werewolf back home: Tina. They all lived together along with a monkey named Marc, who was currently "on shift." It made much sense to Antonia; Michael and Jeannie, her alphas, surrounded themselves with betas. They lived together like a family.

One in which she had no part.

She shoved that thought away and it went, as she was practiced at ridding herself of that particular thought. Instead, she pondered the most fascinating thing about these oddballs: The king, the queen, and Garrett had no scent at all.

She had heard of vampires, of course, but she had never seen one. Nor did she know anyone who had ever met one—or, at least, who admitted to it. According to lore, vampires were territorial to a degree that they had convinced themselves werewolves didn't exist. Which was perfectly fine with the werewolves.

"Well, here I am, then," Antonia said, feeling peevish that she'd assumed the servant was the mistress. "Put me to work."

"If you'll give us a moment, Antonia," the king said pleasantly, in the way leaders pretended like they were asking. "We need to 'catch up,' as it were. You say you're a werewolf?"

"Yes."

"Mm-hmm. And you left your pack to serve our queen? The queen of the vampires?"

"I didn't know she was the queen of the *vampires*," Antonia explained. "That part wasn't in the picture."

"But you believe us? That we're vampires?" the queen asked.

Antonia shrugged. "Sure."

Sinclair continued. "And you get these, ah, pictures of the future? Do you have a camera of sorts?"

"Yes, my brain," she snapped. "Which is overtaxed right now having to go through this again."

"Do not speak that way to the king," the tiny brunette, Tina, warned her.

"Why not? He's not *my* king."

"This is how you serve the queen?" Sinclair asked silkily. Antonia, who hardly ever noticed such things, noticed his suit: black, immaculate, and obviously made for him.

"I'm here to *help* the queen, not kiss your ass. I think 'serve' might be an exaggeration. I'm not a walking TGI Friday's."

The queen burst into helpless laughter, which almost made Antonia smile. Certainly, everyone else in the room was looking sour.

"That's great," the queen said between giggles, "but I already have more help than I can shake a stick at. I mean . . . well, look." She gestured to the kitchen. "I've been trying to get rid of some of these bums for almost a year."

"Some of us," Jessica piped up, "her whole life."

"Well, too bad. I have to help you to—to get something I want, so here I am."

Tina leaned over and murmured something in the king's ear. Idiots. When she said she was a werewolf, did she say she was hard of hearing, too?

"I don't know who Dr. Spangler is, but don't call him. There's too many people for me to deal with as it is."

Tina looked startled, and Jessica, who had only seen Tina's lips move, jumped, and then said, "Well, uh, I think—we think—you might be. Uh. Crazy."

"No no no," Sinclair said smoothly. "That's a harsh word, I think."

"Confused," Tina suggested.

"Oh, come on," the queen said. "Give her a break. She came all the way from Maryland—"

"Massachusetts."

"—right. And she knew George's real name! I mean, hel-looooooo? Am I the only one who thinks that's a really good trick? So why can't you give her a break on this?"

"Because werewolves don't exist," Sinclair explained.

A short silence followed that and then Jessica said cautiously, "But you're a vampire."

"The existence of one does not ensure the existence of the other," the king almost snapped. "And I can assure you, in all my long life, I've never seen one."

Antonia snickered. "So that's why we don't exist? Because you've never seen one? Too bad; I thought you were smart."

He blinked and said nothing.

"Well," the queen said, and Antonia almost—almost—liked her. The woman was obviously pulling for her. She must be used to strangers popping up out of nowhere and making declarations. "When's the full moon? She can, you know, get furry and make believers out of us."

"It's in six days," Antonia said with a sinking feeling. "But the thing is, I can't Change. Into a wolf, I mean."

"Oh?" Sinclair asked with a truly diabolical smile.

"Yeah, yeah, I know how it sounds. My father was a—anyway, the pack thinks that instead of Changing, I get visions. All the disadvantages of being a werewolf, and none of the advantages," she joked. "I might as well be a m—be a regular person."

"Boy oh boy, you're not making it easy for me to stick up for you," the queen commented.

"Sorry," Antonia said, and almost meant it.

"She isn't," Garrett said from his corner, and they all jumped.

"Cripes, George! I forgot you were there, you were so quiet."

"Why are you calling him George?"

"Well, he doesn't—uh, didn't—talk, and 'hey you' got old."

"His name's really Garrett Shea?" Jessica asked, leaning forward. "How did you know that?"

Antonia shrugged. She wasn't about to go into the whole "sometimes in addition to pictures, a whole fact will appear in my head, indistinguishable from something I read" thing.

As it was, they were probably about ready to toss her on her finely toned ass. She was pretty sure. It was so hard to read them! Except for Jessica, who smelled hopeful and interested, an altogether pleasing scent. But the others . . . nothing. It was maddening, and cool.

"Garrett," Garrett said, nodding.

Tina and Sinclair looked at each other and then back at Antonia. "We really aren't in the habit of letting strangers just, ah, insinuate themselves into our lives . . ."

The queen buried her face in her hands. She'd painted her claws lavender, a monkey habit Antonia found completely ridiculous. At least she didn't bite them. "Oh my God, I can't believe you've even got the nerve to say that."

"That was entirely different, my love. As I was saying, this is not our normal habit, but you seem to possess information we can find useful."

"Aw," Antonia said. "Stop it or I'm gonna cry."

They all looked at Jessica, for some reason, who said, "Hey, there's plenty of room for her and then some. She's welcome to hang."

"Jessica owns the house," the queen explained.

"Oh," Antonia replied, mystified.

"And I'm sorry, you probably said your name earlier, but I didn't catch it."

"It's Antonia Wolfton."

For some reason, this made the queen blanch. "No. That's not really your name, is it? Antonia?"

"What the hell's wrong with you? If possible, you just went pale." The woman *did* look ghastly . . . practically unattractive, which was a good trick for a good-looking, green-eyed leggy blonde.

"Nothing. Uh, nothing."

"I mean, you're the queen, your name is Betsy, and you've got a problem with *my* name?"

"No, not at all, it's a great name. Um, can I call you Toni?"

"No," Antonia said. "You can't."

Chapter 3

Okay, so here's your room while you want to stay with us, and the bathroom's right here ..." The queen stepped back out through the doorway, pointed to her left, and then stepped back into the room, a largish bedroom with green and gold–flecked wallpaper. Antonia liked it at once; the walls were the color of the forest in mid-afternoon. "Sorry it's not attached, but it's your own private bathroom so you won't have to share it with anybody. And, uh, I guess that's it. Agh!"

Antonia spun around. Garrett had followed them up. "That's going to get real fucking annoying," she warned him.

He smiled at her in response.

"Bad George! How many times do I have to tell you not to creep around like that? You'll give everybody heart attacks. Bad, bad Fiend!"

"Why are you talking to him like a dog that pissed on the rug?" she demanded.

"Uh ..." Betsy (the queen ... har!) looked flustered. "You're right, I'm sorry. It's just that we're so used to him being more like an animal than a person. Up until a couple months ago, he never talked at all. Not a single word, nothing. Heck, he didn't even walk! Then he said something—"

"What?"

" 'Red, please.' He's into crafts. Long story. Actually, it's a short story: He likes to knit and crochet, and he was out of yarn. So anyway, he says this, right, and we all freak out. Right? Then, nothing. Then you show up, and you're all, hidey ho, how's it hanging, Garrett? And he freaks out and *jumps* you! You gotta understand, in addition to not talking, he's never done that before, either, unless he was bringing down prey or protecting me. He's like a lion with a gazelle when it comes to rapists. I dunno, it's weird. Anyway—"

"Not having to take a breath," Antonia commented, "must come in really handy for you."

"Like you wouldn't believe. Anyway, you can understand why we're all a little freaked out."

"Sure, I guess." She was still mystified. At home, when a stranger showed up, you let them stay as long as they liked, no questions asked. She reminded herself that vampires and monkeys were different. Duh. And Garrett, even for a vampire, was the most different of all. Interesting.

"Antonia," Garrett said. They both waited, but that was apparently all he had on his mind. She took another look at him. Brought down rapists, did he? Not much of a talker?

Mmmmm.

"You've got great hair," she told him. "A girl could fall in love."

He smiled at her again.

"Agh, don't *do* that," Betsy said. "I swear, his grin is as creepy as yours."

"He's got a nice smile," Antonia said defensively. "It's just right: friendly, but not aggressive."

"Uh-huh, sure. Well, I'll let you get settled, and—"

"I don't need to get settled. I need to help you. What are you doing now?"

Betsy looked startled. "Now now?"

"Yeah, now now. Because I'm stuck to you like a squashed bug until—until whenever."

She shrugged. "You know, a year ago, this would have seemed incredibly bizarre to me, but no longer. Now I take it all in stride, bay-bee! You want to help? Come on. Not you, Geor—Garrett. You'll just make a mess of things."

Garrett ignored her, which Antonia thought was just adorable.

Chapter 4

Oh no no no," Antonia groaned. "Isn't there a bullet I can take for you or a knife in the ribs or something?"

"Hey, you wanted to help, so you're helping."

"I don't think so," Jessica said, looking her up and down critically. "The blue makes her look washed out. Which, we can all agree, is not a problem I myself have. But it's not so good on your model."

"Go back and change into the yellow one," Betsy said.

"Fuck this shit," Antonia snapped. "I seriously doubt this is what the gods or whoever had in mind when they sent me a vision of helping you."

"Sez you. Go change."

She stomped back into the small sitting room, ripped the ice blue bridesmaid gown off, and struggled into the piss-yellow one. This, *this* was her punishment for every bad thought, word, and deed she had ever thought, said, and committed. Fucking bridesmaid gowns!

She slouched out into the larger room, and both women immediately said, "No."

"Why'd they even send that one over, anyway?" Betsy asked. "It's awful. Nobody can wear that color."

"Because they want a big fat commission, so better to send too many instead of not enough. Why don't you try the black one?" Jessica suggested.

"Why don't I make a rope out of this one and hang myself?"

"Quit bitching," the queen ordered, "and go change. And hurry it up; we don't have all night."

Jessica laughed. "Actually, we do."

"Well, that's true, but never mind. Change, please." At Antonia's poisonous glare, she added, "I meant dresses. That wasn't some kind of werewolf put-down."

"Better not have been," she muttered and stomped back to the sitting room.

"So, uh." Jessica was speaking with forced casualness, which smelled like oranges on fire. "When did you figure out that you weren't, uh, going to turn into a wolf ever? I mean, you're pretty young."

She had to laugh at that one. "I'm old for an unmated were-wolf."

"Oh. Because I was thinking, maybe you just haven't had a, uh, chance to, you know. Change."

"It happens with puberty."

"Puberty?" Betsy echoed.

Antonia was wrestling with the zipper. "Yeah, you know. Hair in new places, things get bigger, and suddenly you're thinking about boys. Don't worry, it'll happen for you soon."

"Okay, okay, you don't have to be a jerk about it."

"Yes she does," Jessica whispered, having no idea that Antonia could hear her perfectly well.

"So you were a teenager and you never Changed?"

"Not once." At last! The thing was on. Hmm, not to bad. She studied herself in the mirror; she looked like one of those old pictures of a Greek stature. The dress was simple; no ruffles or fluffs. Straight across the boobs, falling to her hips, and then falling to the floor. And the deepest black, so black it made her skin glow.

"This one isn't horrible," she said, stepping out.

"No!" Betsy cried. "Black bridesmaid dresses at a vampire wedding? How clichéd can you get? I mean, it looks great on you, Toni—"

"Stop trying that, it won't work. *An-TONE-ee-uh.*"

"—but I just can't do it."

"Why are you even getting married? You're already the king and queen, right?"

"It's a long, horrible story," Betsy said, "and I don't have any alcohol, so I'm not telling it."

"Maybe that dress in a different color?" Jessica suggested.

"Maybe." Betsy got up and started circling Antonia, which she thought (but didn't say) was extremely rude in her culture. "It does look great on her. And it helps, frankly, that all my bridesmaids are fabulous-looking."

"Well, that's true," Jessica said modestly. "But Tina and I are short."

"Andrea's tall, though."

"Yeah, but still. Tina and I won't look as, uh, what's the word? Stately. With this cut of gown, I mean."

"I don't know," Betsy said, prowling around Antonia like a panther. "It's a great dress. Good cut, good lines. Probably look good on everybody."

"I thought we agreed that no dress looks good on everybody. You've got a short skinny black gal, a short brunette, and a tall blonde walking down the aisle in front of you."

"You *are* really thin," Antonia informed her. "Where I'm from, they'd hunt for you and be sure you ate everything brought to you."

"Thanks for that," Jessica snapped. "I can't help my metabolism any more than Oprah can help hers, so hush up."

"Hey, I was being nice!"

"That's *nice* for you? Jesus."

"What colors do you think we should try the dress in?" Betsy said, jumping in. Too bad. Antonia was hungry for a fight, but a catfight would have been a fine substitute. "Emerald green? Royal blue? Red? No, that's another cliché. I have to say, Antonia," she added, looking her up and down, "you're one of the most gorgeous women I've ever seen. And that's saying something around here."

She shrugged. This was nothing new, and it was inevitably followed by "too bad you're such a grump" or "it's so unfortunate you're not a complete woman" or "at least you've got your looks."

"Too bad you're such a grouch," Jessica added.

Antonia rolled her eyes. "Can I get dressed now?"

"Yeah, I think we're done."

"Don't tease," she warned.

"What a baby!" Jessica hooted. "We've been at this barely two hours."

"We've? You haven't done shit, just stood around running your gums. I've been doing all the work."

"In return for free room and board, which is not such a bad deal, I might add."

Antonia snorted but had no comeback for that, so instead she said, "We're really done? You're not just yanking my chain?"

The queen looked shocked. "Not about wedding matters. Never!"

When she went back to the sitting room, Garrett was waiting for her.

Chapter 5

She blinked at him. There was one door to the sitting room, and he would have had to get past the three of them to get in. She had no idea how he'd slipped by. That lack of scent was maddening, not to mention a real asset.

"Antonia," he said.

"Shhhh," she said, jerking a thumb over her shoulder. "They're right in the next room, I'm sorry to say." She started wriggling out of the dress. "This is so completely not what I had in mind by helping the queen, I can tell you that right fucking now. I assumed she'd be attacked and I'd save her with my superior—" She realized she was standing in her underwear and he was staring at her.

Stupid monkey customs! Apparently it even bothered dead monkeys, the whole no-clothes thing. Although, strange, she hadn't thought of Garrett as a monkey before. But of course he was. Right? A dead monkey was still—

Well, that wasn't true at all, and she knew it well. He was stronger, faster, quicker. He didn't babble until she felt like ripping out her own throat, he didn't fret, he didn't want to talk about her feelings, he didn't make war to get more money and then pretend it was to help people. He was just . . . Garrett.

"I'm sorry," she whispered, reaching for her shirt. "I forgot that—look, where I come from—which admittedly isn't here—nobody really cares about nudity. But I'll try to remember in the future—"

"Pretty," Garrett said and grabbed her arm, which startled her into dropping her shirt. She hadn't even seen him start to move. Now, why was that thrilling instead of frightening?

"Thanks," she said, "but really, I get that all the time."

"So?" he asked and pulled again. Now she was in his arms, and his cool mouth was on hers, and his hands were moving in her hair, restlessly, almost tugging.

"Yeah," she said into his mouth. "That'll work."

"What's taking so long in there?" Betsy hollered.

"And when you're done kissing me," she said, pulling back and looking into his eyes, which struck her now as more chocolate-colored than mud-colored, "could you drive that hanger into my ear until I can't hear her anymore?"

"No," he said and kissed her again. Which she privately thought made the whole stupid trip worthwhile.

Chapter 6

There was a polite rap at the door; she could smell a single youngish man, blood, and vomit. It was six o'clock in the morning; everyone had gone to bed (to coffin?) but her. Jessica, she had since learned, adjusted her sleeping schedule to the vampires', and Betsy usually went to bed early.

With her charge out of commission until dawn, Antonia found herself putzing about in her room with absolutely nothing to do. She cursed herself for not stocking up on magazines before she came to the house.

There was another knock, interrupting her thoughts. "Come," she called.

The door swung open, and a twenty-something dark-haired man of average height (wasn't Minnesota supposed to be the land of blondes? What was with all the brunettes?), wearing pea-green hospital scrubs and scuffed tennis shoes, stood framed in the doorway. Interestingly, his stethoscope was still around his neck.

"You smell like puke," she informed him.

"You must be Antonia," he replied, grinning. He held out his hand, and she reluctantly shook it. "I'm Marc Spangler. Dr. Spangler, which is why I reek. I swear, I thought the nurse was going to grab the emesis basin in time, but, as so often in my life, I was sadly wrong."

She laughed in spite of herself. "That's too bad. So you spend your days getting puked on?"

"And peed on, and shat on, and bled on," he said cheerfully. "But hey, the pay sucks and the hours are horrible, so it all works out. Luckily, my rent is low."

She laughed again. "What can I do for you, doctor?"

"Oooooh, almost polite and everything! That's funny, I was warned about you."

"Pussies," she scoffed.

"Mmm. Well, today I gotta earn my keep—Sinclair asked me to take a look at you. So if you don't mind." He didn't trail off, as people usually did when they said such a thing. And she realized that, in his laid-back way, he wasn't really asking.

"I'm not crazy," she said. "And you're not a shrink, I bet."

"No, just a garden-variety E.R. rez. But what the hell, it'll make the big guy feel better, right?"

She rolled her eyes. "Right. Get on with it."

He took her pulse and blood pressure and listened to her heart and lungs. He chatted with her about this and that, and she wasn't supposed to notice that he was checking for depression, schizophrenia, paranoia, or delusional thinking.

"Look, I'm flunking your little mental health checklist," she told him, rolling her sleeve back down, "because I do believe things most people don't, I do think people are out to get me, and I'm really bummed about my life, which is why I'm here."

"Yeah, but on the bright side, your vitals are all textbook perfect. You've got the heart and lungs of a track star."

"Well," she said, shrugging modestly. "Superior life form and all that."

"Descended from wolves, is that right?"

She rolled her eyes and didn't answer.

"Uh-huh. But of all the werewolves—and there aren't very many—but of all of them, only *you* don't turn into a wolf during the full moon. Instead, you can see the future."

She sighed. "I know how it sounds."

"It sounds like you're loony tunes," he told her gleefully, "but who am I to judge? I live with vampires."

She smiled at him. She liked him, and on short acquaintance, too! Unheard of. "That's true," she replied. "So what are you telling the king?"

"That you're the picture of health, but I have no idea if you're crazy or not. For what it's worth, you don't seem like a drooling psychopath."

"Aw."

"Time will tell," he went on perkily. "Just when I thought it was getting dull around here, too. I mean, how many times can Betsy obsess over her bouquet?"

She didn't answer him; she was looking at the picture that had popped into her head. "Dr. Spangler," she said after a few seconds.

"Hon, call me Marc. Dr. Spangler is—no one I know, actually, but it's weird, anyway."

She reached out and touched his arm, gently, she thought, but he ow'ed and pulled away. "Youch! Hon, you don't know your own strength."

"Call security before you treat your first patient. Have them check his coat pockets. Understand? Because if you don't . . ." She was rubbing her temples in anticipation of the headache to follow if he ignored her, not to mention the aggravation of funeral arrangements and Betsy's hysterics. "If you don't, your first patient will be your last—stop that!"

He had whipped the stethoscope out and was listening to her heart. She pulled away. "Did you hear what I said?"

"Yup. Did you know your pulse goes way, way up when you're having one of those visions or whatever?"

"Yes," she said and escorted him out. "Remember what I said!" she yelled at him and shut the door before he could bug her with more questions.

Chapter 7

And the guy had not one, ladies and gents, but *two* guns on him! And every other word was the 'MF' word. It was like a bad episode of *Deadwood*."

It was the wee hours of the next morning, an hour or so away from dawn. Jessica and Betsy were listening, slack-jawed. Tina and Sinclair were hiding their emotions a little better but couldn't conceal their interest. Antonia yawned, bored.

"A thirty-eight and a forty-five, for the love of Pete! And I'll tell you what, the minute I'dve tried to Foley him, he would have blown my brains all over the wall. Which would have improved the color scheme, but that's about it."

"And Antonia told you this would happen?" Sinclair asked carefully.

"Yes!"

"No," Antonia said. "I told you to have security check your first patient's coat. That's what I saw: them checking his coat. For all I knew, they would have found a pack of Chiclets."

"You *saved* him," Betsy breathed.

"They were only guns." Oh, wait. Guns were taken a little more seriously by the regulars. "Hmm, maybe I did." She waited. They all waited. Finally, she said, "But I don't feel any better. I mean, I don't feel like I got what I wanted."

"Is it an instant kind of thing?" Betsy wondered. "Boom, you're satisfied and you go home?"

"What do you want?" Tina asked.

She shrugged, partly because she wasn't one hundred percent certain, partly because it was nobody's damned business, and partly because the truth—if it was the truth—was embarrassing. How do you tell strangers you want to belong, you want friends and a family who weren't afraid of you?

"Well, saving Marc certainly helped me out," Betsy said. "Thanks."

"No," Sinclair said.

"Oh, *that's* nice," Marc sniped.

"Don't misunderstand, Dr. Spangler, but I fail to see how saving your life directly helps Elizabeth."

"That's a lot better," Antonia told her. "You should use that instead of Betsy. Betsy's lame."

"Oh, shut up," Betsy told her. "And Sinclair, what are you talking about?"

"I guess he's right," Marc said reluctantly. "Me being dead might have bummed you out, but you would have gone on."

"And on, and on, and on," Betsy said glumly.

"So saving Marc was a bonus? You're really here to do something else?" Jessica asked.

Antonia shrugged.

"Fascinating," Sinclair commented.

"Honey, as soon as the bars open tonight, I'm buying."

"I don't drink," Antonia told him. "And you're nuts if you do. You *do* know alcohol is a poison, right? Aren't you supposed to be a physician?"

"Oh, good," Jessica said. "A sanctimonious soothsayer. Those are the best kind."

"See if I ever warn *you* of mortal danger."

"You *do* know I'm the only thing between you and another gown fitting, right, Fuzzy?"

She smiled; she couldn't help it. It was the first time she could recall joking about not warning someone about impending doom, and the someone in question taking it the way she meant it: as a joke.

The pack honestly worried she would see someone's death and not warn them out of spite. This both puzzled and upset her—she might not be Little Miss Sunshine, but she would never, ever keep such an awful secret. How could her own pack so misunderstand her motives and actions? She'd grown up with them. And what could she do about it? She was too old to Change.

"Fine," Marc was saying. "Virgin daiquiris all around."

"Strawberry?" Sinclair asked hopefully, and Betsy laughed and got up and brought out multiple blenders.

Chapter 8

Y ou make him sleep in the basement?" Antonia practically roared.

"We don't make him do anything," Betsy explained patiently. "He's definitely his own Fiend. Guy. Whatever."

"Oh." Slightly mollified, Antonia calmed down.

"Besides, if he's out and about when the sun comes up . . . poof. At least in the basement, I don't have to worry that he's lost track of time. I mean, does he even tell time?"

"Try giving him a watch."

"I guess. In the past, he'd nibble on whatever we gave him . . . books, magazines, clothes. He's way ahead of the other Fiends now, though."

"What is a Fiend?"

They were strolling along Hennepin Avenue in Minneapolis, as far away from the police station as they could get and still be in the neighborhood. Bait. The queen of the vampires, interestingly, had a thing about drinking blood: she only did it in response to attempted assault.

"Well, the guy in charge before Sinclair and I took over was a real psycho." Betsy was tripping along daintily in ludicrous shoes for city-walking: buttercup yellow pumps with black stripes along the sides. "And he was into experimenting on his subjects, like any psycho. And apparently how you make a Fiend is—it's so awful that I know this—you take a newly risen vampire, and you don't let them feed for a few years. And—and they go crazy, I guess. They turn feral. Forget how to walk, forget how to talk—"

Antonia wrinkled her nose; the three punks following them had too much garlic on their pizza. And their guns hadn't been cleaned in forever; they stank of old oil and powder. "But George can talk and walk. Well, he talks a little."

"Yeah, now. See, for whatever reason, George wouldn't stay with the other Fiends. We had them sort of penned up on Nostro's grounds."

"He agreed to this when you took over?" she asked, startled. Vampires were weird!

"He didn't agree to shit; he's dead."

"Oh." Appeased, Antonia hurried her gait, pretending to be nervous. The jerks quickened their pace, whispering to each other. "So Garrett wouldn't stay with the other Fiends . . . ?"

"Right, he kept getting off the grounds. And one night he followed me home. And I let him feed off me—yuck!"

"Yuck," she mused.

"And he started to get better. And then my sister Laura let him feed off her, and he got *really* better—that's when he talked."

"Oh, your sister's a vampire?"

"No," Betsy said shortly, and Antonia knew that was all to be said on *that* subject. "Anyway, he was always different from the others. And now he's really really different. And then you came."

"And then I came." She whirled, picked up one of the thugs, and tossed him. He skidded to an abrupt halt, courtesy of the unlit streetlight.

"Antonia!" Betsy shrilled. "You're supposed to wait until he attacks us!"

"He was just about to," she said defensively. She smacked the gun out of the other's hand, almost smiling when she heard the metacarpals break.

The third, predictably, took to his heels.

"Well, there you go," she said, gesturing to the two moaning, crying attackers. "Take your pick."

"I don't think this is how you're supposed to help me, either," Betsy snapped, mincing over to the one by the streetlight.

"You're right, this was a freebie. *Bon appétit.*"

"Go over there," she grumbled.

"You mean in the corner that smells like piss?"

"I can't do it in front of you," the queen of the vampires whined.

"Are you kidding me? You're kidding me, right?" Antonia paused. "You're not kidding."

Betsy pointed. "The quicker you go over there and don't look, the quicker we can get out of here."

"I think it's fair to say nobody's ever sent me to the corner before."

Betsy snickered. "Nobody puts Baby in a corner."

"What?"

"Nothing. Monkey culture."

The guy by the streetlight groaned and flopped over like a landed trout. The one with the broken hand had passed out from the pain. "I guess I'll be in the corner, then."

"This is quite a life I've made for myself," Betsy muttered and stomped over to the streetlight.

Antonia yawned and ignored the groans and slurping. When the queen was finished, Antonia walked back to her. "Ready to go?"

Interestingly, Betsy looked . . . what was it? Mortified. "I'm sorry you had to see that."

"You sent me to the corner," she reminded her. "I only heard."

"Yeah, but . . . it's gross. It's so, so gross." She covered her eyes for a moment and then looked up. "Except . . ."

"When it's with Sinclair," she guessed.

"Yeah. Yeah! How'd you know?"

Antonia tapped the side of her nose.

"Yuck. I mean, great! Wait a minute. I thought you couldn't smell us."

"I can just barely smell your blood. Which was on him, last night. Don't worry. What do I care? You're vampires, for crying out loud, why wouldn't you share blood?"

"We're not going to talk about this," Betsy declared and went clicking off down the street in her silly shoes.

Antonia hurried to catch up. "You don't have to be embarrassed. It's your nature now. I mean, I like my steaks raw, and you don't see me apologizing."

"Different thing."

"Totally the same thing."

"And already, you've been hanging around me too long. You said totally!"

"I totally did not." She reached out and touched Betsy's chin. "You missed a spot."

Betsy flinched back, newly self-conscious, and then forced a smile. "Thanks."

They walked in silence for a minute and then Betsy asked, "You really weren't grossed out?"

"Are you kidding? My high school graduation was gorier than that."

Antonia was amused to see Betsy could skip in high heels.

Chapter 9

They returned a couple hours before dawn, about the time Jessica brought out a large bag full of yarn skeins.

"I'll take them down," Antonia offered.

"That's all right, I'll do it."

She yanked the bag out of Jessica's hands, nearly sending the smaller woman sprawling. "I insist. Besides, it's another way to earn my keep."

"Yeah, whatever," Jessica grumped, rubbing her elbow. "I hope you trip on the stairs and die."

"Thanks for that."

The funny thing was, she was in such a hurry to get to the basement and see Garrett, she almost did trip.

For nothing: He wasn't there.

She looked everywhere, listening as hard as she could, frustrated because her sense of smell was useless. It was a big basement—it ran the length of the house and had lots of little rooms and nooks and crannies—and searching it took a long time.

Finally, she gave up, left the yarn bag on one of the tables, and trudged up to her room.

To find Garrett crouched on her desk, his toes on the very edge, perfectly balanced like a vulture, his arms clasped across his knees, his gaze nailed to the doorway.

"There," he said comfortably, as she shut the door and tried not to wet her pants in surprise.

"I've been looking everywhere for you, dope! If they knew you were out of your little basement cell, they would fucking freak out, get me?"

"Get you," he said and soared off the desk at her. She ducked, and he slammed into the door and slid to the carpet.

"Ha!" she crowed, slipping out of her coat and dancing around his prone form. "I'm not that kind of girl. Serves you right."

He bounded to his feet in one smooth motion and pounced on her again. Shrieking with laughter, she let herself be borne back on the bed. "Oh, what the hell," she said, putting her arms around him. "I am that kind of girl."

He nuzzled her neck and, though she was expecting it, she was still surprised when he bit her. She was also surprised at how terrific it felt. Always before she'd had contempt for prey, for bottoms, for victims. But letting herself be taken, letting him get what he needed from her—it was exciting in a completely different way. Always before she'd been the wolf; now she was the rabbit, and it was very fine.

She buried her fingers in his long hair, marveling at the feel of it, the silky texture, and he snuggled her closer to him. His teeth were sharp, but his arms around her were gentle, almost careful.

"Wait," she said, but he ignored her and kept drinking.

"Okay," she said, "but I have a limited number of underpants, so don't—shit!" She heard the tell-tale *rrrrrrip* and, out of spite (and, okay, some lust . . . okay, a lot of lust) ripped through his blue jeans in exactly the same way. "If you have any money at all," she informed him, wriggling beneath him so they could match up, "you're buying me new clothes."

She reached down and felt him, cool and hard, which was startling and sexy at the same time. He hummed against her neck, and his grip shifted, from gentle to urgent, and then he was pushing against her, shoving, and she wrapped her legs around his waist to help him, to help herself. They groaned in unison and then she felt him slide all the way home, and that was worth the stupid trip, too.

He arched above her, her blood running down his chin, and she jerked his head down, licked it away, and met him thrust for thrust. He kissed her bite mark, and she heard him mutter, "Pretty."

"Back atcha," she gasped back, her orgasm very close, shockingly close, and then she was clutching at him so hard she heard something snap and realized with dim horror that she'd dislocated his shoulder. Then she realized that he hadn't noticed, or cared, because his thrusts had sped up and his hands were hurting her, bruising her, and she didn't much care, either. Then they were arching together and shuddering at the same moment, and then they were done.

After a minute in which she caught her breath and he popped his shoulder back in without so much as a change of expression, she groaned, "I'm so sorry about that."

"Why?"

"I didn't mean to hurt you. That badly, I mean."

"So?"

She looked at him, and he looked back at her, two night creatures who could see each other perfectly well in the dark.

She smiled. "Boy, you're just the perfect man, aren't you?"

"Yes."

"And so modest!"

"No."

"Want to go again?"

"Yes."

She grinned. "I'll bet. Listen, Betsy said you followed her home . . . you saved her a couple times. It's no big deal, I'm just curious . . ."

"Lie."

"Okay, okay, don't nag. Yes, it's a big deal. Do you love her?"

"Yes."

So. That was that. The perfect man was in love with someone else. Of course. And the queen, of course, thought of him as a highly evolved dog. Of course. And she . . . she was fucked.

Chapter 10

They spent the night together, trying to hurt each other in various ways, to the extreme satisfaction of both. Antonia, who had been warned again and again

(never with monkeys; they're fragile)

found vampires to be fragile, but they healed so quickly it hardly mattered.

And just when she was wondering what to do about the filmy curtains on her east-facing windows, Garrett yawned, showing long, catlike fangs, and crawled beneath her bed.

"I guess that's that," she said. "Hey—there really is a monster under the bed!"

There was no answer, so she got up, showered, dressed in her last outfit (she'd have to shop today—ugh—or borrow something), and went downstairs.

Sinclair was still up, reading the *Wall Street Journal* of all the tremendously dull things. She'd read a shampoo bottle before she'd even look at that paper.

"Good morning, Antonia."

"Hey." She fixed herself a glass of chocolate milk, stirred through the other papers on the counter, and finally picked the *Minneapolis Star Tribune*.

He said, without looking at her, "That's a nasty bite."

"MYOB, king who isn't my king."

"It was just an observation," he said mildly. "But you should know, Tina isn't in, ah, things for the, ah, long haul."

"What?"

"You are a stunning woman, but the very fact that your presence here is a temporary one would be, ah, attractive to her. I hope my candor hasn't offended you."

She sipped her milk dispassionately and thought about what fun could be had if she let him keep his silly idea. Then she compared it to the fun of telling him the truth.

"I didn't spend the night with Tina, numb nuts. I spent it with Garrett. That's all so fascinating about Tina not being able to commit, Mr. Nosy, but I don't swing that way."

"Oh." The paper rattled. Score! He hadn't seen that one coming at all. Har! "Well. That's. Well."

"Not that it's any of your business."

"Right."

"Because it's not."

"Yes."

"The only reason I'm even telling you is because you were nice enough to give me some advice. Totally unasked for advice, but never mind."

He looked started. "Did you just say totally?"

"No."

They sat in silence for a while, Antonia wondering about blood sharing and the nature of Fiends. If Betsy's blood had helped him, and Laura—whoever she was—had helped him, what might werewolf blood do? Anything? Nothing?

She jumped when Sinclair broke the silence. "To answer your question—"

"I didn't say anything," she said, startled.

"—I have no idea what your blood would do to Garrett. Or not do."

"That's really annoying," she snapped. "I wasn't talking to you. I was just sitting here minding my own business. Your problem is, everybody's so busy kissing your ass, they don't tell you to cut the shit."

"On the contrary," he said, completely unruffled—dammit! She was longing for a fight. "My charming bride-to-be tells me to cut the shit on a near-constant basis. My question for you, Antonia, is why you're even wondering about it."

"Why?" She was startled and then angry she didn't see the question coming. "Why? Well, I don't know . . . as long as I'm in town, you know. Couldn't hurt, right?"

He smiled at her. It was a perfectly nice smile, not at all the rich promise of lust he'd given Betsy the night before, but she still felt a stab. Lower. "Do unto others, as we monkeys like to say?"

"You're not monkeys," she said, shocked. "Well. Jessica and Marc—I mean, I'm sorry." She was flustered, and even a little shamed . . . she had obviously been overusing the rude word. "I don't even think of you as—look, can we get off this? If I offended you, I'm sorry."

"You're clueless," he said, picking up the paper with a rattle, "not sorry. You poor thing."

She fumed through the rest of her breakfast and bolted as soon as she could.

Chapter 11

Stop staring."

"I wasn't," Jessica whined.

"Yes, you were."

"Well, I heard you had a bite mark. But I don't see a thing."

"Superior life form," she reminded them. "It's long gone."

It was the next night, and they were going through Betsy's closet, looking for clothes Antonia might borrow. It was all so girlfriend-ish she thought she might puke. But the alternative—shopping—was ever so much worse.

"This is the most ridiculous thing I've ever seen," she said, peering into Betsy's closet and counting at least a hundred pairs of shoes. "Those look expensive. You walk through dog shit in those things?"

"Why do you think she needs so many of them?" Jess asked brightly. She put a rainbow-colored stack of T-shirts on the bed. "Those should work."

"I've got a bunch of leggings and stuff you can borrow, too," Betsy said, muffled from the closet, "but I draw the line at lending you my panties."

"I'll go to Wal-Mart or something later."

Jessica, who was both rich and a snob, was unable to conceal her shudder.

"Knock it off, Jessica. You're in no position to look down on anybody. Not if you can't run a mile in less than a minute."

"I could if I wanted," Betsy bragged from the closet. "I just don't want to."

"You can't do shit in those shoes," Antonia snapped back.

"Hey, there's a perfectly nice Super 8 over on Grand, if ever you feel the need to, you know, get the hell out."

"Would that I could," she grumped, but she was secretly pleased. It was like—like they were friends or something. They were *grateful* she'd helped Marc. They didn't pry (much) into her sex life. Nobody was worried about her having a defective cub. Nobody cared that she was running out of clothes and needed to borrow. It was—er, what was the word? Nice.

"There's something I've been meaning to ask," Jessica said. "Let me see if I've got this straight, calling one of us a 'monkey' is like using the 'N' word?"

"Sure," Antonia said. "Another way to look at it is, if I'm doing it, chances are, it's socially unacceptable. Seriously. I am not the role model for any of you."

"The 'N' word, huh?" Jessica mused.

"I don't think we should be talking about this," Betsy said nervously, emerging from the closet with an armful of slacks on hangers.

"Relax, white girl. I'm curious, is all."

"Look, it's really really rude, and I'm trying to cut down, okay?"

Betsy was too curious to drop the subject. "So compared to you guys, we're slow, and not too bright, and we can't smell at all, and we stink, and we're really wimpy."

Antonia noticed Betsy said "you guys" in reference to herself as well. Interesting. "Well . . . yeah. But, uh, we know you guys can't help it."

"So it's like being born blind?" Jessica asked dryly. "Poor things, blah-blah, better luck next life?"

"Pretty much."

"But where do you fit in? A werewolf who's never a wolf?"

"I don't know," Antonia said and then shocked herself as much as anyone when she burst into tears.

"Oh my God!" Betsy almost screamed. "I'm so sorry! Don't cry. Please please don't cry."

"I'm not crying," Antonia sobbed. "I never cry."

Jessica leaned across the bed and awkwardly patted her on the back. "There, there, honey. It's gonna be fine."

"Totally fine!" Betsy endorsed. "Totally, totally! Please don't do that!"

"I'm *not*," she said, crying harder.

"Okay, so you're not crying." Jessica held up a navy blue tank top. "What do you think of this one?"

"I hate it," she sobbed.

"Not into blue, eh?"

"Jessica, can't you see she's really upset?"

"Can't *you* see she doesn't want to talk about it?"

"Why did he have to fall in love with you?"

"What?" the women said in unison.

"I said, why did you have to show me anything blue?"

"Well, jeez, we didn't think you'd get so upset," Betsy said. "A tough honey like you?"

"Did George hurt you? Is that why you're mad?"

"Of course he hurt me. We hurt each other. That's what— never mind."

"Oh, sorry." Jessica looked away. "It's none of our business."

"I don't have human hang-ups about fucking," she reminded them. "I'll draw sketches, if you like. It's not that. It's something else."

"Do you want to talk about it?"

"No."

And that was that.

Chapter 12

When they came back down to the kitchen, to her surprise, Garrett was sitting at the counter with a weirded-out Sinclair. Waiting.

For her, she was surprised to see. He came to her at once, nuzzled her neck, and then retreated to his stool.

"You forgot your yarn," Jessica said after a long moment in which it appeared someone had to break the silence.

"Not in the mood," he replied.

Betsy started poking through the mail, squealing with glee when she saw the red Netflix envelopes. She ripped them open, and Jessica groaned when she showed them the discs.

"Why did you get *Gone With the Wind* again, dumb-ass? You own the damned movie!"

"Yes, but this is the new special edition with two new deleted scenes."

"There's one born every minute," Sinclair commented.

"You hush up. Where's Tina? She might want to watch it with me."

"She's out."

"Oh."

"Don't you have to do some hunting, too?" Antonia asked her.

"No."

"Elizabeth is unique among us." Sinclair was giving the queen a look that was positively sappy. "Among other things, she doesn't have to feed as often."

"Like you," Betsy told her. "Unique among the fuzzies."

Antonia groaned. "Please don't call us that."

Jessica had been looking at Garrett during most of the conversation, then back at Antonia, then at Garrett. Antonia could smell the woman was stressed and waited for her to say something.

Finally: "Garrett, do you remember, uh, how you became a vampire?"

"Yes."

They all waited. Betsy, also obviously curious, asked, "Do you mind telling us how?"

Garrett shrugged.

Antonia said sharply, "He doesn't want to talk about it."

"I don't think he cares either way," Sinclair replied, looking Garrett up and down with a critical eye.

"Forget it, Garr. You don't have to say shit."

Sinclair raised a knowing eyebrow. "Protective little thing, aren't you?"

"You wanna go, king of the dead guys? Because we'll go."

"Don't fight," Betsy snapped. "Let's just drop the whole—"

"I was acting. An actor. For Tarzan."

An enthralled silence, broken by Jessica's breathless *"Annnnnnnd?"*

Garrett tugged his long hair. "Grew it out. For Tarzan. Picture folded. Felt bad."

"So you got fired, okay, and then what?"

"Producer tried to cheer me up. Had to get haircut ... couldn't walk around like that."

"With long hair?" Antonia asked, mystified.

"Took me to barber. Late. After sets closed. Producer was Nostro. Had barber cut my throat and drank."

"Jesus Christ!" Betsy practically screamed.

Antonia was on her feet. She didn't remember getting up from the stool, and who cared? "Where's the barber? Is he around here? I'm going to pull his lungs out and eat them while he watches."

"Who was making the movie?" Sinclair asked sharply.

Garrett pointed to the *Gone With the Wind* disc.

"You mean . . . Warner Brothers?"

Antonia had an awful thought, so awful she could hardly get it out; it was clogging her throat like vomit. "That's—that's an old movie."

"Nineteen thirty-nine," Betsy said quietly.

"Tarzan lost funding," Garrett confirmed. "Made that movie instead."

Betsy shrieked again and kicked over her stool. The thing flew across the kitchen and crunched into the wall; plaster rained down on the (previously) spotless floor. *"You've been a vampire for almost seventy years?"*

Garrett shrugged.

"What a pity," Sinclair commented, "that we already killed Nostro." But he was looking at Garrett in a new way: intrigued and even a little alarmed. Antonia wondered how old Sinclair was.

"Sing it, sweetheart! God, what I wouldn't give to have him in this kitchen right now. Torturing poor George and the others for more than half a century, that piece of shit! That son of a bitch!"

"Garrett," Garrett corrected her.

"Right, right, sorry."

Of all of them, Antonia noticed, Garrett seemed the least upset. She asked him about it, and he shrugged.

"Long time ago."

"I guess that's one way of looking at it," she said doubtfully.

"Things are different now."

Yeah, she thought bitterly. *You've been redeemed by love. Loving someone else, that is. Fuck.*

Chapter 13

I'm glad you didn't cut it," she said later, after making love. She stroked the long, silky strands. "I like it long."

"Now, yes. Then, no."

"I suppose. That'll teach you to conform to society," she teased.

He made a sound like gravel rolling down a hill, and after a minute, she realized he was laughing.

She supposed she should tell him; he might wonder, tomorrow night, where she had gone. "Just a heads up, I'm leaving tomorrow."

"Why?"

"Because . . . because I haven't been able to figure out how to help the queen. And I can't stay here while you—I can't stick around, let's just leave it like that."

"But if you don't help . . . you don't get what you want."

"So I don't get what I want. My life will remain completely unchanged." She thought she said it with no bitterness. And dammit all, she was about to cry again. But not in front of Garrett. No way.

"Don't go," he said.

Okay, now she *was* crying. "Well, I am, so shut up about it. What do you care? You love Betsy, don't you?"

"Yes."

"So that's all you need."

"No."

"What's the matter with you? Why do you even care? You've got everything you need right here."

"Now."

"Look, Garrett. I guess . . . you don't really love me."

"Wrong."

"What?" Outraged, she sat up. "You just *said* you loved Betsy."

He yanked her back down. "Love Betsy . . . like the sun. Powerful, can't control it. Don't know what will happen."

"Yeah, that sounds about right."

"Love you like . . . air. Need it. Betsy is queen . . . belongs to everybody. Like money. You . . . belong to me. You're . . . only for me."

She went still as stone for a long time, wondering if her ears were defective, wondering if she dared believe what he'd said. But why not believe him? When had he lied?

"If this is your way of trying out telling jokes," she said through a shuddering breath, "I will dislocate *both* your shoulders, *and* your legs."

"Do it, if you'll stay."

"I'll stay."

"Then okay," he said comfortably.

"I'm not sleeping in the basement, though."

"Okay."

"They can give us good curtains, or we can board up the windows in this room."

"Okay."

"I love you, jerk."

He looked surprised. "Of course."

She groaned and punched him, which led to other things. Nicer things.

Chapter 14

You're moving *in*?"

Antonia nodded with a mouthful of breakfast. "As of right now," she added, spraying the queen with scrambled eggs.

"Oh. Okay. You're moving in? Okay. I thought you were going to leave. We all—I mean, we didn't want you to go but didn't feel like we could make you stay. Ugh, don't smile like that! Especially not with your mouth full."

She swallowed but couldn't help grinning. "Better get used to it." They had wanted her to stay? Had talked about convincing her? How charming!

She scooped more eggs onto her plate. Damn, that Sinclair could cook! Where'd he gotten to, anyway? Oh, who cared?

"Don't you have to call your boss, or leader, or whatever?" Betsy asked, sitting across from her and picking eggs out of her hair.

"Did it last night."

"So it's all taken care of."

"Umm-hmm." Michael had sounded almost insultingly relieved at the news that she wasn't coming back. If she hadn't had Garrett, she might have been devastated. But as it was . . .

"I have a new family now. Don't look scared, I'm only going to get sentimental for a minute."

"I wasn't scared," Betsy said defensively. "Just surprised, is all. You have to admit, you kind of pulled a one-eighty in the last twenty-four hours."

"Yeah, well, this is where I'm supposed to be. My lover's here, he lets me be as rough as I want—"

Betsy put her hands over her ears. "Overshare!"

"—you guys don't seem to care if I can see the future or shit nickels."

"I think I liked the gruff, unsentimental side of you a lot better."

"So I'm staying."

"Well, that's great. A werewolf who can see the future will probably come in handy." She gestured to the cavernous kitchen. "And it's not like we don't have the room."

"Yeah, having me around all the time will be a help, get it?"

"Uh, no."

"And by hanging out here, I get what I want." Lover. Love. Family. Acceptance.

"Oh! So—"

"I switched it around by accident. Or maybe I just wasn't paying attention. Bottom line: I get what I want. Then I help you by moving in. Or I move in with you. Then I get what I want. Either way, I was right. Again. I just don't have enough faith in myself, that's the problem."

"Yeah, that's the problem." Betsy looked mystified. "I don't get it."

"If you were as smart as me," Antonia assured her, "you would."

"Oh, goody. Someone else who has zero respect for me. Because there aren't enough of them hanging out in this mausoleum."

Garrett picked that moment to bound in, give Antonia's hair a friendly yank, and bound back out.

Betsy watched him go. "How, uh, sweet."

"Wow! I didn't even hear him come in that time! God, what a man." Antonia sighed and shoveled more eggs in her mouth. "Isn't that just the sexiest, coolest thing you've ever seen?"

"Um. Let me get you a napkin. Possibly five."

"Bitch."

The queen laughed at her. "Sez you."

MaryJanice Davidson is the bestselling author of several books, most recently *Undead and Unreturnable* and *Hello, Gorgeous!* With her husband Anthony Alongi, she also writes a series featuring a teen were-dragon named Jennifer Scales, most recently *Jennifer Scales and the Messenger of Light.* She lives in Minneapolis with her husband and two children and is currently working on her next book.

Visit her website at www.maryjanicedavidson.net or e-mail her at maryjanice@comcast.net.

THE

Science Fiction

BOOK CLUB®

If you enjoyed this book...
Come visit our Web site at

www.sfbc.com

and find hundreds more:
- science fiction • fantasy
  - the newest books
  - the greatest classics

THE SCIENCE FICTION BOOK CLUB

has been bringing the best of science fiction and fantasy
to the doors of discriminating readers for over 50 years.
For a look at currently available books and details on how to join,
just visit us at the address above.